THE FAR-CALLED

Volume Two

STEPHEN HUNT

First published in Great Britain in 2015
by Gollancz
An imprint of the Orion Publishing Group
Carmelite House, 50 Victoria Embankment,
London EC4Y 0DZ
An Hachette UK Company

This edition published in Great Britain in 2016
by Gollancz

A CIP catalogue record for this book
is available from the British Library.

ISBN 978 0 575 09211 2

1 3 5 7 9 10 8 6 4 2

Typeset at The Spartan Press Ltd,
Lymington, Hants

Printed and bound in Great Britain by
Clays Ltd, St Ives plc

www.stephenhunt.net
www.orionbooks.co.uk
www.gollancz.co.uk

To my parents,

who once explained how democracy is mob rule with taxes.

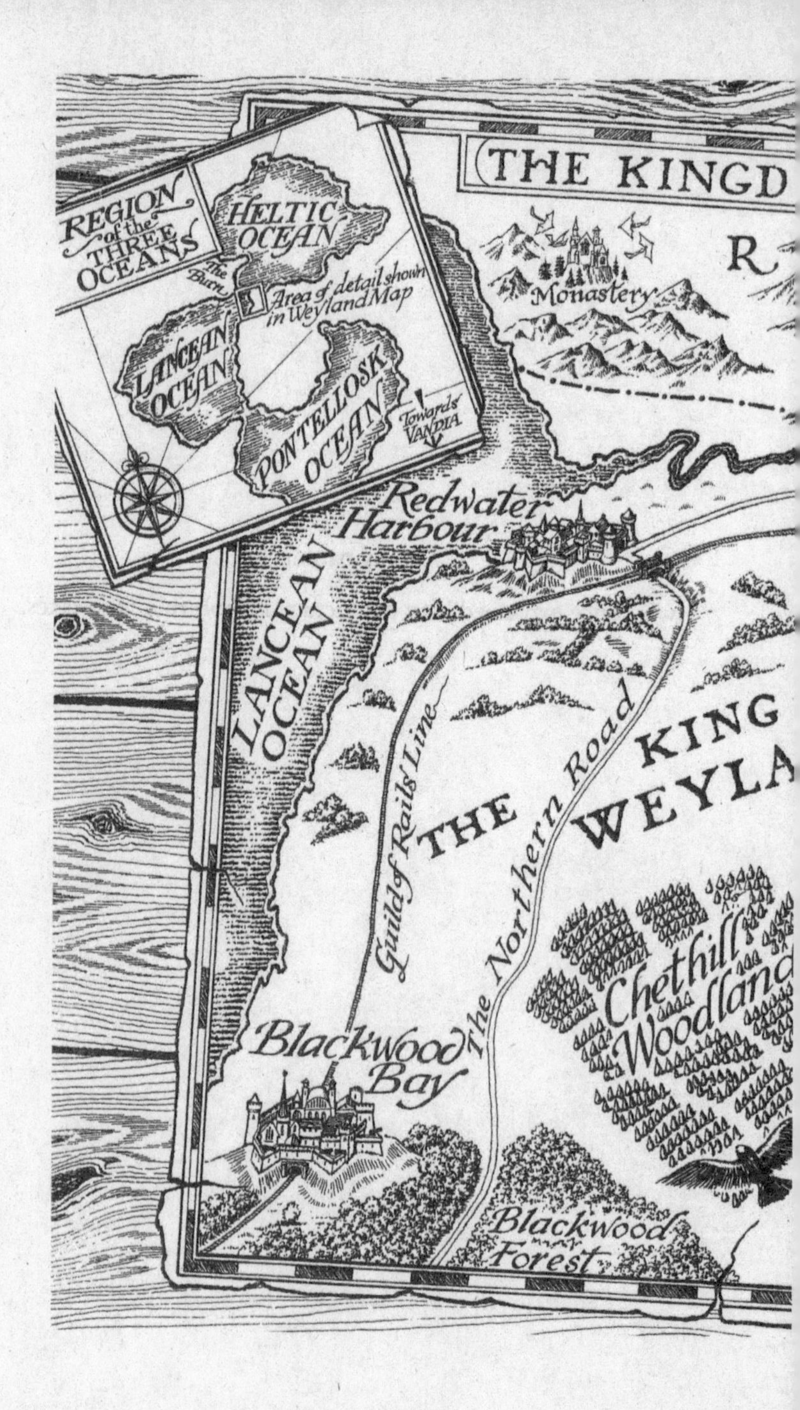
THE KINGD
REGION of the THREE OCEANS
HELTIC OCEAN
The Burn
Area of detail shown in Weyland Map
LANCEAN OCEAN
PONTELLOSK OCEAN
Towards VANDIA
Monastery
R
Redwater Harbour
LANCEAN OCEAN
Guild of Rails' Line
The Northern Road
THE KING
WEYLA
Chethill's Woodland
Blackwood Bay
Blackwood Forest

OM OF WEYLAND

O D A L

Library Hold

Northhaven

Quehanna

NORTHHAVEN and its surrounds

White Wolf River

The Great Gask Forest

DOM OF

AND

WEYLAND and Neighbouring NATIONS

Great Plains of Arak-natikh

The Thousand DUCHIES

RAILWAY

HELLIN

RODAL

Hadra-Haner

Northhaven

Hahellon

Area of detail shown in Weyland map.

TRESTERER

Heshwick

The Rotnest Islands

Navon

Midsburg

GIDOR

LANCEAN OCEAN

WEYLAND

IVAH

Atn

Talekhard

Argoed

Arcadia

RISH

RAILWAY

Tenuthin

MYSA

Chirk

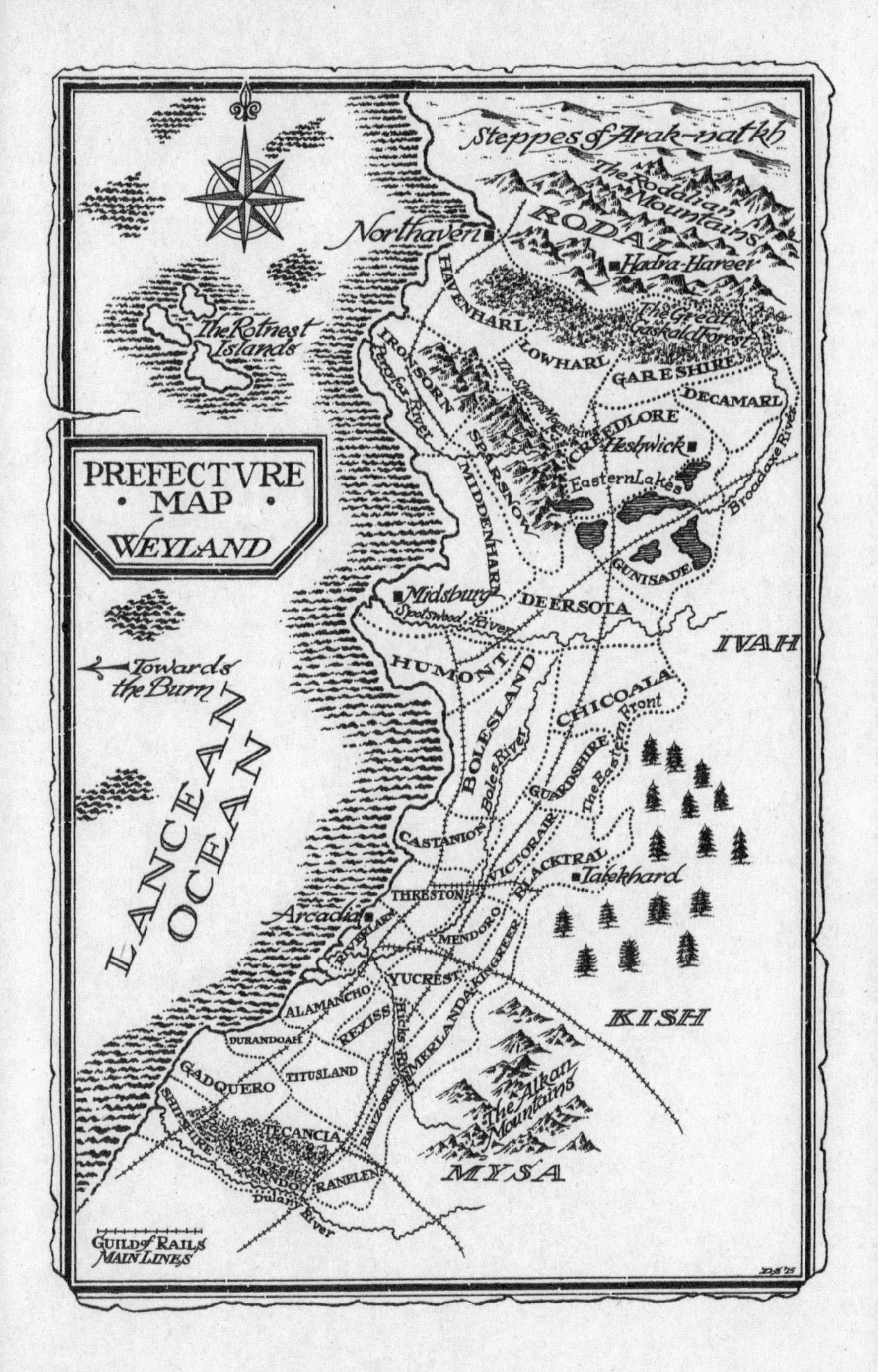
PREFECTVRE
• MAP •
WEYLAND
Steppes of Arak-natkh
The Rodalian Mountains
RODAL
Northaven
Hadra-Hareer
HAVENHARL
The Great Gaskald Forest
The Rotnest Islands
IRONSORN
LOWHARL
GARESHIRE
DECAMARL
The Sharps Mountains
CREEDLORE
Heshwick
SPARSNOW
MIDDENHARL
Eastern Lakes
Broadaxe River
GUNISADE
Midsburg
Spotswood River
DEERSOTA
IVAH
HUMONT
BOLESLAND
Towards the Burn
CHICOALA
The Eastern Front
LANCEAN OCEAN
Boles River
GUARDSHIRE
CASTANION
VICTORAIR
BLACKTRAL
Takkhard
THRESTON
Arcadia
RIVERLARK
MENDORO
KINGREER
YUCREST
ALAMANCHO
MERLANDA
KISH
REXISS
Hicks River
DURANDOAH
TITUSLAND
GADQUERO
BALIZORRO
The Alkan Mountains
SHIPSHIRE
TECANCIA
RANELEN
MYSA
Dulany River
GUILD of RAILS MAIN LINES

ONE

WANDERER'S WELCOME

It was cold coming out of the east in winter, a biting chill that even the flames from the burning, overturned wooden coach couldn't cover, nor the whipping snowstorm conceal. Young Thomas Purdell – Tom to those in his confidence – suspected he might not live long enough to warm himself at the wreckage's inferno, though; not the way the bandits were working their way through the surviving passengers. So far, they had only slit the throats of those travellers who'd put up a struggle while resisting the sudden attack. Tom was far from hopeful he was out of the woods yet. It was hard to question a dead man or woman; and this attack wasn't quite as it appeared. Not that the wilds of Northern Weyland weren't infested with bandits and marauders. But such men usually rode cheap nags and carried old single-shot rifles. These eight killers were suspiciously well-equipped with lever-action rifles from the *Landsman Repeating Arms Company*, and though Thomas wasn't much of a judge of mounts, their horses were healthy grain-fed sorrel-coloured steeds rather than the usual nags rustled as prizes by the likes of *these*. The dirty and well-patched clothes were fully in keeping with their supposed ignoble profession, however.

'You've not got much on you,' noted the bandit chief, placing himself in front of Tom. He carried a short sabre on his belt that lent him a piratical air.

Tom glanced at the prisoners on either side of him; a well-dressed traveller on his left, and one of the coach's surviving drivers to his right. They cowered, not meeting their captors' eyes, and were about as much use to Tom as trying to warm his hands on ice-cubes. As useless in a fight as the two women, a pair of sisters, from a southern city whose name he had already forgotten. Staying silent to avoid attracting attention; as the only two women on the coach, they had already failed in that task.

'I'm a simple journeyman from the Guild of Librarians, travelling to my new order,' said Tom. He tried to keep them talking. Keep them conversing long enough, and they might start to see him as a human being, rather than just another mark that needed robbing and killing. Sadly, Tom reckoned that basic tradecraft might not apply here. These men, he suspected, would share a feast with you, laugh at all your jokes, and then happily slit your throat at supper's end, before lifting your wallet. 'What wealth the guild has sits on its shelves. Archives,' Tom added, 'that are very well protected inside our guild holds.'

'Anyone would think there were thieves abroad,' laughed the chief. He waved a leather tube, the wax seal at the end broken. Tom groaned aloud. That had been well concealed inside his luggage tied to the coach roof. Not well hidden enough, it seemed, from the expert fingers of these dangerous, desperate men. Tapping the tube against his palm, the bandit removed a thick paper scroll and turned it around to reveal . . . a list of numbers scratched by hand in black ink. 'And what the hell is this, then?'

'A cipher.'

'I know it's a bloody cipher. What's it say?'

'I don't carry the means to decrypt it,' said Tom. 'In all likelihood, it's just a message of greeting from the Master of the Codex at my last library to my new master. The old girl was never happy with my work. She's probably telling Master Lettore to watch me like a hawk in case I slack off.'

The bandit leader snorted. 'That's not going to be a problem for your guild boss anymore, *simple* librarian, trust me. If you know anything about what's really written on this, I could make things go a lot easier for you.'

'It's encrypted,' said Tom. 'And you don't send the key with the man. It's not how the guild does things.'

'Pity,' said the bandit. Tom didn't get the feeling he meant it was going to be a pity for the raiders. He swivelled toward the prisoner kneeling next to Tom, a slick dark-haired passenger with a jutting chin and a tanned neck enclosed by a starched white collar and dark red tie. 'What about you, fancy pants? Where're you travelling?'

'Northhaven prefecture,' said the passenger. 'I'm a salesman for the *Turnage Machinery* Manufacturory, selling horseless ploughs and subsoilers to the landowners up that way.'

There was a ripple of discontent among the bandits at this news. 'Ah,' said their chief. 'You'll have to forgive my boys. Many of them were labourers on farms in the eastern plains . . . until their landlords cleared them out and stole their fields when they couldn't make rent. What a hoot, eh? All those machines that can work land using just a tenth of the labour; such generous harvests they produce, and your family still dies of hunger when you can't find work. I think that's what they call irony, isn't it?' He kicked Tom in the ribs; painful, but meant as a gentle nudge. 'What do you say, Mister Guild of Bloody Books? That's irony, isn't it?'

Tom nodded. 'That's one word for it.'

'Yeah,' said the chief, tugging a thumb behind his leather bandoleer. 'I thought it was.'

'Why are you doing this?' asked Thomas Purdell. 'Attacking a coach on the road? If we had money, we'd be travelling with a Guild of Rails train. If we had *real* money, we'd be flying.'

'If I had wings, I'd attack merchant carriers in the sky. If I had a hundred more men and powder to blow the rails, I'd bushwhack a train and damn their high-and-mighty guild. As it is, you grass-suckers are my marks today. You see, there's always someone worse off than yourself,' said the bandit chief, pulling out his sabre. Its steel almost glowed in the white of the snowstorm. 'The trick is to make sure that those worse off stay that way, while stuffing your own pockets. Just ask those landowners out east. Besides, it's not just money that travels by road. Sometimes secrets do, too.' He nodded at his men. There was a scream from the two sisters as the bandits dragged them closer to the burning coach, ripping the women's dresses as they hauled them away. It looked like the marauders intended to stay warm by the coach's wreck, at any rate. Tom cursed the old harpy of a guild mistress who had forbidden him to travel with a pistol. *Librarians are not soldiers*, she had archly instructed him. *Knowledge is our weapon.* Maybe he could try braining the bandit chief with the single book he carried as a gift to the new library. *The Philosophies of Holtus.* God knows, Tom had found it hard enough to penetrate the text . . . maybe its weight would concuss this fiend long enough to escape through the snow.

The travelling salesman tried to get to his feet, mumbling a protest about his ill-treatment after handing over his coins, but the bandit chief merely plunged his sabre into the multi-coloured threads of the man's tweed jacket, adding a spreading stain of crimson to the rich fibres. Tom stared down at the salesman's corpse as it collapsed to the hard, icy ground. Neatly and efficiently done.

The bandit chief winked at Tom, as though they were just exchanging pleasantries at a local tavern. 'That's man's work, sticking someone to put 'em in the ground. Haven't designed any dishonest machine to do that yet. Why waste a bullet, eh?'

Tom heard the words whisper out of the white, like jagged ice pushing in on the snowstorm. *'It's not a waste.'* The wind rose like a detonation. Just as Thomas Purdell thought he might have imagined the words, the sabre clattered to the ground, falling from the bandit chief's fingers; the marauder staring in shock as a pool of bubbling blood spread across his chest, a mirror image of the wound he had just inflicted on his hapless prisoner. A snow-swallowed silhouette moved at the margins of the blizzard, barely visible, and Tom was deafened by the rippling explosions of two pistols being fired simultaneously, little arrows of flame marking each shot. A grey ghoul emerged from the white-out, cloaked in wolf fur, twin long-barrelled pistols smoking, hot gunmetal leaving a trail of vapour drifting behind as though the weapons had sucked up the souls of the departed only to expel them through its barrels. But this wasn't a ghoul. It was a man concealed by a fur cape, only his face really visible. Why was there no return fire? Tom cast his eyes back. Four bandits lay scattered across the snow, crimson blemishes spreading where the men had fallen, three more had tumbled into the blazing shell of the coach, the two sisters shivering in the gusting wind, speechless, too shocked even to scream at the sight of the raiders charcoaling in the flames. Thomas Purdell hadn't registered enough shots to match the number of fatalities. But there must have been, unless the man cloaked in wolf fur had found a way to dispatch multiple victims with a single bullet. It had all occurred impossibly fast... or maybe it was just impossible.

'There's a fork down the road which you passed a little while before the raiders hit you,' said the figure. He had the kind of voice a ghoul should possess. Deep, sonorous, commanding. He crossed to the trees where the coach's surviving horses had been tied up by the bandits, released them and led them back to the driver. 'Follow it for ten minutes... you'll arrive at a farm run by a family called the Proillas. They're good people. They'll take you in until Northhaven Township sends a patrol out to escort you.'

The figure walked back into the white-out and returned, leaning forward on a horse as if he was communing with the storm. Concentrating, in the event more raiders stalked the night. Tom watched the man pass before turning to their surviving driver. 'Is he a scout for the army?'

'That's the pastor of Northhaven,' said the driver.

'Pastor? You mean a churchman? What kind of churchman is that?'

'The kind that's been through hell, I reckon,' said the driver. 'A while back the town was hit by slavers. They killed half the folks and stole most of the rest young enough to be worth stealing, murdered the pastor's wife and kidnapped his son. It was the pastor that went after the missing people. Went out as one man. Came back as another.'

That was a familiar tale. 'What's his name?'

'Jacob Carnehan.'

'He's the man I was sent to find,' said Tom.

He grabbed one of the horse's reins from the driver's hand, mounted it and rode into the snow after the pastor, catching up with the churchman shortly after. Despite the fierce weather, he didn't seem to be in any hurry; just advancing steadily through the storm as though it belonged to him. 'My name's Tom Purdell and I have a message for you. It needs to be taken to the librarian's hold in Northhaven to be decrypted.'

'You knew the message was for me? You should have told the bandit leader. He might have spared your life.'

'He wouldn't have,' said Tom, swaying uncertainly on his borrowed horse. It was still skittish; after being halted, cut from the train, rustled and made a witness to two massacres in a single evening, Tom could hardly blame it. In fact, he knew how it felt. He took a closer look at the man he had been sent to find. As straight, tall and sharp as a razor; a big man in his late middle age with hard, knowing eyes fit to unpeel a man's soul. His movements were careful and close, spare and measured. But he could explode into violence at speeds that should be impossible for anything mortal. Tom had already seen that. *Can a devil be a churchman . . . can a stealer?* Things here weren't exactly what they seemed.

'No,' said the pastor. A voice that was used to being obeyed, the word dragged over gravel. 'He wouldn't have. You're not stupid, boy. I'll give you that.'

'Foxy enough to know those raiders had been told to raid the coach and search it for messages,' said Tom.

'It's not foxes that are needed out here,' said the pastor. 'It's wolves. Wolves to eat wolves.'

'I'm just a simple librarian.'

'I believe that as much as the bandit leader did back there,' said Jacob Carnehan.

'You're a distrusting man,' said Tom.

'I'm *alive*,' said Jacob. 'And fixing to stay that way.' He spat onto the ground; it froze on the way. 'You won't be able to reach the library until tomorrow morning, not without freezing to death. You had better come into Northhaven with me. You can stay at the rectory.'

'My credit's good for a hotel in town,' said Tom.

'And I might wake up tomorrow to find you in a ransacked hotel room with your throat slit and your message vanished,' said Jacob. 'The kind of news that can't be passed down open radio relays for fear over who might intercept it, that kind has a way of attracting trouble.'

'I'll be safe in your rectory?'

Jacob's eye's narrowed to dark slits. 'The protection of the good lord, guildsman, do you doubt it?'

Tom's eyes drifted down to the twin pistols on his belt. *And his tools.*

'I'll stay with you, don't worry. Is it true, Father Carnehan? You were one of the people who brought back the true king.'

'*True* king?' said Jacob. The pastor grunted. 'Seems there are two men who claim that title these days, which one of them did you mean . . . Marcus or Owen?'

Thomas Purdell knew when he was being teased, or perhaps tested. 'Prince Owen. His uncle has to renounce his claim to the throne.'

'I don't suppose the people's assembly is any closer to deciding the matter of who should wear the crown?' said Jacob.

'They're in debate,' said Tom.

'That's what assemblymen do best,' sighed the pastor.

'The assembly is split down the middle,' said Tom. 'People are talking about a war, a civil war, now. Both sides are at odds.'

'Won't be anything civil about it, if war comes,' said the pastor. 'Family against family, house against house. There's no feud quite so vicious as a good clan feud.'

'You didn't answer my question,' said Tom. 'Were you one of the people who found Prince Owen at the end of the world and brought him back?' *Far-called*, that's what people called it. When you went travelling across a world without end, not knowing if you would ever return alive. Or ever want to.

'I left my home to do two things, Mister Purdell. The first was rescuing my son from a slow death in a foreign hell-hole,' said the pastor, 'and that I did. A lot of enslaved Weylanders escaped during the same slave revolt.'

'Some say the prince is mad . . .'

'*Some* do? *They* wouldn't happen to be newspapers controlled by the uncle who took the throne when the young princes conveniently disappeared, would they? Held as a slave for over a decade, watching his brothers worked to death in a mine under the whip? Wouldn't you be mad about that? I'd say Prince Owen's mildly irked right now. When he gets mad, then the country might really be in trouble.'

There was a fury in Jacob Carnehan's words, every bit as cold as the blizzard swirling around them. 'You said you went out to do two things, Father. I know you found and freed your son. What was the second thing?'

'Oh, the second's a-coming,' said Jacob. 'And I'll let you into a little secret, guildsman, by way of thanks for the encrypted message you're carrying. I won't have to travel far for it. This time, it's coming straight to *me*.'

Tom's eyes drifted down to the holstered pistols, steel barrels still warm and cutting a fine mist in the cold. And he thought of the eight dead bandits lying back on the road around a burning coach. Gunned down so fast and quick. *Like quicksilver.* Tom had never seen anything like that before, never even *read* of anything like it. And reading was, in theory, meant to be his trade. How many killers' corpses would you trade for a murdered wife before you counted yourself satisfied? Tom reckoned it would depend on the man. He stared at the shadowy silhouette sharing the road and being knifed at by biting snow, and he saw the pastor as he truly was for the first time. *A shadow on the world, making shadows.* Safe in this man's rectory? Like hell. Thomas Purdell suddenly realized he was caught at the heart of the storm.

When Jacob Carnehan woke up and went downstairs, he discovered his visitor sitting at the breakfast table with his son, Carter.

'Father Carnehan,' said Tom. 'I didn't realize your son was a fellow guildsman.'

Jacob grunted, sitting down at the table. Carter Carnehan was about as much a member of the Guild of Librarians these days as Jacob was a churchman. But they all needed some illusions to cling to, to survive. 'My boy will travel out with you to the librarian's hold in the hills. Let's see if that message of yours was worth an ambush and five dead souls.'

'You shot more than that,' said Tom.

'I was counting the passengers and coach crew, not the wolves.'

'More raiders from the east?' asked Carter.

'On the face of it,' said Jacob. 'But they were taking a suspicious interest in guild ciphers considering they had already stolen all the silver coins going. Take a pistol with you when you travel to the hold and keep a wary eye open for strangers.'

'I think I might still qualify as a stranger,' said Tom.

'Yes, but I can still smell the scent of ink heavy on you, Mister Purdell, not blood. Carter, when you have that message decrypted, commit it to memory. Don't risk travelling back to Northhaven with it on paper.'

Jacob watched the two young men make ready to leave. They would travel up to Northhaven's old city where the Guild of Radiomen's first message cart of the day would be preparing to set out to the librarian's hold, a virtual fortress buried in the slopes of a valley an hour's travel from the town. The two of them would hitch a lift to work. The fact that the librarians were sending physical couriers rather than trusting the radiomen to transmit messages for them spoke volumes for the splits appearing in the nation. Rifts even among the long guilds, which, stretched across the world of Pellas, were meant to remain neutral in such conflicts. A hard thing to manage when many of the guildsmen were locals with divided loyalties. The radiomen backed King Marcus, while the librarians – with their holds packed full of law-books – judged Prince Owen to have the better claim on the throne.

Jacob spoke to Carter before his son stepped out of the rectory. 'You don't look particularly happy this morning. Our unexpected guest worrying you?'

'It's not that,' said Carter. 'I went to visit Willow yesterday evening at the park, but the gatehouse guards wouldn't let me in. Said she was too busy at some social function to see me.'

'Too busy to meet you? That's horse manure.'

'Of course it is. Old Benner Landor's made it clear he doesn't want me seeing his daughter anymore. That refusal was on *his* orders.'

'You and Willow survived a death sentence in the imperium's sky mines,' said Jacob. 'I reckon you can endure her father's disapproval.'

'But we shouldn't have to. After all we've been through, enduring hell at the end of the world, the two of us are just expected to slot back into Northhaven, same as it ever was? Rich man, poor man. Bowing down to the great and powerful landowner, doffing my cap and showing my respect. Benner Landor wouldn't have lasted a week inside the sky mines if he'd been taken by the slavers. It might be the House of Landor's money paying for the town to be rebuilt after the raid, but that doesn't make him my master.'

'Willow's got it worse than you,' said Jacob. 'Living in the great house at Hawkland Park with all the changes up there. And you know

Benner Landor hasn't forgiven any of us for leaving his son behind in the imperium.'

'Duncan chose to stay in the empire. He was a free man while the rest of us were dying as slaves in the sky mine.'

Jacob shrugged. 'I don't think Benner will ever believe it.' The pastor was the only one in Weyland who knew that he'd put a bullet in Duncan Landor's heart before they'd escaped the empire's clutches. The boy hadn't left Jacob with much choice in the matter and the pastor hadn't lost much sleep over it. A boy who had turned against his own people . . . joined the enemy. Become an imperial citizen while his friends and family were dying from hunger and overwork under the whip. No, Jacob Carnehan wasn't going to lose any sleep over a single dead turncoat, even if the boy had been the heir to a great northern house.

'Doesn't want to believe it, you mean,' said Carter. 'The son's not that different from the father, that's the truth of it.'

Jacob worried that the same might be true of him and Carter. Jacob lifted a gun belt down from the wooden wall – a simple rotating chamber pistol slid inside the holster – and passed it to his son. 'You be careful on the road. Some of those marauders haunting the wilds aren't real bandits. They're the king's agents, out hunting for that young imperial noble we took hostage.'

His son examined the pistol and belt. 'I still prefer my knives.'

'Hard to threaten a bandit with a blade,' said Jacob. 'You might have to kill the raider just to prove you can throw faster than he can draw.'

'Fair point,' said Carter, belting the gun around his waist. 'They won't find that little Vandian girl, you know.'

'Not unless they tie you to a tree and light a fire under your feet, to loosen your tongue about where Lady Cassandra's stashed,' said Jacob.

'They won't be reckless enough to do that,' said Carter. 'King Marcus doesn't know we're not bluffing about hanging our hostage if he attacks us.'

Jacob didn't correct his son. There wasn't any artifice in the threat he'd sent south. As far as the pastor was concerned, if there was even a hint of a revenge attack against Northhaven and the escaped slaves, Weyland's treacherous King Marcus would have to explain to his imperial allies why the Vandian emperor's kidnapped grandchild was occupying a grave. Jacob would tie a noose around the young noblewoman's neck and kick the chair away himself. Let the emperor suffer like he'd suffered. Vandia slave traders had murdered Jacob's wife, taken his son and destroyed his life. The empire's suffering for their crimes had only just begun.

'Things will get better soon,' said Carter. 'Prince Owen will replace King Marcus and the country will settle down again.'

'The prince is a good man,' said Jacob. 'But that's my worry. Asking the assembly to force King Marcus to abdicate. Following the due process of the law, always doing the right thing.'

'The law is on the prince's side,' said Carter.

'The law's been bought,' said Jacob. 'Bought and paid for by imperial gold secretly shipped to King Marcus. That rodent on our throne's little better than a puppet ruler for the empire.'

'We're a *long* way from the empire,' said Carter. 'When it comes to raiding for slaves, the Vandians prefer their pickings easy and compliant. If King Marcus refuses to abdicate, the prince can reveal how Marcus arranged for his own brother and family to be assassinated so he could steal the throne. And if that doesn't have the king hanging from a lamppost in the capital by the end of the day, Owen can explain how Marcus has been stuffing his treasury with imperial gold in return for selling his own citizens as slaves.'

'Well,' said Jacob. 'We'll see how much the truth and the right thing is worth soon enough.'

Yes, they would. Trouble was, a plausible lie could travel a million miles around the world before the truth got its boots on. Prince Owen should have listened to Jacob when they'd first returned to Weyland. Jacob's method of abdication would involve a quick bullet in Arcadia City's royal, long before King Marcus realized that the citizens he'd secretly sold off to the empire had rebelled and escaped home. Lord, how he'd love to be the one to do that. Once King Marcus became ex-King Marcus, Jacob would still be aching to try. Not many would miss the damn snake. And their endless world was certainly large enough to swallow a deposed king's bones.

Carter and the guild courier had been gone a couple of minutes when a guest arrived in the form of Thaddeus Castle, the master mason supervising the building of the town's first cathedral. Tanned from long exposure to the sun and sporting muscles built by hauling stone, Thaddeus looked like he'd been assembled from bricks himself; as though he could fill in for one of his crane-and-pulley arrangements. A human building machine if there ever was one. Damned if he wasn't better company than most of the churchmen who'd be filling the new cathedral once it was finished. Jacob had loved the Northhaven of old, when it had been a quiet backwater and his pews the only seats in town. No politics, no interference from the church council; a simple, tranquil life. When Thaddeus departed for his next job, Jacob would miss the master mason for more than the good company the man had provided – it would mark the start of a new stage of existence for the pastor with a finality that he resented.

'You haven't forgotten you're meant to meet the bishop this morning?' said Thaddeus.

'If I had, he surely wouldn't let me.' Jacob gathered his coat and closed the front door of the rectory. The day had hardly started and already he was deafened by the thump of hammers on wood, like a morning chorus of woodpeckers. When Jacob had left to track down his kidnapped son, large swathes of the new town had been nothing but burning ruins. Only the old town, sitting up high behind its fortifications on the hill, had escaped more or less unscathed. Now, the town of Northhaven was being rebuilt on the scale of a city. Bigger, wider, taller, better. Extra streets. Fresh faces. It didn't seem much like the home he had lost along with his wife. What would Mary have thought if she could have seen all the new streets and shops and mills where once there had been meadows and woodland? *Too much noise and too much buzzing without consequence,* whispered his wife's ghost. Jacob couldn't fault Benner Landor on the landowner's ambitions. The man had been given a clean slate to impose his vision across, and he'd taken to the task with a relish and all of his house's resources. Even the great stone cathedral that Thaddeus and his workers were putting the finishing touches to had been paid for by Landor money. The same could be said of Northhaven's new bishop – Virgil Kirkup – Jacob reckoned, even if the bishop had nominally been appointed in the capital by the Synod Council.

'You won't be his only visitor this morning,' said Thaddeus. 'Bishop

Kirkup has himself a house guest too grand to check in at the big hotel up on the hill.'

'Do tell,' said Jacob.

'Arrived last night at the airfield,' said Thaddeus.

Jacob groaned. 'I liked it better when the country didn't have a shiny new-minted skyguard, when anyone who wanted to come to Northhaven had to spend months on a train to get here.'

'Seems that progress is flying in whether you like it or not,' said Thaddeus.

Jacob didn't. Especially not when he suspected that the blueprints for the flying machines and the money and resources to build them had been supplied by the imperium; all part of King Marcus's sly dealings with Vandia. 'Somebody important, then, I'll wager?'

'Won't find me accepting that bet. Nobody more important in this part of the world. It's the head of the prefecture, Hugh Colbert.'

Now Jacob really had cause to be aggravated. Not that he had ever met the politician. But unlike the lower house of the assembly, voted for by its citizens, the nation's upper house was appointed by writ of royal council, which in practice meant prefects swanning around acting as the king's personal marionettes. The apple didn't fall far from the tree, Jacob suspected . . . and this particular apple was writhing black to its core with worms. 'You heard what he's come north for?'

'Your assemblyman's been protesting about the number of vagrants and hobos drifting in from the east to play highwaymen in the prefecture. Prefect Colbert's come up to smooth the ruffled feathers of the great and the good in Northhaven.'

And that meant the House of Landor, since the assemblyman they had voted for was as much in Benner Landor's pocket as everyone else around here. *What are you really here for, king's man? Maybe the kidnapped granddaughter of a very distant, very powerful emperor?* 'Give the poor enough work to feed their families and the royal highways would empty of brigands quick enough.'

'Careful what you wish for, Father Carnehan,' said Thaddeus. 'I heard tell that you were out practising your own version of toll-keeping on the road last night.'

'Just returning home from a farm. The church's work has a greater call on my time than warming my feet around a fire,' said Jacob.

'And there'll be a few souls who won't be returning to the unruly bands roaming the wilds,' said Thaddeus. 'At least, that's the story from a coach driver who rolled into town early this morning with twenty horsemen from the royal cavalry.'

'Those bandits were violating the laws of the nation as well as the lord,' said Jacob.

'I'm sure your lead cure was very effective. You know, people in town are beginning to talk,' said Thaddeus. 'They say that you ain't you anymore. They say that when you were far-called hunting for the town's taken, the stealers swapped your soul for a demon's.'

'Well, they're half-right,' said Jacob.

'Which half?'

'I met one stealer at the end of the world. It didn't take to lead, so we dropped an aircraft full of explosives on its head. That seemed to discourage it.'

'I never could tell when you're joking,' said Thaddeus.

'Not many can.'

'I know that a journey can change a man,' said Thaddeus. 'And you were gone long enough for me to oversee the build of a fine new cathedral while you were chasing down slave traders. But you weren't gone nearly long enough to teach a man of the cloth to wear a holster as easy as you do.'

'I don't wear the pistols, the pistols wear me.'

'I heard you were trained by monks in the mountains,' said Thaddeus. 'Must have been an unusual seminary.'

'I'm an old man, now,' said Jacob. 'But there's a few good works left in me, yet.'

'Who decides what counts as good?'

'Sometimes it's the richest man; sometimes it's the most powerful. Sometimes it's another type of man altogether.'

'Anyone I know?'

'The quickest,' said Jacob, 'and the one with nothing left to lose.'

'You've still got a little left to go on both scores,' said Thaddeus.

'Don't let my enemies know that,' said Jacob.

'How many enemies can a meek country pastor possess?'

Jacob thought back to a burning coach in the snow, surrounded by corpses. 'A few less every week.'

'You're an unusual priest, Father Carnehan; I'll say that about you.'

Jacob stared at the new cathedral hoving into view; its grey stone facade still surrounded by oak scaffolding, masons lifting twisted gargoyles on pulleys. The workers shared their platform with glaziers carefully installing elaborate rose windows under the highest of the five pointed spires. 'That's a fact the bishop in there will be only too pleased to thump in, if you lend him one of your hammers.'

Jacob watched the master mason leave to supervise his team, then entered the cathedral via the west portal. One of the increasingly numerous functionaries hired by the new bishop appeared to lead Jacob under ribbed vaulting still fresh with stone dust, towards the private rooms of this newly installed prince of the church. Bishop Kirkup was older than Jacob by a decade, maybe sixty-five, his forehead shining and a curve of wild white bushy hair clinging to the back and edges of his skull. The bishop possessed a sharp, scholarly manner that verged on the pedantic; allowing no opportunity to pass by without reminding the pastor that Northhaven was now guided by a new lord of the church. Jacob was careful to conceal his contempt for the churchly courtier by affecting the veneer of a provincial hayseed. This fussy martinet could well be one of the many acting in the service of the old king who so desperately wanted to cling on to his crown. So it was that the two men circled each other in these meetings, the bishop prodding and goading, Jacob pretending that he was too much the country bumpkin to understand the subtleties of the bishop's provocations.

'Father Carnehan, this morning finds you well?'

'Very well, Reverend Excellency.'

'I hear the same cannot be said of some of the prefecture's less welcome souls.'

Jacob nodded. 'I would have to say that's about right, Reverend Excellency.'

'We should comport ourselves in the eyes of the saints by conducting services for the departed, Father. Not *creating* them.'

'I've clutched that piece of advice to my heart, Reverend Excellency, since our last meeting. But the trouble was I was out riding late to my parishioners when I was beseeched by a coach full of honest travellers to intervene in their troubles. It just didn't seem charitable to ride on by.'

'Northhaven has a territorial army regiment for such business.'

'I know,' said Jacob. 'I often find myself wondering where they are when I'm out riding. But then it's *very* cold at the moment.'

'You conduct a queer amount of parish business in the small hours . . .'

'Flu spreads like the devil around the farms at this time of year,' said Jacob. 'But then it is *very* cold.'

'Doctor and constable both,' said Bishop Kirkup. 'Have you given any more thought to returning to the monastery in Rodal?'

'I have,' said Jacob. 'And I'm sure I'll head back there one day, but it doesn't seem the right time at the moment. My son is still in a fragile state after his travails as a slave, as are many of the younger members of the parish who suffered after they were taken.'

'The cathedral is nearly finished,' said Kirkup. 'And our generous patron hasn't paid so much towards its completion for the people of Northhaven to continue worshipping at a humble wooden church.'

'Oh, I'm sure the good citizens of the town will come out here to visit your grand vaulted arches and sit in your fine pews. By the size of the city Benner Landor's raising out here, now, I can see the cathedral opening dozens of smaller churches spread across Northhaven.' *All reporting in to you, naturally.*

'We shall see,' said the bishop, as though this wasn't what he'd been planning all along. Of course, the one thing Kirkup wasn't planning was to keep a pastor hanging around who, under ecumenical law, should have been considered for the position of bishop before a certain churchly courtier bagged the role. It was an easy mistake for the church's council to make. Any pastor departed the country to wander the endless lands outside, searching for a scattering of human needles in a haystack . . . by rights, such a man should have ended up dead on the road a hundred times over. That Jacob hadn't, had thrown more than just this opportunist's schemes out of joint. 'Father Carnehan, how does one man manage to slay eight highwaymen in the middle of the night?'

'It wasn't one man, Reverend Excellency.'

'It wasn't?'

Jacob leant forward, raised two fingers and pointed up to the ceiling. 'It was me and *Him*. And only the unholy were smited. Nobody can see much in the dark, of course, so I must have had luck *and* the saints on my side. Our country manners are a little more bluff than I expect you found them down in the capital.'

Kirkup sighed, trying to hide his exasperation. He waved Jacob away, indicating the audience was at an end as far as he was concerned. 'A little more prayer, Father. A little less smiting.'

Jacob stood up. 'Don't worry, Reverend Excellency, I think the marauders are losing their taste for our prefecture's acres. After all, it is *very* cold up here in the north.' *And a lot colder for those planted in the dirt.*

Outside the office, Jacob noted the bishop's secretary coming back with a fresh guest – one sporting the stiff blue uniform of a Weyland prefect, a ribboned silver and gold star over the right breast of the bright tunic. *Hugh Colbert?* His hair was silver, but still as thick and healthy as a lion's mane, tied in a fashionable ponytail at the back. Jacob stopped before the man.

'Prefect Colbert.'

The man nodded. 'Do I know you, sir?'

'Not yet. I don't reckon we met when I was down at the capital, petitioning the king for a company of his guardsmen to help my expedition.'

A look of understanding settled across Colbert's cunning face. 'So, you are Father Carnehan. I understand we owe the return of the man claiming to be Prince Owen to you.'

'*Claiming*?'

'I suspect he is but a poor deluded soul, a commoner driven mad by forced labour in barbaric, foreign climes. Who would not wish to be someone else, someone of consequence, as a way of escaping their true terrible circumstances? The mind is a weak vessel, easily cast adrift.'

'Not everyone Prince Owen knew in his youth has conveniently expired,' said Jacob. 'I reckon the truth will out, one way or another.'

'So it will. Whatever happened to the king's royal guardsmen, by the way? I heard they failed to return from your rescue mission?'

'It was a hard, perilous journey,' said Jacob, 'and they made a serious mistake.' He didn't say that the primary one was trying to murder Jacob and his comrades on the king's orders after they had crossed the border.

'Let's hope it's not one anyone is likely to repeat,' said the prefect. 'So, you've travelled north to help us with our bandit problem? That's right good of you.'

Colbert touched the ceremonial dagger hanging from his belt. 'Oh, I'll think I'll have a stab at it.'

'Good luck, then,' said Jacob. 'But watch yourself while you're here. The north isn't what it used to be. Getting to be as dangerous along the northern frontier as those foreign acres where the guardsmen ended up under the dirt.'

'Thank the saints we have the king to regain control.'

'One of them, at least. I'll be seeing you around, Mister Prefect.'

'I think you should count on it, Father.'

Jacob pointed towards the office. 'One piece of advice when talking with the bishop; he presently seems rather set against people in the smiting business.'

'I fear that's outside his hands, right now. We live in troubled times.'

Jacob grunted a careful farewell at the prefect. 'I keep hearing that.' He could feel the prefect's eyes boring into him as he walked away. And he could almost taste the man's desperation to discover where the Vandian emperor's granddaughter was being kept as a hostage. *Well outside your reach, king's man.* If her imperious little highness Lady Cassandra hadn't been under Jacob's control, he suspected he'd be filling the cathedral's fresh graveyard with the bodies of the king's assassins, killers would be crawling out of the woodwork right about now. Jacob didn't have time for that. It was the head of the snake he needed to sever. He glanced back towards the office's shutting door, the prefect disappearing. *Maybe the tail of the snake requires a little severing, too.* Jacob's mind wandered to his son and the guild courier, safe in the librarian's hold. Whatever the contents of the mystery message Tom Purdell had carried in, Jacob just knew it wasn't going to be good news.

TWO

UP IN THE BIG HOUSE

As always, Willow cringed when she heard her name screeched, hating herself even as she did. Willow Landor was a free woman again, female heir to the House of Landor's considerable fortunes. Should she really feel this helpless? After all, it was ridiculous that she had survived the worst excesses of being held as human property and worked close to death, beaten and starved, yet could still flinch at *that* woman's voice. And this – Willow's position in the family – was really the problem. At least for Leyla Holten. Or should that be, née Holten, now Landor by marriage? Not that Willow would ever recognize the woman's new surname. To her, the interloper would always be Holten.

Of all the shocks that Willow had endured recently, the worst had been returning home to find her father re-married to a gold-digging harpy from the south. A woman almost young enough to be Willow's sister. But give the woman her due, she certainly put on all the airs and graces of Mistress of Hawkland Park, and had taken to ordering Willow around as if she really was her mother. In reality, she was nowhere close. Willow's mother had been a decent, kind woman before she passed away from sickness; she had been the conscience of the estate, keeping her husband Benner Landor's worst instincts in check. What was Leyla Holten? Some ludicrous fortune-hunting stage actress from Arcadia, famed for her beauty and charm. Willow had seen precious little of the latter, although she recognized that the malicious woman could turn it on and off like a faucet, especially when it came to wheedling her way around Willow's father or any other man in her vicinity. *The Songbird*, that had been her nickname in the capital. The journalists who had so named her had clearly never heard her shrieking at them at home. They probably had never seen past the wide blue eyes and long golden hair so fine it almost appeared silver in certain light; just the right height not to appear too threatening to a man – not too tall, not too short.

And the man who had fallen hook, line and sinker for her allure? Willow had hardly seen her father since she had returned. To be fair to him, he was deeply involved in rebuilding the town and improving his house's fortunes in the process. It was obvious that it was his son's continued absence that he regretted. And that had turned into resentment against her . . . that she could have been so cold and unfeeling as to flee the Vandian empire while leaving her brother behind. That was a re-writing of history if ever there had been one. Before the town had been raided by slavers, Willow's brother, Duncan Landor, had been deeply uninterested in managing the family business, preferring to duel and drink his life away, when he wasn't pursuing every unsuitable woman in striking distance. After Northhaven's youth had been sold to the mines by the slave traders, Duncan had impressed another of those unseemly women, being taken away as a plaything for a local princess, eventually deigning to send for Willow and offering her a similar ticket out of the mines. Was it any wonder she had refused the rotten offer and helped lead the slave revolt back to Weyland? But Willow's father would hear none of this. Instead, Duncan's place in history had been rewritten to make him some sort of golden child who had done no wrong while living under the mansion's roof. And Willow cast as the wicked villain for having 'abandoned' the house's young heir in Vandia, while selfishly saving herself and daring to make it back home alive.

'What are you doing here?' demanded Leyla Holten, striding into the house's great entrance hall.

Willow turned around. 'You mean here in the hall, or here in the house?' Given Holten was now female head of the house, Willow should have addressed the woman as *Mistress*, but she'd choke on the word before it crossed her lips.

'You know what I mean. Don't play the giddy goat with me, girl.'

As much a girl as you. 'I am waiting for the ledgers from the bank to be sent over with the morning's paperwork. There's a glaring discrepancy in the last corn oil shipment we sent down the railhead, and I promised the warehouse manager I'd try to ferret it out.'

'Oh, that,' said Holten, sniffing as though Willow had announced she'd lost control of her bowels during the freezing night just passed and soiled her bed. 'They arrived early this morning. I opened the accompanying letter, read it, and sent the ledgers back to the warehouse.'

Willow only just managed to choke back on her outrage. 'You read my post . . . you did *what*?'

'It is not the place of a daughter of this house to sully herself with matters of common trade.'

'*Sully* myself?' Willow fought to hold down her rising temper. 'Even when my brother was here, I was the only one apart from my father to show the slightest interest in the family business. I've been helping him since I was old enough to read. If I'm not going to do it, then who pray tell is? You?'

'We have offices filled with clerks who we pay to watch the accounts,' said Holten, haughtily.

'And just what am I meant to do?'

'I have noted your predicament in that regard. I am not blind to it. I think,' said Holten, 'that you are of an age to be married. If we leave it any longer, people will start to talk. They will think that your time as a slave has left you somehow stained. In short, they will begin to wonder what the matter with you is.'

'I seem to recall that the last time we talked about my "predicament", you and my father almost choked at the dinner table.'

'It is not the institution of marriage we object to, but your ridiculous affections for the mop-haired ruffian offspring of the local preacher. A penniless book-botherer who's perfectly matched to his station buried in the librarian's hold. You are the daughter of a Landor, and that vulgar young man is *no* match.'

'And what in the world do you know about being a daughter of a Landor?'

Holten caressed her pregnant belly, smugly. On Holten, the condition just seemed to accentuate the curves of her hourglass figure. She was no stick from the south, she had a farmer's generous frame around her bones, it was only a northerner's soul the woman lacked. 'I will shortly know what it is to deliver a Landor son, girl. The doctors have promised us a new male heir.' She ran her eyes contemptuously down Willow's plain dress. 'And then you will be perfectly redundant, in both matters of trade and inheritance, when it comes to the course of this house. I am merely suggesting that a well-starred exit before we reach that point will be advantageous to you.'

'Not just for me, I think.' Willow stared in hatred at this interloper who had wormed her way under her own roof. 'I've been through hell. This, all of *this*, is nothing compared to what I survived in the empire. There's nothing you can do to me that isn't water off a duck's back. Not even on your worst day. Just you understand that, Holten.'

Leyla Holten turned around. 'Nocks, where are you?'

Holten's short, stocky manservant came running like a lapdog at the sound of his owner's commands. Nocks never failed to make Willow's skin crawl. You would think the man was a vampire, the way he skulked around the house by day, only venturing out after dark – and then, rarely. He trotted to a halt and stared at Willow, his leer made worse by the ugly red scar across the side of his face, as though someone had once tried to split the noxious servant in half. Unfortunately for her, they had failed. 'Mistress?'

'Miss Landor is to be confined to her bedroom for the rest of the day. I fear she is overwhelmed by the demands of her reduced circumstances in the household.'

Willow snorted. 'Why don't you just let me go and make my own way in the world? We'll both be happy.'

'I don't think you understand what it takes to make me happy,' said Holten. 'Off with her, Nocks. And make sure the gatehouse staff are informed that she's not to ride into Northhaven without my explicit permission. Anyone who disregards that order will be searching for new employment in this prefecture, a territory where *very* few people will be willing to open their doors to them.'

She had that much right. Willow hated the way that respect for the house was slowly turning to fear. Holten swanned off down the corridor. Nocks pushed Willow towards the upper storey, two banks of stairs sweeping up either side of the hall. He placed his slab of hand against the back of her leg, letting it linger there for far too long before she slapped it away. 'You know, you should learn to get along with people, girl. It's a useful skill to have in this world.'

'I've had all the advice I can stomach for the day,' hissed Willow. 'And possess all the friends I need.'

'That's your problem, there,' laughed Nocks. 'None of them are under this roof, as far as I can tell. Now, upstairs with you. It wouldn't look dignified if I slung you over my shoulder and carried you back to your room.'

He shoved Willow towards the higher floor and she glowered at him. 'Where the hell did she scrape you up from, Nocks? Begging for coins around the back of the theatre when she took pity on you?'

The manservant guffawed, as though this was all playful fun. Maybe it was for him. 'In the capital, sure. The mistress has a way about her. She makes friends easily. I was introduced by one such gent, a mutual acquaintance.'

Willow reached her bedroom's door and unlocked it. 'Oh, I bet she had many admirers.'

'The mistress knows how to keep bees buzzing around the honey. I bet you could learn that too, if you tried.' He reached out to brush her cheek and she recoiled, pushing him back out through the doorway. 'Don't be like that, willowy Willow.'

'I'll order you flogged.'

'You won't find any under this roof willing to raise a whip to me,' laughed Nocks. 'And it wouldn't make much of a difference if you did. He tapped the wounded side of his skull. 'Had myself a little accident a while back. Fell against something sharp. It went into my head, straight through the bit of the brain that controls pain. Everything feels the same now, like a dull throb. You could cut my arm off and I wouldn't even whimper. A whipping or a kiss, it all feels the same to me.' He ran his finger down the red weal down his face. 'I thought you might like scars. I see your pretty boy, the pastor's son, has one down his face too. Not as good as mine. Just a scratch in comparison. Overseer's whip, I'd guess, from his time in foreign climes.'

'Carter. You've seen him? *When*?'

'No different to you, girly. We don't let trash onto the estate anymore,' said Nocks. 'Not the beggars who trudge in from the east. Not the ill-mannered plebs from the town, either.'

'You've turned him away! Is that why Carter hasn't been visiting?'

'What makes your buck so precious, eh? His churchman pa and all the others from the town, heading off into the far-called on a wild goose chase to get him back. And get *you*, of course. But not your poor brother. Never mind, petal, you came back with your young buck, didn't you? I bet he kept you safe when you were a slave. The men must have been queuing up to do that. Did you give him a little taste? Is that why he keeps on coming to the gates to be turned away?'

'Get out!' shouted Willow.

Nocks stuck his face far too close to hers. 'You'll need a friend soon. If not me, it'll be someone else. You'll see.' But the odious man finally obliged her by leaving and Willow slammed the door behind him and locked it. Through the wood she heard a strange little song drifting down the corridor, the tune Nocks often hummed to himself. *'Keep a little songbird, feed a little songbird.'*

Willow found herself shaking in anger. At the lewd servant. At her father's new wife. At the ironic idiocy of finding herself as much a prisoner home in Northhaven as she had been when her fingers were bleeding from sorting rock in the Vandian sky mines. Willow fingered her locket and clicked the hidden trigger to open it. Inside was a brown daguerreotype miniature of Carter Carnehan's face. Willow had bought the expensive image from a travelling photographic peddler, and kept it hidden, knowing her father's disapproval for the lowly pastor's son. *He saved me from a life of slavery. Why can't that be enough for my father*? She let the anger pass and then took action. She sat down at her bureau, exposed a tray with pen and paper, and dashed off a letter to Carter and the pastor, explaining her predicament. Then she pushed the letter into an envelope and sealed it with a drop of red wax. After that, it was only a matter of waiting for her young maid, Eleanor Kaylock, to come and stoke the fire in the bedroom, as she always did in the mornings. Not summoned by Willow, but following the daily routine of Hawkland Park. Nothing to arouse any suspicion. When Eleanor arrived, Willow explained what she wanted. But the maid turned pale, quite an achievement given the already porcelain complexion of the blonde servant.

'I can't take your letter through the gate to town, miss,' said Eleanor. 'It's not that I don't want to. But the guards search us when we pass through the gatehouse. It's Mistress Landor's orders. Says we've been stealing the silver and selling it at Northhaven market.'

'She treats people like that and you can call her a Landor?' said Willow. 'That sound is the lid rattling on my mother's coffin in the crypt.'

Eleanor lowered her eyes to the floor, embarrassed and perhaps ashamed. Willow felt her anger rise again, but not towards this kind, honest woman. The shame was all the House of Landor's. 'It's not how things used to be here, miss. I wish things would turn back to how they were. Before the slavers attacked.'

Willow sighed. 'If wishes were silver we'd all be rich. What about this: follow the trail down the hill to the river. It narrows on the bend and freezes as strong as granite this time of year. Cross the river and push my letter into one of the rabbit warren entrances along the opposite bank. Then backtrack, go through the gate and leave as normal – let the guards search you. When they're satisfied, retrieve my letter and pass it to Father Carnehan or his son in the old church. Only one of them, you understand? Nobody else.'

'You don't need to write, miss, I can speak to them on your behalf.'

'Carter and his father recognize my hand. Better they have something in writing in case they need to involve the town's magistrate to force me out of this house.'

'I'll do it for you,' said Eleanor. 'I'd have done it even if you hadn't come back with my husband Garrett freed from the slavers' chains. It's not right the way you're being treated in your own home. But what can the pastor do? Your father is your *father*. Many of the shops, houses and mills that weren't owned by your father before the raid... well they are now. It'll take more than a sermon to turn *that* woman into a decent soul. And your father's under her spell as bad as it gets.'

'The law's the law,' said Willow. 'For king or forester, peddler or plain simple Benner Landor's daughter. I've reached my majority. The pastor will be able to use the law to get me out of here.'

'You can't walk away from Hawkland Park,' protested Eleanor. 'Abandon all of this? Not because of that harpy. She'd have won!'

'Oh, Eleanor. I've seen things, survived things – the kind of fate nobody should have to experience. I've endured the world as low as it's possible to live. Maybe that's only fair after all the years I had living high on this estate, with not much thought given to what life was like for everyone else. But I've no fear left now. Certainly not of losing baubles and trinkets and silks. I know what's important in life and what's not. A woman like Leyla Holten? If you sink into the mud to wrestle a pig, only two things happen. You get dirty and the pig gets happy. If Holten wants to think my rejection of this estate for Carter is a victory, then let it be so.'

'I'm only staying on here because of you,' protested Eleanor.

'Then it's time you got another position, too. One you deserve, where you can be happy.' She reached out to touch her maid's belly. 'You've got a child coming this summer. You'll want your child to have a happy mother and children pick up dark humours like catching a cold. It's only fear keeping you here.'

'You talk just like Garrett does,' said Eleanor. 'It's as if he's a different man now. As though nothing can touch him or ever will.'

'One of the little ironies of life,' said Willow. 'After you've suffered as a slave you can live truly free.'

'I'm glad those dirty skel slavers didn't take me during the raid,' said Eleanor. 'Say what you like, but I'm glad of it!'

Not as glad as your husband. 'I am, too.' Willow closed her eyes, trying to banish all the images of the town's taken who had fallen. Starved, beaten, worked to death and executed.

Eleanor folded the envelope away, hiding it under her pinafore. 'I'll carry the letter to the old church for you this evening after my day's duties are done. I hope you're right about the law.'

'Trust me,' said Willow.

And it wasn't really a pastor Willow was summoning from the old rectory. She had fought alongside the merciless wraith who had travelled to the ends of the world to help rescue the slaves, who had freed her and Carter and their friends. The churchman's clothes and dog collar, they were camouflage. The miles between Northhaven and the big house at Hawkland Park . . . they were nothing. Only slightly further than the distance between a hand and a pair of shining silver pistols. Willow felt a sudden, unexpected brush of ice against her heart. So she was still capable of feeling a jagged shard of fear, after all.

Carter stood alongside Tom and watched the cart from the radiomen's hold trundle away from the library, leaving tracks in the pristine snow. They were shadowed by the concrete grotto in the side of the valley's slopes, the thick steel door still awaiting a gatekeeper's appearance to open their way into the subterranean lair. Both men were surrounded by the crates of leather message tubes they had unloaded for the driver by way of payment for their ride here. Each container was filled with updates. Trade data, cartographic alterations, news – some sent by nations hundreds of millions of miles away, messages that had been passing across the radio relays for centuries before reaching this backward, northern corner of a small nation on the shores of the Lancean Ocean. Growing chilly after finishing unloading, Carter thumbed the intercom again, reporting that the morning's bounty had been dropped off ready for transcribing: and could someone please open the damn door for him. Some things had changed very little during Carter's enforced absence from his reluctantly entered career. He was still the new face in the Guild of Librarians' Northhaven outpost; still the drudge and general run-around. Carter might have travelled as far as some of these radio messages, having been tossed into a skel slave ship's hold and sold off in distant parts, but nobody was going to rush to the entrance to let him in from the cold. His lowly position was just made bearable by the fact that this wasn't his true vocation anymore. He was only pretending to be a librarian while he and the other escapees holed up in Northhaven, waiting for matters down south to resolve themselves one way or another. Carter watched his breath smoke out as though he was part-dragon. Up in the grey gunmetal sky, the high distant black shape of an aircraft slowly tracked across the sky from west to east.

Tom pointed the plane out. 'One of our new skyguard, do you think?'

'Too large,' said Carter. 'That bird's at least five-hundred rotors big. Merchant carrier looking to cross the eastern plains and keep on going, I'd say.'

Tom tapped his padded, fur-lined jacket. 'Should be wearing my eye-glasses, and then I'd have seen that. It's a vanity, I know, but my spectacles make me look too bookish.'

'Can a librarian *look* too bookish?'

'On the road you can. I prefer to blend in. Since the guild interpreted the constitution in favour of Prince Owen, there are many of Weyland's officials who've been acting mighty peevish towards our order. Other guilds, too. I'm surprised that radioman even gave us a ride out here.'

'Peevish, Mister Purdell? You mean like those bandits that hit your coach on the way into Northhaven – *that* kind of peevish? Well, there's not too much by way of politics on the northern frontier,' said Carter. 'People hereabouts are more concerned about laying down enough stores to make it through the winter and keeping wolves away from their livestock. Will you be posted here, do you think?'

'Not long term,' said Tom. He tapped the pocket inside his coat where he'd stashed the encrypted message. 'Our people don't trust the radio relays now. Not the veracity of what passes along them or the privacy of the signals sent by the guild. Boot leather is back in fashion, Brother. I figure I'll be on the road again soon enough. Maybe for as long as these troubles last.'

'Lucky you.'

'What, and you with a nice warm job in the archives? After what you have been through, I'd have thought the guild routine would be a welcome return to normality.'

'This wasn't exactly my true calling before the slavers snatched me,' said Carter.

'And being far-called *was*?'

'It's not the distance we travelled which changed us,' said Carter. 'It was the hell at the end of the journey.'

'The papers say the slaves who made it back were being worked in one of the baronies across the ocean . . . in the Burn . . . held by a local warlord.'

'We weren't sold across the ocean and it wasn't local,' said Carter. But he could understand why the papers were saying it – it was a narrative that made sense, a lie that King Marcus wanted to propagate, while the truth of their return home was so outlandish it might as well be magic. In fact, it probably *was* magic. At least as far as a conspicuously absent and boastful bard-turned-sorcerer was concerned. *What are you doing now, Sariel? Where the hell have you and your ridiculous songs and tall stories and peddler's sorceries gone now that we need you?*

'But it was your father and Northhaven's posse who tracked you down and rescued you? That much is true?'

'True enough,' granted Carter.

But was it *really*? Certainly, a man had turned up inside the empire's vast provinces who had resembled Jacob Carnehan; pastor, recently widowed, father of three sons, two long dead from sickness and one snatched by slave traders. But Carter and his father's mind had been joined in the sky mine, fused briefly; an explosion in which Carter had glimpsed sights of blood and revenge and war that should have had no place in the life of the gentle pacifist who had raised Carter. And what of the man that had returned home with them? Prowling the margins of the prefecture like a wild animal, a shaking kettle of barely suppressed rage waiting to boil over, *wanting* to boil over. Was that man Carter's father, still? There wasn't a day that went by that Carter wasn't reminded of his murdered mother, not a day passed where he didn't ache for the sound of Mary Carnehan, the sight and memory of her. But his father wouldn't ever talk of his mother. Couldn't even abide a mention of the woman he had loved so much. Had her passing really affected the pastor's serenity this badly? It didn't make sense that it should. Carter had many worries right now. That he wasn't good enough for Willow's wealthy family. That the king would send his agents north to take revenge on the slaves for escaping from his secret ally's clutches, to silence the survivors and seek terrible retribution for returning with Weyland's true sovereign in tow. But of all Carter's worries, the greatest was that the shadow of the Northhaven raid could still reach out and claim his father's life. Carter wanted justice for what the town's dead had suffered. But justice wasn't enough for Jacob Carnehan. He needed revenge now like he needed air to breathe, and Carter worried there wasn't enough blood in all the nations of the world to soothe his father's pain. He just wished he knew how to make things better. Carter was left with the terrible feeling that his fate was as much under his control as a raindrop's was tumbling inside a tornado.

Tom interrupted his brooding. 'Maybe the head of hold – Master Lettore isn't it? – would allow us to swap duties. I could stay here in the warm and you can take to the road carrying the communications we don't trust to the open relays anymore.'

Carter smiled. 'Once, I would have bitten your hand off at that offer.'

'But not anymore?'

'I've dropped my anchor here, Mister Purdell. For better or worse. Until I'm blown out of safe waters.'

'*Safe* here? You should try travelling into Northhaven using the land route.'

'I've got the comfort of my friends and family. That's about as good as it gets. Besides, it sounds like the troubles in the land are spreading everywhere.'

It took a few minutes, but the sally port in the large steel door finally opened. Then the two of them carried message crates inside to the dumb waiter system, before travelling the entrance passage towards the library's central core, where Tom introduced himself to Master Lettore, roused from his work in the lower levels. Lucas Lettore took the message tube.

'This has already been opened,' said Lettore, darkly.

'I met a bandit with a taste for reading,' said Tom.

'What happened to him?' asked the master.

'He ran into my father on the road,' said Carter.

Lettore shook his head and removed the message to scan the encrypted text. 'Then it is a wonder the message isn't covered in the sinner's blood.' He beckoned them both to follow him. Given Carter's status as an initiate who hadn't even passed the first stage of his examinations, it wasn't long before the hold master led them to parts of the library Carter hadn't been allowed to stroll before. Stone corridors and metal fire doors sealed with complicated locking mechanisms. Lifts powered by banks of ancient batteries, the green spill of acid on the floor, and the entire reeking apparatus charged by corn-oil generators that could be heard vibrating in a faraway chamber. At the end of a maze of corridors, Lucas Lettore took out a large key that seemed too rusty to be up to the task of opening the iron barrier in front of them, slotted it into a keyhole, twisted it to the accompaniment of unlocking bolts, then let the two younger men drag the door back on its rollers. Inside was a small room lit by a single flickering ceiling lamp. Under its uncertain illumination stood an ancient oak desk holed by woodworm and, on its surface, something that resembled a typewriter.

Master Lettore turned and fixed the two young guild members with his intense, almost hypnotic gaze. 'You already know what this device is, Mister Purdell.'

'I do,' said Tom.

Lettore looked at Carter. 'And so would you, if you had stayed with us long enough to complete your studies.'

'The slavers that took me send their apologies,' said Carter. 'They thought near-fatal mining work would suit me better.'

'Despite all evidence to the contrary, they were wrong,' said Lettore. 'This is a five rotor polyalphabetic substitution cipher machine, made to the guild's design by our own craftsmen. Its existence outside the guild is, hopefully, unknown. No encrypted messages are sent by us over the open relays to make our enemies suspect we possess such a device.'

Carter looked at the box. 'It will allow us to read Mister Purdell's message?'

'That is its function.' The guild master fiddled with the machine, spring-loaded ratchets clicking. Then he took the sheet of unintelligible text and started to type, stopping every minute to read the cylinders and scribble the decoded message on a second page of paper. After he finished, he lifted a pair of reading glasses hanging on a string around his collar, balancing them on the end of his nose, sniffing delicately as he read the unscrambled communication. He passed the decoded sheet to Carter. 'The characters at the end are in a shorthand notation you have yet to master. They refer to the message's provenance. This came from the librarian's hold in Arcadia, passed on to us by a source called *Paterson*. I am presuming the name means something to you, for it does not to me?'

'It does,' said Carter. Paterson was the surname Prince Owen had used in the sky mines when he was held as a slave. Nobody apart from the handful of survivors who had escaped the distant Vandian Empire's hospitality knew that. Carter read the message. It was short, direct, to the point, and oblique enough that even if intercepted and decoded, the contents would make little sense to anyone other than its intended recipients.

Agents have arrived in Northhaven. They seek the girl.
Once they take her, they have been ordered to slaughter everyone.
They will take those you love to force you to release her.

'The source is reliable?' asked the guild master.

'As good as gold,' said Carter.

'I know who the girl refers to,' said the guild master. 'Your father has taken me into his confidence on that matter.'

'Well, I'm glad to see he still trusts someone,' said Carter. He was finding it hard to concentrate on the guild master's words. *They will take those you love*. What if the king's agents seized Willow? She was in danger again. He had to see her, warn her, even if it meant breaking into the estate at Hawkland Park, Benner Landor and his money and men be damned.

'I passed your father our guild's seal before he left the country in search for you and the others who were taken,' said Lucas Lettore. 'It proved to be of some small assistance on his journey.'

'You have my thanks for that. All in all, I've been a pretty poor librarian,' said Carter. He glanced towards the courier. 'Tom here's a lot more dedicated to the calling than me.'

Lettore smiled thinly. 'We're still glad to have you returned to us, Mister Carnehan, even if the rates of transcription errors in the archives have also returned to unacceptably high levels.'

Carter passed the sheet back to the guild master. 'Burn it.'

'I see that you have learnt caution during your troubles,' said Lettore. 'An admirable trait. Your enemies will find it difficult to discover where the girl is being held.'

'That's what I'm counting on.'

'Is there to be a return message, Master?' asked Tom.

'In due time.'

'I need to warn my father,' announced Carter. *And Willow*.

Lettore nodded. 'And speaking of warnings, on the way home to

Northhaven you should make a side-trip to the great forest. Your father is not the *only* one this message is intended for.'

'Should I accompany my guild brother?' asked Tom. 'The roads aren't exactly safe these days.'

'A wise idea,' said the guild master. 'Go as far as the forest and return to the hold when Carter has arrived safely.'

'My new posting is to be here?'

'You shall remain with us a while, I think. Perhaps you will be able to use your time to tutor Carter in such skills as the accurate re-shelving of updated volumes.'

Carter wouldn't count on it, but his failings in that regard were the least of his worries. *Slaughter everyone*. It would be easy enough for the ruthless usurper to arrange a bandit raid on the town – after all, he'd slaughtered his own brother and nephews to seize the crown. There were enough genuine, desperate and hungry wanderers on the road that would be glad to be paid for slitting the throats of every Weylander who'd escaped slavery. He thought again of Willow up in her grand mansion. How could Carter protect the woman he loved if he wasn't allowed to see her anymore? The thugs on the gatehouse were fine for intimidating tramps, but they wouldn't last long if a mob of marauders turned up to loot the estate. Holding on to their hostage was all that stood between them and murder. *I have to get Willow out of the park. Benner Landor will never believe the threat. She'll be safe with me, even if we have to disappear into the wilds for a while.*

Carter left the room with Tom while the guild master reset his code machine's cylinders back to its neutral position. 'You don't need to travel with me to the forest; I'm not quite alone.' Carter pulled his coat back, revealing a holstered pistol and two sheathed steel knifes. He was still more accurate with the throwing blades than the gun.

'I'll come anyway, if it's all the same to you. Two eyes are better than one.'

'What were your eyes doing on the coach when it was hit by those bandits?'

'Closed, sleeping,' admitted Tom.

Carter tried to smile. 'Some sentry you make.'

'I've got a strong pair of legs and some shoe leather that hasn't been worn through yet,' said Tom. 'That's the only qualification you need to be a guild courier.'

When Jacob returned to his rectory after the last service of the day, he discovered Brother Frael waiting patiently outside, visiting once more from the old monastery in the mountains. It had been Jacob's home too, an age ago; its serene heights perched over an almost endless view across the Lancean Ocean's jade-coloured deeps. Brother Frael seemed to bring the scent of the ocean with his humble slate-coloured habit. Below his tonsured hair – a ring of greyed silver like a low-sat halo – lay a pallid but affable face, his cheeks stretched waxen by sun and wind. Like many of the brothers and sisters from the border orders, Brother Frael had a touch of the Rodalian about him: wide, knowing eyes and soft manners combined with a somewhat candid nature. The old man was kindly enough, but his appearance was frequently the foreshadowing of a storm; though if Jacob had been in a better mood, he might have said the monk often appeared to sweep up the pieces of Jacob's life.

'I hear you have been vexing the bishop,' said Frael.

'That's a man easily vexed,' noted Jacob. He unlocked the door to the rectory. The tiny splinter of wood he had left jammed in the frame tumbled to the doorstep. *Alone, then. Just me and my visiting conscience.* 'I don't think Kirkup sits comfortable with the fact that, as the pastor of Northhaven, my name should have automatically been considered for the seat he occupies.'

'Such a nice new shiny seat,' said the monk, standing up and entering the hall. 'But an easy mistake to make. When you left to pursue the slavers, the Synod in Arcadia thought you as good as dead. For that matter, so did the order.'

'Happy to disappoint,' said Jacob.

'Sadly, the bishop is not the only one disappointed,' said the monk. 'When the order discovered you lying half-dead on the beach all those years ago, surrounded by corpses and driftwood, our healing of you went far beyond your shattered body. You were almost dead, but in the end you were reborn. It was as much a miracle as any I have seen, heard, or read of. You came into our order as one soul and left as another.'

'I'm still the same man,' said Jacob.

'I wish that were true.' The monk indicated the pair of belted pistols hanging in the hall. 'Those are not our tools. You should have left them buried in that false grave outside.'

'These are dangerous times,' said Jacob. He took the monk's simple wooden begging bowl out of the man's hands. 'I'm not sure how far I would have travelled on that journey shaking one of these. I'd better fill it for you, though. I'm not sure how many others around the town will honour the old hospitality of salt and roof. Many people still feel forsaken after the raid. By the lords down here and the saints up there.'

'Blood begets blood,' warned Brother Frael. 'I watched you reclaim your old guns from that coffin. I watched you dig them out, unroll them, strap them on before leaving to save Carter and the other children taken by the slavers. I said nothing then. Well, Carter is safe at home again. Is it not time to rebury those hideous instruments in the dirt?'

'You said plenty, as I recall. Carter is home, but *safe* . . . ?' said Jacob. 'Which of us can say that? That damn usurper of a king down in Arcadia is less than happy I returned with a member of his family with a better claim to the throne than his, or that we've made a lie of the story that Northhaven was sacked by the usual pirates from across the water.'

'When has there not been trouble in this world?' said the monk. 'Princes who want to be kings and kings who want to be emperors. Bandits who want to be rich and nomads who want to be conquerors at the head of a horde. There is only one choice to make in this life. Whether you are to fight or whether you are to walk away.'

'Sometimes the fight comes to you,' said Jacob. 'No matter how many cheeks you turn, it comes for you and keeps on coming.'

'Those are not your tools,' insisted the brother, turning away from the twin pistols. 'They are Jake Silver's. Let that man rest, as dead as the thousands he slaughtered.'

'I left my guns below the dirt once,' said Jacob. 'What peace did it buy me? My first two children taken by the plague, my town fired, my wife murdered by the skels, and my last son stolen to be a beast of burden and treated worse than any animal by the Vandians. I watched helpless. Jacob Carnehan couldn't save them. But Jake Silver could have. Except he was gone. Hiding under *this.*' Jacob pulled off his priest's collar from his shirt and hurled it angrily down to the floorboards.

'And would Mary Carnehan have wanted such a path for you?'

'She's dead,' said Jacob. 'She doesn't want anything.'

'Is that true?'

Jacob reached out to hang on to the banister of the staircase. He couldn't walk into a room in the rectory without seeing her ghost. Feeling her presence. But his wife never whispered to him anymore; not like she had on the journey to rescue Carter. *Maybe rescuing Carter brought her shade to peace?* 'True enough, Brother.'

'This is not your punishment, Jacob,' said Brother Frael. 'Neither God nor his saints are so cruel.'

Maybe it only feels like it. 'It's not His vengeance I fear is coming upon us,' said the pastor, 'but a more temporal power.'

'And how many graves do you intend to fill with your revenge?' asked the monk, sadly. 'How many will it take to punish those who slew your pretty wife and burned your beautiful town?'

'And buried half my parishioners. If we're keeping count, let's not forget all our dead friends out there where my guns used to lie. All those good people whose houses you used to rattle your begging bowl in front of. Weyland is as wide as it is tall,' said Jacob, 'I reckon we've got space for a few extra tombstones, as long as the right boots get to fill them.'

'And will you choose the feet inside those boots?'

'No,' sighed Jacob. 'I reckon they'll more or less select themselves when it comes to it.' *At least, that's how it's been working to date.*

'Put Weyland behind you,' urged Brother Frael. 'Cross the border and return to the monastery with me.'

'If I do, trouble will only follow me,' said Jacob. 'I can promise you that.'

'Our deaths are the rapids which await each of us behind the final bend of life's course. All a mortal may navigate is how we choose to meet our end. The order's offer is not unconsidered of the dangers your presence would bring. When death comes, let us meet it serenely. Let us meet it mindfully together, without fear.'

'My fate isn't something I can discard behind me like some old coat. I'll never forget what you did for me. How the order saved me . . . and I won't be the misbegotten soul who brings destruction down on Geru Peak. I forgot the world for nigh on twenty-five years, but it remembered me in the end. It stole into Northhaven and took everything from me.'

'If you believe that, then perhaps it *has* taken everything.'

Jacob reached out, feeling the reassuring heft of the ivory-handled pistols. *No, not quite everything.* Six reasons apiece in each pistol's rotating chamber; that made twelve reasons for going on. 'I don't fear death, Brother.'

'Then you fear something worse. You fear *life*.'

'Fear it?' Jacob snorted. 'I don't even feel it anymore.'

'Is that not precisely why you must return with me?'

'A foul tide is washing in, brother,' said Jacob. He walked from the hall into the pantry in search of a meal for the monk. Something for Frael to take on the road with him, for the brother wouldn't want to spend the night under this roof after he'd heard what the pastor had to say. 'Jacob Carnehan can't turn it. But I figure Jake Silver is a man who might.'

'There are always stealers ready to worm into our soul and hollow it out from the inside,' said the monk. 'Please—'

'Maybe I could turn and run,' said Jacob. 'Forget who I am – was – again. But could my son? Could the woman he loves? Could the hundreds of Weylanders who escaped the sky mines as slaves? Is your monastery big enough to hold everyone in the whole nation? Because that's where this particular cart is rattling.'

'I can only save one soul at a time.'

'Then save someone else's,' said Jacob. 'Because I'm never going to lose my son again.'

'If you plunge down this path you surely will, and take how many other widows and widowers with you?'

Jacob handed back the bowl, full of salt meat and dried fruits. 'I've filled your bowl, Brother. Let fate fill its own as it will. I'm not going to run and hide and watch like a coward for a second time.'

'Then you've chosen.'

'Life's chosen for me, old friend. Fate's chosen.' Jacob raised his hands open. 'I'm just here waiting on the tide.'

'Fare you well then, *Quicksilver*. It seems my brother has already departed.'

Eleanor Kaylock stared back up the hill's stepped grass slope. The windows of the big house were orange with lamp light, warm and inviting compared to the biting cold outside. Hedges ran up either side of the hill, carefully trimmed to resemble ramparts in shape and size. They made the manor house up high look even more like a castle. Rows of trees behind the hedge stood sentry, bare of leaf and dark branches iced with snow. The maid touched the pocket of her coat to make sure she still had the envelope given to her by Willow Landor. Of course it was there. She'd hidden it inside her room in the manor house until the end of the day came and then retrieved it. Calling on the church for help and succour, or at least calling on the old dog-grizzled pastor? Well, it was probably marginally more fruitful than sending for the constables in the old town. The High Sheriff of Northhaven might not be related to Benner Landor by blood, but he knew which side his bread was buttered on, that much was certain. Eleanor comforted herself with the fact that the pastor's son was genuinely in love with Willow . . . for reasons that didn't have anything to do with the fortune she stood to inherit – not that there'd be any money for either of them if Willow defied her old man. Eleanor rubbed her stomach with her gloves. Not until they had some grandchildren to soften him up a bit. Then, the old fool wouldn't much care if Willow Landor was married to the pastor's son or the Grand Duke of Dedovo.

Eleanor reached the frozen river and picked up a stone from the bank that hadn't been concealed by the snow; bring it cracking down hard on the surface. *Good.* Strong enough to have gone ice skating under the bright full moon if she'd brought a pair of wooden blades. Tentatively, Eleanor tried to keep her footing on the ice as she edged across towards the opposite bank. She was perhaps a quarter of the way across when she heard an odd humming at her rear. *'Keep a little songbird, feed a little songbird.'* She glanced behind her. Eleanor started at the sight of the mistress's short, ugly manservant, lurking under the weeping willows. What in the name of the saints was he doing all the way at the grounds' borders . . . ice fishing in the dark?

'I was heading to my father-in-law's farm. It's quicker this way,' spluttered Eleanor.

'You want to be careful, petal. That river ice is mighty thin.'

'In a midwinter freeze?' said Eleanor. 'It's as thick as the walls of the house.'

Nocks leaned forward and she saw what he had been hiding behind his back. A heavy short sabre. What was the devil's intent – did he meant to give her a poke, or worse, skewer her?

'*Please*, I'm carrying my husband's child.'

'Are you sure that's all?' Nocks had the blade out in a second, driving it's sharp point manically into the river's frozen surface, the scar cleaving his features throbbing as vividly as a devil's vein as he laid into the ice. Eleanor stumbled desperately for the safety of the opposite riverbank, trying to stay upright, but cracks in the ice rippled out, flowing below her boots, and suddenly she wasn't standing on a solid surface anymore, but falling through a bobbing tear of crumbling ice shards, the shock of the freezing water so intense it was like slamming into a wall. The water here on the bend was shallow, hardly higher than her hips, but the current trapped below was dragging at her with the full force of a train of horses. She clawed with her fingers at the remaining ice sheet, desperately struggling for enough purchase to resist the force of water trying to drag her under. Nocks reached out and for a fleeting moment Eleanor thought he was trying to help her escape, but he merely tapped his blade against the sheet, as though measuring the distance between her and the river bank. 'You see, petal, when I was listening at the door, I swear I heard you agreeing to carry something to Jacob Carnehan and his young buck.'

'Help me! Don't let me freeze!'

'Bit late for that,' grinned Nocks. 'But don't worry; you'll drown long before the cold finishes you off. And I think Miss Haughty back at the house is due a proper lesson in submission. You're the first part of it. The second part will be a lot more fun. At least, I plan to make it fun for me.'

Eleanor tried to scramble up onto the sheet, but it started to disintegrate under her weight. She was so numb; she couldn't feel a thing below the waist anymore. What was this doing to her unborn baby? 'Please!'

'I'm doing a kindness for your man, saving him all those sleepless nights. He'd thank me if this wasn't to be anything other than a tragic accident. He's going to remember you how you were before you swell up as wide as a whale.'

'It's only a message,' pleaded Eleanor, trying to think of something, anything, she could say to make this foul piece of human flotsam save her life.

'And this is mine!' snarled Nocks. He lashed out with the flat of his blade, striking her fingers with enough blunt force that she screamed, her grip abandoned. The instant Eleanor let go, the river yanked her downstream, striking her head against the sheet, and then she was sucked away, whirling in the darkness, banging uselessly on the wrong side of the ice, a muffled, useless thumping that got weaker and weaker until the bubbles of air obscuring her view slid away, replaced by cold darkness.

THREE

QUADRATICS WITH THE FOREST FOLK

Pah, another morning in paradise. Lady Cassandra Skar might have been one of the Vandian emperor's numerous grandchildren, daughter of an imperial house and heir to more riches, land and vassals than most people could count but, sadly for her, her exalted status meant nothing to the creatures keeping her hostage. She wasn't even sure these people of the forests, these *gasks*, had money. Not amongst themselves, anyway, to be used in the hidden deep woodland city of Quehanna. Perhaps to trade with the common pattern people beyond the green cathedral vaults of their pines; neighbours her ever-present minder, Sheplar Lesh, had to be counted among. The gasks were a nation of many contradictions. The twisted men and women were outwardly peaceful to the point of somnolence – avowed pacifists – but when roused, provoked, they could fire the spines that covered their leathery hides with all the speed, accuracy and lethality of a rifle. She had seen it for herself. During the slave revolt, the battle fought in the shadow of the great stratovolcano and the sky mines, a single gask slave had launched itself at the waves of imperial guardsmen, turning the air around its death dance into a dark cloud of fleeting spines, each spine tipped in natural neurotoxins that sent her loyal fighters' bodies twitching and twisting to the ash to spasm their last breaths away. That wasn't the only contradiction of the gasks' society. They lived in the forest, seeming to do without most of the trappings of high civilization enjoyed by the Vandians – not even the barbarian stone buildings and crude society of the nearby Weylanders. Yet when they chose to, the gasks could produce miniature machines of such delicacy and advanced technology, that, in many ways, they rivalled those fashioned by the empire's scientists. It was as though you were watching a drunk painted savage dancing around a fire stop, fiddle with his spear, and suddenly flourish an automatic rifle conjured from twigs and mud. Frankly, given the gasks' dangerous temper, she did not want to test their nation by offering them physical violence, even though the likelihood was that when she escaped, she would have to. That point was fast approaching. She had waited to be ransomed. And waited. And then waited some more. What, she asked herself, was the point of being taken hostage if you weren't going to be ransomed? Isn't that why foreigners seized notables like Cassandra as hostages? To be honest, given that it was a ragtag bunch of escaped slaves who had carried Lady Cassandra away, she was more than a little surprised they hadn't burnt her at the stake or had her skinned alive out of revenge. It was the fate the emperor would certainly have arranged for any of their number taken alive. With countless slaves in the imperium, not to mention hordes of lower-caste citizen rabble thronging their cities, strong messages needed to be sent that there was no escape for the empire's living property, and that rebellion only led to certain death. So, not executed; not ransomed? At least, not yet. She could add the reasons for her captivity to the list of things she still didn't understand . . . such as how she had arrived here?

Lady Cassandra had absorbed the blast of an exploding shell during the revolt and been knocked unconscious. Delirious and concussed for a few weeks. But that should have placed her location firmly within the empire's boundaries, not here. This was the slaves' homeland, millions of miles away. Territory that should only be reachable in any reasonable timescale using an imperial warship driving onward at full thrust. Even travelling on a merchant aircraft at high altitude, riding the fierce trade winds, Vandia was a decade or so of non-stop rotor-engined flight away. She knew she was in Weyland. Many of the slaves working in her sky mine had been harvested from this state over the years. And she had also learnt that she was being held in the north of Weyland, bordering a mountainous land called Rodal. Her clumsy, stupid minder, Sheplar Lesh, came from Rodal. But could Cassandra find Weyland on a map? *Of course not.* Weyland was just one of countless thousands of faraway states between here and the imperium. It would require a lifetime working as an imperial geographer to even attempt to commit the route home to memory. Cassandra's present distance from home was no accident, of course, but a matter of imperial policy. You didn't raid your immediate neighbours for slaves; neighbouring states gave people willingly as tribute in return for resources. No. Pissing on your own doorstep was never a good idea. Especially not when you possessed brutal proxy forces like the skel slavers, willing to absorb the locals' animosity for the attacks, allies who would sell human cargoes on to the empire. Had the slave revolt ended in the rebellious sky miners seizing a Vandian vessel and escaping back to the lands they'd been harvested from? It seemed unlikely, yet here she most certainly was. And, as worrying as Cassandra found the prospect of how mere slaves had returned home so easily, she presently faced the far more pragmatic anxiety of how *she'd* travel home after she escaped? The best option she had come up with so far was to try to make contact with the empire's agents who should be working here. Have them use their secret radio network to send for a warship. Cassandra knew that the imperium's standard methodology for harvesting human flesh was to bribe a local barbarian warlord to look the other way while the skels raided and seized those young enough to survive the rigours of a lifetime of imperial service. Some primitive ruler around here was no doubt growing fat on imperial gold and silver. But she could hardly escape this forest and walk the streets of the barbarians' capital wearing a sign saying 'Kidnapped Vandian celestial-caste royal: large reward offered for return home,' until she happened across a barbarian on the empire's payroll.

Cassandra cursed herself for her defeatism. She was the heir to an imperial house, trained to rule and command and fight from the moment she had been old enough to walk. What were these gasks? Twisted leather-skinned savages, holding on to her as a favour to hairy-arsed slaves who had somehow got lucky and escaped from Vandia. If she couldn't get away from gutter scum such as this, then she was not fit to be a celestial-caste imperial. She should be considered a mewling disgrace to her blood, breeding and house's name. And rightly so. Her grandfather's harem produced countless grandchildren sprung from his loins, all expected to fight and scrap for a share of what was rightfully theirs. It was how the empire kept itself strong. She was the empire's strength. As far-called as young Cassandra Skar had ended up, she must survive and prosper, or wither and die. Unfortunately for her, Sheplar Lesh had other ideas.

Her minder had just turned up outside her quarters; a store room, originally. The one type of room that used doors in the gask city – to keep rodents away from baskets of pulses and grains that were the vegetarian people's diet. And now, ironically, used to keep a Vandian noblewoman in. Sheplar stepped past the two gasks on guard duty outside, bowing to her. The foolish man had the face of a clown, Asiatic features buckled around a semi-permanent smile. He wore a leather flyer's jacket dyed purple with white sheep-fur trim around its waist, cuffs and collar. An aviator. That was a joke. She had occasionally seen his people's aircraft patrolling the border overhead, through gaps in the trees. Little wooden triangles with a single rotor at the rear powered by a primitive corn-oil fuelled combustion engine. The Rodalian barbarians wouldn't last a minute in the air against her people's advanced forces.

'It is time, bumo. Lessons.'

Cassandra frowned. Always he called her bumo. Or even worse, young bumo. Whatever the term meant in Rodalian, she suspected it wasn't respectful. Sheplar always managed to speak the common language, often known as *radio*, or simply *trade-tongue*, with a thick accent that made him sound more muddled then she suspected he already was. 'As always, Lesh, I find I must consume your insolence for breakfast. Why do you believe your spine-skinned friends have anything to teach me?'

'The gasks believe it is the duty of the young to learn, and so they will teach you, whatever your wishes. It will go easier if you set your mind to humility.'

'Humility is about the only thing a slave has to teach me.'

'The gasks have never been conquered by your people,' said Sheplar. 'You have only ever held one of their kind as a slave. And *that* arrangement did not work out very well for Vandia.'

'All outside the empire are fit only to serve us as slaves. All countries yet to be claimed by Vandia pay tribute to us.' Cassandra jerked a finger to the ceiling of the little wooden room. 'The metal in the propellers on your toy aircraft comes from Vandia's sky mines, even if you are ignorant of its origins. It has travelled along the caravan routes for centuries to reach your foul barbarian lands. When you pay travellers for metal, you ultimately pay us.'

'I think I'm still paying for it,' sighed Sheplar. He lifted Cassandra up by the scruff of the neck and manhandled her towards the door, the two gask guards falling in behind them as they left the room. They passed along a narrow wooden corridor; brown of course, as brown as everything in this cursed forest that wasn't leafy and green. Even the membranes in the wall that admitted washes of emerald light were some form of solidified transparent sap. 'You'll discover this morning's tribute to the empire waiting for you, bumo. Paid in the form of mathematics, I believe. A currency I hope you will find acceptable.'

Cassandra stepped through an open circle carved into the building and onto a swaying wooden walkway suspended high in the trees. She gazed down onto the forest floor seventy feet below. Like all the city's gask hovels, the building she'd left was a shaped wooden pod grown organically around the trunk of a tree, clinging to the bark like some bizarre fungal growth. As far as the young imperial noble's eye could see, hourglass pines rose like columns around her, thick at the base, pinched in the middle, before widening out for a final spurt to their full two hundred and fifty metre height. 'In the imperium I was tutored by Doctor Yair Horvak, one of the greatest minds in the empire, which means the greatest mind in the world, in *all* of Pellas! I mastered weapons at the hands of Paetro Barca, the legion's deadliest soldier and guardsman. Do you expect a herd of gask druids clinging to the trees to have anything to teach me?'

'Teaching is the kindling of a flame, not the filling of a vessel,' said Sheplar. 'I fear that in you, they are kindling with very damp wood.'

Cassandra ignored him. They crossed the walkway on foot, a giddying prospect to someone born to finer things in the empire; where celestial-caste citizens kept air-conditioned helos with trained pilots to ferry them across the vast, towering cities. Not that one of the rotor-topped aircraft could have hovered between the trees. After a few minutes, they arrived at one of the larger communal pods used as a classroom for the younger gasks. Inside, she found twenty or so gask pupils sitting cross-legged in the floor, short bodies covered by identical brown robes resembling togas, each creature's chest crossed by the belt of a satchel that contained their almost-holy calculator machines. In the teacher's position at the front was a gask she recognized. Cassandra bridled. This gask had once been one of the slaves labouring in her mines. Did they really expect her to accept tuition from a lowly miner?

'Do you expect me to accept lessons from this, *this* slave?'

'An ex-slave, technically,' said Kerge. 'Given that I am no longer being exploited as a source of labour in Vandia's sky mines. And in broader moral terms, gask-kind neither recognizes the concept of slavery nor practises it.'

Sheplar leant in behind Cassandra, a hint of menace infecting his usually jovial tone. 'And as Kerge's father gave his life to free him from your cursed empire, I suggest you count yourself lucky that the gasks are not a revengeful people and accept his tuition.'

Kerge indicated the floor. 'Please, womanling...'

Womanling. Hardly any better than bumo. Cassandra snorted, but occupied one of the vacant wicker mats on the floor regardless. That this gask Kerge's heart had not filled with revenge was only a symptom of his nation's weakness. Only the weak practised pity. Those born to rule defended their position without mercy. Of course the gasks wouldn't dare to hurt her. For if the empire ever heard that one of the emperor's own blood had been abused by barbarians, the imperium's forces would arrive here and burn the forest to ashes in punishment.

Kerge shuffled in front of a blackboard while Sheplar Lesh stood guard by the doorway. 'Today,' announced the gask, 'we shall examine measure-theoretic probability theory, looking in detail at sample spaces as applied to Borel algebra and the Dirac delta function.'

'If you expect me to work at your ridiculous mathematical recreations, then you shall issue me with one of your calculation machines,' demanded Cassandra.

'None of those studying here will be using their computation engines during the lesson,' said Kerge. 'Before you pick up the chisel, you must develop enough understanding of form to carve.'

'And what use are your stupid tortuous mind games? Are they rhetoric to allow me to sway minds and lead? Military theory to allow me to conquer battlefields? Economics to help my commercial interests flourish and prosper?'

'Their mastery allows us to navigate the true paths of the great fractal tree.'

Cassandra snorted. The savages' faith that they could scry the future and adjust their behaviour accordingly was no better than shamans swaying on the ground in a drug-induced haze, before emerging from their trance to announce that they had seen the future, and the gods wanted everyone to pay the witch-doctors a *lot* more tithes. 'And do you also expect me also to commune with the heathen spirits of your holy tree?'

'That would be too much to ask. But no learning is ever wasted,' said Kerge. 'As long as you live, keep learning how to live.'

'And what did you learn as the imperium worked you in my sky mine, slave?'

Kerge indicated the oval pod-like room they sat in; the vast, deep forest beyond the sap windows. 'To be more grateful for what is free.'

'You would be well-advised to set *me* free,' hissed Cassandra. 'For if the empire ever discovers I live, they will travel here for me and make a hell of your damn precious forests.'

'You would still be a prisoner, even if you set out today for Vandia on one of your craft. You have not yet learned to discern the bars of your cage. Now, we begin . . .'

Lady Cassandra groaned, but picked up the wax tablet and sharp wooden needle needed to compose answers in the tablet's surface. It wasn't fair. These savages were tutored from their youngest years in such convoluted mathematical bunk. How did they expect a Vandian to keep up, when her superior education to date had been in subjects that really mattered? If only Doctor Horvak was here. He'd understand this abstract nonsense backwards and forwards, and find a way to make it intelligible. But the gasks didn't even begin to try . . . they wanted to humiliate her, to make her doubt her abilities. To keep her a compliant little hostage until she became an old maid, driven insane by captivity and their outlandish, contradictory slave philosophies. At least when the empire made serfs of its barbarian inferiors, the Vandians had the kindness to make it abundantly clear what was required for a slave's survival. Work. Obedience. Loyalty to your betters in the higher castes. Well, the gasks and the dirty human savages they counted as allies wouldn't succeed. In Lady Cassandra, these cud-chewing primitives had bitten off far more than they could handle. She had made her mind up. Escape from this dreary perdition was worth any price, up to and including her possible death. Where there was a will, there was a way. And her will was inestimable. Cassandra set her mind to following this lesson, a confusing fug of concepts and expressions she fought her way through. The class went on for hours without a break. But an interruption did finally arrive in the form of an elderly gask. Veneration of the ancestors was one small thing Vandian culture seemed to share with these tree-hugging natives, and Cassandra could tell from the tenor of the hushed conversation that something of import was passing here between Kerge and the elder. Her suspicions were confirmed when the tutorial ended early and Sheplar joined the conversation, his body stiff with a palpable tension quite unlike the gormless, happy-go-lucky mountain barbarian.

Sheplar walked over and lifted the tablet from Cassandra's hand, placing it in a pile on the side of the room, making no comment on her progress – or lack of it – during the lesson. Of course, the clownish Rodalian could probably barely count beyond the number of fingers on his hand, and was ill-placed to sit in judgement on any work done here. He marched Cassandra towards the classroom's exit.

'Where are we going?'

'I wish to accompany Kerge to his people's council, bumo. And as it is my duty to guard you today, you shall come with us.'

Cassandra stepped outside. The other pupils scattered across a multiplicity of walkways, travelling home or to whatever tasks they had to attend. 'What are the gasks' concerns to you?'

A rare look of sadness creased Sheplar's features. 'Kerge's father, Khow, was a fine friend. He saved my life many times on our journey to rescue the people your empire stole from Weyland. Anything that concerns his child also concerns me.'

Cassandra travelled the roped walkway, boards swaying under her feet as she and her jailor followed Kerge and the city elder. She noted the two gask guards trailing carefully behind her, the pair's weight adding to the path's rocking. 'I saw the old gask die on the battlefield during the slave revolt. He died well.'

'With honour, perhaps. But the gasks are ashamed of giving in to their killing furies. His death was not judged well by the standards of his people. For them, Khow's end was at best a regretful necessity borne of self-preservation and the love he held for his kidnapped child.'

'You are a fool, Sheplar Lesh. Put the gasks in a legion and beat their pacifism from them and you would have an unstoppable force with which to hammer your enemies.'

The Rodalian aviator sighed. 'Perhaps we have fewer enemies than your empire.'

'One enemy is all it takes. You will discover that, when Vandia arrives for me.'

'We shall see, bumo. My country is a member of the Lancean League, as is the kingdom of Weyland. We will fight together if your imperium raids here again.'

'Then you will fall together. Your web of petty alliances will not be enough to challenge Vandia.'

'It is a sin to believe evil of others, but rarely a mistake. That is a quotation you can find carved in the wind temples of my country. I never understood those words until I travelled to Vandia and saw the conditions you held your workers in at the sky mines.'

'And travelled *back* again,' said Cassandra, hoping to elicit some information she might use to help her escape. But her jailor was not to be drawn. Perhaps Sheplar Lesh wasn't *quite* as daft as he looked. They reached a spiral staircase winding around a tree trunk; twisting stairs leading to a series of joined pods raised high above the web of walkways. This, it seemed, was their destination. She began climbing the stairs after the aviator, her pair of native guards treading lightly behind her.

'Keep quiet inside,' ordered Sheplar. 'Kerge's fate is bound to yours . . . by more than the branches of his people's fractal tree. Your generous treatment here has partly been due to Kerge's intervention. If you were being held in a human town by the Weylanders you mistreated as slaves, your education would, I suspect, be more arduous than some classroom learning.'

'If you and your friends ever hope to ransom me, you'd be advised to keep me well.'

'The imperium's gold is just one of the many things I do not require from it,' said Sheplar.

Cassandra climbed upward with renewed interest. So, her ex-slaves weren't holding her for money? No ransom had been sent for, then. Cassandra wasn't sure if her inestimable mother, Princess Helrena, would have sent gold or dispatched the price in steel, in the form of a revenge fleet to burn this barbarian backwater to the ground. It was looking more and more likely that escape was the only sure way Cassandra would depart this dreary place. And her fate was somehow tied to this gask ex-slave, or at least, the clemency of her treatment was dependent on him? She was suddenly alert to the possibilities and pitfalls awaiting her. The stairs rose through the floor of one of the pods. Cassandra found herself standing inside a large oval meeting hall, its wooden walls polished to a burnished walnut shine. She felt like a squirrel inside a tree's hollow. But there were no acorns stored here, only seating built into the wall, some kind of council chamber judging by the number of elder gasks dotted around the room. A case that resembled a wooden cabinet had been constructed slanted across the floor's centre. As Cassandra moved closer, she noted the cabinet was fronted with a thin sheet of glass. A complex wooden labyrinth connected inside its interior, like an oversized version of a child's ball-in-a-maze puzzle, where marbles needed to be manoeuvred towards a maze's centre. A series of seven jars had been fixed to the case near the floor, each a different colour glass. Was this some kind of gask gambling den? Did they drop marbles in the top of the labyrinth and make wagers as to which glass the ball dropped into? If Kerge owed a betting debt to some local lord, maybe she was here to watch the gang break his fingers as an inducement to pay? Cassandra knew such punishments were common among the criminal underworld of Vandia's overcrowded cities, but felt oddly disappointed to think matters might unfold similarly amongst her exotic captors. Cassandra kept out of the way by the edge of the hall, standing by Sheplar Lesh, watching for what was to unfold next.

Kerge took position in the centre of the hall. He bowed towards an elderly male gask who hobbled forward from his seat. Cassandra reckoned the creature would have been better off staying seated. The elder moved slowly, with all the cares of bones made brittle by the passage of time. The old councillor halted before Kerge and reached for the leather satchel dangling from his thin chest. The councillor removed a white ivory box. Flipping its lid up, the elder revealed a row of small brass ball-bearings. Given how rare metal was out here, she guessed they would be worth a fair amount of money.

'It is time,' said the elder, simply.

Kerge took the box and removed a ball. He turned to the case. Before he dropped the ball into the open top, he spoke. 'Blue.' Kerge dropped the ball in at the top of the case. He took a lever at the side and pulled it forward, causing a hidden mechanism to wobble the case left and right, a rhythmic clicking noise like the pendulum of a grandfather clock. The ball Kerge inserted began to drop through the maze, rolling through the labyrinth of slats. What were the stakes of this game? Hopefully nothing that involved Lady Cassandra's good treatment? Kerge was out of luck. A minute later, just as the case's movement stilled, the ball emerged at the case's edge, tinkling into the red jar. The gask repeated the exercise for each sphere sitting in the ivory box, announcing a colour, loading a ball and then setting the case into action until each jar had been filled. Cassandra sucked her breath in. Kerge had truly appalling luck. He hadn't got a single guess right. She didn't know if the gask had much of a family inheritance owing him, but at this rate, he was going to end up a pauper. She could see the gask who had once worked as her slave growing unhappy at this turn of events, turning his face to stare at the chamber's floor as if he might find coins dropped there to pay off his wager.

The gask elder didn't seem pleased, either. He turned to the councillors sitting around the hall. 'It is as I warned you. Kerge's golden mean has been poisoned. I will not humiliate him further by repeating the test. We must now retire to decide his fate.'

Sheplar Lesh stepped forward. 'I would speak.'

'Then do so, manling,' said the elderly gask. 'We shall hear you address our council in respect of the millennia of friendship we have shared with the manlings of Rodal.'

'I ask that you give Kerge another chance.'

'Kerge's fate is not yet decided. We are never hasty in such matters. We shall commune at length and decide where his position should be.'

'His place is here, with his own kind. Alongside you!'

'As an aviator of the Rodalian Skyguard, it is said that you commune with the spirits of the wind to ride the fierce cross-winds of the mountains. This is true, is it not? You studied in a temple as well as studying the mechanics of flight and the engineering that keeps your flying wings aloft.'

'It is so,' said Sheplar.

'In a similar fashion to your fliers binding with the spirit of the wind, we of the gask-kind are bound to the numbers that describe and detail us. What you and your expedition did in rescuing Kerge, son of Khow from being far-called at such vast distances, that was a rare feat. Some would call it impossible.'

'There was no part of the journey that was easy,' agreed Sheplar.

'You observed the testing. Before Kerge left our forest, he was possessed of a golden mean. We could have asked him to roll the ball a thousand times and call the colours, and he would have predicted their true course a thousand times without error. Now? Seven balls and he cannot call one correctly, when crude chance should have given him that blessing at least once.'

'That is no reason to exile him.'

'Kerge's luck has been exhausted by being returned here alive. In surviving his impossible journey, his golden mean has been poisoned. In addition to exhausting his store of luck, Kerge's father died in his arms. Sometimes the shock of grief can unhinge a gask's position in fate. Doubts erode his confidence in his own talents. I fear such an illness has infected Kerge.'

'You must reconsider—!'

'I believe it is now dangerous to Kerge to remain in the great forest. It is dangerous for us, as well. Dark futures multiply, blocking the branches of the fractal tree that lead to life and prosperity. Kerge's presence among us will bring no happiness to either Rodal or the gask-kind. Nor will *that* foreign womanling's presence.' He pointed at Cassandra and she recoiled at being involved in their nonsensical witch-doctory. The strong made their own luck. Only the weak blamed the stars and the auguries of chicken entrails. 'Her place is no longer among us. Neither is the true path of Kerge, son of Khow.'

'It won't be safe to hold the Vandian girl in Northhaven,' said Sheplar. 'You must have heard how the affairs of Weyland turn. The country is deeply divided over who should be king.'

'There is often violence outside the great forest. Those beyond know little serenity. This is not a new thing, is it, manling? As long as your people have lived in the mountains, you have clashed with the nomadic savages of the endless grasslands north of your country.'

'We *defend* ourselves when we are attacked. Rodal's mountains are the walls of the league,' said Sheplar. 'And those walls protect your people here in the great forest as much as we protect the entire league to the south.'

'The trees are our protection,' said the elder. 'And while we offer peace to all, only fools stick spears in a gask to see what will happen.'

Cassandra had to agree with that.

'Please,' begged Sheplar.

Kerge reached out to lay a hand to the aviator's shoulder. 'I thank you for speaking for me, but the council makes its judgements based on the kindest branches of our likely futures. My vision is clouded. They must choose, not I. What they choose will be best for everyone.'

Best for everyone? Cassandra's eyes narrowed. Not, by the sounds of it, anywhere close to the best for her. If Cassandra was thrown on the goodwill of her ex-slaves, ending up dangling at the end of the noose after a lynching might be one of the kinder fates awaiting her. She had to escape. And soon. These barbarians had left her no choice.

Kerge and Sheplar departed down the spiral stairs. Cassandra marched behind them with her pair of native guards. She caught up with the mountain savage. 'Perhaps now you will consider sending a ransom note to my family.'

Sheplar snorted. 'Your price has already been paid in blood.'

'Reconsider.'

'Be quiet, bumo. You mistake me for a merchant. I am an aviator of the Rodalian skyguard, bound by our warrior's code, not one of your tame slave traders.'

She switched her attention to her ex-slave. 'And what do you say, gask?'

'What is to be is yet to be chosen,' said Kerge. 'For me as it is for you. We are on the great fractal tree together.'

Cassandra was about to argue further when she heard a shout from the forest floor below. There were two human visitors walking below, one of them she recognized. Carter Carnehan. Another ex-slave from the sky mines. The one whose father had arrived in Vandia to help lead the slave revolt. Cassandra's mother had ordered this boy whipped more than once, but the only lesson it seemed the young barbarian had learnt was rebellion and insolence. By all accounts, it was this young savage's father who had carried her away from the battlefield, conveying her to a life of captivity here. Oh yes, she had cause to loathe the Carnehan family. They were the authors of all her current troubles and a fair few past ones as well. Sheplar Lesh obviously didn't feel the same way. The clown's face widened into a broad smile and he raced down the stairs to the forest floor to meet the visiting Weylanders. Cassandra was carried along in his wake like an afterthought. For someone who was used to being the centre of attention, able to control lessers with a flick of her fingers, her unacceptable demotion in position rankled like an open wound. She watched them shake hands, the second Weylander introduced as Tom Purdell from the Guild of Librarians.

'How does the day find you, Kerge, Mister Lesh?'

'I have a feeling we will soon need to relocate our guest,' said Kerge.

Sheplar nodded in agreement. 'Our welcome here is quickly being worn out.'

Carter scowled towards Cassandra as if all of this was her fault. The damnable impudence of the slave. The blame for her predicament lay squarely on his broad shoulders in the first place. 'I'd chain her in down in the rectory's storm cellar, but I'd need to employ a food tester to make sure someone in town doesn't poison her.'

'Food tester. A fitting enough position for you, slave,' said Cassandra.

'No sky mines here, your *ladyship*,' said Carter, hooking his finger under his coat and revealing a flash of his holster, 'but we've got plenty of remote farms with cold, hard winter fields that need ploughing. Maybe I can find one of your old mine workers with a swine shed for you to bed down in, a plough harness small enough to fit you, and a soul sweet enough not to impale you on the end of their pitchfork.'

'I don't fear you. Where I stand, the empire stands too.'

He grunted dismissively. 'I've received a message from the capital that you must hear,' Carter said to Sheplar and Kerge, 'but—' he nodded towards Cassandra '—not in front of *her*. Mister Purdell, if you'd be so good as to keep an eye on her little *ladyship* here . . .'

The locals walked out of earshot, deep in conversation. She burned to know what they were talking about. Something that might give her heart and hope, if that damned escaped slave Carter Carnehan didn't want her to hear about it. Perhaps concerning distant Vandia, even? She tried to edge forward, but a hand from one of the pair of gasks behind her fell instantly on her shoulder.

Tom Purdell gazed at her, as insolent as the rest of them. 'You're not exactly the most popular person around here, are you?'

'Do I look like I care what a mere barbarian thinks of me? One day Carter Carnehan will encounter my nation again, and his insolence will be burnt out of him inch by inch by an imperial torturer.'

'That'd be a shame,' said Tom Purdell. 'He seems like a nice enough fellow.'

'He's property which we paid for. His very presence here amounts to theft.'

Purdell smiled. 'Here's a little advice, even if it is unasked for. Never annoy the man who gets to decide the class of pig shed you end up sleeping in.'

'You're correct, it *was* unasked for.'

Purdell shrugged, seeming to find their exchange amusing. More than she did, at any rate. The meeting over, the other two men and their gask ally returned. Cassandra ran forward and grabbed at Carter's coat. 'Don't let them take me away from here! At least these gask savages aren't escaped slaves with a grudge against me!'

Carter pushed her away. 'Please, I've seen better acting during the local amateur dramatics night.'

'That's my fault,' said Tom. 'I told her if she was nice to you, you might find her a sty with a blanket, rather than just straw and wet mud.'

Carter rubbed the scar slanting across his face. Cassandra remembered her mother had laid her whip on the impudent devil to make a point. 'Our hospitality's been a sight friendlier than yours ever proved, Vandian. You'll damn well travel where we send you.' Her escaped slave shook the mountain aviator's hand in farewell, and then the gask's. 'I know this isn't exactly what you trained for in the skyguard, Sheplar, but mind her well. Kerge, look after yourself. Just remember, whatever happens, it'll never be a tenth as bad as what we survived in the empire.'

Kerge nodded. 'You speak the truth, old friend.'

'It is a strange wind that has blown us together,' said Sheplar. He glanced at Cassandra. 'An annoying one, too, at times. But I still follow my honour.' He called out to Carter and the other young Weyland man before they were lost among the giant trees, immense bark columns standing like sentinels in the green cathedral. 'And remember, if it comes to it, there are wind temples in Rodal where it takes half an hour in a basket to be winched up to the monks.' The two men disappeared into the emerald twilight. Sheplar Lesh patted Cassandra on the shoulder in an irritatingly familiar manner. 'Yes, bumo, there are always long corridors that need sweeping and meals of rice and root that require preparing inside the temples.'

Cassandra didn't retort with the first thought that leapt into her mind: that she would find it a lot easier to prepare meals as their drudge, now she had slipped one of Carter's two daggers out of his belt while pretending to throw herself on the barbarian slave's mercy. The blade was concealed up her sleeve. Not that she would be using the weapon to peel vegetables. It was going to come in very useful for dislodging the floor of her makeshift cell this night, and it never hurt to have a blade to dig into bark when scaling down tree trunks, either. Handy for cutting a gask sentry's throat too. Cassandra's acting might not be up to much, but when it came to sleight of hand and armed combat, she had been tutored by *masters*.

FOUR

FOR THE HONOUR OF THE HOUSE

Duncan watched Princess Helrena moving around the duelling hall, sweating and cursing as she thrust and parried, warily circling her trainer. Helrena had been pushing herself hard for the best part of an hour, as though trying to exorcise her demons. The princess's squat, bullet-headed head of security, Paetro, stood alongside Duncan at the edge of the hall, passing little comment beyond a grunt or two as the two combatants whirled around each other. Helrena trained today with a foreign weapons master, a man expert in the fighting style the empire knew as long-and-short-stab; the *long* being a single-edged thirty-five inch long sabre; the *short*, a slightly curved dagger with a basket hilt designed to block a sword. To look at the princess, you would hardly know she'd had her leg crushed, the best part of a warship's bridge crumpling around her when the great stratovolcano had erupted during the slave revolt. Duncan touched his chest at the battle's memory. There was still shrapnel embedded inside him, too close to his heart for removal to be risked even given the almost supernatural skills of the imperium's surgeons. Not shrapnel from Jacob Carnehan's bullet, precisely aimed at his heart, but pieces of the medallion that had saved his life even while being driven deep inside his body. Who would have thought Northhaven's pastor possessed such accurate aim? Not Duncan Landor, certainly.

The wound was part of him, now. A reminder, as if any were needed, to never underestimate your opponents. His friend, Paetro, carried the scars of the same encounter – and not just physical wounds. Paetro's pilot daughter had died, gunned down by Jacob Carnehan as she tried to protect Lady Cassandra. Not a day went by when Duncan didn't regret his little charge's absence. What was the poor girl enduring, now? Nothing good he feared; captured by Weylanders who had been held as slaves. Taken for what? Revenge? Ransom? Protection? Some vengeful sense of symmetry on the part of the pastor? Your empire stole my son for a slave, so I'll take your daughter? Ultimately, Duncan knew the motivation mattered little. Only the perilous pragmatic reality of the situation. Duncan trusted his once-friend Carter appreciated the sacrifice the pastor had made for him. Attempting the near impossible journey to the empire. All that way, all that blood on the road, not to mention the fierce fight at the other end. Duncan should never have expected his father to do the same. Of course not. Why would old Benner Landor bother joining the rescue party when he could stay at home, count his coins, manage his estate and pay for others to go off and do the dying for him? It was *only* his son and daughter that had been snatched during the slavers' raid. Jacob Carnehan had made that trip for his son without a second thought, knowing the odds were he'd die on the way, if not at the destination. He'd turned up a different man, half insane and the remainder feral. But he'd turned up. Carter Carnehan should take time to appreciate what it was to have a real family. Not a father for whom the jingle of silver meant more than the lives of his own blood. Or a sister who Duncan had rescued from the sky mines, only to be betrayed when she threw in with the rebel slaves. It was good to think about them from time to time, Willow and his father, to remember the pain of their betrayal. It made his new life here in the empire all the easier to bear. Not the son of a great man, but his own man. Self-made, become a citizen through his own talents and deeds.

Paetro wouldn't talk about what had happened during the battle. But then, the old soldier had been responsible for Lady Cassandra's protection. Paetro had kept the girl alive from enemies within and without the house from almost the moment she'd been born. And he had allowed her to be snatched out of the empire by nothing more than a rag-tag bunch of exhausted travellers and a dirty mob of escaped slaves. Assisted by Duncan's failure in that battle, too, of course.

Helrena back-stepped on the duelling floor, her trainer's sword sliding through the space her head had occupied a second earlier.

'Too slow,' muttered Paetro.

'She's wearing practice armour,' said Duncan. 'She'd move faster without gel-padding and face guard.'

'Not fast enough,' said Paetro. 'Her leg hasn't healed fully. Look how she becomes unsteady on the left leg when the weapons master forces her to pivot on it. Anyone with half an eye will notice her bad leg in a duel and use it against her. Slide in, exploit the weak spot and gut her.'

'Nobody has managed to do it yet.'

'We've been lucky, lad. The challenges have been fought in private, no one surviving long enough to tell another where our mistress is weak. Circae's not sent her best fighters yet. She's been testing the princess; waiting to see how the other great houses side before making her real move.'

'Given that Circae is Cassandra's grandmother, you'd think that she'd be looking to help us rescue her rather than hindering us.'

'Circae only ever desired custody of the little highness to pain her daughter-in-law,' snarled Paetro. 'Do not mistake anything the old witch does as love or care for Lady Cassandra. The little highness can only rely on us for that. Circae scents our house's blood in the water and plans to strip us of our position and wealth. She will *feed*, and it matters little who gets in the way.'

'Still,' said Duncan. 'Her son's only child . . . taken hostage.'

'A son Circae as good as murdered to get her own way,' said Paetro. 'Circae has played matchmaker for the emperor for generations now, filling his harem with hundreds of wives, producing thousands of children and countless more grandchildren. Everyone within the celestial caste is related to everyone else inside it. Whoever the princess guts in a duel, she's severing a branch of the imperial family's tree. You tread on your relatives to get to the top here.'

Duncan remembered how easily his sister had betrayed him. How quickly she had thrown the freedom he'd arranged for her back in his face. *Not just Vandians, it seems*. 'You were friends with Cassandra's father in the legion,' said Duncan. A statement more than a question.

'Aye,' said Paetro. 'Friends and brothers in battle. I miss poor old Aivas.' He looked at Helrena, clashing steel with the trainer. 'I know the princess still mourns her husband. And there wasn't a week that passed that Lady Cassandra didn't ask me to tell her an old war story about her father the hero.'

'You once told me that Circae had her son stripped of caste and exiled to fight with the army for daring to fall in love with Princess Helrena, but you never told me who Aivas's father was.'

'Not the emperor, if that's what you're thinking,' laughed Paetro. 'The head of the imperial harem doesn't also get to bear the emperor children; although I dare say the old goat tupped Circae, too. Just without issue, is all. If Circae had given birth to children with imperial blood running through their veins, the old witch would have been sure to match the emperor with noblewomen likely to bear inbred weaklings and cripples, and positioned her own children at the front of the queue to seize the throne. *All* the sons and daughters of the empire need to breed strong for the empire to survive. No, the little highness can only call Emperor Jaelis grandfather through Princess Helrena. Her other grandfather was rumoured to be a professional gladiator that Circae took as a lover. He died, I think. Most of them do, sooner or later.'

Duncan watched the fierce training duel continue. 'Can the house's surgeons do any more for the princess's leg?'

Paetro shook his head. 'Not unless they can give us time, for that's what is needed for the mistress to heal.'

Duncan bit his lip. *Time*. Not much of it left, now. Helrena had barely managed to stop her house being stripped of their sky-mining rights after the slave revolt. It was only the fact the ruthless head of the secret police was up to his neck in the empire's failure to control the slaves that had saved them from total disgrace. Exile, execution, worse. Slippery Apolleon had called in many favours to extradite himself from the disastrous revolt, and in doing so, had been required to spare his ally and her forces . . . who had been acting, for the most part, under his command. But the name of Helrena's house was still mud, associated with the only mass escape of slaves in the imperium's history, a revolt which had sparked dozens of smaller outbreaks of violence and rebellion among the easily encouraged slave force and lower-caste citizenry. The imperium of Vandia could be many things, but Duncan knew that as soon as it was perceived as fallible, as weak, the empire would fall in an inferno of ancient grievances. If its own restless masses didn't do the job first, it's jealous, subjugated neighbours would seize their revenge. But it wasn't for the likes of them that the princess trained so hard.

The door at the back of the duelling hall opened and Apolleon appeared, causing Duncan to shudder involuntarily. *Why do I feel like this, every time he visits the Castle of Snakes*? As always, Apolleon wore luxurious civilian clothes. A dark tunic with a wolf-like emblem over his right breast, a velvet cloak lined in crimson. Apolleon's pale white face shone round and dandyish, jutting out from a stiff, high collar where his neck emerged. There was something about the ageless man, something beyond Apolleon's falsely obsequious manners so at odds with his position as head of the *hoodsmen*, the emperor's ruthless secret police. Strange shadows that moved around the edges of the man when you caught sight of him in the corner of your eye; shadows which brought back the memory of the peculiar howls Duncan had heard reverberating through the thick clouds of volcanic ash during the revolt. Inhuman wails. But he needed to put his feelings aside. For without this slippery creature, this menacing, awkward ally, the house Duncan had joined his fortunes to would be destroyed. The man's appearance meant news of import for the house, for if the high-ranking imperial ever socialised for the pleasure of it, Duncan had surely missed the occasion.

Apolleon strode over to Duncan and Paetro and ran a supercilious eye over the princess dancing back and forth across the duelling floor, as though the practice of arms was beyond him. He might have a point there. Apolleon could have most people in the imperium legally executed with just a word – no sweat required. ''Pon my soul, she will tear a muscle if she continues to exert herself so.'

'She trains to help her forget,' said Paetro.

'Better she remembers,' said Apolleon. His mouth narrowed around the edges. 'Better if we *all* do.'

'You have news, my lord Apolleon?' asked Duncan, guardedly.

'Oh, I always have that. I am *very* well informed. The tribunal at the Court of the Grass has ruled,' said Apolleon. 'Helrena can only join the expeditionary force after proving herself through trial-by-arms.'

'A trial she may not survive,' observed Paetro, grimly.

'Another duel?' asked Duncan. 'Does Circae not tire of Princess Helrena sending her cat's-paws back in coffins?'

'This is far more significant than a private challenge,' smiled Apolleon. 'It will be a public contest, fought for all to see in the arena.'

'I do not think this is wise,' growled Paetro.

'It is not your name that needs reclaiming.'

'After all I have sacrificed—'

Apolleon raised a hand, cutting him off. 'I do not gainsay your personal loss, Paetro, but only observe that the emperor doesn't give a gnat's piss about your sad, dead soldier girl. One of the seeds of Jaelis Skar's imperial loins has been snatched, the chastening cherry on the cake after the empire's humiliation at the hands of a motley band of barbarian slave miners. Such a public humiliation deserves an equally public punishment squadron dispatched to extract revenge against those responsible.'

'And Helrena deserves to lead that punishment squadron,' said Duncan.

'Deserves?' Apolleon snorted. 'I can tell that you weren't born to the imperium, my young barbarian buck. Nobody in the empire gets what they deserve; only what they can take and hold.'

'I thought you were fixing matters with the court?' said Paetro.

'The magister in charge of the challenges tribunal has two daughters due to come out next season, and an ambition to have the women installed in the imperial harem, their bellies swelled with potential heirs to the diamond throne before Emperor Jaelis grows any sicker. Let's just say that Circae currently has more influence on his state of mind than my coercions. If Helrena wishes a high command position on the punishment force, she will have to fight for it.'

'And who would challenge her right to hold that position?' asked Duncan.

'I understand it will be Baron Machus.'

'He's bait,' said Duncan.

'Of course,' said Apolleon. 'Circae wants the princess to fight – what better way than dangling Helrena's treacherous cousin in front of her nose to goad her into accepting.'

'And you *still* want her to accept?' said Paetro.

'I *need* her to,' said Apolleon. 'Can you not hear the sound that carries in the air, simple Paetro? It is the sound of this house's wealth draining. If Princess Helrena doesn't secure a commission in the punishment squadron, she will never regain the face she lost during the revolt. Her house will suffer a death of a thousand cuts over the next couple of years; every enemy emboldened to snatch at her territory in the capital and the provinces and the sky mines. But if Helrena fights and wins, if she takes the position and returns victorious, then she will have a good chance at Jaelis's throne after he is gone.'

'She'll fight,' said Duncan. 'Not for the throne – but as a mother who wants her daughter back.'

'How sweetly naive,' Apolleon grinned. 'But so long as she fight and wins, she can be doing it to collect spare silver from the arena's betting touts for all that I care. But fight she will. The alternative will not be pleasant, for *anyone*.' He left the threat lingering in the air like a bad stench from a sewer.

'And what would you ask of an *Empress* Helrena?'

'Only the opportunity to continue serving the imperium,' said Apolleon, 'as assuredly as I have served her father during his reign as emperor.'

Duncan knew there was more to the arrangement than that. Helrena had hinted as much to him when he'd been caring for Lady Cassandra following the last kidnap attempt on the house's young heir. Duncan burned to know more, while fearing what he might discover. It must have something to do with Doctor Yair Horvak, the genius scientist whose work the house sponsored. What might the good doctor accomplish with the entire resources of the empire at his disposal? Why, whatever Apolleon ordered him to, of course. Given that the empire's reach and influence already extended across the almost infinite leagues of Pellas, just how great were Apolleon's ambitions, Duncan wondered? Perhaps almost as far-called as a world so large that a single message took millennia to pass around the relays of the Guild of Radiomen before making a single circumnavigation of the globe. A scale that was almost beyond comprehension. All

Duncan wanted was to make something of his life that stretched beyond the shadow of his family's name. That was far-called enough for him. No, whatever ambitions Apolleon harboured, they obviously required longer to fulfil than the dwindling lifespan of the current half-insane emperor. Apolleon needed a new patron, and it seemed that for better or worse, Princess Helrena was his choice in the race to fill the coming vacancy on the diamond throne.

Helrena strode over; her bout finished. She tossed Duncan the steel-mesh of her face guard and stood there a moment, observing Apolleon as the sweat dripped off her forehead and rolled down the padded white fencing suit. Paetro passed her a towel and she wiped her face before meeting Apolleon's gaze again. 'If you're here, then the decision is the arena...'

Apolleon said nothing but bowed lightly, acknowledging the noblewoman's words.

'Better if you stalled for time, Highness,' advised Paetro.

'The punishment squadron being assembled won't wait,' said Helrena. 'And my enemies certainly won't.'

'Your injury—'

'Shit on my injury,' said Helrena. 'Do we have a ransom demand from the barbarians, yet? Assurances of good treatment for Lady Cassandra? Does my daughter have a year of me lying on my back with my leg tied into a muscle regeneration scaffold?'

'We know she is held in the nation of Weyland, where most of your slaves were sourced from. Our local allies exert themselves,' said Apolleon.

'*I* exert myself,' snarled Helrena. 'To what end? Does my sweat help Cassandra? I want my daughter back safe, not platitudes about how hard the local barbarian war-chiefs are scrambling around in the mud to keep the imperial bribe money flowing.'

Apolleon chuckled. 'It will be Baron Machus that opposes your commission in the squadron.'

Princess Helrena shook her head in bemusement. 'Is Circae that transparent? Well then, she may choose among the fools to enter the arena.' Helrena raised her sabre. 'I shall select our weapons.'

'You'd rely on your bad leg less if you chose pistol-and-paces instead,' said Paetro.

'True enough,' said Helrena. 'But my snake of a cousin is a passable shot, and I intend to give Circae a small parting gift before I travel to reclaim my child. A bloody parcel of filleted baron.'

'What an empress you would make,' marvelled Apolleon. 'As fierce as a goddess. A light to burn so bright that few will dare gaze upon it.'

Helrena's mood didn't appear sweetened by his sugar. 'Who would have ever thought that a poet lurked inside the soul of the imperium's chief torturer?'

'Poetry is about revelation,' said Apolleon. 'Much the same can be said about the intimacies extracted from the empire's enemies when they are tied to our truth tables.'

'Inform the court I still desire a command position in the punishment squadron,' said Helrena to Paetro. 'And I will accept trial-by-arms to clear my way to that commission. We shall see which of us is the prey and which of us hunts. Make sure the court records my choice of weapons . . . dagger and sabre.'

'Capital,' said Apolleon, rubbing his palms against each other as he watched the squat bodyguard stalk away. Paetro glanced back at Duncan and smiled thinly before he left the duelling hall, then Apolleon continued, 'You have made the right decision. This is the first step to recovering your house's name.'

'I will recover more than that,' said Helrena.

Apolleon smiled knowingly. 'I trust so. It would hardly be the same in the fleet without you and your forces.'

'You will be travelling to Weyland too?' said Duncan, surprised.

'Not to help the legion pull the wings off our errant flies,' frowned Apolleon. 'But the outlaw Sariel is lurking somewhere close to that land. The slaves could never have escaped home without his assistance. Sariel must be found and executed.'

Duncan tried to keep the disbelief from his face. *I doubt the elderly vagrant I saw before the escape is dangerous much beyond his malodour.* Apolleon seemed dangerously obsessed with capturing the rascal, almost blind to the fact that it was their precipitate pursuit last time that had ended in such disaster at the sky mines. Apolleon's words sounded deranged. How in the world could some old tramp have helped the slaves escape home? The sky miners must have hijacked a Vandian ship, the way Carter had always talked about doing. *It was my home, once. And the errant flies will be half of Northhaven if Apolleon has his way.* Now Duncan had another reason to make sure that Helrena emerged victorious from the arena. He would travel home and do what he could to moderate the Vandian's retribution. Ensure that the dogs who kidnapped Cassandra took the full weight of the punishment. They deserved all that and more if they had harmed one hair of the precious little girl's head. And Duncan's father deserved to see that his out-of-favour son had carved a future without his controlling, barking, overbearing plans for the heir to the Landor fortune. All the people in Northhaven who had only tolerated Duncan because of his father's position, pretending to be his friend and searching for ways to help him: they would have a *real* reason to show a little respect and obsequiousness towards Duncan Landor when he turned up in Weyland with the forces of the imperium at his back. Yes, it would be quite a homecoming.

'And perhaps my house is not the only one with a reputation that needs burnishing?' said Helrena.

'You may kill more than one bird with the appropriate stone,' said Apolleon. 'But first you must find the right projectile to eliminate your cousin.'

'Killing Machus will be a rare pleasure in this business,' said Helrena. She could barely speak the baron's name without revealing the pain she felt about his betrayal, switching sides to join Circae and attempting to arrange the princess's assassination.

'I never saw the attraction of mixing the two,' said Apolleon. He bowed and departed the hall.

Duncan hardly believed that. There was a man who enjoyed his work, if ever there was one. It was only the title *man* he was uncertain of.

'You are not going to chide me like Paetro, I hope?' asked Helrena, hanging up her weapons on the wall rack. 'For accepting the challenge.'

'I know you're doing it for Cassandra.'

'I'm doing it for the house, too. Hell's teeth, I'm doing it because I have no other choice.'

'You'll get her back. *We'll* get her back.'

'I'll be relying on you more than any of them when we arrive,' said

Helrena. 'For your local knowledge of Weyland and the barbarians there; the damn slaves that stole my girl. Tell me again about the priest from Northhaven.'

'Jacob Carnehan was a good man when I knew him. There was always a harsh edge to him, but he believed in what he preached. Forgiveness and peace and the love of the saints and the compassion of God. He helped people in the town when they were sick. He abhorred violence.'

'Nothing like the imperial cult, then. Here, priests and priestesses of the Imperium Cosmocrator preach only loyalty, fealty and honouring our ancestors.'

'He won't harm Cassandra.' *I hope.*

'Yet he snatched her up from the battlefield.'

'I think he was afraid of the empire's retaliation for inciting the sky mines to rebellion.'

'Your priest isn't stupid, then, for he has good cause in his concern. But I spared his son, didn't I? I gave Carter Carnehan his life in the sky mines. That must count for something.'

You mean you only had him half-flogged to death for trying to escape.

'I wish I could have kept her safe,' said Duncan. *I was there. I should have done more.*

'As do I. As does Paetro. But Cassandra was trained to lead from the front, and she followed her duty during the slave revolt. I did not raise a daughter fit only to cower in safety while the soldiers of her house die on her behalf.'

'But—'

Helrena reached out to him. 'You were gunned down trying to protect her. Hesia died attempting to protect her. Paetro was lucky to live. It is no failure to survive to fight again. The only failure is in giving up.'

'I'll do whatever I can to help you.'

'Then you will come to my bedroom now; rub oils on me to help my muscles relax and recover.'

Duncan knew how that would end, and it wouldn't be *entirely* relaxing. Certainly not for him. There were a great many matters where it was Duncan who was still in training, and Helrena who was the master, or at least, the mistress. Slave or freeman of the imperium, his status now made very little difference between the sheets. Still, you had to be pragmatic about these things.

'I will have Cassandra back at my side, soon. But that is only the first step. My daughter will be truly safe when I am empress,' whispered Helrena as she gazed back at the training hall, leading Duncan out. 'Only then.'

Perhaps she would. But how safe would the rest of them be when Helrena Skar sat on the diamond throne, with malevolent Apolleon hissing suggestions by its side?

Sheplar had only recently made sure that Cassandra Skar was bedded down for the night, secure in the storeroom with fresh gask sentries posted at either end of the pod's corridor, when he saw Kerge heading towards him on the swaying walkway. Night had fallen and the freezing wind whistled in between the trees. It scoured his face, but was unable to penetrate his thick, warm flying jacket. To a layperson, the wind might have sounded like the gusts that roared through the mountainous crags of Rodal, creating twinges of homesickness; but Sheplar was not such a man. He knew each wind by the hundreds of titles his people gave them, and he could name their associated wind spirits, too. This one was *Thagyang*, the winter forest gusts of the gasks which spoke of iced needles and brittle leaves. Its soft song held few memories for Sheplar, even though the wind's touch was as cold as those in Rodal.

Sheplar stopped on the walkway and bowed to Kerge. 'No further messages from the council?'

'In all likelihood, we will loiter here for the rest of the week before a decision is made,' said Kerge. 'But I carry more auspicious news. A party of riders has travelled down from Rodal and been billeted in the halls of Travellers' Tree.'

'Riders?' said Sheplar, 'We are long outside the trading season. Who rides through deep snow?'

'They are not merchants. I believe they are a government party travelling to Arcadia through the Deep-heart Road.'

Now Sheplar was even more confused. The dignitaries described by Kerge shouldn't be riding down from the heights and cutting through the forest at all. Why weren't they flying to Weyland's capital? 'You are certain they are Rodalians? Remember Carter's warning... the king's agents are abroad, looking for the bumo.'

'We recognize Rodalians down from the mountains well enough. These guests are most assuredly of your nation, not enemies masquerading as friends.'

They crossed the walkways between the trees, passing on to larger structures as they walked toward the heart of the gask city – ornate wooden bridges flanked by flickering orange lanterns and elaborately carved palisades. Every now and then they would come across scenes from gask history carved in the wood, but most of the bridges were covered with ornate mathematical script – seas of tightly nestled characters rendered abstract by their density. Sheplar knew the oil burning inside the lamps came from the forest's flame trees; a slightly nutty scent to it that he would forever associate with the gasks. Even as the aerial streets grew crowded with gask families taking the evening air, there was a peace to the city which would have been entirely absent from even the smallest of Rodalian mountain villages. Gasks moved quietly and serenely at an even pace, never raising their voices, never jostling or running. No jabber, no songs, no shouting or raucous laughter. It was like living inside a wind temple where the monks had taken a collective vow of silence. Travellers' Tree was one of the higher, ancient trees standing at the city's centre, its length covered in hall-sized pods, a thick crown of branches at the top raised out to the sable star-lit sky above. Hundreds of windows glowed there in the dark, oblongs of luminescent green attracting swarms of glowing insects around its false, artificial light. They faced a long climb up spiral stairs to reach the chamber where the guests from the mountains were being entertained. Sheplar was accustomed to long climbs in the peaks, though, and his muscles ached only slightly by the time Kerge indicated they had reached the correct pod. Inside, a gaggle of human travellers stood around circular tables covered with dried fruit, vegetables and jugs of honeyed goat's milk. Sheplar recognized some of the gasks' council members among the mingling locals. The visitors had taken off their heavy, padded winter travelling coats and stood in familiar tunics and trousers. They certainly looked like Rodalians. Sheplar peered closer. There was a woman there, her back to him, but it looked like...

Then she turned around as though sensing his eyes on her spine. 'Sheplar!' she cried.

Sheplar's heart leapt at the sight of the familiar soft porcelain skin, ethereal cheekbones and wide brown eyes offset by sweeps of long ebony hair. After all this time. To meet *her* here! It was true then. This *was* a genuine party of officials from his homeland taking a short-cut through the great forest.

'Nima,' said Sheplar. 'It has been many years.' He reached out to indicate the white belt that bound her tunic. 'You still do not wear the black sash of marriage.'

'Nor do you,' said Nima. She tugged self-consciously at her pale belt, tied around a brown single-breasted leather tunic, large white buttons glittering like moonstones, baggy red russet trousers flowing around her legs as she leaned forward, almost close enough to touch.

'Border airfields do not see many marriage festivals,' said Sheplar. 'Only hard landings and cold patrols.'

'The same could be said of embassy postings,' said Nima.

'Of all the people I have known, it is you who most deserve happiness.'

'Better the sorrows of being apart from the right man, than the sorrows of being alongside the wrong one.'

Sheplar said nothing to that. There was little he could say. In their sorrow, as with so much else, they were as one.

'Until recently I had feared you dead on distant soil,' continued Nima. 'I heard you single-handedly engaged the fighter squadrons from a skel carrier in Northhaven's skies, were downed, and then disappeared, far-called, to chase your honour.'

'You heard the truth. But I have returned alive.'

She smiled and it almost melted his heart. 'That much I know. You are the reason we travel south.'

'I am?' His surprise at her words verged on shock. 'Me?'

'Well, more accurate to say, the man you freed from his existence as a slave . . . the one who now claims himself a prince. His appearance is the cause that drags us south.'

'Owen Hawkins? It is no claim . . . he is the rightful heir to Weyland's throne. Owen's uncle is little better than a usurper. The uncle arranged for Owen and his brothers to be assassinated, but one of their killers took pity on the children and sold them on to skel slave traders instead. Owen grew up inside the sky mines – a hellish education I would not wish on my worst enemy. He was the only one among the royal family who survived.'

'So you say. We go south to the capital to help their court and national assembly adjudicate that claim. Many of the countries of the Lancean League dispatch diplomats, now. We all fear a civil war that may drag league members into the conflict on one side or the other.'

'But you travel to Arcadia by horse?' said Sheplar, trying to mask his astonishment. 'Why do you not travel by flying wing?'

'We only journey as far as Northhaven by horse,' said Nima. 'There we will test the newfound skills of Weyland's pilots and engineers on one of their aircraft at the new airfield.' She saw the quizzical look that appeared on Sheplar's face. 'Have you not heard? Our skyguard's patrols are no longer required now that Weyland has an aerial force of its own. Rodal has been forbidden to overfly Weyland territory.'

Sheplar was outraged. 'It seems I have lingered in the gasks' forest too long. Such news is shameful! Our two countries have worked together to honour the self-defence pact of the Lanca for as long as the mountains have stood. Are we simply to be banished from the air here, like an old hound whose master has acquired a new pup?'

Nima shrugged. 'It seems we currently have *our* air and *their* air. Even the merchant carriers that cross Weyland's skies are expected to pay duties on their cargoes, now that King Marcus has discovered the means to dispatch fighter planes up to the clouds to extract fresh taxes.'

Sheplar growled in despondency. If a state was a body, then the world's caravan routes were its veins. You blocked them at your peril. It seemed King Marcus had grown arrogant enough to think his secret alliance with the empire could sustain his nation in isolation. Trouble in Rodal's neighbour would eventually spill over into the fresh air of Sheplar's beloved, high homeland, given enough time.

Nima still read his body language well. 'I feel the same way, Sheplar. But as one of the ambassadors to Weyland, I must arrive with a clean mind.'

'Better you arrive with a sharp sword than a clean mind,' said Sheplar. 'The usurper is *Nyenkha*, the false wind. He pretended to assist the expedition to rescue Northhaven's snatched citizens, but ordered his guardsmen to murder everyone in the party when we reached foreign soil.'

'Predictable,' said a voice behind him. 'For a skyguard to counsel aggression. A hammer perceives all problems as nails.'

Sheplar spun around to discover Palden Tash himself, the first speaker of Rodal. Sheplar bowed as custom and honour demanded, even as his joy at discovering Nima shrivelled. He told himself that he bowed to the position, not the man, before he corrected himself of such unworthy thoughts. *Palden wears his animosity like an old cloak, pulled close by habit and routine*. 'First speaker. Matters must be grave indeed if you travel down to our ally's capital.'

'They are,' said Palden. 'And it also predictable that an ill wind should be preceded by a member of the Lesh family.'

'I followed my honour.'

'And look at what you found. Trouble at best, war at worst. But I expect the skyguard will welcome any chance to fly at an enemy, even one we should be calling friend.'

'I am a true friend of Weyland,' said Sheplar.

'What are you doing here, Sheplar Lesh?' demanded the first speaker. 'Skulking away among the forest people? Is this a voluntary exile for you, for I know that I have not banished you yet?'

'You might say that I am staying out of the reach of King Marcus,' said Sheplar. 'For I understand he is not best pleased that we returned with a member of his house with stronger claim to the throne than he.'

'Then at least one good thing has come out of this foul business,' announced Palden. He turned to Nima. 'You are not to converse with this man again while we remain in the gask city.'

'I am an ambassador!' protested Nima. 'I have rank, mind and a will of my own.'

'I do not command you as first speaker,' said Palden Tash. 'I order you as head of your family and as your father. There is still *dgra shalen* between the Tash and the Lesh, and that is a law I will not allow you to flout.'

Sheplar despaired. *Dgra shalen*, the Rodalian code governing feuds. Always it came down to that. Where opposing families were required to remain at a distance in the claustrophobic mountain holds, lest their meetings break out in disharmony and ultimately, violence and pain for their society. 'I carry no enmity towards your clan, First Speaker.'

'The same could not be said of your father, when he lived. Or your grandparents or your uncles and aunts and countless cousins that breed like hares on the lower slopes.'

'My father gave his life for Rodal, fighting in the skyguard.'

'That he did. But where you find a Lesh on one side of an argument, you will find a Tash on the other. It has almost become a law of nature among the peaks, the spirits' own command.'

'It is the folly of men, not the will of the spirits, which gusts in the chasms between us,' said Sheplar.

'You speak well,' said Palden. 'But then, the blood of politicians and orators courses through your veins as strongly as it does through ours. Always on the opposite side of the council, naturally. Remain here in the shadows of the forest, Sheplar Lesh. And stay away from Nima. We shall be gone soon, to help ease the ruptures your foreign misadventures have caused. Let there be a fast return to serenity and the natural order of things.'

And of course, the natural order of things was an unbridgeable chasm between himself and Nima. Kerge headed back towards Sheplar as Nima and her cantankerous father moved away. 'I overheard a little of what passed there. You have my apology, manling. I thought that meeting your people might bring you some small measure of happiness. It cannot be easy, remaining apart from your home and your countrymen.'

'There are no shadows without sunlight,' sighed Sheplar. 'You have nothing to apologise for, Kerge. Our two families have been tossing stones in anger at each other across the heights of Rodal for a very long time.'

'You know the womanling well?'

'We were tutored in the same wind temple together. She is the best of them.'

'May her embassy bring the peace which was talked of.'

'You were held by the Vandians as a slave,' said Sheplar. 'Do you think peace is likely?'

'I can no longer see the branches of the future,' said Kerge. 'I have my own theories as to why that is.'

Sheplar cursed himself for not remembering the gask's troubles. 'I misspoke.'

'You did not, manling. My theory is that my talents have fled me because of what the future holds. Every potential branch in shadow. *Every* branch. And I can no longer bear to see it. Not after the horrors of working inside the sky mines. All I desire to watch now are the meadows between the trees. Is that too much to ask?'

'After what we've been through,' said Sheplar, 'I think it is not. But it may not be wise to wish for warm winds in winter.' Sheplar had no wish to linger further here among his countrymen; not with Nima's presence to remind him why remote skyguard postings, journeys to distant Vandia and gask forests were not half as hard as remaining in Rodal would have been. He and Kerge exited the hall and were climbing down the spiral stairs around the trunk of Travellers' Tree when a tall adult gask wearing the green robes of a ranger came sprinting up towards them. At close range, Sheplar recognized his features. It was Slell, head of the local ranger force.

Halting, the gask drew a quick breath to recover from his dash, then spoke. 'The Vandian womanling has gone!'

Sheplar spoke first, his heart racing. The shock announcement had driven all brooding thoughts of what might have been, what should have been with Nima, out of his mind. 'Where?'

'Into the deep forest. We track her using wood-sign, but with nightfall we are blind to many of the traces of her passage.'

'Are her guards safe?' asked Kerge.

'They live, if in deep embarrassment. It seems she stole a cutting tool and quietly sawed through the bonding agent of the floor, before using the tool as a climbing axe to assist her descent. Her tree leaks sap from bark cuts all the way to the glade floor. The guards only realized she was gone when they entered her room to clear away her empty supper bowl.'

'Can you not use your future sight to see where she will run?' asked Sheplar.

The ranger snorted at his ignorance and Kerge explained. 'Individual will is too strong to predict in the short term with any accuracy. Her potential escape paths lie north, east, west and south.'

'So she could be anywhere.'

'Correct,' said Kerge.

'But she still has a weight in the world,' said the ranger. He descended the stairs as he talked, Sheplar and Kerge following, all the way down to the distant forest floor. 'And to those whose fate she is bound to, her presence in the numbers may be felt.' He looked meaningfully at Kerge. 'That is the reason I came here, rather than following my nose with my brothers in the forest.'

There was real pain in Kerge's voice as he answered. 'Have you not heard, Slell? My golden mean has been poisoned, my talents withered to darkness. We might as well let the womanling run, for both she and I will likely be cast out of the forest by the end of the week.'

'I have heard what you suffer from,' said the ranger. 'But I do not believe it. I knew your father well, Kerge. I counted him as my friend. He always believed you were to be the greatest of the gift-chosen. As did many of us. Was he wrong?'

'My father is dead,' murmured Kerge. 'He died to free me, our luck depleted. I miss him so much.'

'Spare me your self-pity,' said the ranger, brusquely. 'Do not smother your gifts with doubt. Give me a landmark to track towards. You have at least a chance of getting it right. Your fate and the womanling's are joined together; she snatched you and you in turn took her, your numbers fused heavy on the weave of the world. Now, where does her weight roll?'

'There is bad blood between us,' moaned Kerge.

'It is not blood you wade though,' snarled the ranger, 'it is *life*. I am not asking you to predict future potentials, only to feel for the bindings where your fate has become mutually entangled. Do not think. Do not doubt. Don't you dare reach for your calculator and cloud your perceptions with sums. Just reach for her presence and tell me . . .'

Kerge groaned as though he had been wounded in battle, but at last he spoke. 'The bridge across Byberry Brook.'

'East?' said Slell. 'Clever of the young womanling, then. The initial wood-sign led west, but I suspected it might be a false trail. She has been well trained. She flees for the deep-woods before changing direction towards a manling settlement beyond our boughs.'

'I might be wrong,' said Kerge. 'I probably am. Please do not trust my instincts.'

'I trust them more than you do,' barked the ranger. Slell raced off, and Sheplar and Kerge followed fast after the gask as he called his remaining group of trackers to him; all tall, wiry rangers who moved through the trees effortlessly, slipping through the dark undergrowth like ghosts.

'She must be retaken unharmed,' said Sheplar, feeling like an inelegant bull crashing through the forest in comparison to the locals. But this was not his realm. His sense of smell was a fraction of the gasks', and their eyes could peer far further through a dark forest twilight.

'We shall do our best,' said Slell, not even glancing at the aviator as he ran. 'But her instinct for resorting to violence will be vented more readily than those of gask-kind; she's spirited, even given her common pattern flesh. No offence intended.'

'None taken,' said Sheplar, ducking a thorny bush heading straight for his face.

'You only have to watch how the womanling prowls around the halls of Quehanna, how she holds her balance on her heels. She works to conceal it, but you only need to look at her to know that she's been hard-tutored in the ways of killing.'

'Sadly, ruling Vandia is not a gentle profession,' said Kerge. It almost sounded like an apology for his cruel once-captor.

'I do not doubt it, Kerge. But none among us wish to meet our end with a stolen carver's chisel driven into our heart. Still, we shall first attempt to snare her.' He lifted up the set of bolas he carried, three polished stone spheres joined by twine. It would be enough to twist around Cassandra Skar's legs and trip her. The rangers needed no other weapons aside from the pelt of poisoned spines that covered their bodies. Unfortunately for both Sheplar and the fleeing Vandian girl, such spines were only ever fatal. Gasks couldn't vary the dose of their natural defence mechanism, any more than Sheplar could adjust the charge of his pistol's shells to wound an adversary. Shooting to kill was the only option for anyone in this pursuit.

They ran through the dark for what seemed like hours, moonlight making shadows of them all, the grass as hard as spears and covered with pine cones that cracked like eggs when stepped on. Sheplar was beginning to suspect that maybe Kerge's lack of faith in his abilities might be warranted, but then the rangers suddenly changed direction, announcing they had picked up Cassandra Skar's trail. He could barely keep up with their easy lope through the forest, let along discern whatever comprised the escaped hostage's trail. Even though Sheplar was beginning to tire, muscles in his legs growing heavier and heavier, he allowed himself a brief flash of hope that they could recapture her. Young Lady Cassandra Skar was his responsibility. As long as they held her, the empire and its perfidious local allies couldn't take their revenge on the escaped slaves. Cassandra had to stay hidden away here until the true king of Weyland was restored to his throne. Then the empire would slope away, looking for easier lands to corrupt to feed its slave trade. And Sheplar would gladly release the spoiled little hellcat, ending both her imprisonment and, in a smaller way, his. He broke through the undergrowth and onto a paved path through the trees, one of the smaller tracks that led to the well-ridden route up to the mountains. Had the Vandian girl passed this way? Harder to track her in the open. Wouldn't Lady Cassandra try to keep away from the roads until she was sure she had shrugged off her pursuit? Up ahead, moonlight in a clearing and a damp wind, *Rlonpa-Tsang*, flowing off a stream. Was this the bridge that Kerge had spoken of, fording the river meadow?

A sound carried on the air, cries and shouts, danger and peril . . . a skirmish beyond the bend. Sheplar drew his pistol and he and the gasks darted forward. They came across a scene of carnage at the foot of the wooden bridge, a brawl between Lady Cassandra and a group of men circling her, trying to grab the girl and pull her down to the road. There were seven attackers, not including two on the ground already, face down in pools of their own blood. These travellers had no horses with them and wore tattered clothes with heavy backpacks – outlaws camping in the deep-wood beyond the reach of the law? They had tried to grab the Vandian girl, but found she was better practised in knife work than someone of her age had any right to be. And whether these devils had intended to rob her or rape her, they had bitten off more than they could chew. So far they hadn't reached for the pistols hanging off their belts, but it was only a matter of . . . They caught sight of the local rangers bearing down on them around the corner and fulfilled Sheplar's fears. Gunshots split the night, fierce explosions of flame as the intruders drew and blasted away at the natives. Sheplar's pistol bucked in his hand, the weapon crafted by the skyguard's own workshop, blessed by monks and etched with ornate prayer symbols. His aim was good – one of the invaders nearest Cassandra Skar tumbled back, falling into the stream, his body swirled away with the fast-moving slushy ice flow. Sheplar heard the whistle of the bandits' return fire, an angry hornet buzzing as bullets slid past his ears in the twilight. He took a second shot, the jointed arm of his pistol lock springing up as another cartridge ejected, his aim thrown off as Kerge pulled Sheplar to the side of the road, knowing what was about to follow. 'Stay out of the way, manling!'

For the gasks around Sheplar needed no handguns, and the lethal provocations initiated by these intruders were all they required to respond in kind. A cracking noise accompanied the sudden sleet of spines launched in the bandits' direction, driven by chemical muscle contraction, flying near invisible in the dark without muzzle flash or powder detonation, only its effects could be seen. Marauders fell back, silhouettes spasming as bodies tightened in paralysis, pistols tumbling out of hands, voices croaking as their throats constricted into the last sound they would ever make. The rattle of gunfire died away as the last man standing fell to the ground, the rush of combat replaced by the fire of neurotoxins coursing through muscles turned into burning flesh too heavy to move.

'They should not have fought,' said Slell, simply, regret heavy in his words. 'Have they never heard of gask-kind? Do they not know whose forest this is?'

Perhaps not. Sheplar had never heard of a gask attacking in anger first. And he had never heard of a man surviving a provoked gask's natural defences. He holstered his pistol and covered the grip with the leather holster flap, clipping it into place; intended to keep it by his side during the twists and turns of aerial combat. *Spirits, but I miss my flying wing.* The rangers didn't slow, running along the corpse-covered path and grabbing Cassandra Skar before she could flee the scene of her attack. They seized both her arms and removed the bloody blade from her fingers. It was a knife she had stolen, rather than a chisel. The others fanned out through the corpses, checking to make sure none of the bandits were faking being hit.

'Bumo,' said Sheplar. 'If you wish to take in the night air for a walk, you would do better asking for an escort from our friends. There are scoundrels abroad who will not treat you as well as we do.'

'I didn't require your help. I would have killed them all,' she snarled. 'Gutter-scum, attempting to manhandle my person. No better than the lower-caste mobs that riot in my district.'

Sheplar remembered his glimpses of Vandia's capital – mountains made of concrete and glass and steel, every bit as high as his peaks. Lady Cassandra had lived in a fortress built to protect her family from the restless mobs that crowded that unnatural place. People swarming like ants; fed and bred beyond humanity's natural limits by the imperium's ceaseless wealth . . . much of it paid for by the slaves' toil in the sky mines.

'Look at this,' said Slell; standing over a bandit corpse he had just finished searching. He held up a small strip of paper the same size as one of the fortune blessings that pilgrims to a wind temple were given when making a small offering, but as Sheplar looked closer, he saw this was no augury of auspicious business dealings. It was a photograph of Cassandra Skar, resplendent in imperial robes that made her resemble a doll. Such pictures were rare in Rodal and the rest of the league, the chemicals to process and capture images hard to come by; as were the skills of photography. Occasionally, a travellers' caravan might rattle through a pass, one of its wagons containing a large box on a tripod along with an artisan who possessed the talents to take a family portrait – usually for an exorbitant price. This photograph must have been taken in the imperium when the bumo was younger, and it could only have ended up here through one route . . . passed on to the usurper's hands by imperial agents.

Sheplar looked at the dead men scattered across the clearing. Only *dressed* as bandits, then; or perhaps they were mercenaries. Such men seemed to fill Weyland now. Thrown off the fields and cast out of their acres by labour-saving machines produced by the king's new mills. 'They were here hunting for the bumo,' said Sheplar. 'They must suspect she is being held in Quehanna.'

'Ironic, then,' said Kerge to Lady Cassandra. 'If you were as quick to listen to these men's words as you were in offering violence, you might be beginning your long journey home by now. If you had merely stayed inside Quehanna, they would have raided the city to rescue you. Your escape attempt tonight has undoubtedly saved many gasks' lives.'

Cassandra looked disgusted by the turn of events as she realized how well she had done her captors' work for them. 'They were fools. Shouting to grab and bind me. They should have prostrated themselves on the ground in front of me. Then I would have known they were sent to serve me.'

'How did they come to know her location?' wondered Sheplar.

'We do not keep the womanling chained inside her room,' said Kerge. 'There are travellers who pass through our roads with eyes to see and tongues to wag, loggers and trappers.'

Sheplar scowled at the young imperial. 'More is the pity. Chains would suit her.'

She flashed him a rude hand sign. 'Now I know I have allies among your local tribes, mountain barbarian. Those who would claim my grandfather's favour. It seems that your country is not so different from the empire, then. Men will do anything for gold here, too.'

'Cutpurses may follow their gold,' said Sheplar. 'I will follow my honour, and we shall see which shines stronger.'

'You need no longer wait upon the council's decision,' said Slell. 'You are not safe as long as you remain in Quehanna. The raiders will come searching for the young human again, and likely swelled by additional numbers when their scouts fail to return.'

Sheplar couldn't deny the imperative of the ranger's logic. *We need to move on.* After crossing half of Pellas to reach the imperium, he'd done enough travelling to last a lifetime. But it seemed a foul wind would blow them a little further, still.

FIVE

THE ROAR OF THE KREVHALLE

Duncan walked with Princess Helrena towards the double doors of the lift that would take the noblewoman down to the staging area before entering the arena, the vast Krevhalle. The largest arena in the capital, Vandis, and by the same token in all of Vandia. Duncan could hear the crowd's roar beyond the walls, like the sea's breaking surf. The people watched images of past combats on the giant kino screens outside, duels fought between celestial-caste nobles as well as the general gladiatorial melees laid on to help keep the capital's restless mobs subdued. Two guardsmen waited at the lift doors, as, for some reason, did Apolleon. He strode forward to meet them.

'I thought you weren't coming to watch the challenge,' said Helrena.

'I had a meeting in the vicinity earlier. I won't be staying for the challenge,' said Apolleon. 'I find these tedious physical entertainments a distraction to my work.'

'Even when you have so much riding on the outcome?' probed Duncan.

'What will be, will be,' said Apolleon. 'One will live, one will die.'

'Forgive me if I say that I find your philosophy far from reassuring at this point,' said Helrena.

'Then perhaps you will find my advice more to your taste,' said Apolleon. 'As the challenged party you will have first choice among the pair of weapon cases presented. The sabres inside the boxes will be identical, but if you look closely, you will see a slight difference in the daggers accompanying the swords . . . one with its pommel shaped as the head of a panther, the second hilt's head shaped as a tiger. Select the dagger with the panther-shaped pommel. I presume you can distinguish between the two animals?'

'Well enough,' said Helrena. 'And why should that be important?'

Apolleon smiled cruelly. 'Let us say that I think the right choice will bring you luck.'

Helrena was about to say more, but they were interrupted by the sound of running footsteps echoing down the narrow corridor. It was Paetro, sprinting towards the lift at full pelt. He pulled to a halt, panting, before passing on his news. 'There has been a substitution of challengers! We should have heard hours ago, but news of the amended contest was "delayed". The tribunal courier was found stuffed dead in an alleyway inside our district.'

Helrena sighed wearily. 'Whom now, if not Machus?'

'You will face Elanthra Skar.'

Duncan knew her. One of Helrena's numerous half-sisters from the emperor's army of children. She had been one of the first allies to switch sides and betray Helrena. But Duncan was more than a little puzzled by the development. 'Why? To what advantage? Isn't Machus stronger?'

'Stronger, certainly,' said Helrena. 'But this is not a brute contest of lifting weights. Elanthra is an expert in sabre and dagger work. One of the best in the celestial caste. Her only rivals are the professionals in the arena who specialize in long-and-short-stab style.'

'Can't you switch class? Choose pistol-and-paces?'

'Not allowed at this stage,' said Apolleon. 'Oh, a most adroit move.'

'We should challenge the substitution,' said Paetro.

Helrena shook her head, grimly. 'Not in this world. The challenge was issued on the basis that my house is unfit to contribute leadership to the punishment squadron. If I withdraw, it will be seen as proof of the house's weakness and broadcast for all to see on screens across the empire. Circae knows I have no choice but to fight.'

'Wheels within wheels,' said Apolleon. 'I give the old whore-keeper her due; she does the great game honour.'

'Some game,' said Duncan.

'Best to think of it as such, lad,' advised Paetro. 'The alternative is to live weighed down with fear and worry every minute of the day.'

'One will live, one must die,' said Helrena, resigned.

Duncan leaned in and whispered in her ear. 'Live,' he said, simply.

'I intend to,' she smiled, speaking softly so that only Duncan could hear her reply. 'But if things go badly, stay close to Paetro.'

Duncan wanted to ask her what she meant, but the lift doors opened and the two imperial guardsmen accompanied her inside. Then the doors slid shut and she was gone.

Apolleon looked at Duncan and Paetro. 'So. We shall see. May our ancestors give us lucky allies and clumsy enemies.' He strode away looking as unconcerned as if he was taking in the air at the imperial gardens. There was something deadly cold about that one. As though his emotions were entirely afterthoughts, expressed only for the benefit of his audience and to allow him to fit in better.

From inside the massive, elliptical arena of the Krevhalle there was no sign of the triumphal arcs, squares and wide boulevards that led up to the structure. The Krevhalle stood six hundred yards high, concentric tiers of seats covered by the greatest dome in the empire. Copper-plated on the outside, mounted at its summit by a stone eagle with its claws clutched around a spherical globe representing the world of Pellas, the dome's interior ceiling was a single massive kino screen. Not showing past entertainments. That was left to a series of vast screens furled like banners around the arena walls. No, the dome's interior rippled with colourful murals, ancient artworks of Vandia's long-forgotten victories; scenes rotating every minute through a sequence of panoramic paintings. The imperium's air fleet hovering over cities burning in bright napalm light, her legions raising the imperial standard over mounds of broken bodies; foreign forces fleeing before galleon-sized armoured vehicles and equine cavalry; cannon and lance, blood and death. Duncan gazed out across the arena; completely packed to capacity this day. Two hundred thousand seats squeezed under the massive dome, tier upon tier with acres of additional standing room behind the electric fences that surrounded the arena's walls; so many spectators breathing that the arena's air misted with its own internal weather system.

Duncan stood at the stadium's north end on the celestial caste's private platform. The wide space was conspicuous for its comforts, servants in tunics circulating around the noble spectators, some seated in deep, cushioned seats and attended to by slaves and staff, others standing, like Duncan, behind the glass barrier that afforded them a high clear view of the challenge below. Paetro aside, there were a few familiar faces from their house that Duncan recognized, but one that stood out.

'Doctor Horvak,' called Duncan, spotting the scientist among the milling courtiers. 'I didn't take you for a follower of blood sports.'

Yair Horvak lifted out his monocle and polished it with one hand, pointing with his spare towards the glowing banner-like screens where images of the crowd flashed. 'I am most assuredly not. Trust me; I would much rather be working. But those with standing in the house's ranks are expected to show their faces here today. The alternative is for the mob to think we believe our cause lost and that we cower behind the Castle of Snakes' walls.'

Duncan glanced towards the marble gallery behind them, its floor running with reflections like a river. Crimson-uniformed hoodsmen stood along the length of the galley, the secret police's more visible guardians. 'We have Apolleon's thugs to protect us.'

'Oh, dear boy,' laughed the doctor, his voluminous girth shaking as he brushed his wild silver beard and raised a bushy eyebrows. 'The hoodsmen are only notionally here to protect us from the mob. The officers' function is similar to the stewards' posts.' Horvak indicated spire-like structures built into the arena walls, circling the vast oval of sand like prayer towers. 'Monstrous amounts of money are wagered on the outcome of the games here. The snipers in the towers execute those foolish enough to invade the arena, flash mirrors into the eyes of the contestants or slip stones into catapults smuggled past the gates. But no common arena guard could be permitted to gun down a member of the celestial caste – who knows what assassinations might be attempted in that manner? So the hoodsmen behind us stand ready to execute any noble caught violating duelling law and interfering with the challenge's outcome.'

So, the emperor's law applied to all. Apart from Emperor Jaelis Skar himself, of course. Duncan remembered his last terrifying visit to the diamond palace alongside Cassandra and the princess. The paranoid, skittish emperor taking fright and gunning down a delegation of visiting dignitaries bearing tribute. 'Nobody here cheats, then?'

Doctor Horvak shrugged. 'Nobody is *caught*.'

Duncan listened to the crowd baying, hooting with encouragement, large sections chanting songs at each other. 'They sound as if they actually care.'

'Everyone from our district is here or watching the challenge on the screens of Vandis,' said the doctor. 'What is the saying? They have a dog in this fight, too. If the house falls, our district will be divided up, the fattest slices going to Circae and her allies. The millions of citizens we're responsible for will be expected to switch fealty to other princelings. Those with good positions in our manufactories and businesses and mills will be demoted to make way for the new incumbent's favourites. Even those on the dole, the gratis imperium, will have to scramble for fresh ration cards and fight like dogs to make sure they aren't allocated worse rooms in fouler slums. And that is if it's an *orderly* transfer. If Circae's allies fall out over the choicer spoils, then you can factor in months of bloody violence and skirmishing to any handover.'

All that riding on a single challenge. *And so much more.* If Helrena fell, who would give a damn if Lady Cassandra was returned alive? She would become the notional fig-leaf the punishment squadron was flying out to avenge. Nobody outside of their house wanted a live heir standing in the way of appropriating Helrena's holdings. If Cassandra was rescued alive, the little girl wouldn't stay that way for long. The best that could happen was Circae would claim custody of her granddaughter and use the poor girl to lend an air of legitimacy to the looting of the spoils. And that was a dangerously poor *best*.

'I don't want to lose Helrena,' whispered Duncan. 'I can't. Not now.'

'A word of advice,' said the doctor. 'I know that you have been given your papers; that you are a citizen now rather than a slave. But it would still be better for you to think of the princess as *employer*, rather than anything more intimate.'

'Helrena cares for me, I know she does.'

'You are not celestial caste. The princess cares first and foremost for her house and if she ever takes another husband, it will be an alliance of political necessity. Powerful lords do not care to keep potential cuckolders around, however long and loyal a servant's previous service. Your best fate in that unhappy event would be a new life in a rabble tower inside our district, a ration card and an empty existence spent watching kino screens while trying to steer clear of the street gangs.'

'I'm a free man now.'

The doctor nodded towards the baying crowds. 'They are also citizens for the most part. And the only real difference is that we wait over here on marble, and the mob occupies the cheap seats.'

'I think you are somewhat cleverer than they.'

'How kind of you to say. In possession of a clearer mind, perhaps. But I am not quite clever enough to be safe in my homeland surrounded by family, rather than standing here in an imperial arena praying for the better of two outcomes.'

'Helrena said something about sticking close to Paetro if things go badly.'

The doctor nodded. 'Paetro has a number of helos sitting ready to evacuate us to the house's holdings on the eastern frontier. To wait it out until matters are settled inside the capital.' Horvak indicated the crowds filling their side of the arena. 'If the princess loses the challenge, you will not wish to dally outside the arena. There will be many thousands of severely disappointed citizens spilling out onto the streets of Vandis keen to rip us apart to make their own suffering briefly more tolerable.'

Without Helrena, maybe it would be better if they did? But who would be left alive to keep Cassandra safe, then? He and Paetro would try, surely? There had to be a way they could sign up with the punishment squadron. Thousands of soldiers would soon be shipping out to Weyland. Duncan glanced back, up towards the only level of the arena more luxurious and exclusive than this. The imperial box stood empty. Whatever the Emperor Jaelis's business today, it wasn't here at the Krevhalle. Two of his numerous offspring were about to murder each other over power and territory and petty jealousies . . . but such events occurred weekly here. It was a salutary reminder of how small Duncan's concerns stood in the scope of the greater imperium. To

Duncan, his entire world was at stake. To the imperium, this was just another day at the arena.

Horvak nodded towards the spectators on their side. 'Trouble, my boy. You might wish to make yourself scarce.'

Trouble? Duncan cursed as he saw who the scientist had indicated. Of course *she* would be here. Adella Cheyenne had a dog in this fight too, but on the rival side. Of all the Weylanders to have remained behind when most of the survivors had escaped back home, it had to be the woman he had once so foolishly loved . . . a long time and far too many treacheries ago.

Duncan scowled at Adella. 'You have a nerve coming here to watch this.'

'That's unfair, Duncan. I travel where Baron Machus takes me. Unlike you, I haven't been given my freedom. I'm still a slave.'

Duncan stared at the spectators. He couldn't see Machus in the throng, but the platform was filling up with imperial nobles and their entourages now. Those on Helrena's side, or those who opposed her and supported Helrena's scheming mother-in-law, Circae.

'I know what you did when you visited our castle, slipping the traitor a device to bring our defences down. I nearly died protecting Lady Cassandra when Circae's assassins attacked us.'

'I heard that act of stupidity earned you your freedom,' said Adella. At least the Weyland woman didn't have the nerve to deny the role she had played in trying to destroy them. 'You should be thanking me.'

'You're joking! I could forgive you betraying me – it wasn't exactly the first time, was it? But Cassandra's just a little girl!'

'Circae never intended any harm to the precious little brat,' said Adella. 'The assassins had orders to seize the girl and bring her to Circae, not murder her.'

'What about Princess Helrena? She rescued you from the sky mines. She passed you into the care of her cousin.'

'Care?' Her voice fell to a whisper as she glanced around to make sure they were not being overheard. 'How can you call anything that beast Baron Machus does to me *care*? What about the bloody princess? What are their squabbles to you? Machus fights Helrena, Helrena battles Circae, Helrena confronts Elanthra. A pox on all their houses.

They can murder each other in their stupid, endless feuds until the empire's one big graveyard. I didn't ask to be grabbed by skel slavers and sold at the end of the world to the imperium. Do you think I give a lump of horse shit about what happens to the baron? I'm just a pretty bauble to him. To be toyed with and discarded when he gets bored. Just like you and the princess.'

'It's not like that—'

'Oh, Duncan. You're not that big a fool, are you? A free citizen here is just what the upper caste calls the slave who happens to have been born inside the empire. They're fed and watered like farm animals, worked when they're needed, and culled when they're not.' She pointed to the roaring multitude beyond the almost invisible glass barrier. 'There they are, free citizens all. You're a single droplet of water in the ocean. You're nothing to the empire's rulers and you'll never be more.'

'You know what the real irony is?' spat Duncan. 'If you hadn't got your ticket out of the sky mines by betraying Carter's escape attempt, you would have been on the mining station during the slave revolt. You'd have left with them. You'd be home in Weyland now, strolling the streets of Northhaven and all of this just a bad memory.'

'Perhaps. Or maybe I'd be one of the corpses covered in volcanic ash in the mines' shadow. You still think you're better than me, don't you? So quick to judge. Heir to the mighty Landor fortune back home. The princess's lapdog, here. None of it earned by you. Well, you could be searching for a new kennel, soon, Duncan Landor.'

Her words bit home. 'We'll see. Send word when Machus gets bored of you and wants a new mistress. Maybe I'll buy you myself. The castle's barracks can always use a whore who knows her way around on her back.'

'Better that than a fool who doesn't even know they're a whore.'

'I *chose* to be here.'

'Then you're the biggest fool of them all.' She patted her belly, and for the first time, Duncan noticed the bump below her red silk dress. 'And soon you won't even be the only Weylander freed as a citizen inside the imperium. When I give the baron an heir, he'll make me a gift of my papers. It wouldn't do to have the mother of one of his sons occupying the lowest caste in the empire, would it?'

Duncan reeled back, astonished. 'You're pregnant?'

'You see, there is still something a *mere* slave can do better than you. I'll have a real position inside the baron's house. Secured by blood. Not subject to the whims of that ruthless cow you follow around.'

How could he have been so blind for so long? It was suddenly clear to Duncan, now. All the moments the two of them had snatched together in the grounds of his estate at Hawkland Park, their late-night assignations. Adella refusing to run away with Duncan to build a new life together far away from his overbearing father. To start again from scratch. Duncan had never mattered a damn to her, only his position and inheritance. This was exactly what Adella had been trying to do to him back home. A chancer attempting to marry into a fortune. To snare him. 'You and the baron deserve each other!'

'That's funny,' said Adella, 'I was about to say the same thing about you and your royal bitch.' The woman strode angrily away, quickly lost inside the swarm of nobles and their retainers.

Doctor Horvak reappeared, having been hanging back, a concerned look on his face. 'Do not judge her too harshly.'

Duncan snorted. 'Circae's assassins nearly murdered you in the castle, too. She's the one who opened the door for them.'

'Unlike yourself, I have lived alongside the empire throughout my life. I understand the imperium all too well. The only choice slaves have here is to say yes and choose survival, or disagree and embrace a usually unpleasant end. Would you have had the girl refuse Machus when the baron decided to swap sides and betray his family? She would be dead, as would the new life swelling inside her body.'

Beyond the glass barrier, the crowd erupted with excitement. Portions of the arena floor were sliding back, Helrena and Elanthra rising into the open space. They were tiny in the vast floor, built to accommodate mass battles between hundreds of fighters, war as sport and spectacle. Stewards stood by, ready to offer the long wooden weapon cases, each containing a sabre and dagger. Medical staff advanced with hypodermics and surgical devices to ensure neither party had been doped. The testing was done quickly, and then the stewards offered Princess Helrena her choice of cases to select her killing tools.

Duncan ignored the portentous drone of the challenge commentator warbling over the speakers, treating the coming brutal combat with the fake solemnity of a church ritual. 'Perhaps, Doctor, but how well did Adella choose in the sky mines? Friends of ours were executed when she sold out the escape plot; people we knew, our neighbours, people we had grown up with. All of that, just to leave the mine and become a house slave?'

'She is too young to choose better. She must have been terrified.'

'It's our decisions that define us,' said Duncan. 'Trust me; Adella knows what she's doing. She's probably the only one of us snatched from Weyland who did.'

'We fight to survive and prosper.' The doctor sighed. 'And not just in the slave caste, it would seem. The challenge begins.'

Duncan gazed through the barrier separating their platform from the arena sands below. The banner-shaped screens had stopped showing shots of the baying crowds and moved their focus to the two women. At this distance the two combatants were just black dots, tiny on the sand. But the screens showed everything. The look of deadly calm on Helrena's face, the pinched malice facing her in the form of her half-sister, Elanthra's pale gaze focused on her challenger, both women warily circling each other, a sabre clutched tight in their right hand and a dagger swaying in the left. Elanthra said something to her half-sister, but Duncan couldn't hear either the words or Helrena's response, accompanied by a shake of the head – both exchanges too far from any microphone, lost among the encouraging roars of bloodlust from the crowd and the echoing commentary from the chief adjudicating steward. Duncan tried to clear his head of what Adella had just told him, his burning renewed hatred of her. *This is all that matters now. The future, not the past.* The life he had hewn for himself here, dangling by the thinnest of threads.

Helrena and her half-sister began the combat like a dance, shifting and circling, each making feints to try and draw the other out. It seemed almost choreographed, as if this were a pre-arranged show and not a real duel. But it wasn't. They had both been expertly trained, and neither of them would commit unless they could draw blood, so the false attacks and retreats continued, the crowd's roar rising and fading with each pass. Both women fought unarmoured, wearing white silk-like material wound around their bodies like bandages, all the better to show their wounds for the crowds and the audience to track and follow the challenge's deadly progress. It didn't take long before the first crimson lines stained the clothes. Elanthra drew a cut across Helrena's right arm, the princess a fraction of a second too slow to turn her opponent's blade as the feint became real. Helrena's lips pursed in pain and she drew back as they pivoted smoothly around each other, sabres held high in the right hand above their heads with daggers offered in the left, quivering, like locust antennae trying to sense the direction of the next attack to parry. Encouraged by the initial blood, Elanthra grew bolder, and a couple more flicks of her sabre saw additional crimson stains added to the marks along Helrena's twists of silk – one to the princess's shoulder and another to her leg. Duncan was amazed Helrena's rival struck as fast as she did. Elanthra stood thin and bony. Facing the woman must be like defending against a serpent-fast skeleton. The fight went on in a similar fashion for ten minutes, no fatal wounds, but glancing cuts traded five to one in their foe's favour, and even the Weylander could see that poor Helrena was flagging now. Blood loss, perhaps? In the duels back at Northgate, the cut and thrust of clashing steels was savage, short and brutal; but not often intentionally to the death . . . rather, meant as blunt punishment. If an opponent was killed and the murder publicized, the prefecture's constables would come riding for you quick enough. This arena fighting was highly tutored art; too expertly matched to end quickly with a ring of onlookers rushing in to protect a badly wounded friend or family member. Hell, the crowd would probably rip anyone apart who tried, even if the snipers in the steward towers didn't drop them first.

Duncan heard a braying sound of amusement from the crowd to his side. It was Baron Machus, the princess's hulking treacherous cousin, cheering on Elanthra. The rumours were that the two were lovers, but a more mismatched pairing Duncan could hardly imagine, like a bull and a sickly peahen mating. And the bull should have possessed the courage to face Helrena in the duel, rather than slipping his more proficient lover into his place at the last moment.

Duncan bridled at the insufferable arrogance of the nobleman. Selling out his cousin, then cheering on her death as though this was a horse race. 'That should be you down there, if you had the guts, Baron!'

The doctor reached out to quieten Duncan but it was too late, the baron's attention had been diverted from the challenge, both duellists separated by stewards as trumpets marked a brief rest break. The break was unnecessary, but helped draw out the spectacle for the clamouring mob. Extra stewards sprinted out onto the sands, setting up colourful, quickly erected tents where water could be swigged in relative privacy, out of sight of the loud, jeering multitude.

'So, Helrena's pup is still yapping,' said Machus. 'Swaggering like a citizen with a sky miner's dust still fresh on his servant's breeches. If you had done a little better protecting Lady Cassandra during the slave revolt, perhaps there wouldn't be a punishment squadron being assembled and your mistress's guts wouldn't be about to be spilt into the sand.'

Duncan felt a flash of anger burning across him, his fingers twitching for the ceremonial steel dagger of an imperial citizen hanging from his belt.

'Don't be tempted, lad,' said Paetro, appearing at Duncan and the doctor's side from the crowd of onlookers. He raised his voice loud enough for Machus and his entourage to hear. 'The baron knows the hoodsmen will gun down anyone foolish enough to start an unlicensed duel on the emperor's neutral ground. Find someone else to taunt to their end, Machus. Or better yet, make it formal and have the balls to actually step onto the sands yourself.'

'And here was I thinking the good doctor was in possession of all the brains inside your house,' laughed Machus. 'Yes, Horvak's knowledge is a prize worth having. I'm not sure if there will be a place for you, though, Paetro Barca, in the new order. You've got a habit of always being on the wrong side. You're unlucky. That's a poor trait in a soldier.'

'Maybe it's because I don't switch sides every time the wind blows in a different direction,' said Paetro. 'Or maybe it's because I can't afford to buy women to use as blade catchers when the action heats up.'

Machus's face grew crimson at that last insult, but a tall blond nobleman Duncan didn't recognize appeared to pull the fuming baron away. The newcomer shrugged at Duncan, Paetro and the doctor. 'We'll settle this through the law and the challenge, soon enough.'

The stranger disappeared into the crowd as armoured housemen from both sides interposed themselves along the middle of the elites' viewing gallery. Battle lines had been not so subtly drawn inside the gallery, for and against Princess Helrena, a division as stark as in the arena below. It was all too noticeable how few allies remained alongside their house.

'There's a lie if ever I heard one,' spat Paetro. 'If we win, Circae will never let this rest here. She will keep coming at the house until either Helrena is made a corpse, or she is.'

Duncan had a feeling the soldier was correct. 'Who's the baron's friend?'

Doctor Horvak peered at the man Duncan had singled out through his monocle. 'That's Gyal Skar. Just as Apolleon supports Prince Helrena's cause for the imperial throne in its imminent vacancy, Prince Gyal is Circae's choice as the next emperor.'

'*Choice*,' snarled Paetro. 'There's more to it than that. I swear it. It's whispered in the capital that Circae gave birth to a child in secret and ensured the boy was swapped in the cot for one of the emperor's real newborns, with the poor devil of a true princeling made ashes inside an incinerator to remove any evidence of the crime. Gyal's supposed mother died in a convenient helo crash before his first birthday and after that the lad was raised in Circae's orbit.'

'I thought the empire's surgical machinery could be used to test if an heir is true or a cuckoo?' said Duncan.

'That it may,' said the doctor, 'but the identifying features of an individual's blood can be over-written using high medicine, and it is said the imperial surgeons have such techniques hoarded among their secret knowledge. The code of the blood is like a book whose letters can be changed and swapped around by a competent forger. Whether the rumour about the prince can be substantiated or not, I cannot say. It is certainly true that Circae dotes on Prince Gyal as if he were her own flesh and blood. But then, she has lost one genuine son... Helrena's husband, the tragedy of which finds us standing here today. Perhaps Prince Gyal is a proxy for Circae's maternal feelings.'

'The witch has no feelings,' spat Paetro. 'I don't need your damn high medicine to confirm that one way or the other. Circae is capable of anything. Princess Helrena is the best chance Circae has of recovering her granddaughter alive, but Circae would sooner see Helrena face down in the arena and our house sliced up like old pork roast to scatter to the hyenas than support her in the court.'

But if the bodyguard's scurrilous tale of scandal had a grain of truth, maybe sacrificing a granddaughter from a daughter-in-law she hated to see a closet son ascend the imperial throne . . . perhaps that was the kind of blood offering Circae was willing to make. Duncan was more determined than ever to rescue Cassandra and see her safely home. 'Circae isn't here to watch the fight?'

'Easier to divide the spoils if you're not seen to directly wield the dagger,' said Doctor Horvak.

'Not that she's fooling anyone with her absence,' said Paetro. 'Just observing the forms, is all.'

Duncan's attention was caught by a blast of trumpets from the arena's speakers. The challenge in the Krevhalle was about to restart. Numbers flashed across banner-long screens, imposed above the dance of death the two daughters of the imperium had recently put on for the mob, the combat's moving images slowed to a crawl as a hidden orchestra blasted out a portentous hymn heavy with deep drumbeats. Duncan realized the numbers weren't a count-down to restarting the duel, but the current gambling odds. And looking at the betting, frankly, the wagers weren't flowing in their favour.

Both women emerged from their tents and stood facing each other. A steward raised a pistol in the air and fired to begin the next bout. Elanthra didn't waste a second. She lunged forward with her sabre, but Helrena managed to catch the blow between the crossed blades of her sabre and dagger, shoving Elanthra away, a glancing cut to their foe's shoulder as Helrena's dagger sliced across silk and forced her enemy's own blades against her skin. A single wound among a handful, though; while Helrena's white swathed form was a mass of bloody bandages, not a limb untouched and dripping red. This duel was literally a death of a thousand cuts.

'The mistress is too slow on her bad leg,' growled Paetro. 'Elanthra's marked the limp. Look how she always strikes against Helrena's wounded side, where she can't cover quickly enough. Damn, but I warned the mistress to wait long enough to recover.'

'The celestial caste's prerogative to ignore our advice,' said Duncan, trying to disguise his fear over how badly this was going.

'Don't have to be born a princess of the imperium to do that, just being a woman will do.'

Duncan wondered if the soldier was thinking of his dead daughter. Poor Paetro. He felt a wave of compassion for the man. Duty and honour were all that he had been left with, and if Helrena fell here today, who would his friend owe that to anymore? Who would Duncan, for that matter?

Helrena and Elanthra circled each other, daggers moving as though they were tracing invisible runes in the air, sabres held as high as a scorpion sting. Helrena moved first this time, seeing some subtle sign, an opening in her enemy's defence that Duncan failed to see, either through lack of art or his distance from the duel. Helrena lunged forward and whirled the blade around in a move that would have sliced Elanthra in half if it had connected, but it didn't. Elanthra had already moved, her whip-thin body stepping to the side and pivoting to deliver a bone-cracking kick to Helrena's bad leg, exactly where the worst of the wound had been taken during the revolt. She had either marked her foe's weakness well, or been supplied the tip by a spy. Helrena tried to step back, avoiding Elanthra's counter-strike, but her bad leg seemed to fold under her and as Elanthra lunged again, the only way Helrena could avoid being skewered was to crumple under the strike and fall to the ground. Duncan moaned and he heard Paetro bite back a shout of anger by his side. Helrena had lost her dagger on her left while her sabre had fallen to her right, Duncan's lover scrambling back in the sand as Elanthra swung her sabre down to disembowel the princess.

SIX

THE TRAP OF HOME

Willow sat in the library, oil lamps throwing a warm orange glow across her newspapers as she carefully turned the pages. Her body might be confined inside the house; but given the papers her mind swooped free. It obviously hadn't occurred to Leyla Holten that the library had standing subscriptions with the Northhaven stationers that could be cancelled, otherwise Willow had no doubt the malicious fortune hunter would have taken great pleasure in denying them to Willow. Although that would have entailed the harpy setting foot in a library for something other than seducing the nearest available male, which was probably, on balance, beyond her. These news sheets were weeks old, freighted up from the capital, Arcadia, by the Guild of Rails. Willow's main interest these days was comparing how the nationals' views differed from the local newspapers' stories. It was obvious that the press in the industrial south was in bed with King Marcus and his allies: every story and editorial cast doubt on Prince Owen's identity. An impostor, they thundered, a rescued slave whose mind had snapped during too many harsh years in captivity. The conservative, rural north was still free-thinking enough to print the testimony of retainers and civil servants who'd known the old royal family before their unfortunate 'accident', swearing that Prince Owen *was* the heir they had looked after, a boy now grown into a man. It was growing increasingly clear to Willow that this controversy had divided the nation along pre-existing political fault-lines. The citizens of the north which the Gaiaist Party relied on were its pastoral heartland, pitted against the Mechanicalist Party of the great southern cities. Mill owners against land owners, industrial lords against country lords, conservatives against radicals, guild against guild; the same old sniping that had been going on in the national assembly for centuries. So far, none of the papers had reported that the resources being used to industrialize weren't travelling along the caravan route, but were being supplied by the imperium to King Marcus in return for making his state a slave farm. King Marcus had all the new wealth of the kingdom on his side; Prince Owen wielded only the truth and a superior claim to the succession. Which faction would win?

Willow sighed in exasperation. Mechanisation had caused turmoil, the delicate balance of man and nature so valued by the Gaiaists upended with the trickle of metals made a torrent; everywhere workers displaced from the fields and heading for the cities, the king and his allies growing wealthier than anyone in the country's history, apportioning mill licences and largesse in return for a slice of ever-increasing profits. Willow had never known anything like it and nor had Weyland. The country had become like a prize pig bred for competition, force-fed food until its body swelled to unnatural limits. Her home was, Willow realized, in a small way, beginning to ape their secret master, Vandia. The imperium was so rich it could buy anything, including the slaves it needed to die in harness to keep the empire rich beyond the dreams of avarice. They were becoming a ghost of Vandia, a pale reflection, just as the covetous King Marcus had made himself a second-rate imitation of the Vandian emperor. Willow was stunned by her sudden insight, the new labour laws passed into statute for factory owners thrown into a shocking new light. Indentured servitude to help mill owners absorb the masses being thrown off the farms . . . and it was being heralded as a solution to help the starving unemployed; unfortunate families provided with food, clothing, lodgings in return for working for free for a term of ten years. What was that law but a mannerly form of slavery? And a single decade could easily become five at the stroke of a pen on a government charter. What was the nickname the few dissenting newspapers in the north had given the king? *Bad Marcus*. Never was a title so well earned. She'd heard that a gang of thugs in the pay of loyalist mill-owners had been dispatched to the leading opposition title to smash its printing presses. They'd done the job thoroughly, removing all the lead type used to spell out Marcus's name so they could never abuse the usurper again, before setting fire to the premises.

I've escaped the imperium, and all my miseries as a slave, only to find the empire being rebuilt in miniature here by the shores of the Lancean Ocean. They had to fight. *She* had to fight. Willow had to tell someone. The door opened and she nearly jumped out of her chair, her reverie broken. She had nothing to tell *him.*

Nocks leered at her, the stocky manservant grinning. 'Thought you might be here, petal. I can see why you fancy the pastor's son. Two book-botherers together, a match made in heaven, eh?'

'Unless you've come here to dust the shelves, why don't you push off,' said Willow. 'My attentions are occupied with something more important than your fripperies.'

'Fripperies? That sounds like a right good word. Maybe you've got a dictionary around here I can look it up in. But first—' He pulled out a soggy envelope and slapped it down across her desk. 'I'll thank you to show me a little more in the way of your famous northern manners, given I'm kindly acting the part of postman for you today.'

'What is this?'

'Got it out of the maid's pockets. The woman was found bobbing under the river ice by the weir.'

'What?' A terrible gnawing horror dawned on Willow as she processed the unpleasant servant's words.

'Silly cow; looks like she tried to cross the lower brook last night rather than leaving the estate by the main gate. The ice cracked and she went under and drowned. Eleanor, I think her name was. Mistress reckons she was trying to lift some of the silver from the house. Thieving bitch had this letter on her, though. Ink's run, but we could just make out your name on the front. Thought it might belong to you.'

Willow lifted up the sopping paper envelope, her letter to Carter and the pastor rendered into illegible papier-mâché apart from her faded signature on the front. 'She's *dead*?'

'Course she is. Not a fish, was she? You can have a gander at her corpse if you like. It's in the outhouse behind the kitchen until the undertaker's cart arrives from Northhaven to carry her away. Still as hard and cold as a block of ice. But that's winter for you. Reckon she'll stay like that until the spring melt.'

Tears ran down Willow's face, guilt and horror rising up inside her. *My fault, this was my fault.* 'Eleanor can't have drowned down there . . . the ice is too thick.'

'Oh, but the world's like that,' smiled Nocks. 'One minute you're here, carefree as a bird, and the next the world's opened up beneath you and swallowed you whole. But you and I know that, don't we?' He ran a finger down his hideous scar. 'Me sporting this. You being carried off by slave traders. The ice can *always* crack below your boots, wherever you are.' He raised a fist and pretended to bang an imaginary sheet of ice hanging above his head. 'Help. Help me.'

'Get out!' yelled Willow, throwing her chair back. '*Get out*!'

'No gratitude in your bones, girly,' laughed Nocks, backing away. 'Thank me later for bringing you your post. Don't you worry about matters; it'll just make it all the sweeter when you come around to my way of thinking.'

Willow picked up a paperweight from the desk and hurled it at the door as Nocks shut it, then she collapsed behind the table. Her newspapers fluttered in the rush of air from her body, all the kingdom's problems held in their pages, rendered small and inconsequential by the manservant's hideous news, its mocking delivery. How had Eleanor died couriering the message? It didn't make sense. Willow only knew one thing for sure, and that was that the maid and her unborn child had died trying to help her. Two lives gone, just like that, plus a living hell for Eleanor's husband as long as he lived. *What have I done*?

Nocks was halfway down the corridor when Leyla Landor appeared. 'How did she take the news?'

'Not well,' grunted Nocks. 'Floods of tears and a good bit of guilt to go with it.'

'Excellent.'

'I do hope it's worth it,' said Nocks. 'Having the death seem like an accident. I could've slit the maid's treacherous throat and made it look like she'd run into a gang of highwaymen.'

'And heartily enjoyed yourself before you took a knife to the girl? You're a wicked fellow . . . I really don't know why I keep you around. An accident leaves nobody for Willow to blame but herself. If outlaws had murdered her maid, Willow would hold the gang responsible. I wager her time as a slave left her able to hate quite adequately. She's used to seeing death – not so used to causing it, I suspect.'

'Hating adequately? Not a problem for either of us,' said Nocks. 'A little revenge is good for the soul.'

'All in good time, you horny devil. It's time to accelerate our plans for Benner's daughter,' said Leyla. 'A good marriage will serve all of our interests.'

'And here's me thinking it was going to be a bad one?'

'Willow's husband-to-be's not so bad. Voracious between the sheets, of course, but what man isn't, given the chance?' She reached out to brush Nocks' hair and he shivered at her subtle, knowing touch. 'He'll beat out whatever spirit's left in Willow that we haven't broken. And, if she's lucky, after that maybe he'll sate his appetites on his mistresses rather than her.'

'You're sure old man Landor will go along with the plan?'

'A noble title for his daughter?' smiled Leyla. 'It's what the old fool's always yearned for, and that's the secret of managing Benner Landor. Give him what he wants, not what he needs.' She rubbed her belly. 'First a loving virile wife; then a male heir on the way. Next, a high-born match for his out-of-favour little bitch.'

'How fast can we move?' asked Nocks.

'As quickly as we can. There's a visitor arrived in town who'll be able to help us.'

'You should be thanking Willow,' said Nocks. 'The way she abandoned her brother. What would you've done if Duncan Landor was still hanging around, blocking your new brat's inheritance?'

'Oh, slept with him . . . had you arrange a fatal fall from his horse. Maybe both in quick succession. His portraits make him look like quite the young buck. It'd be nice to think at least one of the Landors was capable of making a woman bite the pillow.'

'The old man doesn't tickle your fancy? You're a right good actress, then,' said Nocks.

'Of course I am. Around a pig like Benner Landor, nothing else will do.'

'I dare say the old man's vast fortune helps,' said Nocks.

Leyla smiled, a cold, cobra's grin. 'Well, it certainly can't hurt, can it?'

Carter glanced around; checking the patrol of armed retainers had rounded the corner before sprinting from behind the hedge towards the house. Benner Landor wasn't taking any chances with his security. Given how many dangerous wanderers were on the road these days, that was a wise decision. The oil lanterns' light swaying in the guards' hands grew dim and he started to climb. In Carter's childhood, he and Duncan Landor had treated Hawkland Park's rooftop escarpments as their private fiefdom, climbing its chimneys and scaling skylights and sloping attic roofs like a pair of red squirrels. Who would have thought that he'd be putting his knowledge of the Landor grounds to this use?

Carter shrugged off the wind on high, iron drainpipes which creaked as they took his weight. The roof tiles were slippery and silver with frost, but he kept his footing until he reached the wing where Willow roomed, and swung himself down outside her window, rapping on the pane of glass, three long raps, three short. Carter waited for the window to open, then Willow helped pull him through the thick winter curtain, her face a muddle of warring emotions – hope, fear, sadness, longing. *Something is definitely wrong.* He hadn't seen Willow this upset since their wicked life-and-death existence inside the sky mines. That was when he noticed the anteroom beyond. She hadn't just bolted the door to the corridor in the house; she'd dragged a couch across the doorway to barricade herself in for the night. *What the hell's going on here?*

'What is it?'

'Everything,' blurted Willow, before unburdening herself . . . the maid's accident, Willow's torments at her stepmother's hands and imprisonment inside the grounds of Hawkland Park.

'You're right, it doesn't make sense,' said Carter, after Willow's voice slowed and she stopped confessing her troubles. 'I crossed the brook myself to sneak up to the house. It's frozen solid. And anyone with half a brain tests the ice first. See if it cracks before you walk on it. Eleanor hadn't been drinking had she, trying to find the courage to help you in a bottle of whisky?'

'No!' said Willow, outraged. 'She wouldn't. Eleanor was carrying a baby, Carter. Two people died out there trying to help me, trying to—'

Carter cut her off. 'It doesn't feel right. There's more to this than meets the eye, I can feel it in my bones.' Carter's sixth sense bordered on the supernatural these days. Heightened vigilance after having survived the horrors of life as a slave; a life where every minor mistake or infraction could mean death? Or something stranger after the many bizarre experiences he'd endured: his mad visions after falling into the Vandian volcano and the brief joining of minds with that sly old road-sorcerer, Sariel?

Willow sunk onto her bed, burying her head in her hands. 'I thought it was odd, too. But I wasn't sure if this was my fault, or if there is more to it. Or is that just my guilt, trying to find someone else to blame. I don't know what to think anymore.'

'Let's make her end mean something, then,' said Carter. 'Just like being back in the sky mines. When one of us drops we don't give up, we go on.'

Willow rubbed the tears from her eyes, and Carter could almost see her body filling with a new-found purpose, laying aside the self-pity she'd allowed to wrack her. This woman had done the same for him back in the sky mines, more than once. The two of them shared a bond far greater than love and heart. It was the connection of having survived the worst possible together and lived to see the light on the other side.

'You're right,' Willow sighed. 'This isn't helping anyone. Eleanor would kick me in the pants if she could see me like this. You need to ride to the magistrates in town, obtain a court injunction to take me out of the park. I'll write you an affidavit swearing that I'm being restrained here by my stepmother against my will.'

'Damn the courts,' said Carter. 'You're coming with me tonight.

I'll take you back to the rectory. Tomorrow we can head out for the woods, join Sheplar and the little imperial girl.'

'You don't know what Leyla Holten is capable of,' said Willow. '*That* woman will lie. She'll say that you've kidnapped me. We'll have enough trouble on our hands without the local constables hunting for us across half the prefecture. We have to do this legally.'

'Your stepmother's less than spit on the wind,' said Carter. 'We escaped the imperium together, remember? Legions and soldiers and warships and the volcano's dead zone. We crossed more miles than there are heads of corn in your father's fields. What's Leyla Holten compared to that? Just a southern fortune-hunter on the make.'

'She's the mistress of this house . . . and she's pregnant as well. A boy, she claims.'

'Pregnant?' Carter had to choke down an amused snort. Who would have thought old Benner Landor still had it in him? An heir to replace Willow's brother, he hadn't wasted much time. 'Then your father shouldn't kick up too much when you leave with me.'

'You don't know my father as well as you think you do, then. If we defy him, even if it suits that cow Holten's plans, there'll be hell to pay. Benner Landor won't let anyone make a fool of him. Just the fact leaving here'd make me happy will probably be enough for it to be forbidden.'

'There was a day when I let people tell me what to do and think and be,' said Carter. 'It was a long time ago. I defied an empire to be with you. An old man who thinks he can own all the land to the horizon and a gold-digger young enough to be his daughter? They can both keep it. You're all I need. And I have news of my own. Prince Owen's sent word from the capital . . . a guild courier came into town carrying a coded warning. Owen believes the king's running out of time down south and needs to make his move quick. He's hunting for Lady Cassandra to keep the imperium sweet. Things are going to come to a head around here real fast, now.'

'Does your father know?'

'Gave him the news before I sneaked out to you. The local prefect's flown into town. Dad met him in the cathedral and reckons he's up to his neck in the conspiracy. Probably arrived to give orders to whatever killers the king's paying to do his dirty work. You've got to come with me tonight. It won't be long before ex-slaves are being snatched from the town and tortured to find out where the emperor's girl is stashed. You're not safe here anymore. Anybody we stay with isn't exactly safe, either.'

'Sweet saints,' groaned Willow. 'Bandits wouldn't attack the estate, would they? We've dozens of armed guards and all the servants have been practising drills with rifles and swords.'

'King Marcus made sure Northhaven's troops were posted well away when the slave traders flew in before,' said Carter. 'And he arranged that just for a cut of their spoils. I don't think he'd shy away from letting bandits murder everyone in Northhaven to shore up his rule. He's backed up against the wall now.'

'Please God, let the assembly vote in favour of Owen's claim,' said Willow. 'A new king and all of our problems will be over.'

'Maybe,' said Carter. He sure prayed that's how things would go; but he reckoned Weyland's current ruler wouldn't go quietly if the assembly demanded he abdicate. 'You know how the saying goes: "hope for the best and prepare for the worst". Leave Hawkland Park with me. For our future and the sake of everyone here. I know I'm not much . . . a poor pastor's son with a trade I'm not much suited to; no property to my name, just the clothes on my back and, it seems, a bunch of real powerful enemies at court.'

'That's more than enough for me,' said Willow. 'I've never cared a whit for land or money or power, and what enemies you have, we share. I'd sooner be by your side in a simple log cabin than inside the greatest estate of the kingdom's wealthiest house without you.'

Carter reopened the window. 'Let me save you from all this disgusting luxury, then, Miss Landor. You can ditch all your servants and silk dresses and silver cutlery; swap hot baths for bathing in cold forest streams; trade stuffed swan breast and honey-roasted pork for snared wood pigeon and hare.'

'Sold,' said Willow, with a faint smile. 'It beats Vandian gruel any day.' She went to a large wooden wardrobe, opened the door and removed a warm brown fur-lined coat that wouldn't have disgraced a mountain trapper. After she'd put it on, she bent down and fiddled inside the back of the wardrobe. There was a click and Willow dipped her hand deep inside, returning with a canvas bag swelled with coins.

'You been helping those highwaymen attacking travellers?' asked Carter.

Willow shook her head, sadly. 'The week we came back from Vandia, I went to town and sold most of the jewellery my mother left me when she died.'

'You didn't have to do that.'

'I'm not a fool, Carter Carnehan. I knew we'd be in danger the moment we arrived home with the true king, carrying the secret that the usurper's court was trading our people for the imperium's riches. If my mother was alive and given the choice between a live daughter and a well-accessorized dead one, I know which she'd choose. The pieces I kept on top of my dresser have disappeared, anyway. The cow's been sending her foul little manservant into my rooms when I'm not around, stealing anything that's not nailed down and fencing it in town. But nobody knew about this wardrobe. My mother had the hidden compartment made for me before she died.'

'A girl has to have secrets,' said Carter, a saying that Mary Carnehan often used to bring out and dust off when her son had been asking too many questions.

'I wish we didn't know the king's,' said Willow. She slipped the coat on, pushing the coins into a pocket. 'No, actually, I take that back. I *am* glad we know what King Marcus's capable of; it's the only way we're going to end his reign. Let's go.' She gazed around her room for a last time, wistfully.

'Anything else you want to take?'

'Only my memories. Damned if this has been any kind of home to me since Leyla Holten arrived. I lost my brother in Vandia, and although I didn't know it at the time, I lost my father back home too. Sod the bloody lot of them.'

Sod the bloody lot of them. There were words to live by. 'I'll climb out onto the ledge first, scramble on top on the roof and then help you out.'

'I swear, the Carnehan family are part mountain goat.'

'Part owl's what we'll need. Plenty of patrols walking the grounds tonight, guarding against trouble.' And Carter was sure they'd find some tomorrow morning when Willow Landor's rooms were discovered empty.

Carter emerged first, the cold biting across his cheeks at this height. He quickly got himself onto the roof. Then Willow emerged. Carter helped her off the window ledge and onto the tiles above, keeping a tight hold as they scrambled across the gables. Willow was never as comfortable with heights as he was. Carter remembered that from their youth. Willow'd been quite a tom-boy, almost as ready for mischief as Carter and her brother, but she had always hesitated when Carter and Duncan scaled the grounds' old oaks. Shouting up angrily as they shook branches and threw acorns down at her. Those trouble-free days seemed a lifetime away, now. The two of them moved slowly and carefully in the dark, checking each icy foothold on the tiles' slope before they reached the edge of the mansion facing the brook. The sentries' lantern light made it easy to mark the servants' position in the grounds. He and Willow waited until the lights had bobbed around the far wing of Hawkland Park and then started to descend using a drain-pipe, moving between the ledges and balconies until they reached the ground. Carter landed first, Willow hitting the flower bed outside the dark dining room next. She groaned, trying to hold her silence but he thought Willow might have twisted her ankle on the final drop. He slipped across to her, but that concern vanished as his heart leapt into his mouth — gravel crackling to their side. Carter spun around, taking in the ring of armed retainers emerging from the mansion's shadows, seven or eight men uncovering lit lanterns covered with black-out blankets. *An ambush, but how?*

A short, evil-faced servant waved a pistol towards the leather belt under Carter's coat. From the wicked scar running down his face it must be Nocks, the mistress of the house's lapdog. 'You can drop that to the dirt, hayseed. And certain careful how you do it.'

Carter did as instructed. His belt hit the floor, one pistol and two knives crunching on the path's gravel. No, just the one blade, Carter noticed his second sheaf lay curiously empty. Not that its loss mattered much given his present circumstances. He heard a deep growl of disapproval and glanced behind him. Damn, but it was old man Landor himself, accompanied by his new wife. Leyla Landor was beautiful, but well-formed the same way a newly minted blade was, the kind that'd cut you even as you held it in your hand. Her face glowed pale and cruel in the lantern light. Benner looked older and more tired than he remembered. Resurrecting his half-burnt town as a city must be proving wearying.

'You've set yourself on a hard path,' rumbled Benner. 'Because if I didn't know any better, boy, I'd say you were running off and taking my daughter with you.'

'Carter wasn't *taking* anything,' said Willow. 'I was leaving with him.' She frowned in the direction of Leyla Landor. 'You've got everything you want right there.'

'On this land, I decide what I want,' said Benner.

'I told you she was playing you for an idiot,' smiled Leyla. 'All you do is disappoint us, Willow.'

Willow angrily tried to push Nocks away as the man dipped a hand into her coat, triumphantly removing the bag bulging in her pocket. 'And they've been thieving from you, to boot. Look at this fat bundle of trading currency. How many silver candlesticks have you and lover-boy here stolen from the park to sell for this? I wager that's why Willow's maid was avoiding the gatehouse and creeping across the brook the other night. Probably carrying a sack full of stolen loot so heavy it broke the ice under her feet.'

'That's not true!' shouted Carter. He stumbled as retainers swarmed over him, grabbing Willow too, forcing their arms behind their back and binding them with rope thick enough to anchor a riverboat.

'This is *your* filthy influence on her,' bellowed Benner at Carter. 'You're as much a thief as your father, boy. Jacob Carnehan's been laughing at me ever since he returned to Northhaven, speaking out against my plans from his pulpit. He bilked me for the money to fund the rescue mission and used it to buy you back, abandoning Duncan to rot in a foreign hell-hole.'

'It wasn't anything like that,' cried Willow. 'I've told you a hundred times. Duncan had been granted his freedom when the expedition turned up to rescue us. Duncan was as good as one of our captors!'

Benner leaned forward and slapped her. 'Liar! Lying to cover up your guilt about abandoning your own brother while you fled for freedom. But now I see why the boy brought you back, even if the coward deserted Duncan. You've been rutting with this bandit against my wishes under *my* own roof; a man who left your brother to die. Have you fallen so far?'

'You mustn't be too harsh on her,' said Leyla with false kindness. 'When Willow was held as a slave, she no doubt submitted to many degrading acts to survive. This low rascal traded on her vulnerability to debase her.'

Leyla Landor's tone only seemed to enrage the old man more, as she'd calculated it would.

'I won't have excuses made for her,' barked Benner. 'She carries the Landor name. That means something in this nation. She's disgraced her family, her house and her honour.'

'Here we are, Mister Landor . . .' Nocks held Willow's coins out to the head of the house.

'No, Nocks, you keep it and divide it among yourself and your men. You were absolutely right to keep a watch on my daughter's quarters from a hide on the grounds. I never thought your fears would be proved correct, but it seems you're a better damn judge of people than I am these days. Work well done, this evening, sir.'

'What about this thief?' asked the manservant, jangling the coins in his hand.

'Apply a good leathering for trespassing,' ordered Benner. 'Then lock him in one of our out-buildings overnight. Toss him out of the park tomorrow morning, after we've left for the airfield. I don't want to see his face again.'

Carter was shaken. *Left for the airfield? Where the hell are they going?*

'What are you talking about? Don't you dare touch Carter!' shouted Willow, writhing in the arms of the servants restraining her.

'Take your hands off her,' pleaded Carter. 'How can you treat your own daughter like this?'

Benner stepped forward and waved a fist under Carter's face. 'Shut up, boy. You had the best of my girl out in foreign parts. I hardly recognize her as a Landor now.'

'Name's the only part of you Willow's got,' snarled Carter. 'Everything else comes from her mother.'

Benner's elbow lurched back and lashed forward, winding Carter in the pit of his gut. 'You're not fit to utter my wife's name, boy. You brought Willow home alive . . . that's the only reason I'm not ordering my men to drop you in an ice-hole like that poor maid you corrupted. My daughter's not for the likes of you. Never was. You might have taken her when she was a slave, but your taint on her skin doesn't make her your property. For the Landor title Willow bears, if nothing else, she's going to be married off well; just as she would have been if wicked fate hadn't snatched her from us.'

'You should be grateful,' said Leyla towards her obviously shocked step-daughter, 'that there's still a man of quality willing to accept you, Willow. But then gossip travels slowly across the nation these days with so many real troubles in the news. I can't say you'll make Viscount Wallingbeck a good wife, but perhaps with enough time you'll make him a passable one. William Wallingbeck's a respectable friend of mine from the capital, so I'm counting on you not to totally disgrace our arrangement.'

'I'll see you in hell first, Holten!' Willow spat and swore at her young stepmother, thrashing furiously and almost breaking free of her captors before extra servants grabbed her and hauled her back. Leyla Landor took a medical bag from one of the retainers, removed a bottle of chloroform and soaked her handkerchief in the sweet-reeking liquid before slipping behind Willow and smothering the girl's face inside the silk fabric. Willow moaned and slowly stopped struggling and slumped towards the gravel. The servants dragged her unconscious body into the yellow light of an open doorway.

'Completely hysterical. Send for the doctor immediately,' commanded Leyla. 'She'll need to be professionally sedated for the trip to the capital. I don't want the girl making a scene along the way. Long journeys are intolerable enough at the best of times.'

'You mad bastard,' railed Carter at the landowner. 'Willow's a free Weylander. You can't marry her off against her will . . . you're selling her like some nomad trading a spare pony for a wife.'

'Hold your tongue, boy.'

'Marriages between people of quality are arranged all the time in the south,' said Landor's new wife. 'Raggedy woodsmen in the wild north may run off at will with penniless field-girls, but those with inheritances to protect must compose suitable matches. The base freedoms of the rutting poor are not, thankfully, shared by sophisticated society. You will understand in time and so will Willow. It is better this way.'

'Better for *you*,' said Carter. 'With a fresh heir to the park filling your conniving belly. You're throwing Willow to a nest of vipers in Arcadia.'

'Have you even visited the capital? Of course not,' said Leyla. 'Your views really aren't worth a damn, hayseed.'

'Get this thieving rogue out of my sight,' ordered Benner Landor.

'You don't know what you're doing!' Carter cried as the servants dragged him away from the house. 'If you send Willow south, it's as good as a death sentence—'

'You're pig-ignorant,' laughed Nocks, the manservant strutting by his side. 'I knew you'd be heading to the estate for willowy Willow. That envelope we fished off the maid was intended for you, and once you've dipped your fingers in that sweet honey, you could never leave the jar alone.'

Carter struggled in the hands of the retainers restraining him, but they were too many men and they were too strong. 'You're evil filth. I don't need Willow to tell me how you've treated her to see you for what you are.'

Nocks laughed as they approached a stable and opened the door. 'Just more honest than most. No need to take against me for that. You'd like to kill me, wouldn't you? It doesn't take much to strip a pastor's son of his civilized coating, does it? You'll feel a lot more vengeful once I've whipped you like the thieving, trespassing dog you are. Old man Landor's too soft for his own good. I'd take a finger or two from you; maybe more. Give you something to remember us by every time you reach for your manhood.'

They pulled Carter into an empty stall and secured him, spread-eagled, to the wooden walls on either side. 'I'll remember you, Nocks.'

'Oh, that you will. And you should remember this,' said Nocks, putting his hand out to receive a horse whip, and then leaning in to whisper in Carter's ear so the others couldn't hear what he said. 'I'm going to enjoy willowy Willow myself, one day soon. I don't care who the mistress marries her off to; that honey jar's just too tempting for these calloused fingers. But I'm going to make sure I have something that your little lady needs first, so I can hear her beg me to open that lovely lid of hers. Any other way would just be too easy, and I do grow easily bored.'

Carter threw a head butt at Nocks, but the manservant was quick, sliding to the side as he tore the shirt off Carter's back. Carter's spine lay exposed to the cold air, a mess of healed scars from his toil in the empire's sky mines. He shivered.

'I can see you've done this dance before,' grinned Nocks. 'I knew you were trouble, pastor's boy. Too wild a buck to be broken by those slave traders, were you? They should have old Nocks working for them. I'd have mastered you. That, or you'd be properly dead.'

'Compared to the imperium's animals, you're just an amateur in Landor livery, a short-arsed tame little monkey dangling at the end of a gold-digger's leash.'

'Going to make you eat those words, boy,' growled Nocks, testing his whip in the air. 'If you don't bite your tongue off first. Maybe we'll get lucky tonight, and your old man will wonder where you are and ride out here to try to rescue you, just like he went out after those slave traders. Then I'll get to give two Carnehans a whipping. Hear you crying for willowy Willow and the pastor begging his God. Wouldn't that be a fine thing?'

'I told my father I'd bed down in the guild's hold tonight. It's closer to here.'

'You like books so damn much; I should've flayed you in the house's library and made your lady watch. Wouldn't want to spend so much time in there, then, would she? Oh well. Just the one thieving Carnehan tonight, then. Can't have everything.'

Carter heard nothing more until the whip cracked, and despite his best efforts to deny the malicious manservant the satisfaction of hearing them, his screams split the air as the cords bit into his back.

Duncan's heart leapt as Princess Helrena scrambled out of the way of the descending sabre, the raw dictates of survival lending her a desperate second wind. She'd rolled every bit as fast as the quicksilver-fast Elanthra moved. Helrena used the ankle of her good leg to strike her fallen sabre's hilt, springing it into the air for her to catch the blade even as she hobbled back to her feet. Elanthra's sabre was still in a downward motion towards the sand occupied by her rival, but she twisted and stamped forward with the dagger in her other hand. Helrena had anticipated the strike and was already in position to block the dagger with her knife, leaving her sabre arm free to feed a foot of shining steel through Elanthra's gut. Elanthra stumbled back, taking the sabre with her, impaled through her stomach and emerging bloody through her spine. She stared down in astonishment at the length of metal speared through her, not quite comprehending the reality of it. Helrena lifted her own dagger in the air like a victory torch, and then threw it full force at her rival, striking Elanthra in the centre of the forehead. Circae's cat's-paw was no longer alive to understand the magnitude of her failure as she fell backwards, smacking the arena floor in a cloud of sand that seemed to belie the weight of her bony body. Duncan hardly believed the speed of the turn-around. Neither could the crowd in the seats, it seemed. Hundreds of thousands of spectators in their house's stalls roared and cheered the unexpected victory, leaping and clapping and taunting the mordant crowds separated by electrified fencing on Elanthra's side of the arena. Circae's supporters on the elite's viewing platform drifted towards the exits. Duncan couldn't see Adella among the entourage, but Baron Machus bustled away in the scrum, swearing and pushing at others in as foul a mood as the Weylander had ever seen the brutish nobleman. Duncan resisted the impulse to toss a few good insults in his direction. Helrena's treacherous cousin might have stolen the woman Duncan had once loved, but in doing so, the baron probably did Duncan the greatest favour of his life. He doubted the baron would shed many crocodile tears over Elanthra's loss; relief rather than grief would be more his style at his high-born lover catching a blade that should have been his. It was relief that overwhelmed Duncan, too. Helrena had survived the challenge, and so, by default, had the rest of them. Helrena had earned her place in the punishment squadron and helped remove the blemish of her house's failure during the slave revolt. Duncan Landor would soon be travelling back to – *no, not home* – the distant nation of Weyland, to help rescue Cassandra.

Among the exiting crowd, Prince Gyal Skar strolled away. He noticed Duncan staring at the losing side, shrugged and gave the Weylander a casual wink as he left. For the handsome prince this was all just a game . . . the same advice he'd passed to Duncan. However long Duncan stayed in the imperial capital, he doubted if he could ever view their vicious machinations so casually.

Paetro sucked in a breath. 'I hope Apolleon is as tight with the triku as he's rumoured to be.'

'What are you talking about?' asked Duncan.

'The triku are the criminal lords who control the underworld in Vandis,' explained the doctor.

'What have the gangs to do with this?'

'Apart from fixing half of the fights in the arena? The edge of Helrena's dagger was surely wiped with toxin. Nothing too egregious; it wouldn't do to have the challenger keeling over frothing at the mouth, but enough to slow Elanthra down or blur her vision, I'd say.'

'Fixing? This isn't a public spectacle where you can buy a crooked trainer,' blurted Horvak, horrified. 'This is a court-licensed duel among the imperial family. If anyone finds out—'

'Let's trust that whatever poison Apolleon arranged is fast-dissolving on blade and in blood, then, Doctor,' said Paetro. 'Or that the stewards who do the official autopsy have been well paid. Otherwise, we'll have won only to lose. The empire would execute the lot of us for this, every caste from top to bottom . . . breaking arena code in a court-sanctioned duel. There's no greater dishonour.'

Duncan thought back to the head of the secret police's appearance at the arena. Apolleon's convenient *meeting* nearby and his equally opportune advice. Circae had tried to fix the challenge, but she'd been outfoxed in turn. 'The dishonour of getting caught.'

'Now you're thinking like a Vandian,' said Paetro.

All three of them here were foreigners inside the imperium, not born to any of this. Duncan really wasn't sure if it was meant as a compliment or not.

'You rigged the damn fight,' accused Helrena, barely able to sit down in her own meeting chamber, pacing around the floor as Apolleon sat coolly unmoved in a chair at the table. Duncan exchanged a nervous glance with Paetro, both waiting alongside the door. Outside, a storm had blown in off the coast, lashing the Castle of Snakes' windows with torrents of water. A reflection of the princess's mood, thought Duncan.

'Let us say I anticipated Circae's tricks and worked to get my retaliation in first,' said Apolleon.

The princess was as furious as Duncan had ever seen her. 'This was my fight, Apolleon, *my* house's honour.'

'A fight with your cousin Machus, as I remember,' said the head of the secret police. 'You were the challenged party. You had the right to select arms and accept or refuse based on your opponent. Would you have chosen dagger and sabre against a trained whiplash like Elanthra? I think not. You would have picked a ranged weapon which she lacked the body mass to wield competently and where her speed could not be brought to bear against your wounded leg . . . the compound bow, perhaps?'

'He has a point,' said Duncan to the bodyguard. Helrena would have been dead without the nobleman's trickery.

'Aye, that he does,' agreed Paetro.

Helrena glared angrily at them both and they shut up.

Apolleon raised his hands to placate her. 'Of course I have a point. And Circae's chicanery has yet to run its course. I have not come calling so you can throw imperial barbs my way . . . save your tantrums for when you occupy the diamond throne.'

'What then?' demanded Helrena.

'The court has ruled in your favour, as they are required to after trial by combat. But they have also announced the leadership of the punishment squadron. Prince Gyal Skar is to be squadron marshal. Baron Machus is to be his second. You are permitted to join, but only as third.'

'Third!' roared Helrena. 'That worm Machus is to rank more highly than me? A mere baron? I fought for this! I am a daughter of imperial blood, a celestial-upper, a princess equal in every way to Gyal.'

'That is what makes the insult so studied,' said Apolleon. 'The military anticipate a magnificent victory and Circae wishes your house to carry no glory back from the battlefield.'

'They might as well put me in command of digging latrine ditches and serving food in the officers' tents,' spat Helrena.

'We could challenge the decision,' said Paetro, 'but the courts would spin their wheels while we watched the punishment squadron depart without us.'

'So, I must choose between accepting this insulting humiliation and retrieving Cassandra?'

'Naturally,' said Apolleon. 'I anticipate a whole wave of new blood in the imperial harem, the way Circae must have been promising the emperor's cock around the court to arrange this.'

'That witch,' said Helrena. She slapped the pane of the nearest window, cold with running water.

'Consider your next move carefully,' said Apolleon. 'If you join the punishment squadron in such a submissive position, you will be seen as subordinating yourself to Gyal, endorsing the fruits of his victory and reinforcing his position. It would not take too great a triumph to consolidate Gyal's path to the throne, and your father's health worsens every week.'

'This is not a decision I need to consider. My house shall join the expeditionary force. Whatever their terms, I will rescue my daughter and avenge the slave revolt.'

'I shall let the magister know,' said Apolleon. 'But I will keep how much you are willing to endure to myself. There are worse positions than third, even if your main responsibility in the squadron will be jumping to obey your traitorous cousin's commands.'

Helrena didn't look pleased by the prospect. Duncan wasn't exactly happy at the prospect of sharing the same air as the baron himself; let alone fighting under the brute's command. 'Do it, then.'

'There is another matter,' said Apolleon. 'When you are fighting far from the imperium, it would be better if Doctor Horvak relocated his work to the protection of my fortress. Circae has already shown she is capable of trying to have him murdered in the Castle of Snakes. She may make a second attempt.'

The head of secret police was mistaken. Duncan had been inside the laboratory when the castle was assaulted. Circae's assassins had been trying to abduct Doctor Horvak, not assassinate him. Whatever Horvak's part was in the various mysterious schemes swirling about, Circae obviously wanted those plans hatched for her, rather than halted with the doctor's murder. *What's the doctor's part in all of this*?

'Better for who?' said Helrena. 'Not for my house. I prefer the doctor working precisely where he is.'

'I am not certain that is wise,' said Apolleon.

'Wise? I shall decide what is wise here. Never make my decisions for me again, Apolleon . . . that foolery you arranged in the arena,' said Helrena. 'Cross me in that manner again and I will have no further part in your schemes. I am nobody's puppet. If you wish to think for me, seize the diamond throne and make *yourself* emperor instead.'

Apolleon bowed. 'And who would wish for that, who was not born to it?'

Oddly, Duncan actually believed the nobleman's words. There was something genuine in the way Apolleon had said it. He really *didn't* desire the imperial throne. Far from finding the statement reassuring, however, it had the opposite effect on the Weylander. It made him fear the unexplainable, capricious head of the secret police all the more. The nobleman strode from the chamber, leaving the rest of them to digest the news.

'Damn Circae,' said Helrena. 'My wounds from the arena are hardly sealed with bandage spray and she finds a way to turn my victory over Elanthra into a resounding defeat.'

'Maybe Gyal's better being considered the front-runner for emperor. Let the assassins' blades be sharpened for his spine instead. The throne's a hard, uncomfortable seat,' advised Paetro, cautiously.

'It's a *safe* seat,' said Helrena.

'Few wish an empress to ascend to it,' said Paetro. 'The power of the imperial harem loses its potency without hundreds of royal brood-mares lounging around in silks to give the empire's great and good their chance to produce a living lottery ticket for the next crown.'

'The rest of the imperium can go hang,' said Helrena. 'The diamond throne's there for whoever has the will to take it. I have as much right as Gyal Skar to rule.'

'Just as long as you're not doing this simply to make Circae unemployed,' said Paetro.

'That's merely a very happy bonus,' said Helrena. She looked at Duncan. 'You don't have to travel with us to Weyland. It will not be a comfortable experience to watch the punishment squadron avenging the slave revolt in your homeland. The empire wants blood spilled, and there is only your people's to sacrifice.'

'I have to go,' said Duncan. 'I was there when Lady Cassandra was taken. It was my duty to keep her safe.'

'No, lad,' said Paetro. 'That duty was mine.'

'If you wish to allocate fault,' said Helrena, 'kindly blame Apolleon. It was his rash decision to pursue the outlaw Sariel into the lee of an erupting stratovolcano that damned our ship. What is done is done.'

'I have to go with you,' said Duncan. 'Don't ask me to stay.'

'Very well,' said Helrena. 'Never give me cause to say *I told you so.*'

'I won't,' promised Duncan.

'In that case,' said Helrena, 'use what time is left before we depart to train with Paetro.'

'I know how to use a sword,' said Duncan.

'May the ancestors spare me your male pride. I am not talking of exchanging sabre blows with villagers, but the full range of skills and techniques legionaries are trained with. Modern arms and equipment.'

'Our job is to protect *you,*' said Paetro.

'I suspect I will need neither a bodyguard nor a food taster for the moment,' smiled Helrena, sadly. 'When we are in Weyland there will be ample opportunity for Circae's allies to have us killed simply by ordering us towards the worst of the fighting. Train hard. My house has lost enough people in this business. I do not wish to add any more, least of all you. Save your suspicious eyes for when we serve alongside Gyal and Machus.' She waved the pair of them out and they left together.

'She meant it, you know,' said Paetro. 'About staying in the imperium when we ship out.'

'You're going,' said Duncan.

'There's not a force strong enough to keep me away,' said Paetro. 'I'm shipping out to bring back the young highness. And I'm going to track down the bastard that killed my girl and make him regret the day he set foot in the imperium.'

'It won't help your family if you die on foreign soil,' said Duncan. He remembered how shockingly fast the deranged, travel-worn pastor of Northhaven had drawn and fired his guns. Duncan left for dead.

Hesia a corpse in the volcanic ash. Paetro wounded. Almost too fast to follow. Not a skill that Jacob Carnehan had mastered behind the pulpit, that much was certain.

'I'm no celestial-upper,' said Paetro, 'but I still have my honour. That's all I have. He won't catch me by surprise again. Won't be a duel. I'm a soldier, and I'll kill him like one.'

'We need Cassandra back alive.'

'I know my damn duty. The young highness returned safe first. Hunting that devil down second.'

'What I don't understand is why the pastor took Cassandra hostage and has made no demands.'

'None that we know about,' said Paetro.

'Did Father Carnehan say anything to you when he took Cassandra?' asked Duncan.

'Nothing polite,' said Paetro. Duncan knew the old soldier well enough to know when he was dissembling. There was something more to this matter that he would not talk of. *But what?* And that wasn't the only mystery nagging at the Weylander. 'What is Doctor Horvak working on for the house that is of such importance?'

'Has the princess not told you, lad?'

'She said to me that there are some things I am better off not knowing, safer not knowing . . .'

'Well, then, there you have it. As far as this matter is concerned, I haven't been taken into her confidence either. But I think we can hazard a guess by the limits of the ambitions of those involved: Apolleon and Helrena.'

'What limits?'

'My point precisely,' said the solider. 'Taking the diamond throne is enough of a game for almost every schemer and celestial-caste nob inside the imperium. But for those two? Taking the empire is only the first part of the equation. The real question is what do you do with the empire once you hold it? When you can answer that, I suspect you will know what the good doctor is beavering away on.'

'Helrena doesn't want Apolleon to lay his hands on the doctor or his work.'

'If the man had the doctor, maybe he'd change his tune about who should take the throne next.'

'Well, at least Helrena doesn't fully trust him,' said Duncan. 'That's something.'

'That's a fine intuition. I'm going to make you a soldier, yet, lad,' said Paetro, slapping Duncan's back. 'You learnt how to spot snares and poisoned plates and explosive trip-wires hidden under a mattress well enough. Let's see how you do with legion training in as short a time as any trainer was ever given.'

It wasn't going to be easy, but then, nothing worth earning ever was.

Jacob Carnehan wasn't having a good start to the day. He looked at Sheplar Lesh, freshly arrived from the great forest with pine needles still clinging to his jacket. 'So if you're standing here, where the hell is the imperial brat?'

'Tied up in a wagon outside Northhaven,' said Sheplar. 'Kerge watches her. We had no choice in our departure, even without the marauders closing in on Quehanna. The gask council did not wish her to remain in their city any longer. They scryed the future and concluded she is bad luck.'

'They got that much right,' said Jacob. 'Don't need their talents to tell you that. We need to get her stashed somewhere, quick. Northhaven is crawling with strangers asking too many questions. One of the king's hands is here as well, a prefect, and I guarantee he hasn't come north to sample the ice wine.'

'I plan to take the bumo north,' explained Sheplar. 'To Rodal.'

'Will your country offer you and Kerge sanctuary?'

'Officially? I am not certain. They are not eager to become embroiled in Weyland's internal politics, old ally or not. But I still have many friends in the skyguard and the temples. They will help me when they understand what is at stake. The key faction that would oppose us travels south to Arcadia in an attempt to broker a peace between Prince Owen and the usurper.'

Jacob nodded. It was the best of a bad lot, then. In the mountain heights of Rodal the king's killers and assassins would stand out like sore thumbs. So would an imperial girl and a gask acting as her jailor, of course, but it had to be safer than hiding her in Northhaven farmland; where he'd need to protect Cassandra Skar from the vengeful locals as well as the ruthless forces looking to free her.

'There is another option,' said Sheplar.

'Speak,' said Jacob.

'The bumo is no longer an effective shield against the king's vengeance. She is like a young hare scrabbling around the bush, drawing predators towards our camp. We could simply release her. Let your king find her and carry her back to the empire.'

'Then what?' said Jacob. 'We trust that crown-wearing viper to leave us alone? I didn't bring back half of Northhaven's children and cut Vandia's chains off them, just to have them start turning up with their throats slit by "bandits".'

'They will keep coming for her,' warned Sheplar.

'Let them come,' said Jacob. 'As long as we have the emperor's granddaughter as a body shield, their aim's going to be off.'

'Or be very careful,' warned Sheplar.

'I'm a careful man, myself.'

The aviator looked at him oddly. 'Indeed. I can see that. There is no more to the matter than this? You have not concocted a plan with that devil Sariel which you have not cared to share with me?'

'As if. I haven't seen Sariel since he left town,' said Jacob. He waved towards the window. 'He's out there, somewhere, chasing the lost memories of his old life.' Always start a lie with the plain truth. Bait, not shield, was exactly what Lady Cassandra Skar was to Jacob. As large as the imperium lay, there weren't nearly enough Vandians in their legions to begin to pay for murdering Mary Carnehan. *Burning my town. Taking my son.* And Vandia was millions of miles away. Only reachable with their own shockingly advanced ships . . . unless they chose to come to him.

'I think I preferred the smelly one when he was half-insane,' said Sheplar. 'Sanity does not suit him.'

'I reckon Sariel's still mad.' *Mainly at our enemies, right now. Which is the way I'd like to keep it.* 'Come on. I'll see you safe out of town.'

Kerge and Sheplar had parked their wagon on the road out to the river, smoke from the warehouses and docks visible in the distance trailing into a cold, clear sky. Jacob couldn't walk this road without remembering the horrific sights he'd witnessed here during the raid.

All the captured townspeople too old or sick to be worth their haulage costs beheaded by the slave traders, the children and young chained and marched out to the pick-up planes, ready to lift off for their carrier bird. His wife, Mary, had endured that sad sight too, before she'd been murdered by the skels. *Lord but I miss you. The sight and sound of you. Having someone to talk to.* The now empty cornfields the covered wagon sat in had grown higher than ever in the summer past, nurtured by the blood of the dead. That was a fair analogy, Jacob reckoned, to the present health of the kingdom. Never richer. Never poorer. And all of it nourished by the people's blood. *I'll bring Benner Landor's fields a fresh crop of fertilizer. All of it Vandian.*

Kerge sat on the cart's tailboard, ahead of a wagon bed with a cylindrical grey canvas cover stretched over arched wooden bows, two oxen in its harness. They had brought a horse along too, tethered to the wagon and tugging happily at the grass along the verge. The gask waved when he saw Jacob and Sheplar approaching.

Jacob drew to a halt in front of the wagon. 'Where's your little friend?'

Kerge reached back into the flatbed and pulled a blanket off a pile of woodchip crates. Lady Cassandra Skar sat there wedged between two boxes, glowering at him. Despite himself, Jacob smiled. 'Take the gag off for a minute.'

The gask did as Jacob asked. The young Vandian indignantly shook her hair. 'The empire has not forgotten about me! They will arrive to free me and you will be skinned alive for every humiliation heaped upon my person.'

'Didn't work out so well for you, last time. I left a couple of legions face down in the ash of that ore-spewing volcano your people value so highly. And this is *my* country, girl.'

'It'll be left as burned-out as the volcano's dead zone once we've finished with it.'

'I should hand you to that serpent sitting on our throne. The two of you deserve each other.'

'The empire has provinces without end, armies without peer. We will be the tide that sweeps your people away.'

'There is no tide that can reach Rodal's heights,' said Sheplar. 'And the rocks of our peaks do not burn.'

'If your savage hill tribes value silver, someone will be willing to knife you in the back and turn me over to my countrymen. It happened in the forests, it will be the same wherever you try to hide me.'

'I got plenty of lead to trade them,' said Jacob. He patted the brace of pistols under his coat.

'You're a fool, Weylander.'

'Your people murdered my wife. Mary's buried next to our two children. My old life's buried down with her and all the townspeople you had butchered. Maybe I am a fool, girl, but that's only because you took everything from me. I've nothing left to be.'

'The empire will find something.'

Jacob raised his hands in the air. 'You've hollowed me out. I'm empty, here. And a man without hope, that's a man without fear.' Jacob climbed into the wagon and re-fixed the girl's gag. Kerge and Sheplar checked the wagon for the journey ahead, inspecting the hooves of the oxen and the grease on the wheel axles. Lady Cassandra Skar glared silent loathing at him. Jacob pointed to the mountain range barely visible in the distance, beyond the river and the hinterland of hills and valleys that led up to the vast heights. The league's stone walls, where the Rodalians kept out the nomad hordes that haunted the steppes beyond. He whispered to her. 'You think those are mountains? They're not, Your *Highness*. They're an empire-sized snare, big enough to bury every legion you've got.' Jacob smiled coldly at the Vandian and dropped the blanket over her, concealing her presence from the prying eyes of other travellers. 'You'll see.'

Sheplar called up to him from the side of the wagon. 'Jacob, is that one of your horses coming down the road?'

He looked out. *By damn, it is.* And Carter slumped wounded across the saddle as the steed was led in by Tom Purdell, the young guild courier riding one of the hold's horses. Jacob sprinted out as the pair crawled into town, grabbing the reins and halting the old nag, Kerge and Sheplar close behind him. 'What the hell's happened here? You're meant to be working in the library . . . were you jumped by bandits?'

Carter was too hurt to do anything but mumble through swollen lips; but the state of his face was nothing compared to the blood-soaked shirt clinging to his back.

'I found him like this in the saddle,' said Tom as Jacob and his companions practically caught Carter and laid him out on the cart's flatbed. 'He's been drifting in and out of consciousness. He didn't show up at our hold last night, so I went out towards Hawkland Park to see if the house had seen him. Carter mentioned he might be passing by to see his lady before heading for the library. Best I can tell from what's said so far, the staff at the mansion caught him trespassing and half beat him to death for it.'

'Benner Landor,' growled Jacob, angrily slapping his holster. By the saints, if the grasping landowner was in favour of hedgerow justice, two could play at that game. *I'll put a bullet in that ungrateful bastard's heart for this!*

'Do nothing hasty,' cautioned Kerge. 'Your country's laws do not stand on your side.'

When have they ever? 'They've been bought and paid for, you mean.' *Rich man's law.* This was all too familiar to Jacob, a little piece of history repeating. *And look how well it ended before when you caught up with the high-born bastards who murdered your mother.*

Carter started to cough as Sheplar pressed a water canteen between his lips. 'Willow,' he spluttered. 'Been drugged. Taking. Her south. This morning. Forced marriage. The airfield.'

So, that's it. And a lowly book-botherer was no longer required on the scene, even if the man in question was the one who'd saved Willow Landor's life. But of course, they'd both saved each other's lives in Vandia. Which meant Jacob owed Willow as much as he owed her father for *this*.

Jacob mounted Carter's mare. 'I'll bring her back if I can.'

'I'm coming,' coughed Carter from the wagon.

'That would be ill-advised, manling,' said Kerge. 'You need to visit a healer in Northhaven.'

Carter shook his head, stubbornly.

'Let him come,' ordered Jacob. He ignored the shocked expressions Sheplar and the gask shot him. 'He's a man, now. He and Willow endured hell out in Vandia. He's earned the right to make a man's decision over the Landor woman; even if it's a damn fool one.'

'I'm coming with you,' said Tom.

'Hell if this is your fight,' observed Jacob.

'You saved my life on the road and Carter's my guild brother,' said

Tom. 'That makes it my business. This started in Arcadia when the guild sent me to meet Prince Owen and pick up your coded message. I promised him I'd deliver it to you safe, so this might as well finish in Arcadia. Besides, the guild takes a dim view of our initiates being seized and summarily beaten.'

'And that's official policy is it?' Jacob shook his head.

Sheplar pulled an aviator's carbine out of the wagon and mounted his horse, pulling at the reins to bring the steed close to the wagon. 'Get Carter up behind me . . . he will not be able to ride unaided.'

'We'll head hard for the airfield,' said Jacob, looking at Carter wincing in agony as he was propped up behind the mountain aviator. 'After that, you're going to the doctor.' Unless things turned uglier than they had to, in which case the doctor might have to be coaxed out at the end of a gun barrel to wherever they holed up. Jacob nodded at Kerge. 'Try not to sell the Vandian girl off to any slave traders who might pass by, however tempting that might be.'

'You do not intend to send for your people's court officials or constables, do you?' sighed Kerge.

'No more than Benner Landor did when his hirelings grabbed my boy.'

'The tenets of your religion,' said Kerge. 'Do your saints and God not require forgiveness?'

'Oh, I'm sure they'll forgive Benner Landor,' said Jacob. *Especially after I've beaten him to within an inch of his miserable life in front of his craven staff.*

Jacob pulled the mare around and set it galloping down the road, the clatter of hooves from the others loud at his rear. He only spared the spurs for his son's sake. The airfield had been constructed on the south side of the waterway, close to the piers where riverboats docked and the Guild of Rails' railhead sat, paid for by government money but serving, like so much else, the commercial interests of the House of Landor's warehouses. A quarter of an hour later and Jacob was looking over the field. Northhaven's new airfield was a simple, unfenced affair. A long cruciform of flattened grass, its main runway ran parallel with the river, while aircraft sheds, hangars and a technical site for the maintenance staff squatted on the opposite side, its passenger hall and commercial buildings close to the riverbank.

Most of the planes on the ground were small fighters, part of the nation's freshly minted skyguard, their barracks, air-raid shelters and bomb and ammunitions stores buried under soil and sod as a series of artificial hills. It was meant to be a source of pride for their nation – Weyland's new-found protection from aerial nomads and raiders, the state's ability to claim sovereignty of the skies above. For Jacob, it was just another reminder of the blood money that had paid for it.

The pastor halted his horse by a worker walking along the perimeter track. 'Where's Benner Landor's party?'

'You mean *Prefect Colbert*'s party?' said the field worker, watching the others cantering in behind Jacob. 'They took off early this morning for the capital.'

Carter groaned in his saddle, the news not helping his injuries. Sheplar reached behind to help steady him. 'Willow Landor, she was— She was with them?'

The worker nodded. 'Daughter, wife, servants, old man Landor himself, the prefect and his aides. Had a bunch of Rodalian diplomats along for the ride, too. All bound for the court, I reckon.'

'Too late,' muttered Carter.

'We might have missed their transport,' said Jacob, 'but we're not too late. We can take another flight and follow them. We've still time to halt the sham of a marriage.'

'It'll be hazardous,' cautioned Sheplar.

'And Northhaven isn't? Prince Owen is down south risking his neck among that nest of politicians, pitting himself against the usurper's interests. If the boy can brave the risk of assassination, so can I.'

'A noble with a claim on the throne going missing would be noticed,' said Tom. 'Even with half the nation's press sitting pretty in the king's pockets. Whereas any of us . . .'

'I'm not asking you to join me,' said Jacob. Although he doubted his ability to stop these fools from trying. He glanced at Carter. 'And *you're* heading for the doctor.'

'Don't leave . . . until I'm fixed up,' grimaced Carter.

'You'll slow us down,' said Jacob. 'Wait until you're patched up; then follow us.'

'Can travel,' insisted Carter. 'Took worse than this . . . in the mines. And I was expected to work . . . the next day.'

'Work until you *died*,' said Jacob. 'I didn't travel all that way to Vandia and rescue you so you could kill yourself at home.'

'Won't abandon her,' said Carter. 'If Willow was . . . Mother, what would *you* . . . do?'

Jacob sighed. *Making another of those decisions.* Just as foolish. 'Carter, you'd charge hell with a bucket of ice water.'

'I'm going after Willow.'

'All right then. Hell if a drought doesn't usually end with a flood. Sheplar, drag Carter to the doctor opposite my church. Tell the man I want good hard alcohol for the wounds. Make sure those scars stay clear of infection.'

'You don't wish me to help arrange passage?' asked the Rodalian.

'No choice how we fly out, this time. Only government birds – skyguard and merchant wing.' More was the pity. When they had needed to get to Arcadia after the slavers' raid, Sheplar's friends had provided the aircraft. Now, the skies above Weyland were being treated as protectively as her land borders. Rodalian patrols, once a reassuringly familiar sight in the air, could only be glimpsed now, confined close to the mountains. Jacob noted an aircraft on the field being refuelled with corn ether, the House of Landor's coat of arms painted on the fuel tank. He recognized the plane from the aircraft silhouettes being published by the jingoistic press, trumpeting the nation's revived power and influence. A Culph and Falcke Berrypecker. A transport aircraft, far larger than the stubby single pilot fighters dotted around the field. The transporter was a wide 200-feet long wing mounted with ten forward-facing engines, stabilized by twin booms and a single large rear-push propeller at her tail. A pilots' cabin jutted from the centre of the wing as proud as a warship's superstructure, aircrew visible moving around inside, a conservatory-style canopy behind it stretching back spine-like across the wing to enclose a hundred or so passenger seats on the top deck, the lower being reserved for cargo. She sat on two massive underwing pods housing fixed landing gear and a gun turret apiece, the gunners' positions open to the air, heavy calibre rifles mounted on swivel mounts. She looked unwieldy compared to the triangular air wings of the Rodalian skyguard and little more than a gnat compared to the vast city-sized six-hundred propeller carriers he'd travelled on after leaving Weyland in search of the slavers. But if she bore him safely to Arcadia, he wouldn't complain. Sheplar cantered away with Carter slung behind him, across the field and towards Northhaven.

The airfield worker pointed out a two-storey building where tickets could be purchased. Jacob and Tom rode for the wooden structure, tying up next door to a six-wheeled spring wagon operating between the field and the riverboat pier. A couple of beggars sat outside, calloused farmworkers' hands reaching out to rattle cups, while a green-liveried doorman eyed them suspiciously, barring the entrance. He opened the door for Jacob and Tom, albeit with an arched eyebrow. Travelling by air was still an expensive novelty. For humble pastors and penurious couriers, the guild's train service was still the style. They entered a hall lit by tall glass windows, rows of seats upholstered in padded green leather; warm and luxurious compared to the bitter cold outside, iron pipes creaking from the weight of heated water. This was the first time Jacob had been inside. Apart from the porters and staff moving luggage around on hand carts, it was only quality inside, the moneyed cream of the prefecture – women in expensive day dresses and long gloves and men in brightly patterned waistcoats and frock coats. Even their servants were expensively attired. The ticket desk was a polished booth manned by a worker in the same stiff green uniform as the porter, the glimpse of a room through the wooden grille hung with wall-maps of Weyland.

With no queue at the booth, Jacob walked to the front and addressed the ticket seller. 'Does that ten-engine bird on the field count Arcadia as one of her layovers?'

'Certainly,' said the seller.

'I'll need tickets for tomorrow morning,' said Jacob.

'I'm afraid we're all sold out, Father Carnehan,' said the seller.

'Is that so? Funny thing is, I don't recall introducing myself,' said Jacob. 'Tickets for the day after, then.'

'Sold out that day, too.'

'And when will you have tickets available?'

'Try coming back in a couple of weeks,' advised the seller.

'This is outrageous,' spluttered Tom, banging the counter. 'Our money is as good as anyone else's. We need to travel to the capital.'

'I'm sure the Guild of Rails will sell you tickets to Arcadia, if you're in a rush,' smiled the seller.

'Travel overland by train? That'll take months!'

Jacob laid a hand on Tom's shoulder and eased the angry courier back. 'Our money might be as good as anyone else's, but our pockets aren't quite as deep as Benner Landor's, am I right?'

'Try the Guild of Rails,' repeated the seller.

Jacob strode out of the hall, Tom stamping behind him. 'This is completely contemptible.'

'The fix has been put in,' growled Jacob. 'Landor's city, Landor's fuel. Benner was counting on me and Carter following after his party. Don't waste your breath railing against fate. Even if that fool in there sold us a ticket, our flight would develop engine problems before it ever left the ground. Or maybe get diverted in the air, leaving us stranded even further away than Northhaven.'

'He can't stop the Guild of Rails selling us tickets south. They're neutral.'

'Maybe. But you're right about travelling overland. Too damn slow. I don't think Carter is fixing to interrupt his sweetheart's honeymoon,' growled Jacob. He stopped by a luggage desk and picked up a discarded customs form and pencil, scribbling a message on the paper's blank reverse. 'You're the courier. Run this to the radiomen's hold in the old town for me . . . tell them it's official business for the Guild of Librarians. Then find me at the doctor's.'

Tom took the sheet and read the note. 'Why transmit a message to a shipping office in the Rotnest Islands? That's in the middle of the Lancean Ocean, isn't it? Faster to catch a train south than board a clipper ship, surely . . . and the Rotnest Islands aren't exactly the kind of place I'd trust to book a safe passage anywhere.'

'They operate real fast clippers out of the islands,' said Jacob, trading the hall's warmth for the freeze outside.

'Yes they do. Primarily to escape being sunk by all those pirates and freebooters.'

'Have a little faith, Mister Purdell,' said Jacob.

'If you think I'll be put off coming with you just because the journey south is dangerous, you're wrong,' said Tom.

'Oh, it'll be dangerous enough for sure,' said Jacob, mounting his horse. There wasn't much he could promise, but he could certainly promise *that*.

SEVEN

THE KELPERS' BOAT

Carter's fever ebbed and flowed, leaving him disoriented. His nausea had grown stronger since being enveloped by the rolling of a vessel on the waves, the toss of spray through gaps in the wooden hull leaving a sheen of salt on his lips whenever he licked them. He tried to find the sleep his body craved, but the timbers creaked noisily as the vessel bobbed in the swell. Was he really travelling by sailing ship? It didn't seem likely. What had happened to his flight to Arcadia?

Carter had started having visions, like faint afterimages that he could barely remember; but they still interfered with what was real, lending much that was mundane a dream-like quality. Willow struggling against her stepmother's servant. Nocks making good on those sordid threats he'd taken such pleasure in whispering to Carter during his beating. Then Willow being dragged down a cathedral aisle, screaming for help as hundreds of nobles cheered and applauded. *Just fever dreams from the darkness. Please.* The medicine which Tom helped Carter sup when he was awake didn't help, a brown glass bottle without a label, but surely laced with opiates. The saints know, he needed it when that clear spirit was poured across his wounds, like acid against his flesh. Hopefully like fire against gangrene, too. His medicine stole the pain across his spine but replaced it with hot hallucinations that had to be sweated away. Carter dimly recalled swaying on his horse while he and his father said goodbye to Kerge and Sheplar Lesh before they rattled away in their wagon towards the mountains. That must have been real, surely? Lady Cassandra Skar's choice, colourful curses before she'd been gagged and covered weren't something Carter's mind could have reasonably been expected to conjure.

He remembered a boat ride down the river towards the coast. But this wasn't a riverboat now, surely? You didn't experience swells like this on the White Wolf River, nor the taste of salt. The truth of his location was only settled when Tom Purdell came to Carter's cabin and helped him out of his hammock, feeling the wet canvas as he helped lift Carter to the floor.

'Salt damp,' said Tom. 'Good for your wounds. You're healing well.'

'Damned if I feel like it,' coughed Carter. 'Have we arrived?'

'Maybe. But nowhere we need to be,' said Tom. 'We've been travelling west, towards the Burn.'

'Willow's been taken south.'

'Don't I know it.' Tom explained how their aerial passage to Arcadia had been stymied by Benner Landor's machinations. Carter tried to take the news in his stride, but it was harder than ignoring the agony clinging to his back. Every hour that passed was another hour nearer to losing Willow for ever. 'Your father's acting as though he knows what he's doing, but I'm fast coming to the conclusion he's a little bit cracked. He got me to send a radio message to a shipping office in the Rotnest Islands for him. Now he's asked for you up on deck. I reckon we're due to rendezvous with a clipper, because this old tub doesn't have the range to travel much further.' Tom shoved the unlocked door open with a boot and Carter saw what the courier meant, drizzle whipping in his face. They had emerged onto the ship's slippery deck. The vessel was a three-masted schooner and a line of burly men and women worked along the length of the main deck under furled sails. Beyond the ship the horizon stretched green and infinite with oarweed, a massive floating forest of it. Each of the sailors worked a long hooked staff, pulling the green vegetation on board where children and kelpers so old they should have been retired heaved it into wooden tubs. Dried and rolled, the oarweed made ready-seasoned noodles: a staple diet along the coastal towns. It could also be fermented into a raw, salty alcohol. Carter twisted his aching neck around. No sign of land, but he spotted his father talking to a sailor on the quarterdeck. He shivered. It was every bit as cold here as it was on land, raining to boot, and he wasn't wearing a sailor's oiled leather raincoat.

'What did the radio message to the islands say?' asked Carter.

'It didn't make too much sense,' said Tom. 'It was about selling a couple of tonnes of kelp in port and the cargo's purity after it was fermented for sea-grape rum.'

'A code, then?'

'That's what I figured. All kelpers are smugglers on the side, aren't they?'

Carter grunted. *So it's said*. He grimaced in pain. His back crackled like dry leather every time his feet shifted across the deck's damp planking.

'Your face looks like Master Lettore's after I told him I was travelling south with you.'

'That I would have paid good money to see.'

'He came around,' said Tom. 'Reckon he's getting used to seeing you far-called. And two brothers can travel more securely than one.'

Jacob Carnehan climbed down to where Carter and Tom waited. 'Good to see you up on your feet, Carter.'

Carter nodded towards the ocean. 'If we can't fly to the capital, how is it we're not taking a train?'

'Officially we are,' smiled Jacob. 'I booked tickets south with the Guild of Rails. The station master told me that an hour after I paid for passage, a whole gang of strangers showed up demanding tickets for the same train.'

'The king's assassins?'

'His silver in their pockets, at any rate,' said Jacob. 'Hopefully they're on the train now, wondering why we never emerge from our locked cabin. I paid the train guards to deliver meals to our empty berth and a little extra to scoff the food down themselves.'

Carter sat down on a grating. Emerging from his hammock had left him exhausted. 'And you trust this crew?'

'This isn't a crew, it's a clan. One of the families which supplies my old monastery in Rodal. These good folk are as tight as a deep-reef clam.'

'A "family" that doesn't just use the mountain coves to land kelp?' said Tom.

Jacob shrugged. 'My old monastery at Geru Peak is the church's last outpost in the north, not a branch of the revenue service. I reckon you can say we're both fairly good at turning a blind eye.' He pointed to the air. 'And that, Mister Purdell, can be a mighty useful talent.'

An antiquated flying boat appeared out of the grey clouds, almost a galleon with wings, four large propellers droning above the fuselage, wing-tip floats on either side which wobbled as the aircraft circled, before skipping down across the waves. This aircraft flew no flag or national colours, but it clearly didn't belong to the Rodalian skyguard or Weyland's new air fleet. As soon as the ungainly flying boat landed, the kelpers launched a series of long boats from their schooner, rowing out for the plane, drums of kelp-derived ethanol in their keels that were carefully winched through a cargo hatch opened along the plane's fuselage.

'More smugglers?' observed Tom. 'Does that antique even have the range to reach the shore?'

'Let's find out,' said Jacob. 'And sharpish. There's a storm brewing, I can taste it in the air.'

'I'm not sure you'd ever make much of a guild courier,' said Tom. 'Your ideas of transportation . . .'

Jacob gave a taciturn smile. 'You might be right, Mister Purdell. And our journey's hardly even started yet.'

Carter's father and his guild friend helped him climb down into one of the longboats, the wind and rain picking up as they approached the plane across the water. As weak as a kitten, Carter ignored his nausea as the boat crawled towards the sea plane. Tom hurled a rope to a man standing in an open freight hatch in the fuselage, their boat's six oarsmen drawing the line as tight as possible to make the perilous crossing between pitching longboat and aircraft possible. His father and Tom crossed first, and then he leapt for the plane. Carter felt as a light as a feather as he flopped into his father's hands inside the flying boat.

Jacob rested his son on a crate inside the hold, airmen tying wooden fuel barrels down for take-off. The crew – two men and a woman – wore no uniform, just a patched collection of fur-trimmed leather air jackets that had seen better days.

'You know who we are?' asked Jacob Carnehan.

'We've been told,' said one of the airmen, looking at Carter. 'Is that one going to live?'

'I'll survive,' wheezed Carter.

'We'll roll you out if you don't. No dead weight in the air.' The airman chuckled at his own observation before the three fliers exited the hold.

'They're real charmers,' said Tom. He turned around and gazed out through a porthole in the fuselage, waves lapping angrily against the glass, their flying boat rocking against the breakers.

'These people believe your spirit flies free in the air after you've passed,' said the pastor. 'Your flesh is just so much worthless freight.'

'Must make for cheap funerals,' said Tom.

Carter was fading as they waited for the cargo hold to fill up with fuel barrels; then the flying boat started to pick up speed, crashing against the waves and jolting Carter back into consciousness. He could hear their engines struggling against the dead weight of the transport plane. She had taken on enough ethanol that she could probably make the journey to Arcadia without touching down to refuel once.

'You need to rest,' said his father.

'Every time I go to sleep, I see Willow. Not dreams, more like visions. Evil visions.'

'I thought that old sorcerer Sariel had drained your mind of those.'

'So had I,' whispered Carter.

'Try and rest. We'll get your girl back. Benner Landor might have a head start on us, but there are trade winds high above the centre of Lancean Ocean, fierce and fast. Merchants call them the *Spear*. That's what we'll be riding south. A spear.'

The cargo hold spun dizzyingly around Carter's head, fears his only anchor. 'What if we're too late? I can't face the rest of my years without her.'

'One way or another,' promised his father, 'we'll make this right.'

Grey clouds disappeared, leaving streaks of water across the porthole, sunshine visible, glinting on the haze below like another sea.

Gravity's hold lightened as the flying boat climbed, the engines' roar dimming as their workload eased. *So light*. It grimly put Carter in mind of his time on the sky mines. No good memories, there, apart from finding Willow.

'Sweet saints!' shouted Tom.

Carter tried to focus through the porthole to see why Tom had suddenly gripped the fuselage so tight his knuckles were turning white, angling his head for a clear view outside. Then Carter saw it – a city-sized carrier in the air above them, four fat stacked wings coming out of the sun, rated at least six-hundred rotors large, squadrons of smaller aircraft circling her like flies on a turd. She sported a blue and white camouflage pattern on her ground-facing fuselage, while painted as dark as night on everything above the keel. All apart from the tail, where a severe white skull and crossbones scowled out of black. There was only one free carrier that matched this sight, and it was a description written in blood across a hundred lurid newspaper reports of shipping raids on the open ocean. The *Plunderbird*. Commanded by the scourge of the Lanca – the vile pirating butcher known as Black Barnaby. It suddenly dawned on Carter why so few aerial merchants braved these fast, fierce trade winds, the answer bearing down on them as inexorably as God's own judgement. Then the black of the approaching carrier expanded across his sight as fever plunged him back into darkness.

Willow glared at Nocks and Leyla Holten from the opposite side of the coach compartment as they rattled along the road. Even with the window blinds down, Willow could tell from the coach's speed and lack of noise outside that they had left the crowded streets of the capital behind about half an hour ago, just the calls of the coachmen outside as he drove his train of eight horses on. It was a good thing Nocks had bound her hands behind her back with rope, or she would have stuck him with the sharp carving knife she had slipped unseen from the dining room and hidden under her dress. After days drugged out of her mind, eating the saints knows what if anything, she had fallen on the small feast they had allowed her in Arcadia like a starving pauper. Now she was suffering the after-effects, unsteady from both the sedatives and dropping half a table's worth of nourishment into her empty stomach.

'Where are we going?' demanded Willow.

Holten sighed and looked at her manservant. Nocks leaned across and slapped Willow hard across the face. 'Where are we going, *mistress.*'

'Where are we going?'

Nocks went to slap her again, but Holten raised her hand, wearily, and her lapdog stopped short of a second strike. 'Let's not mark her too much. We need her looking half-respectable.'

'For what?' demanded Willow. 'You can't keep me captive like this. I've reached my majority, you have no right!'

'She's a right little barracks-room lawyer,' grinned Nocks.

'You were kept as a slave before, my dear. What right did your captors have? Only the right of those in authority to do what is necessary.'

'My father will have you whipped for your effrontery.'

'We're doing this with *my* husband's blessing,' said Holten. 'This, my dear, is your introduction to high society in the capital. Do try to keep your whining mouth shut and mind your manners. I want you to create a good first impression.'

'You do? Then stay behind in the carriage.'

Holten went to slap her then, but pulled back, regaining control of her temper at the last second. 'Not today, my dear.'

They rode on in icy silence. Willow was shivering with cold by the time they eventually halted. Both Holten and her manservant wore warm coats in the coach's unheated compartment. Willow only had her dress. Nocks pulled Willow up and untied the rope around her wrists. The door opened and she was pushed out into the cold. She found herself on a wide gravel drive lined with moss-covered ornaments; overgrown lawns beyond. A group of servants waited to greet them in front of a dilapidated but elegant house, four towering storeys of honeyed limestone, a wide sweeping frontage with two symmetrical wings jutting out at either side. Chimneys poured smoke into the sky, statues of angels striking a variety of positions under cupolas mounted on the roof.

'Welcome to Belinus Hall, Mistress Landor,' said the senior servant, stepping forward from the line of footmen and maids.

Holten raised a hand perfunctorily. 'Take us to the master of the house at once.'

'Of course. This way, mistress.' He raised his eyes uncertainly to look at Nocks and Willow.

'I'm being held against my will by these people,' said Willow.

'As you value your employment, ignore her,' commanded Holten. 'She's a difficult child, highly-strung, lazy and probably better off confined to an asylum.'

'We get all sorts here, Mistress Landor,' said the servant. 'Our discretion is renowned.' He beckoned to the line and four burly, broken-faced retainers stepped forward who wouldn't have looked out of place as bareknuckle boxers in a ring. 'No trouble today, miss, if you please.'

Willow groaned as the retainers fell in behind the visitors. Whatever help she might receive, it obviously wasn't going to come from these southern bruisers.

They entered through the house, moving quickly across a chequered diamond-patterned black and white floor, then through narrow wooden-lined corridors, staff bobbing, bowing and curtsying towards the visitors everywhere they went. It was almost as cold inside the house as outside, despite the dark smoke Willow had noted emptying towards the sky from the hall's stacks. *I thought the south was meant to be warmer than Northhaven*? Willow was marched into a large drawing room on the ground floor, still cold but at least well-lit by a wheel-like gasolier. She stood there a moment, lost among the octagonal oak tables and slightly tattered sofas. At the other end of the room sat a man, looking small under an ornamental plastered ceiling shaped with spirals of vines and fir cones. Nocks pushed Willow across the carpet towards him, and as she drew closer, she saw the chamber's occupant was anything but small. He was six foot of arrogance, sprawled lazily across a chair, lacking even the courtesy of getting to his feet to greet his visitors. He possessed the thick, curled black hair of a dandy. His face was blocky and handsome in its way, perhaps thirty years of age, but the noble's expression seemed to alternate between languor and bitterness, and that was enough to make Willow take against him even without the dishonour of her present company.

When he opened his mouth to speak in a deep growl, the impression wasn't softened. 'Leyla, or should I say Mistress Landor now? Always a pleasure. You have done well for yourself.'

'And so, shortly, will you. With my assistance, it goes without saying. This man,' said Holten to Willow, indicating the nobleman sprawled lazily across a chair, 'is your future. Treat him very well. It will be your privilege to provide Viscount William Wallingbeck with an heir to his house.'

'More than one,' drawled the viscount. 'My mother lost two of my brothers and three sisters here to cold and illness before I was ten. Need to lay down a good crop to prepare for wastage. Hope for the best and prepare for the worst and all that.'

'You're insane if you believe I will have anything to do with this charade,' spat Willow. 'I don't know who you are, I don't love you and I won't marry you.'

'Love has so little to do with this affair that a college scholar with a magnifying glass would be hard pressed to uncover it,' said the viscount. 'As for introductions, you are I take it, the Willow Landor whose dreary farming father is one of the richest men in the north? While I am Viscount William Wallingbeck, title-holder to one of the oldest houses in the kingdom. Your children will have such honours it will wash away the stain of your low birth, and in return, your house's dowry will help alleviate my gambling debts and repair the leaking roof at Belinus Hall.'

'There is *no* stain in my birth. And I am not a cow to be traded at the local fair!'

'I find breeding bulls an agreeable diversion,' said the viscount. 'From your comportment so far, I fear I will not be able to claim the same of lying with you.'

'And we are in Arcadia now, my dear,' said Leyla Holten. 'This is *very* far from local.'

'Divorce my fool of a father and marry this high-born pig yourself, then.'

'Alas, my dear, I find myself far too comfortable with my present circumstances. And William is correct; his gambling debts really are rather severe. Why, my personal funds would barely cover the silver piss-pot his maids use to catch rainwater from the hall's leaking battlements.'

'And I do take exception at being characterized as a swine,' said the viscount, standing up to admire himself in a mirror between two notably empty bookcases. 'I'm a strikingly handsome fellow.'

'Indeed so,' said Holten, reaching out to run her fingers through his hair. 'And quite the brute with it.'

Willow backed away from them. 'You think there's a priest in the capital who will marry me against my will?'

'Oh, I'm sure we could find one or two,' smiled Holten. 'But I don't have time to waste, and a formal ceremony is no longer necessary. You were probably too drugged to remember the flight south. We shared the transport with Prefect Colbert who had a suggestion that is simply perfect for our predicament. An obscure four-centuries-old law still vested on the statute book from the reign of King Morlan. If you recall your tutoring, Morlan was the dirty dog who enjoyed divorcing his wives almost as much as he disliked listening to churchmen lecturing him about why taking fresh queens was out of the question. His solution was ingenious. Divorces exclusively by royal decree . . . with a marriage licence on the bill's opposite side. William's never been married before, so the palace clerks only had half the paperwork to prepare, for which I'm sure they'll thank you.'

Willow felt a rising sense of dread. 'It's not true!'

'You've been married by *decree regius* since this afternoon,' laughed Holten. 'Consider the rest of the evening your honeymoon, my *lady*.' She gave a mocking curtsy towards Willow. 'I'll have to arrange a proper title for your father too, now, I suppose. I would so hate to have the misfortune of sharing a table with you, and be embarrassed in public by being seated with lower precedence.'

Willow seized a vase from a nearby table and hurled it at her stepmother, ceramic smashing across the woman's chest and sending her stumbling back into a panelled wall. Holten recovered herself, shaking with rage. 'You little bitch! You dare strike me, mistress of your house!'

'Well, you did warn me she would need breaking in,' said the viscount, amused. 'I trust the dowry is as large as your husband promised. It seems this will be a tiresome amount of work.'

'Half now,' said Holten. 'The balance when she's provided you with an heir.'

Willow suddenly realized how very alone she was, surrounded by Holten's place-men and the poisonous woman's friends. She backed away towards a high glass window, drawing out the stolen knife she had hidden under her dress. 'I swear, I'll kill the first one of you who tries to lay a hand on me.'

'It won't be me to do it,' said the viscount, sounding bored. 'A dreary rural maid like you, you must know how a recalcitrant cow is led to service the bull, and it's never the bull that's expected to tie a cow to the frame. That's what farm-hands are for.'

'Nocks,' commanded Holten. 'It's time for you to earn your pay.'

The malevolent manservant shook his head in mocking sadness, signalling the viscount's burly retainers to move towards Willow and seize her. 'I did warn you, girl. You're shaming your marriage with this disobedience. It's a pity I didn't bring my horse whip down south with me, or I'd use it to whack some sense of duty into you. Had to throw it away, though. Too much blood on it, after I beat your pastor's son to death with it.'

'You're lying,' cried Willow.

'Didn't mean to, but I mistook him for one of those wild marauders out on the road, sniffing around the park. Easy mistake to make, in the dark.'

'You knew who he was!' shouted Willow. 'You took him prisoner alongside me.'

'Really? My eyes aren't so good,' said Nocks, derisively apologetic. 'He died moaning your name, if it makes you feel any better.'

'There's no one coming for you,' said Holten. 'No one! You're alone and this is your new life. Thankfully, it's a decent distance from Northhaven.' She contentedly rubbed her engorged belly. 'Don't trouble yourself to visit. We'll be quite busy enough without you. Enjoy the season here; there's so much to see and do in the capital.'

Willow glanced down at her knife and then rushed at Leyla Holten with the blade, incandescent with rage, imagining plunging it in and out of her chief tormenter's heart, but Nocks was too fast. The manservant stepped into the path of her attack, throwing one of the viscount's retainers in front of him as a human shield. Willow tried to halt, but only stopped as her knife met the man's gut, a soft slap as the sharp blade buried itself smoothly into his flesh. Viscount

Wallingbeck's servant collapsed screaming onto the carpet, the blade lodged inside the man's body as Nocks and the retainers swarmed over Willow, pinning her down.

'How tedious,' said the viscount, looking at the man dying on the floor. 'That carpet's been in the family for generations. In the name of the saints, drag him outside before he bleeds all over it.'

Willow looked down in horror at the man. 'You've done it now,' growled Nocks. 'You'll swing if he dies.'

'No,' commanded Holten. She clapped her hands and the retainers bound the struggling Willow across the largest of the tables, legs and wrists tied so tight that her circulation was nearly cut off. One of the retainers handed the stolen blade to Holten, the metal still slick with blood. 'If she's tried, Benner Landor might read about the court case in the papers. I've promised him a title for his grandchildren, not a noose for his disobedient little spare.'

'The court can try me for three bodies, because I'm going to slit your throat, Holten,' swore Willow. 'I don't care how long I have to wait. And I'm going to hunt your lapdog down too, for what he did to Carter.'

'Oh, my dove,' said Holten. She stepped to Willow's side and ripped her dress away, then used the knife to slice off the corset, exposing her cold skin to the eyes of everyone in the room. 'Much better. You'll find yourself far too occupied for such nonsense after you have been bred a few times. You won't allow her any maids, will you, William? I believe she'll benefit from looking after her brood herself. Nothing like exhaustion to clip a shrew's feathers.'

The viscount stood up. 'More like my kennel of hunting hounds, I'd say. Need to be run out daily to stop them barking and biting.'

'Mount her and consummate the marriage,' ordered Holten as she and Nocks followed the noble's servants dragging the groaning retainer through the door. 'Do it now, William. I don't want to leave any holes in the decree that can be challenged later.'

'Perish the thought, Leyla. You have to appreciate the irony of the situation,' said the viscount as he advanced on Willow. 'Normally I toss coins at whorehouse wenches to have them bound to a frame for my sport. And here we are, the tables turned. A pity I won't be so handsomely paid every time I have you. Still, we'll just have to make the money last, my dear *wife*.'

Willow shook with horror as she felt the viscount running his hands admiringly down her spine, but that revulsion was nothing compared to the outrage of thinking of Carter murdered by Nocks. Left for dead in a stable at Hawkland Park. All the miles the two of them had covered out and back again from Vandia, all the terrors they had survived together. The skels. The empire. The sky mines. The slave rebellion. All of that only to be killed in Northhaven, in her own home, by a sadistic servant? Could fate be ludicrous, so random? *Please God, I can survive anything, I will survive this, but how can I survive losing him?*

'Another problem solved,' said Leyla Landor as she walked down the corridor. 'The line of succession at the House of Landor has just been enormously simplified. If my son ever requires a half-sister, I'm quite capable of providing him with a brat myself.' She halted, irritated. 'Do come along, Nocks. I'm sure you've been party to such recreations frequently enough that you're not required to hover outside the chamber.'

'You're just spoiling my fun,' said the manservant from outside the closed door.

'I enjoy playing the voyeur, but only when I'm loitering to be pleasured myself. That girl's whining grievances are grating at the best of times, and these are a much greater irritation. If Willow thought being a Landor under *my* roof wasn't to her taste, let's see how she likes being Willow Wallingbeck of Belinus Hall.'

'I thought they needed a witness?' laughed Nocks, abandoning the door behind him.

'Don't be boorish,' said Leyla. 'You know the presence of the Privy Council by a marriage bed's reserved for royal marriages. If there was a marriageable prince going spare, I certainly wouldn't be wasting that impudent girl on him.'

'Or a king going spare?' grinned Nocks.

'Don't over-reach yourself,' warned Leyla. 'You've proved yourself very useful to me. It would be a shame for our association to be terminated now.'

'I'm not going anywhere,' said Nocks. He halted by a branch in the corridors. Down the side passage, the wounded retainer had been laid across the floor. Willow's knife wound bubbled in his chest, the man attended by two of the viscount's staff.

'Isn't he dead yet?' asked Nocks.

'We've sent for a doctor,' said one of the staff.

'Then go and fetch bandages and hot water for when he arrives,' ordered Leyla. 'Quick, quick!' She waited for the pair to scurry away and then turned to Nocks. 'I've just found a way for you to be useful to me again. Save William the doctor's bill. Having a murder with commoners as witnesses might be a useful threat to hold over the silly girl in the future.'

'You like to plan ahead, don't you?' Nocks bent over the semi-conscious retainer and placed a hand over his mouth, then closed the retainer's nostrils with the other, leaning on the man's body as he shook and shuddered, suffocating, until it was a body no longer, just a corpse. 'There we are . . . she's a murderer, now. Crowds in the capital always do enjoy seeing a rich girl swing at the gallows.'

'Vicious little thing. Who would have suspected it? Willow would have buried that blade in me without a second's regret. Still far too trusting, though. She appeared to swallow what you told her about the pastor's son. Without hope, she should prove a lot more pliable. William will break her in a few months, and if I know him, once the thrill of the hunt has vanished, he'll go back to leathering fresh whores. She'll end up confined to the hall's top floor, wet-nursing an ever expanding brood.'

'Good for her, but I don't give a shit about the little sweet-meat if she's not going to end up on my plate.' said Nocks. 'We've got *another* problem for now.'

'The lure's been well baited.'

'Maybe a little too well,' said Nocks. 'The pastor's boy will pursue the girl. And the pastor will travel with him. He crossed a world to follow the lad before. What's the trip down to the capital compared to that?'

'I would have let them follow us by air,' said Leyla. 'But my dear interfering dolt of a husband had other ideas.'

'A slow guild train'll do nicely,' said Nocks. 'Old Benner doesn't know it, but he did us a favour. We're not hunting rabbits, this is a mountain cat. You put a snare in the open and bait it with a handsome young doe, and the cat's going to get suspicious. It needs to believe taking the doe is its idea, not the hunter's.'

'He's just one man,' said Leyla. 'And I know all about men.'

'Not this one you don't,' said Nocks. 'Jacob Carnehan's the wildest mountain cat of them all. Taking him down is going to be as far distant from easy as both Poles of Pellas.'

'You mistake me for someone else,' said Leyla, coolly. 'I always get what I want and I never fail.'

'How nice that must be for you,' said Nocks, running his finger down his scar. 'When you do fall short, you'll know it. That you will. A burning pain that you go to sleep with and wake up with just the same.'

'Ah, my poor dear revolting little Nocks.' A muffled scream of rage escaped into the corridor behind them. 'There, you see. You have to earn everything in life,' said Leyla, a smile twitching at her full lips. 'Every penny, every title. Just ask *Lady* Wallingbeck.'

Carter awoke with a start. He was in a cabin, but not the schooner he had dreamt, wet with kelp and sea spray. A dry, warm cot, rather than a hammock. One of many in the room, alongside well-scrubbed carving tables. *A sickbay, then.* He could feel the distant drone of a hundred propellers, their vibration feeding through the fuselage. *Just like the skels' slaver carrier. But healthier quarters.* An old man Carter didn't recognize sat opposite him, a portly chap balancing on a stool, pushing a jelly paste around a clear glass dish. Whatever the substance was, it didn't look fit to eat, covered in a mottled fur of coloured mildew.

'Awake, are you? I am Mapple, the ship's surgeon.'

'Ship? This is the *Plunderbird* . . . or did I hallucinate that too?'

The surgeon nodded and tapped the side of his jelly, before sealing it with a transparent lid and placing it in a black surgeon's bag by his boots. Carter noted the more traditional bone saw jutting out and was all too glad he wasn't suffering from gangrene. 'Aye to the matter of your location. But no more hallucinations for you. Not unless you're partial to a pipe or two of strong dank. Mapple's medicine has seen you cured. And a word to the wise . . . carriers are known as "ships", by those that fly on board them.'

Carter reached behind his shirt and touched his back. It was crusted over, most of the pain gone, just a dull itch remaining when he touched the scar tissue. 'If that's so, what do you call sailing vessels?'

'Boats,' said the surgeon. 'Or on the *Plunderbird*, "marks" or "catch" will do nicely.'

'I'm a poor catch,' said Carter.

'That much I don't dispute.'

'You have my father and friend hostage?'

Mapple snorted. 'Hostage? Worth much silver, are you?'

'I must be, or why would a crew of pirates hold on to me – or cure me?'

'Pirates? Oh, we're never airbooters,' said Mapple. 'We're *privateers*.'

'Is there much difference?'

'The difference between a prison cell and a gallows, in the right company. Or perhaps the wrong one. We only swoop when we hold letters of marque from a powerful patron. So, you're really the pastor's son, are you?' He chuckled to himself. 'There's a thing, now.'

'My father is alive – he's here?'

'Both, last time I checked. Same for that itinerant book-botherer travelling with you.'

Carter didn't understand any of this. *Patrons? Pirates? Privateers?* He should be dead, a bloated corpse bobbing on the ocean's surface. Unless the aircrew were planning to sell him off as a slave for a second time. Or receive a fat purse from King Marcus for turning them over to the usurper's forces. 'Why am I alive?'

'Too deep a question for me, young-un,' said the surgeon.

'You know what I mean.'

'That I do, but it isn't Mapple's place to tell you.' The portly old man stood up and stretched. 'I can tell you one thing. The dog that did that to your back didn't want you dead. He was an expert at his craft. A minute or two more of the lash and you wouldn't be here. He teased you right to the edge and then intentionally stepped back from the brink.'

'He was an amateur flogger,' said Carter. 'But a professional bastard.'

'No, I don't think so. I was trained in the Burn. Surgeon and torturer are two sides of the same coin out there. The man that did this to you has mastered his trade.'

'He's a dead man, either way.'

'That's the spirit, young-un. Show a little gumption and folks on board might keep you around, rather than casting you out with the contents of last night's piss-pot.'

'Not much point in healing me for that.'

'Mapple serves his captain. On your feet, lad. Black Barnaby wanted to meet you when you're fixed, and you're as fixed as my sickbay is going to see you.'

It proved to be a short trip between the sickbay and the pirate commander; narrow corridors, cold fuselage, riding a series of room-sized elevators transferring flying boats and fighter planes between hangar decks and the carrier's repair workshops. Crewmen, all armed, swaggered around as though they were the lords of the sky. *Maybe they are at that*. The surgeon led Carter through a hatch and into a substantial hall that wouldn't have looked out of place inside a castle. Walls hung with hunting trophies, not the usual bears' heads and stags' antlers; instead, carved wooden figureheads taken from sailing ships. Eagles, curly-haired maidens, sea gods, dolphins, unicorns; multiple painted eyes seeming to follow Carter as he advanced towards a throne at the far end – simple dark oak with a fan of wooden propeller rotors rising out of its rear. Doors opened to either side of the throne, giving on to the aircraft's bridge, airmen manning long banks of instruments, spotters on swivel-mounted telescopes while crew strode across the floor's planking. Power here, it seemed, resided close to the cockpit. The black-bearded man who filled the throne wore a crimson jacket, brown trousers with a military stripe, long leather boots draped insolently over the throne's side; one hand clutching a glass of red wine, the other with a thumb tucked behind a military leather clip holster holding two pistols and multiple ammunition pouches. There weren't many privateers idling in what passed for the *Plunderbird*'s throne room, a cabin boy and a scattering of officers, and a woman that was hard to miss . . . an exotic-looking privateer who looked to have a mixture of Weyland and Rodalian blood. Around Carter's age, she stood alongside the throne, her dark hair tied back below a crimson aviator's wedge cap, the competitive gaze of her fierce clever eyes tracking Carter's entrance as closely as the ships' ransacked figureheads.

The ship's surgeon bowed before the throne, indicated the Weylander by his side, and then departed.

Carter gazed carefully around him before speaking. 'You're Black Barnaby?'

'I much prefer *Brave* Barnaby,' laughed the man. 'But for some reason the name never sticks.'

The pirate looked oddly familiar, although Carter had never met him. *Must be his portrait drawn on all those newspaper covers.* 'Try painting your carrier yellow instead.'

The woman reached for a dagger on her belt. 'Do you call us cowards?'

'Peace, Aurora. You must forgive my daughter. She gets cabin-fever when she hasn't killed a groundling for a few weeks. Our crew are traditionalists and they prefer to fly with traditional colours.'

'Yet here you sit on a throne.'

'Just another wooden seat, whelp. We elect our leaders,' boomed Black Barnaby. 'And bow before no one.'

'That's good,' said Carter. 'I won't curtsy before you, then.'

'He's got spirit,' said Aurora, 'I'll say that for the dog. Is he a groundling noble?'

'Another book-botherer,' said Black Barnaby. 'If the pastor and the young guild courier are to be taken at their word. And who would doubt a priest?'

'Such broad shoulders,' said Aurora, admiringly. 'That's a waste of a life, buried in a hold with only paper and dusty groundlings for company.'

Carter nodded in her direction. 'I always thought much the same thing.'

'Ha! I only had to gaze upon your spine to know you were an awkward sod,' announced the captain. 'Nobles still like to whip manners into their peasants, I see. Groundlings have to be expertly acquainted with bowing and scraping to survive. That's why I'm up here.'

'And why am I?'

'Let's call it idle curiosity,' said Black Barnaby.

'Why don't we call it an obligation, instead?' spoke a familiar voice behind Carter. He turned around. His father had entered the chamber. 'I thought we agreed that my son would stay in the sickbay for the flight.'

'You expressed that wish,' said Barnaby. 'I don't recall agreeing to it.'

Carter was confused. From their tone, it was as though his father and this rogue had more of a history together than merely hostage and captor. Had the pastor's monastery been involved with the kelpers' fuel smuggling out to the *Plunderbird*? 'You know this airbooter?'

Black Barnaby laughed and spoke for Carter's father. 'Me and this *good* man? Can't a privateer occasionally request the mediations of a pastor, or are we also godless in your eyes, whelp?' Black Barnaby's needling brought back memories to Carter, a time when his and his father's minds had fused under Sariel's sorcery. He had recollections of blood and fighting; terrible and blasted. But none of this pirate, no memories from the air or of the *Plunderbird*.

'That's enough,' said Jacob.

Carter looked at his father in astonishment. 'Is *this* our ride south?'

Black Barnaby stretched languidly out in his throne. 'Eventually the light dawns on even the dimmest horizon.'

'We need to follow fast, and a carrier plane riding the arrow is the best I can do. Beggars can't be choosers, Carter.'

'And all priests are beggars,' grinned the privateer captain. 'On your knees to the saints, on your knees to the church and its bishops, on your knees to your congregation with the church plate extended and rattling. It's a surprise you can still stand with the sores you must have developed on your knees.'

Carter felt a flash of anger. 'Better an honest parish for a trade than raiding innocent merchantmen.'

'*Innocent?*' Black Barnaby rocked with laughter at Carter's words. 'What do you think the main trade east to west across the Lancean Ocean is? Fine silks and spices? They don't have much call for extravagances in the Burn. It is guns and arms and sharp steel that flow, along with men who're desperate enough to sell their skills across the ocean *and* know which end of a pike to stick a peasant with. This month, the *Plunderbird* flies as the skyguard of the Three Cities of Abbarriss, hunting for boats running supplies to their most troublesome neighbour, the Dukedom of Opard. There are Weyland clippers sailing west with cargoes of greased rifles and crates of bullets paid for in blood, because that's all they have left to pay with in the Burn. And after all those centuries of war, even the ruins of the ruins being fought over, it takes a *lot* of squeezing to ring blood out of that much ash.'

'You freely admit to hunting Weyland vessels?' said Carter.

'Compared to your state's arms trade, what we're about is almost missionary work,' grinned Black Barnaby.

'Maybe you should apply to the church council and study to wear the black.'

'He's your son, all right,' said Black Barnaby to the pastor. 'The *good* man you are presently, of course. I can hear your cant in every word he utters.'

'You don't know who I am, now,' growled Jacob.

'I can't predict what you're going to do next,' said Black Barnaby. 'But then, which of us ever could? What the hell do you think you're doing travelling south? Into the mouth of the shit-storm brewing down there, and for what? A young noble-woman your whelp fancies?'

'It's true then?' said the captain's daughter. 'These fools are following a girl? I thought the flying boat's crew were joking when they spun me that yarn.'

'No joke,' said Black Barnaby.

'Not to me,' said Carter.

'I hope she's beautiful, groundling,' said Aurora.

'She's the right woman,' said Carter. 'The only one. It took me a long time to realize that. I would cross all of Pellas on foot twice over to find her again.'

'Then I hope you know a good cobbler,' said the pirate captain. 'You understand it won't matter soon, even if you succeed. I foresee a long stream of boats sailing from west to east; carrying tutors to educate soft Weylanders in how centuries of war have elevated conflict into a higher form. That's all you'd be rescuing the girl for. The way things are going in Weyland, it won't be long before there are prefects and assemblymen breaking off and titling themselves kings and dukes, offering me letters of marque to hunt for *them*.'

'There's only one true king in Weyland,' said Carter.

'You're a believer, whelp? You share that in common with your old da, then. I find kings are a lot like gods. So many to choose from, and believing in exclusivity is never as profitable as embracing the many. Poor Weyland . . . a boy the king calls pretender and a king the boy calls usurper. And freemen of the air who only care which noble will pay most to guarantee sole use of the title. King, king, *king*. Such a stubby little word, given how many lust after it. Maybe if it was longer and harder to pronounce, the Burn wouldn't be the Burn and we would all live in a land of milk and honey.'

'Forget her, book-botherer. Fly west with us, instead,' invited Aurora. 'You'll meet few nobles on the far side of the ocean that don't style themselves kings or queens.'

'This whelp's not for you, Aurora. Can't you see he's fixing to die nobly? Along, I suspect, with a great many others. Famine is coming for Weyland,' said the captain, swigging from his wine cup. 'But it'll be a feast for us. Nothing drives up the price of our services like a bit of honest competition.'

'The word honest doesn't belong on your lips,' said Jacob. 'That's the province of people who rise with the sun and break their backs in the field every day to provide for their children.'

'Yet, neither of us are farmers out a-toiling,' said Black Barnaby, indicating the trophy-heavy walls of his chamber. 'And do I not provide handsomely for my children?'

'I can't complain,' said Aurora.

'You do. Frequently and loudly. I suppose you must have hundreds of bastard half-sisters and brothers scattered along the coastline who might take issue with my generosity. Of course, if I knew who they were, I'd do more for them.'

'Try flying over the port-side whorehouses and bombing them with coins,' said Aurora.

'And how then would I pay you and the rest of my valiant crew?' laughed Black Barnaby. He raised his cup and called for more wine, a young cabin boy rushing forward with a crystal decanter. 'Will you two groundling rascals not drink with me?'

'Carter's barely out of the sickbay,' said Jacob, 'and wine dulls my wits.'

'That's rather the point. And you can hardly grow much duller, *good* man.' He waved them away. 'Go. Go. I was in a happy mood before you came in. You drain my natural cheerfulness as fast as an engine with a spray of bullet-holes in its fuel chamber. Away with you, before you convert me into a dour saint-loving pilgrim and I swap my carrier for a monk's coarse robes.'

'Why's he flying us south?' asked Carter, once they had put the chamber behind them, exchanging it for a narrow corridor with port-hole views out of the fuselage. They were in the heart of the spear, fast-flowing winds shredding the clouds, rivulets of water running across the glass. No fighter squadrons or flying boats circling around them in the air now, all the little birds landed inside the flight decks under the carrier's monstrous wings.

'Pirates are romantics at heart,' said Jacob. 'Maybe your story touched his heart.'

'He has a heart?'

'Barnaby has a sense of honour, in his way. Let us say that this passage on his carrier helps settle some debts that were long resting in the dust.'

'Please tell me you never served with this crew,' said Carter, wishing his suspicions away.

'I don't have to lie to you to tell you that. Barnaby has only ever fought for money and wealth. And wealth makes a good servant but a poor master. I'm going to remind King Marcus of that fact one day very soon.'

'We're travelling south for *Willow*.'

'You don't need to remind me, boy. But it won't just be Benner Landor and his house's hirelings facing us in the capital. The usurper has too many scores to settle with us to simply let matters rest.'

'Damn him. I've never even met the man.'

'He sold you and countless thousands of Weylanders he was sworn to protect into slavery for imperial silver. He's as responsible for your mother's death as the skel slavers and the imperium. That's all you need to know about the usurper.'

'Sometimes I—'

'—wish you had taken up Sariel on his offer?' said Jacob. 'Allowed him to carry you and Willow away to some quiet far-called country where news of our home's troubles might drift in over the radio relays in five hundred years' time as distant history.'

'Something like that.'

Carter's father halted him in the corridor. 'Maybe that would have been for the best. I know I'd sleep easier knowing you were safely out of Weyland. But you're a man now, and I won't demand you do the wrong thing just because it's the easy option. Doing the right thing often comes with a cost. It sure as hell comes with no guarantees. Bad men can end up occupying thrones and good men can end up face down in the dirt with a dagger in their back. Your mother was the best woman I ever knew, and she died at the hands of slavers she'd never heard of, by arrangement of a king she'd never met, in exchange for wealth she wouldn't have given a damn for, along with half the friends and neighbours she loved buried with her. There was no fairness, no sense, and if anyone could call that justice I'd damn them as a devil.'

'And you? Are you a good man? The one that pirate scorns.'

'I'm good enough,' said Jacob, patting his twin pistols. 'Or we're all in trouble.'

'And if not?'

'Man's got to die doing something, Carter. You have something else you need to do?'

No. On reflection, he really didn't.

EIGHT

THE WALLS OF THE LEAGUE

Lady Cassandra Skar sat, shivering, in the rear of the wagon. Her legs were manacled together, but with enough play on the chains that she could shuffle about the wagon if the mood took her. Her hands were still bound behind her back, chafing, gloveless and chilly. It was freezing in these monstrous damned Rodalian Mountains and it didn't seem to matter how many layers you wore or blankets you wrapped around yourself, the winds would seek you out like snakes of ice, slipping through the smallest gap to bite into your bones. She could see why superstitious savages like Sheplar Lesh treated the winds as spirits and worshipped them. You always worshipped the things which had power over you. In Vandia that was the emperor and the Cult of the Imperium Cosmocrator. Here it was the high winds. That she was born of divine blood was of little concern to the weather as she rattled through the mountain passes. They travelled at such altitude that the air had thinned out, Cassandra having to breathe faster and harder, even gravity's touch not as strong as the forest where she had been held previously. *If only the local fools who tried to rescue me had made a better job of it.*

As if the cold wasn't bad enough, there was a constant whistling in the air that only varied in intensity as it slipped through the cracks and crags. Cassandra could tune it out for large periods of time, background noise she hardly noticed. And then suddenly it would reappear randomly at night when she was trying to go to sleep, or when she was eating a bowl of rice, and when it was there she would hear nothing else. It was almost enough to send her insane. It probably explained much about the demented Rodalian flyer and his people. When she complained to Sheplar Lesh and demanded something she could plug her ears with, he only laughed and told her that it was the spirit called Naimzeraw the Prankster, welcoming her to Rodal and trying to gauge the measure of a Vandian.

'You are probably the first Vandian to visit, bumo,' said Sheplar. He huddled next to Kerge on the wagon's footplate while the gask held the reins. He sported a rabbit-fur-trimmed aviator's hat, the fur dyed purple, with its leather earflaps worn down. She was more than a little envious of its obvious warmth. 'Naimzeraw merely wants to test you. To see what sort of person comes calling.'

'Why would any of my people want to come to this barren, forsaken place?'

'The clear air and a view from heaven's doorstep?' suggested the Rodalian, condescendingly.

'These winds are intolerable.'

'These are hardly winds, bumo,' said Sheplar. 'We call this Sogo, the windless region of Rodal. In trade tongue, *porch*.'

'You are joking.'

'He does not joke,' said Kerge from the front of the wagon. 'Rodal is not known as the walls of the league just because it holds back the steppes' nomads. It's also a containing chamber for weather systems that form when cold air from the league nations meets warm air from the steppes, mixed in with massive quantities of moisture from the Lancean Ocean to the west. Rodalian winds are a thing of legend and terror.'

'Not to us,' said Sheplar. 'We respect the spirits, but we never fear them. This is our home and they are our guides. Rodal has given me everything.'

'You must forgive me my apprehension, then,' said Kerge. 'Given the choice, we gasks prefer not to venture far from our forests. We live in the shadow of the mountains but few of our traders travel this far. As much as we appreciate the protection of your heights, Northhaven streets are as far-called as we wish to explore.'

'Given the choice.' Sheplar glared back at Cassandra.

'You should have stayed in Vandia,' she goaded. 'You could have joined the spiky one as a slave in the sky mines. You keep boasting about what an excellent pilot you are. You could be put to service flying transporters between our mines.'

'It is not a boast when it is a statement of fact,' said Sheplar. 'And Kerge, son of Khow, will never be your slave again. He is a free gask.'

'That is so, yet I may never be considered a gask again,' said Kerge. 'The universe moves, but my mind may no longer move ahead of it. Without the gift of prediction, what am I? Little more than a common pattern manling with a few poisoned spines running along his skin.'

'Your future sight may return to you,' said Sheplar. 'Your ranger friend Slell was hopeful.'

'I fear he is too optimistic. To survive in the sky mines is to have your soul stolen. I, among very few, escaped. My lifetime's luck has been depleted,' said Kerge.

'It had better not be,' said Cassandra. 'For when the empire comes for me, you will need a great deal of good fortune.'

Sheplar shook his head. 'There is nobody on the road to hear her cries, but I am sorely tempted to gag her.'

'Find cloth to cover my ears rather than my mouth and you will find me silent enough.'

Sheplar pulled himself off the footplate, rummaged around inside the covered wagon's boxes and came out holding a cape with a fur-lined hood. He dropped it over her head and re-joined the gask at the front of the wagon. 'Keep to your word, bumo.'

She snorted but held her peace. She had been filled with hope since realizing that the imperium's local agents were sweeping the land for her. The very fact these barbarians had moved her so suddenly from the gasks' forests spoke volumes of how much they feared she would be located, secured and returned to the empire. It didn't matter where they took her now. Vandia would not give up on her. Not, she understood, out of any deep or abiding love for her. But because Lady Cassandra Skar carried divine blood, the *emperor*'s blood. To be held like this was to insult Vandia and all that was Vandian. Her only worry was that the empire's agents would prefer see her dead than left a living hostage to remind Vandia's enemies of the empire's fallibility. It was all too feasible that if she was chained in some Rodalian mountain nest and proved too hard to rescue alive, the alternative – a little poison slipped into one of her meals – might seem a pragmatic solution to the kind of foreign intelligencers kept on the imperium payroll. Still, if her mother had anything to do with the matter, being retaken alive would be the only scheme they countenanced.

They rode on for the best part of the day. The back of the wagon's cover was tied up against the elements but she could see well enough out of the front between her two captors. Green grassland covered the lower mountain slopes and valleys between the rises, giving way to mottled white where snow covered dark rock. They rattled slowly along a high path carved out of the mountainside, barely wide enough to accommodate the wagon. A vertiginous view to the left, only a few wooden markers with colourful pennants whipping in the breeze to mark places where they might fall to their deaths, wispy clouds drifting past below. There was little sign of the aviator's countrymen along the path. Only the flags showed that anything sentient had passed this way or considered it, literally, a highway. The sun was going down, snow along the distant peaks glowing orange, when she spotted what looked to be a town or perhaps a large village. Blocky white-washed buildings had been carved out of the slopes of the mountains opposite, flat vertical walls dotted by hundreds of narrow windows sealed by sliding stone storm shutters. There were a few slanted lines where external staircases ran and a long flat stretch of rooftop for a skyguard plane to set down. The bulk of the space was no doubt burrowed inside the mountain face itself. Cassandra could hear a constant clacking from exposed rotating cylinders turning in the wind. No sign of electric lights, though, so the drums weren't wind turbines. Prayer wheels, perhaps. Rice terraces sat in the shadow of the town's underhang, narrow ledges as carefully carved from the mountainside as the buildings. There was no bridge across the chasm to the town, however. It seemed the three of them wouldn't be spending the night there, whatever that place was called.

'Your artisans have yet to master suspension span engineering,' said Cassandra.

'We can build bridges when necessary,' said Sheplar. 'But they are more use to our enemies than us.' He pointed towards the town opposite. 'To reach Salasang we would need to take a road down to the valley floor, cross the valley and then travel up again. Maybe two days, by foot. That is two days in which we can see our foe approaching and prepare for attack.'

It was a good point. Although who was around to attack this godforsaken land apart from mountain goats and eagles, she did not know. If it had been closer to Vandia she supposed they would have conquered it, installed an imperial governor and extracted annual tribute from the kingdom. The barbarian country would be considered a hardship posting, though, and thin pickings for the calculators of the empire – unless you valued snow, ice, granite and baskets of rice. They could always have found a use for Rodal's pilots in the legions' levies, she supposed. Anyone who could set an aircraft down on that thin long building in the gusty winds and survive the landing might make a passable pilot for imperial service. Maybe they were all mad, though, like poor clown-faced Sheplar Lesh. She almost laughed at the thought. An air legion of loons. Mad enough to call these bleak rocks home. Crazy enough to fly here.

They rode on, leaving the mountain with the town behind. The party continued their slow, careful journey through the high mountains for days, passing small villages and towns in the distance but never stopping. At one point they crawled past a structure she mistook for a dam, a sloping wooden structure built across a valley between two mountains, squatting in the shadow of a stone temple nearby. But when Cassandra asked about the angled doors opening and closing in the wood by a complex system of rope pulleys – with no sudden torrents of water released – the aviator told her it was one of the nation's many wind walls. They channelled and managed the worst of the winds that flew through Rodal, mitigating the gales that would otherwise lash the valleys. Priests here, it seemed, did more than pray for clemency from their gods, they also operated as wind keepers on their high walls. A primitive solution compared to the cloud seeding that the empire used to guarantee the provinces' harvest, but a reminder that you underestimated barbarians such as these mountain tribes at your peril.

It was getting close to dark when they took a fork in the road and headed away from the cliff edge, rock walls on either side of them, following a winding path until they reached a dead-end – a circular space for a caravan halt with a single building. They drew to a stop in front of a low brick building that resembled a windmill, stripped with vanes replaced by rope webbing hung with dyed pennants – devoid of houses' arms and sigils, but fluttering in every imaginable colour. It was as though a party of children had descended on the bleak place and decided to decorate it with silks cut from their mothers' dresses. The high rock walls and the winding road managed to cut off the worst of the wind, and the building, while simple grey brickwork and little more sophisticated than an oversized kiln, would keep any rain and snowfall off their heads. There was a small well next to the building but, given the small stream running down one of the walls, it seemed superfluous. Then she realized it must serve as a toilet. It seemed they were not the only travellers staying over. A horned yak had been tied up outside, its flanks warmed by a woollen saddle – a patchwork of colours every bit as bright as the fluttering flags – thrown across the leathery-skinned creature. It must make for an uncomfortable, slow mount. But then, what use a fine racing stallion on these dangerously high roads? The dull creature chewed at mossy grass that grew from cracks in the walls, oblivious to the newcomers.

Kerge gazed at a line of firework-like rockets dangling from a basket on the yak's side. 'A military patrol?'

Sheplar Lesh shook his head as he dismounted. 'There is a hold of the Guild of Radiomen on one of the peaks nearby. What you see are postal rockets to fire bundles of messages across to villages and towns too small or poor to have their own guild receiving station.' He left Cassandra's leg irons on but untied her hands so she might eat, administering a stern warning about what to expect if she tried to escape. She shuffled after them. There was no door, but a blanket had been hung over the entrance. It was warmer inside the squat domed building than outside, if a little pungent. There was a single room with a lonely fireplace, and what she took to be dried yak shit acting as fuel for an iron pot simmering with rice. The room's sole occupant glanced up from stirring the meal. An ancient man with lazy eyes, smothered in a brown fur coat that looked like the best part of a bear wrapped around a bony, wrinkled old stick.

Sheplar bowed towards the guild courier and introduced the party, one by one, condescendingly omitting Cassandra's titles, as though she were no better than a common goat herder. The postal courier's name, it transpired, was Gephal. He introduced himself by sweeping off his embroidered hat that had a wide white-fur brim and a tall crown elaborately sown with yellow and black mountain peaks.

'You come from Weyland,' said Gephal, more of a statement than a question, his curious gaze taking in the gask and Cassandra.

Sheplar nodded. 'That is so.'

'An aviator without a plane is a rare sight,' said Gephal.

'I buried her bones in the mud of Northhaven,' said Sheplar, sadly. 'Lost in combat.'

'There will be more of that in the south,' said Gephal. 'I read many of the messages sent by the wireless voices. Hopefully their troubles will stay far from us.'

'We travel to the skyguard station at Talatala,' said Sheplar. 'For passage on to the capital.'

'The roads are open. Snow has been light here this winter. The winds from the steppes have blown angry and warm. That is never a good augury. Still, share my rice, Sheplar Lesh, you and the bumo and the man of the deep forests.'

'You are kind.'

The old man handed the wooden spoon to Sheplar to stir and used a metal-tipped walking staff to hobble over to the door to check his yak. On the way he stopped and gazed thoughtfully at Cassandra. 'You are not a Weylander.'

'I am a noble daughter of the imperium, old man. One day I will be a princess.'

He grunted. 'I have three daughters. They are all princesses. And my wife acts as if she is the greatest empress of all the ages.'

'It is *true*,' said Cassandra, irritated by the thin old man's lack of respect.

He raised a bony finger to point at the cloak she wore. 'Is that why the skyguard keeps you chained . . . you are so royal that you will float away, otherwise? Wear your clothes looser. Allow air to circulate, or you will sweat, and sweat turns to ice here, bumo. Unless princess's bones have special protection against the mountain spirits.'

He grunted again and walked outside, muttering in a sarcastic imitation of her voice.

Dogs, I am surrounded by low-born dogs. She cursed him but sat down to eat his simple brown rice. It was astounding how hungry you could get when your body had to work so hard to stay warm. She drank from a clay pitcher of water filled from the mountain spring outside, so cold that it was almost hot. After the meal she lay down on one of the mats on the hard floor and covered herself in rough woollen blankets. Sheplar Lesh made the small concession of binding her hands in front of her rather than behind her back, so she could at least pull the blankets closer as she tried to sleep through their racket, the two Rodalians jabbering like monkeys as they supped warm rice wine from a glazed clay bottle. At least the gask did not join in their antics, happy to sit by the fire and drink spring water.

When she woke again it was the dead of night. The fire had gone out under the metal pot and she could feel the winter cold from outside pressing on her face. She was dog-tired, but her bladder was full and demanding a trip to the toilet. Cassandra really didn't want to leave the warmth of her blankets, but the pressure was too great, there was no way she was going to sleep comfortably now. She kept the blankets wrapped around her as best she could as she shuffled slowly outside, pushing under the heavy blanket acting as door. It was every bit as freezing as she'd been dreading with little light from the stars and moon, the sky hidden by clouds. Her chains clinked against the rocky ground as she sat down and fumbled for her belt, shivering as she balanced on the primitive well-like structure. Her business done, she stood up, and suddenly noticed something was terribly wrong. The yak had vanished, its basket filled with postal rockets resting on the ground accusingly, chiding Cassandra for her woeful lack of observation. That was when a tattooed hand clamped a damp, sweet-smelling cloth around her mouth and an almost impossibly muscular arm yanked her off her feet as easily as a hurricane ripping a leaf from a tree. She struggled, trying to let out a muffled warning scream. But it was lost to the spinning blackness as the sweet hot stench of the cloth overwhelmed her.

*

Carter was getting used to moving in the shadows. At the end of their journey, the pirate carrier *Plunderbird* had unceremoniously set Carter, his father and Tom Purdell back down on the waves in the same flying boat which had picked them up; a night-time rendezvous with a crew of thoroughly anonymous smugglers inside a fishing boat. The boat sailed them to Weyland's capital along with their catch – legal and illegal – before the three of them travelled by wagon to Arcadia's fish market, merging with the early morning crowd of merchants and traders. They booked rooms in a cheap guesthouse frequented by market workers and porters and remained inside their rooms, Carter chafing to take the next step. To do something – anything.

Somewhere in Arcadia and its environs, Willow was being held against her will, drugged and insensible, waiting to be sold off like a prize cow by her family. It seemed like an age before a nameless messenger arrived carrying details for a meeting between Jacob Carnehan and their old patron and protector, Prince Owen. When the party left the guesthouse, Carter's father led them around the corner to an army wagon waiting for them with two horses in front that had seen better days, a single army teamster in its seat. They sat under the wagon's canvas bow as they rattled through the cobbled streets and Carter had his first proper look at the capital by daylight. There were no dirt roads here, every street either cobbled or covered in a smooth coating of asphalt. Arcadia would have counted as a *proper* city even before an army of navvies had set to improving it. Northhaven could have been squeezed into the corner of a single district. Wide boulevards, paved streets flanked by oil lamps, trees and statues; all of the roadways were congested with streetcars, riders, carts and private carriages. Mansions and gardens in the shadow of the dust and flurry of fresh building works, new metal-framed buildings rising above the city like the skeletons of giant beasts. Below the new works sat the old, street after street seemingly without end: hotels, shops, pavilions, churches, monuments, stately apartments, galleries, stables, guild railway termini, partially concealed courtyards and open sweeping crescents. Carter realized he felt ill staring like a rube at all this conspicuous wealth. *How much of this was unknowingly purchased with human lives? My mother; all of my friends murdered in the sky mines.*

Arcadia's noisy crowds had other concerns; gentry and workers, shop assistants and hawkers, all utterly oblivious to a far-called northerner's disquiet. Not just ignoring his worries, either. There were far too many people begging in the gutter, as well as long lines of unemployed men and women lined up for wagons that might come calling for day workers in the fields and factories. Carter's love and life with Willow had seemed as large as the world up in Northhaven. Down here, it was too easily diminished; swallowed by the racket and throngs of the endless populace. He tried to stop himself brooding and worrying. If he was going to help Willow, it had to be done in the present, not a past he couldn't change or in a future that had yet to arrive. The wagon brought the three travellers to a massive five-sided fort overlooking the capital's harbour, high sloping granite walls lined with heavy guns protruding from fire holes, a wide sweep of fire over the navy's monitors and ironclads resting in the water below alongside hundreds of trading vessels, starlings sweeping through the sky above. Gates opened in the gorge wall and gave them access to a parade ground the size of a small village. There was an efficient bustle about the place far removed from supposedly sleepy garrison life: cavalry horses being exercised in fenced paddocks, companies of crimson-uniformed soldiers drilling with rifles, artillery-men cleaning the large cannons and mortars on the ramparts above. They were preparing for trouble, Carter realized. And try as hard as he could, he couldn't see a future where their efforts would prove unnecessary. A large sergeant appeared, to lead them inside the fort, taking them to a room filled with old friends for such unhappy times. Prince Owen and Anna Kurtain. It felt strange to greet them like this, in normal clothes rather than the slave's robes they had all worn when he had worked and fought alongside them in the sky mines. They waited around a large wooden table with an obviously important officer, white haired, ruddy faced and perhaps seventy years old; he had enough medals and braid across his green uniform to drown him if he fell into the sea outside.

Carter bowed towards the prince, but Owen waved him up. 'None of that, Mister Carnehan. I would still be stranded and far-called at the dark ends of the world if it wasn't for you and your father.'

The prince indicated the officer. 'This is Field Marshal Samuel

Houldridge, commander of the standing army. It's the field marshal and his officers who have kept me safe since I arrived in Arcadia.'

'It is no more than my duty,' rumbled the portly old warrior. 'Your father appointed me head of the army during his reign, and despite the best efforts of that bloody shoemaker, I still command the army, rather than whichever jumped-up aviator from Marcus's new skyguard the devil'd like to stick in m'post. Over these dead bones! Yes, I recognized the boy in the man as soon as I clapped eyes on his highness here. A man of honour and the best man for these difficult times.'

'You're willing to fight for Prince Owen when the time comes?' asked Carter's father.

'I used to allow the prince and his two brothers to ride my horse when they were no higher than m'knee,' barked the field marshal. 'I'll lend his highness a massed cavalry charge, if that rascal of a usurper doesn't step down when he's lawfully commanded. He'll discover why my men call me Hard Charging Houldridge.'

Owen looked older than Carter remembered. It was odd that the cares of the world in Weyland's so-called civilized circles could have aged him more than a near lifetime of captivity as a slave inside the sky mines. 'It seems a long time ago now.'

'I suppose it does,' said Owen. 'Back in Vandia, always dreaming of escape, I thought my troubles would be over when I returned home. How wrong I was.'

'The troubles aren't with the country,' said Anna. She was wearing civilian clothing, but she had a large army pistol holstered around her thigh. She was obviously still acting as Prince Owen's bodyguard. 'They're with your damned uncle.'

'True enough,' said Owen. 'I'm glad to see that Mister Purdell here made it through with the message I entrusted to the Guild of Librarians, though. I was worried that my uncle's agents would act against you before you received my warning.'

'Oh, they certainly tried,' said Jacob. 'Of course, if we had done things my way when we first returned to Weyland, that "problem" of ours would be a surprised corpse occupying a shallow hole in the ground.'

'I won't begin my reign with regicide,' said Owen. 'Not when the throne is mine by right and the laws of the kingdom.'

'It's a pity that Marcus wasn't so scrupulous about the niceties of the law,' said Jacob, 'when he arranged for the rest of your family to be buried in an avalanche so he could steal the throne and pocket the Vandians' blood money.'

'All the more reason to seek justice in the right way,' said Prince Owen. 'I am not my uncle. Tell me, is Lady Cassandra Skar still safely in custody?'

'For what it's worth, the imperial brat's on her way to Rodal by now,' said Jacob. 'It might have been more fitting if we'd shipped her across the ocean to the Burn's slave markets . . . give her a taste of her people's own medicine.'

'You do not defeat your enemy by stooping to their methods, Father Carnehan. It is not merely an exchange of tyrannies I seek here.'

'Those are fine words, but I'm a pragmatic man,' said Jacob.

'And still a vengeful one?' asked Owen. 'Do I not have that right too, after all I suffered as a captive? My brothers worked to death. My youth wasted. Put it aside, Father. Nearly all men can withstand adversity, but if you want to test a man's character, give him power. My uncle has failed that test and he must be removed. But he must be made to abdicate by the just laws of our land and the will of our people. Emissaries from the League of the Lanca have been here all week mediating between the two sides. The People's Assembly will vote tomorrow on the matter of succession.'

'And how many assemblymen have been bought and paid for by the usurper, Your Majesty?' asked Tom Purdell.

'Not nearly enough to save my uncle's skin,' said Owen. 'Sons and daughters who have followed their parents into the same living for fifty generations find their old trades dead; the only work available to them is on terms that would shame a poorhouse foundling's keep inside mills owned by Marcus's cronies. Prices soar beyond the common people's means to feed their families. But the workers still have the vote and their voices shall be heard.'

'I've seen a few of those common people up north,' said Jacob. 'Hungry and jobless and desperate and roaming the roads like wolves.'

'Common people are the best in the world,' said Owen. 'Surely that's the reason the saints make so many of them in Weyland.'

'I've had a gang try to pull me out of a coach and gut me, Your Majesty,' said Tom. 'I didn't think so kindly of them, then.'

'I appreciate the Guild of Librarians' interpretation of the constitution in favour of my claim,' said Owen. 'And your personal efforts, Mister Purdell. Would that all our guilds were so partial to my cause.' He returned his attention to Jacob. 'Father Carnehan, I will ask you to testify about the king's treachery tomorrow in the assembly if the vote is looking in the balance. How his guardsmen betrayed you and attempted to murder Northhaven's rescue party.'

'They won't believe Marcus allowed the slave raids in return for silver,' said Jacob. 'Not with most of the newspapers in the king's pocket and printing his lies.'

'The truth can meet any crisis,' said Owen.

'We'll have to disagree about that, but don't doubt I'll do whatever it takes to shove Marcus off his stolen throne,' said Jacob. 'You received the note I sent this morning?'

'Indeed,' said Owen. 'I'm sorry to hear about Willow's difficulties. She was the best of us inside the sky mines and she deserves far more than a loveless match with her consent provided by a bottle of laudanum and a bribed priest. Although the saints know, that's hardly a unique tale in the south these days. I have investigated matters and the Landor family are staying in the Winteringham Hotel; the grandest in the capital. The hotel is hosting a ball tonight in favour of my uncle's cause, and the man you say Willow is to marry, the Viscount Wallingbeck, is going to attend as one of the speakers. It seems his house is permanently impoverished and he's looking to the king to reward his loyalty, no doubt in equal measure to the Landor dowry. He's a lieutenant-colonel in the Territorial Army down here and commands a good-sized regiment of irregulars.'

'A rank amateur,' said Field Marshal Houldridge. 'Commanding pasty-faced loom workers who can barely march in order, let alone load, sight and discharge a rifle under fire. We'll see them off in quick order if the usurper has the gall to defy the assembly.'

'I'll pay Wallingbeck what he's due,' growled Jacob. 'Damned if it'll be what he's expecting.'

'I ask you not to act rashly, Father Carnehan,' said Owen. 'Matters are finely balanced inside the capital, it's a veritable tinderbox. Party marches of Gaiaists and Mechanicalists clash regularly; mill owners pay thugs to act as regulators and go on the streets to keep order with whips and clubs. The labour combines and little guilds have lost their power with so many unemployed workers flooding in, and they're champing at the bit for a quarrel too.'

'We won't do anything rash,' promised Carter. 'I just want Willow to be free to choose her own future. That's her due under the law.'

'You've arrived at a bad time, Northhaven,' said Anna. 'King Marcus is a cornered fox, now, and you know that's the biting kind. One of his hirelings tried to slip poison in Prince Owen's supper last week and damn how his death might look to the rest of the country. It's getting to be we'd be safer having stayed back in Vandia breaking our backs for Helrena Skar.'

'Bide your time,' advised Prince Owen. 'Soon enough I'll have the throne. I'll make the viscount an ambassador and order him dispatched to the ends of the league, and if old Benner Landor gives you any trouble, I'll appoint him governor of the Rotnest Islands and he and his wife can retire to a sea-view of a couple of thousand screeching gulls and damp sheep.'

I can't wait that long.

Anna noticed Carter's poorly suppressed anger, and she shook her head sadly. 'There never was a bigger fool in the sky mines, or a man who took more whippings and created more trouble for the Vandians.'

'I see that Carter hasn't changed,' said Tom.

'No, I'm not that slave anymore,' said Carter. 'I won't fight unless I'm forced to. But there's no way in the world I'm going to allow Willow to come to harm, that much remains the same.'

Jacob bowed towards the prince. 'Thank you for pointing us in the right direction, Your Highness. We're just going to make sure the viscount doesn't hang his washing on someone else's line, is all.'

'Be careful,' called Prince Owen, somewhere between pleading and ordering, as the three men left the room. 'For all of our sakes.'

'I'll go ahead to the Winteringham Hotel,' volunteered Tom as they walked through the barracks. 'None of the Landor family or their staff know me. I can scout around and make sure that your lady will be attending the dinner before you turn up for her.'

Carter removed the portrait miniature of her from inside his pocket watch and passed it across to his guild friend. 'This is Willow.'

'You don't get many red-heads down south,' said Tom. 'It won't be so hard.'

'Don't be too eager, boy,' warned Jacob. 'With so many of Marcus's high-born allies in one building, that hotel'll be locked down tighter than a drum.'

'I still have my guild credentials,' said Tom. 'There should be dozens of runners carrying packets in and out for the librarians and radiomen. I'll just be one more face in the crowd.' He reached out and put a hand on Carter's shoulder. 'We'll get her out of their hands. You'll see.'

'You've been a good friend to me, Tom,' said Carter. For the first time since Carter had set out from Northhaven, he allowed himself to feel a sliver of hope that things could work out for Willow, and for him.

Willow found it hard to concentrate on what the maid was saying as she rocked with the carriage's motion, the clatter of metal-rimmed wheels against cobbles throbbing intensely inside her head. The male servant seated opposite kept his hard, cold eyes resting on Willow, reaching for the pocket under his coat, tapping the little glass bottle whose contents he forced down Willow's throat when she proved uncooperative, as if to make sure he hadn't left it behind in the viscount's estate. Willow's mind was returning to her now, slowly, even if her body still drifted, detached. Whether it was the result of the 'medicine' or her brutal so-called marriage, she couldn't say.

The maid raised a privacy blind on the coach's window, checking their progress through the jammed streets. 'We'll be there soon enough. We would have arrived already if the police hadn't turned us away from those strikers on Maddox Street.'

'Dull-witted loafers,' said the servant. 'I should be so lucky as to get paid a little guild rate working for the viscount. Here now, make Lady Wallingbeck's hair presentable before we arrive. She looks like she's been dragged through a hedge backwards.'

Willow tried to push the woman's hand away as it snaked towards her with a brush, but the servant opposite dragged her hand away and patted his coat again. 'You want to enjoy the evening, don't you, your ladyship? Or do you need another swig of hysteria's helper to help settle your nerves?'

'Let me brush your hair,' hissed the maid. 'Don't be a fool. If you keep acting like this, his lordship will have you committed to an asylum.'

'I'm already in one,' muttered Willow. She heard a peal of laughter from the rear of the carriage, the two footmen clinging to it exchanging levities with a servant sat next to the driver. A full complement to chase her down if she tried to lurch away from her 'fine new life'.

The maid pawed at her hair. 'It's a mistake bringing her to the dinner.'

'All she has to do is sit at a dining table,' said the man. 'How hard is that? Anyway, it's nothing to do with me. His lordship's orders. This'un's parents are going to be at the banquet, too. Want to make sure their dowry is well invested, I reckon.'

'My mother's long dead and my father might as well be.'

'I'm still owed five months' wages,' complained the maid, ignoring Willow's slurred mumbles. 'It had better be invested in my direction pretty soon, or I'll be seeking fresh service.'

Willow tried not to gag. 'Take me with you.'

'Oh, do be silent, your ladyship,' said the maid. 'Do you realize how selfish you sound? How many people have what you have? Half my brothers and sisters are forced to lodge with my mother with no work or prospects, and you're whining about spending a warm night in fine silks, dining in the company of lords and ladies to the accompaniment of a chamber orchestra.'

'You know anyone hiring?' said the servant. 'Because I don't.'

Willow clung to the carriage's seat, feeling queasy and coughing faintly. 'No better than a slave.'

'Here now, if a night at the Winteringham is slavery, you can drop those chains on me,' guffawed the male servant. 'You're to be on your best behaviour this evening, your ladyship. If you try to run again, we've got his lordship's blessing to give you a proper chastisement. He's going to be too busy with his tongue up half the court's arse tonight to be bothered with your peculiar little fevers.'

Willow rested her head against the seat's padding in misery. There was none of the kindness of the servants at Hawkland Park at the hall, not even during the strange diminished period of her stepmother's regime. These hirelings weren't part of the house's family, because what fool would want to claim Viscount William Wallingbeck as kin if they had a choice in the matter? They took his money and did what they had to, which was a greater choice than Willow had been allowed.

'Don't give her the rest of the bottle,' said the maid. 'She can hardly stand as it is.'

'Good,' said the servant. 'We can't have her scarpering tonight. You heard about old Luther? Broke both legs when he was thrown from his horse trying to chase her through the orchard. Poor bleeder's laid up in the stable as useless as an ice teapot and I hear he's going to be dismissed. A new groom's already been hired.'

'I wish I was in service to a proper lady,' said the maid, finishing mauling Willow's hair. 'Not asylum keeper to a mad hare.'

'Mad hare's father is good for a few coins, though,' said the servant, grudgingly.

'That's as maybe, but you keep your eyes on her ladyship every second during dinner,' said the maid. 'Don't move away from behind her. No sharp cutlery to be slipped out; or there'll be more than broken legs for one of us at the hall tomorrow when she recovers.'

The servant sighed. 'By the saints, I'd let the bloody viscount jigger me for just a tenth of what he's been paid to take this loon on, and I'd thank the dirty dog kindly for his troubles.'

The carriage lurched to a halt, side-mounted oil lamps illuminating the face of the liveried bruiser who swung the door open; two men jumping down from the rear to make sure the House of Wallingbeck's prize new possession didn't abscond. Willow shivered uncontrollably as the cold breeze came from outside and cut straight through the ridiculous clothes she had been forced into. Her copper-coloured corset bustle dress with more sequins than stars in a sky might have been all the style inside the capital, but it was in no way practical against a hard winter. A hand from behind shoved Willow down into the waiting servants' grasp, a wary loathing for her written across their features. Willow's carriage was one of a line drawn up inside the courtyard of the same grand hotel where she'd stayed when she first arrived at the capital. Golden light spilled from its tall windows, but there was one new addition – the doors into the lobby now stood guarded by tall blue-uniformed soldiers from the king's own guard, a stiff yellow stripe down their trousers as they stood ramrod straight.

Two footmen opened the doors of the carriage in front of Willow's and she swayed groggily on her uncomfortable shoes as she watched Leyla Holten step daintily down its folding steps, swathed in an even more ludicrous dress than Willow's, a mound of purple satin above a billowing underskirt and a corset so tight it was a wonder she could still breathe. Benner Landor exited the carriage behind her, Willow's father looking pompous and stiff in a dark heavy tailcoat and curling green cravat. The haughty woman had, it seemed, finally had her way and successfully remade the Landor patriarch as a southern gentleman. Even slowed and fogged by the servant's sedative, Willow found the hatred she felt for the interloper who had invaded her life still burned fierce and strong. Willow thought that the misery she'd suffered in Vandia had made her compassionate towards the worst mankind had to offer, but she realized that given the strength and opportunity, she'd happily strangle this malicious woman as though she was no more than a wounded animal.

Leyla Holten turned and spotted Willow, a look of cunning triumph slipping across her face and then disappearing almost as quickly as it had appeared. 'Ah, my Lady Wallingbeck,' announced Holten, loudly, the master of the House of Landor swivelling around to spot his daughter. 'Ready to hear your husband speak for the loyalist cause this evening? You must be so proud of how essential he has become at court.'

'Husband,' said Willow, her voice barely escaped her throat, as though the servant's foul concoction had sapped her voice. '*Beast.*'

'You'll have to forgive her ladyship,' said the servant as his men manhandled Willow swaying towards the steps to the hotel lobby. 'She's taking poppy tincture for her nervous attacks.'

'Fish oil is the cure for melancholy,' said her father, sounding saddened. 'Have the viscount's doctor contact mine in Northhaven. Willow, hold yourself steadier than this. Stand straight, girl. Half of the realm's most powerful leaders are gathered inside. You will bring dishonour to your new name in front of them unless you can master your dark humours.'

'She will settle given time,' said Holten, affecting concern. 'I told you, husband, it is natural she should be jealous of my state and yearn for children of her own. When she is pregnant, her body's changes will bring her comfort naturally without the need for further medical remedies.'

'What have you done to me?' Willow croaked.

'You have a title,' said her father, as if this was the most precious thing in the world, 'you have a house of your own to call yourself mistress over, and a generous financial settlement in the bank. We've prevented you from throwing your life away. I would say our work's been well done.'

'You've *destroyed* my life.'

'I had hoped she would come to understand the importance of her new position,' said Holten, tugging at Benner Landor's walking cane, 'with the fate of the country swinging in the wind. Her husband may have embraced the king's cause, but your daughter's still behaving no better than a petulant child denied a bag of sweets. The pretender's rabble is breaking windows in the streets, the nation's order hangs in the balance, but Willow's self-indulgent whims must be met or she'll be sure to sulk and swoon until she gets her way.'

'Yes, you were right about bringing her to Arcadia before it was too late,' said Benner. He waved at the servants. 'Drag the frivolous creature inside and ensure she doesn't disgrace us any more than is necessary to see this evening through. Thank the stars that King Marcus isn't attending tonight to meet her like this.'

Holten and her father passed Willow as the servants escorted her towards the entrance and she was about to pass the doors when she heard an explosive cry behind her. Her first thought – that the trouble on the streets nearby had spilled outside the expensive hotel – was replaced with a ferocious surge of hope as she turned and saw who it was yelling. *Carter*! And Carter's father sprinting fast behind him, along with a young man she didn't recognize. Willow staggered, shocked. She only realized it was no drug-addled hallucination when she heard Holten gasp; her father growling, 'How in hell's name did *they* get here?'

'Willow!' yelled Carter. 'Let her go, damn you.'

Willow's father barked at the guardsmen advancing down the steps. 'Throw these men out – they have no part in tonight's business at the banquet.'

Jacob Carnehan pushed past one of the retainers trying to hold him back, waving a sheet of paper towards them. 'I have an affidavit of legal majority for this woman, duly notarized by the circuit court of Northhaven,' said Jacob. 'She's free to come with us and return to Northhaven. Ask the lady what she wants to do . . .'

The soldier's captain took the paper and examined it. 'It's as he says,' nodded the officer, confused by the unexpected turn of events.

'Let me go!' demanded Willow, trying to struggle free. 'Take your hands off of me. I'm leaving with Carter.'

Her father shook his head in fury. 'So, the northern magistrates are still trying to tweak my damn nose? They're nothing but jealous buffoons in dusty wigs and fancy gowns paid for by *my* taxes.' Benner Landor snatched the legal paper from the guardsman's hand. 'Let me see that!' He scanned the document rapidly, before flourishing it with a look of triumph on his face that Willow knew well. So, that was all she was to him now? *Trade. A successful trade deal.* Her surge of hope retreated as rapidly as it had appeared. 'This judgement is made out in the name of Willow Landor, and my daughter is a Landor no longer. She is the Lady Wallingbeck! This document carries as much validity as a handbill blown down the street.'

Carter's face distorted as if someone had plunged a dagger inside his chest. '*Already?* No, she can't be married.'

'It certainly wasn't the grand affair that would have been worthy of my house,' snarled Willow's father. 'But by the saints, the marriage papers are legally lodged. She's not for you; boy. I told you that back in the park. You've come a long way south to be disappointed.'

'Was that before or after you had Carter whipped like a dog?' spat Jacob, and for a terrible moment Willow thought the pastor might reach for one of the pistols swaying by his side. There was a clatter of rifles from the guardsmen protecting the hotel as they realized the confrontation might turn into more than angry words between two bickering families.

'I gave your son what he had coming for trespass, breaking into the house and trying to steal my daughter like a bandit in the night,' shouted Benner. 'My retainers would have been within their rights to gun him down in the dark. There are enough marauders scavenging about the wilds close to home to have justified it.'

'We saved Willow's life,' said Jacob. '*Carter* saved Willow's life. We returned her to you from the sky mines.'

'And you abandoned my son in that far-called hell-hole as though my boy was no more than a tainted barrel of corn oil!' shouted Benner Landor. 'You stole my money to fund the rescue expedition and left the heir of my house behind to rot. Duncan's blood is on your hands. Maybe my treacherous daughter deserves no better than your thieving wretch of a boy, but the name she carries does, and by God that's what she's been given. She's Lady Wallingbeck now, so you can bugger off back to the north and your whelp can rut until he's dry with fishermen's girls and tavern owners' daughters. Willow Landor's been taken from you every bit as surely as you stole my son from me.'

Carter tried to fight through the line of servants around Willow, but they were picked for their size and strength and held him back. 'Please tell me this isn't true, Willow. That you're not married.'

'It . . . is true,' cried Willow, the admission nearly breaking her as she tried to struggle free of the hands restraining her. 'They forced me, tricked me. He's—' She broke down, overwhelmed by trying to express all the evil that had been done to her.

'She's been drugged,' said the young man wearing a librarian guildsman's livery. 'Look at her, Carter. She's barely conscious.'

'My stepdaughter has sadly been overwhelmed by the demands of her elevation to high southern society,' said Holten, standing haughtily astride the steps. 'Society with whom we have an engagement to fulfil, alongside Willow's proud new *husband*. See this beggarly rabble far from the Winteringham, Captain. They have no lawful business with those gathered here tonight, no business at all.'

Before the guardsmen could react, a commotion began beyond the railings separating the hotel from the street. A sizeable group of constables in the bright green uniforms of the capital's police pushed through the people on the pavement, emblem plates on their pillbox-style hats glinting in the lantern light. Willow hadn't heard anyone at the hotel whistle for the police. Were they here to help the pastor enforce his court order? *Please*. She felt her desperation to be free of her forced marriage rise overwhelmingly. *Let them be here for me*. Shadows bobbed behind the hotel's high windows, curious faces against the glass wondering if the capital's troubles were about to spill into their privileged enclave.

Benner Landor raised his voice as though he spoke to a group of his estate's tenants, pointing at the three northerners. 'These wretches are in breach of the peace. See them off.'

'I have an order from the Northhaven circuit court concerning that woman,' said Jacob, his deep reverberating voice demanding he be instantly obeyed. 'She is in her majority and being held here against her will. You *will* enforce it.'

Willow watched a police officer – the commander from his plumed custodian-style helmet – wave away the document offered in his direction by the pastor. 'I have an order, too, Father. And mine's from the People's Assembly with the seal of the High Court of Arcadia stamped on it. You and your son are called as witnesses to the assembly tomorrow morning. We are commanded to take you into custody to ensure your attendance.'

'Damn Prince Owen,' said Jacob. 'That isn't our business.'

'But it's mine,' said the police commander. His constables had their pistols raised in the group's direction. 'I'll relieve you of your sidearms, Father, as slowly and carefully as you like.'

For a second, Willow saw a flash of the terrible figure she had glimpsed in Vandia during the slave revolt – the man who had no right to be a pastor or Carter's father – absolutely not the peaceful, gentle man she had grown up with in Northhaven. A shadow who could draw his pistols and walk their fire across every constable and guardsmen here like an angry hell-storm, dodging and weaving, enemies dropping to thunder faster than dying men could possibly react to. A corpse-maker, a hungry devil given flesh. But that evil alien shadow passed as quickly as she'd glimpsed it, the young man in librarian's livery resting a hand on the pastor's wrist. 'That's not the way. Not yet.'

Carter lashed into the servants blocking his path as the constables seized him from behind, dragging him away. 'I'll come for you, Willow. I don't care what they do to me or what any court in the land decrees. You're not staying in the south with that bastard. I'll come for you, wherever you are, wherever they take you . . .'

Willow struggled to break free, to call to Carter; to tell him she'd fight for as long as she endured and that she'd escape time and time again, however much filth they poured down her throat, whatever they did to her, however much pain they subjected her to; but the servants clamped their hands tight over her mouth and dragged her through the hotel doors. Into polite company, gossiping ladies in bell-shaped dress whispering at the shocking disturbance outside. Her father had stormed away down the corridor, furious at being embarrassed by the interlopers in front of the great and the good.

Leyla Holten strode forward, Willow gripped vice-tight from behind by the servants. Holten had the servant's bottle in her hand and she forced the neck into Willow's mouth, making her stepdaughter gag as the bitter liquid rolled down her throat. Holten smiled for the benefit of the chattering aristocrats in the lobby. 'There we are my dear, that should help calm your nerves for the evening,' Holten bent in and whispered into Willow's ear as her feet swayed beneath her. 'But don't think you won't feel anything when you're taken back to the hall after the banquet. My fingers will make sure that William is wound as tight as a bow-string for his sport tonight. There won't be enough laudanum in the kingdom to deaden your pain.'

Willow's dulled gaze focused on Holten's face. 'I swear . . . I'm going to see you dead, you bitch.'

Holten kissed her gently on the cheek, turning to smile at the onlookers and whispering back. 'And I swear I'm going to keep you alive, *Lady* Wallingbeck. For just as long as I can, right up until the moment you decide to slit your wrists to end all of this.'

Cassandra's eyes opened blearily, her face left itching by the sleep draught. For a brief moment she allowed herself a flash of elation at the possibility that she had been followed from the great forest and rescued by the imperium's agents. But her hands were still tied behind her back. Then she saw she was not the only prisoner huddled under the camouflage net strung between boulders, she was one of three women, the other two Rodalians by the look of them. And the men that had taken her were nothing like the ragtag bandits back in Weyland. Her kidnappers were bare-chested above brown leather trousers and covered in a whirl of abstract tattoos, a tanned blue tinge to their skin that seemed natural rather than dye or woad. They had sword scabbards strapped to their backs, and a couple carried large wooden crossbows as well, quivers filled with ugly barbed-head bolts tied to their thighs. All of them had dark hair, short-cropped, but the most remarkable thing about her new captors was how muscular they were – they would have embarrassed the professional gladiators of the empire, warriors who spent all day with weights and training, fed like prize cattle to build fighting bulk. It was unnatural! Muscles upon muscles, looking more like shaped rocks than mortal flesh.

'Do not make a noise. Do not stare at them,' hissed one of the Rodalian women. 'Try not to attract their attention.'

Cassandra snorted. 'As these dogs have already seized me, I don't think they have much to fear from my gaze.'

'They are Nijumeti . . . nomads from the Arak-natikh steppes,' said the woman. 'Do not anger the warriors.'

'To hell with them.'

'Your accent is far-called. You are a traveller with a caravan?'

'Prisoner seems to be my permanent trade at the moment.'

'I am Dolki.' She indicated the other woman, who smiled thinly back. 'This is Inmu. She is a river washer. She speaks no trade tongue. Until she was captured, she hadn't even left our valley.'

Cassandra introduced herself and shivered in the morning's cold, a single blanket left from the night before. Her leg irons had been struck off, ankles now unencumbered, although her hands were bound tighter than ever behind her back.

Cassandra moaned in pain. Her ankles burned. 'Do they hold us for ransom?'

Dolki shook her head. 'What ransom would the daughter of a postal rider be worth? They will carry us back to their clans in Arak-natikh.'

'Those big brutes will freeze to death before they take us anywhere.'

'They will not,' said Dolki. 'They are able to lie down in night snow and treat it as we would a soft down mattress. Cold does not affect the Nijumeti. Heat does not bother them. Pain much the same. It is said they can ride a week in the saddle and still fight a battle at the other end. You will find out . . . your children will be half-Nijumet.'

'I will have no children by these barbarian dogs!' said Cassandra, outraged.

'Why do you think they have snatched us?' said Dolki. 'They are a raiding party and this is their final rite of passage as clan riders. They must steal wives from Rodal so that they have less need to raid rival steppes clans for women, causing feuds and bad feeling.'

'I thought your cursed freezing land was known as the "Walls of the League", holding back such savages?'

'The major passes are fortified by great walls,' said Dolki. 'No horde can force entry. But our border with the steppes stretches for thousands of miles.' She nodded her head up towards the camouflage netting. 'The Nijumeti scale the mountains in parties of less than a hand, and those who survive enter Rodal to search for wives and booty that may make their boys into men. Even the skyguard's patrols cannot stalk and strafe them all.'

'I will make no boy into a man!'

'In that much you are right,' said a voice. It was a female Nijumet, her azure face half-hidden in the shadow of a hooded leather cloak. 'There is hardly enough meat on your arm to lift a feed bucket up to a pony.'

Dolki moaned in fear and fell into silence.

'And have you come looking for a husband, barbarian? Or would you have me as a wife, too?'

The Nijumet yanked her hood down and slapped Cassandra hard across the face. Her arm was as bare and strong as the male warriors. 'I am a witch rider, whore-child, and you will show me respect.' She seized Cassandra's face and turned it left and right, then dug her blue fingers into Cassandra's mouth to inspect her teeth, 'Incredible teeth, like those of a four-year-old. What manner of creature are you, wide eyes? No Rodalian, that much is certain.'

'You will not have heard of my country. When you do encounter Vandia, you will have cause to lament its name.'

'Brave talk for a little sow taken so easily.'

'In case you didn't notice, I was chained, tied and sat on a shit hole in the middle of a night when your barbarian friends grabbed me. If it were otherwise, you would not have a prisoner. You would have your friends' corpses to drag back to the dirt of your home.'

'I saw you were chained. It was I who melted your restraints away with my magic,' laughed the witch rider.

'Use a less powerful acid for your "magic" next time. My ankles are raw and bleeding.'

The witch rider crossly pushed Cassandra away. 'Rodalians do not keep slaves, so I would know you for a convict even without my dream-travels. What are you? A whore being dragged to trial? A caravan traveller caught stealing horses? A murderer? A poisoner?'

'I am the granddaughter of the Vandian emperor, a hostage of war and of immense value. If you return me to my people you will be made rich beyond dreams.'

'I may actually believe such words, slipping through those expensive, shining teeth. But your foreign titles are horse shit to me. Nijumeti count nothing of value unless it is stolen by guile and can be packed on the back of a saddle.' One of the male nomads slipped under the netting and the witch rider turned to speak urgently to him. 'Do not take this strange one for a wife, Alexamir. She is a soft noble who knows nothing of cooking and healing and keeping a tent. Any of these Rodalians are a better match. At least they know how to clean trousers in a stream. Would you have your children be weaklings or, worse, stillborn?'

'Was it not your dreaming that led us to the caravan halt?' said Alexamir. 'I followed the wagon, and it was exactly as you dreamt. An aviator of the skyguard and a forest man transporting a beautiful female prisoner. She is a fine little thing. Like a golden furred fox, ferocious and sleek.'

'Try to drag me to your bed and I will snap your neck,' swore Cassandra,

'See,' laughed Alexamir, winking down at his prisoner. 'What could be better than her, Nurai?'

'You carry back a foreign sow, a couple of horses and a single yak, and you count your trial complete? That is still a boy talking!'

'I cut the wagon's horses out and left her Rodalian guards snoring inside alive to spread word of Alexamir's mischief and reputation. The skyguard's prize is now *my* prisoner. We will eat yak meat until we return home. And my little golden fox will give me many sons. Your dreaming has proven true and you will surely be anointed as the High Witch Rider when old Madinsar passes. Is this not the perfect little journey into the mountains for us?'

'I have dreamt false,' said Nurai, scowling at Cassandra. 'She will bring us nothing but trouble and death.'

'Have you dream-walked this?'

'No, but I can feel it by the power of the land. The bad omens that circle her sing in my very bones.'

'Ha, it is the power of aged yak liver talking,' said Alexamir. He crossed his massive arms and did a wild kicking dance, cheered on by the other brutes along for the raid. 'By Joni, perhaps I should have cooked one of the foreign horses instead. The scald-crows wouldn't carry word to the Goddess of the Night: she must forgive a great many offences in an unholy land like Rodal. I have a wife! The goddess loves a lucky rogue!'

Cassandra suspected it was the power of jealousy talking as far as Nurai was concerned. And the witch rider could keep her capering barbarian horseman and breed as many blue-skinned brats as her womb could stand before it broke. Cassandra would be having *none* of it. It seemed that trading Kerge and Sheplar Lesh for these brutal savages was a bargain badly made. Nurai obviously felt the same. The witch rider glared in hatred at Cassandra and fingered the handle of a curved knife hanging at her side. Her notched blade looked as if it had seen more use than just slicing herbs and berries for these barbarians' ceremonies.

Carter stood alongside his father and Tom Purdell in a witness box inside the People's Assembly of Weyland. A group of people called to testify earlier filed out past the three newcomers, most of them elderly ex-palace servants who had served Prince Owen and his brothers. The assembly sat perched on top of a hill in Arcadia, the largest domed structure in the country, so it was said. Inside the chamber's vast circular space, the voices of hundreds of assemblymen rose past multiple galleries and levels held up by cast-iron columns and hung with crimson and gold drapery. The space was as bright as day inside, the large central skylight in the dome above encircled by twelve smaller circular skylights, their illumination augmented by dozens of gas-fed brass chandeliers.

Carter was still fuming at being held in police cells overnight, marched here in the early afternoon like a common criminal called to the dock. He waited wearily. Carter had hardly slept all night, tossing and turning in the hard cot, trying to banish the sight of Willow's stupefied, drugged face; the anguish written across her features as she was dragged into the hotel and the brutal 'care' of her aristocratic new husband. Carter had tried to tell himself that there was nothing he could do. That even if the police hadn't turned up to take him into custody, he would have been hard pressed to face down the company of royal guardsmen and Benner Landor's servants protecting the banquet. And the staff of Willow's new *husband*. Even the thought of the word made him sick.

'We should hold our damn peace,' said Carter, looking out across the amphitheatre-like arrangement of seats, all fully occupied for the nation-shaping vote. 'Refuse to speak here. Prince Owen had no right to have us dragged into custody.'

'The boy's desperate,' said Jacob Carnehan. 'The vote is resting on a knife-edge and he needs the assembly's support if he's going to have his uncle removed from the throne.'

'That's no excuse,' said Carter.

'No, it isn't.'

'You need to speak here if you are called as a witness,' urged Tom. 'You *must*. Remember what Prince Owen said. When he's king, he'll help save Willow. If Benner Landor and Viscount Wallingbeck want any sort of preferment under Owen's reign, they'll bend to his will or suffer the consequences.'

Carter knew the guild courier was right. But damn it all, he just wanted to do something – anything. To shout and rail against the heavens for this unkind fate. All Carter needed was to have Willow with him, the two of them left alone, finally free. But now there were chains weighing down on them that were never forged in Vandia's mines. The name and title of a Landor. A great house's expectations. A marriage without consent. Right now, Carter felt like a leaf, powerless and unable to influence events. Blown compassless in the winds of war and helplessly caught up in the fierce political machinations of a man who would be king and his rival who would stay one.

A rumbling undercurrent of conversation rose and then fell as the speaker of the assembly stepped up from his podium at the front of the chamber. Unlike the neighbouring mahogany desks, the speaker's platform had a fabric cover, and two Weyland flags on golden staffs crossed behind the awning – each a field of royal red behind a blue cross filled with the prefectures' white stars, a silver crown and pelican in the flag's upper corner next to the staff.

'We have heard this day the testimony of many servants from the royal household, both current and retired, testifying that the man who calls himself Owen Hawkins is the true son of the old king. We now call Father Jacob Carnehan of Northhaven to give evidence in the matter of the succession and claims of precedence to the throne,' intoned the speaker.

Carter watched his father advance to the wooden rails at the front of the stand and take the oath over a weighty leather tome. There was a similar stand opposite on the other side of the chamber, presently empty.

'Augustus Sparrow shall question the witness first, for the Gaiaist Party,' announced the speaker. 'In favour of the claim of precedence made by Owen Hawkins.'

The assemblyman who stepped before the house had a long, gaunt face, a tall starched shirt collar covering his neck, dark receding hair curling around the back of his skull, leaving a high domed forehead shining in the light from the cupola above. Watching him walk forward through the graduated semi-circular platforms filled with politicians was like watching a strange bird strut around the grass, pecking. 'You, Father, were a member of the expedition who pursued the skel slavers that raided Northhaven, seeking to liberate the Weylanders captured during that foul incursion?'

'I was,' said Jacob.

'Tell us about the expedition's route and the manner of your pursuit. Including where your hunt ended.'

Carter listened to his father's long story. It was a tale familiar to Carter from many tellings back home, but the pastor glossed over many of the more outrageous elements and truths, while sparing nothing about the brutal conditions the rescuers had discovered in the Vandian imperium at journey's end. They were conditions that Carter remembered all too well. He, Willow and a few others had suffered and finally survived them. Many of his friends had not.

'And it was in Vandia that you liberated the slave we now know as Prince Owen Hawkins, returning with him to Weyland?'

The pastor grimly nodded his head. 'Along with survivors from Northhaven and other towns and prefectures raided by the skels.'

'Do you have evidence pertaining to Owen Hawkins' claim of royal title or true identity?'

'I cannot speak directly to that,' said Jacob. 'I lived in Northhaven and prior to the raid, my previous dealings with the royal family were wholly limited to newspaper reports and the features of monarchs past and present on coins and bank notes. But I can tell you this from my time fighting alongside Owen. He is a good and true man, better, perhaps, than the evil times we find ourselves in. I believe he is Prince Owen Hawkins, son of the old king and our nation's rightful monarch.'

There was a murmur of approval from the Gaiaist side of the house, a few hisses of disapproval from the massed ranks of the Mechanicalist party. Next, Carter found himself called to take the oath by the speaker, and questioned as witness by the assemblyman. Carter told the council about his time working in the mines and the terrible conditions he and the other Weylanders had struggled to survive under. And he talked of the clandestine circle of slaves who knew of Prince Owen Hawkins' real identity, acting as his protectors in the sky mines, keeping safe the secret of his name and title from their Vandian captors, who would have surely executed him for it. Finally, Carter told to the assembly how he had heard that the other two princes taken as slaves, Owen's brothers, had died in captivity before the slaves from Northhaven had arrived.

The speaker stepped forward again. 'I now call Herschel Pharlann for the Mechanicalists to examine your evidence, their party declared in favour of King Marcus's claim.'

An assemblyman rose from his party's mahogany benches, of late years, dark hair, smooth almost oily skin, with shoulders so broad he could have sat a child on either one of them. 'I will address the testimony of Father Carnehan first. I find many inconsistencies in your testimony, Father,' drawled Pharlann. There was a self-satisfied tone to his examination that immediately irritated Carter. As though everyone should stop what they were doing and pay the closest attention to his deep well of wisdom. 'Chief among them the nature of the buyers of those poor unfortunate Weylanders forced into slavery. Our country still suffers from periodic slaver incursions by sea and air, despite the league's stance in stamping out this foul practice and the best efforts of our royal navy. Most Weylanders taken as captives end up transported west and thrown into battle as slave soldiers for the many pocket kingdoms of the Burn, is this not so?'

'Not in this raid.'

'So we are to believe that you led your pursuit to the south, against all logic, travelled further and faster than can be easily explained in such a miraculously short time, and amazingly found the near-mythical end of the caravan route where a mighty empire prospers on the back of human suffering?'

'I'm standing here, alive, to give voice to the truth of it,' said Jacob. 'As are hundreds of freed slaves. Not just those taken from Northhaven, but men and women seized in earlier skel attacks.'

'As you say,' noted Pharlann. 'And I haven't been to Northhaven to examine first-hand the testimony of those supposedly rescued by your expedition, so I shall need to call one who has to the stand... Prefect Colbert of the upper house.'

Assemblyman Sparrow leapt to his feet. 'I protest! We have not allowed King Marcus or Prince Owen onto the floor today to sway the vote, for neither king nor prince must play any part in parliament that is not defined by the royal binding. The appointees of the king's council have no voice here. We are a free assembly elected by free Weylanders.'

'The prefect is another witness, no more,' said Pharlann. 'Are our liberties so precious that they are threatened by the words of a single man?'

'Admit the prefect and his delegation,' ordered the speaker, sternly. 'A prefect is as much a subject, humble under our nation's laws, as the grooms, wet-nurses and country pastors we have heard testify here today; let the prefect speak to this issue as both a man and a Weylander.'

Hugh Colbert appeared at the witness stand on the opposite side of the chamber, clutching the wooden rails as tall and haughty as a captain at the prow of his vessel. The prefect spoke the oath over the tome of limitations of royal power before he submitted to Assemblyman Pharlann's questioning. So, this was the man Carter's father had met at home. It was a wonder he didn't choke on his words.

'You have returned this month from Northhaven, prefect?'

'I did, sir, I did.'

'And the purpose of your visit?'

'To investigate the matter of the returned slave who calls himself Owen Hawkins, a man who claims to be the only surviving issue of King Jevan and thereby the rightful heir to the throne of Weyland.'

'And did you reach any conclusion from your researches across the north as to the veracity of that man's disputed identity.'

'One: That he is indeed the only surviving child of Jevan Hawkins, our previous king.'

There were gasps of astonishment around the chamber, shouts of anger and catcalls tossed between the rival parties, but none was so shaken by the shocking admission than Carter. *Can it be so easy?* Prince Owen handed the crown, able to keep his word to Carter and free Willow from her cursed marriage; proud, querulous Benner Landor and his spiteful new wife forced to submit to royal authority. King Marcus tossed off the throne and unable to pursue his revenge against Carter and his father? *Let it be so, saints let it be so.*

The speaker had to smash his gravel into the mahogany surface in front of him to restore quiet back to the chamber. 'Order in the assembly! Order I say!'

'And what led you to this rather surprising conclusion, prefect?' continued Pharlann as some measure of quiet returned.

'I must beg the assembly's indulgence to tell a wider tale. What I uncovered through the testimony of the poor devils returned from captivity is, I believe, no less than a conspiracy against every Weylander in the nation.'

At this, the chamber broke out in uproar, only quelled by the speaker's mad hammering against his desk.

'Continue, please, Prefect Colbert.'

'Through careful interviewing of the escaped slaves, it became evident that what I was investigating was far more than the random raids of skel brigands. Those here today must prepare themselves to hear a most monstrous truth.'

'Speak, Prefect, speak...'

'It was not the skels alone who sold our poor people across the ocean to the warlords of the Burn. There were also many traitors from Weyland acting as agents of this foul slavery, profiting by it. Chief among them, Prince Owen Hawkins!'

'Lies!' yelled Carter, shaking his fist at the prefect's stand. 'We were never taken to the Burn.'

'Witnesses called here for the Gaiaist Party will be silent!' shouted the speaker, his breath growing short with irritation.

Prefect Colbert held his hands out beseechingly to the gathered assemblymen. 'This whole monstrous scheme was set up by the previous king in return for generous payments from the slavers into his private account. When Marcus Hawkins – then one of our leading merchants – heard some outlandish rumours he investigated and discovered the evil truth. His own brother was auctioning off our people. Marcus naturally did not want to believe it and confronted the old king with his evidence but, forewarned, the majority of the conspirators escaped justice by fleeing into exile across the ocean, where they have been directing subsequent raids against our shores in revenge for being unseated from the throne. King Jevan chose to take his own life by suicide rather than flee, but the conspirators ensured his three sons were smuggled across the water to continue their father's foul trade as slaver lords.'

'This is outrageous,' spluttered the speaker. 'Why has the assembly not been informed of these facts before?'

'King Marcus did not wish these revelations to undermine his efforts to bolster our defences against the skels and the nation's traitors. Would King Marcus have been able to push through the skyguard's formation to keep our acres safe from the skels' predations with this deplorable scandal still echoing loudly through our land? In addition, our new ruler had to proceed warily. Who could King Marcus trust?

The court and government was riddled with traitors complicit in the slavery ring.'

'We never voyaged across the Lancean Ocean!' called Jacob Carnehan, his voice boomed across the chamber. 'We travelled south to Vandia! That's where the slaves were taken.'

'No more than a clever half-truth,' laughed the prefect. 'There is indeed a powerful empire in the distant south called the Vandian Imperium. It is where the skel brigands' homeland used to be, and the empire suffers more revenge slave attacks for chasing the skels into the air than any nation in the world. That is the price of their people's defiance. The Vandians are why Prince Owen now has the barefaced cheek to stride the capital's streets whining about his lost crown. Vandia dispatched an expeditionary force to the Burn to recover thousands of their citizens seized in skel slave raids. It was Vandia's military power that freed our people, not some insignificant rescue party from Northhaven. Prince Owen and his skel-loving nest of traitors-in-exile were smashed by Vandia's legions, forced to sail back to their old homeland. This black-hearted prince has cruelly been claiming to have been one of the *very* unfortunates he preyed on.'

'None of that's true, it's all lies!' yelled Carter. 'I was there. I was one of the slaves snatched from Northhaven!'

'Those poor unfortunates enslaved,' continued the prefect, 'did not know where they were held or taken. They had no compasses, no charts; they were locked up for months in cages inside a skel carrier. Slaves see only their chains and the degrading, murderous work they are forced to undertake under the whip. If the warlords of the Burn told any of our people they were held in some far-called land, it was merely an easy lie to deter them from escaping.'

'You dare speak of working under the whip,' called Assemblyman Sparrow, trying to break the spell the prefect's words had cast over the people's council. 'You whose friends are sweeping the hungry and unemployed up from the streets and into their mills; forcing Weylanders to work as indentured labour? It is your class that should be charged with slavery, every bit as severely as our forces interdict the skels.'

'I have friends who generously offer food to those who are hungry, provide warm cots in clean new barracks for citizens made homeless through no fault of their own. Is it too much to ask that those accepting such charity work in return? Or are the unpaid apprenticeships of the little guilds only to be gifted through nepotism to the friends of the Gaiaist Party, now? I know my friends, Assemblyman, how well do you know yours?' He cast an accusing finger towards Jacob, Tom and Carter in the opposing witness stand.

'I know you, Hugh Colbert, for what you are,' retorted Jacob. '*King*'s man.'

'You do not know me, Father, for if you did, you would know that I am remorseless in ferreting out the truth. Is it not true that you were in league with the slavers, acting as one of their paid informants? You sent word to the skels after Northhaven's territorial regiment left on manoeuvres with the fleet. You told them that here – *now* – was the perfect time for the slavers to attack your town.'

'Those skel bastards stole my son and *murdered* my wife.'

'The wages of sin, Father – an irony that has not escaped me. It is very hard to control the direction of a fire after you have set it, isn't it? Did you not think people might wonder how conveniently your son returned? Sadly for the nation, the company of royal guardsmen King Marcus sent to assist Northhaven's rescue mission did not survive your journey. You arranged for the skels to ambush Weyland's soldiers, did you not? You betrayed your military escort and had the slavers kill them all.'

'The only traitors with the rescue mission were those damned troopers of yours.'

'Is that the best lie you can come up with, Father?'

'You want the truth? King Marcus is the beast behind the slave raids! Your high-born hound murdered his own brother and family; he climbed over their corpses to reach the throne.'

'Murdered, you say? Well, perhaps we should trust the word of a simple country pastor when it comes to such fancies. After all, churchmen are known to be universally reliable and virtuous, are they not? Mister Speaker, will you allow me to call forward a witness of my own? One who can offer key testimony uncovered during my investigation of the Northhaven raid.'

The speaker nodded and Hugh Colbert ushered forward a woman Carter had never seen before – or at least if he had, he had forgotten their meeting. She was in her early fifties, a handsome proud face still littered with freckles, her cheeks obscured by a bonnet set above a conservative grey dress. She took the oath and gave her name as Miss Minerva Paulet, current mistress of a place called Mounteagle Manor in one of the southern prefectures.

'Do you see the man in the stand opposite you wearing the churchman's shirt?'

She nodded, solemnly.

'You know him?'

Again Minerva Paulet nodded gravely.

'Is that man Jacob Carnehan, the pastor of Northhaven?'

'He may wear a pastor's collar, but his name is not Jacob Carnehan. It is Jake Silver.'

'And how do you know him?'

'His family were tenant farmers on my family's land in Mounteagle. But they ran into hard times during a famine when I was sixteen years of age. Jake Silver ambushed my father and an estate worker while they were out riding, murdering them both.'

'If only the murders had stopped there,' said the prefect, his voice rising in righteous fury, throwing an angry hand out towards the stand opposite. 'Jake Silver and his younger brother fled an arrest warrant for the murder of Lord Simeon Paulet and twelve other men, taking passage across the ocean where they served as mercenaries in the Burn for many of the most unpleasant rulers on that bleak, misbegotten continent. Jake Silver grew *very* proficient at murder and brigandage, but then, his education had an excellent start in our own acres, did it not? This vile villain became known as *Quicksilver* and secured a position as a warlord in his own right, one whose crimes and cruelty became legendary. Eventually Jake Silver was defeated, as all such tyrants must be, and escaped back home across the ocean to the hinterlands of the north where he adopted a new trade and name. One that would place him beyond reproach or suspicion . . . a simple country pastor.'

'Simeon Paulet was a filthy killer and a rapist who murdered my mother so he could steal our family's water rights,' called Jacob. 'Putting him and his killers in the dirt wasn't a crime. It was a reckoning he wouldn't have got any other way, not with his wealth and power.'

'Please! You cannot but open your mouth and the lies spew forth. Nothing of your testimony is true, Father,' said the prefect. 'You impugn a good man's memory even as you try to launder an evil one's. You helped your slaver paymaster Prince Owen find exile in Weyland after he was chased out of the Burn by the Vandian military; you even helped him abscond using the same escape route you yourself had fled by.'

Jacob Carnehan shook his head. 'I found Prince Owen as a slave. Only alive because he'd escaped assassination as a child by your master, Marcus.'

'Is it not true that your own brother flew you down here to Arcadia? Your brother, who keeps the family trade of brigandage going... Black Barnaby, that cursed scourge of all honest mariners? As much a pirate of the air as the skels. Barnaby *Silver* to use his family name. Yes, *your* murderous brother, Jake Silver.'

There were gasps around the assembly at the infamous pirate's name, then a rising clamour as both sides of the assembly began throwing furious insults and curses at each other, some of the assemblymen aiming punches at rivals from opposing parties, assembly guards trying to intervene as the speaker smashed his hammer almost unheard.

Carter swayed on the stand, rocked by the revelations he had just heard. 'It's not true?'

'Barnaby's your uncle,' said Jacob. 'That much is no lie.'

'What the prefect said about fighting in the Burn, your name? Are those the things I saw back in the sky mine's fever room when our minds were joined? The blood – the battles?'

'Leave,' whispered Jacob. 'Find the prince. Things are about to turn as ugly they are going to get. You suffered as a slave in Vandia for long enough to know the truth of matters. Marcus has laid his own crimes on his nephew. No amount of talking or voting will see justice done here now.'

'What about you, Father Carnehan?' asked Tom Purdell.

Jacob nodded towards blue-uniformed troops appearing at the entrances to the great chamber. 'This was obviously planned some time ago. You two haven't been directly accused, yet. Run. Find the prince. If you can't find any regiments still loyal to his cause, perhaps the Guild of Librarians can help you escape.'

'I won't leave you and I'm not going to abandon Willow.'

'You can't help her escape if you're a corpse or a prisoner at best,' growled Jacob. 'If you love Willow, if you can still love me, then leave.'

'I won't,' said Carter, a surge of unsettling anguish rising inside him.

'You're one of the few people who can speak to the truth, boy; that makes you dangerous. If I try to leave here with you, they'll arrest us all.'

'They'll kill you.'

'I was called here as an unarmed witness,' said Jacob. 'Recover my pistols and your arms from the assembly's guard post. You're going to need them before the day's out. See him safe, Mister Purdell.'

Carter grabbed his father's arm. 'They'll try you for the gallows.'

Carter Carnehan gazed sadly over the assembly – royal guardsmen shoving politicians down to the floor with their rifles; his father staring across the chamber towards the daughter of the man he had slain. Assembly guards struggled against the king's soldiers, but they were only carrying ceremonial daggers and slightly more practical billy-clubs. Carter could hear Assemblyman Sparrow yelling that this was an unlawful coup while many from his party fled for the numerous exits, trying to scuttle to safety. 'Jake Silver was a killer. That's the only truth that escaped Colbert's lips today. A man has to answer sometime for what he's done.'

'You're not him. You're not! You're my father.'

'Save Willow, Carter. Whatever else happens will come about whatever you or I do. The tide is coming in now, and it'll sweep away all before it. Keep safe what matters.'

Tom seized Carter's arm and started to yank him down the steps, through the scrum of brawling assemblymen. Circling troopers came sprinting down from the chamber's walls towards the witness stand. A rifle butt drove into Jacob Carnehan's gut, winding him, troopers seizing the pastor and forcing his hands behind his back, locking wrist chains on him. A sudden surge of brawling assemblymen sent Carter stumbling back, Tom Purdell lost among the cascade of humanity. Carter tried to drive forward but a wildly swinging rifle slammed hard into the side of his skull, sending him tumbling across the wooden floor, dazed. He rested on his knees for an unknown time, his head aching as angry politicians, chamber staff and soldiers pushed back and forth, toppling mahogany desks and chairs; until a pair of arms lifted him back to his feet. It was Assemblyman Sparrow. 'Follow me, son. There are still a few ways out, left over from ages when the kings used to regularly dissolve councils and send troops in for recalcitrant assemblymen.'

Carter clutched his pounding head and let himself be led through the melee by the politician. There was no sign of his father on the stand or of Tom Purdell.

'How much of what the prefect said was true, son?' asked Sparrow.

'I don't know,' moaned Carter. Far more than either of them wanted to be, he suspected.

'It doesn't matter,' said Sparrow, shoving and squeezing through the struggling mob. 'The truth will be whatever King Marcus says it is, and he'll even provide the ink free of charge to his newspaper-owning cronies to print it for everyone to read. Let us hope that Field Marshal Houldridge's regiments prove loyal to the assembly, or our struggle for freedom will be over before it has begun.'

Sparrow fell against the curving oak-lined walls of the chamber and fiddled with the door of what looked like a service cupboard, the door swinging inward on to a long narrow corridor. Carter risked one last look back at the near riot erupting behind him. Still no sign of his father or friend. Carter suddenly realized how alone he was here in the far south. His father dragged off by King Marcus's soldiers, the usurper only too glad to pay the pastor back for returning alive with his troublesome nephew. Willow forced into a loveless marriage with a high-born bully and king's man. Carter realized he was terrified by the future. This was only the start of a war and already Carter had lost everything that meant anything to him. What was left for him, now? *Only to fight.*

Cassandra had been travelling for days. Travelling didn't prove particularly exerting in the nomads' company. Not when Cassandra was strapped across the horses stolen from her wagon with all the dignity of a grain sack, trussed up alongside the young Rodalian women, their numbers now swelled to five females thanks to the raiders' continued attacks along the way. They usually trekked by night and hid by day, stretching camouflage nets across boulders in the valleys and passes. The bloody yak meat would be cut into thin slices and buried in the thin soil inside a mirror-lined wooden box which acted as a solar oven, the meat baked by the fierce light of the high altitude sunlight. These Nijumeti weren't quite as simple as their appearance suggested. The witch rider Nurai acted both as a living map and compass; the heights, twists and inhabited regions of Rodal committed to memory, bypassing valleys where the distant roar of the winds sounded like thunder gods smashing away at each other. Leading them to easy pickings; small villages away from the skyguard's main patrol routes.

'The Nijumet will make us climb down the heights to the steppes,' said Dolki, bemoaning their fate under the netting as they rested. 'They will have left a boy in a ravine to guard their horses. They will strap us across their saddles and ride into the plains. We will be lost to the world!'

'Your soldiers never pursue the raiders?' asked Cassandra.

'Not far. Nobody crosses the steppes but the riders of the Nijumeti,' cried Dolki. 'Not even the guilds. The Guild of Rails tried to build a line along the coast centuries ago, but their trains were attacked and the rails torn up for blade metal. The radiomen keep no stations there. You will find no librarians' holds across any of the hills of the Araknatikh. Trading caravans bypass its shores by taking ferries along the ocean or travelling overland far to the east. Once we are taken there, we are lost. I will never see my father and mother again. If I should ever meet my sisters, I will feel only sorrow, for they will have been snatched by the hordes too.' Dolki brushed her ears and then yelled in fright as she realized someone was blowing softly against her lobes.

Alexamir rolled off a boulder behind them, roaring with laughter. 'I thought you Rodalians worshipped the gusting wind. Do you not regard me as a god now?'

Dolki muttered something in her own language and shrank away from him.

'What, not even a small god? Joni the Trickster, perhaps? I have always felt a powerful affinity for Joni. I have a taste for shenanigans and guile that would make even the trickster blush.'

'How can anyone tell when you blush, you blue-skinned savage?' spat Cassandra.

'I grow a horse's tail and it swishes coyly behind my arse,' said Alexamir. He patted the front of his trousers, fondly. 'Or is that something else that swishes down there, I never can remember.'

'It is so small you must lose it constantly.'

'You are a tiny creature, golden fox. That thought must cheer you somewhat, even though it is wrong.' He reached down and scooped her up as easily as his knapsack, tossing her over his back and howling with laughter as she struggled like a fish in an angler's net. Alexamir strolled across the heights for a few minutes before he swung Cassandra down off his shoulder and slid her body along the frost-covered granite. 'I am only sorry that you cannot see the steppes from here. We are still many weeks from the cliff-edge. Why anyone should want to live in this high, rocky storm-maze when the steppes lay beyond is a mystery beyond even the understanding of our witch riders and sorcerers.'

'Perhaps the Rodalians prefer the company here,' said Cassandra, struggling along the rock. 'Even among barbarians, I can tell that your kind is benighted.'

'Ha, to be Nijumeti is to be blessed by the Goddess. When the greatest warriors of Pellas die, they are rewarded by having their essence poured into the flesh of Nijumeti babes. When warriors' champions die, their souls flow into our horses' foals. That is why we have never been conquered. That is why there is nothing freer than a Nijumet.'

'You confuse having a quarrelsome nature with nobility.'

'Well, we even have nobility this season. Our clan is pledged to follow a king, now. A lord of clans called Tragmass. I do not think I like kings. The Weylanders call their nobility blue blooded . . . but all Nijumeti bleed blue. No, even a great horse king is a king too much for the Clan Stanim. But I am not yet lord, and so my words do not bear the true weight of my extraordinary wisdom.'

'Then you should cut me loose, for I am the granddaughter of an emperor. If the ancestors smile upon my house's strategy, my mother will be empress one day. And even kings must bow before an empress.'

He growled with amusement and sat alongside her. 'My land is too big for kings or emperors. They are too quick to develop a taste for taxes over a raider's honest spoils. You should never steal from your own people, only others, or however will you take your fun? And taxes can only be paid by tying yourself to the land and making the dirt your master. What man should be slave to another? What man should be kept by the dirt, rather than keep the dirt for his cattle and his horses as he wanders?'

'Said the nomad stealing a woman for a slave.'

'Stealing? To be a thief is a *high* calling. Kingship is the whore's trade. Those who call themselves kings will sooner or later demand you invade some country or another and trick you into believing their ambitions are your own. When you want to steal a fleece, it is best to leave the sheep alive to grow a fresh coat for the following year. Even the most stupid goat rustler knows that. Kings usually fail this test at the first hurdle.'

'I will never be your slave.'

'You misunderstand your position – you will not. I shall elevate you, golden fox. You were born a mangy royal in some ugly far-called land. But you will die a Nijumet wife with many fine healthy Nijumeti children around your tent weeping for your passing. You may thank me later. In fact, I will probably insist upon it.' He leant across and pressed his lips to hers. Despite Cassandra's best intentions, she felt her heart racing. His skin might look like he had expired of cold in the night, but his kiss was hot and passionate. In a certain light – one that didn't make him look like he was dying of hypothermia – he might even have been considered handsome, in a ridiculously blocky kind of way. 'There,' grinned the young nomad. 'I have stolen a kiss from you.'

'Lay me down on the rock,' said Cassandra, 'let us see what else my sly blue thief can steal.'

'Ah, you see, these charms rarely fail me. Please me eagerly and I will venture out in search of new wives only occasionally.'

'Only *occasionally*? Truly my ancestors have blessed me,' teased Cassandra.

'Many wives make light work for the camp. Does your nation not have this saying? But you do not need to fear you will go unattended in later years. I could tup twelve women a night and not think it too much. I may be young, but already I am a legend among my people. I strangled a lion in the long-grass when I was twelve. When I was thirteen, we were attacked by the Clan Menin and I cut down twelve riders fighting on foot. My stallion Astultan was probably one of your emperors in his last life, for he can gallop for two weeks and sleep while we travel.'

'Cut the ties behind my back so I may use my hands properly.'

'Is this the face of a fool?'

'One lives in hope.'

Alexamir jumped to his feet and drew a long sword from the scabbard on his back and held it out before him, glinting in the high clear sunlight. 'This is what I cut with. Have you ever seen the like of it before?'

Cassandra had to admit, she hadn't. The cobalt metal of the slightly curved sabre seemed to shimmer the same shade as the nomad's skin, and the shining blade was etched in a script she did not recognize. Its hilt looked like a ridged white spine-bone.

'I was riding among the hilltops when a snake leapt at Astultan. He reared to crush it. I was thrown off and fell not into the grass but through the roof of a burial mound. This sword was there, as bright and new as the day it came from the forge. The bones of the warrior below must have been eight foot tall – a giant from the ancient times.'

'It's an interesting blade.'

'*Interesting*? It shakes in my hand when my anger grows, almost humming. I think the soul of the warrior it was buried with lies in the blade, and shakes with envy when it sees how well I fight. Yes, it is envious of the glorious life that stretches out before Alexamir, the lord of thieves.' He slid it back into his scabbard and winked at Cassandra. 'If there is a luckier woman than you in Pellas, I would not care to throw dice against her, for she would sweep the stakes on every game.'

'I have been trained as a thief too,' said Cassandra, laying her back against the hard surface. She raised her legs and wrapped them around the nomad's ribs, caressing him as his weight slid down towards the granite. 'From almost the moment I could first walk.'

'I thought as much. The skyguard of the mountain people are soft and do not imprison people lightly, preferring banishment. What can you steal from me, my little golden fox, apart from my heart?'

'Your weight and your strength,' said Cassandra, twisting and converting his momentum, throwing the descending brute's weight against the boulder to her side. His skull cracked against the stone and he tumbled down to the rock moaning but still conscious. 'There was a reason my previous captors kept my feet chained, Alexamir.' She stood up and lashed out with her boot, catching the nomad in the side of his cheek with a crunching sound. Now he was rendered properly unconscious. 'Four gask guards with broken ribs, you overfed blueberry.'

Cassandra heard pebbles dislodged behind her and ducked just as a blade so curved it was almost a scythe cut through where she had been standing. Nurai, the cursed witch rider.

'Why my dreams led me to you, wide eyes, I will never know,' growled the woman, circling Cassandra. She knew what Nurai saw. A soft foreign noblewoman with her hands still bound behind her back, a quarter of the weight of the muscled nomad.

'Well, a Vandian is surely your people's best hope of improving your bloodline,' said Cassandra. 'But on balance, I think you can keep that one for yourself. Did you come sneaking here to watch us? To see what a Vandian woman has to offer that you do not?'

'I'll leave Alexamir your entrails for a belt!' Nurai lashed out at Cassandra, but the Vandian had already stepped to the side and brought her boot down on the woman's knee, shattering the bone. Nurai crumpled to the mountaintop, yelling in fury.

'You're about four times stronger than a Vandian,' said Cassandra. 'But you strike at the same speed as my people. And whatever blue piss-water you're pumping for blood, your bones are no harder than mine. Let's make this a fair fight, shall we . . . you can tie my legs together and I'll hop around you.'

Nurai roared at being so mocked. She came in faster than she should with only one working knee, her knife curving in low for a proper gutting, bellybutton to throat. Someone had at least taught the nomad how to do that correctly. But only if the blade connected. Cassandra threw herself down, sliding across the frost-driven rock, kicking Nurai's boots out from under her and rolling back to her feet in time to add a leg behind her spine and speed the witch rider's impact with the ground. Nurai's knife slid away towards the unconscious raider, but Cassandra stamped down and broke most of the fingers in the nomad woman's right hand to be certain.

'You'll be mixing potions with your left hand for a while, witch.'

Nurai was trying to struggle to her feet when Cassandra heard screams from the direction of the camp. It sounded like Dolki and her friends panicking. The thought that the other Nijumeti were claiming their wives before they reached the steppes vanished as an aircraft burst out of the slopes, roaring into the sky above, its wing guns smoking. Not much of a fighter aircraft at all. A small triangular flying wing with a single rear-mounted propeller, a combustion engine burping corn oil as it weaved through the air. She caught a glimpse of one of the horses bolting away, terrified, the nomads leaping and fleeing, shards of rock erupting into the air under a fusillade. There was an explosion behind Cassandra, but it was no bomb launched from the aircraft. Green smoke drifted with the stench of a child's stink bomb bought from market. As the wind from the heights shredded the mist she realized there was no sign of Nurai or Alexamir. Cassandra grunted. *Smoke cover. Not much of a witch, either.* But Dolki had been proved right about the nomads' capacity for pain. A Vandian would have been laid up for months with that shattered kneecap, absolutely unable to scamper away carrying a monstrous brute like Alexamir across her back.

'Well, that was a thankfully brief engagement.'

The witch rider's knife had been scooped up too, so Cassandra wouldn't be using that to free her hands. She sprinted back towards the camp. *If I can get to the remaining horse . . .* She turned the boulder. The camp was devoid of nomads apart from a couple of bleeding corpses left across the hard ground, and while a horse was still tied up, there were others inside the camp. Sheplar Lesh, Kerge, men in Rodalian aviator's uniforms and the old postal courier from the caravan halt, Dolki in his arms crying. He had lost a yak but regained a princess, it seemed – his daughter. Cassandra felt a sad stab of regret that she would never have a similar reunion with her father. Not until she slept with her ancestors, at any rate. A couple of flying wings had touched down on the flat ground ahead while two more circled in the sky above. Cassandra tried to back away but Sheplar came sprinting over the second he saw her, a pistol clutched in his hand.

'Tracking men over granite is never easy,' said Cassandra, grudgingly. 'Those savages underestimated me and I have made the same error with you.'

'Easier from the air. Hunting border reivers is bread and water to the skyguard of Rodal,' said Sheplar.

Cassandra scowled at Sheplar Lesh, a grudging newfound respect for the Rodalian clown. 'And you came after me.'

'You are under my protection as well as in my custody,' said Sheplar. 'My honour would never permit me otherwise.'

'I would have allowed the nomads to carry me away and make my presence here the clans' problem.'

'Then there stands the difference between your people and mine.'

'You are a fool, Sheplar Lesh,' said Cassandra. 'But a brave one. I must give you that.'

'Not so big a fool as the Nijumeti,' said Sheplar, holding up a pair of manacles. He tossed them across to her and gestured at them with his pistol. 'Lock them around your ankles. I would hate to have you run away and slip down a ravine.'

She sighed and did as he had ordered. 'You owe me a husband, I think.'

'And you owe me a life, bumo.'

'I'll relinquish your debt if you relinquish mine.'

Sheplar grinned with weary resignation and indicated the two empty cockpits of the nearest plane. 'And how then could you afford to pay me to fly you to Hadra-Hareer?'

So, my trade stays the same. For the moment. Maybe she would have been better off being carried away to the steppes by the nomads after all.

Carter watched the streets in resignation as his taxi cab rattled over the cobbles. The police were out in force, chasing down looters and protesters, and his carriage had already been forced to divert four times on the journey to the sea fort as barricades rose up across the streets, furniture being thrown out of windows, crates dragged out of shop fronts, mobs of angry workers reacting to the news that the king had dissolved the national assembly. It wasn't just mill workers raising barricades against the king. The wealthier areas had barricades of their own, citizen militia composed of shop workers and house servants; armed civilians chasing away looters and opportunists in search of plunder, the flag of Weyland fluttering over overturned wagons as they bellowed support at passing police and threatened to lynch any rebels that strayed into their territory. *Civil war, then. So easily started.*

Royal guardsmen swarmed across Arcadia's lanes too, blue-coats dragging angry yelling labour combination men out of cheap apartments and shackling them in ankle chains to the back of army wagons. Luckily for Carter, he travelled in a civilian vehicle and the troopers left him unaccosted, their attentions focused on rounding up everyone listed as enemies of the king from their known addresses. Carter shared his cab with Assemblyman Sparrow and two other Gaiaist Party politicians, their chatter about the implications of this situation arcane compared to the chaos on the streets. How the prefects would need to be removed from each territory and the assemblymen rule alone; which assistant assemblymen would need to take over to replace loyal northerners arrested up on the hill. Which prefectures would declare for the prince and which for the king? Their gassing continued, apparently oblivious to paving stones being ripped up from the road around them, piled up by citizens to be used as crude ammunition between the rival forces vying for power. The ride passed a timeless haze. As they reached the sea fort, Carter saw the soldiers loyal to Field Marshal Houldridge arrayed in long lines, boarding civilian ships down in the harbour. Men, horses, artillery, all being loaded along the quayside. In the distance, he could just hear the dim rattle of small-arms fire, the barricades' rise being opposed, grey lines of smoke drifting up from the proud city.

Carter stepped out of the carriage and he and Assemblyman Sparrow found Prince Owen in the sea fort's courtyard with Anna Kurtain, supervising the embarkation.

Owen nodded gravely towards them. 'Is it as bad as we thought, Assemblyman?'

'I fear it is, Your Majesty,' said Sparrow. 'Marcus didn't even allow the vote to go ahead before giving credence to our worst fears. His troops dissolved the assembly by force. Half the party are heading towards the usurper's cells and awaiting his "mercy", now.'

'I sent a warning to you on the hill as soon as we heard the southern armies had disobeyed the field marshal's orders to stay in barracks. They're advancing on Arcadia and seizing all the bridges along the Boles River.'

'I'm afraid I never received your note,' said Sparrow. 'Marcus's soldiers invading the council served as warning enough of the usurper's intentions. He planned this devilry well in advance, that much is certain. Marcus's troopers are scouring the streets, arresting our people house by house. It's a damned premeditated coup is what it is.'

Prince Owen sighed. He indicated the vessels at harbour. 'My uncle has his plans. We have ours.'

'What are you doing escaping by sea? Why aren't you making a stand?' demanded Carter, looking at the vessels below. 'This fortress controls the harbour. Thick walls guarded by heavy cannons. If you control access to the ocean, you control the city.'

'In the days before the skyguard, perhaps,' said Prince Owen. 'But now? This isn't a tenable position anymore, however thick our bulwarks.'

'Arcadia isn't just the capital, anymore, Northhaven,' said Anna. 'Arcadia is the *enemy* capital.'

'We have to fall back north,' said Owen. 'The saints know, I don't want to. But if we fight now, here, we'll lose before we've even started. This is the heartland of the usurper's support. We intend to declare a Provisional Army of the Northern Prefectures and establish a new national assembly at Midsburg. We'll organize ourselves there and push back to the capital eventually.'

'I don't have that long! Damn your eyes, my father's in Marcus's hands.'

'It is true,' said Sparrow. 'Prefect Colbert appeared in the assembly to name Father Carnehan kin to Black Barnaby and a few darker things besides. In the end, it was as though the father wanted to be arrested... to give himself up.'

'Barnaby the pirate?' said Owen, shocked. 'You cannot mean the pirate raider?'

'My father's the man who brought the slaves back from Vandia,' protested Carter. 'The *same* man who saved you, Anna, all of us. Half of what was said by the prefect was lies.' *It must be. It has to be.*

'The prefect also accused you of being in cahoots with slavers in the Burn,' said the assemblymen. 'Colbert claimed your father was behind the skel attacks and that he took his own life when Marcus courageously uncovered the conspiracy, before driving you and your brothers across the ocean.'

'I must have missed that part of my life,' said the prince.

'I reckon we were too busy starving in the mines to notice,' said Anna. 'Marcus has surely spent some of his Vandian silver on a brass neck. Your uncle's pissing on the nation's back and telling us it's raining.'

'We live in strange days,' said Sparrow. 'When monarchs become tyrants and pastors become pirates.'

'Well, I guess we're all rebels now,' said Anna. 'Not much choice in the matter.'

'I wanted the crown by law, not by war,' said Owen, sounding anguished.

'Any blood is on the usurper's hands,' said Anna. 'No different from when we were dying for Marcus's damned gold in the sky mines.'

'Forgive me, Carter. Perhaps I should have listened to your father's advice,' said Owen, his voice wracked with regret. 'Had a blade slipped into my uncle's spine before he learned we'd returned alive. I could have let that sin rest on my head alone, not involved the rest of the country.'

'There are no words that rest more bitterly on the tongue than "I might have", Your Majesty,' interjected Sparrow. 'We are where we are. Your uncle seizes power in the south and raises steel against the nation. If we are to cast the usurper off your rightful throne, it will be a long, hard pounding between here and seeing the devil unseated.'

Carter's hands tightened on the handles of his father's pistols. Their weight felt strange and uncomfortable around his waist. *They're not all I'll take with me to remember him by*. 'The past is gone. But today? How can I leave Willow here, married against her will to that bastard Viscount Wallingbeck? I won't just abandon my father. What kind of man would I be?'

'The kind who's still alive to fight for your family's freedom,' said Owen. 'If you stay, you'll face nothing but southern regiments loyal to

Marcus for a thousand miles in every direction. Your father's probably locked up tight as a tick in the palace dungeons and heavily guarded by my uncle's forces. The best fate you'll meet hiding in the capital is to be swept up from your lodgings and chained inside an aristocrat's arms mill or conscripted to fight for the south. The worst is someone will recognize you and turn you in for the price on your head and you'll end up in Marcus's hands.'

'Listen to the prince,' urged the assemblyman. 'Your name's sure to be on the arrest lists the guardsmen are scouring the capital with. A man's got to use his wits to fight as well as his heart.'

'If I can't free my father, maybe I can rescue Willow. We could board a plane north and follow you.'

'You won't be flying anywhere until the skyguard's engineers flush their planes' engines. The teamsters' union are presently busy spoiling every fuel drum in the capital's airfields with tar,' said Owen. 'I can't risk the skyguard attacking our fleet as we sail back up the coast. They're my uncle's creation. Don't expect safe passage from any airfield in this half of the nation.'

'My father came for us,' said Carter, trying to keep his voice level. 'Against all the odds, he crossed half the world, stood against an entire empire. Everyone at home said he was insane, a dead man seeking suicide on an impossible journey. But he still came for us in Vandia . . .'

'Son,' said Sparrow, 'if half the things Jacob Carnehan stands accused of are true, he had a unique talent for raiding and an enemy that wasn't expecting him at the far end of his travels. Your pa chose to surrender in the assembly so you could escape. Don't let his sacrifice be in vain. Your father made his choice, and as for your lady, Arcadia is going to be a long way from the frontline. Think things through. If you grab her, what then? Your lady travels with you and has to survive a string of bloody battlefields up north, dodging cannonballs, bayonets and strafing runs by the skyguard? She's a good deal safer down here in some aristocrat's warm mansion than she would be back in Northhaven alongside a man whose cards have been marked by the usurper.'

'Live to fight,' said Prince Owen, almost pleading with the pastor's son. 'Sometimes, it takes far more courage to retreat than advance. You saved my life once, Carter Carnehan, and I have to believe it was for this task. The seeds of despotism have been planted at our door and we must stamp them down. I have as little choice in the matter as when we were slaves struggling to survive in the sky mines. Sail with me to Midsburg and we'll fight, I promise you that. For your father, for Willow, for a free assembly and for everyone in the land. There'll be fighting enough until you're sick of it. That I can promise you – perhaps it's all I have to promise you.'

Carter's skull felt as heavy as lead as he slowly nodded his agreement. He tried to tell himself that he was a rebel, not a coward. But however much sense it made to fight another day, he was still running away. So much fear, so many worries blistering away inside his heart. Only today, none of his dread was for himself.

Cassandra gazed through the narrow window at the high white-topped mountains beyond, pale and shining in the bright moonlight. It was too narrow to lean out of and see the other buildings clinging to the mountain side in the Rodalian town. Too narrow to feel the wind on her cheeks, but she knew it still blew here, angrily hissing and shushing beyond Talatala's thick stone walls. If the near gale serving as her constant companion wasn't annoying enough, there was the persistent clacking of prayer wheels mounted on the town's exterior, turning, turning, turning like the sails of a windmill. Even closing and locking her wooden shutters couldn't dampen the relentless background noise. Cassandra was locked in a cell-like room, simple and spare, intended for skyguard staff. A bamboo cot with a stuffed mattress and a black walnut wood table with a small stool, the monastic room's cold stone tiles warmed only by a square woollen rug with a blood-red amulet pattern which wouldn't have looked out of place as a nomad's saddle. A single door, always locked; with a basic and somewhat rickety cupboard to its side. And a single arrow slit of a window, no glass of course, opening on to her soaringly cold view. There was a pair of iron oil lamps mounted on the wall, their flicker and burnt grain stink giving her a slow but unremitting headache. Cassandra was loath to turn them off, though. Something about this place left her with a nagging unease. It was as though the previous occupants of this harsh, rocky outpost of Rodal still lingered in the stone, standing sentry over her. She would wake up sometimes, shivering, convinced that someone was watching her. Perhaps a guard had opened the door to the room and checked she was still securely imprisoned inside. But they were never present when she opened her eyes, neither closing the door nor locking the latch outside. *How long have I been here now? A week? Waiting for permission to be dispatched to Rodal's capital; ferried there with as little respect as a sack of grain.* The gask, who still insisted on tutoring Cassandra in uselessly abstract arithmetic, had told her she was to remain in Talatala for one more night before departing at daylight's first gleaming. *Another flight. I hope I won't be sick this time.* Cassandra had gained an unexpected respect for the talents of the Rodalian skyguard pilots on her journey to the town. Flying through insanely strong winds that would have grounded most modern imperial craft, risking their necks – and hers – in a fierce aerial dance across the canyons and peaks. Cassandra was fairly sure she could pilot one of the triangle-winged aircraft if it came to it. Rodal's pilots talked a good talk about how they could only fly by communing with the spirits of the wind, but she was fairly sure it was just sharp flying instincts supplemented by the barbarians' false local religion. Their planes were basic enough to embarrass even the humblest imperial trainer. Wood and fabric rather than an armoured metal fuselage; a rear-mounted propeller and engine which stank like a kitchen range from the organic ether poured into it. Although Cassandra had to admit, she had never before seen an airfield like the one the skyguard squadron plunged into. Hangars driven into the peaks with long tunnels for runways to land and launch, then a maze of turns and twists to deprive the winds of their terrific hold, the bulk of the field's facilities carved into the mountain's heart. Like the town itself, what you saw clinging to the slopes' surface was just the silver plating on a cheap goblet. Cassandra had caught glimpses of Talatala on the way to her current chamber, carefully memorizing the route in case she could slip her captors. She'd seen buildings which scarcely differed from the brick and wood constructions of Weyland, except they clung to rock walls of vast hollowed-out spaces inside the mountain, carts, yaks, horses and people crowding the enclosed stone streets, cold light from shuttered openings in the slopes entering like spears of illumination through a forest. Cassandra passed temples, shops, homes and bazaars; the smell from the food sellers overwhelming the cloying sweetness of incense candles and reminding her just how poor her rations had been during her captivity among the nomad raiders. She looked hungrily at dumplings bobbing in rich beef and potato stew, sizzling yak strips and golden-coloured fried flatbreads stuffed with spiced meats. Flickering lamps and warm air from inside the tiered buildings lent the place a surprisingly homely feel – well-insulated from the mountain winds beating down beyond their half-buried town. The subterranean spaces were intertwined with corridors, buildings and chambers constructed on the mountain slope itself – which were chillier and exposed to the whipping gales. Much like the mountain people's nature, the Rodalians kept the greater part of themselves hidden and out of sight. Certainly, she'd find it easier to wring blood out of a stone than get any useful information from Sheplar Lesh. But Cassandra was canny enough to know that her captor still intended to imprison her inside the Rodalian capital. And everything she learnt of this country made her realize how hard it would be for Vandia's agents to winkle her out of the stronghold she would end up trapped within. Bad enough if the imperium's local sell-swords tried to assault a provincial town like this tonight. Talatala could give the Castle of Snakes and her mother's formidable defences a run for their money. How much stronger was Rodal's capital? *They have to come for me again. They found me in the gask forests: they can find me here, surely? And next time, I'll try not to cut them down before I hear them out.*

Cassandra sat on her cot and pulled the blankets around her. It was never warm here, this close to the town's overhanging exterior. Why couldn't they have made her a captive in one of the chambers deep inside the mountain? She imagined feeling the corridors' warmth again, as she marched from the aircraft hangars. It would be superior to her present accommodation, at any rate. Her last visitor of the day was due shortly. Eventually Sheplar Lesh arrived and came into her quarters bearing a wooden plate of food and a jug of cold water. Nothing like the tasty fare she had seen the locals enjoying. More dried fish and tofu. Military rations, she suspected, designed to make sure those consuming them never turned too soft. No danger there. If Cassandra never saw another helping of the revolting curd-like food again, it would still be too soon. And the fish was so salty it had almost ossified on its plate.

She moved to the table and balanced on the stool. 'It is cold here. Why is there no fireplace?'

Sheplar placed the food on the table, crossed to the cupboard, opened its door and indicated three thick crimson robes hanging there, piped yellow around their edging. 'There are fire spirits who would be delighted to show you what they might do with hot cinders this near the wind, bumo. Besides, why would you need a roaring fire when you have these to wear? Put on one and if you are still cold, pull on the other two.'

'They look like the cassocks worn by the priests I saw chanting in front of your temples,' said Cassandra, suspiciously.

'Skyguard pilots spend at least a year studying alongside our priests,' said Sheplar. 'Otherwise, how could they read the winds?'

'Keep your priests' robes. I would look absurd in them. What if I give you my word not to escape?' said Cassandra, tugging her leg at the uncomfortable manacles around her ankle, making the chain links clink where they were fixed to the wall.

'The chains are for your protection, bumo,' said Sheplar. 'The winds which bide outside Talatala are known as the *Shi'pa*, the spirits of the fallen ones. There are stories here of parents walking into their children's bedrooms and finding babies floating in the air, being sucked towards an opening by malicious shades, their babe only saved by the chains of their cot. The winds of Talatala call many ghosts to the slopes outside, ghosts that may make the living dead too when they grow cruel and bored.'

'Ridiculous man! I can't even get my face through this slit of a window.'

'The *Shi'pa* possess ways of squeezing a soul. That is what is said.'

Cassandra snorted. 'Spare me your crude barbarian superstitions.'

Sheplar pulled up a single leather strap dangling from the end of her cot. 'This is what a pilot uses to secure one leg while they sleep here. It lacks your chain's lock, but serves the same purpose. Tightening if a sleeper is dragged from the bed while deep in sleep.'

'You lie!' said Cassandra. 'That's for securing a spare bedroll.'

'It is the truth,' said Sheplar. 'I was posted to the skyguard station at Talatala for a year. I slept in a room down this very corridor, and was long warned by a temple priest of the ghosts here. Once, when I was walking back alone to my bunk after a day's hard duty, every shutter on the corridor's windows banged open behind me, in perfect order, as though turned by an invisible hand. I fled into my room and bolted the door. I have never since known the terror I felt trying to sleep that night, not even when I flew against an entire skel carrier squadron. I would sooner face a sky full of slave raiders than encounter whatever I sensed that night.'

'Your phantoms would not find a Vandian soul to their taste,' said Cassandra. 'I am protected by my ancestors, the blood of emperors and empresses counted among my line.'

'A rich delicacy, perhaps,' smiled Sheplar, 'compared to the life that pumps through our thin mountain veins.'

'You are trying to terrify me into submission with ancient camp-fire tales,' said Cassandra, struggling to ignore the uneasy feeling she'd become so familiar with before the Rodalian ventured in bearing her supper. 'You should know me better than that by now.'

'In truth, I scare myself when I remember my time here.' He left the meal on the table for her, opening the door. 'Be glad of your chains, bumo. And be glad we fly you to Hadra-Hareer tomorrow morning.'

Cassandra heard the clack of the latch as the mountain man secured her inside her cell. She moved the stool around and sat with her back to the door, keeping a wary eye on the window as she crunched into the over-salted fish. Cassandra doubted if a stall selling hot Rodalian food would prosper inside one of the imperium's covered markets, but the cold had a way of firing her appetite all the same. She finished the meal, left the plate largely emptied, and began to return to her cot. Cassandra was halfway across the room when a sibilant hissing drew her attention towards the window slit. She froze, fighting down a rising sense of dread. *I am Vandian, heir to an imperial house. Foreign spirits will not paralyse me with fear.* There was the sound again, accompanied by scratching and scrabbling. Her hands flashed to her ivory-handled chopsticks, one for each palm. Not exactly a brace of matched duelling daggers, but she might put out the eye of any vampiric shade that was corporeal enough to do her injury. As she had the thought, a hideous bleached face came into view, its malevolent features filling the gap outside.

NINE

ROYAL HOSPITALITY

Jacob Carnehan paced the windowless confines of his cell, a substantial space large enough to hold twenty prisoners, his boots scraping granite flagstones covered with a scattering of dirty straw, a couple of tattered old blankets in one corner to serve as cot and cover, both. He was penned in by three featureless stone walls with a line of thick iron bars as the fourth. As best as the pastor could tell, these were the dungeons beneath the palace at the centre of Arcadia. All the jailors he had seen wore the blue dress uniforms of royal guardsmen, a single yellow stripe down their trousers. The troopers wouldn't talk to him, and only visited to pass plates of food and jugs of water through a flap in the cell door twice a day. No news of his son or the prince or the progression of events in the wider world. Only rodents for company. Little grey mice exactly the same shade as the rock floor, which streamed out of nowhere when Jacob's back was turned, heading for what few crumbs he'd left of his meagre rations.

His captors left him to stew here for days, imagining the worst of what might have transpired in the capital. With no other prisoners in the adjoining cells along the chill stone corridor to distract him, Jacob's imagination was prey to his worst imaginings. He hated himself for it. It was exactly what his captors wanted. He was given time to let his fear and apprehensions build. Like leaving a blade resting in the coals to make it malleable when the smith finally beat it with his hammer.

It appeared that Jacob was being singled out for special attention;

a suspicion that was confirmed when King Marcus appeared beyond the iron bars, maybe a week into the pastor's captivity. The usurper looked little changed from when Jacob had last met him, petitioning for his help to chase down the slavers. The fastidious grey man still seemed anonymous, even in the military-style uniform he now sported. A blue tunic with brass buttons, braid, medals and a patent leather cross-belt with sabre on one side and pistol on the other. The usurper didn't wear it comfortably. Marcus looked like a clerk forced into a uniform for a wager. Sadly, the fate of the kingdom hinged on this particular bet.

'Father Carnehan. It seems like an age since you first arrived at my palace, begging me for a company of royal guardsmen to rescue your friends. And here we are again, in much altered circumstances.'

'Your troopers didn't prove to be much use,' said Jacob. 'I had to let them go.'

'Yes, the imperium's agents in Hangel sent word about Major Alock's sad fate before the city fell. Wherever you go, trouble seems to snap at your heels.'

'Alock met the same fate as the Vandian's puppet king in Hangel. Puppet kings are never missed much.'

'Is that what you think of me?' smiled Marcus. 'I am no puppet. I'm using the imperium as much as they use me.'

'To get rich by selling your people into slavery.'

'Personal riches?' Marcus snorted. 'Is that the dreary limit of your vision? I may be king now, but I was a prosperous industrial lord long before I rose to the throne. Did you by chance pass a vast stone tomb in the capital raised to contain my corpse, gold-plated ziggurats as large as mountains to honour my reign? No, of course not. That is not how I have used the crown. I have old-fashioned vices which I have always had ample means to indulge, although I dare say the imperium might serve as an example. Do you know the Vandian emperor keeps a harem filled with hundreds of wives? How economical, to store all your mistresses under one roof. I will have to introduce something similar after I've crushed the pretender.'

'Well, why the hell not?' said Jacob. 'You've already screwed the country. *Bad Marcus*.'

'Don't call me that!' The usurper lost his temper with the yell, before recovering. How quickly the mask could slip. 'And how, pray, have I done that? With thousands of new roads; trade metals flowing towards us for engines and machines and girders; freshly raised mills; newly constructed hospitals and schools; our recently formed skyguard's contrails trailing proudly across the heavens? This is where the imperial largess has been invested. Weyland is being remade as a modern, prosperous nation; the most powerful force in the league. Able to withstand the worst that nature and our enemies can throw against us. That will be my legacy to this land.'

'Blood and suffering and war are all you've given us.'

'They should make you head of the Gaiaist Party, Father. *Live within the circle of existence on Pellas; prosper alongside nature and accept life as it is*. I'll tell you what nature is, Father. It is sickness and poverty and early deaths and hard, heavy lives. It's the need to have seven children because two thirds of your young ones won't survive into adulthood. As you noticed during Prefect Colbert's performance in the assembly, your carefully concealed past has been exposed. You might have lost one child to slavers, but you lost two more during the epidemic. Those sums are writ large across the realm. My wife blessed me with eight children. Only four are alive today, and I am the bloody *king* for the love of the saints. Who is the real enemy? The imperium, your king, or the cruel randomness of the world and its blind, uncaring nature? Everything we possess, everything that separates us from beasts, has been laid by the ingenuity of our minds and hands. All I demand is that we build better, further, faster.'

'You pious bastard! You had my wife murdered, my town burnt and my child sold like a sack of wheat.'

'A handful hurt so that many thousands more may prosper. That is the arithmetic of morality when you rule. You've frustrated my schemes so adeptly. Bringing the taken back from the sky mines when you should have been left a corpse out there. Returning with my cursed nephew in tow. I expected better of you. I expected you to have a plan, a vision, something greater than revenge.'

'I'm happy to disappoint you. Sinking my blade through your throat is all the legacy I need carved on my gravestone. *Jacob Carnehan. He once slew some useless sack-of-shit usurper.*'

'Carnehan was your wife's family name,' said Marcus. 'Your

tombstone should read *Jake Silver*. Aren't you curious how I unmasked your criminal past? How I was always one step ahead of you?'

The king's commanding voice echoed down the dungeon corridor and two figures approached; both of them men that Jacob knew. Tom Purdell, the guild courier. The second a figure that Jacob recognized despite the new scar splitting his ugly face; but *this* man should have died in a dark forest a long way from Weyland. Jacob's palms went white as he gripped the metal bars, desperate for a way to reach his tormentors, imagining squeezing the life out of their throats.

'Captain Purdell is an officer of the army intelligencers,' laughed the king. 'Placed inside the Guild of Librarians long before their dusty order declared for the pretender's cause. My other comrade I believe you also know, although not by the alias he adopted in Northhaven.'

'Nix!' spat Jacob. 'I left you for dead.'

'*Nocks*, more recently,' grinned the royal guardsman. 'I've been serving as loyal retainer to Benner Landor's wife . . . That little hellcat's one of His Highness's mistresses. Your son has good cause to know my new name. I gave your lad a few stripes across his spine to make up for this . . .' The soldier ran his hand down his disfigured face. 'As for my still being in this mortal coil . . . That last bullet you so generously left me to end my life? I used it. The shot passed through my head and left me looking like this. But it didn't finish me. Nor did those twisted forest cannibals when they captured me and tried to cook me. The dog-riders couldn't kill old Nix. You couldn't. Seems like nothing can.'

'Even the stealers don't want your soul polluting hell, Nix.'

'They'll take yours, though, Father. I'll make sure of that.'

'Sergeant Nix returned alive from the expedition. He was the regiment's only survivor, bringing me the secret of your true name,' said the king. '*Jake Silver*. A murderous killer on both sides of the ocean.'

'I should apologize, Father,' said Tom Purdell, stepping forward. 'For flying false colours in Northhaven. But unlike you, I'm a loyal servant of the state.'

'Shut your face, boy,' said Jacob. 'When I come for you, I'm not even going to waste a bullet on you. I'll snap your treacherous neck.'

'I do hope not,' said the king. 'Captain Purdell's proved terribly helpful to me. Did you think it was my foolish nephew who ordered the police to hold your party as council witnesses? It was *I* who had you taken into custody, after the good captain advised me you'd be visiting the Winteringham in search of your boy's errant lover.'

'It's a pity my hired swords failed to take Lady Cassandra in the forest, Father Carnehan,' said Tom Purdell. 'It would make your interrogation go a lot easier for you. Still, one girl in a rickety wagon riding north with a gask and a Rodalian flier. How far can they get?'

Jacob cursed himself. The night ambush of the coach and the attack on the passengers, Tom Purdell's execution only just averted by Jacob. All staged solely to make him trust the king's duplicitous agent. The bandits slain by Jacob that night probably hadn't even known that the courier they had captured was one of them. All a ruse calculated to earn Jacob's trust. And he had fallen for it. 'They'll get further than you, boy. I'll see you meet a turncoat's end.'

'Empty threats are all you have left,' King Marcus sighed. 'Your brute savagery pitted against my intellect – hardly any contest at all. I planned everything, you dolt. After Nix returned alive bearing news of your survival, I dispatched Leyla Holten to worm her way into the House of Landor and be my eyes in the north. I arranged to have her stepdaughter dragged to the capital, knowing the boy would follow *her* and that you'd follow *him*. I calculated that your notorious past would cast doubt on the pretender's claim to the throne. Now the traitors in the assembly are retreating north while I rule absolutely through a reformed parliament led by my prefects, unencumbered by the opposition's liberal bleating. Vandia's embassy informs me that an imperial armada will be arriving shortly to punish the escaped slaves for their revolt, and my precious nephew has kindly gathered every rebellious opponent to my rule in the north, ready to receive the empire's retribution. Not to mention being a handy target for the people's hatred once they learn how my brother arranged the slave raids. I could have destroyed Owen's rebels here, but why waste the army's bullets when the Vandians need to taste a little Weyland blood? The imperium will do my killing for me. *All* of this, all to *my* plan.'

'To hell with your schemes. Reformed parliament?' snarled Jacob. 'One man, one vote . . . and you're that one man?'

'I am the monarch and I shall rule in a royal style. I really should thank you for your invaluable assistance, Father. You've proved yourself almost as useful to my cause as the captain here. All the southern factories and mills packed with indentured labour, their votes passed to their masters to exercise. Block voting is so much easier to coordinate for the greater good. A man always rules alone, you must remember that from leading armies across the ocean?'

'I only remember the blood. You've nothing but lies to offer, usurper.'

'You are wrong about that, too, Father. You see, I am here with a generous proposal for you. Owen's rebels won't last long against the army and the skyguard; but I cannot risk the rebels scattering into the wilds to fight a protracted guerrilla war. This rebellion would be ended decisively with a brute of your ilk as my general. Quicksilver, the Hammer of the Burn. The greatest mercenary commander of the war-with-no-end. Every battle you fought you won, no matter the odds. And when your noble patrons grew jealous of your success and turned on you, you destroyed them too. Yes, I know all about your history, Jake Silver.'

'I haven't been that man for decades.'

'You might have fled your responsibilities and buried your soul under a false name, but I think you're still that creature,' said the king. 'Serve in my guard. Replace Major Alock whose corpse you so carelessly misplaced on your journey to Vandia. All you have to do to secure your position is tell me where in Rodal the emperor's grandchild is being held. Help me retake her unharmed. In return, I will permit you and your family to prosper. I shall have to let the Vandians burn Northhaven to ashes in punishment for the slave revolt, but if there is anyone in the region you are particularly fond of, I can have them spirited away before the slaughter begins.'

'I stashed the imperial brat up your hairy arse while you were asleep last night.'

'And that is really your final answer? You *have* changed, Quicksilver. You've become a weak-blooded fool without the will to do what is necessary! A waste, indeed. With my acumen and a brute like you as my hammer, I could have forged a future so great our praises would still be sung at the far end of Pellas millennia from now. Oh well, I shall just have to rely on soldiers like Nix here. But, as you might recall, he is something of a blunt instrument.'

'Give me the job of making him talk, Your Highness,' begged Nix, hatred distorting his grotesque features. 'Old Nix was about to warm his flesh when he escaped me last time. I was fixing to get Carnehan to tell us how he knew to set his compass for Vandia.'

'Yes, that is still rather a puzzle.' King Marcus placed a hand on Nix's shoulder. 'But he's not for you, at least, not yet. A tortured man will invent anything to make his pain stop. Isn't that right, Captain Purdell?'

'Indeed so, Your Majesty,' said the officer.

'Before the captain infiltrated the long guilds, he served as an interrogator for me. The answers he obtained weren't nearly as important as the fear he spread among the rebels. But it's not fear I need now. Lady Cassandra must be returned unharmed, or the Vandian emperor will have *my* skull for a feasting cup. We live in a modern age and so we should rely on modern methods.' He waved a hand at Purdell. 'Captain, send word to the imperial surgeon. He has a new patient.' The king returned his attention to Jacob. 'It's not only metals and raw materials the imperium supplies us with. Among their agents and advisers serving in the kingdom, Vandia's embassy keeps an expert in making people talk: an imperial surgeon with techniques so advanced I can only watch in awe.'

Jacob watched the treacherous guild courier scurry away. 'You wouldn't recognize the truth if it spat in your eye.'

'But I'll know it when the Vandian brings it to me.'

Jacob shook the bars, as though fury alone could twist them out of place. 'You had better put a bullet in my head right here. Because I'm going to come for you, Marcus. It doesn't matter how many sell-swords like Nix you surround yourself with, how many Vandian allies you buy with our people's blood. None of them will save you when I come for your filthy carcass. I'll make you suffer. I swear it by the saints and my murdered wife and my last living son. Life in the Burn as the lowliest trodden-down serf soldier crawling through the mud will be a paradise you'll beg me for before your pain's done.'

The usurper raised his hands mockingly towards the cell. 'Charity, charity, Father. *Please*. What a wasted opportunity.' Marcus strode off, turning back just before he exited the corridor. 'You're standing in the way of progress, and so it's only right that progress should take everything from you. The pretender, his rebels and his lost cause. Your son. Your home. Your last pathetic secrets, and finally your life, too. He is all yours, Sergeant Nix, just as soon as the Vandian has loosened his tongue.'

Nix leant in towards the bars and looked Jacob straight in the eyes. 'I'll do it the old-fashioned way, myself, for old time's sake. Shit on progress. It'll be like being back in the Burn, two old comrades with a white hot fire to toast your hide on. You remember what I did to your friend Wiggins, don't you? How loudly he screamed as I warmed his old bones.'

'I haven't forgotten,' said Jacob. *I haven't forgotten a thing.*

Leyla Holten found King Marcus in front of an orchard on the eastern side of the palace gardens. She stepped off a gravel pathway flanked by expensive bronze monuments to Weyland's previous monarchs. An octahedron-shaped wooden pavilion stood between the trees and a lake with a serene view over a double-arched bridge, a gentle slope with well-tended green banks on either side, the structure built to accommodate a band to play for the pleasure of king and court. Today it featured a rather different kind of entertainment. A man was bound to a chair on the oak platform, while the king pecked at his lunch from inside the cover of a canvas pavilion, fires burning in braziers to either side of him. It was no normal seat placed on the bandstand, though. It held a condemned man, while an officer slowly tightened a silk scarf around his neck using a poorly oiled crank wheel.

'You remember Captain Purdell, my dear?' said the king, indicating the officer gradually twisting the crank.

Leyla nodded. 'Of course. I have the captain to thank for bringing me your instructions to return to Arcadia.'

'Yes, the good captain has proved himself highly useful. This entertainment is partly to reward him for his labours. He is like one of my hunting hounds. He needs a little blood every now and then to keep him prepared for the actual hunt.'

'I can't see any blood yet,' noted Leyla, stepping close to the warmth of the brazier.

'Wait until the end,' said the king. 'You will not be disappointed.

Unlike your king, who *is*. It would have been far better if you had returned bearing the Vandian emperor's missing granddaughter.'

Leyla felt a bristle of indignation but did not rise to it. This had always been the king's way. To undermine her achievements and confidence. He did it with all of his subordinates. Marcus clearly felt it was the way to get the most out of people – like squeezing a fruit for the last few drops of juice.

'I brought you the people who took the brat hostage,' said Leyla. She nodded towards the prisoner moaning in the garrotte chair as the silk tightened around his neck. 'I'm sure they can be induced to cooperate.'

'Oh, our friend here hasn't come to lunch to be tickled into providing us with information,' said King Marcus. 'This is Harland Stanbury, retired colonel of the royal guard.'

'I thought you needed every officer with experience to crush the rebellion?' said Leyla, curiously. 'God knows, there are enough factory owners and aristocrats joining your army who are hard pressed to distinguish a rifle from a riding whip.'

'I need officers I can rely on,' said Marcus. 'Loyalty above all else. Not a quality I can accuse Colonel Stanbury here of. He's been on the run for quite a while, until he was found by a recruiting party. And Stanbury knows he disappointed me. Betrayed me, if I am to be brutally honest. He was one of the royal guardsmen who set the charges that brought the avalanche down on my brother and his family. For which I made him a colonel and gave him a very generous settlement. But it transpired that the colonel's workmanship was rather shoddy. He only did *half* the job he had been paid for.'

'I couldn't do it,' croaked the prisoner, shaking his chair. 'When I found them alive in the snow. For the love of the saints, they were only children.'

'So instead you handed the three princes to the skels to sell as slaves,' said Marcus, 'which was as good as a death sentence. You didn't want their blood on your hands. If there're two things I cannot abide in a man, it is squeamishness and hypocrisy. One sin by itself I can stand, but both? Too much.'

'Two of the princes died,' begged the prisoner, 'only Prince Owen who survived. And I did for your brother and the old queen.'

'That's all right, then,' said Marcus. 'Centuries ago, the crime for treason was to be hung, drawn and quartered. Severed heads were spiked on the bridge for courtiers to see as they arrived at the palace. Seeing as only *one* out of my three nephews is still alive, I'll spare you the drawn and quartered portion of your punishment.'

'I didn't know he'd come back alive,' pleaded Stanbury, his voice cracking. Or was that his throat? 'How could I have known?'

King Marcus waved wearily at Thomas Purdell who began turning the crank again. 'Yes, yes, imagine my surprise, also.'

The guardsman's desperate pleas became a strangled gargling, his frantic words punctuated by a choked hacking. King Marcus offered up a woven basket filled with warm chicken legs towards Leyla. She demurred. 'We might not have the snow they do up north, but it's still a little cold to eat outside.'

'Have you never seen a man garrotted?' said the king. 'They splutter and spit blood everywhere. The dining room has some very expensive carpets and we'd never get the blood stains out.'

'It's not as if you would have to clean it yourself, my darling,' said Leyla.

'I would still have to walk on it.'

Leyla shrugged. She had forgotten how fastidious the king could be. When she had been kept as a mistress in apartments not far from the palace, Marcus had always insisted she dispose of any dresses she had worn during their love-making, going out quickly to purchase new ones – in case a worn dress became contaminated with the vapours and pollution of the capital's mills in-between their trysts. She hadn't minded spending the king's vast fortune, of course, even though indulging his hypochondria quickly grew tedious. Benner Landor might be a common-born bore, but at least he tolerated a little rural dirt on a girl.

'I have done everything you asked of me,' said Leyla. 'Married that old fool up in Hawkland Park. Kept my eyes and ears open. Used Nocks as your dagger in the north; sifted the returned slaves' dull stories of misery in Vandia for useful intelligence; helped your agents search for Lady Cassandra and goaded Jacob Carnehan and his son into coming down to Arcadia. When will it be *my* turn, Marcus? My time to be with you again?'

'You've done very well out of your intriguing for me, *Lady* Landor,' said the king, 'and you may yet do even better.'

'I have kept my side of the arrangement,' said Leyla. 'If I had wanted to be a mere lady, I could have married any number of titled suitors in the south.'

'You have done what was needed, that I agree. And I still have need for your artifice,' said King Marcus. 'More people for you to coax into doing their duty. Benner Landor and his daughter have a further part to play in my plans.'

Leyla bent down to stroke the king's hair. 'And do you have a part to play in mine?'

'This war will change everything,' said Marcus. 'The powers I will claim to win it will allow me to do whatever I need to, to give us the nation we truly deserve. Nobody will dare to speak against the new order. I will only have to speak for it to be considered law.'

'You will make me your wife, as you promised,' wheedled Leyla.

'Of course I will,' said Marcus. 'Although you should expect a little company. The Vandian way seems to have much to recommend it. Every one of our children will rule as grandly as kings and queens in our land. And when our acres are all taken, we shall turn our attentions to our neighbours in the league and add their strength to our own.'

Leyla's gaze frosted. She didn't tolerate competition. Her rivals had suffered a rather statistically-unlikely series of fatal accidents.

Marcus laughed as he saw the look in her eyes. 'I'm told that in Vandia, the role of mistress-keeper of the imperial harem is one of the most powerful positions in the imperium. All those well-born ladies grovelling and bribing and ingratiating their way into the keeper's good graces, so that they may give birth to heirs with imperial titles. Can you think of anyone suitable for such a high station in Weyland?'

Now, that is honey for the toast. Leyla Holten immediately saw the possibilities; particularly the humiliation of every noble-blooded, wealthy heiress in the capital and court who had snubbed her as another common mare in the king's stable of mistresses. Given the king's appetite for variety, it was guaranteed that theirs could never be an exclusive relationship. Better that she gain immense power through directing his lusts, rather than be run ragged trying to stop his ardour lighting on someone who could entirely displace her. Landing the king was one piece of work, keeping him interested was entirely another. With such a position, she could keep herself in favour indefinitely. She would be safe from poverty for as long as she lived. Perhaps the mores of distant Vandia were superior, after all? 'Of course, my love, I already have a husband, with a child for him on the way,' said Leyla.

'War is a wicked business,' Marcus smiled. 'It claims many husbands, especially when the husband in question has been commissioned as an officer by royal warrant. And as for your little bastard, after the rebellion is crushed, there'll be a harvest of youthful missing soldiery left as worm-food under the battlefield's churn; with legions of northern widows only too glad to take on a bawling little responsibility to help them forget their pain. It would hardly be the first whelp you've farmed away, would it?'

Leyla rubbed her swollen body, as if just the act could wipe away her painful weight. The saints knew, she would just be pleased to get rid of *it* from her and onto a wet-nurse. Slowing her down, making her stay in the vicinity of comfortable plumbing. And how could she wheedle men to do her bidding when she resembled a whale dragging her belly down the street? No, the end of this particular 'favour' for the king couldn't come too soon.

'But,' added Marcus, 'a ruler's favour is not lightly given, it must be indulged . . .'

Leyla smiled, her happiness not conjured for artifice's sake this time. So, the king's lust for her even stretched into her present condition. *Reassuring*. Well, Marcus was a connoisseur of novelty, and this wasn't something readily available in any bawdy house. Courtesans in her unhappy condition were usually tossed out on their ear. Luckily, she knew exactly how to please the king. Leyla bent down, hitched up her skirt and offered herself to Marcus, watching the prisoner's dreary death throes in front of her with as much detachment as if a cow was being milked in a field. Life and death. Two sides of the same coin. The trick was in making sure the coin toss always landed in your favour.

'Have you washed this morning?' demanded King Marcus.

'Come closer and find out,' she laughed.

Soon, the final croaking shudders of the dying guardsman weren't the only moans drifting across the palace gardens.

Willow waved at her maid and the woman immediately had the carriage halted in the middle of the street. Willow flung open the door, stumbled outside to be sick across the pebbles. Four weeks into her pregnancy and the terrible nausea seemed to rise every afternoon in heavy waves before returning twice as bad during the evening. Breakfast was the only meal she could face and keep down. At least she could handle that solitary meal with a clear head. Since Willow's condition had made itself known, the viscount's servants had not dared use sedatives to keep her manageable, for fear of poisoning the nobleman's firstborn inside her womb. And Willow's pregnancy had the additional benefit that Wallingbeck's foul attentions had drifted away from her and back onto the capital's courtesans. But the servants at Belinus Hall watched her even more closely now. She had only been able to make one attempt to flee her despicable so-called husband, during a night of patriotic music performances at Arcadia's concert hall, and the staff hadn't even felt they could beat her when they caught her trying to slip out, disguised in a silk shawl she had stolen from another private box.

'You make such a damnable noise when you're sick,' said Leyla Holten, sticking her head out of the open door. 'It's unladylike and really quite disagreeable.'

Willow glared back at the carriage. Her stepmother was as swollen as a whale, only weeks from giving birth. Perhaps Holten felt the need for company in her misery. That would be one explanation for the unwanted marriage slipped like chains around Willow's neck – beyond Holten's need to expel the previous brood from the Landor nest. 'Then you should have left me to throw up in my bedroom.'

'I couldn't do that,' said Holten, her eyes flashing with dark mischief. 'I have a couple of highly congenial surprises planned for you this afternoon.'

'Keep them,' said Willow.

'Where would the fun be in that, your *ladyship*?' Holten kicked the maid's ankles and indicated Willow on her knees in the dust of the street. The servant went to help Willow to her feet while a couple of footmen from the back of the carriage stood sentry around her. They needn't have bothered; not on her account – she could hardly stay away from a bathroom for longer than an hour – and the brutes didn't need to shield her modesty from onlookers. All the crowds were at a crossroads down the street, lining the pavement and cheering a regiment of blue-uniformed soldiers marching off to war, the crunch of boots in unison and the rap of drums at the side. There were only loyalists to King Marcus left inside Arcadia. What happened to any gainsayers didn't bear thinking about.

They rode on, eventually pushing through a crowd of onlookers surrounding a square. There was a fountain in the middle pouring water into a round pool, a crust of ice around its edge, but the rest of the scene was anything but peaceful. A long wooden gallows had been raised, men suspended from ropes hanging dead in the breeze. In the platform's shadows, women had been lined up, guarded by a company of soldiers, waiting their turn for their heads to be shaved to the jeers of the mob beyond.

'What is this place, why have you brought me here?'

'I promised you a couple of surprises today,' said Holten. 'This is the first of them. Those being hanged are looters and rebels, traitors who have given succour to the enemy. The women having their heads shaved are the traitors' abandoned wives . . . every treasonous dog fled north to fight for the enemy.'

'Does this foul sight amuse you? The suffering of poor unfortunates drawn into this awful conflict?'

'I think it's an excellent lesson to see what happens to those that rise up against their lawful assembly and king.'

'I need no lessons in cruelty from you or your royal warmonger.'

'I disagree. But I haven't brought you here today to see Gaiaist conspirators swing in the wind, as much as the sight warms my heart.' Holten swung open the door. 'Out with you.' The footmen entered the cab and practically lifted Willow off her feet, forcing her into the open square in front of the gallows. She averted her eyes from the women being humiliated, a carpet of their hair blowing across the paving stones and across her shoes. Holten dismounted and crossed to the company's officer, pointing back at Willow and saying something sternly. The captain frowned, but reluctantly submitted to whatever sly scheme Holten was about today.

'Here!' said Holten. She indicated a wagon being loaded with the bodies of those hanged. Its back-board bore the little guild sigil of the barber-surgeons. The cadavers were to be used for practice by surgeons in training. No doubt the nation would develop a strong demand for freshly qualified doctors in the months ahead. 'You have been writing incessantly to poor Benner, driving him to distraction with your maddening pleading for news of what happened to the Carnehans . . .'

'No, please!' Willow stared at the mound of bodies, fresh corpses tossed onto the flatbed as she watched. *He can't be dead*. Willow couldn't let their last meeting be when Carter had stumbled into the fact of her forced marriage.

'Not the looters, you foolish girl,' snapped Holten. *'Them.'* She indicated two workers loading the wagon. They wore drab convict's clothes, little more than uncomfortable hemp sacks with sleeves and course leggings. Neither of the two men were Carter or his father, though. Willow drew closer, uncertain what painful humiliation her stepmother could have planned for her here. Then she realized she recognized the men, if barely. Their heads had also been shaved to ugly stubble, presumably to ward off lice. The first man was the young courier from the Guild of Librarians who had arrived with Carter and Jacob Carnehan outside the Winteringham to try to free her. The second man was someone she knew from frequent visits to Hawkland Park. Charles T. Gimlette, the assemblyman who had long represented Northhaven. She rushed towards the cart despite its awful cargo. Willow nearly gagged when she stopped. Flies buzzed over the bodies despite the cold, and the stench of it was sickening.

The guild courier stepped forward, his forehead pale and sweating from the hard labour. 'I'm Tom Purdell, I travelled south with Father Carnehan and Carter.'

'I remember your bravery well from the hotel, guildsman. And Mister Gimlette! What in the name of the saints are you doing in a convict's rags?'

'Miss Landor! A bad bargain, I say,' wheezed the assemblyman. He was a lot thinner now; she remembered an overweight politician during his stays at the great house. 'Here I am hauling dead Weylanders, branded a traitor over a terrible misunderstanding. Condemned solely for my party membership. But all those who sought office in our prefecture embraced the Gaiaists. There hasn't been a Mechanicalist elected in our neck of the woods for three hundred years.' He noticed Holten standing behind Willow and fell wearily to his knees. 'Please, madam, you must tell Benner Landor that I'm still his man. Haven't I served his interests well? Done everything he ever asked of me?'

'Stand up,' barked Holten. 'You're not even an assemblyman anymore, you fat fool. Those traitors back home have cast you aside and installed another turncoat in your place to conspire against the kingdom. What good are you to me now?'

'I can still be of use to your house,' pleaded the broken official.

'You may,' said Holten, imperiously. 'You and your courier friend here, tell this girl what happened to Father Carnehan and that impudent whelp of his.'

'We were in the national assembly, Miss Landor,' began Gimlette, 'when—'

The captain in charge of the detail drew his pistol and whipped the assemblyman across the side of the head with the grip, sending the politician stumbling down to the street. 'This is Lady Wallingbeck you address, you rebel dog. You will use her title.'

Willow helped the courier lift the old politician back to his feet. 'Leave him alone! It's no title I ever asked for. Please, Assemblyman, tell me what happened to Carter and the pastor . . .'

Gimlette moaned, clutching his bleeding head. 'The king ordered in his guardsmen to dissolve the council. There was a huge fracas between the parties. Father Carnehan and his young fellow had just finished giving evidence when the troopers marched in. Your people were swept up by the king's men and arrested. Everyone in my cursed party, too, that didn't take to their heels fast enough. Ah, curse my comfortable belly. I'm no sprinter, not after a good lunch, not young or spry enough anymore to outrace a battalion of brutes armed with rifles and bayonets.'

'It's true,' said Tom. 'I was in the witness box with Jacob and Carter; I heard them testify for Prince Owen's claim. But nothing went as it was meant to. The father was dragged away as a wanted murderer on the run. The assembly was dissolved before it could vote on the king's abdication. We were unarmed – we didn't stand a chance. The usurper's soldiers surrounded us and gave us a beating for our troubles. Then we were dragged away and locked deep below the palace. The king's men tossed me out of the dungeon and transported me to one of the regular prisons when they realized I was merely a guildsman travelling with your friends. Carter and Father Carnehan are still under the palace, enough chains piled on them to anchor a frigate in a cyclone.'

'Please,' pleaded Gimlette, 'beg your father to release me, your ladyship. I am loyal to him still.'

'He won't listen to me anymore,' said Willow. 'I'm sorry, Mister Gimlette. I'm as much a prisoner in the south as you. Captain, what is to happen to these two poor gentlemen?'

'The rebel sympathizers in Arcadia have been routed, your ladyship,' said the officer, indicating the dead dangling lifeless from the gallows. 'After tomorrow, these two dogs and a good few like them will be transported east to the stockade at Greealamie to build a prisoner-of-war camp to hold the rest of their disloyal friends. The cowards will be surrendering by the battalion-load as our boys press north.'

Holten thrust a finger at the two convicts. 'Tell Lady Wallingbeck what you heard from Prefect Colbert inside the assembly.'

'There's no need to repeat the newspapers' foul propaganda,' said Willow. 'It'll sound no truer parroted by a prefect. I *know* the truth, Mister Gimlette, Mister Purdell. I survived as a slave, with Carter, struggling to stay alive while I watched my friends and countrymen worked to death, beaten and executed for attempting to escape. I know all I need to know about Carter and Owen Hawkins, as well as the pastor and his people who arrived to rescue us from the sky mines. Our feet never touched an inch of soil in the Burn, and the Vandians were only ever our captors, not our rescuers.'

'But the prefect's accusations weren't all lies,' said Tom. 'Black Barnaby gave us air passage when nobody else would thanks to the father's influence. I heard the pirate leader himself call Jacob Carnehan "brother". The pastor fights like no priest of my acquaintance

– I think he must have been a mercenary across the water. And if that much was true, what else . . . ?'

'Do you see what I and your father have saved you from?' said Holten in triumph. 'Carter Carnehan is not merely some ruffian commoner, he's the son of a murderer, convicted in absentia after fleeing our lands to slaughter foreign peasants for money. Carter – son of a murderer and nephew to a pirate. That's who we saved you from.'

'Carter still loves you,' said Tom, the soldiers preventing him from reaching out to touch her. 'That's what matters, Willow. Whatever Carter's father has done, he hasn't forgotten or forsaken you. Carter understands your marriage was forced on you against your will.'

'By the saints, I'm pregnant now, Mister Purdell. How in the world will Carter feel about—?'

'Enough,' snapped Holten, snapping her fingers. Her footmen dragged Willow away from the wagon, leaving behind shocked expressions on the politician and courier's faces. 'Now you may rest secure in the knowledge that your thieving commoner lover has found his level: in the king's jail and the king's chains.'

'Why?' demanded Willow. 'Why tell me he's still alive? There's not an iota of mercy to be wrung from your heart.'

'You may yet find out,' smiled Holten. 'Now, on to your second surprise of the day.'

Willow was bundled back in the carriage and as they rattled through the streets, tried to hold back her renewed nausea. She wasn't just suffering morning sickness. The stench of dead bodies seemed to cling to her. And yet . . . *Carter's alive*. She felt joy at the unexpected news; clung to it tight through the waves of biliousness; a tiny pearl of hope. But they were still apart, each weighted with very different chains. Holten and the viscount would never agree to let Willow visit Carter in prison, even if the authorities proved willing. Maybe that was for the best? Carter wouldn't have to see her condition; suffer the torment of seeing what Willow was suffering at the hands of another man; worry that she had embraced her marriage and abandoned him to his fate. But wasn't abandonment exactly what she had done to Carter? Not willingly, but did it matter, when that was the reality of her situation?

They entered a richly appointed shopping district, luxury arcades nestling inside five-storey-high facades of white stone, tall glass windows shaded by colourful awnings. Their four horses clattered down a road of drapers, cloth merchants and tailors, with prices no doubt as exclusively costly as the private carriages idling along the street while wealthy clients perused within. Willow was forced out of the carriage and into a tailor's shop called *Nimrod Lock and Company*. A narrow wooden corridor and then a large room surrounded by shelves filled with fabrics of every type from tweed to silk, measuring tables in the middle, tailors and customers milling at the far end.

'And here we are,' said Holten, indicating two men in uniform. The pair turned around to reveal her father and William Wallingbeck, as proud as peacocks under the weight of braid, epaulettes, sashes and shoulder boards. Blue double-breasted frockcoats with two lines of silver buttons, each with a white sword and holster belt, a bold stripe of yellow-piping on their trousers. 'See how well they stand. Benner has been elevated as Marquess of the Northern Borderlands and also granted a colonelcy in the army by King Marcus; while William has been made a lieutenant-colonel attached to the general staff of the Army of the Bole.'

Willow ignored the brute Wallingbeck, incredulously approaching her father. 'A uniform outfitters? Tell me you're not really going to fight in this insane war?'

'The insanity is wholly that of our neighbours,' said Benner Landor. 'Northhaven has declared for the pretender. I leave the prefecture alone for a few months and you see what evil flourishes in my absence... madness and rebellion. But I will quash the troubles. Hugh Colbert has been made General of the Army of the Bole. We intend to travel home and restore order rapidly. Northhaven's own prefect marching at the head of the lawful forces sent to root out rebels and criminals, with myself and your fine husband by the general's side.'

'Are you not gratified by your father's achievement?' said Holten, her voice swollen with a pride so false she could have buttered bread with it. 'A peerage as grand as any, and made responsible for crushing the rebellion in our home acres? It is recognition of your father's talents that the House of Landor has deserved for decades. Think of it... Marquess of the Northern Borderlands! Your family now has title to a tenth of the north.'

'And you a lady with it,' added Viscount Wallingbeck, slyly, as if the thought wasn't uppermost in the mind of the scheming bitch.

'Far more importantly, a son shortly to be born to wear the title of the second marquess,' said Holten, smiling at Benner Landor. 'This happy age.'

A tailor stepped behind Willow and began to measure her. She pushed him back. 'What is this?'

'For our dress shop next door, your ladyship,' said the tailor. 'Your travelling clothes.'

'What? Travel where?'

'The ladies of the court are to tour with the army,' announced Benner Landor. 'They have elected to show their support. You shall accompany us on the campaign. You will not disgrace your husband and your family again, old or new.'

'I will play no part in your war, this madness!'

'Silly goose, you do not need to fret for our safety,' said Holten. 'We will have grand picnics overlooking the battlefields, well beyond the range of stray bullets and shells, as we watch our fine gentlemen rout the rebels. It will be glorious. I will have given birth before we leave and the war will be over long before your child arrives.'

'To hell with your "surprise" and your war, both.'

'Oh, but the Landors' rise at court *isn't* your surprise, my dear. That is only testament to Benner's dedication to his duty, which can be of no surprise to anyone who knows and loves your father. Do you wish to tell to Lady Wallingbeck the happy news we have received, husband?' There was a little twitch of Holten's mouth as she spoke, making Willow suspect that Holten might not find the news quite as welcome as she was pretending to.

'The Empire of Vandia is dispatching a force to assist us in chasing the pretender and his slavers and his filthy rebel friends all the way back to the Burn,' said Willow's father, grandly. 'And the Vandians have rescued Duncan from the slavers. The king himself gave me the joyous news at the palace when I was elevated to the peerage. Do you understand, girl? Your brother is coming home.'

'No!' said Willow, rocked by the news. 'The Vandians are coming . . . ?'

'Did you not hear what I said about Duncan?'

'You damned fools; they're coming for their revenge! To execute every escaped slave and make an example of us . . .'

'Are you mad, girl? Do you care nothing for your brother?'

Duncan Landor. No wonder that Holten was less than happy about this turn of events. Just as she was about to produce a new heir to the Landor fortune, up popped the previous one to spoil her plan. The saints must have been laughing in paradise. 'Duncan made his damned choice when we were slaves, the stealers take his soul.'

'Forgive Willow, please, Benner. This must be her guilt and shame talking,' begged Holten. 'It can't have been easy, living every day with the knowledge that she abandoned Duncan to rot in the Burn while she escaped with her crooked lover . . .'

'Your heart is too soft, my love. Lord Wallingbeck, if your wife was not with child, I would urge you to have her committed to an asylum,' Benner told the viscount, shaking his head. 'My own daughter . . . It's unimaginable, unpardonable. It's those filthy Carnehans. That murderer's son has utterly corrupted her.'

'Yet, she will still be the mother of my child,' said the viscount, reaching out to rub Willow's stomach even as she recoiled in disgust from him. 'So we must be merciful. I will see the mistress of my house has every assistance needed to support her, and that my heir is given many siblings for playmates as soon as possible.'

'You're the ones that belong in an asylum. I know you for what you are. All of you!'

'Remove her ladyship,' ordered the viscount. 'If my wife can find no joy in the news of her brother's return, she can seek out her pleasures back at the hall.'

Willow jerked back in horror when she saw who appeared from the side of the shop. Nocks, the stocky brute's plain manservant livery swapped for a sergeant's cobalt-coloured uniform. 'Don't I look fine, Lady Wallingbeck? Once a soldier, always a soldier. All them lawyers and mill owners made officers in the new army; they'll have need for a little experienced grit and ballast to steady them.' He pulled Willow out of the shop, frog-marching her back to the carriage. 'You're going to be a perfectly behaved little dove for us,' snarled Nocks. 'No more running away and spouting the pretender's cant. Or your precious Carnehan boy will taste more than the whip from me. I'll visit the palace cells with my knife and slice off a finger for you as a keepsake every time you cross me. And when I run out of fingers maybe I'll find something else to slice off you'll miss more.' He guffawed at his own crude humour.

'Leave Carter *alone.*'

'Then you'll do what's needed,' said Nocks. 'When Duncan arrives, you'll do everything you can to keep your dear brother sweet. King Marcus needs the Vandians on our side. You're going to play your loyal part in that arrangement. So is your old man.'

'The imperium only has one side, you idiot . . . *their own.*'

'Then they'll get along fine with me, because damned if that isn't my philosophy as well. War's as fine a time as God ever created for men like me. We're fed well and we get to fight, and at the end of a battle, if we're the ones left standing, we take anything and *everything* we want. If there's someone else eager to do the killing for us, so much the better. Let the Vandian legions be first in the line. They'll take the bullets and I'll take the widows in their own beds. As long as old Nocks gets to join in the sack of a good few rebel towns and villages, he'll be happy as a pig in the proverbial.'

'You turn my stomach.'

'Need much help in that regard, lately? I see Wicked William didn't waste any time planting his harvest in your orchard, eh. Back to the old dog's whoring for him now that you're marked. I'm not a fussy bugger like his lordship, though. Beggars can't be choosers. That's the good thing about them that's in the family way; you can't be made double-pregnant, can you?'

She lunged for the knife on the side of his belt, but he grabbed her wrist and turned it so hard she had to bite back a scream. 'Nocks hasn't forgotten about you, my little weeping Willow. The time will come when you look to me to keep you safe. And I will . . . for a price. Yes, war's a fine thing.'

'Give me your knife and I'll pay you in steel.'

Nocks snorted in amusement as the servants took Willow from his hand and hurried her up the steps into the carriage. 'I see your belly hasn't slowed you down yet, girl. It will. You'll be waddling like Lady Landor back there soon enough. Let's see how much spit and fire you have then. Your brother anything like you?'

'Duncan's only ever been his father's son – a selfish fool who never sees when poisonous women are using him.'

Nocks grunted, running a finger thoughtfully down his scarred face. 'So? You'll find a way to get him to help us. Or I'll make your lover a cripple and you a present of a finger bone necklace. The Carnehan boy won't miss 'em much where he is, anyway.'

Cassandra staggered back, a cry freezing in her throat as the disfigured face swayed outside her window. Suddenly, fingers appeared – all too human – and pulled away the leering face. *Straps*? A wooden wind mask, and she realized she was looking at the grinning and triumphant features – albeit upside down – of the nomad Alexamir. She dropped the chopsticks she had been wielding in surprise.

'This is a windy nest you have found for yourself, my little golden fox,' said Alexamir.

'I only have to cry and the Rodalians will peel you off your rocky perch quick enough,' threatened Cassandra. As the shock of seeing the barbarian hanging outside diminished, she suppressed a small glimmer of satisfaction at realizing how many risks Alexamir must have braved to follow her. He must have been tracking her since she was taken from the raiding party. Or had he known the Rodalians would take her to the nearest skyguard station?

'Cry out if you will,' said Alexamir. The young man lowered and righted himself so he was no longer conversing with a rush of blood towards the head. 'But if the mountain people chase me away, you will still be in your nest with those pretty little chains around your ankle. That is not how the Rodalians treat their guests. You must be quite a thief for them to take so much trouble over you.'

'Hostage,' retorted Cassandra. 'Of noble birth.' Of course, he wasn't so dull-witted as to have forgotten. He was teasing her.

'And does your fine noble blood allow you to pick the lock holding you in there?' said Alexamir. 'Better an honest thief.'

'And have you come to steal dried fish from the kitchens of Talatala, honest thief?'

'Indeed not. I have climbed these cursed crags with a generous offer, golden fox. To escape with me to the north.'

'As the first of your newly minted harem? I think I prefer the over-salted taste of Rodalian hospitality to *that* cruel fate.'

'My proposal has been improved. Come with me and I shall show you the majesty of the steppes without end. But you must accompany me willingly. If you do not find the free life of a Nijumet to your taste, you can contact the horse traders of the Thousand Duchies and send word to your people using one of their far-talking devices. They may dispatch galleons to the dunes of the eastern coast for you, or divert one of the aerial traders to the plains to pick you up. I will allow my golden fox to slip back to her distant warren if you choose to; though you steal the best part of my soul should you slip away from me again.'

'Willingly?' snapped Cassandra. 'You need me willing to descend this mountain. After that, I wager I'll be trading my leg irons for a barbarian's rope bindings, with my royal personage as your saddle accessory.'

'I swear I will allow you to leave if that is your choice,' said Alexamir. 'By the Black-God and the Six Huntresses, may they devour my horses, scatter my clan and cast me into the darkness of the night if there is a lie to be found hiding in my heart.' He reached behind him, slipped a knife out and offered her the dagger through the narrow gap. 'This is the only weapon I could climb with. Descend alongside me and keep its sharp edge as my true faith.'

Cassandra took the hilt of the dagger and slid it through the gap. Obviously Rodalian and stolen. But worth a fortune out in the steppes. Alexamir might not realize it, but dagger or no, with Cassandra's training, she could snap the nomad's neck and break his spine a dozen different ways in unarmed combat. Her mother had paid for only the greatest tutors, with a sprawling empire of millions of fighters and exotic battle styles to select them from. The nomad might possess well-developed muscles and overconfidence, but neither would prove much of a shield against a dangerously honed Vandian royal.

'And what of your friends . . . that foul witch rider?'

'Nurai thinks me a fool for coming here,' said Alexamir. 'Even as she revealed where in the city I should search for you. But poor Nurai needs a victory to carry back to the clan from our foray, lest her dream sight be doubted. And not once has a thief broken into

Talatala before, let alone to steal such a fine prize. But then, there has never been a legend among our ranks as audacious or courageous as the magnificent Alexamir.'

Cassandra pointed the dagger's threatening tip towards the nomad's nose. 'I am no treasure to be stolen.'

'Doubtless, the mountain folk have you chained up here for the thick milk of your banter,' said Alexamir, tapping a finger against the inclined stone slit between them. 'You have my offer and my blade. Now, I would appreciate your answer. The wicked Rodalian spirits play most cruelly with my body out here. This climb has been a feat of fable rivalling that of the White Slywolf's ultimate trickery, and I would rather have the tale end with a fine feast in a tent-hall, than a body badly broken over a granite ledge.'

Cassandra stared at the dagger's gleaming steel as though her answer lay engraved along its length. *Should I trust him?* What was the word of a lowly barbarian worth at the best of times? A self-admitted thief and nomad reiver. But then, Cassandra understood what fate awaited her with the ploddingly honest and dull Sheplar Lesh. Another cell, and next time in a mountain citadel where her every choice would be removed from her. Remaining a hostage of the slave revolt, where the best outcome was being ransomed back to her house in disgrace; the worst, exploited as leverage to force imperial diplomacy towards the barbarians' favour. What was it that Paetro used to tell her? *The risk of wrong decision is always a thousand times preferable to indecision's dangers.* 'I accept your bargain, thief. But play me false, attempt to make me a prisoner again, and I will steal your horse and make you a present of your own manhood with this steel before I ride off. That *I* swear. By *my* ancestors and the shades of the emperors who stand behind me.'

Alexamir's smile gleamed back at her as white as bone. 'A vow for a vow. Wait for me, golden fox. Think on our splendid reunion, fated in the stars. I may be gone a little while. There is nothing as confusing as dead stone corridors to the fine free men, but I shall follow your agreeable scent and see what mischief I may make on my way.'

Fated in the stars? Fated by jesters, more like. Cassandra grimaced as Alexamir tugged the leering painted wind mask back over his face and disappeared from view. It would be just her luck if the daring buffoon was caught sneaking through Talatala, just because the barbarian was hard pressed to recognize the purpose of a stout wooden door or understand what stone stairs were for. But how many could have made that climb? *And how many would have bothered*? Alexamir was either deranged or possessed of a death-wish; she stamped on the warm feelings of flattery lurking at the edges of her chilly prison. *You should not be complimented by the novelty of his boldness. Remember, you are the daughter of an imperial house, not a common milkmaid to be charmed by the likes of him*. Certainly, she had known few genuine suitors in Vandia. Doubtless, had Circae forced custody of Cassandra from her mother, matters might have been far different. Circae stood well placed to arrange pacts between the great houses of the empire, with few wishing to burden themselves with the ire of Cassandra's malicious grandmother. It was thanks to Circae's scheming that Lady Cassandra had been left alone, an undervalued pariah at the imperial court with dreams of how matters might change should Princess Helrena became empress . . . and Cassandra the sole heir to the diamond throne. She'd need a legion of bodyguards just to fight off the dutiful sons of the imperium who would arrive calling on bended knee with hollow promises and dishonest assurances. How they would fight for her hand, for there could be only one prince-consort. There would be no harem for an empress. For what would be the point of it? Entertainment, but no longer a mill to churn out heirs to the throne. If Helrena seized the throne, Circae would lose all position and power as keeper of the emperor's broodmares, and maybe Cassandra's father could rest pleased among the ancestors, his death by Circae's scheming avenged at last. *That would be a fine thing*.

But none of it would come to pass if Cassandra remained far-called, rubbing goat-milk cream on her saddle sores in foreign parts with some barbarian chancer, however proud the rogue strode and however tall his largely self-authored exploits. She was beginning to wonder if Alexamir had indeed got caught or hopelessly lost, when a scraping came from outside the door as the bolt drew back. The nomad entered smoothly and closed the door behind him. He prowled to Cassandra, waiting on the side of her bed, and knelt down, inspecting her ankle chain. Alexamir pulled out a pair of thin iron rods from a leather pouch at his side and started to probe inside the keyhole. 'A treasure is worth double when it is stolen. Did you know that?'

Cassandra prodded him in the shoulder with the dagger's tip, but held back from drawing blood. 'Beware, barbarian, this treasure is protected by a sharp-staked pit.'

'All treasures worth the taking should be. Or where would the joy be in their theft?'

A clink sounded as the shackles fell to the floor and Cassandra rubbed the itching skin when she felt the cold air against her bare skin for the first time since she had arrived in Talatala.

'We should be climbing down the mountain before my mischief makes itself known,' said Alexamir.

'Mischief?'

'I left a fused pouch of gunpowder in a carpet-weaver's shop,' said Alexamir, looking exceptionally pleased with himself. 'Sheep shearings and dyes burn most splendidly, and guards passing water buckets are too hard-pressed to notice a golden fox descending the slopes of Talatala.'

Cassandra groaned. 'Better we departed quietly at night and left the town sleeping. One of my captors is Kerge, a twisted forest dweller . . . a gask. Gasks possess a homing sense they can use to follow people they've spent time with. I suspect that is how the skyguard tracked me down before.'

'I have heard songs of the gasks and their poison spines and strange spells, making luck as a smith forges horseshoes; but they hold to the southwoods – I have yet to meet one.'

'Kerge's natural talents have grown somewhat sickly and shaky, but I would not wish to put them to the test again. We need a faster way to cross Rodal than pony and foot,' said Cassandra, 'or we may wake in a ravine one fine morning to find a flock of Rodal's canvas-covered crows circling us, with skyguard pistols jabbed against our chests.'

'Sadly, all my rustled ponies have been reunited with their owners. I have two feet, and luckily for you they belong to Alexamir. When I run, Kalu the Apportioner himself rises in the sky and gazes down towards the plains to see whose cheeky sandals wake him with such thunder. I can sprint for a week and still not think it too much.'

'Running towards capture or death?' said Cassandra, uncertainly.

'Best I handle the planning, blue boy, along with the navigation.' The boasting she would leave to the nomad. Alexamir seemed more than capable of handling outrageous claims for them both. She opened the cupboard and removed two robes, tossing one at the nomad before slipping her robe over her body and raising its hood to cover her head. 'Keep your face lowered and pretend you have taken a vow of silence.'

'I will itch as though tied to an ant-hill,' complained Alexamir, examining the wind priest's garb.

'You will itch more from a pistol shell. Put it on!' Cassandra waited for him to do so, then opened the door and checked outside. A long empty stone corridor lit by a couple of flickering oil lamps, no sign of the ghosts Sheplar Lesh had spoken of, although the hackles rising along the back of her neck told another tale. *Curse the Rodalian and his stories.*

Alexamir shivered as he followed her out. She trusted her disguise appeared more priestly than the nomad's robes, his broad shoulders rolling with the strangeness of the clothes. 'All towns are tombs to a free man, but none more so than a Rodalian's settlement. A burial mound's rock between us and the clear air. They have no riders' blood; they are jackrabbits who stuff their high stone burrows with treasure to tempt honest thieves to die against their crags.'

'The crags won't be a problem. Now, battle silence.'

There was nobody in the corridor, although Cassandra heard snoring from one of the cells as they slipped into the mountain passages. There were few people about at this late hour and the lanterns in the cavernous streets had been allowed to burn low, presenting long shadows to add to the escaping pair's disguise, a slow, stately shuffle with bent heads, retracing her steps through Talatala. The town looked different with moonlight spilling through the cavern's light ports, the mirrors used to defuse the natural illumination dark now, with only a reflected scattering of the stars visible hanging outside. Cassandra had mastered her urban orienteering training long before she had needed the skills... counting the steps between each turn and marking the time passed during their passage, memorizing the shape of the streets' rooftops as well as the foreign shop signs cloaked by night-time. Now, she rewound that memory like a yarn of string and led them silently back towards the hangars carved into the mountain.

They passed few Rodalians, and those they did ignored the sight of two priests returning home. Cassandra and her companion halted in the shadow of a warehouse-like building close to the skyguard's mountainous launch tunnels.

'How long for your fuse to run?'

'I trimmed it long for two leagues,' said Alexamir.

Cassandra cursed his time-keeping system, almost as barbaric as the nomad's manners. If a horse could gallop a league in ten minutes that made his fuse burn twenty, and with at least fifteen of those already lapsed, then there should be a healthy blaze erupting in town in less than five minutes. 'This way. Follow me.'

'You mean to slip through here? There are two sentry towers on the slopes outside these tunnels, with skyguards watching for friends who wish to land – or their foemen among the pirates of the air. Better to descend from the town. We can squeeze through their sun slits after climbing the cave.'

'We are unlikely to be challenged inside the skyguard's airfield,' whispered Cassandra. 'When I landed I saw their priests blessing planes and chanting for friendly winds.'

'Priests do not scale peaks here,' said Alexamir, stubbornly. 'There is a long winding road outside Talatala that leads down to the villages of the valley. We could hazard that, but it has many guard posts on the way with fighters who will be curious why two timid temple chanters dare to venture out at night. I could easily defeat them, but not before they fire a warning beacon and bring the entire town down the slopes for me to slay.'

And I'm sure you could handle them and not think it too much. 'Just follow me. Your golden fox knows all there is to understand about burrows.'

Alexamir muttered under his breath, but did as he was bid. She would have to work on his slowness to obey orders. Cassandra would happily defer to the nomad when it came to which local mosses it was safe to pick from the rocks for food, or even which horses were likely to possess the most endurance. But the wild thief needed to realize that when it came to matters of strategy, the planning was best left to superior Vandian intelligence. *Mine, in fact.*

There was no sign of sentries in the opening chamber of the

skyguard. Most would be back with their families or abed by now. She could hear a distant clink of tools and muffled voices. Doubtless, a maintenance hangar with some final duties being completed by ground staff. Alexamir was right. Any watchful eyes would be in the fortified positions on the slopes outside, scanning the skies and crags and mountain road for enemies, for what danger could rise from deep within their town's stone heart? She would give them cause to regret their complacency. Inside the first tunnel, Cassandra located and quietly opened a round wooden door in the wall and discovered what she had thought would lie inside – a narrow fire fighters' passage, just as you would find on a Vandian carrier. When damaged aircraft crashed hard in the landing tunnels, the ground staff needed a way to bypass the flaming wreckage and tackle the full extent of the blaze. She lifted a torch from the wall and indicated to Alexamir that this was their way to pass unseen through the stronghold. He was clearly uneasy about entering a place even closer to a tomb, but she knew he wouldn't make a lie of his boasts. The nomad ducked through the doorway with a vexed shake of his head. Ventilation ducts running to Talatala's slopes made the fire tunnel as chilly as a food cellar, and she held up her flickering torch and counted down the paces to a chamber she remembered passing. When she reached zero, she found the nearest door and pushed it open a sliver to check for Rodalians. None that she could see, so she opened the door and stepped out into a large circular chamber. She could feel bitingly cold air from outside drawn down the five tunnels that branched out in front of the space. Above Cassandra, a framework of well-greased wooden rails rested with a turntable mounted in the ceiling's centre. And behind her a series of side-chambers, a number of the skyguard's small triangular-shaped aircraft hanging suspended from rope cradles inside each space.

Cassandra found a likely-looking two-seat kite in one of the hollows, and indicated to Alexamir that they should drag it along the rails towards a launch tunnel. 'This will do just fine.'

Alexamir's cyan face had suddenly turned as pale as Cassandra's. 'You cannot mean to fly the Rodalians' wooden pigeon?'

'That's exactly what I intend to do,' said Cassandra, starting to heave against the plane. It rocked in its rope cradle, but began to slip along the wooden rail. 'You don't need to worry. I mastered simple mono-winged craft before learning to pilot a helo.' She felt a stab of sadness at the memory. It had been Cassandra's personal pilot, Hesia, who had trained her to fly. And she had betrayed them to the house's enemies at court and then a second time during the slave revolt.

'Flying is only half their magic,' spluttered Alexamir. 'We may wear their priests' robes, but we cannot command the winds as the mountain dwellers do. We will be smashed to splinters against the rocks.'

'There's demon turbulence outside, I grant you. But I'll climb high for altitude and leave the worst of the weather below. We'll be safe enough. I'm planning to push north on a trade wind, not strafe their valleys and villages.'

'Even the great merchants of the air do not risk Rodal's skies,' warned Alexamir. 'They pass over the marshes of Hellin.'

Cassandra bit back a sharp reply. *All of a sudden the horseman fancies himself an expert airman*? The insufferable arrogance of the nomad. She was the one trained to fly this kite, not him. Cassandra could see she would have to goad him into the spotter's cockpit. 'I think that the great Alexamir is scared of a steed made of canvas and wood. Perhaps he was pecked by an eagle during one of his raids into Rodal and does not fancy taking to the sky in case he meets the bird again?'

'I fear nothing and no one, but I show respect to power by saying what is famously known,' grunted Alexamir, 'that the spirits of the mountain are unfriendly and ill-disposed to foreigners. Rodalians may tame the winds, but only because they respect their spirits' power.' Despite Alexamir's protestations, he helped her push the aircraft towards the turntable and lower it into the middle of the circular platform, before throwing his back against a wooden wheel meant for a harnessed pony. He groaned with exertion before slowly cranking the turntable and plane's weight towards a launch tunnel. The plane she intended to steal would do. Two open cockpits in a line in the centre of the triangular flying wing with a rear-mounted propeller behind them, while protruding from its domed nose, a gun barrel riddled with ventilation holes to cool the heated metal parts. The fuselage was shaped in an oddly organic way, with curves and protrusions where she wouldn't have expected them, more like a hand-carved musical instrument than the product of a factory line. Cassandra went to the rear, removed a fuel stick, opened the engine's reservoir hub and checked its fuel level. *Fully fuelled*, she noted with satisfaction.

Cassandra left the kite and headed towards a chart she had noticed pinned to the hangar wall. It showed the territory's trade winds marked in standard library guild script. Alexamir's words proved correct. The main trade winds passed over a country called Hellin lying to the east of Rodal. This region of Rodal rose as a maelstrom of swirling air currents, tight against each other like a thousand furiously twisting serpents. A single high altitude current passed over Talatala heading north, another forking west towards the Lancean Ocean, none marked flowing south. Even if she had been minded to break her oath to Alexamir and try to make for Weyland, a single tank of fuel wouldn't be nearly enough against the headwinds. *And I doubt the locals will refuel me when I land, however I flutter my eyelids at them.* She checked the wind speed of the north-bound current and her eyes widened. She examined the chart again, but she had read true the first time. *Nearly six hundred miles an hour*! That was approaching the speed of a Vandian warship. She glanced nervously at the flimsy-looking triangular aircraft. *How is that going to stand up to such velocities*? The high altitude wind was marked as The Bdur'rkhangmar and nothing about the name augured well to her mind. Well, they wouldn't need more than a tank of fuel to put Rodal behind them, but judging from the chart, a vast area of still air squatted over the steppes north of Rodal's tall mountain ranges. Rodal's ravines and canyons had sucked up all of the hot dry air out of the Arak-natikhan plains, leaving its northern neighbour effectively becalmed. Any merchant carrier crossing far above Arak-natikh's flat open expanses would need to ensure it was fully fuelled before attempting the journey, for the nomads surely grew no fuel crops to sell to traders. As for Cassandra, she'd get as far as the steppes in her stolen kite, but not much further before needing to switch to horseback. She watched Alexamir despondently walking the length of the aeroplane, tapping its canvas fuselage as though checking for tears. *You'll earn your passage soon enough*. She discovered an aviator's cap and goggles and was searching the hangar for a spare flight jacket to protect against Rodal's cold when distant bells started to clang a strident warning from the direction of Talatala. *Damn, we're out of time.* Alexamir's parting act of arson had been detected. She sprinted back to the turntable as the clatter of approaching boots grew louder, more than one set of feet. Locals. Probably looking to secure the planes and fuel in the event the fire spread out of control. Cassandra climbed up toward the plane's forward cockpit, taking seconds to inspect the strange, foreign controls, a few simple dials and a wooden flight stick, but before she could mount the cockpit she realized that it was too late. Talatala's ground staff were upon them.

Jacob had never felt more tired. He had endured weeks with hardly any sleep, even though he was lying horizontally, manacled to a hard wooden table. Every time he tried to close his eyes, freezing cold water was hurled over his face, and when even that wasn't enough to stop the fitless bursts of sleep which overcame him, he was wired up to a cart-like machine with a sulphurous-smelling battery lodged on its platform, burning his skin every time he nodded off. Jacob lost all track of time. Days, weeks, maybe months of such treatment, until he started seeing visions. His dead wife Mary standing in the corner, crying, and she wouldn't stop however much he begged her. Weeping for . . . Carter's two beautiful brothers sprawled across the cell's straw, every bit as pale and trembling as when the fever had claimed them in their final hours. Constable Wiggins came to him too, the old lawman laconic and scathing of how easily Jacob had let him die at Nix's hands. *All of my ghosts*. No, not all of them. Not even a fraction of the true tally. All the soldiers he had put in the dirt in the Burn. There were countless phantoms, far too many to fit in a punishment cell under the palace. King Marcus was right. It didn't matter what name he took. *Jake Silver, Jacob Carnehan*. Both were butchers. The only thing he regretted was that there weren't more corpses to add to his reckoning when he finally went before the saints. *King Marcus, Tom Purdell, Benner Landor, Sergeant Nix*, he whispered the names to stop himself going insane. Clinging to his hatred like a cork raft in a raging sea.

By the time the man in the white surgeon's apron appeared, Jacob was so tired and ragged he needed every iota of his will just to focus on what the visitor was saying.

'Yes, yes, I'm real enough,' said the surgeon. 'What things you must have seen over the last few weeks. The mind is so predictable when stressed. My name is Keall Merrisor; I am a doctor of the College of the Snake and Purple, an imperial surgeon. Do you understand what an honour this is? We normally only minister to the emperor, his family, and any allies whose lives the emperor wishes to preserve.'

'Vandia's found a real snake in our palace,' growled Jacob. 'I wouldn't count on King Marcus's loyalty, though. It's for sale to the highest bidder.'

'Now then, my friend. I'm not terribly fond of my posting here either. A year in your dreary, foul-stinking barbarian backwater. This city has only recently introduced electricity. Do you know how hard it is to read by oil-lamp at my age? I pray every day to my ancestors for my tedious service here to be done.'

'Keep talking, torturer,' said Jacob. 'Please. You're sending me to sleep.'

Keall placed a black bag on the platform where Jacob lay bound. 'I am no imperial torturer, my friend. They're a separate college. I demand the truth. Their disciples demand an example, a slow excruciating spectacle. The two matters are mutually exclusive. But your presence here *has* done me something of a favour. This element of my work has been sadly neglected of late. Your chieftain has only drawn on my healing skills – primarily for the pox he catches from his predilection for sexual congress without prophylactics. Almost as dull as the host of illusory diseases he imagines himself struck by . . . every sniffle a fever and every rash the onset of a plague.'

'I should be so lucky. Let him die. You'll get home faster.'

'And wouldn't my enemies in Vandia love that,' said the surgeon. 'The same resentful bastards in the college that encouraged my posting here. But I will show them how ingenuity may prosper, even in adversity.'

'I know what you've been doing,' said Jacob. 'Tenderizing me like a piece of steak. And now you're here to fry me. I've had people interrogated, Doctor. Maybe it's only fitting that I should get a taste of my own medicine.' The Vandian just chuckled and made no comment; and when Jacob's vision started to fade, his own screams woke him. The machine he was wired to had detected his slumber and burned into his flesh like a vat of acid.

'No dropping off, please. Duty, duty,' said Keall, removing a glass hypodermic from his case. He found a small vial and carefully began to charge the needle. 'Duty is what we must remember. Now, I'd like to know where exactly in the Rodalian Mountains the Lady Cassandra Skar is being held hostage. An expeditionary force will shortly be arriving from Vandia and after I play my part in rescuing the emperor's granddaughter, I hope to be recognized as a champion of the imperium. The great houses will vie with each other to have me select a high position among their ranks.'

'You don't need to fill me with that poison,' said Jacob. 'Just let me rest. Your royal brat's being taken to Rodal's capital, Hadra-Hareer.'

'So easy?' Keall held the needle up to the light as he tapped it. 'Shall I trust you? I think not. You're one of the leaders of the slave revolt. A barbarian who helped crush a legion in the shadow of the great stratovolcano. And you simply give me her ladyship's location like that? Why?'

'Lean closer, I'll tell you.'

Keall frowned, checking Jacob's manacles were fully secure before he bent down. 'Why, then, my friend?'

'Because one legion's not nearly enough.' Jacob found the purchase to whip his skull forward, striking Keall's nose. The imperial surgeon stumbled back indignantly, raising a hand to staunch the blood fountaining across his chin.

'Healing that should make a change from curing Marcus's mangy trouser sword, Doctor.'

'Filthy savage!' Keall leaned over and struck the cart's control panel, sending Jacob's back arching up in agony as current lashed his body. The surgeon's blood-stained fingers settled around Jacob's arm and with the other hand, he drove the needle into the pastor's flesh. 'I'll have the truth from you now.'

Keall paced up and down the cell for a couple of minutes, angrily staunching his own bleeding, waiting for his drugs to work their way through the pastor's body. Jacob found himself drifting, losing all sense of weight and place. He had been remade as a barrage balloon floating over the battlements of Northhaven.

'Where is Lady Cassandra Skar?'

'The capital of Rodal,' moaned Jacob. It was as though he was watching someone else speak. Not his lips moving at all. 'In the custody of the skyguard and Sheplar Lesh.'

'That was the truth after all, then?' said Keall shocked. 'Why?'

'Because one legion isn't enough.'

Keall shrugged, sadly. 'You are nothing but a dirty savage . . . an ignorant fool. They'll drag you back to Vandis for abducting the emperor's granddaughter and record your punishment. In countless centuries' time, imperial torturers will still be watching your pain during their apprenticeships as a demonstration of how one man can be made to suffer so much and for so long. But first our legions will arrive in your barbarian land and you will be witness to a kind of hell that you have never seen before.'

The surgeon faded from sight, replaced by darkness, then burning agony as Jacob rode a series of shocks back to consciousness.

'What was that you were mumbling?' demanded Keall.

'You're wrong,' said Jacob. 'I have seen it before. The hell was mine.'

'Too high a dose,' said Keall, annoyed. 'I must have given you too much. You're babbling. Focus, now. I have more questions for you. There was an outlaw who fought alongside you when you led the slave revolt. An outlaw carrying many names . . . Sariel Teller. Sariel Player. Sariel Skel-Bane. Where is the devil now?'

'Here,' groaned Jacob.

'Yes, he's hiding here, but where in Weyland? What city, what region?'

'Here.'

'Very well. I shall wait until the dose weakens,' sighed Keall.

'I won't,' a weighted staff came crashing down onto the surgeon's skull. Keall crumpled to the floor, striking Jacob's restraining table on the way down.

Sariel leant against his staff, satisfied, wearing his brown leather coat etched with hundreds of intricate pictures as though they were tattoos in leather. The sorcerous vagabond had changed little since he'd vanished from Northhaven. His ancient face even more sunburnt by travel and lined with age, the same raggedy bleached white beard. Sariel wiped a tear of sweat from Jacob's forehead and licked his finger, before his bright, devilish eyes flashed. 'Aha. Severe neural hyperpolarization through sodium thiopental, a highly potent truth serum. The quack has injected you with far too much serum, though. Enough to make a bull-shark sing the truth, and sharks are renowned as the greatest liars in the ocean. It's a wonder the fool's allowed to practise.' The old sorcerer reached out to seize Jacob's hand and the pastor's skin prickled as Sariel's golden skin glowed like a swarm of fireflies. The warmth swelled, comfortable at first, then rising higher and higher through Jacob's flesh, a raging heat that left him moaning and trembling. Jacob plummeted landward from the giddy clouds where he had just been drifting, but his mind was clear again.

'A blood heat to purge the poison from your system.' Sariel lifted the fallen syringe from the cell's floor and his hand flared with light again, the liquid inside the glass bubbling as it changed colour. 'There . . . a small transfiguration. Far more useful, now. A dose of armodafinil, mother maiden's little helper.' The sorcerer jabbed the needle in Jacob's arm, drawing blood as the potion entered his flesh. 'You'll stay awake for another day and a night, now. But when you next sleep, it will be for the best part of a week.'

'I'll sleep when I'm dead, you old dog,' groaned Jacob. 'Where the hell have you been?'

'Chasing my memories,' said Sariel. The old man found the key for the manacles on the surgeon and released Jacob. The pastor pulled himself to his feet, suddenly dizzy, his flesh creaking and weak after the saints knew how long being held here. All desire for sleep had fled, though.

'The same memories your son carried to me in the sky mines,' added Sariel. 'I have been learning which of them are true and which of them are false and which of them merely echoes of the great might-have-been.'

'You *might-have-been* with us a little earlier,' said Jacob. 'That would have been just dandy. There's a war breaking out in Weyland now.'

'You're quite welcome, your excellency,' said Sariel, his voice dripping with sarcasm. 'I only live to release you from capture by your enemies. This land is but a small corner of a much wider war. One that has been going on for far longer than Weyland's current troubles.'

'The rest of Pellas isn't my home. Shit on them.'

'That's fine then,' said Sariel, picking up his traveller's staff. 'All those countless baronies and kingdoms and states out there, everyone with its share of envious fools who believe they're stronger, cleverer, more popular, wiser, better looking and more entitled for the job of ruler than the incumbent. We'll forget about them, shall we?'

'No,' said Jacob. 'I won't even think about them to start with.'

'What a fine representative of your people you are,' said Sariel. 'I should send a portrait of you to every librarian's hold in the world and ask them to record it under the entry, *Man; common pattern.*'

'Ask the guild to record it under "regicides",' said Jacob. 'Because I've a king to kill.'

'First you must choose which monarch to slay.'

Jacob bent down and checked the imperial surgeon. 'This leech's master will do.' Keall still possessed a pulse. 'Excellent. Their pox doctor is going to live.'

'Still a remnant of a priest's compassion then,' said Sariel. 'Even for a Vandian.'

Jacob shrugged. *He'd better live. I'd hate the empire to get lost when it comes hunting for me.*

Sariel took his staff and scratched a symbol on the wall; two circles joined together, a *lemniscate*. 'There, every artist should sign his work.'

'You want them to know you broke me out?'

'Oh yes,' Sariel smiled, although there was only coldness in the old man's eyes. 'The Vandian secret police, the hoodsmen, they would grow idle if I did not poke them every now and then. It's a game we have been playing for a long time. We are all used to our traditions, and I wouldn't wish to disappoint them.'

Jacob couldn't help but wonder how long. *Longer than I could accurately guess, I suspect.* They exited the cell. Jacob found himself in a wide corridor with metal doors, ancient and rusting. No sign of the royal guardsmen acting as warders, but he could hear people talking somewhere in the distance, echoes drifting to his ears. 'How did you know to come for me here?'

'My friends the sparrows told me to visit your son, the Lord Carnehan, much suffering over the loss of his beloved. The son informed me of the father's predicament and so here I am.'

'Carter, thank the saints! Where is he?'

'Thank Prince Owen Hawkins' forces, instead, for he is with

them.' Sariel explored a side corridor and passed into a largely empty storeroom. He placed his hand against a wall, as though feeling for something. Then he found it. There was a sharp crack and a line of bricks swung inward on a sliding wall. 'These hidden passages were put in by King Theron. He had similar appetites to King Marcus, but was married to a queen who was far less forgiving of his philandering ways. Queen Henrietta's suspicious vigilance necessitated that he sneak out unseen by his own servants, who were, wisely, far more afraid of *her* than of *him*.'

'My son is safe?' asked Jacob, already impatient with the old man's tall tales. The passage beyond was narrow, little more than a gap between the walls, lit by tiny arrows of light reflected by mirror-lined channels that emerged somewhere on the palace roof.

'And where would you consider safe, now, your grace? Your son lives. Does that sit well enough with you? The northern members of the People's Assembly have declared for the pretender and retreated to the city of Midsburg. That is where Lord Carnehan waits. The southern assemblymen and the majority of the prefecture support the usurper and advance towards your people's positions. It isn't just *your* revenge that is worked out here. There is no conflict bloodier than a civil war. Brother against brother. Friend against friend. Gaiaist against Mechanicalist. Reformer against traditionalist. Party against party. Guild against guild. Families torn apart. Old feuds settled and every festering spleeny hag-born jealousy given its vent through violence.'

Jacob watched Sariel close the hidden door, sealing them into near darkness. He waited for his eyesight to adjust to the gloom before moving off, the elderly sorcerer in the lead. Jacob had a feeling that the old man could see just fine in the darkness. But then, he'd watched the strangely twisted traveller reattach his own arm after it had been torn off by a fighting cat inside an arena with as little trouble as fixing a child's broken toy. 'Who is winning?'

'Winning?' laughed Sariel as he eased his way through the narrow passage. 'Each field fertilized by the flesh of the fallen, that's your victor. But you mean which side will prevail? Who is to know that? Even the finest soothsayers among the gasks would be challenged. Your northerners are wily landsmen familiar with the ground over which they fight, while the southerners field soft city boys who have only ever known mill-work. Numerically, more regiments declared for the north, with many of the eastern prefectures also siding with your boy king. But that long-tongued oath-breaker King Marcus holds the south with its arsenals and manufactories and the easy means to restock them. Apart from a few border squadrons, the skyguard is largely loyal to the doghearted incumbent who founded it. Weyland's navy is as split as the rest of the country and has so far remained in port. Who is to win? Toss a coin.'

'This was always going to happen, even without Prince Owen's return.'

'A lie you must tell yourself daily,' said Sariel. 'Standing so tall in front of the blaze, with the fuel oil and matches still clutched in your hand.'

'Marcus started this fire, on the day he decided to assassinate half his own family and take imperial silver for selling his people.'

'Well then, my grace, let's set our compass for Midsburg. We may watch the flames lick around your land together.' He laughed, cruelly. 'Maybe someone will even *win*.'

'I'll tell you how we win,' said Jacob. 'We withdraw from Midsburg and mount a guerrilla campaign. We draw the southern armies into the high north, into the mountains; extend the usurper's supply lines. Then we crack them like eggs on the rocks of Rodal.'

'If only you were in charge of the rebellion, your excellency,' said Sariel. 'Sadly that task is entrusted to a callow youth in the form of Prince Owen. And he trusts his advisers in parliament's army, officers who have demonstrated their loyalty to both him and the assembly. Their thinking shows a rather conservative dint. In this civil war, it is King Marcus's loyalists who show a glimmer of original thought when it comes to strategies and skyguards. You would be better off commanding the southern forces rather than Prince Owen's.'

'The boy would still be a slave in Vandia if it wasn't for me.'

'Owen has a prince's weakness for following his own mind. And what part will the imperium play in this grand plan of yours?'

'They're here to revenge the insult of the slave revolt. They'll take their blood price, grow bored, and leave. Even with all of Vandia's might, we're too far-called to be made a province of their empire. It's Bad Marcus who we have to live with. Who we have to defeat,'

'I have lived too long a life,' sighed Sariel. 'I have seen so much. And one thing, one lesson I have taken to heart. People are never game pieces to push around the board. No battle plan ever survives contact with the enemy.'

Jacob felt his way down the narrow passage. 'I have never quit the field in defeat.'

'Jake Silver has never quit the field in defeat. Which of you is to fight this war? The pastor or the killer?'

'You know the answer to that question, old dog.'

'I suppose I do. And how will you take charge of parliament's army?'

Jacob didn't answer. The question was a terrible one. Or perhaps it was the price that was going to have to be paid that was terrible. *Saints forgive me. Because after this, nobody else will.*

The Vandian surgeon, Keall Merrisor, clutched the back of his bleeding head in the empty interrogation cell, withering under the gaze of the foreign monarch he had been sent to serve. Captain Thomas Purdell had never seen the king in such an obviously foul mood. But then, having a prisoner escape unseen from the palace's dungeons was a unique occurrence as far as the officer was aware, even if Father Carnehan did supposedly have the assistance of the most mysterious of the expedition members – unless the doctor was lying to cover his incompetence. *That's always possible. A man will tell any lie to save his own skin.* The king's guard were out of sight, having sealed off the lower level of the palace and discovered precisely nothing. Thomas imagined the troopers scurrying about in the grounds above, desperately searching for the missing captive. They wouldn't find anything. The chickens had well and truly flown the coop.

King Marcus stopped questioning the doctor and turned his attention to Thomas. 'What do you know of this man Sariel?'

Depressingly little, although that was nothing the king wanted to hear. 'I combined the intelligencers' reports with a handful of second-hand accounts from the escaped slaves, Your Majesty,' said Thomas. 'But we still know almost nothing about the man. We have no record of his birth on Weyland soil, so he probably isn't a Weylander. Sariel affects the appearance of an itinerant vagrant, as addled as most gentlemen of the road; he joined the Northhaven expedition at the free port of Talekhard; and there were those outlandish reports that he practised sorcery during the slave revolt and drew on strange powers to assist the miners' flight home.'

'Sariel is a dangerous outlaw with a long history of fermenting trouble inside the imperium,' said Merrisor. 'His presence in your country is of vital concern to the emperor.'

The captain stared coldly at the Vandian. 'What can you tell us of this infamous outlaw, then, Doctor?'

'I did not say he was infamous. Our press isn't like yours,' said the surgeon. 'Our newspapers and kino screens do not report tittle-tattle and gossip, they announce only what the imperial censors deem to be in the people's interest to hear. Sariel is known to the authorities. To the people he is nothing.'

'How refreshing,' said King Marcus. 'As always, we have so much to learn from our dear allies.'

'The embassy briefed me to interrogate Jacob Carnehan about the bandit's whereabouts,' said the surgeon. 'The outlaw has many aliases . . . Sariel Teller. Sariel Player. Sariel Skel-Bane. The order to discover his whereabouts originated from the hoodsmen, the emperor's secret police. That tells me all I need to know about the level of threat Sariel poses to the empire.'

'Was he schooled as a hedgerow magician?' asked Thomas.

'On that I have no information,' said the doctor. 'Beyond the obvious observation that many travellers who pass through the imperium claim spurious powers of witchdoctory and offer quack remedies whose only real magic is to relieve the gullible of their coins. One thing I can tell you for certain, Your Majesty, our hoodsmen do not waste their time hunting charlatans who sell sham wart cures and love potions.'

'Well, it seems he's a sorcerer indeed,' growled the king, 'to be able to pass through my palace like a ghost, pick my dungeon's locks and walk out unseen with Jacob Carnehan.'

Thomas Purdell felt a frisson of fear at the thought of the pastor on the loose. The captain had seen the murder Jacob Carnehan had worked on the bandits paid to attack the Northhaven coach. *I've never seen a man kill as fast and effectively as him.* And now the pastor was free and fully aware that Thomas was a loyal officer of the king's forces. Jacob Carnehan knew Thomas had slipped the king secrets that put the pretender's cause at risk, not to mention endangering the life of the pastor's only surviving son. Nothing Thomas knew of Jacob Carnehan suggested the pastor was a forgiving sort of man.

'Jacob Carnehan broke under questioning,' offered Merrisor, triumphantly. The doctor was all too eager to gloss over his incompetence in allowing the prisoner's escape. 'Just as I promised you he would. It was only a matter of time, as it is with all men, however strong of will and fierce of spirit. I have the location of Lady Cassandra from the pastor's own lips. She is being taken to the Rodalian capital of Hadra-Hareer.'

'That's a small crumb of comfort, Doctor,' said King Marcus.

'I think we can assume that Sariel and Carnehan's intention is to flee north to Rodal and use her ladyship as a hostage against the emperor,' said Merrisor, speaking quickly, still trying to appease the king. 'Carnehan threatened to assassinate Lady Cassandra if Vandia dared pursue its escaped slaves. He may yet make good on his threat.'

'I have daughters myself,' said King Marcus, sympathetically. 'I can only imagine the anguish your emperor must feel over his missing granddaughter.'

'It is different inside the imperium,' said Merrisor. 'Emperor Jaelis has many hundreds of heirs from the imperial harem and, thank the ancestors, his healthy grandchildren number in the thousands. Lady Cassandra is just one of royal birth and from the moment she could walk the girl has been taught to sacrifice herself for the imperium. No. It is the empire's honour that has been insulted here. That mere slaves dare raise arms against their lawful owners, seizing the emperor's blood and presuming to dictate terms to the imperium as equals. Such a stain cannot be allowed to stand.'

'Nor will it. In this, as in all our previous dealings, Vandia and Weyland are firm friends.'

'I shall return to our embassy,' said Merrisor. 'The emperor must be radioed the news that the outlaw Sariel and Lady Cassandra can be hunted in Hadra-Hareer.'

King Marcus nodded at Thomas, a pre-arranged signal. He slipped behind the imperial surgeon.

'You are in no fit state to use your embassy's radio, Doctor,' said the king.

'I do not understand?' said Merrisor, raising a quizzical eyebrow.

Thomas Purdell took the knife he had drawn and plunged it into the Vandian's spine, a bloody stain left spreading across the back of the jacket as he withdrew the steel. Merrisor fell onto his own interrogation table, hardly able to gasp. He just managed to turn over, and Thomas shoved the blade into his heart, once, twice, thrice for good measure. The Vandian tumbled off the table and slapped down against the floor.

'You see,' said the king, kneeling down beside the dying Vandian, 'sadly you were unfortunately murdered by your prisoner during his escape. But with your dying breath, you valiantly managed to inform us that Lady Cassandra Skar is being held prisoner by the escaped slaves at Midsburg. Don't worry; we'll "discover" that the emperor's granddaughter was moved to the Rodalian highlands just before the city falls.'

'You'll be a hero of your nation at last, Doctor,' said Thomas. 'Just a posthumous one.' Purdell observed the doctor's final moments with a connoisseur's attention, before kicking the Vandian's corpse to ensure he really was dead. It was strange how easily he could affect the emotions that took hold of others. All Thomas really felt was fear or joy. Fear for his own skin and joy, usually, when the fear was someone else's. Otherwise he was more or less a hollow core, but one easily covered over. He understood how to indulge himself, and how to attach himself to those powerful enough to offer him such opportunities. Not even the king knew what Thomas was capable of. Perhaps that was what made him such a good agent, able to deceive others with ease. Thomas was a blank canvas, projecting back exactly what a person wished to see. 'A hero's corpse, ready for the Vandians, Your Highness.'

King Marcus shrugged. 'A pity. I do hope his embassy is able to offer the services of another surgeon just as talented.'

'Vandian medical techniques may seem miraculous to us, but they are, I suspect, commonplace in the empire,' said Tom.

'They will be inside Weyland, too, one day,' said King Marcus. 'Now, Captain. Have you finalized your scheme to "escape" north?'

'Some of my people are at the stockade acting as prison guards. They're turning a blind eye to an escape tunnel being dug. When the tunnel's completed, I will lead a group of prisoners in an escape and head to an aircraft positioned on the edge of the Greealamie airfield. One of my agents is the pilot who helped us murder Chicola's rebel skyguard squadron in their beds. She's currently held in the camp as a downed rebel flyer and will pilot us to Midsburg. With that fat fool Assemblyman Gimlette and a few genuine prisoners alongside us to vouch for the details of our escape, the pretender will suspect nothing. The only fly in the ointment will be if the pastor arrives in the north before I do. In that event, I'd be greeted with a firing squad rather than open arms.'

'Have no fear, you'll reach the north long before the pastor and his vagabond friend,' said the monarch. King Marcus appeared satisfied with the arrangements. 'Carnehan cannot return by air. Thanks to your timely identification of the smugglers who trafficked you inside the capital, every contrabandist in Arcadia working with Black Barnaby is dangling from the end of a gallows. With the skyguard patrolling the ocean for the *Plunderbird*, there will be no quick and easy passage to the north for Father Carnehan and his mysterious tramp. Stay focused on your task after reaching Midsburg. I trust you will prove more adept at poisoning my nephew than the fool on the field marshal's staff you paid to carry out the task.'

'There are other ways than poison for your nephew to die,' said Tom, tasting the doctor's blood on his blade, before bending down to wipe it off on the Vandian's corpse. Vandian blood tasted identical to Weyland blood to him; just like everyone he had murdered for king and country. 'And I will be there to aid Owen's cowardly exit from the hardships of the war.'

'Excellent,' said King Marcus. 'Make it appear a suicide and I shall leave the fine details to you, Captain. I require the rebellion's morale to be utterly broken by Prince Owen's betrayal of their cause. The rebels are too well dispersed across the north and the east. We may rely on the Vandians to smash the bulk of the uprising at Midsburg but, in the long term, the imperium is nobody's lapdog. Once the Vandians have recaptured their slaves, taken their revenge and extracted a heavy blood-toll, the empire will depart. The ruins will be left for me to rule over with little care as to how difficult the destruction may prove to govern.'

'Let the Vandians sack Northhaven,' said Tom. 'I've been there. Nobody will miss it. Nor Rodal or the great forests . . . Nothing there but foreign mountain tribes and twisted gask-kind living as low as squirrels in the trees.'

'You're a pragmatic man, Captain,' the king smiled. 'You could always return to torturing enemies of the state; after the rebellion is over, there will be a surfeit of examples needed to be made. But I sense the butcher's table would be a waste of your skills. I shall have to locate a duty worthy of your talents when these troubles have been quelled.'

Captain Purdell considered his answer. Taking a hot questioning blade to traitors was excellent sport and he had shown a high aptitude for such duties. He joined with his victims; became whole through them in a way he could never recapture after their suffering ended. However, infiltrating the guild had revealed a different side of the service's work. Burying himself in a role and winning others' trust, before arranging the dissidents' disappearance. That yielded a different sort of sweetness. The look on his victims' faces as they realized he'd betrayed them was something to treasure and keep him warm on long cold nights. But this last mission had been a long posting, slow, with limited opportunities to torment turncoats. And his current role as a rebel convict held even less appeal. 'I will go where I am needed, Your Majesty. But if I never have to spend months inside a deep dusty guild hold again, I will count myself a happy man . . .'

'Easily granted,' said the king. 'The long guilds will be an irrelevance in my new order, as immaterial to us as they are to Vandia; while the small guilds have sided with the prince and will be repaid with dissolution. There will be a fortune in confiscated property and titles available after the rebellion has been put down. None who have proven their loyalty to me will have cause to be disappointed, Captain.'

Now, there was news to warm his heart. Like the pretender Thomas was being dispatched to assassinate, Captain Purdell was an ambitious man, and this rebellion was full of opportunities to be seized. 'I have never killed a prince before.'

'I once believed I had successfully disposed of three of the pests. On reflection, it seems that I missed one. How careless of me.'

But Thomas Purdell would not miss. The failure of the king's previous assassins would be the captain's greatest chance. It was good to enjoy your work; to reach the top in your chosen profession. How much better if you grew filthy rich through murder, too?

TEN

UNDER A RODALIAN SKY

Cassandra turned, still half-mounted against the side of her aircraft as three Rodalian ground crew sprinted forward, armed with hand-tools, shouting above the racket of the fire bells at her and Alexamir to stand down, and then the men were upon the them. Two wrestled furiously with the nomad, ripping at his false priest's robes, while the third, a serious-faced young engineer in stiff grease-stained overalls, rushed at Cassandra, attempting to brain her with an iron mallet. Her foot lashed out, catching him on the nose with a crunch as she drove the bone back and the man twisted down unconscious. When he came to, he'd feel the shattered bone and wish he'd stuck to fixing aircraft engines or whatever task had been interrupted by the alarm. Cassandra's hand snaked down to the dagger Alexamir had offered as a token of his faith, about to toss it in his direction, but the nomad was deploying his muscular physique to good effect. His boot lashed into the larger of his assailants, winding him, before the nomad seized the second man and twisted him about in the air, driving the Rodalian's head into the engine block at the back of the aircraft. The Rodalian jounced against the flying wing with a fearsome crack and joined Cassandra's victim on the floor, insensible. The last of the ground crew recovered enough to swing a large metal spanner towards Alexamir's skull, but the nomad swayed back, caught the tool and the man's hands both, and then spun him like a child, tossing him high into the nearest wall. By the time the Rodalian crashed into a tool cabinet and tumbled off towards the turntable, he was well removed from the field of battle.

'Those rice eaters will have a fine tale to tell their friends,' Alexamir laughed as he approached the aircraft, 'of how they were fed their hangar's stone floor for daring to wrestle a hearty Nijumet thief.'

Cassandra vaulted into the cockpit, desperate to start the engine before better armed sentries showed up. 'Get to the back and turn the propeller for me when I shout "contact". Then make sure you're standing well back, or you'll be filleted by the blade.'

She pumped the fuel, engaged the ignition and sounded the cry, hearing Alexamir's grunt as he spun the rear-mounted rotor and the engine growled into life. 'Mount up! It's bad luck to fly in a plane with no name, so I'm calling our bird the *Lightning Gull*.' That was the emperor's private flagship, and while Cassandra's kite was a splinter of wood in comparison to such a leviathan of the skies, maybe some of her grandfather's luck would rub off with the name.

Cassandra felt the shift in weight as the nomad dropped his heavy bulk into the rear cockpit. She released the plane towards the launch tunnel and checked behind to make sure they were escaping unaccompanied by their hosts, noting that Alexamir was wearing his wooden wind mask again. *Not a bad idea*. She tugged on the aviator's cap and secured its goggles over her eyes. Cassandra nosed the jouncing aircraft through the twists and turns intended to cheat the gales of their power inside the dug-in airfield, familiarizing herself with the controls as they went, getting a feel for the responsiveness of the stick and bird both. Compass, altimeter, air speed, engine gauge, tachometer, climb-type and bank-and-turn instruments, everything she would need up in the air. Despite the familiarity of the dials, she quickly realized that flying a skyguard aircraft was to pilot a work of art, untouched by the empire's impersonal mills and manufactories. The *Gull*'s dial glasses were hand-cut gems, the wood carved and polished by temple priests, and its fuselage's canvas fabric had been covered with the elaborate calligraphy of dozens of prayers. The stolen kite was primitive in more ways than she could count. An elegantly curved dark-mahogany propeller rather than two symmetrical straight steel blades; a piston engine rather than an air-breathing rocket engine; the nose-mounted cannon's trigger not set on the stick, but mounted as a separate wooden grip below the dials. No radio set, either. Instead, a set of chopstick-sized signal flags resting in clips to her left, no doubt backed up by a complex battle code to communicate with fellow pilots in the air or their ground forces. *Simply built means simple to fly. Come on,* Lightning Gull, *take wing and see me safe from my captors.*

'Command your pigeon to fly steadier,' moaned Alexamir from behind her.

'This isn't flying; it's taxiing for take-off.' As she spoke, the maze gave way to a long straight launch tunnel with an oblong of light at its end, easily long enough to leave the mountain town with the fifty-five knots they'd need to start the climb. She felt the warmth of the oak engine throttle lever in her fingers and gunned the *Lightning Gull* towards the light, the tunnel widening before her as the piston engine's idling hum rose into a full-throated roar. Cassandra approached the light and realized the tunnel's ceiling sloped higher to accommodate the *Lightning Gull*'s final lift, so she raised the plane's nose a few degrees, feeling the lift swell beneath their triangular wing, and then they broke into the cold, open air, and she immediately found herself straining against the insane pull and throw of the angry winds, ripping them left and right while Talatala's dark heights shrank behind them. Cassandra's arms already ached from clutching the stick, climbing for the mad fury of the trade wind marked on the charts. Gain it, and they would be riding an arrow shot straight against the north. Miss it and they'd be quickly cornered by the local skyguard squadron. She climbed to the sound of Alexamir's wild swearing, his words muffled by mask and gales both. Promises to his pantheon of savage gods that he would make offerings every day if only he returned to the ground alive. *All you have to do is gain altitude. Not scout the territory below. If that clown Sheplar Lesh can fly one of these kites nap-of-the-earth, then at the very least you can pilot it above the worst of the weather.*

Her teeth rattled in her head, but the erratic turbulence began to diminish with every extra minute they climbed, the rudder pedals' violent jerks against her boots growing gentler too. The weight on her body gradually eased as gravity's hold grew lighter and lighter. It became warmer too, even in winter's night, the heat of the radiation belt girdling Pellas replacing the sleeping sun. Cassandra mumbled a blessing to her ancestors that she wasn't required to swoop low over Rodal, but she recognized there was little heathen magic to mastering these winds. *If I had grown up flying in such atrocious conditions, I'd be an ace of the gales down below too.* Pretty soon her breathing began to run shallow and laboured. Cassandra's fingers quested under the wooden seat until she found a leather air mask with fur-lined ear covers, dangling tubes trailing away to a concealed oxygen tank. Cassandra brought the mask up and pulled the mouthpiece over her face, then turned to Alexamir and was surprised to see he'd spotted what she was doing and had copied her motions, swapping his climber's mask for the plane's breathing apparatus. *He might be a boastful horse-stealing barbarian, but I shouldn't underestimate him.* Alexamir's mumbling profanities sounded rudely against her ears, and she realized one of the mask's tubes must be a primitive communication conduit between pilot and spotter.

Cassandra tapped the compass, fixing their direction. 'I told you I could fly this kite.'

'You spoke true, golden fox. But it is not such an extraordinary feat.'

Was that a nomad's insolence, or just masculine wounded pride? 'I'd like to see you try!'

'My uncle owned a pterippus,' said Alexamir, his words uncharacteristically wistful. 'One of the magnificent winged horses of Persdad Beyond the Plains, a great and rare prize. It was an ancient stallion, but before it passed, my uncle let me ride it. That was an excellent way to take to the air. Not like this dead rattling wooden pigeon.'

'You have yet to see one of my empire's aerial warships,' said Cassandra.

'Hah, the Persdadians style their chief an emperor too, but his imperial scouts' stables can still be raided for their expensive winged steeds. And the shadows of many of the great traders of the air pass over our grasslands, but they trouble us not.'

'I don't suppose they need to trade for grass,' said Cassandra. 'It grows free throughout Pellas.'

'You may mock,' said Alexamir, 'but you will see, golden fox. I will show you the glory of the plains and what it means to be *free.* To own the land and never have the land own you. To wake up and follow the sun and the breeze with your family and clan by your side. We suffer no chains and pay no taxes and owe no homage to any chief we have not chosen.'

Cassandra glanced down and snorted. She saw the reflection of the moon on bodies of water stretched between the snow-topped mountains, pale against the darkness of the valleys and lower peaks, thin white blankets of cloud obscuring large tracts of Rodal. She glanced up to take a direction from the starry sky's constellations and inspected her altimeter. If those charts had been marked accurately, they would be entering the northerly trade wind soon, and she would see how her little *Lightning Gull* stood up against the fierce Bdur'rkhangmar. *You've no choice here. As soon as Sheplar and Kerge realize you've escaped, the gask will be on your trail like the twisted bloodhound he is, with half the skyguard in train. You've got a single tank of fuel and this six-hundred-mile-an-hour tailwind is your sole chance of putting Rodal far behind you.* Cassandra would need to carefully navigate the turbulence gradient when entering the current, for if her entry proved too abrupt, she'd see the fine craftsmanship of the *Lightning Gull* ripped into a stream of gale-torn splinters and fabric. If there was any silver lining to such a cloud, it was that she and Alexamir would be buffeted into oxygen-starved unconsciousness long before their final impact against a mountainside ended this journey.

'Pray that we don't meet the glory of your plains nose-first,' said Cassandra. The flying wing had begun to shake, the fuselage palpitating as though alive. 'Hold on.'

Cassandra felt the force of the air currents lifting stronger against her elevator flaps and rudder, and suddenly she realized why the Rodalians crafted their kites as a triangular flying wing, fuselage and wing fused as the same beast. *The force of shear against the ailerons would rip a pair of wings straight off!* And their propeller was rear-mounted for the same reason. She imagined watching her twisting prop torn off and drifting away inside the intense trade wind, then blinked the defeatist vision out of her mind as she struggled against the stick and controls, attempting to angle the *Lightning Gull* safely into the force of the current. Whipping winds roared intermittently, the hump of raised fuselage behind Cassandra's head directing airflow away from her in turns as their angle of ascent shifted, the best she could hope for, given an enclosed cockpit would have been ripped from any kite entering this maelstrom. *Not so savage after all, the Rodalians. Clever. Damn clever.* Everything about her little bird was designed to help it survive these dreadful conditions. Cassandra altered the angle of ascent, using the noise generated by the curve of fuselage behind her head as her guide. *Quiet, good. Roaring, dangerous.* Keep the roar to a minimum and follow the passage into the Bdur'rkhangmar just as the flying wing's craftsmen had intended. Those sly priests of the temple. This was their magic and now she was making it hers.

'Kalu the Apportioner spare us this one time,' lamented Alexamir. 'Do this for your brave son and I will steal a thousand horses for you and consider my toil only half done.'

And then they were in the main flow of the trade wind, the turbulence zone left behind. But still, Cassandra felt her cheeks quivering in the force of the warm blow; goggles and face mask biting into her skin. But slowly, that pain began to diminish. Cassandra watched an unexpected counter-current swirling around the plane, and it quickly became apparent that the strangely organic shape of the flying wing she had noted back in the hangar had been crafted to redirect and fold currents in ways that allowed the *Lightning Gull* to survive this velocity of travel. She held the flying wing in the centre of the trade wind, burning precious fuel with every hour, keeping a wary eye on the fuel gauge. Like flying on glass, every push of the stick or squeeze of pressure on the pedals skidding them across the fierce Bdur'rkhangmar, the vast tunnel amplifying her flight controls' movement. It was hypnotic, a false calm that lulled Cassandra and her unwilling spotter into silence, arrowing ahead for the best part of the night. Star-speckled darkness above them, clouds below like an endless sea, pierced irregularly by the tallest of the peaks, so high that no Rodalian could inhabit them. Cassandra dared not fall asleep though, however heavy her eyelids. A minute of delicious sleep and they might find themselves in the margins of the trade wind and snatched out of all control by the turbulence.

'Sing for me,' she demanded, stifling a yawn. 'Give me a tune to keep me awake up here. If I grab a nap, it'll likely be the end of us.'

'I am no bard,' growled Alexamir.

'That canvas bag beside your feet is a parachute. Would you rather be a pigeon with a silk parasol?'

He took the hint and let loose with a number of coarse and lusty ditties – mostly involving the superior horse-riding skills of the Clan Stanim and the sickly breeding potential of many warriors' mothers from the Clan Menin and other rivals. Alexamir belted out how the merchants of the Thousand Duchies were so dull-witted that a blind drunk horseman might outwit them without recourse to his dagger or bow, and warbled that the women of Persdad walked so proud that a wild stallion might be easier tamed. Cassandra was beginning to think the parachute might be a preferable fate after a few hours of his crudely unmelodic voice, when she registered the trade wind tapering away. The mighty Bdur'rkhangmar would soon be funnelling them towards the becalmed steppes. Its strength dropped off surprisingly fast. Her flight stick grew heavier, the drone of the engine roaring louder as it worked to keep the *Lightning Gull* powering forward rather than just holding them inside the fierce tunnel of wind. The sun was rising, fingers of light on the horizon, welcoming her to a new future. *We've done it. Goodbye Sheplar Lesh. Goodbye stinking Weylanders and twisted forest men. Goodbye rebellious slaves.* She'd suffer Alexamir's overpowering boasts and nomad reek for a week or two and then hold him to his blood oath and ride for somewhere civilized enough to send word to Vandia's foreign agents. Free by her own cunning, escaped with honour from her house's enemies . . . no ransom paid. And best of all, Lady Cassandra's return would be a cause for grave consternation among Princess Helrena's numerous rivals, the young heir's reappearance strengthening Helrena's claim to the diamond throne when it came time for her grandfather to sadly join their ancestors. Circae would be utterly furious, while Cassandra's friends in the house – Paetro, Duncan and Doctor Horvak – would be exultant and proud that Cassandra had conquered the punishing challenges of her foreign odyssey. The dreams of her victorious return were shredded by Alexamir's warning yell. She returned to alertness on a rush of blood and spotted what had alarmed the nomad: two dark triangles, drifting and turning above the clouds. A skyguard patrol, and their duty up here no coincidence. *Damn Sheplar Lesh.* He must have reached a radio guild station and sent word to the border fields to watch for Cassandra riding the trade wind north. She'd hoped he'd think navigating the Bdur'rkhangmar beyond her, searching the south instead for a ditched flying wing. How far did Kerge's tracking sense extend? No matter: she had to deal with the situation as it was, not as she wished it.

Cassandra spoke to Alexamir. 'I spotted a telescope clipped back there with you. What do we face?'

Alexamir found the leather-lined tube and extended it in the direction of the two aircraft. 'A pair of wooden pigeons. Rice eaters inside, a single pilot in each kite.'

Skyguard fighter craft rather than spotters. They'd have the edge in manoeuvrability – she checked her dwindling fuel reserves – as well as more time in the air. The Rodalians wouldn't even need to force the *Lightning Gull* down; they could just wait her out on their full tanks and anticipate her landing. 'We have to take them on, no choice.'

'Rodal's spirits have cursed us,' said Alexamir. 'Jealous of the greatest thief to climb her cliffs and steal across her cold, hard stone.'

'The greatest in self-conceit, perhaps,' said Cassandra, before barking a warning. 'Clearing the gun!' She pressed her hand around the cannon grip mounted below the dials and squeezed its trigger for a test burst. Nothing apart from dull empty thuds inside the nose cone. Cassandra groaned. She had checked the flying wing's fuel reserves, but the nomad's ill-judged act of arson and the rapidly arriving airfield staff had thrown checking the ammunition out of her mind. Nearly out of fuel and not a single shell for the gun. *Cursed indeed.*

How very strange, mused Duncan, *to be in Weyland at last. And nothing like I'd imagined.* Every night while imprisoned as a slave he'd dreamt of returning home. Long febrile nights, hungry and tired beyond exhaustion, sweating like an animal in the furnace-like sky mines above Vandia's great stratovolcano. During those hard, endless days, Duncan's lost life in Northhaven had seemed impossibly distant. Another age. But his conditions had changed: he'd risen to the rank of free citizen of the imperium through his own efforts. Of late, he rarely, if ever, dwelled on his old life. And now he was back in Weyland, everything about his old land felt unreal. Was it that Duncan was finally home, or that he was flying towards Arcadia's royal palace that made a dream of the sights fleeting past his helo's porthole? Arcadia, a city resonant with memories, even though he had never set foot in the capital before. Benner Landor deeply regretted not dispatching his children here to be educated; keeping to the last promise he reluctantly made Duncan's dying mother. In another life, Duncan would have visited the palace on different terms... attending a coming-out celebration, introduced at court by one of Benner Landor's well-greased political contacts. Instead, he was here as – what? – a conqueror, a rescuer, an avenger or perhaps, an ally? Duncan had arrived with three vast Vandian warships, steel cathedrals turned horizontal and made thundering javelins powered by engines that flung them through the sky faster than sound itself – the *Warhawk*, the *Empress Gauntlet*, and the *Fleetwing*. Inside those three warships, the fleet transported nine legions – veteran troops of the imperial army augmented by house forces and levies – their long hangar bays crammed full with helo squadrons and a full armoured battalion's worth of hulking mechanical vehicles. Before landing, the fleet had passed low over Weyland's capital, no doubt throwing its citizens into a fine panic. Vandia's expeditionary force had settled in the vineyards outside Arcadia, leaving some poor landowner's living a smoking stubble, a gale of crisped leaves blown towards the endless green horizon of the Lancean Ocean. So it was that on this strange day, Duncan found himself accompanying Princess Helrena and Paetro on a troop transport leaving the princess's ship, the *Fleetwing*. Their helo sported four vertical blades whirling above its metal fuselage, forty seats at the rear and a cockpit for two pilots and a couple of high-born passengers; just part of a squadron heading towards the palace at the city's heart. Blade-topped aircraft skimming the capital's rooftops as they buzzed towards the ancient bastion. Duncan wondered what the locals made of the sight; Arcadians rushing out as small as ants below, filling the streets, gawping at the humming helos darting across Arcadia's skyline. None of his countrymen had seen anything resembling a helo before, let alone the vast metal behemoths used to ferry Vandia's legions to landfall, each vessel twenty times the length of a nautical frigate, bristling with cannons, gun turrets, bomb-bays and rocket mountings. Craftsmen in the imperial foundries had shaped the vessels' prows into long, sinuous dragon-skulls; lighthouse-sized lanterns for eyes which glowed bright demon-crimson when flying at night. An unimaginable fortune in metal forged in the form of destructive steel dragons. After taking in the fiery engines at the stern and blasting stabilizing jets below her triangular steel fins, most nations' locals fled in terror at the first sight of a Vandian warship. Duncan had laughed when he had first noticed Weyland's newly formed skyguard trying to keep up with the Vandian warships – completely unaware they were only matching the fleet's sluggish cruising speed in preparation for landing. Twenty-rotor aircraft trying to keep pace, the royal black boar of Weyland painted proudly in the centre of yellow and green circles on vertical rudder tails, the craft little more than canvas stretched over pinewood frames, tiny engines belching corn ether as they swerved out of the way of the metal monsters invading their airspace. Once upon a time such aircrafts' presence above Weyland would have made Duncan's heart swell with patriotic pride. Now they were a reminder to him of how very far he had progressed from his undistinguished beginnings. Primitive toys buzzing modern vessels, when each warship was capable of razing Weyland's capital city to the ground and salting its ruins in a barrage of deadly, fiery rain. Up in the helo's cockpit, Princess Helrena seemed oblivious to the stir the empire's arrival had caused. She was in a sour mood and Duncan couldn't blame her. Despite Helrena's hard-won position among the fleet's command, Prince Gyal and her brutish cousin, Baron Machus, missed no opportunity to exclude the princess from their councils and the planning for the Weyland expeditionary force. It was only because Helrena had resorted to bribing naval officers for information that should have been hers by right, that the princess was even aware there had been radio contact between the expeditionary force and Vandia's local embassy. It seemed there was trouble in Weyland, and Prince Gyal was eager to capitalize on it to ensure his return to the empire was properly triumphant . . . a silk carpet rolled out all the way to the impending vacancy on the imperial throne. Helrena had told Duncan that just the thought she might have to bend her knee as a subject of an Emperor Gyal – and by extension, to the princess's deadly mother-in-law, Circae – was enough to make her redouble her efforts to take her fair share of glory from this campaign. If her exclusion wasn't enough, the camp followers travelling with the fleet included Adella, simpering at the baron with the brute's other mistresses. A constant reminder to Duncan of how foolish he had been in once trusting her, loving her. *I'll make my fate here. And a better fate than hers.*

Paetro sat perched on the seat next to Duncan's in the helo's troop hold. 'Does returning to your home make you yearn for your old life, lad?'

'Hardly at all, to tell the truth. It's as though I don't belong here anymore.'

'Aye, visiting the imperium will do that to a man. You come back home and all those grand houses you remember have been turned into wooden-walled hovels, all the wide streets remade as mud tracks while your back was turned.'

Duncan nodded toward Prince Helrena's position in the cockpit. 'I feel the same as the princess . . . somewhere out there we'll find Lady Cassandra. Scared. Fearful. Praying for us to come for her.'

Paetro grunted in amusement. 'I doubt that. The more scared she is, the more she'll take it out on whatever poor unlucky bastard's got her in chains. That's the young highness I helped raise.'

'Her captors are about to get a whole lot unluckier,' said Duncan.

'About that, I'd say you're right,' said Paetro. 'But you remember something, for Prince Gyal and the baron, none of this is about bringing the young highness back alive. Lady Cassandra's little better than a standard to be sliced out of the hands of the slaves who revolted against the empire, and if that flag comes back broken in half and blood-soaked, that's just part of the butcher's bill. It's the insult against Vandia's reputation that can't be allowed to stand. The imperium's like one of the triku crime families. It's been disrespected, and should the empire let that dishonour go unpunished, its rivals will start to wonder what other indignities it might permit, and pretty soon it won't be able to walk down the street without someone trying to stick a blade in its belly. Vandia's surrounded by enemies, and they're carrying a lot more than daggers.'

Just the thought of Lady Cassandra coming to harm was more than Duncan could bear to dwell on. 'She's a lot more than a flag to me,' said Duncan. *But surely it won't come to that?* Father Carnehan had grabbed the girl from the battlefield. The long journey from Weyland to the empire had clearly left the pastor unhinged. There had been no ransom demands. It was just a mad act of defiance, petty revenge for the skels' raid on Northhaven. Paetro was right. Cassandra was likely tied up in some barn in Northhaven, swearing at her captors, making their lives hard in every way possible. 'And damn the empire's revenge.'

'That's why we're in a troop transporter on the way to this little covenant,' said Paetro. 'Someone with Lady Cassandra's interests at heart has to attend, because it certainly won't be Prince Gyal or Baron Machus.'

Yes, they needed to push for Cassandra's safe release. And if Duncan got a chance to blunt the worst excesses of the empire's mission to punish the slave revolt, he would be doing both nations a favour. Not that Duncan would receive any gratitude or recognition for it, but someone had to try, and Duncan Landor was the only one with the fleet who cared a damn for Weyland. He stared thoughtfully through the gun port. The concentric rings of street-lined canals below were tightening to a single bull's-eye in the centre of Arcadia, a high crenellated wall protecting the royal palace, and then their squadron's fleeting shadows were passing over private orchards and gardens, ornamental streams brittle with broken ice. The squadron slowed. Ahead, King Marcus's palace stood three storeys high, honey-coloured brick punctuated by hundreds of tall oblong windows running across the lower two storeys, circular ornamental windows up on the third, three wings of stone and terraces reflected in artificial square lakes surrounding the palace. To Duncan's eyes, Weyland's palace resembled an elaborate version of the doll's house that Willow used to play with. He had grown accustomed to the imposing and functional might of the Castle of Snakes, surrounded by the cloud-scraping towers of Vandis. The empire's capital city was like an ants' nest, crowded, packed, and climbing hungrily towards the sky. Duncan's helo set down in flower beds across from an orangery, rotors blowing away clouds of light powdered snow before slowing to a stop. Baron Machus and Prince Gyal had already disembarked from their craft and were striding towards a gathering of dignitaries on the palace terrace to welcome the newcomers. Princess Helrena left the helo flanked by her troops with as much dignity as she could muster, trying not to look like a child hustling after the adults as they gathered to discuss the business of grown-ups. *We're as welcome here among the expeditionary force as our legions must be in Weyland.*

Duncan and Paetro climbed out of a sliding cabin door, joining the train of Vandians at their rear. They entered the palace through a balustrade graced by sculpted figures, vaulted ceiling held up by columns of veined pink marble, the Vandians' boots echoing down the corridor as they paraded along its length. This sounded very much like a conquerors' march to Duncan's ears. Paetro pushed through the crowd, guarding Helrena's back and leaving Duncan with soldiers and assorted staff officers from the command. *We should be safe enough in the king's palace.* Although it had occurred to Duncan that on the battlefields to come, that would not be the case. How easy for Helrena to catch a 'stray' bullet in the fog of war, or be ordered to assault a well-defended position with a force not up to the task. How much easier for Prince Gyal to leave his main rival to the imperial throne as a corpse on foreign soil. Weyland's courtiers and palace staff milled around in clusters, staring curiously at the foreign force marching through their palace. One of the courtiers, perhaps bolder than the others, came quick-stepping after the Vandians, falling in alongside Duncan, moving quickly despite her obvious pregnancy. A pretty young woman in her early twenties wearing a cream dropped-shoulder blouse designed to flatter her extended stomach, her pale shoulders covered by a burgundy-coloured courtier's cloak.

'Duncan Landor? Duncan of Northhaven?'

'You know me?' asked Duncan, surprised. He was sure if he had ever met a woman as attractive as this he would be able to put a name to her face.

'It would be hard not to,' said the woman, twisting coyly at the golden locks of her hair, 'for there is a painting of you hanging in my husband's hall.'

Duncan gazed uncertainly at the woman's mischievous face. *Has she taken leave of her senses?* 'Next to a bust of myself in marble, perhaps?'

She smiled sympathetically, a sweet flash of white teeth surrounded by her winsome face. 'I'm sorry. I forget; you don't know me at all, when I have been told so much about you. I am Leyla Landor, Benner Landor's new wife.'

'New *wife*?' Duncan was astonished. Ever since the death of

Duncan's mother, there had been women calling at Hawkland Park, huntresses hoping to tempt the rich old widower back into matrimony. But Duncan's father had sent each fortune-seeker packing, anchoring his life around the estate and his house's holdings. How in the world had this woman convinced Duncan's father to marry her, however beautiful and comely she was? The answer struck Duncan with the force of a landslide. After the slavers' raid on Northhaven, when Benner Landor had lost his son and daughter, he hadn't just suffered the loss of his children . . . old man Landor had also forfeit his house's heirs. And this young attractive woman looked to be heavily pregnant and near to her full term. *Yes, that makes sense.* Leyla Landor wasn't a replacement for Duncan's mother: she was a replacement for *him*. Duncan didn't know how to feel about that. He had chosen to stay in Vandia, to carve out a new life for himself, far removed from everything that was familiar. And even before that, back in Weyland, Duncan had been planning to strike out on his own with Adella by his side. Shouldering the heavy role of heir to Hawkland Park had hardly figured in his plans, and yet . . . finding himself so easily replaced; that was a bitter fruit to suck on.

'I understand it's a lot of news for you to take in,' said Leyla. 'But it's been a long time since you disappeared. Even when Willow returned alive carrying word of your achievements in far-called lands, we were never sure how you really fared. Your father's been terribly concerned for you. Despite my best efforts, I fear he rather blamed Willow for returning without you.'

As well he might. Duncan frowned. 'Where is Willow now?'

'Your sister's here in the capital with your father. Willow will be eager to see you again; and I can't wait to tell Benner of your safe return . . . he'll be so happy.' Her face turned thoughtful and concerned. 'But you should understand that there have been a great many changes in Willow's life. She's now Lady Wallingbeck, the wife of the Viscount of Belinus Hall.'

'A lady . . . and married? Now I know I'm dreaming.' Duncan didn't know whether to laugh or cry. Shock after shock, in rapid succession, and nothing that could be called a true homecoming. It was as though he had slept for centuries and awakened to find everything familiar changed, with just enough left to confound him. But then, what had he expected? His father to go into mourning at the park, turning away all visitors and neglecting his business until he died of a broken heart? Willow playing the part of grief-stricken sibling for escaping to join the slave revolt, well knowing how damaging her treachery was to Duncan's prospects. Actually, that was more or less how he had imagined matters progressing at home; but never *this*. How easily Duncan Landor's presence had been supplanted, his existence lost among Weyland's daily business. If Duncan had ever entertained any doubts about staying in the imperium and refusing the princess's offer of passage back to Weyland, they vanished now. *I'm not home anymore. I'm as much a visitor here as Helrena and Paetro are.*

'Willow is expecting her first child,' said Leyla. 'The next Viscount Wallingbeck, with God's benediction. Due to arrive a little after my own birth. Willow's child and your new stepbrother will be small blessings in very troubled times.'

A child on the way already? Saints, how Willow's suffering in the sky mines must have changed her. No longer satisfied with her stupid library and a quiet, bookish life at home, she was married for position and title to an aristocrat? Expecting a child? The only way this was going to seem stranger was if it transpired Willow's husband had been born in the Lancean Ocean and his sister was due to give birth to a mermaid. He sighed. *What in the world has been going on here in my absence?* 'My sister makes her own decisions. Always has and always will. On the way here I heard there was trouble in Weyland, but very little concerning its source?'

'You will hear more of our troubles when the king speaks with the Vandians,' said Leyla. 'Our peace has been sundered by rebellion. The northern prefectures have declared for a pretender and are raising armies to fight King Marcus.'

Duncan concealed his shock. He had been raised in the most boring province of the most uninteresting country in the whole Lancean League, and yet, as soon as the slavers flew him over the border, the nation plunged into madness! 'How can that be? Weyland's been at peace for centuries. Has everyone gone mad while I've been away?'

'When people forget their loyalty and chase ambition and greed instead, it's easy enough for treachery to prosper. This must seem terribly strange to you. You arrive back home to find little is as it once was.'

'Actually, there's far too much that is the same.' *I never mattered a damn, here . . . only my position as heir to the Landor pile. With that gone, I might as well not have existed at all. But they'll know me in Weyland now. That they will.*

'King Marcus feels similarly to you,' said Leyla, misunderstanding his words. 'The king is a modernizer, and it's the advances he's gifted to our nation that have fed the traitors' loathing and jealousy of his reign.'

Duncan bit back the cruel retort that any advances the king tried to make in Weyland were just a high-born savage playing with mud castles compared to what Vandia had achieved – all the resources of the world at the imperium's command, born of fire in the great stratovolcano and captured in its net of sky mines. 'Weyland should tread carefully, Mistress Landor. The imperium's arrived to punish the indignity of the slave revolt. They want blood, and they won't be too fussy about whose they need to spill.'

'We have a Vandian embassy here now. From what little I know, we have tried to be good allies to the imperium.'

'Vandia doesn't have allies,' said Duncan. 'It has supplicants and it has foes.'

'And how do you tell the difference?'

Duncan remembered the horde of foreign nobles lined up to bow and scrape before Emperor Jaelis in the Diamond Palace at the heart of Vandis. 'One has kings on their knees; the other has monarchs cut off *below* the knees.'

'That sounds less than ideal. Can we still count on you, Duncan Landor? Your people, your father, your house?'

'I answer to a different house now. An imperial one. But I will do all I can to help Weyland. I wish no ill to anyone here.'

'I am glad to hear it,' said Leyla. She gently patted her wide belly. 'And your father will thank you too, although you might have to wait a few years for your little brother to voice his gratitude. You are every bit as fine and brave as Benner described you.'

'He said that about me?'

Leyla nodded. 'Of course.'

'Not so fine that he risked his neck to pursue the slavers that kidnapped me,' said Duncan, bitterly. 'Instead he paid Father Carnehan to come after us, a mere pastor, in his stead; Carnehan driven half-mad and become a wilding by the time he caught up with us.'

'Do not tell Benner I said this to you,' said Leyla, 'he is too proud to have it known. But I was at Hawkland Park comforting your father when you and your sister were believed lost, far-called, in some hellish slave pit at the other end of the world. He wept every night, cursing the slavers and his family's unkind fate. Benner would have joined the pursuit if he could have, but he had a wrecked town to rebuild, a prefecture full of broken families missing children, brothers, sisters, parents – either buried during the raid, or slaved and lost. To be the head of a great house is to be responsible for more than just his own blood. He carries that burden and he had to live up to it, whatever the personal cost.'

Duncan felt a twinge of guilt. Could it be true? Had Duncan really mattered to his father, beyond his obvious utility as heir to the house? Perhaps he had misjudged the man; believing him so ready to abandon his son and daughter to the slavers while he attended his all-important holdings. Duncan's disconcertingly young stepmother took his hand and squeezed it kindly, joining the courtiers in the throne room after they entered the substantial chamber. Vandia's visitors marched down a wide aisle at the centre of the hall towards the throne at the far end. Weylanders gawked at the interlopers from either side of the room with a mixture of fear, curiosity and uncertainty, splendid tapestries gazing down on them from the walls. Paetro hung back alongside Duncan, the imperial troops halted ahead of them. Helrena strode towards the throne with Prince Gyal and Baron Machus, although the two high nobles paid little heed to the princess by their side; not a single glance in her direction. Duncan could feel the chill under the high hammer-beam roof.

'That's the king of this land?' whispered Paetro, staring with clear disbelief at the man seated on the throne. 'He may wear a set of royal furs, but his face puts me in mind of a chief justice, thin ink running through his veins.'

Duncan shrugged without comment. He couldn't deny it; whoever had illustrated King Marcus for the country's newspapers had taken more than a few liberties to make that plain, pinched aspect look substantial and gallant. On Marcus, the crimson ermine-lined robes of the monarch were like too many clothes layered across an aged sickling relative to warm his bones against the winter.

'Welcome, noble sons and daughter of Vandia. In comparison to Vandia we are but a poor land at the far end of the caravan routes,' announced King Marcus, rising to open his arms towards the delegation. 'But we have this to offer you . . . the hand of friendship raised against our common foe. Those that have struck against you have also struck against us . . . the traitors have raised a rebellion in the north of my realm, where they hold your noble emperor's granddaughter as hostage.' He was trying to sound commanding, but Duncan detected the anxiety in the voice. *Let him fear us, and with good cause.*

Helrena Skar stepped forward, her cousin Machus glancing coldly at the princess for interrupting. 'Lady Cassandra is of my line, my daughter and heir to my house. Where is she to be found?'

'Your noble daughter is being held prisoner in the city of Midsburg . . . the rebellion's stronghold. Those that have plotted against me and conspired against the people of Weyland are the same rebels you pursue for their crimes against the Vandian people. Chief among them, the pretender to my throne, Owen Hawkins. He has fled his nest of villainy in the Burn, fearful of your justice, and even as we speak, he spreads his poison among my citizenry.'

Duncan didn't know what the king what talking about. *Owen Hawkins*? The only Owen that Duncan had served with in the sky mines had been a grizzled survivor called Owen Paterson. And what did the war-wracked ruins of the Burn have to do with the empire? Whatever was going on, Prince Gyal appeared to be complicit in the scheme. This wasn't so much diplomacy being conducted as a choreographed dance between two nations. Gyal pushed his cloak to the side and indicated the forces ranged behind him. 'We require all those that have insulted the emperor's honour to be returned for punishment in the imperium.'

'I require my daughter returned, *alive*,' Helrena interjected.

Prince Gyal waved her to silence with a stern stare.

'I too have daughters,' said King Marcus, nodding gravely. 'And I completely understand your concern, Your Grace, which come honourably as both a mother and a loyal highborn of the imperium. You shall have the full weight of Weyland's forces in returning the young woman to your care. My regiments have driven north, but we have not yet assaulted Midsburg for fear of inadvertently wounding Lady Cassandra or inciting her kidnappers to defile her person. My intelligencers believe she is in the custody of a notorious outlaw . . . a wretch called *Sariel*.'

'Sariel Skel-Bane? He is wanted for execution,' growled Prince Gyal. 'The empire seeks that devil for a lengthy list of crimes . . . robbery, murder, rebellion.'

'And I urge you to seek *peace* here,' called out a man, emerging from a line of ambassadors waiting among the gathered courtiers. 'Not seek brigands.'

'This is Palden Tash,' said King Marcus. 'First Speaker of Rodal. His nation is also a member of the Lancean League.'

'I know of Rodal,' said Prince Gyal, his voice dripping with arrogant disdain. 'As far as your coastal kingdoms' local alliance is concerned, the embassy's reports from the region have been acceptably thorough.' He swivelled to look down on the Rodalians' head of state. 'Your advice is of as little concern to me, Rodalian, as the winds that beat upon your land's barren peaks.'

Duncan frowned. Yet none of the embassy's thoroughness had been directed towards Princess Helrena or her staff. Duncan could see Helrena fuming about being marginalized by Gyal and his minions, her cheeks burning bright with indignation. She was not used to being a spectator to affairs of state, but the would-be next emperor of Vandia was treating her with little more courtesy than the legionaries he had marched into the palace at his rear.

Palden Tash rapped his cane of office against the marble floor, the sound echoing across the throne room like a pistol report. 'Then you should know Rodal and the Lanca have strongly counselled for an end to these hostilities. The league nations have held back from intervention. We do not wish to incite further escalations in fighting. Your forces must leave Weyland's shores. From what I understand, you have arrived from a region of Pellas far-called beyond the reach of normal trade and common alliance. It is not your empire's place to support one side or another in a remote civil conflict. Return to your homeland in peace and allow the Lanca to mediate a lasting settlement here.'

Duncan winced. The first speaker shared his people's reputation for blunt talking, but you did not address a member of the Vandian celestial caste in such a haughty manner. Unfortunately, Palden Tash seemed blithely unaware of his miscalculation.

Prince Gyal nodded, thoughtfully. '*Must depart*? You make an interesting point. Allow me to counter it.' Gyal raised his arm and his troops surged forward, seizing Palden Tash. Before Duncan could gather his thoughts, the soldiers had gagged the Rodalian and dragged him struggling furiously across to a high wall. Gyal's legionaries untied the rope holding a pennant aloft and wrapped its cord around the Rodalian's neck, hoisting him up inside the chamber between two tall stained-glass windows. Tash's boots whipped about as the politician hung above the floor. Many among the group of ambassadors rushed forward to try to cut him down, but they were beaten back by the legionaries' rifle butts. Chief among the would-be rescuers was a young Rodalian woman flourishing a dagger who attempted to stab the Vandians, but the armoured troops easily overpowered her, beating her savagely to the floor and laying into her until she was stretched out beaten, bleeding and still. Duncan noted that none of the king's guardsmen – the only other force bearing firearms inside the palace – attempted to intervene. Short of a threat to the life of Weyland's monarch himself, they had clearly been instructed to offer no resistance to their powerful visitors.

Prince Gyal indicated the desperately shaking Rodalian hanging above the courtiers, his face turning purple; the Vandian noble was oblivious to frantic shouts and yelling from the league's diplomats. 'There is *no* limit to the imperium's reach or imperial law. We suffer no commands from barbarian councils. Those who offend against the emperor or the empire's rule will find immediate execution is their only reward. The King of Weyland has offered the hand of friendship in punishing criminals sought by Vandia, brigands who are now making mischief in his land, and I as the empire's appointed legate have accepted his cooperation. If any bordering barbarian realm believes it can gainsay the imperium's will, step forward now. After I have improvised a gallows for your insolent necks, I shall locate your piddling satrapy on a map and burn whatever open-sewered slum masquerades as capital of your sty to ashes.'

Duncan heard moans and saw wringing of hands, but there were no more takers for the prince's justice.

'Gyal has his father's knack for making friends,' whispered Paetro.

Duncan shook his head, sadly. 'This is badly done.'

But the reality was that the princeling could no more afford to lose face in front of his subordinates than the empire could appear weak before its neighbours. Palden Tash finally stopped struggling at the end of the rope, his corpse swaying limply in front of a religious tapestry of *The Saints' Seven Mercies*.

'Cut him down!' barked Baron Machus. 'Draw and quarter the dog's body, load his remains in a fast patrol ship and drop them over whatever piss-hole he hails from.' Machus's legionaries obeyed with the kind of alacrity that only the truly terrified could show. They knew what their celestial caste masters were capable of: the nations of the Lanca were only just beginning to learn. *That poor Rodalian fool should have kept his mouth shut.*

Prince Gyal indicated the king seated on the throne of Weyland for the benefit of the league's ambassadors. Marcus had broken out in a cold sweat despite being swaddled in so many robes. 'This is what an ally of the imperium looks like.' Then Gyal's hand jabbed towards the corpse tumbling toward the floor. 'While that is how those who oppose us look. Send word to your barbarian chiefs that they must choose which they wish to be considered; but have them know it matters naught to me. My fleet carry shell and fire enough to leave every kingdom of the three oceans nothing but burning dust.'

A clear example had been set. Duncan worried it would not be the last one he was forced to witness before Vandia's expedition left his homeland's shores.

Carter rode ahead of the force of mounted soldiers, carefully following a rutted earthen road through the woods, bristlecone and limber pine that had hadn't been cut back for a long time; dark needle leaves giving the place an ancient, haunted feel. Carter sat astride a black mare called Peppercorn almost as ancient and slow as his father's old horse at Northhaven. But then horses, like so much else, were in short supply among the Army of the Spotswood, and though Carter was a newly minted captain under Prince Owen's command, the steeds allocated by commissary staff reflected the beggarly nature of their war. Horses that had been pulling wagons across Middenharn's farm fields one month had been requisitioned as reluctant cavalry mounts for the Second Royal Cavalry Brigade of the Army of the Spotswood the next. The *royal* in their title was all that was regal about the brigade, and that only to remind everyone who fought under the rebels' banner that Owen was Weyland's true heir. The riders' rough woollen uniforms had been left grey, not enough dye available in the north to colour their coats the southern forces' proud blue. Half Carter's troop fought with a mishmash of weapons collected from above their own mantelpieces, the rest carried notoriously unreliable rifles shipped west across the border from Gidor. If only that had been *all* that had slipped across the border. Battle hardened royalist cavalrymen from the Eastern Frontier, the Fourth King's Mounted Riflemen, had ridden north from the prefecture of Victorair and flanked the prince's defensive line, passing unchallenged through Gidor and striking deep into rebel territory. The unwelcome visitors from the Army of the Bole were acting as marauders, riding and hiding, striking and burning, leaving random northern farms and towns in ashes behind their passage, refusing engagements with the prince's regiments, disappearing like ghosts whenever they were pursued. These soldiers had hunted bandits for decades along the perilous frontier region, and they were proving themselves adept now they'd switched from gamekeeper to poacher. Carter found himself riding eagerly to encounter the marauders, though. A small recompense for champing at the bit in Midsburg while the country was turned into a patchwork of confused, contested, warring territories. He'd seen nothing of battle beyond sad wagon trains returning overladen with bandaged soldiers, many missing arms and legs, their faces tired and hard and blank. Carter pushed the war's victims out of his mind. He needed to know he was making a difference, pushing the enemy back, pressing towards the day when he stood again in Arcadia, his father freed from a royal prison and Willow unshackled from her forced marriage. *I'll go mad riding around in circles up here. Waiting for the fortunes of war to hand me a chance to liberate my family.*

'The fight will come north soon enough without us seeking it,' Carter's sergeant told him. Arick Densen had been an innkeeper before the war, as dry-humoured, dour and flinty as the Sharps Mountains he hailed from, as did the majority of their company. Pragmatic, independent-minded people, and as tough as the Rodalians in their down-to-earth way. Thin and rangy, not an inch of spare fat on the lot of them. Fine shots, too, even with the unreliable foreign rifles in their hands. Carter half-thought his soldiers might be eating the same grass as their mounts when he wasn't looking; such was their endurance on sparse rations. Not for the first time he wondered what the soldiers really thought of him and his competence as an officer. Carter had ended up with the nickname of *Cap'n Warrener*, the rough and ready soldiers taking the two knives tucked into his riding boots as a sign his previous employment had involved skinning a warren of rabbits. Every time they stopped to make camp, Carter suffered a barrage of joke apologies about the lack of rabbit with the rations, and how they'd try harder to capture loyalists for some shaving.

'You brooding about your father again?' asked the sergeant, noticing the far-called look on Carter's face.

'And my girl,' said Carter.

'Best not to dwell on it,' said Arick. 'Ain't any of us riding a gravy train with biscuit wheels in this war.'

'Have you had any more news from your brother?'

The sergeant shook his head. 'Don't reckon northern crewmen are being allowed shore leave now, in case they split for their home prefectures. And even if Jarret got a pass, every Guild of Radiomen's hold would be closed to him. Bad Marcus doesn't want sympathizers sending messages our way . . . too many chances for spies to slip us a few coded words.'

Bad luck for Densen's brother to be serving on a ship declared for the south. The royal navy was the last of the nation's fighting forces to fracture, the tradition of discipline at sea a strong anchor, but its ships and sailors had finally taken sides, the captain and officers' decision – mutinies aside – depending on where a skipper called home. There was a loyalist fleet in Arcadia and a rebel fleet moored in Midsburg to oppose it. 'Least ways you won't be facing him across a northern wheat field, bayonet pointed in the wrong direction.'

'There's that. Might be that old tramp will return with word of how your family are doing?'

'Here's hoping, Sergeant.' *Sariel.* Sariel's surprise visit to the company in their Midsburg barracks had allowed Carter a brief glimmer of hope, but it seemed no sooner had Carter told the sorcerer about Willow and his father's miserable fate, than the mysterious man had disappeared again. Among the vagrant's outlandish boasts and unlikely anecdotes, there had been a vague muttered promise that he would do what he could to put matters right, but Carter had focused more on his rambling account. It had been half an apology and half bragging, that there were greater affairs of man and wider wars that needed to be fought. *Wider than this? If there's any more trouble in the world, I hope it stays well clear of my shoulders. I'm stumbling here as it is.* Sariel understood how to open hidden portals in the ancient standing stones raised around Pellas and travel vast distances as easily as stepping through an open doorway, and the vagrant frequently used them to disappear for seasons at a time, fleeing the demons he claimed still chased him. Carter suspected Sariel was merely a hedgerow magician and itinerant medicine man who had come into genuine arcane knowledge at some point and been driven half-mad by it. *Maybe wholly mad after Vandia?* God knows, Carter could still feel the suppressed shadow of the strange visions which had plagued him. Sariel had cured Carter somehow, reclaiming the madness from his mind and absorbing it into his own; yet the bizarre residue still tugged within the young Weylander, a hidden tide dragging at his mind. Carter could still feel the dreams' dead fingers clutching him, even though he was troubled less by insane hallucinations. It was Sariel who had changed after administering Carter's 'cure', as though the extra madness he'd soaked up had shocked the vagrant out of himself. Sariel could still be wildly boastful, embroidering the truth into fanciful tales, but at times he forgot and something darker and more malevolent stared through the performance. *I may not know which is the real Sariel, but I know the old dog abandoned us fast enough after we escaped from Vandia.* 'Judge a man by his deeds, not his words.' That was something his father had often preached in Northhaven. Sadly, Jacob Carnehan had fallen prey to his own advice. Named as kin to a notorious sell-sword and a pirate. *What does that make me?*

Carter wished his mother was alive. He could have counted on the good-natured, ever-practical Mary Carnehan to counsel him. But she had been murdered by the slavers, along with her son's chances of understanding who and what he was, it seemed. His mother's absence still seemed unnatural, even after surviving as a slave in Vandia and a rebel at home. He'd walk into rooms in the rectory, expecting to find his mother standing there, before recalling she was buried in the churchyard outside, a cold wave of remembrance that seized him like a riptide. *What would she say if she could see me now? Call me a damn fool for signing up, I suppose. Demand I abandon the fight and head home.* But the fight was coming for him, wherever he travelled in Weyland. *It's already cost me my parents and Willow.*

'Lord, but I'd welcome the chance to happen across those raiders,' said Carter. *Anything to take my mind off what I can't change.* 'You reckon they've passed this far west, Sergeant?'

'My, but you surely are an eager one. Prince Owen promised you a bounty I don't know about?' Densen shrugged. 'Hard to say where those bushwhackers are. Right now, planters no sooner spot a peddler's silhouette on the horizon than they start hollering and ringing the church bells, lower storm shutters and bring down their crow rifles. So many alarms across the prefecture, it'd be easier to tell you where the frontier mounted *aren't* than where they *are.*'

Carter thought he heard something and fell silent. He drew in the reins, stopping Peppercorn. An angry hornet buzzing somewhere beyond the enclosed ceiling of evergreen leaves, dull and distant. 'Do you hear that?'

'Royal Sharps Greys, halt the line,' ordered the sergeant, raising his hand in air.

The sound hummed again, clearer without the clatter of their hooves on the road. 'That's a duel in the air,' said Carter.

'I swear, Bad Marcus's skyguard are growing bolder every week,' said Densen. 'We hold every airfield north of the river, and with fighting beyond the Spotswood so fierce, the usurper's pilots can't be sure the dirt they put down on'll still belong to them when they climb out of a cockpit.'

'Might be one of ours intercepting a long-range resupply kite looking for the King's Mounted?' guessed Carter. 'Those bushwhackers can't be finding too many bullets in their raids.'

Sergeant Densen rattled the half-empty ammunition pouch dangling from his belt. 'If they are, they're better at finding rounds than we are.'

Carter rested a hand on the gun belt with his father's expensive twin pistols; their weight a memento every day of all he had lost, as though he needed an extra reminder. *I'll hand them back to you, one day, Father. Just stay alive*. 'Let's ride clear of the woods and have a look. If we're lucky the usurper's plane will put down on pasture and lead us to that band of roof-burning bluecoats from Victorair.'

'Not sure I'd call that luck,' said Densen, 'but the job needs doing, and we're the only fools on the hunt for them in this forest.'

In truth, hunting any band of marauders in Weyland was tough work; there was so much empty territory for bandits to hide in while towns and villages had to stay put, plump poultry marked on the map for every fox with a hunger to steer towards. When you were dealing with professionals like the Frontier Mounted, you could take that work and multiply it tenfold. Carter's Royal Sharps Greys put the woodland behind them, leaving the road and taking a direct path through the trees, cold dead leaves heavy with hoarfrost whirling around their steeds as they pushed on as fast as they dared across the frozen ground. When they broke the treeline they faced rolling flat land filled with prickly green shrubbery rising as high as a mounted rider's boots, a log fence close to the woods marking where a local landowner's territory started. Clear of the shrubs and further back the landscape sat broken by hills topped with more trees, thin stands of red and orange woodland, and above it all the aerial combat they'd heard. True to Carter's guess, one plane appeared to be a fighter and the other a larger, slower transport kite. Their exhausts had left white contrails scratched against the cold sky, doodles on a sheet of paper pointing to the combatants. Carter pulled his battered brass telescope from the saddle and extended it towards the wheeling planes. The fighter was a sleek twin-engined monoplane, outsized compared to the Rodalian flying wings Carter had grown up watching in the air – maybe a fifty-foot wingspan. Someone had painted a leering wolf's muzzle on the front of the plane and it was living up to its predator's colours. Wing-mounted cannons blazed away at the transport kite, a slow, heavy five-engined tri-plane with a sealed cabin at the front, a few portholes for passengers along its length and an open cockpit gun turret twisting at the rear of the fuselage, trying to discourage the pursuing fighter with insignificant bursts of fire. The transport plane weaved from side to side while the fighter spun around it, swooping in and out to leave traces of flapping fabric holes after each attack. *Wouldn't want to be a passenger inside that bird*. The tri-plane began to dodge erratically, a pair of engines on either side smoking as a matched set, leaving only three rotors to carry the large plane forward. Carter growled as he took in the planes' insignia. *Not what I was expecting*.

'Are we winning?' asked Densen.

Carter passed him the telescope. 'Hard to tell. Both kites are flying loyalist colours.'

Arick Densen looked through the eyeglass and nodded in surprise, seeing white tails with Weyland's royal black boar on both fighter and transport plane. The north didn't possess an abundance of squadrons, not when the skyguard owed its recent founding to the usurper's coin, but those that did fly for Prince Owen had painted their tails red and displayed the national assembly's flag as a token of support for Weyland's lawful heir. 'White on white, hell if that's something you see every day. If one of those birds is defecting to our side, it must be the transport plane. The fighter could outpace it in less than a minute, no need to engage.'

'Long guns to the fore,' Carter ordered. 'Let's see if we can't drive that loyalist hawk off our acres. Everyone else back in the treeline . . . the fighter doesn't appear to be short of ammunition. I want pickets behind us, too. If we pitch a picnic blanket below these two jousting skyguards, might be Victorair's bluecoats will join us while we're watching.'

Three men smoothly separated from the company. They dismounted and removed the company's precious *Landsman* single-shot long rifles, a separate holster on their saddles for extendable tripods that allowed them to shoot steady at a distance. The snipers needed tripods to bear the weight of the elongated, reinforced steel barrels designed for heavy powder charges and long-range ammunition.

Against the polished red mahogany butts and furniture, the plates and barrel on their rifles glinted as grey as the company's uniforms. Lacking the resources to mount a skyguard in Weyland, for centuries, the only carriers in the air had been nomads, traders and slavers, and the nation had grown expert in discouraging unwelcome aviators from its skies. His marksmen were careful and taciturn men, set up close enough to the treeline that they could retreat out of sight of an angered pilot. Carter trotted Peppercorn back towards the trees' cover, halting just short of the pines. His three target shooters were all ex-hunters from the mountains, tough and stringy even for Sharps Mountain men, well-used to bringing back rare pelts for trade, as well as claiming farmers' bounties on the lions that slunk down from the upper heights to decimate the cattle. *This lion's got wings, though.* Carter reckoned they could handle the famous *Landsman No. 3 Grade Long* when it came to striking a target in the air.

'Aim only for the fighter,' barked the sergeant. 'That fat pheasant it's chasing might be carrying right-minded Middenharn boys flying the usurper's coop.'

Carter heard the tone in the sergeant's voice and he knew what the man was thinking. That if a lone kite dared desert the usurper's command; maybe his brother's frigate would mutiny for Prince Owen and sail north too. *We cling to what we can in this war, however faint the hope.*

No sooner had the marksmen raised ladder sights on the rear of their rifles than they began to bang out shots towards the wheeling fighter, swivelling barrels and making each shot count between reloading. Despite using the tripods, the recoil blasts were almost enough to throw the heavy weapons off their mounts. The long guns made enough noise to raise the dead, but it was impossible for Carter to see if they were striking the fighter at this range, even with his eyeglass fully extended. He and his troops were being ignored by the pilot at any rate, worms beneath contempt in this duel of angels. Whoever was in the cockpit, they would have to be blind not to see the drifting smoke trailing from the land below. It wheeled tight after the transport craft. Being mostly plywood and fabric; the troops needed to hit pilot or engine to bring this hawk down. The long triplane started to lose height towards the grassy flats between woodland and hills. From its erratic wobble and the streaming flames clinging to the wings between its engine mounts, Carter reckoned it didn't have much choice in exiting the ill-matched aerial combat. If the transport plane didn't land now, it wasn't going to land anywhere except hell . . . and this kite was coming in hot enough that it might not make much difference. The skyguard fighter turned in fast behind the triplane's tail, trailing the transporter, but then suddenly pulled up and began to angle away, setting its compass for south of the Spotswood River. *South. Definitely not on our side, then.* The few precious kites operating in Owen's service were stationed north of Midsburg, away from the risk of being burned on their airfields by raiders paddling across the Spotswood. A lusty cheer rose up from the soldiers as the fighter dwindled to a dot in the sky, but Carter reckoned it hadn't been driven off by ground fire. It had held back from an easy final kill of the descending transport plane. *Out of ammo.* The enemy pilot was heading home to re-arm, paint a crossed-out kite below his cockpit and feel a few congratulatory claps on his shoulder from the squadron's officers. Carter turned his attention back to the triplane. *Damn – it's not going to make it.* One of the engines exploded as its undercarriage bounced off the ground, showering the icy flats with fragments of wing and engine, rising weakly into the air again before the plane's left wing started to fold in the final few feet of its glide, fixed gears collapsing as the kite's wreckage ploughed across the plain. The whole aircraft spun around, engines disconnected and wooden propellers severed by the impact. If there was any mercy to the landing, it was that the transport plane looked to be operating at the end of its range, not enough fuel left for fires to turn the debris into a flaming comet. The triplane slowed to a halt along the lowland, a carpet of wreckage in its wake, the triplane's body remade as a beached boat; the distant, desperate banging sounds carrying to Carter as whatever passengers and crew survived tried to smash their way free of the fuselage before they became engulfed in the final conflagration.

Carter stored his telescope. 'Let's go.'

Densen drew his rifle out of the saddle. 'Keep the long guns set up and trained on what's left. I don't want to dig up more snakes than we can kill this fine morning.'

'You're a cautious man, Sergeant.'

'Captains get paid for glory, sir. Mrs Densen won't thank me if I return to Highbend Springs less a leg and up a crutch. More work for her at the inn.'

And I doubt if she'd like it much if you never returned at all. 'Hell, most your customers are riding with us, aren't they? Fan out. Let's see who's worth a whole drum of skyguard bullets.'

'Those hares aren't going coursing,' someone hooted along the line of horses. 'Not after a landing like that.'

Carter kicked Peppercorn forward, the horse deeply reluctant to approach the fire. 'Less'n they're friendly, we'll skin them just the same.'

Horsemen from the Royal Sharps Greys galloped forward and surrounded the plane, rifles and sabres readied by the time the passengers desperately kicked their way through a broken door in the fuselage. Four men and a pilot, female, stumbled into the grass. The men all wore convict's shifts, plain coarse woollen shirts and trousers with heavy boots, all of them ragged enough to put a vagrant to shame, unkempt beards hanging from chins and cheeks, with thin, hungry faces dirty from engine fire smoke. The woman wore a leather flying jacket, but it was pulled over the same convict's clothing as the others; and she was standing next to a man . . . who Carter never believed he'd see again until war's end. He barely recognized his old friend now, malnutrition and maltreatment having taken its toll. 'Thomas Purdell!'

'Carter, is that actually you up there? Thank the saints! I thought you were being held at the king's pleasure. You look like a real soldier up on that horse.'

Carter dismounted. 'I might even do some real soldiering, Tom. But I'd thank an empty drum on that kite pursuing you sooner than I'd thank the saints.' Carter stopped. The gaunt man next to Thomas wheezed like a chimney, and he seemed oddly familiar too. Suddenly realization dawned. 'You're Assemblyman Gimlette!' He had been a whole lot plumper when he toured Northhaven, campaigning in the hotels and taverns of the territory; never known to refuse any plate of food or cup of beer.

'Charles T. Gimlette,' coughed the politician, raising a weary hand. 'Returned to the cause with a tale of travails on the way that would make a song fit to bring tears to the eyes of every true Weylander who hears it.'

'I'm weeping already,' muttered the sergeant.

'The captain here is Father Carnehan's son, assemblyman,' said Thomas. 'Carter Carnehan.'

The gaunt politician stared at Carter as though he was being presented with a ghost. 'So this is the one, eh. I helped your father on his way to rescue you and the others taken from Northhaven by the slavers, that I did. And what reward did I receive? Cursed as a traitor by a mad king. Locked up and kept on rations so tiny they wouldn't keep a street hound alive.'

Arick Densen glanced at Carter. 'This crew are for Owen, then?'

Carter nodded. 'Mister Purdell here is a courier for the Guild of Librarians. Mister Gimlette is Northhaven's elected assemblyman. Both of them seized during the coup at the assembly building.'

'And my two comrades are from the 13th Battalion, Humont Light Artillery,' said Thomas, indicating the men in convict's rags behind him. 'Bombardiers Kimple and Oatman. Our pilot is Beula Fetterman, flying for the rebel skyguard squadron in Chicola until she was shot down.'

'We were captured when the fort at Grand Valley was surrounded,' said Oatman. 'Didn't even hear the national assembly had been dissolved until a loyalist bayonet was shoved half up my nose.'

'Marcus ordered the survivors seized during the coup interned in a prisoner-of-war camp at Greealamie,' said Thomas. 'We were made to build it and then we were made to occupy it.'

'Only those the king didn't hang as traitors,' added Gimlette. 'I was forced to bury many an old party friend in ditches outside Arcadia before I was tossed inside that muddy camp, left to shiver in a tent in this foul cold.'

'And there we were stuck until a party of us dug an escape tunnel, slipped our leg-irons, and escaped under the stockade one night,' said Thomas. 'Reached the skyguard field outside Greealamie and Miss Fetterman here stole us a plane. Sadly, one of the loyalist skyguards patrolling the waters of the Spotswood proved less than cordial about letting us pass.'

The pilot shrugged sadly, looking back at the wreckage of the aircraft. 'Any landing you can walk away from . . .'

'Saints, but it is good to see you again, Tom' said Carter. 'Do you know what happened to my father?'

'Marcus has him tight as a tick in the palace dungeons,' explained Thomas. 'I thought you were rotting with him. I heard that straight from your Willow.'

Willow! 'She came to see you? How, when—?'

'Willow came a-visiting when we were on burial detail,' cried Gimlette. 'Along with that wicked-minded harpy who married Benner and turned the man against me, his oldest most loyal friend in the capital! I won't talk of her evil; she as good as wished me dead, said I was useless to her, party and parliament dissolved, with no home for Charles T. Gimlette save a loyalist prison.'

'It's true,' sighed Thomas. 'I got the feeling Leyla Landor's using your father's captivity as leverage to keep Willow in line.'

'Poor young woman,' wept the politician. 'Willow and her impending babe both hostages in the hands of the mad king.'

'Babe?'

Thomas glared at the assemblyman. 'I had hoped to give it you gentler, Carter. Willow's husband, the viscount, he's . . .'

Carter held on to Peppercorn's reins, his world spinning. But what had he expected? Benner had finally gotten his way. Carter had been driven away from the Landor's precious daughter, the woman given a patrician marriage the family approved of, and marriage not the only thing forced unwillingly on her. 'He has his heir.' It came out as half a sob.

'At least Willow's safe from the fighting, man,' said Thomas, but even those words seemed uncertain. It was the same platitude Prince Owen had offered before they'd fled the capital, and as true as it was, Carter's failure still felt like a knife filleting his soul. *I let you down, Willow. You were relying on me to protect you. All those times you helped save my life in the sky mines, and I couldn't even protect you from a marriage forced upon you by your own family.*

'And there's still plenty of food in the south,' added the sergeant, kindly. 'The League might not allow arms shipments in from the Lanca, but Bad Marcus won't let his court go hungry while he can ship up steak and potatoes.' Densen stared at Thomas, the politician and two artillerymen from his horse. 'Four more mouths to feed at

Midsburg. Well, if we can scare up a cannon, you boys'll be needed soon enough.'

'We didn't just escape to add four extra backs to the cause,' said Thomas. He pulled out a sheaf of crumpled, snow-stained papers secured together with leather twine. 'This is a sworn list of names compiled by the prisoners at our stockade. Every man and woman the camp's captives had to watch hung, buried or bayoneted in Arcadia by Bad Marcus's forces. Assembly staff and councillors murdered, army officers and constables who refused to bend the knee during the coup, small guild officials that stood against the new indentured labour laws, editors too friendly to Prince Owen's claim to the throne. There's enough blood here for even a false king to drown in.'

'It was a wicked terrible risk we took,' moaned Gimlette. 'If we'd been discovered, the usurper's soldiers would have hung the lot of us for treason and added our bodies to our tally with a grin. But we found some bravery in our bones, even behind the stockade, freezing in our tents with no fuel for a fire and the water rationed to us frozen in barrels.'

'We're lucky they didn't hang us for rebels,' murmured the captured pilot.

Carter ignored her. 'The assembly's never executed a king before.'

'This is all you need to make it legal,' said Thomas, flourishing the document.

'Might be it is,' said Densen, thoughtfully. 'What do you say, Captain?'

'That I hope the Frontier Mounted is riding a long way from here,' said Carter. Because his company was striking out for Midsburg, now. Battles could be won with words and hope and legitimacy for a cause as well as by bullets, and the saints know, the north had few enough rounds. The prince and the assembly needed to see this. Carter remounted Peppercorn.

He didn't catch the sly, imperceptibly quick glance exchanged between Tom Purdell and his pilot. *Just as they had known.*

'My gun's as empty as our fuel tank,' cursed Cassandra, watching the pair of Rodalian flying wings break patrol formation and curve away to intercept the *Lightning Gull* from two directions simultaneously.

Alexamir answered with an apprehensive grunt and she didn't dare take time to check the look on his face, probably not much different to hers. *So, what are the pilots' orders?* Talatala's citizenry would have found the remains of the nomad's primitive incendiary device in the burnt-out shop by now. Sheplar wanted her taken alive, but the rest of the town would want her— Tracer rounds cut through the dawn air, a dull staccato thud of shells flickering out seeking the *Gull*. But they were still too far from each other for the rounds to find their mark. *There's my answer.* Cassandra could almost taste her desperation, a hard breakfast to stomach; that she should have made it this far only to fail now. *Focus. Focus on the enemy, not your fears and fate's poor draw.* Should she attempt a landing? Cassandra glanced down. Whatever passed for ground lay cloaked by a mixture of cloud and early morning mist. She couldn't see mountain peaks breaking through like rocky islands anymore, so were they above the steppes? She fancied risking Rodal's mad mountain winds even less than the thought of having to abandon their plane in some valley while being strafed by vengeful pilots.

'I'll try and lose them inside the clouds,' announced Cassandra. She checked the fuel reservoir and made a quick calculation inside her head. Perhaps ten minutes' more flying time. *They'll still be scouring the clouds for us while the* Lightning Gull*'s sucking on vapours.* But it was the only way. Maybe she'd get lucky. Run them into a concealed peak. Cassandra would play hide and seek and land when she had no other choice. She began gliding lower, using the remaining force of the faltering trade wind to drive them down, the two wheeling birds of the skyguard having to push against the headwind. They'd stopped firing, saving their ammunition for when they drew closer in a minute or so. That opening burst was just to clear their guns. It didn't bode well. Cassandra remembered her flying lessons well. Every ace shared a common trait. They closed almost to ramming distance before opening fire. It was a sure-fire way to bring an enemy down, as long as you were certain of your manoeuvring skills. Only fools treated kites as aerial snipers, wasting shells on long distance fire and hoping for a lucky shot to find their mark. *Skill beats luck. Hold your nerve and hold your fire.* These weren't fresh-faced pilots straight out of the temple, then.

'Our pigeon passes over the steppes,' said Alexamir, his voice crackling hopefully in her ears. 'Their spirits cannot protect them here.'

'How can you tell?'

'Can you not smell the earth below the mist, green grass fit to feed your steed?'

She could smell the rich leather of her air mask. Her own fear, maybe, but no dirt. 'Are your people below?'

'Those left to guard our party's horses, perhaps. These borderlands are within range of the rice eaters' wooden pigeons, and there is nothing their patrols love so much as diving down to show their claws to fine horsemen. They fight like cowards, little golden fox. Only raiders as courageous as Alexamir dare to pass so close to the mountains.'

Cassandra doubted a few arrowheads would prove much deterrence to their pursuers, even if she could draw the skyguard close to any nomads. She remembered the jealous glances Nurai had thrown her way after she had been taken by the raiders. The witch rider was as like to aim an arrow shaft into the *Gull*'s pilot. But then, the woman had told Alexamir where to find her in Talatala. Perhaps the need to return with a prize was greater than the acerbic seer's jealousy of her?

She encountered no turbulence gradient as they dropped towards the white sea below, the heat of high altitude replaced by gravity's salutation and a cold touch of cloud vapour. In front, the two flying wings had marked what she was attempting and one pilot dived into the clouds to seek her within and below, while the other stayed steady, maintaining a bird's-eye view of the duel, ready to put a burst into her cockpit if she tried to climb for height. *Are they aware the plane I stole has no ammunition*? There was a good chance that information had been radioed through. Ammunition was clearly carefully accounted for in every barbarian army and skyguard, the lands at the far-called end of the caravan routes doubly so.

They were sinking like a submarine below the white vapour when the climbing plane finally found the range for a burst of fire. Cassandra felt a shudder at the back of her flying wing, a sudden unresponsiveness to the stick. One of the *Lightning Gull*'s two elevator rudders had been half shredded by the stream of bullets, pieces of fabric left flapping loudly behind them, and Cassandra was suddenly left flying a tractor rather than a scout craft, every move sticky and reluctant.

'That is not good,' said Alexamir.

'Thank you for the mechanic's report!'

She could hear the drone of the ascending fighter growing louder even if she could no longer see it, a triumphant tone to its roaring engine. No sign of slowing, it sounded as though it was still climbing. *I know what you're doing*. The pilot had marked their position in the cloud and was preparing to turn and swoop in a high-side gun pass, looking to place a second, fatal burst into the *Gull*'s rear quarter. She pulled the leather mask off her face, breathing hard in the thin air. She needed to hear what was coming next. Alexamir's muffled yells came in reaction to her seemingly insane decision, but they were no longer clear enough to understand without the ear-phones of her breathing apparatus. The enemy fighter's engine pitch changed into a scream as it began its dive and she counted the seconds down in her mind, before pulling the stick back hard and early, giving the *Gull*'s damaged elevator the time it needed to commence the first half of a loop. Her engine screamed in protest at the turn, not the healthy sound of a fully working engine and she prayed that it hadn't taken damage in the initial volley. *Come on,* Lightning Gull, *see me clear*.

Suddenly they broke free of the cloud's chill, pulling up and over in the open blue sky, Cassandra waited for her stolen plane to hang inverted in a half-loop before throwing the stick and stealing momentum, rolling the *Gull* into an upright position and leaving them facing the diving fighter head-on. She could see the skyguard pilot's surprised face, shocked that she should dare to pull such a manoeuvre – meaningless without a gun to unload into her rapidly closing attacker. The skyguard's features grew even more surprised as he dived past and her hurled dagger found its mark in his chest under his throat. As the flying wing was absorbed by the cloud it began to spin uncontrollably, telling Cassandra that the pilot had more important matters on his mind than shooting her down. Choking for breath she tugged her air mask back on.

'My knife!' Alexamir sounded indignant. 'That belonged to my grandfather!'

Cassandra turned them back into the cloud, before the second fighter realized the broken, corkscrewing plane fleeting past him was his wing-man, not the *Lightning Gull*. 'A stolen Rodalian blade . . . and now it has found its way home. Have you another dagger on you?'

'No! And you are very careless with my gifts.'

She could hear the drone of the remaining fighter, muffled by the clouds and seeking them out. A break manoeuvre might see them safe once or twice from its weapons, but they had nothing left to fight with, and time was on the enemy pilot's side, not to mention a fighter's swiftness and pair of working wing guns. 'That was the gift of life, for the both of us.'

'You are a worthy sky rider,' said Alexamir, grudgingly. 'Do you ride a horse so well?'

Cassandra remembered the largely ceremonial training she had received from a foreign cavalryman called Kele. Vandians valued practical, modern fighting skills, as well as the unarmed combat expertise needed for duels and the arena. But she'd yet to witness a duel fought on horseback. 'I won't fall off.' *Too often.*

'That is good to hear. Silence your engine,' said Alexamir.

Glide right past the enemy fighter inside the clouds? No engine noise for its pilot to track. It might work, but there was a fatal risk. 'If I switch the engine off, I might be unable to start it without someone to turn the propeller on ignition.'

'Restart the engine on a dive,' said Alexamir. 'The force of passing air should rotate the wooden blade on this pigeon's beak well enough and breathe life back into her.'

How the hell do you know that? He was suspiciously well informed about aerial tactics for a barbarian. Such advice would never have worked on a decently modern rocket craft, but on this rickety, hand-crafted hunk of carpentry? *It just might.* She reached out to the control panel and felt a shiver of apprehension as she switched the engine off, the reassuring vibration replaced by the hissing passage of wind across the flying wing's body. Apart from the flapping of their shattered elevator rudder, there was only the enemy fighter's whirr, buzzing louder as it drew close.

'Glide above him,' said Alexamir, whispering through the communication tube, even though there was little chance any pilot could overhear them in the air. 'He will be looking down, not up, seeing if our silence betokens the wooden pigeon remade as cruel wreckage on the ground.'

Cassandra took his suggestion and started a gentle climb. The erratic warm updrafts made for a choppy rise, especially on a single elevator flap, pulling the *Gull* over at an angle.

'There is only one rice eater's neck for me to break,' announced Alexamir, before ripping his mask off and standing up inside the spotter's cockpit. Cassandra barely had time to register that he'd strapped his parachute on, and then she was watching the insane nomad leap into the white ocean towards the passing shadow below. His final battle yell faded into the clouds. 'Not too much for Alexamir!'

Judging by the unexpected pitch-turn the shadow executed as it vanished with a throaty engine growl, the single-man fighter had unexpectedly found itself flying with a dangerously deranged stowaway. This had been Alexamir's real plan all along. Climb for height. Leap across and kill the enemy with his bare hands. How often had he made such a leap from a horse? *Idiot man. Is this my fault? Did I shame him into suicide by taking down the first skyguard*? But she felt nagging doubts. Alexamir's clever scheme for killing the engine and gliding past. And someone had trained him how to use a parachute, and that someone wasn't any blue-skinned savage expert in breaking unridden foals. She pushed the puzzle out of her mind. *I need to restart the* Gull; *follow him down and hope his mystery tutor showed him what the chute's ripcord is for*. She heard a chatter of wing guns. A dying skyguard accidentally kicking the trigger in his final death throes, or a vengeful pilot opening up on a lone descending parachute? Cassandra tilted the plane down, wind rushing fast past her head in a roar. She fired the ignition switch, checking the rear of the *Gull*. Windflow turned the single rotor fast and it spun back into life, but her engine's reassuring hum was replaced by a coughing rumble and then a thick black cloud trailing like a banner behind her, flames leaping along the broken elevator's loose fabric. *Oh my sweet ancestors, that first burst did find more than an elevator flap*. She killed the engine before the fire spread any further, reaching under her chair and locating the canvas pouch for the pilot's parachute, the *empty* pouch. Her only means of escape was resting on some bench back in Talatala, probably awaiting a safety inspection for tears and rent in the silk. A safety check that had just killed her. She burst out of the clouds, scattering a flight of kestrels, a view of green plains and endless rolling hills with a few stands of larch jolting beyond the nosecone, her broken flying wing trembling with turbulence. Rodal's mountains stood like a row of black rotten teeth far behind her, sharp and cannibal. She tried to ignore the heat at her back, the crackling flames fanned by the wind of her diving aircraft. No sign of downed debris from her enemies or Alexamir's floating chute. Cassandra attempted to level up in the glide, but her remaining functional elevator flap hung jouncing in the wind, become a fiery, useless mass. Prayers in elaborate temple script burned black along the length of the wing around her, Rodal's spirits casting their final curse. If the engine's fuel reservoir hadn't already been drained, her poor wounded *Gull* would have been a blazing ball of wreckage scratched across the sky by now. *I escaped. I escaped, and I did it on my own.* How proud her father would have been of her. *I'll know for sure when I meet him.* She finally lost command of the plane, not enough of her rudders, flaps and control pulleys left to influence the gliding *Lightning Gull*.

The wild grassland rose up to welcome her uncontrolled and spiralling dive.

ELEVEN

FAMILY REUNIONS

Willow was about to walk into an expensive restaurant high on the hill overlooking the capital when Nocks grabbed her arm; the odious man's fingers biting into her flesh. 'You remember the mistress's commands, girly. Give your brother honey and spread it on thick. I'll be standing behind old man Benner and listening to every word you say; his loyal old sergeant watching his back. One word against us or the king, one word for the rebels, and I'll finish the job on your precious Carter Carnehan that I started in Hawkland Park. A whipping will be the best of it for him.'

'Your mistress will have her words,' spat Willow. *May she choke on them in childbirth.* Willow chided herself for her malice. *At least, let the witch perish in childbirth after her poor baby's delivered.* Another innocent was about to enter the world; Holten had been confined in her rooms and surrounded by experienced midwives and the finest doctors the Landor fortune could command. Willow had a greater appreciation of the fragility of life since her own condition had made itself known. She could no longer read the stories of fighting in the newspapers without weeping until the sheets were soaked through. Combat fiercest in the contested central prefectures split between Owen and Marcus, Humont, Chicola and Bolesland. Each soldier – rebel or royalist – was the child of some mother somewhere, praying for her child's safe, unwounded return. Nocks conversed with the coach driver and the coach rattling away down the street, then the odious little manservant ventured inside the restaurant to check their reservation. Willow stared at the view. She was close to the top of the hill where the cathedral stood like a citadel, Arcadia spread out before her under a cold, clear sky. The canals' concentric rings dotted with flat boats, smoke from hundreds of chimneys rising up above the city, a couple of tri-wing aircraft patrolling over the harbour and the sea beyond, the sound of engines lost on the slope. Across from Willow on Assembly Hill, the domed parliament building sat empty and silent. Most of the honest assemblymen had fled north while the remainder languished in jail or prison camps. No, from up here you wouldn't know the deep trouble the realm was in.

Willow walked into the restaurant entrance hall, removing her coat as the warmth rose. One of the staff took the coat and cloak from her. She could see into the three dining rooms ahead, two with hillside views, a cheaper chamber looking out on a street – and even its menu expensive – a high desk with a reservation clerk behind it standing sentry for all three rooms. Willow could see many diners seated in the establishment wore similarly silly uniforms to the clothes her father had ordered made. Mill overseers one day, majors and captains the next, swept up in the patriotic fervour fanned by the king's allies and the press. *Like children playing at killing, except the murder is real.* If that wasn't bad enough, half the remaining tables were filled by Vandians, even the empire's common soldiers living like lords in the capital. Unlike the other locals here, Willow knew the true cost of the coins those troops threw around with such abandon. *Blood money. Paid for by the lives of their slaves in the mines.*

As Willow entered she almost collided with a group of laughing women withdrawing, obviously the worse for wear from drink. They wore green Vandian fleet uniforms, ill-fitting to match their ill-discipline and raucous laughter, like girls playing dress-up in their fathers' clothes. The only way they could have looked more ridiculous was if they'd come into the capital wearing the armoured breastplates of the imperium's legionaries. Steel-backs, as the newspapers had nicknamed the imperium's common soldiers. The legionaries might look oddly archaic, but Willow knew from bitter experience how well the light artificial material the armour was formed from could slow and halt a bullet. These women's dress and their flawless beauty marked them out as a party of Vandian camp followers, one of many currently carousing across the capital while their officers plotted and planned their coming victory. *Welcomed by the locals for their money if not for their manners.* A wild voice among the group soared in Willow's direction and she was shocked to realize that she actually knew the woman braying at her. *Adella Cheyenne!*

'Willow Landor. Little Willow!'

'Adella, I never thought I'd see you again,' said Willow. 'Certainly not here . . . in Weyland.'

'I know,' Adella giggled. 'It's so dull and provincial. But I'm to be a wife to Baron Machus, and he's second-in-command of the fleet. Machus is here and where he travels so must I.'

'A *wife*? But the baron grabbed you from the sky mines? You're home now. You could slip away, travel back to Northhaven?'

'And why in the world would I wish to set foot in Northhaven?' she slurred. 'To have your marvellous father tell me I'm not good enough to marry his precious son again? To have the great Benner Landor stare down his fat nose at me? I have moved on so much from those sad old days. My star's risen far into the firmament, my fortune as good as the baron's gold.'

'To see *your* family, Adella. Don't you know how they suffered after you were taken by the slavers? More than any family in Northhaven, especially when so many of us came home and you weren't among those rescued.'

'I don't require rescuing,' spat Adella. 'Not then, not now.'

'They need to hear from you again.'

'You dare to lecture me?' Adella's words escaped in a shriek. 'You look to your own family first. It's no wonder that Duncan decided to stay in Vandia; caught between your constant carping and your father's smug humbug. But then, Duncan receives other rewards, I believe . . . He's a sleek little pet for Princess Helrena to cuddle when she's bored.'

'How can you be so cruel? You loved my brother once.'

'Did I? Perhaps. Even I can make a mistake, I suppose.'

'Go home, Adella. Your parents are old and heartbroken. They deserve to know you're alive and safe before they pass.'

'Maybe I will,' Adella tittered as her companions grew bored of the distraction and started to tug her outside with them. She called back, 'They'll bend their knee to the baron quickly enough when the fleet flies north to smash the rebels. It'll be fun to have all the commoners in Northhaven bowing and scraping before me.'

Nocks came into the hall from a serving corridor, alongside a waiter who surreptitiously slipped the manservant a coin. *A little scratch for booking the reservation here, no doubt.* The wretch stared appreciatively at the bevy of beautiful women swaying uncertainly outside. 'Those Vandian lords know how to live. Of course, a man has to be richer than chicken gravy to take on more'n a single wife. And it's a fool who keeps a stable, when he can rent his ride by the hour.'

'Fools all over,' said Willow, watching Adella depart. And she was willing to bet that every whore who'd ever lain with a pig like Nocks had a special price just for him. *Double or treble*?

Nocks grabbed her arm and squeezed her flesh. 'Just you bring a little of *their* attention to your brother when he sits down. Duncan hasn't arrived yet, but your old man's waiting inside for you. Now, move.'

Willow shook his grip off and followed the head waiter inside. Benner Landor had a fine view of the city below and the Lancean Ocean beyond. He was seated at a round white linen-covered table large enough to host a party of ten.

'Have you seen the prices?' grumbled her father, tapping the oblong of card. 'Even I won't be able to afford to eat here soon.'

'I'm sure you'll cope,' was all that Willow managed as she sat down. Prices had risen rapidly as the civil war's flames fanned higher; from horses to flour, clothing to milk. Those that should be working in factories had been conscripted into fighting regiments and marched north. Hands that should be tilling soil, turning bullets on lathes instead. And that had been before the Vandians arrived . . . even the lowliest legionary was flush with enough silver and gold to make the king's already heavily adulterated currency look as devalued as a barbarian's wooden trading coins. Willow knew things would grow far worse if the fighting wasn't over by spring, when Weylanders fighting the war would be needed in the fields and farms.

Nocks picked his way through the restaurant and took up position behind the table. 'I asked the coachman to return to the hotel, Colonel, and come back when there's news about the mistress.'

Colonel. How strange her father's fresh title sounded to Willow. At least the *'my lord'* Nocks once parroted was the same for a squire or a newly minted Marquess of the Borderlands. *Well, that's the least of this bloody war's changes.*

Benner Landor waved his hand perfunctorily 'Leyla's in the hands of the midwives, Nocks. Let them earn their fees. I asked William to look in on my wife, too.'

A duty that Willow's unwanted husband was no doubt all too happy to perform. Willow suspected that the twin evils of her life, Leyla and Wallingbeck, had been far more than just political allies in the past. But it would be pointless to present such suspicions to her father. Willow had little proof, and any complaints she voiced would be taken as further evidence of malice towards her stepmother. *In the hands of the midwives.* Was that a slight coolness she detected in her father's words regarding his young wife? Willow felt a surge of hope. Was Duncan's return undermining that foul woman's position in the house already? *Saints, let it be so.* Willow glanced at Nocks hoping to find some hint of disapproval, but the face of Holten's creature, ugly as it was, gurned back at her, unreadable. He'd make a fine card-sharp around the gambling table.

'You were present when I was born, Father,' observed Willow, trying to sound neutral. No doubt every word she said would find its way back to Holten.

'In those days we lived too far from town for a doctor to reach us,' said Benner. 'And we could hardly have afforded their services, besides. Things have changed for the family now.'

Willow remembered her mother and could hardly contain her tears. Her father's large hands enclosing hers during the funeral; Duncan by their side, no amount of wealth or land held able to induce Lorenn Landor's return from heaven. *Things have changed.* Everything from that moment had been a slow slide into decline. And now the country had joined Willow in her misery, as fractured and cracked as what passed for her family these days. *I'm glad you're not here to see this, Mother.*

Married off to a foul instrument of Holten's malice. The product of a rape swelling her womb. Willow as good as disinherited. *And those I do love?* Carter and Father Carnehan at the mercy of the king and his brutes. *And now the prodigal son had finally returned from his self-imposed exile*. Well, Willow would have to see if she could turn her brother's reappearance to her advantage. With Holten in her rented townhouse, grunting and screaming as a new beneficiary to the Landor fortune found himself squeezed into the world . . . well, the birthing stool was no place to play games against the House of Landor's true heir.

Willow sat alone with her worries, struggling to make small talk for half an hour with a father she scarcely knew anymore, until Duncan walked into the restaurant. How different he was from their last angry meeting inside the empire. Her brother wore a dark green velvet Vandian fleet jacket with a high collar, an ugly-looking pistol hanging from a copper-coloured belt with a gold metal hook buckle, his stride stiff and proud in black cloth trousers.

She thought she could cope with seeing Duncan again. Wearing the uniform of the empire. But the bile that rose inside Willow as a reaction to her brother surprised even her. 'Why have you come to Weyland, Duncan? As you can see, the country's got enough problems of its own to deal with.'

'Your brother's come *home*,' said Benner Landor, his face colouring with irritation at her greeting.

Nocks bent down to refill Willow's wine glass and whispered, 'Careful, girly,' in her ear. Willow did her best to ignore the blue-uniformed beast.

'Weyland doesn't feel like my home anymore,' said Duncan. She noted a distance in his tone, as though he was hardly present. 'I have made a new life for myself in the imperium.'

'You're not coming back to Northhaven?' said Benner, unable to conceal his disappointment. 'You are my first-born . . . boy, you are the heir to Hawkland Park and the house's holdings.'

Duncan shook his head. 'No. I *was*. I'm not that Weylander anymore. Now I'm Duncan Landor, a citizen of the Vandian imperium, in the service of Princess Helrena – a daughter of the emperor and empire both. You should see Vandia, Father, it's like a dream. You could hide Weyland inside a single imperial province. Buildings there are as high as mountains and cities are as large as prefectures, food and entertainment free for the Vandian populace. They have machines and skills that the average Weylander would think magic.'

'A dream for *some*,' said Willow. *Every idleness and whim serviced by foreign slaves and serfs*. 'You didn't have to fly here with the Vandian fleet.'

'Your brother needs no invitation to visit us,' interrupted Benner.

'I came to help rescue Lady Cassandra Skar,' said Duncan. 'Jacob Carnehan should never have taken her.'

Maybe he shouldn't have, at that. 'What is the girl to you?' asked Willow, curious at the change in the Duncan she remembered.

'She is my duty and far more than that. She was under my protection when Father Carnehan took her hostage. I have to bring her back. I owe it to Cassandra and I owe it to her mother.'

'The pastor,' growled Benner. 'All those years living among us, and not even his name was true. The hypocrisy of that devil, preaching compassion to our people while his words were tainted by the blood of hundreds of innocent victims. Jake Silver, brother to Black Barnaby. A murderer, a Burn sell-sword and a bandit. To think that his thuggish son believed he could marry you, Willow . . . it makes me shudder.'

'His son?' said Duncan, confused. 'You mean Carter? He asked to marry Willow?'

'He never asked,' snarled Willow's father, his voice swelling louder on anger and thick red wine. 'The boy broke into the park and tried to carry her away, as bold as any highwayman or scavenger plaguing Northhaven. We sent him on his way after a good flogging.'

'The apple never falls too far from the tree, Colonel,' noted Nocks, his sly eyes almost daring Willow to gainsay him.

'Never was a truer word spoken, Nocks,' grunted Benner. 'The Carnehans attempted to corrupt Willow's soul, but their wicked schemes were foiled by my vigilance and the kindness of my dear wife. But that's the past. Now Willow's been blessed with a husband worthy of the Landor line. Her firstborn is to be the next Viscount of Belinus Hall.'

'Then you all have what you want,' said Duncan. Willow suspected her father missed the trace of sarcasm she'd heard there. 'I require your help.'

While the only thing I want is to be far from here with Carter.

'Naturally you will have our every assistance,' said Benner. 'The land's gone to hell in your absence, Duncan. Rebellion and banditry and traitors at every turn; our own Gaiaist Party and assemblymen supporting the claims of some far-called pretender, seeking to turf the lawful king off his throne. But the saints are on the side of the righteous, or why else would they have sent the Vandians from their distant shores to make common cause with King Marcus? Between our armies and your foreign friends, we'll set matters right here. Restore peace and order and punish every rebel who has dared to raise arms against the king.'

Willow wanted to scream at her father. Call him for the fool he was. Tell everyone in the room that the South's precious monarch was a regicide who had murdered every member of the royal family blocking his way to the throne, and then sold off his own people like cattle so he could swell his coffers. Instead, Willow met Nocks' malevolent stare and bit her tongue.

'Not the house's help. *Your* help, Willow,' said Duncan. 'Where is Lady Cassandra being held prisoner now?'

'I don't know,' said Willow, sadly. 'She was in Northhaven, being moved around to stop the king's agents from finding her. Maybe she's still there. Nobody ever hurt the poor girl. She was very well provided for. A lot better than any slave was ever treated.'

'You were aware of this?' said Benner Landor, outraged. 'Of the wickedness of that pirate of a priest . . . of this abduction and hostage taking?'

'I didn't know anything about Jacob Carnehan's past,' said Willow, realizing how weak she sounded even as she said it; the testimony of the imprisoned guild courier Thomas Purdell returning to unsettle her. *I heard the pirate leader himself call Jacob Carnehan 'brother'. The pastor fights like no priest of my acquaintance – I think he must have been a mercenary across the water.* 'I still don't know if I believe what they said about the father,' Willow added.

'Damned if it's not the truth,' said Duncan. 'I was there when the pastor abducted Lady Cassandra. I tried to stop him seizing the girl, as did your friend Hesia. He put a bullet in both our hearts for our trouble. If it wasn't for a medallion slowing the slug and the wonders of Vandian medicine, I'd be filling a grave. I came as close to dying as a man can before the empire's doctors brought me back.'

'Father Carnehan shot Hesia?' said Willow, hardly believing what she was hearing. 'But she helped us escape!'

'When it came to it, Hesia knew what was right and what was wrong,' said Duncan. 'And what seizing an innocent like Cassandra for a hostage counted as. I've read the local news. The papers say the pastor was known as *Quicksilver* when he led his army of hired killers in the Burn. It's as good a nickname as any. I'd never seen a man move so fast with a pistol. Carnehan gunned us both down as cold as a hound's nose. I survived, but Hesia wasn't so lucky. I've stood over her grave with my friend Paetro and watched him weep for hours for his dead daughter. I came back to Weyland to save Cassandra, but Paetro's here to slay Jacob Carnehan. I wouldn't stand in the way of his revenge.'

Benner Landor banged the table fiercely, the others in the restaurant turning around at the noise. 'By the saints, he shot my son, did he? Tried to murder my boy! I'll leave Carnehan's bones swinging in a gibbet at Northhaven until my great-grandchildren can stare at them; have everyone understand that no man wrongs a Landor with impunity.'

'Are you sure of this?' said Willow, searching her brother's face for any hint of a lie. But she knew Duncan too well. She had grown up with him, and for all of his many faults, he rarely lied. Willow recalled the fleeting glimpses of the pastor's memories she had experienced in the sky mine as a by-product of Sariel's strange sorcery. *So much darkness, so much blood.* More than she could bear to examine at the time. Jacob Carnehan had told Willow that her brother had been left unharmed in Vandia, and that Hesia had chosen to hide in Vandia rather than becoming an exile in Weyland. *All lies.* And if so much was false, what else were lies?

Duncan undid a button on his shirt and pulled the fabric aside, revealing a terrible scar across his chest. 'That's where the Vandian doctors cut his bullet out of me. Put there by Jacob Carnehan or Jake Silver or whatever his real name is.'

'I'm sorry,' said Willow. 'Carter and his father are prisoners inside the king's own dungeon. They were taken when the national assembly was dissolved during their testimony. There'll be no blood or revenge . . . not for you or for your friend.'

'I don't give a fig about revenge,' said Duncan. 'Not over what the pastor did to me . . . a wild dog only knows how to bite. As soon as I've helped free Lady Cassandra, my business in Weyland is done. Perhaps the empire's business, too.'

'You may have forgiven Carnehan, but by the Seven Saints, I'll see the man swing for this,' swore Willow's father. 'I'll present Northhaven to the king, turn it into a royalist city, and His Majesty will hand me that bastard's neck for the magistrate's gallows.'

Duncan looked like he didn't care either way. 'Why bother? The pastor was a shattered man when I last saw him; as dangerous as a spitting snake and as insane as a hornet. I just want Cassandra back, alive and safe.'

'Weyland's enemies are Vandia's, now,' said his father. 'We're allies. If your abducted Vandian girl is being held in our acres, I'll recover her safe for you. You have my word. Perhaps when you've done a man's duty for these foreign allies, you'll reconsider your place among your real family. I can see that your travels have hardened you, changed you. You're your own man now. The decision will be yours to make and you'll call it true whatever may come to pass.'

Duncan nodded, seemingly satisfied by their father's offer and his fawning words of support. Willow was anything but satisfied. Her father's lips moved, but all she could hear was Leyla Landor's words. Willow tried to bring forth some platitudes of flattery and encouragement, but they choked in her mouth. *Oh Carter, we should have left the country when we could. Abandoned it to its madness. Taken Sariel up on his offer and escaped to some far-called land a million miles from this evil and insanity. This isn't my home any longer, no more than it's my fool of a brother's.*

Cassandra's muscles were stiff from the cold as she pierced the darkness of unconsciousness, discovering she had merely traded it for the dark velvet of a night sky spotted with silvery stars, more stars than she had ever seen before. Whole whirling constellations scattered above her head. She lay under a coarse blanket and a crackling fire burned nearby, the smell awakening a rumbling hunger deep in her gut, voices filtering in from unseen speakers. They didn't sound happy. *Who, then*? Cassandra gazed around. She was surrounded by wreckage, aircraft wreckage, but not the *Lightning Gull*... there was too much of it, a twisted wooden airframe with ribbons of fabric rotted by age rising up around her, clawing towards the starlight. Like camping in a broken, tumble-down castle. This had been a merchant carrier once, one of the slow nomadic cities of the sky. Cassandra remembered the still air above the steppes; there were few trade winds to ride and even fewer places to trade for fuel, making it a dangerous crossing indeed. *I'm still on the plains of Arak-natikh*. She remembered the last few seconds of her descent, but not the crash itself. The pain throughout her body spoke well enough for how hard that had been, as though she was lying in a bath of scalding water despite the freezing night; but there was little warmth from the burning, she was numb and shivering. A reaction to shock or something worse? She tried to get up, but while her arms twisted out from under the blanket easily enough, finding purchase on the icy grass in the hollow of wreckage, she couldn't stand. That was when she realized that the pain across her body burnt everywhere except her legs, cold and numb from more than the cloudless night air. *They're paralysed*. She tried to move her legs again, and when she failed, she slapped her thighs with her fists, trying to feel something, anything. But she might as well have been beating the ground for all the sensation that came from the strikes. Cassandra swore in frustration, moaning as she tried desperately to roll over, stand, but her legs dragged around below her torso; a useless weight of meat, no feeling there, nor the slightest evidence of obeying her urgent commands.

A figure appeared, tall and dagger-thin and almost as dangerous. The Nijumet witch rider, Nurai, drawn by Cassandra's convulsions across the dirt. She called out. 'It is as I warned you. The useless foreign sow is broken. Better to have left her in the Rodalian machine to burn... that would have been a clean death, at least.'

Alexamir appeared, looking as hale as when he had leapt out towards an enemy flying wing with only a parachute for company, but his solid face was creased with worry. 'Is it true, golden fox? Can you not stand?'

'My legs,' said Cassandra, trying to keep the rising terror from her voice, 'they're dead below me.'

'You are a healer,' spat Alexamir towards the witch rider. 'Use your skills.'

'It is not my healing skills that whisper of her fate, it is my Sight. She will not walk. I saw that when we warmed our skin around the fires of her wooden pigeon.'

'If she cannot walk, she will ride. Or let us signal one of Temmell's chosen.'

Nurai did not look happy. 'There are none due here for many weeks.'

'You used one to reach the steppes,' accused Alexamir.

'I foresaw where one of the chosen would be passing, as is my gift.'

'And you will not use your Sight for her?'

Cassandra did not know who the chosen were, but she guessed they had something to do with how rapidly Nurai had put Rodal behind her.

Nurai shook her head in contempt. 'To what fate, what end? Abandon her here. Perhaps the rice eaters will follow after their pink-skinned sow. The mountain folk seemed eager enough to recapture her the first time. What victory would it be to return with *this*?'

'You're lying to me,' said Alexamir. 'You saw this fate before I stole her from Talatala! You knew she would be broken in the crash. This is what you wanted all along.'

Nurai pulled the hood of her cloak back up around her head, but not before Cassandra saw the sly look she stole toward her, and she knew that Alexamir had the right of it. This had been the witch rider's plan all along. Alexamir would have gone raiding to steal Cassandra back whatever the witch rider had said or done, so she had reluctantly facilitated his strike on the Rodalian town, knowing that their escape would leave Cassandra a cripple out in the steppes. Useless to the nomads, and useless to Alexamir. Nurai had managed to keep the wild barbarian horseman for herself after all. Cassandra was cursed as surely as if the witch rider had slipped a blade into the Vandian noblewoman's spine.

She groaned in agony, reeling with the implications of her condition. It was more than her future that had ended out on the plains.

Princess Helrena Skar could not possibly hope to seize the diamond throne with a crippled daughter. Lady Cassandra would not be seen as a marriageable match for any alliance beyond the truly desperate. Bad enough that as a woman, Helrena Skar couldn't treat the great houses of the empire as endless breeding stock for the imperial harem . . . her mother was limited to the heirs she could personally produce. With a cripple as her only current heir, what would the house's chances be of prospering? *Next to none. I have to die here tonight.* 'Leave me. Take the blankets, kick out the fire and ride off.'

'Then you will surely perish,' said Alexamir. 'This cold is nothing to me, for Alexamir this is as warm as summer, but you will not last the night.'

'That is what she wants, you fool,' said Nurai. 'She knows what she is now and what she must do. Leave her a knife to make an honourable end.'

'I gave the golden fox my oath to show her the life of the free people, and if she did not like it, to send her on her way home via the traders of the thousand duchies.'

Nurai struck a hand out towards Cassandra. 'And how well do you think she likes that life?'

'Do what she says,' begged Cassandra. 'Give me your blade.'

'I will not. You may yet be healed.' Alexamir glared at the witch rider. 'This one is a base apprentice to Madinsar. If Madinsar says you cannot be healed, I will trust her judgement. But not Nurai.'

'You did not give your oath to this broken sow,' spluttered Nurai. 'You gave it to a whole woman, and a dirty *foreigner* at that. Let her die as she wishes.'

'No . . . as *you* wish,' said Alexamir. 'You see, but you do not say. Is there any crime worse for a rider?'

'Indeed there is. Being enchanted by a foreign sow who makes you forget you are a free man. Will you plant this broken thing in the ground like a root, build her a dirty wooden shack and grow crops around her body? Will you be known as Alexamir, Prince of the Farmers?' She hooted in derision at the notion.

'There's none among your people that can heal me,' cried Cassandra. 'I've seen injuries like this before, pilots dragged from crashed helos. Even the emperor's surgeons can't make such wounded veterans walk again.'

'She knows the truth of it, at least,' said Nurai. 'Though you would make yourself a fool for her. Return with this damaged flower as a prize from our raid and the clan will fall off their mounts with laughter. You will wake to find your horse stolen and replaced with a mule and a child's saddle.'

'My horse may yet be stolen by them, but a rider's honour is only his own to steal, nobody else's. She has my oath, and you, witch rider, have the only answer I shall give.'

'A laughing stock's answer,' spat Nurai, turning her back on them and then flouncing away from the nook in the wreckage.

Cassandra tried to move again, yelling in frustration when her body failed to respond.

'You can still ride,' said Alexamir. 'I will strap you into your saddle and you will not even think of your legs. This is how the free people cross the steppes. We do not walk like rice eaters hiking up and down their high mountains.'

'I release you from your oath,' said Cassandra. '*Please.*'

'You speak with the alarm of your pain,' said Alexamir. 'You are not used to what you are and yet may be.'

'I speak with a sense of realism,' said Cassandra. 'You would not let a wounded horse suffer like this would you? You'd say a prayer, take a knife to its throat, and put it on a spit for your people.'

'The free people ride fine horses, yet we are not horses,' said Alexamir. 'I know outsiders call us savages, but that is only because they are ignorant in slaves' chains, bending their knees to fools who have never earned the right to lead. When our elders grow old, they sit among councils of the wise and are attended by their sons and daughters. We do not push our people out on a cold night with a rusty blade and our best wishes for many good memories and the lives of those they have birthed.'

'I am not infirm at the end of a life well lived,' insisted Cassandra. 'I am young. My life's finished before it has begun.'

'I say it is not.'

'My mother's enemies will use my condition against my house,' said Cassandra. 'The imperium—'

'Let them bend their knee to another, then. What do I care? You foreigners would hammer a single fence pole in the mud and call it an empire, before proclaiming the closest rice-eating white-beard your king. You are alive, golden fox. Few could have survived that crash. There is a reason for your life's gift that only Kalu the Apportioner knows. And my oath is my oath.'

'I do not want it. I absolve you of it.'

'Then run away,' said Alexamir. 'For we ride for my clan with the morning.'

'You don't want me, you *can't*. What good am I now? Nurai spoke truly the first time I was your prisoner. I will curse your fate just by crossing it. I cannot go home now. I can never go home. You take me for your own and someone will slip a dagger between your ribs as a weakling.'

'I am my own man, golden fox. And you are wrong, just like the witch rider.'

Cassandra sobbed. *Run away*. That was one thing she would never do again. What good was a fighter who could no longer fight? A Vandian celestial class who could no longer rule? She was as broken as the ruins of this once mighty carrier that had crossed the skies of Pellas. How many centuries had it drifted in the high altitude trade currents, beating a course between nations and giving a good living to its people? Like Cassandra, it had been smashed on the windless steppes, no future beyond being slowly picked apart by rodents with its wooden bones a home for snakes. Alexamir left as well and Cassandra howled in fury and vexation, cursing the fates and the barbarians for hours, ignored by the nomads until the weariness of her wounds finally claimed her.

Carter stood in one of the mayor's chambers inside Midsburg, the room remade for a war council by Prince Owen. The city outside the grand palace-sized building showed little of the tension inside the council, but that, Carter reckoned, seemed par for the course here. Midsburg had been protected by two imposing battlements for centuries; an outer curtain wall sixty feet high, thirty feet thick at the base, that stretched for thirty miles, then a far older inner rampart half that height. Those defences and the protection of the enclosing forests and sentry tower-lined hills had bred an insular, independent-minded citizenry who found it hard to believe that anything other than peace was their lot, holding to the comforts of their wealthy city. Fed by the wealth of the Lancean Ocean to the west and the mighty Spotswood River to the south, Midsburg's sophistication – its burghers boasted – rivalled even Arcadia's; a prosperity that now fed close to a million mouths inside the city. *They might have a point*. Despite the number of grey-uniformed soldiers visible from the outlying military camps, you still couldn't walk through Midsburg without being accosted by flower girls and street walkers, or fight off stall vendors trying to force illustrations of the city on visitors. Since being garrisoned here, Carter had grown used to the wide network of canals iced over by winter hoarfrost, broad boulevards and park promenades blown golden brown with leaves dropped by long lines of horse chestnut and sycamore trees. Sewers ran under the city so grand and wide that locals even offered boat rides through them to complement walking tours of the cathedrals and galleries. Just to reach the council he'd passed glass-roofed pavilions filled with meat and fish markets as grand as cathedrals, marble fountains where city employees cracked the coating of ice each morning to let the fish inside prosper, and a greater number of imposing monuments than any visiting soldier had the time or inclination to spend their leave visiting. Theatres and opera houses inside the city offered entertainments ranging from the commonly lurid to chamber music recitals which could only be afforded by the most affluent nobles and merchants. Saloons, restaurants, cafés and taverns by the thousand catered to every purse – even, as he'd discovered, to a cavalry captain's meagre pay.

Inside the war chamber, multiple maps of the northern prefectures were stitched together and covered with wooden counters representing the rebels' regiments and the best guess at where the usurper's loyalists were advancing. *Like some damn elaborate game of draughts. Except thousands of real lives are lost with every move*. On paper, the royalist forces and the assembly's army were evenly balanced. Three armies apiece were raised along the nation's great rivers and the prefectures they streamed across, as well as named after them. The armies of the Dulany, Hicks and Boles serving the usurper in the south. The armies of the Perryfax, Spotswood and Broadaxe fighting for the north and the assembly . . . and the man who represented their cause: Prince Owen. The true heir to the throne stood alongside Anna Kurtain, listening solemnly to Carter's request, just as he had promised. The very least he could do, after Carter had presented parliament with as great a gift as it had received since being chased out of Arcadia.

'I'd like to take my company back out onto the road,' said Carter. 'Being in barracks here makes them itchy.'

Prince Owen suppressed a smile. 'Makes you itchy, might be truer to say?'

'Those marauders from the Frontier Mounted are still running merrily across our acres,' protested Carter.

'Not at present. They were sighted by one of our skyguards fording the Spotswood in Deersota,' said Owen.

'Looking to rendezvous with a supply train from the Army of the Boles,' added Anna.

'All the more reason for you to send my company east. They'll be back soon enough, with fresh ammunition packs and kindling for every town on our side of the river.'

'We have another job for you,' said Owen. 'Far more important than chasing down that gang of bandits in uniform. I have a pilot ready to fly you north to Rodal.'

And that's my reward? 'You want me to act as a damn courier for you?' spat Carter. 'Send poor Tom; that's his vocation'

'War hasn't rubbed the edges off you, has it, Northhaven?' said Anna. 'Just listen to the prince.'

'Mister Purdell is otherwise engaged alongside Northhaven's assemblyman,' said Owen. 'Parliament is acting on the evidence of the mass murder in the south and passing a bill declaring my uncle a traitor, guilty of high treason with a price on his head.'

Carter laughed. 'Bad Marcus is going to love that. Every poacher and vagrant in the south free to stick a knife in his spine and collect a big fat purse for his murder.'

'Sadly, the north will need every lift in spirits it can get. Our spies have sent news of worrying developments from Arcadia. Vandia's arrived outside the capital in force and struck an alliance with Marcus. There are imperial boots swaggering about the streets and Vandian gloves spreading a fortune in silver around the bawdy houses of the south. When the Army of the Boles comes at us over the river, they will be attacking with the support of Vandian legions.'

Carter growled at the news. 'Then you need me *here*!'

'I need the Vandian emperor's granddaughter here,' said Owen. 'As a hostage to blunt their assault.'

'That's a new tune I'm hearing,' said Carter. 'You told my father that taking the girl was a mistake.'

'You don't defeat your enemy by becoming like him,' said the prince. 'I still believe it was wrong to take her hostage. But I fear events have proved your father correct about my uncle and his loyalist supporters. I should have taken a blade to his throat before he realized we'd returned from the sky mines.'

'And *you* would be called traitor and hated for it,' said Anna.

The melancholy words from Carter's father echoed in his head as though Jacob Carnehan was in the room with them. *Owen's counting on too many bought people doing the right thing. I'm counting on them staying bought and loyal to all the money and position that's come their way. That's the difference between us. Though I surely pray he's right and I'm wrong.*

'No worse than being called a pretender in the south. And perhaps we wouldn't have a civil war sundering the realm,' said Owen. 'It doesn't matter. We are where we are. I cannot change the past. Your father dragged Lady Cassandra to Weyland with us and I am unable to alter the fact of her kidnap. But if she were held in Midsburg, the girl's presence may at least give the Vandian fleet pause from circling above the city and burning it to ashes. She may buy us a fighting chance against their ground forces. We beat them before . . .'

Carter held his peace and didn't speak what was on his mind. *We beat a hastily scrambled mix of house levies, mine guards and secret police. If just half the rumours we heard about the imperial legions are true, we're in for a whole different sort of war.*

Anna tapped a map. 'Head north and find Sheplar and Kerge in Rodal. Start with their capital, Hadra-Hareer, that's where your father asked them to take her. Find Lady Cassandra and fly her back here.'

'What if the south advances across the river before I return?'

'We have a volunteer locked up in a cell at the government building,' said Anna. 'An orphan girl the same age as the Vandian, with a similar build and face.'

'Midsburg's crawling with spies in the pay of Bad Marcus,' said Owen. 'My intelligencers believe they've already learned we're holding a young girl in custody who matches Lady Cassandra's description. We need you to return with the genuine item so we can present her during a parlay. The imperium will ask for proof the emperor's granddaughter is unharmed and being treated honourably.'

'And when I bring the girl back,' said Carter. 'Are you willing to back your threats against her with action?'

'If our fate hangs on murdering a foreign child, Carter, then we've already lost.'

That's what I was afraid of. 'I'll go to Rodal for you,' sighed Carter. He glanced across at Anna. 'You're wrong about me. I lost all the taste for scrapping I had in the sky mines. I'm only fighting now because I have to.'

'I understand,' said Owen. 'Though I do believe I can hear a "but" rolling about on your tongue.'

'*But* I'm never going to be a Vandian slave again,' said Carter. 'And we all know that's what the imperium has really come to Weyland for. Revenge and slaves, in lieu of all those they lost . . . and it's never going to be me and mine again. I'll fight until every mile of Middenharn is cratered and smoking and I've one bullet left, and that last round won't be for any blue-coat or Vandian legionary.'

'It won't come to that. A house divided against itself cannot stand,' said Owen. 'Our people will see what Vandia's arrival means soon enough. And when Weyland does, it'll finally turn on my uncle and cast him off his throne.'

Not if the usurper hangs us for his own crimes first. Carter said his farewells to Anna and the prince and stalked out of the room, biting his tongue and swallowing what he would say if he stayed. Carter was haunted by a terrible premonition . . . that believing the best of people was going to lead Prince Owen to a southern gallows long before the assembly could execute the usurper.

TWELVE

A SISTER'S SUPPORT

Princess Helrena stared out of the porthole in the *Fleetwing* while Duncan and Paetro rested on iron seats in front of her map table. Its surface had been covered with maps of the country; local charts secured from the southern army, marked with the war's initial skirmishes between rebel and royalist forces. Helrena's bare metal cabin inside the warship was as safe a place to plan unobserved as any.

'Did your family have anything useful to say?' Helrena asked.

'My darling sister told me that Carter and Jacob Carnehan are prisoners of the king,' said Duncan.

Paetro's eyes narrowed at the very mention of the pastor, hatred burning deep for the priest who'd gunned his daughter down during the slave revolt. 'Her account's been superseded by events. I bribed the news from one of our embassy's residents. The priest was recently broken out of the palace dungeons by Sariel Skel-bane . . . an imperial surgeon supervising the interrogation was slain during the escape, but he lived long enough to name his attackers. Carnehan and the Skel-bane are believed to be fleeing north to join the rebellion.'

'Did Carter escape with them?' said Duncan.

'I heard nothing of the whelp,' said Paetro. 'Just Jacob Carnehan and the Skel-bane. Perhaps the lad's being held in a prison camp.'

'That wild, hot-headed boy concerns me less than the Skel-bane's involvement,' said Helrena. 'I am beginning to understand Apolleon's obsession with seeing Sariel's neck stretched.'

'It was Jacob Carnehan who seized the young highness as a hostage,' said Paetro, 'not some hedgerow trickster with a history of tweaking the hoodsmen's noses.'

'Did your sister tell you anything new about Cassandra's circumstances?' Helrena asked, trying to keep the worry out of her voice, but failing.

'According to Willow, Cassandra was being held prisoner in Northhaven and treated honourably . . . but she doesn't know anything about her current whereabouts.' Duncan snorted. 'Willow abandoned her old friends in Northhaven just as easy she left me behind . . . she fled south and married a loyalist ally of King Marcus. Willow obviously saw which way the winds of war were blowing. She's ashamed of it, though. She could hardly meet my eye.'

'Your sister has much to answer for when it comes to loyalty towards my house, Duncan of Weyland, but I won't condemn her for pragmatism. I understand all too well what a woman needs to do to survive in this life. You lived alongside that cursed priest. Where would he take Cassandra?'

'It's possible Lady Cassandra's confined in Midsburg, as the king believes,' said Duncan. 'That's where the rebel forces have massed. She would be too easily recaptured in Northhaven now the fighting's begun. My town couldn't even stand up to a single skel slave raid, let alone a siege by the royal army.'

'Yet, how convenient it is that Vandia's legions must be deployed to break the back of the king's enemies at Midsburg,' said Helrena. 'I trust coincidence as much as I trust any word that passes through your barbarian lord's lips. Let us say she is there. Will the priest and his rebel friends harm her if the city is attacked?'

Duncan frowned. 'The man I grew up with at Northhaven wouldn't suffer a hound to be kicked in the street. But—'

'He's not the prayer chanter you thought you knew,' said Paetro. 'I warned you in Vandis when I first laid eyes on him. Jacob Carnehan's a killer. I fought with the legions long enough to recognize the breed.'

Duncan touched the scar across his chest. 'The journey from Weyland to Vandia must have broken him.'

'No,' said Paetro, 'it just ripped away his disguise and revealed who he always was. Your king accuses Carnehan of murder along with his brother, a blood-drenched local pirate.'

'The wretched man's past is irrelevant,' said Helrena. 'Carnehan didn't carry Cassandra away for a ransom. If the dog dared send a ransom demand to me, I would have paid him off in secret and arranged his execution the moment my daughter was returned to me.'

'So, we can't be sure Father Carnehan and his rebel friends will treat Cassandra honourably when the war turns against them,' said Duncan. 'What will Prince Gyal and Baron Machus do if the rebels threaten Cassandra? Would they offer guarantees and terms of surrender to Midsburg?'

'Baron Machus will march blindly wherever the prince orders him to, an obedient hound to the last. As for Prince Gyal, I cannot be certain. He relies on Circae's support to win the diamond throne, so the real question is, does Circae feel a shred of love for her granddaughter, or were the battles for Cassandra's custody only ever a ploy to punish me? Which force is stronger? Circae's supposed love for her dead son's only child, or her loathing of me? What instructions did she press on Gyal before we left the imperium? End my house's line or help save Cassandra?'

'Whatever Gyal's strategy for the coming battle,' said Paetro, 'it's obvious that we'll be the last to find out. I hardly dare visit Arcadia's taverns with the lads in case I come back and discover the fleet departed without me.'

'The day will come when Gyal is repaid for his insults,' swore Helrena. 'Every slight and snub. And my treacherous cousin Machus twice over.'

'Damn them all,' said Duncan. 'The prince and the baron, Circae's schemes and Weyland's rebels. We must make our own luck... rely on none but ourselves.'

'I agree with those sentiments, lad,' said Paetro. 'If we infiltrate the rebel stronghold before the assault begins, we can locate the young highness and free her.'

'A small band of raiders might meet success,' said Helrena. 'But we need current intelligence from inside the rebel city: where Cassandra is being held; how many guard her; what are the jailors' orders in the event of siege or assault?'

'My sister can help us save Cassandra,' said Duncan. 'She's well known by the rebels.'

'Well known? In the name of the ancestors, she helped ferment the slave revolt in Vandia. Willow Landor betrayed our house!' said the princess. 'It was for your sake that I offered her freedom and safe passage home, and she tossed it back in my face. Why would I ever trust the foolish woman?'

'Because she has no choice now,' said Duncan. He took heart as he remembered his father's offer of assistance, not to mention how eager Benner Landor's beautiful young wife had been to support the king's powerful new allies. Benner had much to gain from this civil war, and as much to lose if he fell from the monarch's grace, and Leyla Landor knew it. 'My family serves the king's cause. They'll pressure Willow to assist us. My sister is pregnant and vulnerable. If she refuses to help . . . well the fleet can return to Vandia with two extra prisoners for the price of one. Willow *and* her child. Between the threat of returning to the sky mines and my family's insistence, Willow will help us.'

'Our chances would be better with her to scout for us,' said Paetro. 'We can take a patrol ship from the *Primacy of the Sky*. Fly in high altitude at night, put down unseen close to Midsburg and cover the rest of the distance on foot.'

'Gidor is trading with the rebels as well as the loyalists,' said Duncan. 'They're a nation to the east and not a member of the Lanca. If we entered the city posing as a Gidorian caravan, we'd find a welcome selling rifles and supplies. There are plenty of Gidorian traders in the local market selling provisions we could buy to make our masquerade authentic. They're exactly the type of people Willow would take passage with to return home.'

'It should work,' said Helrena, thoughtfully. 'Yes, especially with your sister's condition showing. Who would suspect a pregnant woman if she turned up in Midsburg professing loyalty to her old allies? They'll dismiss her with the same arrogance with which Gyal slights me.'

'I'll speak with my father,' said Duncan. Willow had carved out a comfortable existence for herself as a pampered southern noblewoman. Make her work to hold on to her affluent position. It would be a fair repayment for Willow's betrayal in Vandia. Let her help undo a little of the mischief she had made for him, by leading them straight to Cassandra Skar. There was a justice to his scheme that could not be denied. *Your first betrayal nearly finished me, Willow. Your second is going to bring me everything I ever wanted.*

'I have never been comfortable in a flying wing,' said Kerge, bumping in his saddle, 'but travelling with the skyguard would be preferable to this.'

Sheplar Lesh understood how the gask felt. But it was not for nothing that the steppes were called the *Rlung'kyang* by his people – the windless ground. With no trade winds to carry them and an absence of towns willing to sell fuel, he and the gask could fly no further into the steppes than the range of a flying wing's tank. Thus it was they both found themselves in uncomfortable saddles on unaccustomed steeds, pursuing the bumo and the nomad raiders who had abducted her. Two dirty grey mares ridden out of the walled castle at Dalranga, a great craggy fortress and series of high buttressed walls blocking one of the few accessible canyons from the plains into the mountains. Rodalians did not like horses, preferring sensible sure-footed yaks, and Sheplar's steed seemed to sense his unease. *The feeling is mutual. My mount is as vainglorious and unreliable as the nomads we pursue.*

'Sadly, my flying wing cannot eat grass,' said Sheplar. 'Or we would be high in the air and not on these halting nags. Can you feel the girl's presence yet?'

'My talents have withered,' said the gask, sadly. 'I fear they may never return.'

Sheplar didn't like pressing the gask to use his tracking sense. Whenever the skyguard raised the matter, Kerge would retreat into a reflective, maudlin mood. Kerge barely bothered to pray in the direction of the universe now, while back in the forest, Sheplar had been able to set a clock by his strange worship of the fates. 'Time will heal all things.'

'It will *end* all things,' said Kerge, glancing back at the wreckage of the merchant carrier spread across the plains. They had discovered a camp fire inside the ruins, ashes fresh enough not to have blown and scattered, while cold enough not to have been residue from the previous night. At least the *dokhyi* sniffing ahead of them was proving its value. A monstrous shaggy pale red mastiff known as a door-guard by the mountain people, it was almost as big as a pony and used by Rodalian shepherds to keep wolves and leopards from their herds. As the soldiers at Dalranga had promised Sheplar, Golden-ears was an exceptional tracker, and whenever the young hound grew uncertain of the bumo's scent, Sheplar just dangled a piece of Lady Cassandra's clothing in front of it to sniff, and the dog would renew the hunt with fresh vigour. Golden-ears was also cunning and stubborn and demanded to be fed from Sheplar's saddlebag at ever more regular intervals the closer they drew to their quarry. Given the amount the hound ate, Sheplar wondered what would happen when he ran out of dried meat. Would Golden-ears abandon the hunt and head home for the large frontier fortress in disgust, abandoning his two useless new masters?

'You have a fine set of eyes, Kerge,' said Sheplar. 'Keep them watchful. We are beyond the skyguard's patrol range, now. Every mile we travel is claimed by the clans. Hunters may become hunted here faster than a biting grass viper should we falter in our vigilance.'

They pressed on for the best part of the morning, low grey hills split by plains covered in bushy grass. It felt warmer than inside the mountains while the sun was up; even in winter, a constant dry breeze kept the grass quivering like a living brush; the sun bright above them. When night fell here, the clear skies stretched wide and you could navigate by starlight as easily as if the spirits had laid out a celestial map in the heavens. In summer, many of the clans did exactly that. Pitching tents, hunting and sleeping by day, keeping warm by travelling the steppes during the freezing nights. By late evening silvery mists covered the plains, and crossing such ground in twilight was like fording an insubstantial white river flowing around their legs. It was queer having the mist close enough to chill you, rather than gliding over it from the safety of a flying wing. Sheplar had flown many night patrols from Dalranga during his years of service . . . the preferred time for nomads to penetrate Rodal in search of plunder and pillage.

Afternoon arrived and Sheplar and Kerge trotted up a hill to see if there was any sign of the raiding party before them; but they found only another empty horizon. The gask discovered something else by accident, his horse stumbling on a boulder. On closer inspection, the rock proved to be the lower portion of a fluted marble column, the rubble of an arch it had once supported long buried by dirt and grass down the slope.

Kerge stepped his steed carefully around the debris. A broken leg for either of their horses now would mean an inglorious return to Rodal. 'I thought the Nijumeti founded no cities?'

'They never have. These are ancient stones from long before the riders' conquest. It is said the nomads arrived here from the Karabak Ocean some six thousand years ago. Before their arrival, this land was a vast sweep of civilized kingdoms happily trading with us, but they were all lost beneath the thundering hooves of the great horde. Only Rodal's natural walls stopped the Nijumeti sweeping across the lands of the Lanca and conquering us all.'

'These are sad stones,' said the gask.

That much is true. These peoples had dreams and gods and families and legends and many languages. All had been lost, aside from what little of their bloodlines survived among the horde that conquered them. Dozens of civilizations, their songs reduced to a couple of inches of debris inhabited by chirruping cicadas.

'A lost age of peace,' said Sheplar. 'As golden as the fur of our hound, here. My people have only known raids and blood, since then. Every few centuries, the Nijumeti forget their ancestors' harsh-learnt lessons and mass to try to invade Rodal. Every time their hordes smash against our heights and we drive them off.'

'Peace,' said Kerge, wistfully. 'There is precious little of that outside the happy shade of the forests.'

'Your council will relent,' said Sheplar. 'I know it. Your banishment will be revoked. You will dwell among your forests again.'

'I do not share your confidence, manling. This is no easy expulsion to bear,' said Kerge. 'I was raised with the promise that I carried a golden mean, would make a significant contribution to gask-kind. My father said he had seen it on the great fractal tree, but he scryed it false. Any talents I had died with him. Did he see his own end in Vandia? He did not.'

'Or Khow saw truly, but kept silent and pressed ahead all the same. Your father gave his life to save yours,' said Sheplar. 'He knew what he was doing.'

'It was bargain poorly struck, then.'

'All fathers would strike a similar trade without hesitation,' said Sheplar. 'Jacob Carnehan crossed the world to save Carter when many voices derided his task as impossible and named him a desperate fool for attempting it. My own father's blood soaked the ground we crossed yesterday. He was a great pilot of the skyguard who gave his life to keep Rodal safe and free. I live and breathe because of his sacrifice, as do we all.'

Including you and your forest people, living safe in the shadow of the mountains, thought Sheplar. But he left the words unsaid. Kerge had enough troubles to dwell on. *I hope you are proud of me, Father. Rodal faces many new threats you never had to face. Civil war among our old friends and allies. Vandia preying upon the league like a leech. Lend me the strength to face my enemies, old and new alike.* When the other pilots training at the temple had wished to wound Sheplar, they had called him *togam'nagum*, little shadow. But if Sheplar lived in the shadow of his father's legend, then it was a shade he was proud to embrace.

'That is why you are here, to follow after your father?' asked the gask.

'I follow my honour.'

'It takes you on a curious path,' said Kerge. 'First the hard journey to Vandia to help free me as a slave, and then all the way home again. You know that the womanling may not have flown from Talatala with a nomad knife at her throat. Perhaps it is time to let her follow her own path.'

'The bumo is not just a prisoner, she is under my protection,' said Sheplar.

'Then this is not simply a matter of revenge? Redressing the insult made to Rodal by a barbarian who dared to climb into your town and steal back something your people had taken from him? Besting two of your skyguards in a duel he should not have been able to win.'

'Not for me,' said Sheplar. 'I follow my honour.'

'You are stubborn, even for your people,' said Kerge.

'Rights are stubborn while wrongs are oft pliable,' said Sheplar.

'No doubt that's carved into many a manling temple,' muttered the gask, but Sheplar ignored his words. 'If you wish to go back, Kerge, I will not hold it against you. Perhaps it is better if I ride on alone.'

'As I recall telling you in your mountain fortress, that I shall not do,' said Kerge. 'I may lack my mean, but I know my fate is bound to your cause and the Vandian womanling. If I am to find my path again, I must journey with you.'

Sheplar grunted by way of acknowledgement. Gasks were different people in the forests. Twisted far from the common pattern as they were, Kerge found the wide open spaces of Arak-natikh almost as uncomfortable and unfamiliar as the cold elevations of Rodal. Though probably preferable to the hot hell of the Vandian sky mines. *It's easy to forget that Kerge is still young*. The leathery skin and formal manners of Kerge's people made him appear older than his true age. Easy for Sheplar to confuse the boy with his dead father; even after he put aside their strange skin and pelt of spines, the two gasks looked very alike. Kerge had been snatched as a slave during his vision quest, the rite of adult passage among the forest people. Poor Kerge had asked for none of this. Still suffering from the aftermath of his father's death; acting as jailor to the bumo, then banished because of the gasks' bizarre superstitions. *Perhaps he really did use up all his luck escaping from the sky mines.*

They kept travelling, Sheplar feeling strangely adrift under the wide, open sky. This constant warm breeze would have been described as gentle by many visitors, but Sheplar knew it for what it truly was. An angry, unfriendly, alien thing. Back in Rodal you could navigate by the direction of a storm, even tempered and tamed where necessary by the temple priests. You felt winds rubbing against your coat and knew which mountain you climbed, which valley you crossed and which canyon you found yourself in. Here, the unceasing wind seemed to crawl from every direction, only reminding Sheplar that one compass point was as deadly as the next. This wind had nothing to say to him. Every mile they travelled carried them further into the riders' territory, making it more likely that they would run into a clan and be chased and harried to a fatal end; where Sheplar's bones would join his father's in this exposed, endless land. Taunted by a breeze that had expelled all spirits and only carried its own incessant refrain.

I think this wind is insane. No wonder the Nijumeti have been made savages by it. But then, the nomads had arrived here as savages. The horde must have pillaged countless kingdoms through the millennia on their journey overland from their far-called foreign ocean. Something about this land had sung deep to them and made the horde halt here. *You should have kept going, following the sun, you damn wild Nijumeti. Then Rodal would be a quiet, contented land, rather than the ramparts of the Lanca. And perhaps my father would still be alive for my family to honour.*

Sheplar made his decision. 'We must close the gap between ourselves and the raiders. If they reach the main body of their clan, the task of retaking the bumo will be made many times more dangerous. Their campfires' ashes are yet to blow away as we happen across them; they can be at most no more than a day or two's ride ahead of us.'

'Golden-ears seems eager enough to race forward, but I do not think our mounts will suffer a long gallop,' said Kerge.

Sheplar's horse snorted irritably as though it could understand the gask. 'I agree. These two mares are better used to a slow ranging in the shadow of Dalranga's earthworks. But they are not short of stamina. We must ride day and night until we catch up with the raiding party.'

'Will our steeds not then be too tired to carry us home?'

'Then we shall steal the nomads' horses.' Sheplar burned with pleasure at the thought of that. There was no worse insult to a Nijumet, and such a theft coming at the hands of a trespassing skyguard would be the greatest disgrace of all. His own raid would teach them a long overdue lesson about the price of attacking Rodal. 'The nomads we chase are diminished in number. Most of their band perished when the skyguard attacked their raiding party the first time. There are only a handful of weary survivors left, their numbers swelled by whatever children and elderly picketed their horses outside the mountains.'

'Those *weary* survivors broke into Talatala and carried Lady Cassandra away,' said Kerge, 'and not before they tried to burn your town to the ground.'

'The Nijumeti are a brazen, foolhardy people,' said Sheplar, 'who enjoy treating death like a game. I have seen hundreds of cheering Nijumets charge cannons on Dalranga's walls as though they were racing towards a market stall offering free samples of rice wine. But chain-shot brings down their mounts and makes blue-skinned corpses of the pests just the same. The clansmen are mortal and I intend to treat them to a mortal chastisement before we depart.'

'And such are the people we pursue?' said Kerge. 'I wonder who is the more foolhardy . . . them or us?'

Time will tell. They put ever more miles behind them, their hound bounding ahead, weaving through grasslands green then brown then green again, until it grew silver-tipped with seeds, swaying in the breeze like the surf of an endless living sea. When night fell, Sheplar and Kerge unpacked fur-lined cloaks and wore them wrapped tight around their clothes, continuing to ride, kicking their reluctant steeds on. Golden-ears understood what they were trying to do, raised as he had been on night-time sentry duty over herds of mountain goats. The rusty-furred hound continued, uncomplaining, even nipping at the two horses' heels when the steeds proved reluctant to ride on. Luckily they travelled under a full moon, and with the plains flat and uniform, they passed around the steppe's rolling hills and hardly faltered in their pace, never stumbling. With no fire and blankets this night, Sheplar came to appreciate how cold it became on the steppes, a harsh chill rivalling the heights of home during winter. If anything, the cold made it harder to stay awake rather than easier. At least their horses and hound had the exercise of the chase to engage them. For Sheplar and Kerge it was just a numb, cold pursuit above chafing saddle leather, swaying as they fought exhaustion. Thankfully, night proved short, sharp and quick, its rapid retreat surprising the two weary travellers, yawning and trying not to fall asleep in their saddles. Dawn's diffuse orange light glowed almost unnaturally, scuffing clouds crimson and so forked with blood-red that Sheplar prayed the sky was not an augury of grim events yet to come. Sheplar ached when it came time to eat breakfast in the saddle, his legs and spine burning hot with a hundred invisible fissures. He tossed strips of dried beef down to Golden-ears, who bounced happily around the irritable horses. Sheplar wished he had been born a great lumbering hound of a door-guard.

How can just sitting on a horse be so painful? I've stayed aloft in a cockpit for three days riding tall winds without half the cramps spawned by these cursed nags. Perhaps that is why the Nijumeti are so ferocious? Life in the saddle has made them tetchy enough that stampeding towards our bullets and blades seems a blessing by comparison. Hah. If I have my way, the wild rascals will have an extra reason for irritability soon enough.

It wasn't long before the last stars faded in the sky and the ghost of the moon dwindled away too, a warm sun sliding up to follow them in their pursuit. The pair's passage took them past more hills covered by overgrown mounds – rubble no higher than a traveller-on-foot's ankles – but judging by how far the ruins extended, these must have been once mighty cities of the long vanished local kingdoms. *What fools the nomads are. They could have kept the cities whole and made subjects of those they conquered. Lived like kings. Instead, they are still here millennia later, cooking meat on dried horse dung, stealing foreign brides and enduring every winter in draughty tents.* The evil dry breeze returned and whispered the answer in his ear. *Except then the land would have conquered them. Made them no different to the people they ruled.* All the cities had lost, the kingdoms faded. Only the Nijumeti remained. Sheplar leant over and removed the rifle from the saddle, checking it. Along with the pistol and knife in his belt, he was undoubtedly better armed than the nomads. Kerge had refused all weapons back in the fortress. Not that he needed them with his poisoned spines. How much use would Kerge really prove should their rescue attempt turn ugly, Sheplar wondered? The pacifistic gasks refused all violence, acting in defence only when battle was forced upon them. But when roused, they could slaughter every foe in the field with their toxin-tipped spines. The rage that allowed the twisted men's blood to quicken and release their spines also drove them into a killing madness to match any berserker fury. *Only the dead prod a gask*, was an old saying in Rodal's southern heights. It was no wonder the forest people were so calm and reasonable. Their spines were as poisonous to each other as they were to their common pattern siblings. A single loss of temper by one of their kind could leave scores slaughtered. Murderous gasks never lived long enough to marry and bring children into the world. Those who prospered were people like Kerge and his brave dead father. Sheplar wished he could do more for his old friend's child. It was a painful thing to watch Kerge when they halted, unwrapping the calculation device from his saddle and tapping numbers drawn from his mysterious fractal tree, cursing softly as the results failed to resolve in the manner his mathematical faith anticipated. Kerge could not see the future. Left cut off from his place in the tapestry of existence. Sheplar could only understand the pain of it by seeing how badly it affected his gask friend. *I wish you were here, Khow, to tell me how to help him. I crossed Pellas to help rescue your son from the slavers. But he thinks himself broken, and as long as he believes it, it will be true. How can I help heal him? I am not a gask doctor. I am barely even a skyguard these days, judged unworthy to marry the only woman I ever loved. How can I fix your son? If your shade is out there, watching us, send us a sign.* Though if any sign came, it arrived a few hours later and was not a good one.

They came across one of the circles of standing stones, lonely black sentinels covered in strange runes. A cold shiver passed down Sheplar's spine. This was a dark, ominous place, made more so by his knowledge of the stones' true purpose. Even the superstitious nomads had left the ancient stone circle untouched, though in truth, there was probably little they could do to destroy it. The circle in the shadow of the great Vandian stratovolcano had survived generations of eruptions and magma outflows. A nomad's chisel would, he suspect, make little difference, even if the Nijumet managed to overcome his superstitions long enough to raise his hand out here.

'If Sariel rode with us, he could open a portal here and we might travel back to the forests in an instant,' said Kerge.

'Then I am glad the thieving old rascal is far-called,' said Sheplar. 'I have ridden on the back of his strange sorcery twice already and I do not care for a third such voyage. Even the smelly one is loath to use the gates . . . he says these passages cross hell and each opening calls demons to the destination.'

'The venerable manling claims many curious truths,' said Kerge.

'If you mean he cannot but open his mouth for demented tales to spill out and build a hill of lies, then I agree with you. But Sariel did not lie, I think, about the demons. I caught a glimpse of the strange creature he battled in Vandia during the rebellion. If it was not a stealer broken free of hell, then it was doing a most fine impression of one.'

'You speak of dark attractors,' said Kerge. 'I wish I could find the truth in my numbers.'

'Perhaps be glad you cannot. We have enough problems with blue-skinned raiders and our troublesome little bumo. Let the stealers coil under hell while we mortals scurry on the ground below heaven. Should we never meet, I will count myself well satisfied.'

By the time the distant horizon had called down the tumbling sun, Sheplar and Kerge faced a second hard night's ride, and Sheplar doubted whether they could ride further without falling asleep in the saddle – assuming their exhausted horses didn't collapse first. Even their exuberant hunting hound showed signs of losing his will to continue, no more springing around their steeds. Golden-ears' snout was low to the ground in a slow, plodding pace. They needed to make camp this night. Sheplar urged his horse to climb one last hill to search for ruins they might shelter in, Khow close behind him. And that was where he spotted the camp fire of those who halted before them. Sheplar carefully led his horse back to the lee of the hill and returned with rifle and telescope.

'Is it those we chase?' asked Kerge, crouching down besides the skyguard.

Sheplar extended his eye-glass towards the distant crackling fire, focusing on the silhouettes of tethered horses. Six mounts. Too many to be scouts, far too few to be stragglers from a clan. Just about the right number for the raid's survivors. As Sheplar stared, he spied the dark shape of a flying wing's propeller strapped to one of the steeds. No doubt broken from the aircraft they had escaped Talatala in. So, it still amused the chieftains to use skyguard propeller wood to carve their seats? Warming their savage arses inside their tents on a trophy taken from their enemies. He saw shadows sitting around the fire. No doubt bragging of their daring attack on Talatala and how easy it had been to steal Rodalian women for wives. *I have extra booty for you; a little sharp Rodalian steel you left behind.* 'Fate smiles on us.'

'Is Lady Cassandra among them?'

'I can see only shadows at this range. But they have the propeller from the flying wing they stole, so I do not doubt they have our little bumo, too.'

'How are we to do this, manling?'

'Let us stake our nags and Golden-ears out of sight and then crawl towards the camp. You hide by the horses, ready to cut them loose, saving three mounts for us. I will grab the bumo. If the Nijumeti get in our way, they will meet my bullets; if our surprise is complete, we will leave them horseless. A long walk back on foot and songs of shame will await them at their clan, rather than proud boasts of how they set fire to Talatala.'

'They will die out here without horses.'

'I doubt it, but they will surely wish they had,' scowled Sheplar. 'Save your kind thoughts for the bumo. She may have been dishonoured by these devils.'

Golden-ears wanted to come with them, but Sheplar muttered one of the instructions the fortress soldiers had passed on to him, and the hound sunk to his belly, watching the pair of secured horses with raised ears. *Silence to protect the herd.* He and the gask stalked around the low hill before sinking into the grass on the other side, crawling slowly through the sward towards the fire ahead. With their heads by the rich dirt of the plains, waist-high grass swallowed the two rescuers whole. Sheplar needed to halt every few minutes, gently raising his head above the grass line to ensure that they were still navigating true. The land, already damp from evening's dew, grew moister still as a mist started flowing around them. *All for the good.* It took twenty minutes of careful skulking, the rifle clutched in Sheplar's hands, before they gained the camp. Sheplar jabbed two fingers towards the tethered mounts, and Kerge split off to flank the horses.

Save for the dull crackling of the flames, Sheplar heard only heavy silence from the camp. No boasts. No songs. No curses. Had the nomads fallen asleep huddled around their fire, not wanting to roll out bedrolls in the mist and wake soaked? *Spirits be kind. Let these dogs be insensible with pipe weed.* If the raiding party's survivors had been celebrating their victory, Sheplar should be able to lift the bumo's bound form over his shoulders, leaving the nomads to wake with throbbing skulls and minus their horses and prizes. It might even be worth abandoning his fine dagger impaled in the dirt of the camp, as a message that a Rodalian had stolen their precious steeds and left their pitiable throats unslit. *They'll weep tears of shame when they spy it.*

A little way back from the main fire there was one traveller stretched out under a blanket, and Sheplar recognized the long lustrous hair of the bumo. There was a stake in the ground close to her. *Hah, they have tethered her like their precious horses, and do not care to share the warmth of their camp fire with her.* No doubt the nomads did not find the haughty Vandian girl's constant complaints any more to their taste than Sheplar had. He crawled closer to the ground where she lay, taking his dagger out to slice the rope, and then bent over her huddled sleeping form, turning her body ready to clamp his hand over her mouth should she call out in fright. Except that her mouth had been gagged and the bumo was wide awake, her eyes stretched wide in alarm with her hands bound behind her back.

Sheplar felt the jab of the spear against his neck before he could raise his rifle. Nomads rose like wraiths from the grass around him.

'As I dreamed for you,' called a female Nijumet. 'A rice eater and a forest devil.'

'Find their horses,' whooped the muscled young male by her side. He swivelled one of the hunched figures sitting around the fire around, a tunic and cloak stuffed with dried grass, raising the arm mockingly in salute of his two new prisoners. 'These two won't be worth much as thralls, one is too old and the other is as prickly as a porcupine on the spit. I'll count their mounts and weapons as our night's prize.'

Sheplar groaned. A witch rider, and an obviously powerful seer. Kerge might not be able to scry into the future any longer, but the raiders could. And the witch had delivered them to her prancing savages like a gift.

Duncan found Princess Helrena alone in her chambers on the great warship, no guards, no Paetro. She appeared in a pensive mood, pacing along a series of portholes, the view over Arcadia's distant sprawl across the hills little distraction to whatever really occupied her attention.

'You have talked with your father?' asked the princess as she noticed his presence.

'Yes,' said Duncan, bowing. 'I met with him again in private last night. He will ensure my sister helps us. I am to meet with him later today to hear of Willow's . . . cooperation.' There hadn't been much joy in the exchange, but if there was one thing Duncan could always trust in, it was Benner Landor's desire to further his house's glory.

When Willow returned from Midsburg with the emperor's granddaughter, King Marcus would grant Duncan's father a lot more than a noble title to half of Havenharl. Willow would have no choice. Not if she valued the new life swelling inside her belly. 'And it seems I have a new half-brother . . . a babe called Asher.'

'Congratulations to you and your family. I have many hundreds of them, thanks to the imperial harem,' said Helrena. 'As well as many half-sisters who would happily slip a dagger into my spine if it meant they could steal my house's holdings.'

'Young Asher Landor won't have to fight me for title to Hawkland Park,' said Duncan. 'He can have it. My place is in Vandia.'

'It is of your place that we must talk, Duncan. I too have been in counsel, negotiating with Prince Gyal,' said Helrena, her words slow and serious. 'Seeking his assurances about Lady Cassandra's safety in the coming assault on the rebel capital.'

What did Helrena mean by *your place*? Duncan didn't like the sound of that. 'And were any guarantees forthcoming?'

'At a price,' said Helrena.

Duncan heard the apprehension in her words, his unsettled feeling swelling. 'What has he asked for?'

'My support in his bid for the diamond throne.'

That. This was the moment that Duncan had always dreaded. Would Helrena choose her daughter or her ambition? *Saints, please let her choose Cassandra.* She had to. This was all for Cassandra, wasn't it? Helrena had said as much. But Duncan knew how strongly she saw the imperial throne as her destiny. 'Gyal would have you forswear your claim for his own?'

'In a manner of speaking.'

Now Duncan was really worried. What had she promised her rival? 'You can't allow Gyal to usurp your claim. You must have heard the rumours that Gyal is actually Circae's son.' He reached out for Helrena's cheek, but she pushed his hand away. 'What is it? What has—?'

'Prince Gyal has said that I may yet be empress. By marrying him and ruling by his side when he is emperor.'

Duncan swayed with shock at the news. He always knew this day would come – Helrena having to make a marriage match to secure some vitally important alliance – but not with Gyal. *Not so soon. How could she*? 'This is madness. Circae loathes you. She would never allow this.'

'Prince Gyal calculates that with his house and mine joining together, his allies plus my own, the wealth from both our holdings in the sky mines, we could gain the throne even with Circae's opposition. In that calculation, he is likely correct. Apolleon and the hoodsmen will undoubtedly support me, and very few will wish to cross the head of the secret police. And of course, Cassandra would remain in line for the imperial throne, Circae's own granddaughter. In time, perhaps Circae and I could overcome our animosity.'

'Prince Gyal would keep the imperial harem,' said Duncan, casting about for something, *anything*, to make Helrena change her mind. 'How many other claimants to the throne would Emperor Gyal produce during your joint reign? You have but one womb to produce heirs to the throne with Gyal, and he would have every determined daughter of the emperor throwing themselves at him. How many of those houses would be content with Cassandra having precedence over *their* heirs? Cassandra would never sleep safe from an assassin's blade again.'

'She has never slept a night safe yet,' said Helrena. 'And Cassandra would have Circae scheming on her behalf, watching her back. Circae would keep her position as mistress of the harem, which is all she really desires. She would have her chosen piece occupying the throne, albeit at a price. Everyone wins. It is how the game is played.'

'How can it be worth the price?'

'The trajectory of my life's course was set long ago,' said Helrena, sadly.

'And us?'

'You always knew that this dalliance would have to end. Did I not warn you?'

Dalliance. Had he mattered so very little to Helrena? 'I see nothing good coming from an alliance with the prince.'

'I must set you aside, Duncan. There is always one rule for an emperor and another for an empress. Gyal might tolerate his first wife seeking solace in other arms for a brief period, but he would not suffer a long-term lover walking by my side through the years. Through such understandings are plots fermented and weaknesses opened at the imperial court. I have too much care for you to allow you to be shoved off a walkway in Vandis one dark night when nobody is watching.'

'Too much care for that to happen, but not too much to do *this*,' said Duncan.

'This is the way it must be. I will gain the throne and Gyal will strain every sinew to ensure that my little girl is returned safe to my house. Cassandra will be as safe as she ever will be, protected by both an emperor and empress in Vandia. And there are so many other considerations. Everyone in my house will flourish and prosper under the arrangement. You, Paetro, Doctor Horvak, the millions living in my district and across my holdings in the provinces.'

'I don't want money or power,' said Duncan, choking back a sob.

'And that is why I trust only you to look after my daughter and my life,' said Helrena, gently. 'And why I must set you aside from my heart. From now on, you are Duncan Landor of my house, not Duncan Landor of my bed chamber.'

'I have given up everything for you,' said Duncan. 'My country, my old life, the chance to return to Weyland.'

'You are a citizen of the imperium,' said Helrena. 'There is nothing grander in all of Pellas.'

'I love you,' said Duncan, his heart breaking.

'And when I am empress you and the whole empire will love me,' said Helrena. 'There is so much I have yet to do. There are things you know nothing of, that I must keep to myself, battles yet to be fought—'

'You are talking of Apolleon's schemes?'

Helrena nodded. 'I am.'

'To hell with him. Nothing can be worth this.'

'*Everything* is worth this. You have to trust me, Duncan. I must take the throne, whatever the cost.'

'So, I am to trust you, but never to love you.'

Helrena kissed him; a sad, lingering thing, and somehow Duncan knew it was the last time he was to feel her lips against his. 'Love me if you will, but take care never to show it in public. If you do not feel you can do it, then stay here in Weyland when the fleet flies home. It will be safer for all of us.'

Duncan didn't know what to say. He had been holding on to Helrena for so long, even knowing this day would arrive. *But never so quickly.*

'Do not think I am suggesting you leave my service for convenience's sake. I still have great need of you,' said Helrena. 'Now and later. As will Cassandra. As you point out, when we return to Vandia, the need to have eyes in the back of my head will increase not lessen. There will be threats everywhere in the last months to claim the diamond throne. Those who have set their sights on the throne for their own houses will be desperate to break my alliance with Gyal, and they will come at me twice as hard when they see how close we are to taking the empire. Will you stay with my house, give me your loyalty?'

Will I? Paetro's words during the flight to the palace in Arcadia had been proved prophetic. A life in Weyland seemed small beyond insignificance after living in the imperium. Arcadia's canals were open sewers compared to the endless towering majesty of Vandis, Arcadia's buildings a lean-to of foresters' hovels compared to the imperial capital. The House of Landor's grasping avarice was almost a joke compared to the power wielded by the most minor of the imperium's families. Vandia was the centre of the world. Weyland and the league, the whole Lanca, nothing but a distant backwood at the nub-end of the caravan routes. What counted as civilization here only subsisted on scraps from Vandia, passed between rattling traders' caravans for centuries until the metals finally drifted through Riverlarn and Creedlore and Havenharl. Duncan had seen the wide expanse of the world. His eyes had been opened. Living in Northhaven would be life in a cage; it would be no life at all, a mere existence, savage and constricted and forever haunted by the glories of the empire. *I can never go back*. Paetro had seen the truth of it, and perhaps Willow had too, when she'd treated him like a stranger. Even Benner Landor had forgotten he possessed a son, handling Duncan like an ally to be wheedled to his side.

'I'll stay,' said Duncan, reluctantly. 'With your house, not here.'

'Then we have our life,' said Helrena. She sounded as if she had known all along that this was the decision Duncan would make. *She's surer of me than I am*. 'And we will spend it well,' she added.

And how hollow will our victory be? Duncan had never realized he could feel so conflicted. Helrena was right. This unholy alliance would help bring Cassandra back unharmed. It might even bring Helrena the throne, albeit as only half its owner. And after that, the risks would never be greater . . . and *he* could play a part in it. Duncan Landor, former slave of the imperium, now a free citizen. And the woman who would be its mistress would embed him in the centre of all this, astride history, seizing the chance to shape the world, or as much of Pellas as truly counted. *And all I have to sacrifice to rise high beyond mortal dreams . . . is my love for her . . .*

Duncan walked through the corridors of the house behind a servant, marble floors and oak panels absorbing his footsteps. It was the first time he had visited Willow's new home. A fine old pile, but crumbling around the edges, scaffolds still up where repair work was being undertaken. In wartime such labour was hard to find, and no doubt they were paying a pretty penny for their workmen. They climbed a wide set of stairs and turned towards the front of the house and its commanding views over the grounds below. Distant music tinkled down the corridor, growing louder as they approached a double set of white-painted doors. The servant knocked, opened the door and bade Duncan enter.

'See that we are undisturbed,' commanded Leyla Landor, the servant bowing in response and closing the door to the music room. She had been playing at the piano situated in the corner, surrounded by leather divans for an audience that was wholly missing. Apart from Duncan, of course. It was probably true then, the rumours he had heard, Benner Landor's new wife had been on the stage at some time in the past. *She's certainly pretty enough.*

'I expected to see my father here,' said Duncan. 'To hear his answer and to meet with my sister.'

'I know all about the need to secure your sister's help. Your father asked me to ensure Willow's cooperation. He has other matters on his mind of late. Benner is helping the wet nurse take little Asher around the grounds for some air,' said Leyla. 'Benner is quite besotted with his new son. He even insists on swaddling the babe himself rather than trusting our nursery staff.'

'I can't remember him ever setting aside his business for myself or my sister.'

'He is older now,' said Leyla. 'A man's perspective on such things changes with age. You should not hold it against him.'

'You have softened him.'

'Perhaps. A female touch has long been lacking at the park. A house with no mistress is a sad and lonely thing.'

'My father can play happy families all he cares to,' said Duncan, not bothering to hide his bitterness. 'And my new half-brother is welcome to Hawkland Park and all it holds. My life lies in the imperium, now. Where is my sister?'

'I asked my manservant Nocks to escort her to a public execution outside the capital's eastern gate. Six would-be rebels who were caught distributing pamphlets denouncing the loyalist cause. Willow has agreed to help retrieve Lady Cassandra from Midsburg, but I detected a certain reluctance in her tone. A demonstration of what will happen to her old friends if she doesn't cooperate may help *soften* her.'

Duncan snorted. 'As I understand it, the Carnehan family are not in the king's gift to hang anymore.'

'Oh, but they will be again, if they're not caught escaping north first, or shot fighting for the assembly and the rebels later. A useful half-truth that will serve us well in rescuing poor Lady Cassandra from those who hold her captive.'

'You sound as sure of victory as I am,' said Duncan.

'Naturally. I was at court long before I travelled north and married your father. The north is rich in land and peasants required to farm it. The south is rich in mills and forges and such produce that may be manufactured. You can eat wheat and you can burn corn oil, but it takes bullets and iron to kill your foe. Even without the Vandians supporting King Marcus, the loyalist cause would have swept the north before it, iron against wheat, grinding them into dust. This is a rebellion with only one outcome.'

'And you don't question where all this new-found wealth comes from?'

'You sound like a harping Creedlore news sheet. You're not a stupid man, Duncan Landor; wealth comes from power and those who wield it. In this century as in any moment selected from the last ten thousand years. The only question is whether you wish to be the noble who owns the plough, or the back bent working behind it. I had to answer the same question many years ago. As did your father. And you know what answer he reached.'

'I was half expecting to arrive to find Willow had refused me,' said Duncan.

'I hold another card to play,' smiled Leyla, toying coyly with her long blonde ringlets. 'Willow has been unkind to the domestics here, letting her temper fly. One of our men ended up on the wrong end of a blade and did not survive the altercation. Willow could probably plead her belly and be forgiven by a magistrate; especially as she is Lady Wallingbeck now. But luckily for you, Willow is not willing to take that chance.'

'Willow?' said Duncan. 'Willow *murdered* a man?'

'What Willow endured as a slave has left her unhinged,' sighed Leyla. 'Full of strange fancies and seeing threats behind every curtain. Your sister has become a very different creature to the girl you grew up with in Northhaven. It is understandable. What a terrible trial she endured. Some people emerge from such a tempering as steel,' she touched Duncan's sleeve and squeezed his muscles, 'others are fractured by the same events. But if her crime gives us the chance we need to save your poor young imperial noblewoman then some good will yet come of this.'

Fractured. Duncan remembered the almost feral pastor of Northhaven, facing him below the volcano's eruption during the slave revolt. 'Some good, perhaps. You make it sound very practical.'

'Women always are, in the end. I have done what is required. I have bent Willow's will to aid you,' said Leyla, 'and I would have my reward.'

'Your reward?' said Duncan. 'When King Marcus can tell the Vandians that Cassandra has been freed from the rebels, I am sure the king will grant my father all the titles he desires. Maybe the old man will be made a prefect of the north.'

'He *is* an old man,' said Leyla. 'And the reward I have in mind isn't his to claim.' Leyla pulled Duncan close by the shirt, kissing him passionately until he pushed back in surprise verging on shock.

'In the saints' name, what are you doing?'

Her eyes glinted impishly and challenging. 'Am I so unattractive with a few extra pounds still upon me? I thought you northern men liked their women cushioned against the chill.'

In truth she was far from unattractive, but still. 'You are my father's *wife*.'

'Benner has not visited my bed once during my pregnancy or in the days after,' complained Leyla, her cheeks flushed with mischief. 'Was not this arrangement always about producing a new heir to your house? Well, Asher is produced. I know Benner would never have married me otherwise, not if he had not believed both his children enslaved and dead. He refused every suitor from the court for decades.'

'My heart lies with another,' said Duncan, but his heart had quickened at her touch, the hesitation in his words telling another story. Leyla was closer to his age than Helrena by many years, and her face was so pretty it could have been fashioned from porcelain. *And she has not rejected me.* Unlike the mistress of his house, this lady was a beautiful young woman who seemed to appreciate his virtues.

'I do not speak of hearts here, Duncan. I am still cursed with the blushing fire of a woman's youth. I have seen how these matters run many times at the court. Old men take young brides to continue a proud family's line, but spend more time with their estate's ledgers and the stable's hunting hounds. Those young brides eventually end up pushing around their husbands in a wooden nursing chair. I do not begrudge Benner this. I went into our union with open eyes. It is almost the natural order of events. I love him and will look after him until the bitter end. But I care for Benner too much to cuckold him with one of the park's staff. You may not want the house, but it is still your duty to step in as the heir where he falters. I have given you my support in everything, now it is time to seal the union with more than fine words.'

'I am not certain, this—'

'This only tells me how wisely I have chosen. Soon enough you'll be laying siege to Midsburg alongside Benner and Willow's husband, Lord Wallingbeck, alongside almost everyone in Arcadia I have ever known or cared about. Who is to say which of you will return, or how badly injured? I am a full cup which Benner does not wish to drink. We're both alive now. Let us live . . . you deserve this too.'

Those words sounded uncannily like Helrena's, remade as a command, and Duncan felt the truth of them as Leyla tore at his clothes and he gave up trying to hold on to his own self-control, pushing her down against a divan and drinking from her glass until he had to clamp a hand around her mouth to still her cries. *She's right. I do deserve this*. Duncan had set aside the house of his birth, but it seemed it still had duties to tire him. *Such delicious ones*.

All across the warship's hangar were engineers checking helo engines and cannons, blades suspended above the fighters' fuselage hanging still and quiet as ground crew drove silent electric wagons between the aircraft, long trails of trolleys winding behind them, loaded with grey-metal bombs and rockets, warheads painted with concentric yellow circles like the angry warning stripes on a bee.

Regimental standards hung from the walls, triangular tapestries on ornamental silver staffs; partially obscured by crates of supplies covered in black netting, officers in green uniforms with stiff, high collars, supervising lines of sailors passing the materials of war in chains towards the helos. Squatting amongst this organized chaos was the long-range patrol ship to be used to land in the forests outside Midsburg. Not for the first time, Duncan wished he would be going with Paetro's legionaries to rescue Cassandra. *I'll have to trust Willow*, he sighed. *And look how well that worked the last time you put your life in her hands*, mocked the malicious voice inside his mind. Unlike the other military craft crowding the hangar, the patrol ship was being stripped down by its engineers, everything heavy that could be removed ending up in a heap alongside the long steel-hulled dart. They were planning a night flight and stealth, the faster the better. Everything after that would be in the hand of the saints – and the loyal old fighter checking a line of guns on a folding table. These were tools of the legions' trade, not the primitive single-shot rifles procured from Gidorian merchants as their ticket of entry into the enemy city. Duncan drew closer. A legionary was demonstrating the hidden compartment they had added to a trader's cart, for concealing the deadly Vandian weapons until they had infiltrated Midsburg. Each gun had something resembling a large metal can screwed to the end of the barrel, to silence the gun's otherwise explosive fire.

'Are these those famous weapons the legionaries carry?'

Paetro quietened the other soldier with a wave of his hand and turned to Duncan. 'They're still under lock and key, lad. The imperial armourers travel with the fleet and they're always picky about when and where they release the emperor's bounty. This one's designed by Doctor Horvak, though . . .' He passed a bulky hand weapon to Duncan, a weighty pistol with a magazine jutting from a smooth steel handle; its black barrel flared and slashed with vents. 'It has the range of a rifle. Each shell is powered by a rocket and explodes with a grenade's force. Keep it for luck.'

Duncan took the gun. 'Doesn't seem like a fair fight.'

'That's my favourite sort – as long as the odds weigh heavy in my favour. I know this isn't what you wanted, lad.'

Duncan understood Paetro wasn't talking about the raid to free Lady Cassandra or Willow's reluctant participation in the rescue. 'You always told me the day would come when Helrena would set me aside.'

'I did and there's nothing personal in it. Helrena Skar was raised to be a princess of the celestial caste first and a woman second.'

'How far do you think can we trust Prince Gyal?'

'Well enough up until the point he calls himself emperor,' said Paetro. 'Beyond that? Only the ancestors know. It's been a while since an emperor's ruled Vandia with a first-wife calling herself empress. Sharing power is like sharing a good pie. Someone always ends up with the pastry while the other steals the juicy meat. It'll be interesting times for us, that much is certain.'

'And I was rather hoping for a few boring years.'

'The Skarol dynasty has ruled the empire for millennia,' said Paetro. 'It'd be a brave man who bets against them reigning for a few years more. Princess Helrena has promised my sick daughter the attentions of an imperial surgeon when she becomes empress. One of the high ones reserved for the celestial caste.' He turned to his legionary and ordered the force's weapons concealed inside the cart and then the wagon was pulled behind two others waiting by the patrol ship.

Duncan was glad for his friend. Paetro's daughter Hesia had betrayed their house to secure a similar promise from Circae. It was fitting that surviving these troubles would bring the old soldier and his family some measure of happiness. 'They'll be able to treat your daughter, I know it. If a regular battlefield surgeon can snatch me back when I was so close to death . . .'

'I don't doubt their sorcery. I'll do my best to bring your sister back alive, as well as the young highness.'

'You do that,' said Duncan. 'I'll watch Helrena in your absence. Don't take any risks in Midsburg.'

'You mean beyond walking into an enemy stronghold disguised as a peddler with nothing but a few crates of antique guns as my passport?'

'I mean like trying to hunt down Jacob Carnehan and settle your score with the pastor.'

'I understand my mission well enough. If I'm blessed enough so that dog's guarding the young highness, Carnehan's a dead man. But I know there's trouble enough on the table without me seeking out an extra helping.' Paetro pointed to Willow standing by the fast patrol ship. 'And keep your voice down, man. Your sister still believes they're enjoying the king's hospitality. It wouldn't do to disabuse her of such notions now. And I still say you're a fool to trust her. She betrayed us in the slave revolt. She betrayed *me*.'

Duncan reached out and patted the man's arm. Paetro's daughter had died thanks to Willow's foolishness, but Hesia had sold the house out and would have been executed if she had stayed in Vandis. Yes, Hesia had been murdered. But it was Jacob Carnehan who'd pulled the trigger. Duncan and the old soldier headed for the patrol vessel. Its rear cargo ramp was lowered, carts and horses ready to be led into the back, their soldiers dressed as traders from Gidor, wearing long green cloaks with hoods that made them look like foresters. Paetro went to supervise a legionary working on removing a large mounted gun from behind the cabin door. Willow was looking very alone among the burly men, and her gaze was cold and unfriendly when she saw her brother.

Duncan met her misery with a grin. 'Why so sad, Willow? You'll be fêted as a heroine of the royalist cause when you return.'

'This was your idea, wasn't it, not Father's . . . How could you?'

This is more like it. Plain speaking, not biting your tongue back on the hill in that restaurant. No false courtesies or sullen silences. My old sister's back just in time to help me. 'I might ask you the same question. I arranged for your freedom from the sky mines and you repaid me by joining the slave revolt. Do you have any idea how badly it could have gone for me in the imperium because of that?'

'You'd chosen your side, and you look to have survived well enough.'

'Says the southern duchess from the comfort of her husband's mansion.'

'You think I care for *that*? I'm not helping you rescue Lady Cassandra for me. I'm doing this for Carter. That witch Holten made it clear enough what the king will do to Carter and his father in the royal dungeons if I don't cooperate.'

'I'm sure Carter'll thank you for it when the civil war's over, he always was a grateful soul. Maybe he'll leave you a thank-you note after he's broken into your rooms and stolen your jewels.'

'You don't know anything about my life, or his!'

'I've read enough about who Father Carnehan really was, just like you. A filthy murderer and brother to Black Barnaby. That explains a lot about Carter, doesn't it? Bad blood follows bad.'

Willow snorted. 'You dare call his line bad and talk of murder? Between the usurper's war and the empire's revenge, you're going to leave a mountain of corpses in Weyland and our nation the imperium's dark reflection. Every worker a vassal and a handful of nobles living as high as slave masters.'

'Easy platitudes when spoken from the comfort of a southern lord's table, groaning heavy from food while half the nation's going hungry on war rationing. Spare me your judgements and your hypocrisy. You and your rebel friends abducted Lady Cassandra,' said Duncan. 'And now you're going to see my charge returned safely. If you fail, I reckon you'll be dining around a different table, the kind stamped out of Vandian steel in a sky mine . . .'

'I'm your sister!'

'And you're going to help your brother,' said Duncan. 'Just like a *real* family. After that, you can go back to your carriages and your operas and restaurants in Arcadia and all the rest of your high living.'

'I don't want any of it.'

Willow sounded so desperate and genuine that Duncan almost believed her. 'Really? You seem to have an uncanny knack of backing the winning side, Willow. Unlike the rest of the yokels in Weyland, you've actually seen what Vandian warships and their legions' weapons can do. With the imperium supporting King Marcus, the civil war is only going to end one way. We both know that.'

'The way the slave revolt ended?'

'A couple of hundred miners who murdered their supervisors and slipped the yoke? You were lucky. Finding a ship damaged by the stratovolcano's eruption and using it to escape home.'

Willow sneered at him. 'Is that what they told you? You really don't know anything.'

'I know you'll be returning with Lady Cassandra,' snarled Duncan. 'I know that much. The north will surrender soon enough. And for once, you'll be standing by my side. You *and* the young southern gentleman in your belly.'

'I thought that you were a fool for chasing Adella. But compared to that imperial bitch you're bedding now, Adella is almost up there with the saints. I hope Princess Helrena is worth it.'

'You're not fit to talk of her! Now get on board,' snapped Duncan. Part of his anger came from his guilt at betraying the princess in Leyla's arms. But then, Helrena had spurned him first. What was he expected to do? Moon after her while she took Gyal for a husband and seized the throne? 'And make right what you've done wrong.'

'If only I could.' Willow boarded the patrol ship. Duncan was almost tempted to tell Willow how well he had satisfied the new mistress of Hawkland Park, just to needle her. Duncan knew Willow loathed 'that Holten woman' for deposing her as the queen bee of Hawkland Park. But how Duncan had sealed his alliance wasn't for Willow's ears. There was too great a chance Willow would find a way to use it against him, given her intense jealousy of her brother. 'It was wrong for Father Carnehan to take the princess's daughter as a hostage. I begged him not to at the time. He said we needed her to stay the imperium's vengeance, and look how true those words have proven. But Cassandra's imprisonment is one wrong, like a leaf in a storm, compared to the empire's sins. Our king's little more than the emperor's puppet now, and Weyland is going to end up just another vassal province.'

'Our family is a loyalist house, Sister. Father got that much right, at least. But you keep bleating the pretender's traitorous propaganda,' said Duncan. 'The rebels should believe you, right up until the moment you betray them. Just as you did me.'

'Please, for the love of the saints, I'm your sister—'

'You keep saying that. Yet, Cassandra has proven more of a sister than you ever were. Help Paetro find the poor girl and bring her back. She has no part in this fight. You free her, and I'll forgive you. You can go back to your southern estate and write pious histories about the wrongs of the civil war while your lucky servants carry you trays of chilled wine in summer and mulled wine in winter.'

'Go to hell,' spat Willow. 'You've escaped the slaves' perdition and made your own while out far-called. A self-made man at last, master of your own destiny just as you always wanted.'

Duncan watched the final loading in disgust. *How dare she judge me?* Soon enough the patrol ship was riding a rippling curtain of fire into the dark night sky, heading for an altitude far above the skyguard's aircraft and even the great free merchant carriers, a shooting star looking to land in the north. Willow might have cast herself as a southern lady by marriage, but you didn't have to scratch deep to find that old jealous sibling, still resentful of Duncan's success, trying to sabotage him at every step. At least Benner Landor's naked self-interest was rarely dressed up with such cant and false piety. Their father acted for the family and made no disguise of the fact. Willow had tried to ruin him in the imperium; of that much Duncan was certain. But he had outwitted her. *The House of Landor is behind me at last and I've shackled her to my cause. If she fails me this time, she'll suffer far more than I will. Yes, I can count on my family's greed to bend them to my will.*

And perhaps, when Helrena's daughter was returned safely, the princess would be made to understand the true value of Duncan's place in her household. *She won't be blinded by the lure and novelty of the diamond throne for long.* After Helrena saw how dutifully the new emperor was fulfilling his obligation to fill the imperium with high-born heirs through the imperial harem, no doubt encouraged by scheming Circae, Helrena would remember Duncan Landor more kindly than she did now. If the rumours were true, and Circae had used some trick of science to slip her son into the cuckoo's nest, then perhaps it was a trick that Duncan could repeat with Helrena? Wouldn't that be a thing? *To father the next ruler of the imperium with the woman I love.* It would be the ultimate revenge to take on Gyal, for stealing the woman who should have been Duncan's.

THIRTEEN

MISSION IN THE NORTH

Carter walked through the city on his way to the airfield, the skyguard station a long stroll beyond Midsburg's northern gate, winding his way below three-storey brick and timber buildings on either side of a wide boulevard crowded by carts and wagons and travellers on horseback, all mixed with soldiers from the dozens of tent camps set up in rings around the city. Anna Kurtain strolled by his side, Prince Owen's bodyguard and confidante filling out a long grey overcoat with two series of copper buttons, a worn leather belt with a pistol on one hip and a sheathed sabre on the other. People were flooding in from all over, and not just politicians from the rebel prefectures. Traders and merchants and locals who wanted to witness history being made. There was an almost carnival air to the proceedings quite at odds with the desperate fighting raging along the Spotswood River to hold back the southern armies. There was to be a vote later on in the reformed assembly, demanding the usurper's head for crimes against the people. Could a sitting monarch, even an usurper like Marcus, really be found guilty of treason as a tyrant, traitor, murderer and public enemy? If he could, it would prove a powerful rallying call to the rebellious north. *The world is turning, and what's my part in it to be? Ferreting out Kerge and Sheplar and bringing that imperial brat back to Midsburg. I never asked to be a soldier, but even that's honest duty compared to playing jailor to a sullen little hostage.* As unasked for as his service as a soldier had been, Carter still didn't like abandoning his company. There was a bond between those who served and fought together, and he was breaking it. Its severing left a bad taste in his mouth.

'How long do I have to return the girl?' asked Carter.

'Try to be back within a week,' said Anna Kurtain.

'That soon?'

'That soon, Northhaven. Our spies report that the Vandians have started leaving Arcadia's bawdy houses and taverns untouched. When a soldier forgoes drinking and whoring, he normally has other things on his mind, such as sobering up to be somewhere else more important.'

'We whipped the Vandians in the sky mines,' said Carter. 'And we were just slaves.'

'We beat a handful of hastily scrambled soldiers while they were being rained on by magma and rock,' said Anna. 'What we face now is a full imperial squadron, warships packed with trained fighting men and helos and armoured vehicles. The imperium's sent their best. Veterans. We're barely holding Bad Marcus's boys back in Humont and Bolesland as it is, and now we've got the armies of the Hicks and Dulany linking up in the east to pound us in Chicola. Even if we burn every bridge across the Spotswood, they'll ford the river and flank us through Deersota. It's what I would do.'

Carter halted among the crowd with Anna. A caravan of wagons was being waved through by the gate's harassed sentries. He caught sight of Thomas Purdell riding in behind the caravan. The guild courier slipped through the gate and stopped his horse in front of Carter and Anna.

'You come to see me off?' asked Carter. 'Or are you kindly offering to take my place?'

'Oh, this one's all yours, Brother,' said Tom. 'I was waiting at the airfield for you, but you're late, so I rode back to make sure you hadn't forgotten the prince's orders.'

'I've got Anna to march me to my duty.'

Tom moved his horse in from the cobbled road to make way for the caravan. Merchants in green Gidorian cloaks rode the carts, the wagon's flat-beds covered by bundles of spindly single-shot rifles tied together like fire-wood... and almost as useful as a stout branch in beating back the southern armies. Traders hunched over the riding step, flicking their reins, burly men and what might be a woman seated next to them, her face enveloped by an emerald hood. The Gidorians would find a market for their wares readily enough with the thousands of fresh green recruits being drilled outside the city, Carter didn't doubt. *Cheap rifles for cheap lives, and how many will be spent in the next few weeks?*

'Lend me your horse, Mister Purdell, I'll get there faster.'

The guild courier seemed distracted, staring at the caravan going past.

'Tom?'

The guild courier turned his attention back to them. 'I'm in the wrong trade. I should be selling cheap arms to the prince for inflated prices, rather than running coded messages between the guilds. I thought you were a cavalry man now, Carter, you must have a stable full of horses.'

'They're all needed for the north's real business. My company leaves in a few days,' said Carter, sadly. *And damn me for a coward for not leaving with them.* 'They're under orders to slow down the Army of the Boles and buy me extra time to return with the hostage.'

'You'll be back in time for the fun here,' said Tom. 'Count on it. I'll make sure your kite's running and ready.' He kicked his horse into action and went galloping through the gate and down the road. A gap had opened in the crowd flowing into Midsburg. Carter and Anna took the chance to slip through the gate.

'Does Prince Owen still believe the north can win?'

Anna shrugged. 'Owen's busy believing for the rest of us, just as he did in the mines.'

'My father said he's a better man than the times we find ourselves in.'

'I hope he's wrong,' said Anna, 'as much as I hope he's right.'

'It must rankle,' said Carter, 'being blamed for the crimes his uncle committed.'

'You have no idea,' said Anna.

'You should tell Owen how you feel about him,' said Carter.

'And how would that go?' she said, a measure of hostility creeping into her voice.

'The obvious was sitting under my nose for a long time, too,' said Carter. 'It took Willow tweaking me by the nose to waken me to it.'

'Owen was born a prince,' said Anna. 'His family's murder brought him Weyland's lawful crown. And me? I'm just a Lakes girl from Heshwick, the daughter of a clockmaker.'

'Then give him something to live for, beyond hard duty and a harder war.'

'I'll keep Owen alive no matter what. Just as I did in the sky mines.'

'How many thousands of soldiers do we have fighting for the north?' said Carter. 'All looking to do the same thing for the assembly and our lawful king. And with all those troops to choose from, Owen still keeps you by his side. You should ask yourself why.'

'I'm like a trusty dagger,' said Anna. She tapped the pair of knives hanging from Carter's belt next to his twinned pistol holster. 'One you keep around even when you've found something more accurate to shoot with.'

'You're more than a habit,' said Carter.

'Kind of you to say so, Northhaven. But I don't think so. The only good thing I can say about the sky mines, you got to know the people you survived alongside. That hell surely revealed the character of everyone taken as a slave.'

Carter thought of Willow and Duncan and Kerge and all those who had met their end in the mines, bravely or cowardly, sadly or resigned. So many perished he could barely recall their faces. 'I'm never returning to Vandia.'

'I don't think there's a single one of us who survived who hasn't put one last bullet aside, just in case the worst comes to pass,' said Anna. She glanced sadly back at the city walls. 'I know who you are, Carter Carnehan. You and your father, both. I don't need show trials or loyalist propaganda to tell me what kind of people I'm keeping company with. We kept each other alive in Vandia, and we'll do the same here, whatever direction the winds of war blow.'

Carter nodded. There were bonds far deeper than soldiering.

They came across a wagon travelling from the town's garrison to the airfield, a sentry relief party in the back, and hitched a lift with them. There weren't many aircraft on the field as they arrived, and those that were were barely air-worthy. The few kites the rebels had flying for them were desperately engaged in the fighting along the Spotswood, acting as scouts and trying to avoid the superior numbers of the loyalist squadrons. Anna led Carter towards a Culph and Falcke Berrypecker, the very large transport aircraft denied to their party when he'd tried to follow Willow to Arcadia. Standing in front of the heavy aircraft was Beula Fetterman, the rebel skyguard pilot who had escaped with Tom and flown the prisoners out of the south. Tom was there too, his horse tied up, waiting for them to catch up with him. As good as the guild courier's word, the kite was ready to take off.

Carter eyed the aircraft. *It's too big for the task*. 'Isn't there anything smaller and faster?'

'Corn fuel we've got to waste a-plenty,' said the female skyguard in frustration. 'Pilots and planes are rare. Me and *Raven* here are what's going spare so count yourself lucky.'

Raven? Fat Old Goose would be a better name for this crate.

'You'll be in good hands with Miss Fetterman here,' said Tom. 'She flew our escape party clear of the south's hospitality quickly enough.'

'I requested combat duty,' said Beula, 'but they've stuck me with transport flights.'

'This is a vitally important mission,' said Anna, her ebony cheeks flushing with irritation. 'You wouldn't even be on this run if Mister Purdell here hadn't vouched for your skills.'

'I've just been saying the very same thing,' said Tom.

Beula raised her hands in surrender. 'Don't worry. I'll fly you safe to Rodal and back again. The sodbuster and this secret passenger both.'

'Make sure you do,' said Tom, sounding uncharacteristically intimidating.

Sodbuster. That's all that the people of Havenharl were to the rest of Weyland, simple hick farmers. *Who would have thought the day would come when I wished that's all we were. Not soldiers. Not rebels. Just farmers.* Carter slapped Tom's arm. 'Enjoy the celebrations tonight. Between you and Assemblyman Gimlette, you've stoked the assembly into a fighting frenzy.'

'It won't be the politicians doing the dying when the southern armies come at us to rip apart that declaration of treason against the king,' said Tom.

'Sadly, that's true enough,' said Anna. 'God speed, Northhaven. Prince Owen is counting on you.'

'He's counting on both of us,' said Carter. 'You remember what I told you, Anna.'

'Still trying to look out for me?'

Carter shook his head and climbed up the steps into the plane. 'I gave up trying to do that back in Vandia.'

'I'm not going to be around to pull you out of your hare-brained scrapes in Rodal,' said Anna. 'Nor is Owen for that matter.'

'I'm a different man, now, haven't you heard?'

'It's the pirate blood I'm worried about.'

Thomas watched Carter Carnehan say farewell to the prince's bodyguard and climb on board the aircraft. *How much of a problem will the bodyguard prove, I wonder*? Anna Kurtain was a large woman, strong and quick and lithe. But an unexpected thrust of a blade into her lungs would leave her choking on her own blood easily enough. Thomas planned to make it look like the prince had argued with the woman and slain her in an argument, angry lovers squabbling over an uncertain future. That would add an extra frisson of scandal for the news sheets to pick apart when they proclaimed how the cowardly pretender had hung himself upon hearing how close the king's forces were to poor outnumbered Midsburg. King Marcus was a clever dog. It wouldn't be seemly for Marcus to execute his own nephew, making the boy a martyr for the rebellious north to use to question Marcus's claim to the throne. Nobody liked a kin slayer. *So hard to kill a dead man, unless you murdered his reputation first*. Thomas had already arranged for two of his agents in the town's garrison to be on sentry duty tonight. Both sides had people hidden in the other side's camp. That was the problem with a civil war; everyone looked the same and you could never tell what was in a person's heart unless you cut it out slowly. *I'm proof of that*.

Kurtain waved at him and he waved happily back. *I'm planning your death, you stupid bitch*. Yes, a tincture of poison for the prince and his woman first, to paralyse them. Thomas always worked best when he had a silent audience to appreciate his skill. *This is the work I was born for*.

Beula Fetterman checked the wooden fuel barrels as she knelt beside him, speaking low. 'Where should I land when I have the emperor's granddaughter on board?'

'Not this side of the Sharps Mountains,' whispered Thomas. 'Midsburg will be a charnel house by the time you return. There'll be so much blood running here, the wheels of your undercarriage will spin and you'll crash a second kite. Land west of the Perryfax River by the coast and find a radiomen's hold to signal the capital with your location. We'll send a ship up the coast for you. The Vandians need to believe the girl's a hostage in Midsburg until they've done our killing for us. After the imperium's crushed the rebels, the king will make a great show of handing her over safe to her family.'

'And how grateful will they be?'

'Don't worry, Fetterman, you'll receive your reward,' said Thomas. *And so will I.* 'The Vandians are keen enough. I just saw one of Princess Helrena's killers slip into the city dressed as a Gidorian merchant. And he's got Lady Wallingbeck on the step beside him as a guide. I'm willing to bet the whole caravan is actually a Vandian raiding party.'

'They're here hunting for Lady Cassandra?'

'I doubt they're here to celebrate the traitorous assembly's vote against King Marcus.' *This could be a problem.* It wouldn't do for the Vandians to discover that the girl being held in the city was an impostor. The imperium might divert to Rodal instead and deprive Marcus of his allies just when he was counting on them to win the war for him. *I suppose I'll have to kill them too, now.* It would mean diverting all the southern spies and saboteurs inside the city, but their loss to the loyalist cause would be worth it. He imagined Willow's pretty eyes bulging as he slipped a cord around her neck and strangled her. A pity Carter Carnehan wouldn't be around to hear the news of her death. That would be a fine parting gift.

'What about the Carnehan boy? Should he have a reunion with his true love?'

'Keep Carter Carnehan alive long enough to find Lady Cassandra. But don't bother bringing him back,' hissed Thomas. 'The imperium will be given all the rebel armies' survivors as slaves. They won't need a wild fool who's already escaped the empire's shackles.'

'It's always risky flying with Rodal's storms gusting against your tail,' said Fetterman. 'Easy enough to tumble out of a kite when you're not a trained skyguard.'

Thomas imagined the shocked look on Carter's face as she asked him to check the plane's fin rudder, before resting a hand on his spine and shoving him through the open hatch. *Precious*. A pity Thomas would not be there to claim that memory as one of his trophies. *Still, there'll be more than enough sport for me in the next few weeks*. The end of the rebellion would sate even his refined tastes.

Cassandra swayed on her horse, miserable to her core. Bad enough that whatever her tenuous status with the nomads, she was also a prisoner inside her own body; but she now had to share that misery with Sheplar and Kerge as prisoners of the Nijumeti. Lady Cassandra should have been saddle-sore after weeks riding north towards the heartland of the clansmen, but if there was one silver lining to having both legs paralysed, it was that the cramps and aches of life on horseback had even less effect on her now than the people of the plains who were born to it.

Sheplar and Kerge shared a single horse, one of the nags they had ridden out of Rodal, all the better to slow them down if they attempted to bolt for freedom. Not that they would, with their hands securely tied behind their backs and their horse flanked by nomad guards. A couple of days before, the small band of raiders had linked up with a bigger band from their clan, and now the combined force were riding towards whatever passed for the main encampment of Alexamir's people. Cassandra's ruminating was interrupted as the witch rider drew level with her and the two prisoners. Nurai seemed well-satisfied with Cassandra's broken body. *She obviously thinks that Alexamir will abandon me soon enough. No threat to her, now. No threat to anybody*. Not that Cassandra's feebleness was enough to stop the female nomad from flinging barbed comments at her.

'I heard a thump in the night,' said Nurai, gazing coldly at Cassandra. 'I thought perhaps you had slipped your belt and slid off into the grass. But I see your saddle is still occupied.'

Cassandra didn't bother to dignify that with a response.

'Why have you kept us alive?' demanded Sheplar. 'It's your tradition to mutilate Rodalians and leave our bones where we fall.'

'That is not tradition, rice eater, that is practicality. The gods demand your sacrifice or your servitude.'

'Your tribal group is no longer so . . . practical, womanling?' asked Kerge.

She ignored the gask.

'I will make a poor slave,' said Sheplar.

'Of that I have no doubt. Three broken foreigners,' laughed Nurai. 'A skyguard without his wooden pigeon, a forest man who cannot dream-walk, and a pampered chieftain's daughter who cannot walk at all. The girl is only alive because of Alexamir's foolish oath. As for you two, there are many reasons to keep breath in your lungs. You shall see how my people have changed soon enough.' She laughed wickedly, and Cassandra had a sinking feeling that the two prisoners would not thank the witch rider for their survival when they reached their destination.

Kerge eyed the witch rider warily. 'You caught us through the gift of future sight. Do you scry the branches of the great fractal tree and study its periodic boundary conditions?'

'So, it is true then?' said Nurai. 'The forest people on the other side of the mountains can dream-walk without dreams, during the day?'

'Through meditation and prayer in the direction of the universe,' said Kerge, 'usually. If you removed the bonds from my wrists and returned to me my calculator, I could show you our practice.'

'We do not need your strange abacus machines or any knotty contortions of the mind to gaze into the future. It is a gift to the chosen from Kalu the Apportioner.'

'If it is a gift from your deity, then the boon has been withdrawn from me,' said Kerge. 'My luck is depleted. I have been cast off the great tree and banished from the forests.'

'I do not need to hear your tale to see your pitiable turn of fate,' sneered Nurai. 'Poor unlucky gask. Fate wishes you here, it seems. A nest full of cheeping, defective chicks that cannot take to the sky. But for what purpose? That we shall see.'

Nothing good for us. Cassandra watched Nurai spur the horse forward to reach the head of the nomads' column. 'You should never have come back for me.'

'That Nijumet rogue didn't carry you off, did he?' said Sheplar, accusingly. 'You left Talatala with him willingly.'

'Alexamir gave his word that he would free me when I asked; that he would see me returned to the imperium.'

'A nomad's words are but hot breath against a cold wind,' said Sheplar. 'And carry as much weight. How could you believe that blue-skinned dog?'

'Well, I have been punished by the ancestors for my foolishness,' said Cassandra, slapping the unfeeling calf of her leg. 'I will never escape from you or anyone else again.'

'I was taught the art of the flying wing by a master of the skyguard, Konadun, who earned such an injury,' said Sheplar. 'On the ground he was pushed in a wheeled chair by one of his pupils who fought for the honour, but in the air, our venerated flight master was a hawk, the equal of any of us. Konadun taught himself to fly again after his injury, using a flying wing with rudder pedals modified to hand controls.'

'No one will fight for the honour of shoving me around,' said Cassandra. She remembered what was expected of the celestial caste crippled duelling in the arena. A short-sword slid into the gut by the injured noble's own hand, the stoicism of their end broadcast across the kino-screens for the education of the teeming populace. *Maybe Nurai will slip me my dagger back if I beg her. Or maybe she will just mock me and leave me like this. She'll enjoy watching Alexamir abandon me.*

'Konadun used to say that if the spirits had wished to stop him; they would have broken his neck, not his legs. 'And that his will was still his to command, not fate's to snap.'

'I can't even ride a horse properly,' said Cassandra, dangling her reins in frustration. 'Even kicking it to a canter or squeezing it to a halt is beyond me. Every day I must sit lashed up here like a sack of barley.'

'Yet there you sit.'

'Be quiet, mountain man,' said Cassandra. 'You have failed in your mission to recapture me as surely as I have failed in my duty to return to Vandia a free woman. My mother will never ransom my return now, nor my grandfather, nor anyone in the empire. They would only ask why I have not ended my life. My use to you and your savage friends as a hostage is at an end. If you see a chance to flee, take it. If you attempt to carry me with you, I will howl so loudly you shall think your ancestor's spirits have breached the earth. I have no place in the world, now. I might as well be here as anywhere else.'

'I have no place, either,' said Kerge. 'Perhaps we are all exiles, now.'

'I follow my honour,' said Sheplar, a touch too proudly for his reduced circumstances.

What fools these Rodalians are. Stubborn as the goats that climb their mountains, and about as attractive. 'Find me a knife and I will follow mine,' said Cassandra.

'If I see you try,' said Sheplar, '*you* will hear a yell as if my ancestor's spirits have breached the earth.'

I'll bear that in mind, if it comes to it. 'If you will not help me, then leave me be.'

'What makes you think we can escape?' asked Sheplar.

'I have seen the eyes of your slinking dog glinting in the dark as it prowls around the camp,' said Cassandra. 'It is not a wolf, although it looks as large as one. A wolf would attack the picketed horses at night. You used a scent hound to track me, didn't you? And the creature is still on the loose, following us. It is clever and well disciplined. Perhaps clever enough to slip in one night when the guards are asleep and chew through your ropes?'

'You have seen nothing but a hungry grass leopard, bumo,' said Sheplar.

'I have lost the use of my legs, mountain man, not my mind,' said Cassandra. 'My house's hold, the Castle of Snakes, boasts high walls patrolled by guards with hounds every bit as loyal and wily as your dog. I can tell the difference between a leopard and a mastiff well enough.'

'Believe what you will.'

'I will not tell the nomads,' said Cassandra. 'You thought you were tracking me to save me. But nothing can do that, now. Leave with your spiky friend. But do not try to take me with you.'

'These nomads are not a people to trust,' said Sheplar.

'I trust them to grow bored with me,' said Cassandra. 'And I trust their witch rider to end me sooner or later.'

'There are no good ends out here.'

'I will take an honourable one,' said Cassandra. 'And I have seen enough of those to know they are never easy.'

Sheplar shook his head sadly but kept his peace.

Cassandra slumped in the saddle. *I wonder if I will have my legs returned to me when I am reunited with my ancestors*? It seemed likely. No daughter of the empire would wish to exist for eternity as they were when they died an old crone. A pity that there were no priests of the Imperium Cosmocrator here to ask; although their answers, in Lady Cassandra's experience, were suspiciously close to what the celestial caste desired to hear. *Of course the emperor is the highest of the gods; he deserves your fealty, as does your house from those you shepherd.*

They rode for another four days, a slow but relentless pace every day until it was too dark to see the ground, making camp in the deep of night. This was the riders' way in winter. During the summer, they switched to travelling by night and resting during the baking heat of the day. After staking the horses and penning their sheep and goats, the nomads established a circle of dome-like tents, circular frames quickly set up with wooden poles unpacked from their saddle bags, woollen and sheep-hide felt stretched over as the tents' skin. Each dwelling became a wheel-like home, exterior and interior both coloured with stitched patterns representing the six elements of life: fire, water, metal, wood, earth and flesh. The hide fabric also contained leering gargoyle-like visages of their gods, each heathen deity remade as an abstract symbol. Alexamir would appear in the evening and point them out to Cassandra, naming the gods and explaining their place in the Nijumet pantheon.

'Why do you bother to carry me with you?' asked Cassandra one evening, huddled under the warmth of a pile of blankets. *It doesn't matter how many blankets I cover my legs with. They always feel cold now.* She shivered constantly; perhaps it had something to do with her injury. 'Does your oath mean so much to you?'

'My golden fox is still my golden fox,' said Alexamir, squatting by her side inside the dome-like tent. 'Even with her feet caught in a jaw-trap.'

'If a horse was as lame as I, you would say a prayer, slit its throat and cook it.'

'I do not think you will taste as good as horse steak,' smiled

Alexamir. 'But perhaps when we reach the clan, they can find the salt to season you?'

'I see my fate in your people's eyes,' said Cassandra. 'In your witch rider's.'

'Nurai glares at everyone the same. She has a sour disposition. It is my eyes you should look at,' said Alexamir.

'Why do you take me with you?'

'When you know the answer to that, you will know where you belong.'

'I belong nowhere. I am not one of your riders. At home, I would be the shame of my house. I am no longer even a useful hostage for my enemies.'

'This one,' said Alexamir, tapping one of the symbols on the tent's circular wall, 'is the god of the grass, Atamva. His is the saying "Atamva always remembers". It is taught that winter comes when Atamva forgets his love for his wife, the moon goddess Annayla. Spring is when his love stirs, and summer when he truly remembers his love. Atamva always remembers. This is your winter, golden fox. If Atamva can remember, you shall remember where you belong too.'

'You are insufferable.'

'Does that mean that Alexamir is faster and stronger and more daring than all lesser men?'

'No, it means you have the sense of a horse.'

'Good,' smiled Alexamir. 'Horses are far cleverer than they look. They can find hidden water where a man will die thirsty, and understand enough serpent speech to know where a viper is hiding in the grass ready to strike.'

'Your insufferability stands, but perhaps I was overstating your good sense.'

Alexamir leant across and kissed her, the first warmth she had felt all day. Cassandra would have resisted more, but she could barely even roll out from under her blankets. *And I need the heat, surely I do.* She was drawn to it, despite her best intentions, like a moth to the camp fire's light and heat outside. 'How can you still want me?'

Alexamir got to his feet and bowed towards her before he exited the tent. 'Dwell instead on how could I not?'

Despite herself, Cassandra felt a twinge of regret as the warrior departed. *You are a fool. So grateful for kind words that you can find false affection in your heart for anyone who speaks them to you.* How far had she fallen? *Atamva always remembers.* Cassandra rubbed her cold, dead legs. *And how can I ever forget this? A useless weight, worse than any slaves' chains.*

Their journey continued each day, much the same as the last, save for a couple of nights when a pack of hill wolves started trailing the column across an undulating expanse of land the nomads called the Copper-barrows. There were too many riders during the day for the wolves to muster the courage to attack, and at night the camp fires burned and held them back, fear of bush fires greater than any hunger they might feel. Cassandra heard a fierce howling one night, and after that she no longer glimpsed the scent hound she suspected belonged to her would-be rescuers. The wolves had claimed their meal and slunk away to leave the nomad party unmolested. The sad look on Sheplar's face the next morning confirmed her suspicions. The aviator's last hope of rescue had vanished, too, along with his luckless dog.

Every evening Alexamir appeared in her tent and attempted to amuse Cassandra, make her forget her broken body and pointless existence. Briefly, she might succumb to the diversion. But each morning she awoke, forgetting who and what she was, until she first attempted to stand. Then her misery would come bursting upon her with all the fury of the flood waters of a broken dam. She came to depend on his evening visits, even as she loathed her weakness for doing so. *Was there ever so ill-fated a match?* A daughter of the mightiest imperium on Pellas and a ragtag rogue with barely a saddle and steed to his name. Except she was no longer the granddaughter of an emperor. She was an end without the knife to bring it about; dishonour awaiting a blade. She came to despise herself for the eagerness she felt when Alexamir arrived to talk with her. Lying there, trembling for his presence. The anticipation, followed by sorrow when he departed. Worst of all was when he left for a day or two to hunt wild steers with a few others, ranging off before returning. *What am I doing here? Why am I thinking about him so much?*

Hers was a strange, intense sort of freedom. Exactly what the nomad had promised when he talked wildly about the joys of life with the Nijumeti, apart from the fear and bitterness of her crippled future. Cassandra had been raised on a merciless schedule without a free second to her name. When she hadn't been training in armed and unarmed combat, physical skills of balance and poise, she had her nose pressed to books under the tutelage of the great Doctor Horvak, or was shadowing her mother to learn the duties of leading the house – commerce and trade, strategy and politics, ploys and scheming in the imperial court. Now the weeks were hers to do nothing but live and wander, without much purpose, without any hope. *What's the use of being free without ambition or merit? At least with a schedule from dawn to dusk, my place was certain. I was what I did. What do I do now? Push on, broken.* She did. She had no choice.

When they finally reached the main body of the clan, the meeting was almost unexpected; such had been the slow drift of the days and Cassandra's life. Oddly, the journey's sudden end was the least of her surprises. They rounded a low rolling hill and Cassandra found a number of things before her that she had certainly never expected to see of a Nijumeti clan. From the gasp of shock from Sheplar Lesh and Kerge, mounted pillion to her right, what lay before them was obviously a revelation to them too.

A laugh rang from behind them. *Nurai*. 'There,' smirked the witch rider, cruelly, 'did I not say you would see what we have become . . .'

FOURTEEN

TO KILL A PRINCE

Assemblyman Gimlette raised a glass of wine in his fat fingers while Thomas Purdell lifted his own, content to listen to the plump politician fill the air with bluster. Nobody had noticed that the main beneficiary of Thomas's glass was the spittoon behind his divan. The windows of the prince's quarters held the reflection of fireworks in the glass, a distant sound of cheering and singing from the streets of Midsburg. *This is a triumph, fat man. But the rebels outside are cheering for the wrong side.*

'I told you, Your Highness, Charles T. Gimlette is just the man to bring you victory, and may this be the first of many.'

'We need victories on the field as well as on paper,' said Prince Owen from the divan opposite the politician's seat. He raised a glass to Thomas and the assemblyman. 'But I am grateful to you both for this. The assembly had been arguing about whether to offer peace terms before you escaped, but your testimony concerning my uncle's crimes has stiffened their backbone.'

'Bad Marcus dissolving parliament should have been sufficient warning of his intentions,' said Anna Kurtain. She was sitting next to the prince, her face as worried and furrowed as always.

'Ah, assemblymen, they love to bicker,' said Gimlette. 'That they do. Not all of my brothers and sisters in the party are for such decisive action. But you can count on me to herd them towards the right decision. You are Prince Owen no longer, sir. You are King Owen of Weyland, and we will bend our knees to you.'

'I won't be crowned a king until the usurper languishes in his own dungeon,' said Owen. 'And I will be King of the Weylanders, not King of Weyland. It is not I who has been elected sovereign, but the constitution. There will be no more prefects by royal appointment. Only the assembly and a lawful monarch governed by our laws. Never again will any citizen of this realm have to suffer from an unfit monarch's whims.'

Thomas ignored the nobleman's whining rebel treachery. He got to his feet and walked over to the table to lift the wine decanter, using it to refill the glasses of the assemblyman, prince and his woman. The only people who weren't drinking were the two sentries standing sentry inside the double doors to the prince's apartment. Loyalists, just like the soldier holding on to the reins of four fast steeds outside the mayor's mansion. They'd be back in the south soon enough, escaping the siege at Midsburg before the town was cut off.

'With such freedoms to lift our sails, the party will never let you down, Your Highness,' drawled the assemblyman. Gimlette started to raise his fat hand in toast again, but the glass began trembling and he stared at it as though bewitched by the contents suddenly spilling across his wrist. Prince Owen had stopped pontificating too, his head falling against the leather of the divan and shaking madly as though in a fit. Assemblyman Gimlette attempted to stand, but he collapsed back, his heavy arms raised high as though in prayer, then slumped sideways, drool foaming across the seat.

'Run for the garrison—' snarled Anna Kurtain swaying up, but she dropped to her knees as she lost her footing, '—doctor.'

'Did you hear something?' laughed one of the sentries.

'Not me,' said the other. 'Must be all that larking outside, I reckon.'

'What is this?' croaked the bodyguard, clutching at her throat as she tumbled off her knees. Kurtain lay sprawled across the room's carpet, her hands twitching as she vainly attempted to move them towards her holstered pistol.

'Tincture of Belladonna,' announced Thomas, brushing his trousers as he stood up. Anna Kurtain had lasted a little longer than the fifteen minutes it should have taken from the first toast to paralyse her. The benefits of her size and muscles, no doubt, just like the fat fool's cushioning. 'Strong enough to make granite of your flesh for the rest of the hour. It'll deaden your feelings, but not enough, I fear, to completely banish the pain of what this wicked pretender is about to do to you.'

Kurtain just managed to croak *assassin*, before Thomas's poison fully froze her throat.

'More of a torturer, usually,' said Thomas. 'I regret, sweet lady, that expediency requires I forgo my exquisite craft tonight.' Thomas walked across to the king's treasonous nephew, sprawled on the divan, and lifted the royal's dagger from of his belt, inspecting its keen edge with interest. 'You see, you've just presented the pretender with the shocking news that the Army of the Boles has crossed the river at Humont and is advancing on Midsburg. You and the good assemblyman tried to talk Owen out of abandoning the city and fleeing east like the coward he is. But the pretender took your advice as badly as your news.'

Thomas walked across to where the assemblyman sat slumped, eyes frozen wide and startled inside Gimlette's heavily jowled face. He drew the blade across the assemblyman's throat, stepping aside as a jet of blood spurted across the carpet. A vicious kick of Thomas's boot sent the politician tumbling off his seat and into the floor's embrace. 'Calling for the true king's death? You signed your own death warrant today, Gimlette. Along with everyone else sitting in your rebel's parliament. How strange, I was certain it'd be hot air that escaped your foul fat neck, not blood. It's the only surprise I ever had from you . . . everything else you did was so entirely predictable.'

Thomas clutched the king's dagger and crossed to where the woman lay trembling on the floor. There he plunged the dagger deep into her chest, being careful to avoid the heart and leaving the blade's hilt embedded inside her. Even paralysed, her face contorted in agony. *So beautiful. And so little time to play.* Thomas unholstered the bodyguard's pistol and tucked it behind his own belt. A memento of this moment he would be sure to treasure. He signalled the two sentries. 'Carry her to the bed chamber and toss her across the mattress. Make sure she bleeds copiously across the sheets. I want a nice dramatic death scene for the servants to discover tomorrow morning when they arrive to empty the fireplace. After you're finished with her, come back and help me hoist the pretender's flag.'

'Sir.' The soldier kicked the politician's prone body as he passed it. A river of blood soaked the carpet around Gimlette. Thomas trusted it wouldn't leak through the floorboards and bring the staff up early. 'This one doesn't just eat like a pig, he bleeds like one too.'

'Leave him,' said the other sentry. 'He's filling his face in hell now, right enough.'

Thomas watched in satisfaction as the soldiers dragged the dying bodyguard into the adjoining rooms. He ripped a cord from the curtains alongside the window, flexing it between his hands. *Fine thick knotted cotton.* A balcony lay beyond the cold pane of glass, a view of the city stretched out in the flicker of lamp light and fireworks. He slipped the rope around the pretender's neck and tied into a neat noose while the prince glared hatred up at him. *Too late, my treacherous friend. The truth always appears too late.* Thomas smiled back and patted the pretender's cold cheek. 'I can see the disgrace now, killing your woman and the fat man for daring to bring you the truth. Don't worry; your dishonour will be banished soon enough. Along with the last flickers of your failed rebellion. My two friends here will travel south and inform the news sheets all about your double-murder and shameful suicide. Their distress when Miss Kurtain arrived with the news of the southern advance. How the men heard a struggle and had to break the doors in. Your guards discovered you dead, your friends' corpses scattered around you, before they fled the city for failing in their sworn duty. You'll be remembered as a slaver and a coward who led the nation into destruction, following his mad ambitions. How do you think scholars will record you in the annals of history? Insane Owen, the one-day king, the pitiful pretender? You won't care after you're in the dirt with the worms, I know. But I'll peruse those books. When I'm an old man. I'll read about you and remember the fine sight of your boots jerking as my men tug on your feet to finish you off. It's not every day I get to watch a prince hang, even a treacherous pretender like you. How well do you think the king will reward me for this night's work? I'll live like a prince, I reckon, for executing one.'

Thomas's soldiers returned, the pair's grey uniforms stained crimson with the woman's blood. *Well, they'll be turning those coats for the blue soon enough anyway.* 'She's not dead yet, I hope?'

'Still shaking,' said one of the men.

Excellent. Thomas tossed the cord over the heavy chandelier above. Six brass arms bolted into the ceiling in a dozen places. It wouldn't do to allow such expensive crystal to fall and shatter. *More than strong enough to break this dog's neck.* 'Let's raise our royal standard, then. I'd best take my sport quickly before we quit this place.' *I'll give the woman a traitor's end for daring to call the king Bad Marcus.* A swift leaving present to stir the salacious pens of the newspapers.

Each sentry seized a leg and began to lift the pretender up while Thomas hauled on the rope. Owen was starting to gargle, and the sentries hadn't even dropped him yet, let alone heaved on his boots to speed the process. Well, the noose had to be tight to kill a man.

'That's it, my lord,' said Thomas, dragging the rope back as the sentries lifted Owen high. 'You're the standard saluting our true king.' The tincture of Belladonna would keep the traitor from singing properly, but that couldn't be helped. This night's work was more functional than for Thomas's amusement.

'He's bloody heavy,' complained one of the sentries. 'When do we let him go?'

'A condemned man often is,' smiled Thomas. He left the two dolts struggling to hold the prince while he mounted the table to tie the noose off against the chandelier, then jumped down to remove a chair and overturn it below the rebel leader. Setting the stage, everything had to appear just so. 'And a dead man, always. You'd think that a corpse should be lighter, when its soul blows out, but the bodies of the dead are always so heavy. I wonder why that should be?'

The soldiers were still clutching Owen when the door splintered behind them. Quick as a snake, Thomas had the pistol out and spun the nearest sentry in front of him as a human sandbag, just in time for the turncoat to shriek as a pistol fanned through the room, a volley of shots walked expertly across the soldiers, missing Owen by a hair. The sentries weren't holding the prince's legs anymore; they were tumbling dead to join the assemblyman across the carpet. Thomas Purdell back-stepped and hurled himself through the window and out onto the balcony, shards of glass biting and slicing at his body.

He shot widely as he rolled, not trying to aim, but accurate enough to give everyone breaking into the quarters pause to do something other than worry about him. After all, they had the choking traitor dangling from the chandelier to worry about. He raised his pistol to put a bullet into the prince's heart and had a second to realize that it was Jacob Carnehan he faced. *How did that devil get here?* The pastor clutched at one of Owen's legs, trying to save the choking traitor from death. A man Thomas dimly recognized as the speaker of the assembly, Augustus Sparrow, was mounting the table to cut the cord. Jacob Carnehan swivelled the pistol towards Thomas with his spare hand. Thomas shot wildly at the pastor as he hurdled the balcony, wood splintering where the agent had just been kneeling. Quicksilver, that had been Carnehan's name when he'd fought as a mercenary commander across the ocean. *Well earned*. More shots cut through the air as Thomas spun towards the hedges in front of the mayor's mansion, gravity only just faster than the pastor's aim, a bullet grazing Thomas's shoulder in mid-air. He grunted as he collided with the greenery, hardly feeling the impact with the burn of adrenaline coursing through his flesh. The gunfire merely added to the explosions of fireworks above the grounds. Oil-fired lampposts lined the wall inside the grounds and Thomas shot them out with his stolen pistol's remaining shells, plunging the lawn into darkness as he limped as quickly as he could towards the street corner where the horses waited. *So close*. How would King Marcus reward him now? As the man always rewarded failure? A garrotte screw turned by another torturer's hand? Thomas cursed the pastor. A blunt, brutal savage. Not an inch of sophistication in his methods. To be stymied by such a brute, to have a so-nearly slain prince's fortune snatched from his fingers. *I'll be back for you, Quicksilver. After the siege, if not before. I'll take my time with you. Yes, I think there's a way I can even the score*. Thomas disappeared into the night, where he was wholly at home.

The *Raven* followed the line of mountains on Weyland's side of the border until they reached the ancient trade road north running towards the Rodalian capital, Hadra-Hareer. It seemed a sensible course to Carter, avoiding the unpredictable winds over the sharp heights of Rodal. Below their aircraft, the trade road snaked like a river through the thick forests of Gaskald, a veritable green sea, impenetrable to caravans hoping to make anything approaching a decent pace of travel. Skyguard officer Beula Fetterman hadn't proved good company. Maybe it was Carter, or perhaps it was her resentment of flying cargo, rather than combat, with her comrades in the rebel squadron, but she refused to engage in banter with Carter. In the end, he stopped bothering to try. Beula didn't even show any curiosity about who it was they were flying to collect. *It's almost as if she already knows*. The *Raven* was oversized for their mission. Large enough to carry twenty passengers in comfort, plus an empty cargo hold. Even their cockpit had positions for three crew and a gunner for the rear-facing turret, currently shut to the cold and the wind. Beula had made sure Carter couldn't sit next to her by folding out her navigation charts across the spare pilot's seat. If he wanted to watch the landscape slide by, he had to take the seat behind her or climb up into the gunner's position. They weren't about to encounter enemy kites flying along Weyland's northern border. Every plane either side's skyguard possessed was wheeling above the Spotswood River right now, scouting for ground forces trying to sally across the water, or the regiments trying to halt them . . . looking to blind the enemy and notch a few kills on the side of the fuselage. Eventually the trade road ran into the mountains of Rodal proper, winding its way through the valleys and canyons of their northern neighbour. *The Walls of the League. Well named*. Carter wondered how well named the mountain nation's capital would prove. *Hadra-Hareer, the Valley of the Hell-winds*. His father had talked about his travels to Hadra-Hareer, but Carter had never seen the city. Beula took the *Raven* higher to avoid the turbulence below, growing with every mile north they flew until the plane was trembling as though it was alive, fierce winds making the canvas around their plane's wooden frame undulate and snap. Skyguard Officer Fetterman was attempting quite a balancing act, keeping the plane intact and an eye on the trade road winding below. Gravity's hold lessened as they climbed, leaving Carter with a familiar sick floating feeling in his gut. No wonder he didn't like it. *Too similar to being on the sky mines*. They were flying solely by chart and compass now, lost in the cloud cover.

'We have company,' announced Beula after three hours, breaking the frosty silence between them.

Carter followed her gloved finger through the condensation-covered cockpit canopy. Three Rodalian flying wings had emerged from the cloud cover and were arrowing towards the *Raven*, triangular planes with a single rear-mounted propeller. Two of the skyguard kites were small single-seat fighters; the third sported twin cockpits, an aviator in the rear chopping the air with a colourful pair of signal flags.

'Do you understand signal semaphore?' asked Carter.

Beula shot him a cold look. 'I even understand blinker lamps. Do you think I'm flying this crate solely for my looks, Captain Sodbuster? They're ordering us to follow them to the ground.' She tapped the chart sitting on the spare aviator's seat by her side. 'Their capital should be below us by now.'

The skyguard in the rear cockpit made another series of cutting motions with the two flags. Beula frowned as two of the three planes turned behind the *Raven*'s tail, leaving a single flying wing wobbling in front of their nose.

'What's the matter?'

'Something else. They signalled if we try to turn away or fly off on any other course, they'll shoot us down.'

'That's not very friendly,' said Carter.

'You're sure the passenger we're meant to bring back to Weyland is down there?'

'That was always the plan.'

Beula Fetterman arched her neck to try to see the two Rodalian fighters sitting on her tail. They were in perfect position to bring the *Raven* down in a flaming ball of wreckage. 'Maybe you need a new plan. This one seems to have a few holes in it, as will the *Raven* if one of those pilots' nerves fail.'

What in the name of the saints is going on here? Have the Rodalians been attacked by aerial nomads? Carter wouldn't put it past the Vandians to throw their skel slavers into the current troubles. He began to jounce in his seat as the *Raven* spiralled down, the air currents growing wild and unpredictable. They left the clouds above them. A maze of canyons squatted below, and Carter saw buildings clinging to the canyon walls on both sides, an entire metropolis carved out of, and into, the rocks; just a small fraction of what lay protected within the rocky mass. *Just like my father said*. Jacob Carnehan hadn't described the lack of vegetation below, though. No trees, just moss and scrub clinging to the bottom of the gorge and a few roots protruding from the chasm walls. Carter stared down at the buildings. White stone walls with thick red tile roofs, multiple storeys nestling above each other, rounded to turn and shape the winds that gusted through the canyons. None of the entrances into the city were on the gorge floor. They were all located midway up the rift's walls, accessible by bulky stone staircases, a long climb towards portals which – where open – looked thick enough to put any gatehouse in Northhaven's walls to shame. The windows in the structures were little more than arrow slits, shuttered from inside with metal screens. Nothing lay above the plateau-line, not a single structure to defy the wind. Rodalian flying wings took off and landed from launch tunnels drilled into the canyon walls, like sparrows entering a tree trunk. The gorge had a few paved roads crossing the narrow pass, bridges for a river that meandered along the chasm, but it seemed devoid of carts and foot traffic.

'Why would anyone want to build a capital here?' complained the pilot, following the twin cockpit flying wing's twists and turns. 'It's desolate, nothing growing, no terraces.'

'It's where the winds are most powerful,' said Carter. 'So where their spirits are strongest.'

'Sweet saints, these mountain people are crazy. They want us to put down outside their hanging city,' said Beula, jabbing her hand towards an airfield strip running down the canyon's centre; empty of planes. 'I'd rather the storm-break of one of their tunnel hangars.'

That was worrying in itself. Carter realized that if they set down inside the city, they would qualify for the tradition of salt and roof: hospitality to visitors. Landing outside Hadra-Hareer was entirely different. 'Can you set us down safely?' asked Carter.

Beula peered out of the cockpit and inspected the wind-speed indicators on either side of the cabin. 'It's dangerous, but not fatally windy at the moment. This area is marked on the charts as one of the most treacherous storm sites. They must be stalling the gusts using their famous wind walls.'

'There's a crowd gathering down there alongside the strip,' said Carter.

'Will our embassy staff be among them?'

'Hopefully,' said Carter. 'They're almost all northerners, and they were one of the first Lanca embassies to declare for Prince Owen when parliament was dissolved.'

On their final approach the *Raven* shook violently; Carter dug his nails into the side of his seat, fearing they might flip and be driven to shatter against the canyon's walls. This place was literally a wind tunnel, and it was only the Rodalian priests on the wooden wind dams who were briefly restraining the power of the spirits. *For how much longer, I wonder?* They hit the simple stone runway with a crack of their undercarriage that should have sheared the wheels off, but somehow they held instead. Beula had to keep all their rotors turning just to power them to where the flying wing had halted. They climbed towards the passenger cabin and broke the seal on the hatch, fierce winds pushing them back as they struggled to drop the stairs to the ground. Carter stumbled against an iron ring on the rock, heavy enough to anchor a battleship, as he emerged. Outside they were met by a Rodalian army officer and a company of soldiers. Carter raised a hand, as much to protect his face from the gusts as to salute the officer, but one of the soldiers ran forward, seized his hand, and twisted it brutally behind Carter's back. Carter tried to fight them off, but there were too many soldiers, and they quickly had his arms pinned behind his spine, a similarly restrained Beula Fetterman, cursing the guardsmen for all she was worth.

'What is going on here?' demanded Carter, shouting above the gale. 'We're from Weyland; we are members of the Lanca.'

'We know where you are from,' yelled the Rodalian officer, clamping hand chains across Carter's wrists. 'But you are misinformed. You *were* members of the Lancean League. Weyland has been expelled by unanimous vote of the other Lanca nations.'

Carter reeled in surprise at the news. 'That is nothing to do with us. Let us go!'

'Nothing? You dare to land here in an aircraft of the Weyland Skyguard and proclaim your innocence? At best you will be interned in a prison cell. You shall stand trial for complicity in the murder of the speaker of the winds, Palden Tash.'

'Murder? What in the world are you talking about?'

'Your king's execution of a diplomat travelling under the safe conduct of the Lanca charter, the speaker of the winds.'

Damn Bad Marcus. Even here, his poison reaches out to sicken us. 'We're fighting Marcus. We're flying for Prince Owen and the north.'

'Our borders and airspace are closed to you,' said the officer, 'for your safety as much as ours.' The soldier waved towards his soldiers struggling to hold back a pack of onlookers with their rifles, the citizens of Hadra-Hareer shoving against the guards as the troops thrust back. For the first time, Carter noticed the looks of fury etched across the crowd's faces, dimly heard the cries of *hang them* and *make them pay* above the cutting wind.

'Lock us up, then,' said Beula, ducking as objects began to be hurled over the throng. The missiles were seized by the gale and cracked against the fuselage of their transport plane. 'And be quick about it, man.'

Carter side-stepped a hand-sized rock arcing through the air towards him. 'I need to speak with Sheplar Lesh; he's an aviator of the Rodalian skyguard. He's my friend.'

'I don't recognize that name, but you surely need a friend now, bumo.' The officer snorted while his men dragged Carter and Beula back behind the cover of the aircraft, the patter of projectiles against its airframe a shower turning into a storm as savage as the winds roaring past. 'You'll be lucky if you live to speak with the rats in a dirty cell. The mob looks like they mean to hurl you off the escarpment and we're under orders not to fire on the crowd, no matter what their provocation.'

All around them the winds swelled in ferocity, a mounting whistling that made Carter's ears throb. Whatever trickery the Rodalians had used to placate their spirits, it was finished now. The troops threw the chains over the *Raven*, and Carter realized what the iron rings driven into the runway's surface were for. *Securing aircraft against the gales*. Carter ducked to look under the aircraft. Some of the soldiers had tumbled, shoved over, comrades trying to drag them back behind the crumbling line as the angry mob vented their fury, howling over the ever-growing wind. *And all this time I thought we were cowards flying away from death in Midsburg. Damn me for a bloody fool. We were only ever flying towards it.*

It was crowded in the garrison's mess-hall, the chamber remade as a planning centre large enough to accommodate all the grey-uniformed officers, sentries, runners for the Guild of Radiomen, the senior politicians of the rebel assembly, and of course Jacob Carnehan and Prince Owen. Even more sentries were now posted around the room. Jacob knew the assembly's army was doing its best to flush subversives out of its ranks, as well as among the citizenry of the city, but it was a hard, thankless task. The Weylanders who supported the loyalists looked and sounded identical to those who supported the assembly. They might even be members of the same family. *How can you gaze inside a person's heart and know if they believe Bad Marcus's lies or not, or have developed a taste for his Vandian silver?* The traitor Thomas Purdell had either fled Midsburg or was still inside its walls, being sheltered. In either event, he had evaded capture and the justice of the rope. If it had taken a day longer to reach the standing circle of stones, or if Sariel's mastery over the sorcerous gate had faltered, then the prince would be a corpse and the rebellion's hopes buried alongside him. And if he had reached Midsburg sooner, he might have been reunited with Carter; accompanied his son to Rodal to find their little hostage and bring her back here. *I doubt the prince has the stomach to do any more than bluff with her life.* As it was, Jacob had only encountered Carter's cavalry company in the city garrison, his son's comrades happy to provide him with lodging above their stables and finally meet the man they had heard so much about. He had watched them ride out earlier in the morning. Jacob prayed it wasn't to their deaths. *But what right do I have to pray for anyone now? You're well out of this, Carter.*

'Here,' said a colonel in the field marshal's staff, tapping a map on the table. 'This is where the Army of the Boles broke across the river in Western Humont, supported by the usurper's fleet bombarding the coastal towns. Our scouts report they're marching north-east directly towards Midsburg now.'

'What of the Vandians?' asked Jacob.

'Our spies in Arcadia believe that their aerial force has departed along with the bulk of their legions.'

'The imperium's expeditionary force is heading towards us,' said Prince Owen. 'It will link up with the Army of the Boles and mount a joint assault on our positions around the city.' There was a worrying detachment in Owen's voice, as though he was describing a strategic reversal found in some military history text, rather than the fate of his rebellion.

'How has the assembly reacted to the news of the break across the river?' asked Field Marshal Houldridge.

'The assembly is worried,' said Augustus Sparrow. The party leader's haggard appearance gave weight to that statement. He looked as if he hadn't eaten or slept properly in days. 'I cannot say otherwise. We thought that Bad Marcus would be halted by the waters of the Spotswood; that after the assembly mustered its armies, we would push them steadily back down south towards Arcadia. How can soft mill-hands stand against sturdy northerners who grew up in the woodlands and wilds with a hunting rifle in their hands? That's what we said. But now? Half the assemblymen have left Midsburg for the territories, fearing being caught in a siege and wanting to fortify their home towns against the raiding southern regiments.'

'We need to follow their example. Pull out of Midsburg and disperse the army,' growled Jacob. 'Each company to scatter into the countryside, head to their home territory and mount a guerrilla campaign against Marcus and the Vandians.'

'We are the royal army, sir, not an unruly mob of bandits,' said Field Marshal Houldridge. 'We shall fight as one.'

'You will die as one! The south had the mastery of the sky *before* the Vandians showed up as their allies.'

'You understand nothing of military matters,' spluttered Samuel Houldridge, banging the map with a heavy fist. 'Weyland's skyguard is newly minted, a service that didn't even exist a decade ago. For centuries our army and navy have been high masters of seeing off troublesome aerial nomads, smugglers and sky pirates. Our city walls can release barrage balloons; our ramparts are drilled with heavy rifle mountings that will put a shell through the cockpit and skull of any pilot foolish enough to try to count our guns; our regiments are highly trained in wide-line marching to minimize strafing and bombing casualties. Merchant carriers may buzz around the clouds like oversized bumblebees, scrounging for fuel and never daring to land, but it is on the ground that victories are won. Boots, sir, boots and blood and bayonets.'

'I led men,' said Jacob. 'I never lost a battle, and I'm telling you that the assembly's three armies will only survive through scattering, hitting and running.'

Houldridge puffed up like a crimson-cheeked partridge. 'You led brutes and killers, sir. A taste of mercenary raping and murder across the water in the Burn is not what I would class as quality soldiering.'

'You want to keep the Armies of the Spotswood, Perryfax and Broadaxe intact, then leave a quarter of their companies dispersed across the west to harry Bad Marcus's advance, spread the rest over Havenharl, Garsehire and Lowharl. If you can hold the southern armies back, you will have proved your point. But if the three armies are in danger of being overrun at any point, then withdraw north into the Great Gaskald forest and the mountains of Rodal and live to harass Marcus's forces.'

'Do you hear this?' the field marshal bellowed at Prince Owen. The prince looked withdrawn to Jacob's eyes, as though he had barely heard a word of the heated argument. *He's tired. He might have survived decades as a slave in the sky mines, but none of his old life prepared him for this*. 'That is *Father* Carnehan's sage advice: we should abandon the citizens of seven prefectures to the usurper's forces; let Bad Marcus fire our towns and slay our people while we cower in the far north, waiting for our chance to flee the country should the fighting grow too fierce. That is a coward's way . . . marauder and bandits' tactics. It is not the fashion of a true Weylander, or the tradition of the royal army.'

'To hell with grand traditions,' snarled Jacob. 'We need to fight to win, not to draw the crowds' applause for your shiny, polished lines on the parade ground.'

'You, sir, mistake the battlefield for a tavern brawl over a spilled drink,' barked the field marshal. 'If you had ever served with a real army, with men of honour, you would understand that. Flee to your damnable air pirate of a brother, sir. Fighting for gold and booty seems to suit your blood. Leave the theatre of war to professional soldiers.'

'I owe you my crown, Samuel,' said Prince Owen. 'Without your early support against my uncle, half the regiments which answered parliament's call would have split and wavered.' Owen glanced sadly towards Jacob, hardly seeing the pastor. 'And you have my thanks for journeying to the sky mines and supporting the slave revolt, Father Carnehan. You have my gratitude, too, for saving my life from that traitor Thomas Purdell. If by the grace of the saints Anna survives her injuries, I will grant you any reward you ask for once this terrible war is settled. But in this matter, I must heed the army's advice. Fortify the city as best you can, Field Marshal. Muster every soldier in the prefecture. We shall make our stand at Midsburg. Where we still hold the northern shore of the Spotswood in Deersota, order our regiments to contain the Army of the Boles as best they can. If the river should be crossed in force, our forces must pull back towards the eastern lakes and prevent our being flanked by the loyalists.'

'I understand you're hurting over Miss Kurtain,' said Jacob, 'but you're not the only one who was taken in by Thomas Purdell. The traitor fooled me and my son; he took in the guild and Assemblyman Gimlette. You're not thinking straight. What you're planning is no way to beat your uncle or the Vandians.'

'Hold your tongue, Father. I know what part my failures have played. I still have my conscience.'

'You and your precious, high-born conscience,' spat Jacob. 'If you had listened to me when we returned, I could have slit Marcus's treacherous throat before he realized you had escaped Vandia. Your uncle would be dead, you'd be king, and when the Vandians arrived spoiling for revenge, they'd be facing a nation united, not a country divided and tearing itself apart.'

'Hold your tongue!' shouted Owen, before swaying down to his chair again; almost confused, as though pondering his outburst.

'Enough,' barked Field Marshal Houldridge. 'Sentries, remove this *gentleman*. His presence here dishonours honest fighting men.'

'I couldn't save her,' murmured Owen. 'That was my mistake.'

Not your biggest one. Jacob reached for his pistols by pure reflex, but felt only their empty holsters. *Carter still has my guns.* Soldiers surrounded the pastor and encouraged him out of the mess-hall with hard prodding rifle-butts. Jacob ignored the field marshal's final disparaging remark as the guards marched him out of the room. 'Nothing but a common murderer. Better off without him sullying the council.'

I'm not the common kind; I'm the breed that gets it done. Outside, Jacob found Sariel waiting for him, wrapped tight in his story-teller's coat against the cold wind, its weathered leather covered with illustrations of the tales he told, but none so outlandish, Jacob suspected, as whatever the hedgerow magician's true story was.

'I could have done with your presence inside there,' said Jacob. 'It might have been better if I'd just let that bloody traitor Purdell hang the boy prince. He seems intent on committing suicide for real and taking the cause down with him.'

'Do matters really stand so perilously?' asked Sariel.

'Between Prince Owen's precious honour and the general staff's ignorant stubbornness, the war's just been lost. The Vandians are coming; the southern army's forded the river and is marching towards Midsburg. And what is our fool of a field marshal's brilliant strategy? To pack the regiments in as tightly as possible to make the fattest target for the imperium's weapons. Is there nothing you can do?'

'Alas, I cannot cast a glamour over men's minds, and even if I could, such trickery would not be permitted,' said Sariel. 'I am no plume-plucked puppet-master.'

'What the hell are you, then?' said Jacob.

'A watcher and a waiter, for the most part. A tardy-gaited meddler only when I must be. There are far wider concerns to worry me than those that preoccupy your nation. Weyland is but a small corner of the tapestry of Pellas.'

Jacob bit down a curse. 'So what good *are* you?'

'The good I am allowed to be.'

'This city will fall, the rebellion will be lost.'

'We wade through the dust of fallen empires and lost causes. The very constituent particles of your flesh once existed as part of countless other men and women who passed this way before you; kings and queens, peasants and poachers, stardust delivered through the circle of existence and fired with the spark of the holy. An atom here, an atom there.'

'I don't need your tall tales. We'll be dust again soon enough, you damn rogue. Soon after the Vandian legions arrive outside Midsburg.'

Sariel's elderly face looked serious above his long white beard. 'You saw what we faced in Vandia at the end. Demons, *stealers*. You heard their cries again yesterday when we travelled north through the gate, howling at the surrounds of my tunnel, battering against the very walls of the world. Weyland is but a very small part of the stage.'

Jacob remembered their supernatural journey from the south to Middenharn all too well; but he had hoped against hope that his memories of those furious screams were a phantasm of travelling across Pellas using Sariel's sorcery, a price for transgressing the laws of motion, distance, time and God. Sariel was growing more certain of his powers, that much Jacob could see. When he had first opened up a gate towards the imperium, the effort had nearly killed the tramp and the entire rescue expedition. Yes, the strange man was growing certain and sure of his abilities. But what was the use in that, if every memory that returned to the amnesiac vagrant merely drove Sariel further away from the concerns of mortal men?

'I need your help.'

'That help will come at a price, your grace.'

'Name it then, damn you.'

'Your son, Carter Carnehan.'

'Dear saints, do you think you are God above now, you old rascal? Sending me visions of how I must sacrifice my boy to prove my faith? If so, you are more than insane. Everything I have done I have done for Carter.'

'*Everything*? How easily you lie to yourself. Your mutable conscience may rest easy. I do not require Carter's death. Quite the opposite, in fact. I require your son alive, I require his assistance.'

'Have mine instead.'

'Yours, sadly, is of limited use to me. Carter was given a gift in Vandia. The ability to restore the knowledge of who we are to those of my kind. To return our soul and the reason for our existence. I have been searching for my people, and have happened across rumours that others like myself yet survive. One in particular. I require Carter's gift to heal my old companion as he healed me.'

Healed you? Released you back into the world, is more like. A dreadful thought occurred to Jacob. 'That's why you came to Arcadia for me, isn't it? Why you rescued me from the usurper's jail. You knew Carter would never travel away with you while I was stretched out on one of Bad Marcus's torture racks.'

'What an untrusting rough-hewn fellow you are, your grace. Why, the very milk of human kindness runs through my veins.'

'Your blood's white, thick and milky, I remember that much. I watched you reattach your ripped-off arm in the arena. Better if Carter had left you thinking you were a hedgerow magician and wandering potion peddler,' said Jacob.

'Oh, but you must never wish that,' said Sariel. 'Without my intervention, all your runaway Weylander slaves would have been recaptured on the long flight from the empire. Your son and his young friends would be decorating trees along Vandia's roadside, nailed to the oak as a warning to any slave who dares to rebel against the imperium.'

'You've travelled on a fool's errand, then, freeing me. When Carter returns with Lady Cassandra, you can ask him to travel with you, with or without my blessing. But I know exactly what my son will tell you. He won't be setting a foot outside the nation until Willow's safe.'

'Willow Landor will be protected enough. The ladies of the court are throwing picnics on the hills overlooking Midsburg, hoping to applaud the spectacle of the burning of the city. Willow's father and her blue-blooded new husband are among the officers overseeing the abolition of your rebel assembly.'

'Benner Landor is coming here?' Damn the landowner. *Benner always did know when to trim his sails to chase whatever wind blows strongest.* 'Are you certain?'

'I had that titbit for the price of a major's uniform in Arcadia. The things a client's proud tailor will boast of are almost unlimited—'

'All for the good. I'll kill Benner for what he did to Carter and Willow.'

'Killing is your answer to so much,' said Sariel. 'And you are in the right place at the right time, *Jake Quicksilver*. A siege always brings out the worst in soldiers on either side. There is something final about a good siege, isn't there? A binary proposition. One side wins, the losers are slaughtered. No quarter given or asked for after the first shot is fired.'

'I'll ask Carter to travel with you,' said Jacob. 'I'll even sally out to the southern camp and carry Willow back over my shoulder if needs must. In return, this is what you will do for me . . .'

Sariel listened to Jacob's scheme, and when the pastor had finished, the hoary old vagrant grinned. 'And to think that you had the audacity to call me a devil, your grace. Yes, the right man for the right time, indeed.'

'Believe what you want.' *So, it's to be here. Midsburg. This is to be Vandia's blood price. And mine, too. All I have to do is survive an assault by Bad Marcus's already superior southern army assisted by the most powerful empire Pellas has ever known. And if I can do that, see out the siege, then this will finally be my war.* As Jacob gazed across the parade ground he saw the ghosts of the warlords he had fought and killed in the Burn, hundreds of walking corpses lined up in formation, uniforms torn in the fray, powder-blackened and blood-stained. *You never frightened me. You're my legion. Hell's company. And your numbers are about to grow.*

FIFTEEN

WITH FRIENDS LIKE THESE . . .

Willow stared around her as she walked. Midsburg was clearly a city preparing for war. There were soldiers everywhere, marching in columns or riding in cavalry squadrons, parading past a steady stream of Weylanders leaving the city with all their worldly goods piled around them, weighed down like peddlers. In Arcadia, uniforms had been worn as badges of honour; bright, colourful symbols of status like a fashion; the boast of supporting the loyalists and the winning side. Here they were just drab grey functional coverings needed to hang rifle slings and army packs from, signalling that hope hadn't entirely been snuffed out in the north yet. Willow travelled toward the city's council hall where the reformed assembly sat in war-time session; where she hoped to find Owen or Anna or any of her old friends. *To find them and betray them*. Her brother's parting words rang in her mind, mixing with Holten's threats. *Find and free Lady Cassandra, or watch Carter swing before being sent to Vandia as a slave*. Paetro and his brutes waited in the city market for her; selling rifles and conducting their false business while she was about hers. Willow was started out of her shame. Someone had stepped in front of her. Dressed as a soldier, it was the young guild courier who had travelled with Carter and Jacob. 'Mister Purdell, I nearly didn't recognize you under that regiment cap.'

'A soldier's what I need people to see. I might note much the same for you, dressed like a Gidorian caravaneer.'

'How did you get here? The last time I saw you—'

'Myself and Assemblyman Gimlette escaped the prisoner-of-war camp we were interred in. We managed to steal a skyguard kite and fly north.'

Willow summoned the story she had prepared and launched into it. 'It was the same for me.'

'Don't lie to me, I know why you're here,' said the courier. 'I saw the "merchants" you came into Midsburg with, and if they're Gidorians, then so am I.' He reached out to catch Willow's arm as she turned to flee. 'You don't have to run. Carter made me swear I'd keep Lady Cassandra safe. The assembly's soldiers took the Vandian girl from Sheplar and Kerge's custody by force in the north. They half-killed the Rodalian and are keeping the gask drugged so he can't harm the guards. I tried to break all three of them out of a cell under the town council, but I failed. Look . . .' He dragged Willow over to a lamppost. A sign hung there, a poorly rendered drawing of Thomas's face along with a reward of a thousand shillings. *Wanted for treason.* 'Sweet saints, that's you.'

'I told Prince Owen we could trade the emperor's grandchild for Carter and Jacob. Owen wanted to, but the field marshal in charge of the army, a dolt called Samuel Houldridge, he refused. The field marshal promised Lady Cassandra would end up dangling on a rope in front of the city walls as soon as the first shot was fired in the direction of Midsburg. The assembly and the army are in charge now, not the prince. Owen's as much a prisoner of the assembly here as Carter and Father Carnehan are down in King Marcus's dungeons.'

'None of this is how it was meant to be,' cried Willow. 'I just wanted to escape home and live in peace.' *We should have never taken Cassandra hostage. That poor girl. Carter and I should have travelled into the Lanca and vanished; left the world to its madness.*

'Wars are a damned messy business,' said Tom. 'But have heart, Willow. If we work together, we can still break Cassandra, Sheplar and Kerge out. Where are your "Gidorians"?'

'They're selling rifles in the market.'

'You mean they're travelling the city shouting their wares, looking for weak points to blow up when the siege starts. Distractions from your real business.'

Willow nodded, sadly.

'I still have friends in Midsburg, the true kind who won't be trying to collect on that reward. I'll arrange somewhere safe to room you and your Gidorians. I know the layout of the public halls. With your raiders' help, we can seize the girl. We'll see Carter and Jacob free, yet.'

'If we succeed... what will Carter think when he sees me like this?'

'He will think you are brave beyond measure,' said Tom. 'For travelling into Midsburg and risking *two* lives for his family's freedom. Carter couldn't save you from being married against your will, but you can save him now, and he would never hold a child against you. You must know the sort of man Carter Carnehan is by now. He'd even treat an enemy's child as his own.'

That was what Willow needed to hear, more than anything. *I pray you're right.*

Prince Gyal and Baron Machus stood inside the command room of *The Primacy of the Sky*, as did Princess Helrena and the general of the Army of the Bole, Hugh Colbert and his staff. Not Duncan's father, however. Benner Landor was off riding around the artillery, currently preparing the bombardment of the northern regiments encircling Midsburg's walls. A pity that Leyla had gone with him, the accompanying courtiers eager to see their first battle and make it part of the winter social season. Duncan had grown well used to arranging trysts with the young woman and satisfying the fire that burned in her blood. *My father was a fool to take on such a young wife. He was only ever interested in the house's business when we were growing up and he's no different now. Riding around, pretending to be a gentleman of the south and a leader of men, neglecting Leyla and his new child just like he neglected Willow and me. As soon as the war's won, he'll be busy with his ledgers again. It doesn't matter how many honours he wins or lands he conquers, the house will always come first. Leyla is just another trophy. It is victories the old man is addicted to, and there can never be enough of those.* Duncan could foresee problems ahead for his father when he wasn't around to keep that young woman pleasured. Sadly, Duncan suspected he'd have enough of his own when he returned to Vandia. He stared angrily at Prince Gyal. *An accident of birth, that's all you are. You never would have prospered without your noble blood behind you. Not like I did. You wouldn't have survived a month in your own sky mines.* Outside the landed warship, Duncan could still hear the rumble of Vandian tanks backing off hangar ramps and forming up into neatly armoured columns. He had been watching the tanks disembark before walking with Helrena to the battle congress, each one a mobile steel fortress with high metal ramparts and multiple cannon-spined turrets, twin sets of rotating tracks on both flanks, the tracks grinding higher than Duncan's head. The legions' fighting vehicles growled like animals in the dirt, festooned with colourful pennants, battle standards flapping in the exhaust fumes as they formed up for action.

'These are most excellent defences,' laughed Prince Gyal, thumping the map, 'for someone planning to defend against infantry and horse and a little light land artillery. I'm almost tempted to order one of our capital ships to circle the city and reduce it to rubble with fire bombs and main batteries.'

'*Almost*,' said Princess Helrena, in a cold tone.

'You need not fear for the Lady Cassandra. There is more than one way to skin a cat,' said Gyal. 'The enemy forces are dug in strongest in the east and south, and weakest in the north where they expect the forests outside Midsburg to slow down our advance. They are not used to fighting a mobile war against helos and armoured vehicles. Let the Army of the Boles give these rebels the conventional war they expect, horse and foot advancing against their lines with a baggage train of siege engines to do things the traditional way. When the rebels are fully engaged fighting the conventional war they anticipate, we will land our legions behind their lines with rotor-craft, under heavy air cover, and cut their defences apart. At the same time, our armoured columns will drive through their eastern flank. Then we shall see how long it takes before the city collapses in disarray. Shall we make a wager? Half an hour?'

'Twenty minutes!' hooted Baron Machus. At least Helrena's brutish, treacherous cousin had the good sense to have left his harem behind today. The last thing Duncan needed now was Adella Cheyenne and her sharp comments.

Twenty minutes. Why not make it ten? Should I be insulted Weyland's rebels are thought so easy to defeat? Despite these soldiers' contempt for the Weylanders, Duncan decided he approved of the plan. Paetro and Willow would have all the distractions they could wish for to divert the defenders' attention while Paetro's raiding party went about its business. *Even you can't mess this up for me, Willow.*

'To show forbearance you will take prisoners by the tens of thousands,' said Prefect Colbert.

You wouldn't be so eager to get rid of your enemies if you knew what they'll endure in the empire. The northerners might be rebels who had raised arms against their lawful king, but they were still Weylanders. The lucky ones would end up as house slaves in the mills and crop fields of Vandia. The unlucky slaves would find themselves labouring in the hellish sky mines for the few years they survived. Not everyone had the skill and aptitude to raise themselves out of that hell, as Duncan had. And the imperium would never allow a second slave revolt on its watch, that much Duncan understood. He decided he really didn't like the arrogant prefect put in command of the largest southern army. *Marcus had better find superior men than this to win the peace, or the country will have rebels acting as brigands up here until the king's grandchildren hold the throne.*

'I suppose the captured fighters will make for a worthy triumph when I return home,' said Gyal. 'Although such sudden numbers will depress the price of labour, and I will surely have the controllers of the bondservant market complaining endlessly.'

'There is only one prisoner who concerns me,' said Helrena to Prince Gyal. 'You return her to me as a corpse and our arrangement will be at an end.'

'The emperor's grandchild is the child of us all,' said Gyal, somewhat unctuously. 'And after our houses are joined, I will treat Lady Cassandra as my own daughter.'

Right up until the moment you have your own child by Helrena, thought Duncan. *But I'll be there with Paetro to watch for your assassin's blades and poisons. Helrena doesn't love you, she doesn't even like you. You're just a human-shaped stepping stone dropped in front of the imperial throne.*

Princess Helrena turned her gaze on the prefect. 'What of the pretender? Despite your newspapers' reports of his suicide, the rebel leader appears to still be alive inside the city and planning its defences.'

'We should give the doctor who saved him a medal,' said Gyal. 'For keeping the bulk of his army concentrated inside a single city for us.'

'I believe the pretender was once one of your mine workers,' said Prefect Colbert. 'If the impostor survives the assault, drag the lying dog back with you to Vandia and try him for his crimes against your people. Give him a flogging for escaping, and then another for impersonating one of our poor dead royals.'

'The punishment for revolt in the imperium is far harsher than the whip,' said Gyal. 'The emperor cannot afford to show mercy. There are too many distant provinces of Vandia that show many of the same insubordinate tendencies currently inconveniencing your king.'

You say that like you're emperor already.

'He is my worker,' said Helrena, testily.

'He *was*, indeed. So you shall be the one to hand him over for a very public and very slow execution,' smiled Gyal. 'I'm sure your friend Apolleon will be suitably grateful for the chance to give his hoodsmen and imperial torturers the chance to demonstrate their skills on the kino screens; the hostile caste always appreciates a lick of blood to keep them docile.'

Duncan felt a hand land on his shoulder.

'Ah, m'dear brother-in-law,' said Viscount Wallingbeck. Duncan wished this preening aristocrat hadn't been appointed part of the army staff. What Willow saw in the rakish southerner, beyond his house's ancient title, Duncan was hard pressed to say. The viscount raised a suggestive eyebrow. 'These Vandians know how to handle their workers and enemies both, by the saints they certainly do. An example to our prefects. We'll come out ahead in this game when the rebellion is crushed. The power of the long and little guilds will be broken, and all the whining, bleating proles in the assembly will be dangling from the end of a rope, where they've always belonged.'

'Those rebels are still our countrymen,' said Duncan.

'Agitators and mutineers . . . Who will miss a man jack of them? Are you to be in the first assault?' brayed the viscount.

'Maybe even earlier,' said Duncan. 'As long as Paetro's mission,' *please the saints*, 'meets with rapid success.'

'Lucky rascal,' said Wallingbeck. 'It's unsporting of your Vandian friends to be first through the breach. Just leave some of the spoils for us, eh?'

'And some of the dying, too?'

'We'll leave that task to the pretender's rebels, ha! Have you seen the giant steel bone-crushers rolling off your carrier? How can an honest fighting man stand against that kind of infernal device?'

'Find me one and I'll ask him.'

Wallingbeck winked at Duncan. 'And with my wife helping your Vandian friends, this victory will be a family enterprise; what with old Benner's cannons thumping the rebels and the two of us cutting our way through Midsburg's streets, sabre in one hand and pistol in t'other. I trust the imperium will reward you as handsomely as King Marcus'll recompense Benner and my house.'

'Your concern for Willow's safety does you credit, sir.'

'The Landors are loyalists, just like the Wallingbecks. Duty first, always.'

'You have noticed my sister is pregnant?' said Duncan.

'As I said, Brother, duty first. For myself as it is for Lady Wallingbeck. You can always trust your father's wife to arrange things to our two houses' benefit. She's the cleverest of us all.'

In your case, that's hardly a feat. Duncan watched the officer strut away. If the viscount was as impervious to bullets and blades as he was to irony, then Willow would have a long marriage indeed. Leyla's heated attentions were about the only thing he would miss when the fleet left Weyland. He checked the time on his pocket-watch. *Come on, Willow. Flee the city with Lady Cassandra soon. You can be reunited with this smirking dolt and play lady of the manor down in Riverlarn to your heart's content. Just free Cassandra.*

Princess Helrena left the map table and took Duncan aside, the officers clustered around the table behind her, discussing the finer tactics of the coming assault.

'Matters here are as good as settled . . . this battle can have only one outcome now. I am trusting you to stand ready with the helo squadron, waiting for word from Paetro.'

'He'll free Cassandra,' said Duncan. 'And I'll be ready to bring them out, *all* of them.'

'Thank you.' She glanced back towards Prince Gyal stretched over the command table, moving the counters around like a child playing with toy soldiers. 'You saved Cassandra once in the sky mines and again in the Castle of Snakes. This will be the third time.'

'There are some habits that I find hard to break. Please tell me you are still certain about this arrangement,' said Duncan.

'We must deal with the world as we find it, not as we wish it.'

Duncan nodded, sadly. 'If "as we find it" is all we can hope for, we had better make the best of it.'

'Return Cassandra to me unharmed, Duncan. This victory might help give Gyal the throne, but it will be dust to me if my daughter is not there to see me sitting by that dullard's side.'

'I'll get her and Cassandra will be empress after you,' Duncan swore. *And I'll still be at your side when Gyal is under the dirt.*

Jacob was in his quarters above the garrison's stables, empty since Carter's cavalry company departed for the field, when he heard one of the gate's sentries calling for him. *What now? I doubt the field marshal's had a change of heart and requires my services.* Houldridge might not know it yet, but he soon would. The shells landing inside the city's walls spoke volumes for how poorly the battle was progressing for the assembly's forces. *The south's driven off our regiments thoroughly enough to set up their batteries on those hills to the east.* Projectiles were landing every minute now. Whistles as they flew, followed by the deep thud of impact and a distant detonation, then a column of black smoke drifting into the cold air. *Those are the southern batteries. The Vandians haven't even bothered attacking yet.* The far-off cordite scent brought back the memory of other battles, other sieges. Usually, Jacob had been on the other side of the besieged walls.

The soldier ducked into the stable and located the pastor in the hayloft. 'Father Carnehan, there's a boy arrived outside the gatepost. Says he has a message for you.'

Jacob grunted and followed the soldier out to the keep's wall. A boy in a patched wool jacket waited there for him, a leather satchel for selling the city's newspapers slung around his shoulder. He beckoned the street seller to enter through the gatehouse. For a moment, Jacob wondered if the lad had been dispatched by Sariel with a message, but instead the young newspaper seller wordlessly handed Jacob a silver-plated locket. *I know this.* Jacob searched for the hidden clasp and opened it up, staring down at a familiar miniature brown-tinted photographic portrait of his son.

'Who gave you this?' demanded Jacob.

'A man, sir, dressed as a house servant. He said the locket belonged to his mistress and she needs your help.' The boy's voice dropped to whisper as he glanced around the parade ground in front of the stables. 'The servant said there're people in the city who might think his mistress an enemy, but that you'll know the truth. She's being hunted by both sides.'

'Describe the man.'

'Short, sir, not much taller than me, but as big as a bull. Red hair and a fine thick moustache the same colour. Perhaps forty years of age on him.'

Nobody Jacob recognized. *A loyal retainer, perhaps?* 'Willow,' sighed Jacob. Carter would be overjoyed to find the woman he loved had fled here from Benner's forced marriage, but the pastor felt a heavy weight settle on his shoulders. *You might have been better off laying out picnic hampers with the courtiers outside the city, Willow. The assembly's soldiers will have you in jail for the sake of your southern lady's title, and you'll only end up ducking your husband's shells and bullets in here.* Willow's life was in his hands once more, and he doubted Carter would speak to him again should he allow any harm to come to the young woman.

The boy handed Jacob a folded sheet of paper, the expensive vellum kind that might have been taken from a lady's writing bureau. He unfolded the note to discover an address written inside. 'Where's Kemble Yard?'

'On the south side of the city, sir . . . the tannery district. Cheap rooms around there, if you can stand the stench of the works. You want to visit, just follow your nose.' The boy halted. 'The servant said you'd give me a coin or two for safe delivery of the locket, but I'd sooner take a rifle from the armoury for the battle. I want to be up on the walls.'

Jacob gazed up at the sky, streaks of smoke from the shells coming in, felt the ground trembling from the impact of explosions inside the city. 'This isn't the battle yet. This is just the orchestra warming up for the main dance. You don't want to fight,' said Jacob. He tossed a coin at the scruffy street vendor and the boy caught it. 'Trust me.'

'That's what a pastor's meant to say, even an army one . . . sermons about the peace of the saints.'

'It's the *army one* that's telling you, lad,' said Jacob. 'All that talk of honour and glory in the papers you've been selling, that's all it is, talk. The real thing is just blood and dust and pain.'

The boy snorted and ran off through the gatehouse. *There's no fool like a young fool.* But Jacob had been little different, once. *He'll find out, if he lives long enough.*

Jacob set off across the city, walking hand-in-hand with his old friend. *Carnage.* Plenty of citizens left inside Midsburg to run panicked through the streets, yelling for fire buckets and carriages to drag the wounded to the by-now overrun hospitals, pushing their way past wagons arriving in from the trenches and defence lines outside loaded with maimed and dying soldiers on the flatbeds. Some of their coarse grey tunics were almost dyed brown with blood, grown men screaming and howling like babes for laudanum to ease their agony. The wounded had to compete for the road with private buggies loaded with Midsburg's citizens maimed in the shelling. *Why do they never leave in time? Are their homes and family heirlooms ever worth more than their lives?* Dying for a cabinet full of patterned porcelain and a chest full of clean sheets and blankets. But some people preferred to stick with what they knew. *And may the saints forgive me, I'm no different.* Jacob Carnehan was gone and Jake Quicksilver was back. *This isn't my doing. The Vandians would have come seeking revenge whatever I did or didn't do in their empire. Bad Marcus would have fallen out with the assembly sooner or later. Some people, they just require killing.* If Jacob had acted on that impulse with Bad Marcus, he'd only face half the enemy numbers presently tossing incendiary shells into the city. *Marcus and his Vandian dogs, they're no different to the scum that drove me and Barnaby from our farm and murdered our mother. Just standing up to evil is enough of a reason for evil to seek you out. I was happy in Northhaven. I had a wife and a family and friends and the respect of the people I lived with. Everyone but Carter's dead now. They did this to me, not I to them.* Still, Jacob was glad that he had sent Sariel out of Midsburg; Jacob's cawing conscience absent for this portion of the siege.

He rounded a street and walked into a wall of smoke from buildings burning on both sides of the boulevard. As the rolling cloud cleared, Jacob found himself standing in front of a young costermonger not much older than Carter, the young man clutching his cold, dead wife in his arms, lying together in the wreckage of their barrow. It was as though Jacob was forced to relive his final moments with Mary, murdered by the skel slavers. The costermonger's tear-stained face twisted up to face Jacob, but he saw the wrong man . . . *the pastor, not Jake Quicksilver*. But neither who Jacob was or who he had been could do anything for this poor slain woman.

'Why?' yelled the man. 'Why were they aiming at us?'

They weren't.

'Because you're here,' said Jacob.

'What can I do, Father?'

'Go to the ramparts and put a bullet in the head of the first of the bastards that tries to storm the wall.'

'Is that what the scriptures teach?'

'No, I reckon that's a lesson from an artillery shell.'

'I don't want to fight them; I don't want to kill anyone.'

Jacob knelt down beside the weeping husband. 'Get into a cellar. I'll fight them for you.'

'But you're just a pastor, what can you do?'

I'm not even that. 'They murdered the priest. I'm all that's left.' Jacob reached out to touch the man's arm, as though sharing a confidence. 'I'm going to kill Bad Marcus. I'm going to kill his Vandians and his slavers and every one of his filthy allies. I'm going to kill so many of them that the Broadaxe is going to turn red with their blood.'

'Father, please, you've gone mad, the bombardment's snapped your mind.'

'No,' said Jacob, blinking away the tears for this man's love lying in the ground, missing an arm and half her face. 'But they'll wish I had when this is over. I'm sorry they butchered your wife, but I'll make it up to you, I swear it.'

He pushed away the costermonger's trembling hands. The man started begging the pastor to join him in a cellar, shouting that Jacob would die outside. 'I've already died twice. What's a third time?'

muttered Jacob. He stumbled back into the smoke, heading for the address on the paper.

He heard Mary's voice calling through the cinders and the choking clouds. *How many corpses do you need to pay for mine, Jacob? A hundred?*

'More,' he coughed.

A thousand?

'More.'

A hundred thousand?

He wiped the tears from the biting hot smoke out of his eyes. 'Quicksilver's just getting started.'

But I didn't love him. I never loved him.

'I know: I changed for you. And I grew soft enough to lose you. You had the wrong man protecting you, Mary.'

How many's enough?

'How many do Bad Marcus and his Vandians have to send after me?' Jacob yelled into the flames. 'Three armies and an empire's worth! And when they get truly desperate, they'll send their skel slavers too. Everyone, I need every last one of them!'

How can I ever love you again?

'You can't. You— Can't.' Jacob weaved his way through the city, grabbing fleeing soldiers and citizens, seizing those fighting the fires in lines with fire buckets, shaking the directions out of their confused mouths. 'I'd come back for you, Mary, if I could.'

But she was gone. *Almost everything is.* Hard to tell which way was which when the city was burning. 'This will be my war,' he muttered. *Soon enough it will be mine. Just survive the siege. A little bit longer.* But Jacob had one life to save, one life for the empty side of the ledger before he began adding to the already packed tally on the opposite side. The newspaper boy was right about one thing... the stink of the tannery district was enough to banish the cinder and gunpowder miasma of the siege. Jacob followed the scent and found the address. Wedged in between the tanneries and warehouses stood a tall tumble-down three-storey building wearing moss-covered slate tiles like a worn hat, a hanging sign swaying in the wind with the painting of a bed, and an equally faded wooden sign above the door which bore the words *Mrs Sackville's Workingmen's Boarding House* for those who could read. This was the address. The front door swung inward, not locked and hardly on its hinges. A hallway. An old woman sat behind a wooden porter's booth in the entrance, presumably Mrs Sackville, a staircase on her right leading up to the rooms. Another thing that could be said of the stench of the tanneries outside: it masked the damp wood and musty unclean smell inside the flophouse.

'You have a lady staying here on the third floor?' Jacob's voice was hoarse and just talking hurt.

'I'd say I do,' said the old woman. 'Along with a bunch of cheap Gidorian traders. They've all gone, but she's still here, dearie. Knew she wasn't any Gidorian. Weylander, same as you or me, what with that fluting north-country accent. You come to take her away before the loyalists come marching through? You tell her that she has to pay for her rooms, you hear! She's staying in my most expensive accommodation. Half my tenants have skipped their bills, off with the first whiff of grapeshot in the air.'

'Take me to her,' said Jacob. He placed a silver shilling on the guest book right in front of the owner. He hacked and cleared his throat. Raw from the smoke of the burning city; as though he'd been drinking cheap whisky for the best part of the day. 'I'll give you another just like it to cover her rent. But I need her. I need to save her.'

'Do you, you say? Better you should chant your prayers for the whole city, Father.' The old woman whistled unhappily, but opened the swing door inside her porter's booth and came out to tramp up the rickety staircase, her bones creaking along with the floorboards.

'I'll give you some advice,' said Jacob. 'Follow your tenants and get out of the city while you can.' *I don't want to slay you too.*

'I'm of no age to be bothered by the likes of those fine southern gentlemen outside the city,' said Sackville as she opened the door while knocking on it and calling out, 'A visitor for you, dearie!' She moved out of the way and indicated the pastor could enter.

'This place will burn like tinder before you ever put the manners of those fine southern *gentlemen* to the test,' said Jacob. 'I know them.' *I was them.* A wooden-floored room sat inside, three doors leading off to other quarters. An expensive purple dress was stretched out on the bed next to an open travel case, shot silk, next to a couple of long Gidorian cape-cloaks. 'Willow?'

'Here she be,' cackled the old woman. Jacob felt the cracking impact of a lead sap swinging against the back of his skull, his vision darkening as the floor rose up to greet him. The last thing he heard was Mrs Sackville's crowing laugh fading into the darkness.

Duncan had been present at the final battle of the slave revolt as well as the slavers' raid on Northhaven, so the siege of Midsburg might be counted as his third experience of warfare, but the vista stretched before him bore little relation to his previous two experiences. This was war in all its organized, terrible panoply. Midsburg's high outer stone walls stretched out a mile in front of Duncan, manned by soldiers and cannons, the walls' frontage a blackened, ash-scattered landscape where cheap wooden slum dwellings had been cleared to give the defenders a clear line of fire. Hastily dug defensive ditches, trenches and triangular dirt-packed bastions had replaced the slum town and encroached into the farmland beyond. Midsburg was protected to the north by forests and enclosed on the east and south by a rolling hogsback called Signal Hill, which had fallen to the southern regiments the day before and was now occupied by the best part of the Army of the Boles' artillery; cannons and limber at the front and cauldron-shaped bombards behind, lobbing shells in high arcs onto the city's battlements, redoubts and counterscarps.

The horse artillery fired from behind the ruins of round stone towers, strongholds which until recently had stood as sentries over Midsburg. Now they were little more than granite roundels, mounds of shattered stone and brick, the first line of Midsburg's defences to feel the force of the siege. Duncan's father rode grandly up and down behind the gun carriages, barking orders and encouragement – both largely superfluous – at the gunners. *They know their business.* As soon as one of the twelve pounders bucked and sent a shell spinning towards Midsburg, an artilleryman came sprinting to swab the barrel while his comrades lugged the next round forward. Perhaps seventy cannons were rippling in unison while their shells broke against the walls a mile away. Their horse teams and ammunition piles lay safe on the southern side of the slope, inconveniencing the train of courtiers and camp followers taking their refreshment around burning braziers, frolicking as though this battle was little more than a stage play laid on for their diversion.

Across the flat land on the southern side of the hills, protected from the wall-mounted batteries' counter fire, a vast tented encampment had been set up by the Army of the Boles, guarded by the attackers' reserve companies and the bulk of Vandian legions in the field: soldiers, armoured vehicles and grounded helo squadrons. Prefect Colbert and his proud southern gentlemen hardly needed the imperium's forces to win this siege, not that they had any choice in the matter. The rebels fought bottled up in the city and operating without a functioning skyguard; Midsburg was protected by walls built to discourage periodic strikes by bandits, slavers, barbarians and nomadic horsemen, not its own royal army.

Duncan almost pitied the pretender and his rebellious assemblymen. *You're lucky Lady Cassandra is inside the city, or furnace shells would be raining down on you, too, by now.* But there was no fire storm in the city yet. Prince Gyal needed the empire's blood-price paid in flesh. Midsburg's citizenry and the rebel survivors would be the main payment. Duncan experienced a twinge of unease but shrugged it away as quickly as it rose within him. *I shouldn't feel pity for them. They're rebels, traitors to the lawful king. A life sentence of slavery inside the imperium is better than they deserve.*

King Marcus's loyalists and their Vandian allies hadn't had things all their own way, however. It was too cold for the southern regiments to easily dig their own siege works in the farmland between the city and the hills, but they had done their best to complete their encirclement anyway, using the questionable cover of the farms, hedges, orchards and field walls to mount their attack. The bodies of dead sappers in royal blue uniforms scattered in front of the rebel bastions spoke volumes for how fierce the opposition still was. A number of downed helos cratered the landscape, too; smoke rising from blackened wreckage. Duncan could tell that the Vandians had initially underestimated the northerners' skills in shooting down attacking aircraft, paying a heavy price for their arrogance. The sport of firing the heavy tripod-mounted anti-aircraft rifles had been practised for centuries in Weyland, and while the helos could hover and skim low to the earth, landing and taking off vertically, they were still slower than fast-moving skyguard fighters. The large spinning rotor on top of a helo presented a most attractive target for marksmen. Weylanders trained on geese, wild duck, waterfowl and pheasant; in times past, the nation's sovereigns had offered royal bounties on any bird brought down by powder and ball, merely to encourage commoners to regularly practise with their fowling pieces. In the normal course of events, this siege could have lasted for weeks, many months even, if the rebels showed the spirit to go to ground in the city's rubble and make the attackers fight for each street. *Not this time.* The king's foreign allies would ensure matters moved far faster than that. Duncan approached the staff command post, set up inside the cleared ruins of one of the defensive towers, seeking out Princess Helrena among the banks of Vandian radiomen, loyalist staff officers and their noble allies.

'Still no word from Paetro and his raiders?' asked Helrena.

Duncan shook his head forlornly. *What's happened to you, man?* The soldier was always so unswerving, a rock you could rely on to bear any weight. The same worries crawling through Duncan's mind must be going through Helrena's. That Paetro or Lady Cassandra, or both, were dead. *Why haven't the rebels demanded terms and threatened their hostage yet?* He bit his lip. *Has Willow found a new way to ruin me? Wrecking the rescue mission despite everything she thinks is at stake for her?* Duncan wouldn't put it past his sister.

At the foot of Signal Hill, six southern infantry regiments assembled behind the cover of a series of apple orchards. They were out of sight from the ramparts, but not entirely out of danger, with shells from wall-mounted cannons falling short of the hilltop's batteries and exploding among the gathering battalions. Nothing risked the sky, scouting for the assembly's side, now. The paltry few skyguards flying for the north had either been shot down in the opening hour of the siege or withdrawn to safer airfields in the shadow of the Sharps Mountains.

'This is taking too long,' said Helrena. 'Paetro is beyond overdue. Midsburg is going to fall shortly. Have you ever seen the aftermath of a siege? It is never a pretty sight. We usually have to hang a few of our own legionaries just to send them the message that it's time to halt the slaughter and drag their spoils back to barracks.'

'If Cassandra is inside there for that . . .' Duncan couldn't bear to imagine what might happen to his young charge in such carnage.

'I want you to be one of the first through the breach,' said Helrena.

'The Twelfth Armoured Legion is to be given that honour, I understand. Join them. Your king's intelligencers believe that Cassandra is being held in the cellars below the state building where the rebel assembly holds its congress.'

My king? Hardly that, now. Duncan glanced over towards Prince Gyal. He was laughing with Baron Machus and the prefect in charge of the southern army, Hugh Colbert. 'Have orders been passed to the legionaries to bring Cassandra back alive?'

Helrena nodded grimly. 'So I have been informed.'

They both knew what had been left unsaid. How much cleaner for Prince Gyal if his marriage to Helrena began unencumbered by complications, by past burdens. And the winds of war, well, how many sad fates were caught in such gusts? A bullet in the head. A knife in the heart. Ashes in the ruins of the cellar and they would never know what had happened to Cassandra. Gyal might be holding back from ordering his capital ships to flatten the city, but there were still plenty of ways for Helrena's daughter to meet with an unfortunate 'accident'.

'I could take a helo and have it drop me inside the city,' said Duncan. 'As long as we're not shot down, it'd get me there faster . . .'

'And then what, Duncan? The time for subtleties is past. I don't require diversions and raiding parties, now; Paetro and your sister are already playing that hand for us and I fear they have failed. We must move and move with force. Pound Midsburg into rubble and park our armour on what remains of their streets. Hang the rebel politicians, officers and nobility from the lampposts one by one until someone hands her over.'

'Very well. I'll join the Twelfth.'

He gazed down towards the legion he was to serve with. On the southern side of the hills, the armoured column carried by the Vandian punishment fleet had turned the fields into churned mud with their tracks, metal colossuses surrounded by companies of waiting Vandian legionaries playing cards and tossing dice. There were sixty or so large tanks, each a mobile fortress on steel tracks and each slightly different, a personal expression of their engineers' skill in the weapon mills of Vandis. Some mounted two turrets on the front, as well as a pair on the rear and a central rotating cannon turret; others had a massive squat single mortar-style cannon, or a single round rampart with a porcupine-configuration of multiple cannons aimed in every direction. He could hear the rumble of engines coughing out smoke, setting the farmland a-tremble, steel hulls painted in a mixture of camouflage patterns from previous campaigns as well as prows rendered as fierce animals – turrets with tiger eyes and jungle stripes, armoured skirts covered with swirling dragon hides, and all with flags and pennants snapping in the cold wind. Scattered among the idling metal vehicles sat lines of landed helos, rotor blades turning slowly, ready to lift in support of the ground-based armour. These helos weren't troop transports, but dedicated attack machines, craft of war heavy with rocket pods and armoured gun turrets, nicknamed *pepperpots* by the legions after the large fuselage-mounted missile tubes.

Duncan shook his head sadly, pitying the northerners inside Midsburg. *You've never fought anything like this before. If you knew what was awaiting you, you'd toss the rebel assemblymen out on their ear, fall to your knees and surrender now.* While the Vandian fighting vehicles were an eclectic assortment of designs, the imperium's infantry marched in a more uniform fashion. Vandia's legions appeared oddly archaic on the surface, perhaps fighters from the Empire of Persdad beyond the plains; each legionary heavily armoured around the chest, greaves for the legs as well as armguards, with a shining helmet protected by long cheek-guards. At first glance the steel-backs' armour might be taken for the silver breast plate and helmets worn by one of Weyland's elite mounted lancers, but in reality it was far lighter, not metal but a hardened artificial substance that could slow, turn and even stop a long-range bullet. Their helmets, similarly formed to the breastplate – proof to sabre cuts and spear-heads and anything other than point-blank pistol discharges – fielded transparent bubble visors to protect its occupant's eyes. Each helm had been mounted with a brush-like crest of crimson hair; the only difference between soldiers and their commanders being longitudinally-mounted crests for humble legionaries while officers wore transversely-set plumes. Every legionary carried a short-sword for hand-to-hand fighting, but the real force they wielded was a heavy metal rifle slung over their shoulders, fed by clip or drum, and at least thrice the weight of a simple *Landsman* lever-action rifle. Duncan had considered the automatic weapons used by Helrena's house miraculous enough compared to the firearms he had grown up with, but they were next to nothing compared to the guns issued to the imperial expeditionary force. Each weapon a factory of death, able to spew bullets at a speed capable of decapitating an enemy warrior at close range: a single legionary was capable of laying down the fire of an entire Weyland company. Two cables joined the rifle to a backpack carried by the legionary; the first supplying water to cool the rifle's barrel, the second a cable connected to the battery pack, powering a complex automated loading and firing mechanism. Duncan had heard from Doctor Horvak that there was nothing the imperium's neighbours feared so much as Vandia's armoured legions and their deadly rifles, all such guns strictly controlled by the emperor's armoury inside the capital and only issued when his legions and house troops marched to war under the imperial banner. *Better you had handed over the rebellious slaves and Lady Cassandra and begged forgiveness, emptied your prisons and turned your inmates over to Prince Gyal as his blood-price. Now everyone will pay for the crimes of a few reckless fools.*

Duncan heard a rise of voices from the command post, and as he turned to see what had engaged their attention, he realized someone on the northern side had reached the same conclusion as Helrena about the time for subtleties. Two gates in the wall's nearest side swung open, streams of cavalry sallying forth and forming a line almost as long as Midsburg's outer ramparts, three horses deep, ridden by grey uniformed horsemen spattered by mud and dirt and blackened by gun smoke, soldiers drawing sabres and the horse-mounted carbines favoured by the cavalry. They advanced slowly through the northern trench works, reforming in the clear flat fields beyond the cheap wooden town burnt to ashes as a killing zone by the assembly.

'Are they insane?' spluttered Helrena, hurrying back towards the observation post with Duncan by her side.

'The ancestors have blessed us,' laughed Prince Gyal, pointing at the city. 'These rebels are led by a *traditionalist*.'

Baron Machus practically bayed in triumph. 'By the emperor's blood, we shall show these fools *our* traditions, then.'

Prefect Colbert waved one of his runners forward. 'Order the batteries to retrain their guns from the walls and the town . . . lower all batteries towards the farmland below.'

'Belay that order. Your loyalist guns have as good as completed their task, Prefect,' said Gyal. 'You have duped our enemy into believing that this battle is the kind of work they are familiar with. But the rebels have *never* faced the emperor's wrath before. Put down smoke in front of the battlements instead; let their cursed heavy rifles shoot blind for as long as your smoke grenades last.'

Colbert bowed. 'It shall be as you command, Your Highness.'

Exactly as you command. Despite the fact that King Marcus and his loyalist forces were allied with Vandia, Duncan couldn't help but despise the so-called 'supreme commander' of the Army of the Boles. *A politician only risen to rank through his obsequiousness.* Colbert jumped to the imperium's tune with all the eagerness of a corporal obeying a field marshal, despite the Weylander's supposed high rank. Colbert had clearly realized that he was fighting alongside the next emperor and empress of Vandia and was eager to prove his usefulness. If Prince Gyal requested the services of the prefect's own grandmother as bayonet fodder in the front line, Duncan didn't doubt he would see a silver-haired old lady stooped inside a blue-coated uniform in short order. *I picked this side despite the cost to me. But you, Hugh Colbert, you contemptible lickspittle, you're happy to pay with the lives of as many Weylanders as it takes, loyalist or rebel alike.*

'This is it.' Prince Gyal thumped a fist into the palm of his other hand. 'Radioman, order the helo squadron to return loaded with *treacle*.' He turned to grin at Helrena. 'We shall lay a carpet of bodies down there, a carpet leading all the way to the diamond throne.'

'The battle is not won yet, my Prince.'

'Watch and learn, my darling.'

Duncan glared jealously from behind the prince as he watched the massing attack below. *One lucky cannon shot from the battlements, is that too much to ask for? See if Helrena wishes to marry a bag full of body parts.*

A couple of minutes later the southern batteries along Signal Hill rocked on their carriages, while curls of white smoke spread out in front of Midsburg's walls. Bugles sounded the charge below, and the cavalry's centre moved first, a slow canter initially, then a fast canter before reaching a full gallop, until a 'V' of horses and men hurtled full pelt across the southern trench works, hurdling the occasional low stone wall and hedge, hooves a thunderous clatter on the hard frozen soil. The switch from stone shattering shells to smoke canisters only seemed to encourage the ranks of northern cavalrymen. *Perhaps they think we're preparing to switch to grapeshot for their charge and want to gain the slope before the batteries are fully prepared to meet them?* Duncan looked on with a mixture of horror and amazement. *You'll never get close enough to the batteries to taste grapeshot, you crazy dupes.* Southern soldiers leapt up from behind the shelter of walls and hedges, long rippling lines of rifle smoke rising up as they poured fire into the charging horsemen, but the assembly's cavalry were charging as though possessed, convinced of their immortality. The southern attackers' forward ranks crumpled and fell, slashed by sabres from on high or cut down by carbine bullets; those that turned and fled only running far enough to be trampled under the thundering press of hooves. Some of the southern infantry ignored their hollering sergeants and broke and ran, unwilling to fall under the next sabre.

'Messenger!' barked Colbert, 'Ride down there and tell whichever dolt is in command of those cowards to hold fast.'

'Better you should order your soldiers to pull back,' said Helrena. 'They are too close to the enemy now.'

'Too close for what?' asked the prefect.

'*That.*' Helrena indicated a wave of perhaps thirty helos flying in low and fast from the west, drawn in on the prince's orders. No bigger than dots coming in over the forested hills.

As Colbert jumped to do the princess's bidding, another rider came galloping up, this one a colonel whom Duncan knew only too well. *Father.* Benner Landor halted his steed in front of the prefect, a mist of warm air fountaining from the horse's nostrils. 'Sir, we have nearly exhausted our stock of smoke canisters. Permission to load grapeshot when depleted!'

Colbert turned to the prince and princess, uncertain whose advice to seek first. Prince Gyal waved an imperious hand, as though the matter was of little concern to him.

'Wait five minutes and then return to counter-battery fire,' ordered Helrena. 'Keep the defenders' heads down on the ramparts as the Twelfth Armoured swings east.'

Colbert nodded as if this had been his intention all along. 'As Her Majesty said, Colonel.' He extended a leather-tubed telescope towards the charge. 'Sweet saints, I do believe that is Field Marshal Houldridge himself leading the charge. He's certainly determined to live up to his nickname.'

'Shall I order our cannons to aim for him, sir?' asked Benner Landor.

'That would be far too coarse,' said Colbert. 'The leaders of armies have better things to do with their time. You have your orders, Colonel.'

Benner rode away, nodding down towards Duncan as he passed. 'We're giving the pretender and his grubby rebel friends a hard pounding this day, son.'

Duncan watched the helo squadron growing larger. Down below, the northern cavalry charge had covered half the farmland between the city's walls and Signal Hill. 'You're about to have company in that,' muttered Duncan. *And I suspect the Vandians will pound harder.*

The charging horsemen were sweeping all before them when the helo squadron passed low and fast, the chop of rotors mixing with the din of hooves, and then a series of black metal ovals fell tumbling from the helos and the landscape changed, converted from empty wheat fields and icy orchards into an ocean of fire. Flowering hot flames rippling with blackened bodies and whirling horses, a surf of devastation which swelled down to reveal a flat plain of clinging, cloying fire, most of the charging horsemen incinerated while the remainder, the outriders and laggards, turned and twisted enveloped in fire.

Oh dear God. 'What is that?' asked Duncan, staring horrified, trying to unhear the pitiful high-pitched whinnying of blackened horses and strangled cries of dying riders.

'The legions' treacle . . . a mixture of jellied naphtha, pine resin, quicklime and nitre,' said Helrena. 'It is a fire that is fed by water. Try to extinguish it and it only burns stronger.'

On the other side of the hill, safe from Midsburg's diminished battery fire, the courtiers travelling with the army had abandoned their picnic blankets, winter braziers and hampers, strolling up to discover the source of the artillerymen's wild cheering. A polite clapping joined the yells and hollers of the Army of the Boles, the men and women of King Marcus's court applauding the end of the rebellion.

'How can anyone call that war?' said Duncan, sick to his stomach.

'War is victory. All else is defeat,' said Helrena. 'How do you think the imperium prevails, Duncan? Surrounded by enemies for tens of thousands of miles, every nation desperate to steal the riches of the stratovolcano from us; jockeying for position, planning and plotting, waiting for the day we grow soft and weak? If we cannot win, we are nothing. The day the imperium cannot win is the day we will be extinguished and the light of our world will go out.'

Booming laughter from Baron Machus echoed down the hillside, bellowing for the armour behind the hill to sweep across the barren, burning vista.

'Bring my daughter back to me, Duncan. It is time.'

Duncan left to join the tank column, only too glad to put the sight of devastation behind him. Halfway down the hill he came across Leyla returning from the brow of the hill with the other courtiers. Her face lit up as she saw him.

'I'm leaving to push my way through Midsburg's defences,' said Duncan, halting her. *Better she doesn't see what victory looks like.*

'You're hunting for Willow?' asked Leyla.

He shook his head. 'Damn my sister! With Willow's luck, she'll probably crawl out of the ruins married to Prince Owen and calling herself queen,' said Duncan. 'It's Lady Cassandra and Paetro I'm going in there for.'

'I hardly think Viscount Wallingbeck would approve of such bigamy,' said Leyla. 'But Willow promised your father she would help return Lady Cassandra to the emperor. I'm sure your sister remembers her duty.'

'If so, you're the only one who is sure.'

Leyla reached out to touch his arm, tenderly. 'Let someone else go through first, Duncan. You know what the soldiers first to breach a town's walls are called in the army? The *Forlorn Hope* . . . almost certain death in exchange for duty and glory. You don't have to risk your life.'

Duncan felt a wave of passion rising inside him. An unexpected reaction to the death behind him. For half a crown he'd shelter the woman behind one of the gun carriages and take her on a courtier's picnic blankets. 'I'm going. Not for glory, but for my house.' *For Cassandra.*

Leyla glanced over towards Princess Helrena. 'Your house? Haven't you heard the rumours that your mistress is sworn to marry Prince Gyal?'

'I have. They're more than rumours.' *Sadly.*

'She does not deserve your loyalty, my brave fool. If you are to attempt this perilous thing, take your father's sergeant with you. Nocks.'

'That short cut-faced lout who used to be a servant in Hawkland Park?'

'The same.'

'I don't know the man very well; he was hired after I left the Park. But he acted far too familiarly where Willow is concerned. You didn't see the way Nocks was staring at her inside that restaurant in Arcadia.'

'Nocks is not entirely to blame. He was one of your sister's many servants in Northhaven,' said Leyla. 'Willow teased him constantly, leading him to draw conclusions beyond his station about their future together. The important thing is that before service with the Landors, Nocks served with the royal army on the Eastern Frontier; a hard commission which breeds even harder men. Nocks has kept Benner alive for me throughout this terrible rebellion. He knows his way well around a battlefield and will be only too happy to help save your sister. Mixed feelings for Willow are understandable given your sister's betrayal of you, but I am the mistress of Hawkland Park and I still feel a duty to her, even though she is now Lady Wallingbeck. Please, do not make me watch Benner grieve for another lost child.'

'It is you that my father doesn't deserve.' Duncan glanced around and pulled the woman tight, resisting the urge to kiss her.

'Not here,' said Leyla. 'Later, after the battle. Find me. There will be hundreds of empty tents in the southern camp where we can meet.'

And how many of them were just emptied by the Vandian skyguard? 'I won't be among the missing,' promised Duncan. 'I'm planning to return. Send Willow's servant to the Twelfth Legion. We're advancing soon.'

'Follow your duty, then. May it lead you straight to all that you deserve.' Leyla gave him an enigmatic smile and left to locate Duncan's father along the artillery line. Duncan watched her go with hungry eyes. His father's young wife wasn't who he really wanted, but she certainly helped fill the hollow void left by Helrena's rejection. *It will take returning Lady Cassandra to Helrena to show the princess my true value. I'll do my duty. I'll follow it through every damned traitor the rebellion has to throw at me.*

Leyla Landor left Benner to his bombards and cannons and walked away with Nocks by her side. It hadn't taken much to wheedle her husband's trusted sergeant away from the landowner's command. A hint or two about protecting Benner's son combined with the advantage of helping return the emperor's kidnapped granddaughter and he had practically shoved Nocks in her direction.

'I can hardly ensure Benner steps in front of a bullet if I'm not beside him,' complained Nocks as they walked towards the Vandian armoured column. 'This siege is the first real action we've seen.'

'There will be time enough for my darling husband's ultimate sacrifice for the loyalist cause,' said Leyla. 'I require a casualty of war on Vandia's side right now, and this might be our only opportunity before Duncan departs for the empire.'

'The Landor boy? You sounded eager enough to protect him just now in front of old Benner. I thought you had the whelp compliant between the sheets?'

'I needed Duncan biddable, but his usefulness to the cause is coming to an end.'

'Never could tell when you were acting,' snorted Nocks.

'Duncan's mistress is planning to plight her troth with Prince Gyal. Duncan Landor is foolish enough to think there will still be a place for him in their combined house; but I foresee him returning home in exile with a broken heart, seeking to take up his old station at Hawkland Park.'

'And *he*'d be head of the house after Benner's crushed by a gun carriage.'

'I think my son deserves to be sole heir to the Landor fortune, don't you?'

'You could always marry the whelp after Benner's accident.'

'Mercy me, I think not. Husbands are far too unreliable in the long term,' laughed Leyla.

'You should know,' grunted Nocks. 'How many of yours have fallen under the wheels of a carriage or died from food poisoning?'

'I would consider it common to count,' said Leyla. 'Benner is under orders to lay down a wall of smoke to mask the assault on the city walls. That is where Duncan Landor intends to be. Nobody will be able to see anything in the thick of it, all those bullets whistling though the air. A pistol shot in the back of the skull, to be sure?'

'And the whelp's sister?'

'I doubt Willow's still alive in Midsburg, but if she is . . . ? Well, I understand the most dreadful things can happen to women when a city is sacked.'

'That's always the way of it,' grinned Nocks. 'And I can I feel in my bones that willowy Willow wouldn't be able to live with the shame.'

Leyla nodded with satisfaction. *And you, my odious brute, are going to make sure of it.*

SIXTEEN

WHAT YOU CAN DO IN A TANNERY

Willow woke up, her head spinning. She was inside a works hall, a tannery, filled with great bubbling oak vats of foul-smelling chemicals; each smelt as though year-old carcasses were being rendered inside the tubs. She sat bound painfully to a chair with rope, and opposite her she could see Paetro, feet and legs secured against a similar wooden seat, his arms tight behind his back. A third chair lay between the two of them, unoccupied.

'What—' Willow tried to speak but coughed, retching and only just holding back the vomit.

'Take a minute, lass,' said Paetro. 'We were poisoned. Do you remember? Inside the rooms your so-called friend found for us. We were studying the layout of the city hall Purdell sketched for us when supper arrived. The food was obviously laced with something.'

'Where are the others?' Willow gasped.

'Inside these vats,' said Paetro. 'I woke up in time to see Purdell sliding my boys' dead bodies into the chemicals. The murdering turncoat bastard has other plans for you and me. Our dose wasn't strong enough to kill us.'

Willow retched again, twice as strong. 'Why? Why would he do that? Tom's a friend of Carter; he said he'd help us?'

Paetro spat across the floor. 'Purdell's sold out to the locals rebels, I would say. We're his ticket off that wanted poster you showed me.'

'Right idea but wrong side, Vandian.' A voice growled behind them. Thomas Purdell strode into view. Willow shivered. His voice had changed. Even his walk was wrong. It was as though the guild courier had been possessed and replaced by someone entirely different. Purdell came closer and inspected Willow as though she was meat for his table. 'You two are my ticket to so much more than a mere pardon.'

Willow struggled in the chair but her bindings were too tight. 'Mister Purdell! You don't have to do this—'

'No, I rather think I must. A trap needs to be baited with cheese, and you're all the cheese I currently have.'

'I don't understand. You're Carter and Jacob Carnehan's friend? You said you would help me free them; trade Lady Cassandra for their liberty!'

Purdell reached and stroked her cheek gently. Willow flinched away from his icy fingers. *Why are they so cold?* 'But they are already free, you little fool. Jacob Carnehan escaped King Marcus's cells with the assistance of a vagrant hedgerow magician called Sariel Skel-Bane; and Carter fled north with Prince Owen when the assembly was outlawed. You don't believe me? Ask your Vandian friend here. I'm sure he knows the truth. He was watching you like a hawk in case you ran into any of the Carnehan clan inside Midsburg. I spotted one of his soldiers tailing you the morning we met.'

Willow glanced at Paetro, but he just spat on the floor again, staring in hatred at the guild courier. *For nothing. So this was all for nothing?* Willow felt sick to her stomach. She had been betrayed and duped by her own family. *And not just me. My unborn child, too. How could they do this to us?*

'If you're really one of King Marcus's hirelings, then you had better let us go,' said Paetro. 'Haven't you heard, man? Emperor Jaelis and your King Marcus are allies now.'

'Do I look like I care, imperial? I was dispatched to the north to find and free Lady Cassandra,' said Purdell, pacing between the prisoners like a cat choosing which mouse to devour first. 'You might say we are hunting the same stolen treasure, although only one person can claim the reward for finding it. If it is any consolation, you had failed in your duty from the start. The emperor's granddaughter was never here – she was packed off to Rodal by Father Carnehan.'

Willow groaned. 'Then Sheplar and Kerge aren't prisoners in the city?'

'Your two mongrel friends never even set foot in Midsburg,' laughed Purdell. 'After my agents failed to capture Lady Cassandra in Northhaven, Jacob decided to move the girl to safety in Hadra-Hareer. The brat the pretender has imprisoned here is some northern maid masquerading as the imperial for the benefit of the king's spies. Prince Owen recently dispatched Carter to retrieve the Vandian brat from Rodal; Carter doesn't know he's bringing Lady Cassandra back to *me*. He was walking out of Midsburg when your caravan came rolling into town. If you hadn't been hiding under your cloak you might have spotted him. How differently might things have worked out for you, then?'

Willow sobbed in frustration and impotent rage.

'Don't give this bastard the pleasure of your tears,' said Paetro.

'Shut up!' yelled Willow. 'You and my brother tricked me into this. Everything you told me was a lie. I expected as much from Holten and my father, but *you*, I helped you—'

'Helped me?' snarled Paetro. 'How did you do that? You lied to me in Vandia, Willow Landor. I allowed you to escape from the Castle of Snakes for just one reason, to take my daughter to safety with you. And in return you got Hesia killed.'

'I didn't know Father Carnehan had shot Hesia, not until Duncan came home and told me,' said Willow. 'I thought she had chosen to stay in hiding in Vandia.' It was the truth, but her words sounded like the feeblest of excuses, even to her ears.

'She died true, at least, attempting to protect the little highness,' grieved Paetro. 'Hesia is at peace with the ancestors, her betrayal of her house forgiven. Lady Cassandra was under my daughter's protection, as she was mine, as precious to me as one of my own. I'd cut a deal with a thousand demons if it meant saving the little highness.'

'Then fate smiles on you, Vandian, for this day you only have to deal with one,' said Purdell. He lifted up a hand-sized radio. 'Your people possess such amazing crafts. An entire Guild of Radiomen's hold squeezed into a single device as small as a tinder-box. I require you to surrender your pass phrases to arrange your escape from the city. When your soldiers come for me, I will tell them how valiantly you died trying to free the fake hostage, and how the real Lady Cassandra will shortly be returned to your people from Rodal's peaks. Both our assignments will be complete.'

'Yet only one of us will be alive to benefit from it,' Paetro snarled.

'Quite so, but the manner of your departure is still under your sway. I understand that employment as an imperial torturer in Vandia gives the practitioner great status. Shall I show you how the craft is practised here? We must seem like savages to you, but I may yet surprise you with my talents.'

'I've already glimpsed your foul handiwork. I caught sight of my soldiers' bodies before you rolled them into the vats. They knew nothing you needed, did they? Does your king pay you more to skin enemies alive before you murder them? I knew creatures like you in the legions,' said Paetro. 'No honour, broken in every way a man can be broken. You'll take what you want and carve us up anyway. Die in the siege, you hound; you'll hear no secrets from my lips.'

Purdell shrugged. He didn't seem bothered by the soldier's defiance. 'A challenge given is a challenge accepted.'

There was a noise from outside the hall of vats and two thuggish-looking men in grey uniforms entered, dragging a body between them, an old woman hobbling behind. Willow cursed. It was Mrs Sackville, the landlady of the accommodation Purdell had arranged for Willow and the raiding party. The man the soldiers clutched swayed as they dragged him, and Willow groaned out loud as she realized it was Jacob Carnehan. This at least, had been no lie on the part of the treacherous courier. *The father's really here, not in Arcadia. What Purdell said about Carter is likely true, too. They were free in the north all this time. I could have escaped the viscount and joined Carter. Damn them all: my family, the king, Holten and my so-called husband.*

'It's getting hairy outside,' announced one of the bruisers, a short, stout soldier with a long ginger moustache. A large hunting knife hung from a leather holster across his chest and Willow guessed it had never been used for the tanner's trade. 'A mortar shell nearly landed on the wagon during the ride over here.'

'You'll be deserting soon enough,' said Purdell, 'along with a crown agent's warrant to guarantee you safe passage from the royalists tossing those shells. Secure the pastor well in his chair.'

'I think I've harboured my last crown agent in Midsburg, dearie,' said Mrs Sackville, watching the soldiers bind the unconscious pastor in the seat.

'You'll be well provided for,' said Purdell. 'You can buy another house to run soon enough.'

'Such a pity,' said Mrs Sackville. 'It was convenient owning the tannery next door. Cattle blood and traveller blood: identical when it's flushed down the drains.'

'Help me,' Willow begged the old woman. 'Don't leave us here. Please, send word to Prince Owen.'

Mrs Sackville turned her gnarled face to the wooden roof above, eddies of dust falling down as the structure trembled with the bombardment. 'Not today, dearie. The pretender and what's left of his staff have more pressing things on their mind. They're somewhat distracted by the guns of the south, and the Vandians' peculiar hovering aircraft landing legionaries inside the city.'

'Please, this madman is going to kill us.'

'Oh my dove, *kill* isn't the word I would use. Thomas Purdell is the finest torturer I ever trained for the service. Would you believe that our skills were almost a lost art when King Marcus took the throne? But I'm keeping the flame of the old ways alive now, passing them down through the generations. You should be honoured to help us.'

'Prepare my tools,' Purdell told the old woman.

'Yes, it's time. It must be good for you to have worthy quarry on the slab again, dearie. All those guests I drugged for you, I fear you were growing jaded practising on travelling merchants and foreign caravaneers.'

'Quite true,' said Purdell. 'But these three will more than make up for my lack of sport.'

Willow watched in horror as the despicable old woman shuffled out of the hall like a living corpse. *But she's not the corpse. We are. She's killed us all.* Purdell crossed to a stone washing sink and drew a bucket of water, returning to toss it over Father Carnehan's head.

The pastor struggled awake, groaning. 'Willow.' Jacob turned from her to take in Paetro. '*You*. So you came to Weyland after all. You took your time about it.'

Paetro shook his chair in rage. 'I'm going to kill you, Carnehan.'

'You have missed your place in that queue,' tutted Purdell. 'Give me the details of your escape plan, empire man, and I promise you'll live long enough to watch the priest die in agony.'

Paetro merely spat at the guild courier's feet by way of answer. A shell fell close enough to blow out one of the tanning hall's windows. Willow raised her head and heard the distant thud of the southern batteries loud through the broken glass.

'It seems a fair proposal, Vandian. You help me, and in return I'll show you how much pain the man who murdered your daughter can endure? No? Duty before pleasure, then.' Thomas Purdell sighed, allowing a hint of irritation to slip through his easy demeanour. He signalled his two thugs. 'Drag the Vandian to the cattle skinning room and make sure he's well strapped, then hold him down for me. He looks as strong as his brutes, and one of the imperials nearly slipped his restraints before I stuck a scalpel through his forehead.'

'I'm sorry about Hesia,' Willow cried to Paetro. 'I'm sorry I couldn't save her.'

If Paetro heard Willow's words, he didn't acknowledge them. Purdell's lackeys dragged the Vandian away, the soldier cursing and thrashing and still bound to his chair, out through a doorway into another part of the factory.

'Better he had heard that from me,' muttered Jacob.

Thomas Purdell turned and slapped Jacob in the face, not particularly viciously; more like a butcher gauging the toughness of the meat he was planning to tenderize. 'Except that from you the words would have been a lie, wouldn't they, *Quicksilver*? You deprived me of my sport with the pretender and his woman, so you owe me two bodies. I'll take yours and Carter's little sweet-meat in exchange. Willow went to some trouble to save you, so you obviously care for each other. She will be next, I think, after I've finished with the Vandian. You deserve to watch my artistry so I shall save you to last.'

Jacob glowered at the king's man but refused to give him the satisfaction of answering.

'Silence can be a challenge too. Before I'm finished with you, you'll be more than willing to speak. And we have so much tittle-tattle to catch up on. Wait until you hear how I've arranged for your idiot son to die, you're going to love that. Poor Carter. Had I realized you'd be joining us, Father, I'd have considered allowing Carter to live long enough to be reunited with his girl. Then you could have watched me work on both lovebirds together before I send you on your way. I would have enjoyed giving Carter the news that his girl has a bun in the oven from the noble dolt we bred her with.'

Jacob's eyes opened in shock. 'Willow, you're *pregnant*?'

Willow could only nod in confirmation.

'It doesn't matter,' exhaled Jacob, 'none of it matters.'

'It matters to me,' smiled Purdell. 'King Marcus had a pregnant woman in the dungeons he wanted questioning once. But one of my rivals drew the interrogation, I'm sad to say. I don't mind telling you that I'm fascinated to learn if there's any appreciable difference in such a novelty. What do you think, Lady Wallingbeck? Will you suffer enough for two?'

'I think you'll discover a demon's torment in hell one day.'

'Discover it? I expect to be running the place!' Purdell hooted with amusement and strode away.

'I'm sorry you have to be here for this, Willow,' said Jacob, watching Purdell exit the hall. 'This is a just end for the man I was. But you deserved far better with Carter.'

'No,' said Willow. 'My family traded me off like a cow to be bred before tricking me here to aid their advancement. If anyone is to blame for this, it's the much vaunted glory of the House of Landor, not you.'

Screams started a few minutes later, from outside the vat room. Willow shuddered. The treacherous Thomas Purdell had started his foul work with Paetro.

'You don't understand. I planned for this. I *wanted* this,' moaned the pastor. 'Not you here, Willow, but all the rest. The Vandians, they were too far away. The imperium had to come to Weyland so I could avenge Mary. That's why I took the emperor's granddaughter as a hostage. Not to use her as a shield, but as bait to draw the imperium's killers down on me.'

'Vandia's legions would have come anyway,' said Willow, 'to punish the slave revolt.'

'Who's to say that's true? It was in the hands of God and fate. I should have left it there, been the man Mary married, not the devil that washed up on Weyland's shores half-dead. I deserved to die before, and I deserve it twice over now. Thomas Purdell is only my due.'

'Weyland doesn't need a pastor to pray for our souls,' said Willow. 'It needs the man you once were to fight for us. You must have known that when you left Northhaven to find us, when you set aside your prayer-book and picked up your pistols.'

'You don't understand.' Jacob shuddered in the chair as though he was already feeling the turncoat's blade against his skin. Jacob Carnehan began to speak to Willow of the acts he'd perpetrated as a mercenary officer across the ocean in the Burn. Fleeing over the water as a fugitive murderer alongside his young brother, serving with mercenary companies until they had both fully mastered the fighter's trade. Hundreds of nations wracked by bloody warfare which had endured for centuries: nation against nation, region against region, then finally town against town and family against family; until all that was left was hatred and feuds and warlords and the ashes they fought over. Everything else forgotten... no cause but death without end, purpose or sanity.

Jacob's tale, his terrible choked confession, came out between Paetro's stifled screams. Until Willow had to close her eyes, trying to will away visions competing in her mind, choosing between Paetro twisting in agony just beyond the hall and peasants slaughtered by a warlord nicknamed Quicksilver. Starving farmers' flayed for hiding crops. *Please stop*. Innocent women raped with every village sacked. *End this*. Children pressed into service and marched against enemies just as young. *No more*. Battle after battle and victory after victory until the skies danced dark with crows. *No more*. So much blood that even Jake Silver's own brother abandoned him and found greater peace in piracy. *It was all true, the king's lies. Not propaganda, but the truth. How can this be the man I grew up with?* The acid drip of the tale continued until everything she had ever known about Carter's father had melted away. And by the time the confession had finished, Willow drifted as hollow and light as a leaf blown on the winter wind.

'Is that what Weyland needs?' pleaded Father Carnehan, his eyes as wild and fierce as a wolf.

Willow could hardly speak. *The choice is mine. Why should the choice be mine? Haven't I done enough? How can this possibly be Carter's father?*

'Tell me, Willow Landor. The countries west of the ocean weren't much different to the league of the Lanca once. Shall I remake Weyland as similar ashes?'

'You never lost?' asked Willow.

'I lost *everything* I had,' cried Jacob.

She forced herself to look into the pastor's eyes. 'You never lost a battle?'

'Quicksilver never lost a battle,' admitted Jacob.

Sweet saints forgive me. 'Then the man the north needs is here.'

Jacob Carnehan's head lolled back and a tearing scream escaped his lips – a horrible, unholy mix of agony and pain and primeval rage. Willow had never thought such a torn sound could issue from anything human. *Perhaps it hadn't.* Slowly the sound died away and his tired crazed eyes focused solely on her. 'How will I know when to stop?'

'You must know.' *You must.* Tears spilled down Willow's cheeks, but she was no longer sure who she wept for. *Myself, Carter, his father? Maybe even the Vandians.* Vandia's slavers hadn't murdered poor Mary Carnehan, nor had King Marcus sold Willow and her friends into slavery. No. They had just broken the lock on the cage, and the imperium and the usurper had stepped into the trap. *And I opened the door for them.*

Jacob rocked and scraped his chair back towards the end of the hall, inch by inch, shaking the wooden frame and his bonds, and then he shoved back and overturned the chair, landing in the litter of broken glass with his arms tied behind his back, choking down a cry as it sliced his back, head and hands. *They'll have heard the chair scraping, surely?* But the thud of the distant guns and yells of the tortured Vandian were too loud. The pastor writhed on the floor, trying to clutch a shard of glass with his fingers, cutting at his rope even as blood from his wounded hands slicked across the floor. He was silent with his pain, working to Paetro's screams. Willow watched the scene in horror, waiting for the moment when Purdell or one of his lackeys would return and discover Jacob and Willow trying to escape. And then two did, the pair of bruisers in northern uniforms, probably released from holding Paetro by the fact the Vandian was no longer in any fit state to struggle. Jacob still lay bound to the chair, thrashing on the floor among a wash of his own blood.

'There's a rum sight,' hooted the ginger-haired soldier. 'Trying to slit his wrists before Mister Purdell takes his entertainment.'

'That's a pastor for you,' said the other soldier, 'ain't no fun a man can make that a churchman can't come along and spoil it.'

They moved across the hall. The ginger-haired soldier knelt down to haul Jacob's chair back up while his comrade just stood and shook his head sadly, eyeing Willow, a look of lust burning in his eyes. 'Don't reckon the God-botherer will approve of our turn with his pretty little parishioner, then. You ever tidied it up with a lady viscount?'

'Don't reckon I've had the pl—' The soldier's banter gurgled to a halt, a shard of glass embedded in his throat, collapsing to the floor as Jacob seized the hunting knife from the soldier's chest holster and hurled it into the other man's face. The second soldier almost turned a cartwheel with the blade's impact, his arms flailing in the air like a marionette with severed strings, and then he thumped down on the floor with the knife's hilt quivering deep inside his right eye socket. *Dead, just like that. As easy as breathing for him.* Willow gagged and barely held down her retch. Jacob Carnehan brought a fist down against the chair's frame, splintering wood. He released the ropes around his ankles and lifted a revolver from the closest corpse's belt, before rising, as a shadow might rise. He walked over, drawing the knife out of the second soldier's skull, wiping the blade carefully on the corpse's grey tunic before using it to slice away Willow's ropes.

'Save Paetro,' pleaded Willow. *I opened the door, I opened it. There's nobody but me to blame.*

Jacob looked like he wasn't going to answer. He tugged a belt studded with bullets away from the second corpse and clipped it around his waist instead, but finally he spoke. 'He's a Vandian killer whose daughter I shot dead for stepping in front of me.'

'Then you owe him.'

'Only the first bullet.' Jacob passed Willow one of the brace of pistols he had stolen from the dead thugs.

So heavy. She inspected the metal weight uncertainly. 'What do I do with this?'

'There are six answers to that question inside there.'

Jacob stalked towards the doorway Paetro had been dragged through. Willow hardly dared follow, but she forced herself to. *He's our beast, my beast.* And if she was not his keeper, then nobody was. They passed a series of smaller vat rooms and storage chambers, following the sound of the Vandian's anguished moans, growing louder and more pained, until they found what they were looking for. Willow wished they hadn't. An abattoir chamber with a series of slabs large enough to hold cattle, easily large enough to accommodate Paetro's form staked out naked in a horizontal 'X', the slab's surface crusted with the blood of decades of work. Mrs Sackville hobbled between a stone sink containing the instruments of Thomas Purdell's trade as well as a tanners'. The turncoat glanced up in surprise at being interrupted, a hooked blade hanging in his hand and a brown leather apron to protect his uniform from the worst of the butchery.

'If you had worn that uniform for real, you'd know a soldier expects a little blood,' said Jacob.

Purdell lifted the blade up high in the air carefully, moving it to the side of the slab. 'That's hardly fair, is it, a gun against a feather dissection blade?'

'That's why I'm going to shoot your over-the-hill tutor first, to give you a chance to go for that pistol tucked in your army holster.'

Purdell snorted. 'You never did possess any flair, you dolt.'

Willow had to give Mrs Sackville her due, she ducked fairly spryly when her life was on the line, but Jacob's pistol tracked her dipping form viper-fast, the barrel jouncing with a single shot. Sackville screamed as the bullet's impact twisted her wizened old body and sent it spinning to the floor. Purdell's revolver was in his hands and coming up towards Jacob as the first of the pastor's volley caught the traitor in the chest. Maybe if Purdell's hands hadn't been slick with Paetro's blood, he might have drawn faster. Jacob strode towards the traitor, shot after shot, fanning the pistol and emptying his chamber into the treacherous guild courier, Purdell stumbling back, striking the wall before slipping down the back of the abattoir, sliding on a trail of red strokes, painting the bricks behind him.

An unholy scream of rage tore out of Sackville's wounded throat as she picked herself up and came charging towards the pastor waving a meat cleaver sharp enough to sever a cow's heavy head. The pastor turned and fired, but the pistol chamber clicked uselessly. *Empty*. Willow winced as the blade came arcing down towards Jacob Carnehan's skull until Mrs Sackville went dancing sideways under a volley of fire, her old body fountaining with entry wounds before she tipped over one of the spare slabs. There she lay, a slight trembling and a moan before all life was extinguished. Willow stared down in shock at the pistol in her hand, its barrel warm and a tail of gun smoke stinging her eyes.

'That's your answer,' growled Jacob, looking sadly at Willow. 'And it'll go hard on you.'

There was another groan. Thomas Purdell tried to get to his feet, but he failed and collapsed. 'No . . . style, no . . . sophistication,' Purdell hissed from the floor, the words bubbling from his lips. A hand reached towards Mrs Sackville, but if his teacher had a human soul, it had already departed. 'I should . . . have gone . . . first.'

'Nobody ever dragged a mace to a duel,' said Jacob.

'Mace? You're . . . little different . . . to me,' spluttered Purdell from the floor. 'You need . . . this as much as I do.'

'There's one fundamental difference,' said Jacob, reloading the pistol's chamber with a single shell before lowering the gun towards the prone traitor. 'And it's the only one that ever counted.'

Willow jumped despite herself as the weapon's barrel bucked with the explosion. *He didn't murder Purdell. I did. Just as surely as I sent that wizened old demon back down to hell.*

'Finish me,' moaned Paetro from the tanner's slab. 'For the love of the ancestors . . .'

Jacob brought his pistol around and rested its barrel against the soldier's forehead. It was hard to believe that Paetro could be harmed any more than he'd already been hurt, a web of crimson lines bleeding across his face which were so fine they might have been pencilled on.

'No, please,' begged Willow, stepping forward between the pastor and the slab. 'I promised Paetro I would save his daughter.'

'Then I've made a liar of you twice.'

'*Please*. I came to Midsburg to save you, Father!' Willow thought briefly about turning the gun in her hand on the pastor, ordering him to stop. But she knew Jacob Carnehan would turn and gun her down before she could summon the speed or will to squeeze the trigger. *Like Quicksilver*. Some storms you couldn't stand in front of – you just had to wait for them to pass. Willow felt like a coward, standing there paralysed with a fear far more raw and primeval than when Purdell had held her prisoner. Willow watched the pastor struggle with himself, his finger white and tight around the trigger, stealing herself for another sudden explosion. But the shot never came. She allowed her breath to escape in a deep rush.

'Hadra-Hareer is due north of here,' said Jacob, uncocking the hammer and lowering the pistol at last. 'It's a bleak, rocky place, the capital of Rodal. But men like you and I can always find a way to make such places bleaker, can't we?'

'Why won't you finish me? You want to watch me bleed out slow, you bastard?'

Jacob leant over and unstrapped Paetro's legs before releasing his arms. 'Your wounds are bad, but hate can goad a man into surviving almost anything. And if that's not enough, I figure the duty you owe Lady Cassandra should be good for the difference.' He pushed the radio into Paetro's blood-covered fingers. 'Tell your legionaries to come for you.'

'You can't save me. Not *you*. Not you. *Damn you*!'

'Damn me?' Jacob laughed. 'That ship's already sailed. Tell your mistress not to bother using her carriers to transport prisoners to Vandia. You're going to need every last vessel . . . every soldier and gun and murdering imperial noble you shipped here, as well as all those turncoat southerners your blood money's paid for.' Jacob bent down beside the weeping soldier, whispering so low Willow could barely hear the rest of the exchange. 'Remember your duty to your house. And the look of surprise on your girl Hesia's face when I drew on her. I'll never be far from you.' He turned to Willow. 'You're my conscience, now. You and Carter. There's nothing left in me but you.'

I don't want that. But she had it. She had opened the door to the cage. Willow bent down and helped Paetro sit up, picking up his clothes piled on the floor and passing them to the Vandian. 'If you care anything for Duncan, tell him not to follow me. Give that message to my father, too.'

'You're a fool if you go with the priest, lass,' moaned Paetro, glaring in revulsion at the pastor. 'Death follows him like a shadow.'

'I know.' *My shadow too, now*. Stretching long across all of Weyland.

There was a rattle from the roof above, shaking from a nearby explosion. 'That was one of ours,' said Paetro, glaring at the pastor. 'We're going to win here, Weylander.'

'Break the city, crush parliament's army, smash the rebellion,' said Jacob. 'Yes, that was inevitable. Even without the Imperium's might, Bad Marcus would have starved and shelled Midsburg into submission within a few months.'

'We've won,' snarled Paetro.

'No,' said Jacob. 'Because this city's fall isn't just Vandia's blood price. It's mine, too.'

What does he mean? 'I don't understand?' said Willow.

'All we need to do to win here is survive,' said Jacob, prodding the traitor's corpse with his boot. 'And we have.'

'I'll chase you to the ends of the world,' snarled Paetro.

'With your empire's might, you probably could, if you set your mind to it,' smiled Jacob. 'But you won't have to. This is my war now. You're not facing Prince Owen and his po-faced general staff's noblemen anymore. This defeat will end their control over the army. Don't you see? I couldn't seize command of the northern army in a coup. How could I do that? Who in our undefeated army would ever follow a bandit chieftain and murderer? But if I find the army lying beaten, lost in the gutter like a dropped dagger and bend down to pick it up . . . ? The fall of Midsburg isn't *your* victory. It's mine. I should thank you, Vandian. I should kiss your emperor's arse, because you've done everything I needed you to.'

Paetro groaned in pain.

'And you'll never have to look far for me, Vandian. I'll be your shadow. I'll be your night and your day. And if you ever get lost, just follow the sound of the screaming. That's where I'll be.'

SEVENTEEN

THE FALL OF MIDSBURG

Duncan surveyed the landscape from one of the Vandian tanks, standing on the relative safety of its iron ramparts, fifteen feet above the ground. This particular machine of war was named *The Wolf of Soarspur* by its crew, after some distant province of the imperium. It sported one large turret at the front, two smaller turrets at the rear and a series of heavy guns mounted on the ramparts that ran above its armoured skirt for the accompanying company of legionaries. These gun mounts were clearly designed to take down attacking skyguards, but with Midsburg's air cover shattered or fled, the tank crew had to be content to pick off defenders along the curtain wall. Snarling white fangs were painted on its forward turret, grill-meshed lanterns on its flanks remade as two evil red eyes. At the very front of the vehicle a wickedly-spiked steel roller rotated between two metal arms, felling trees inside the orchards as if that was its purpose. Apple and pear trees crunched before them in splintered streams of timber, bloody red streaks twisting on the drum speaking for the few Weylanders who had survived the empire's 'treacle' and been foolhardy enough to charge the *Wolf*. Barns and farm buildings exploded in clouds of brick, timber, masonry and tiles, singled out as though the tank drivers in the glacis-plate-mounted cockpit were seeking out fresh challenges for their amusement. Duncan's unsolicited bodyguard, Nocks, leant lackadaisically on one of the mounted guns as though the farmers' fields they tore up were his. He had made no comment beyond a little half-amused grunt when they'd crossed the smoking blackened hell where the northern cavalry charge had ended. As if to say *here's something new and the rebels should have expected nothing less*. Duncan had smelt nothing like it before. Churning through bones, hot mud, ashes and the leftover tar of a charnel pit. A stench he'd carry to his grave. Death as a sweet, sickly aroma; *treacle indeed*.

They picked up speed. The entire Twelfth Armoured Legion driving forward like a steel javelin hurled towards the city's eastern flank. There was little opposition worthy of the name left outside, only fountains of cold soil erupting occasionally where Midsburg's wall-mounted cannons spoke. The *Wolf* rumbled forward with its main turret rotated towards the city. The entire tank rocked with each shell launched, a flower of flame and smoke from the big gun and then a shattering explosion and blast of masonry answering from along the curtain wall. Fire rippled the length of the armoured column, ear-splitting big guns detonating, rolling thunder as the war machines tossed their lightning towards Midsburg.

It'd be less noisy inside the tank. Except Nocks and the legionaries seemed to think nothing of riding outside and risking a shell or a sniper's shot from the city. *Hell if I'll have them think me a coward*. A line of horses came galloping up alongside their tank tracks, more than fifty steeds seemingly oblivious to the line of loud rotating track-drive wheels powering the treads. These were Weylanders, blue-coated cavalrymen with a thin yellow stripe down their trousers and a long rifle tucked into each leather saddle. The officer at the front of the riders lifted up his cap as he pulled to the side, and Duncan stifled a groan as he saw it was his brother-in-law's face.

'Those kettles are fine for Vandian steel-backs to rattle around in,' called up Wallingbeck, slowing and allowing his riders to pass him by. 'But you need to be seen up high on a fine stallion for the common herd to know you're a man of quality. These horses hail from m'own stables, corn-fed and groomed by the stable-hands at Belinus Hall.'

I'm sure the snipers up on the wall will be only too glad to see you coming. 'You're riding with the Twelfth Legion all the way to the wall?' shouted Duncan.

'General Colbert doesn't want all the glory of the fall of Midsburg going to the king's allies,' said Wallingbeck. 'Did you see the assembly's army ride out? Have you ever seen anything so magnificent? I won't have it said that any Riverlarn man was less brave than the pretender's dirty rebels.'

Magnificently stupid, perhaps. 'I don't think you will hear any slights cast by the northern cavalry.' *And you had your chance to hear first-hand, as you rode over their baked bones on the way to the city.*

'Damned fine day for riding,' said Wallingbeck. 'Have to give the court a good show.' He nodded and spurred the horse on fast, re-joining the company.

Glad to see that your wife and child's well-being inside Midsburg is still gnawing away at you. Well, it seemed Willow had developed a knack for survival. Her marriage spoke volumes for that. It was his friend Paetro that Duncan was worried about. Things must be dire inside Midsburg for the old soldier to break off contact, failing to report in. *You survived the legions, Paetro. You survived everything that Helrena's enemies threw at the house over the years. Surely you can survive a backwater like Weyland, too?*

'There goes a future field marshal,' said Nocks, dryly. The scar-faced sergeant watched the viscount gallop towards the head of the column of cavalry.

Duncan turned his attention to his father's servant. 'Lady Landor told me that you served on the Eastern Frontier?'

'Did she now? True enough,' grunted the sergeant. 'We taught all the bandits and bushwhackers out Ivah and Kish way that they'd be better off hunting for pickings on the opposite of the border, leaving the kingdom well alone.'

'And how did you do that?'

Nock's eyes glinted malevolently. 'Oh, we had our little ways.'

I'm sure you did. 'I'm not interested in scalping rebel prisoners, Nocks. Willow may or may not have her liberty inside the city; but my sister isn't the reason we're heading to Midsburg. Only Princess Helrena's daughter matters. Lady Cassandra's our duty.'

'Don't worry, boy,' said the sergeant. 'Old Nocks knows what to do. The daughter of a princess trumps the daughter of a northcountry nobleman, even if the northern wench is willowy Willow.'

'She's the wife of that future field marshal, Nocks. Lady Wallingbeck. You'd do well to keep that in mind.'

'Oh, I'm just a simple man with simple tastes,' said the servant, the scar on his face glowing crimson as his face scrunched up in a wicked grin. 'Yes, Nocks knows his place. Lugging a bucket around Hawkland Park in Landor livery or dressed in the royal blues of an artillery sergeant . . . I'm a humble soul.'

'It may be that it'll take hanging a few northern officers and rebel assemblymen from the lampposts to free Lady Cassandra.'

Nocks grinned even wider at that. 'Won't be much different from hanging farmers caught harbouring outlaws. Ain't a lesson that ever needs repeating, in my experience.'

Duncan nodded, glad that the stout leering servant might have his uses after all. *Let Nocks do the deed, he looks like he might even enjoy it. I thought I was coming home to help temper the imperium's vengeance. Instead, I'm crunching over the bones of Weylanders to save Cassandra. Well, the rebels' back-stabbing stupidity sowed this harvest, now they'll have to reap it. I did my best for my old country.* Everywhere Duncan turned he saw foolish choices. The northern prefectures and national assembly choosing to rebel against the king. His sister choosing a dolt like Viscount Wallingbeck for her husband. His father choosing a woman young enough to be his daughter as a wife and then wilfully ignoring poor Leyla to manage the house's affairs. And now those errors were leaking into Vandia with Helrena trying to convert an untrustworthy foe like Prince Gyal into an ally through marriage. *Why does the weight of making things right always fall on my shoulders?*

'I like the way these Vandians make war, that I do,' said Nocks. 'Wagons like land-based ironclads to keep a man safe inside. Skyguards able to hover as still as a hawk and turn battlefields black with dragon-fire. I can see this alliance going a long way. Maybe they'll start recruiting for legionaries inside the kingdom, too?'

'We'll be gone,' said Duncan. 'The imperium will extract their price, free Lady Cassandra, and Weyland will just be one of a thousand distant lands desperately clamouring for the empire's bounty.'

'You sound like one of those steel-backs, right enough, strutting through the streets and throwing your gold about,' said Nocks. 'Weyland's muddled along just fine for thousands of years with only the ocean for company. I reckon King Marcus will muddle on a while longer after you've gone back to Vandia.'

It'll go to hell without me . . . and the nation's welcome to it. I'll have enough on my plate trying to keep Prince Gyal from poisoning Cassandra and Helrena.

A steel hatch opened in the rear turret closest to Duncan and he saw it was the legionary from the vehicle's communications room: A Sig in the military jargon of the legion. 'Any answer?'

'No, sir,' said the legionary. 'The raiding force is still silent. Their only calls are from the city's Guild of Radiomen hold, the rebels requesting help and reinforcements from other towns.'

'Keep trying to reach Paetro,' ordered Duncan and the hatch clanged shut. *As silent as death.*

It grew harder to see the city through rolling waves of smoke snaking out from straw-packed shot; then, as one, the column pivoted, heading directly for Midsburg's eastern corner. They only had the trench works, embankments and traverses between them and the curtain wall, dirt-packed slopes and soil-filled bags proving as insubstantial as mist to the Twelfth Armoured. A roaring chopping noise passed overhead as a squadron of helos arrowed over the war machines, adding their weapon pods to the fusillade of artillery from the ground vehicles, rockets arcing out and disappearing into the murk as showers of stone and brick fountained out of the fog of war. A line of grey-uniformed northern soldiers emerged from of one of the trenches, rifles abandoned and hands high in the air. Nocks saw the rebels first and swivelled one of the mounted guns around, the heavy steel weapon recoiling as he fired burst after burst of shells into the line. Men crumpled like rice paper caught in a threshing machine, the remains of those that turned and ran showering into the trench they had unwisely abandoned.

'They were surrendering!' protested Duncan.

'Can't have them making trouble behind us,' growled Nocks. 'And we don't have time to stop. Not if you want your imperial girl back alive.'

'Where's your honour?'

'Honour? You want honour, boy, read a book to find it. Old soldiers' tales grow as cloudy as wine over time. Out here there's only coming back alive with the job done, or leaving your corpse in the field for crows and looters to pick over. Nocks, he's only ever favoured the first option.'

Duncan heard a noise behind him and turned just in time to see three grey-uniformed rebels climbing up over side of the moving tank. Nocks swung the mounted gun's muzzle down, but it couldn't depress to a low enough angle to shoot them off and then the rebels were swarming aboard the *Wolf.* Shouts and shots sounded from the other side of the tank. They were being boarded on all sides. *The surrendering soldiers were a diversion!* Duncan fumbled for the heavy pistol in his belt, its cold steel grip slippery in his palm, raising it like dragging lead into the air. Almost instantly, Nocks was wrestling with a bayonet-tipped rifle in the hands of a giant of a rebel. One of the grey-coated rebels had his rifle off his back and fired it wildly, the bullet whining past Duncan's cheek. There was an angry roar of electric rifles from the legionaries, the chatter of weapons fire echoing across the tank among the screams of dying men. Duncan triggered the pistol and blinked in the bright explosion of flames from its barrel vents, hardly any recoil as the rocket-propelled shell found its mark almost instantly, spinning the rifleman around so violently he collided with another rebel and they both collapsed to the steel floor behind the ramparts. Nocks twisted the contested bayonet down into the fallen soldier's chest, leaving it impaled and the victim yelling in agony. With his rifle trapped, the big rebel stepped back and reached for his pistol holster, but Nocks was on top of him, head-butting the rebel's face, using the second of confused pain to draw his dagger and shove it through the grey coat and into the enemy soldier's heart.

A fourth rebel had climbed onto the war machine unseen, raising a cavalryman's carbine up behind Nocks. Duncan yelled and brought his rocket pistol around, the artillery sergeant flinging himself down and to the side as he saw Duncan's gun swinging towards him. The pistol roared and the rebel was punched back five feet, the part of his chest that wasn't caved in, aflame. As suddenly as the hand-to-hand fighting had started, it was over. Only Duncan's rapid breathing and the rattle of fire from the battlefield beyond.

Nocks picked himself up and bad-temperedly booted the dead soldier. 'I'm obliged, boy.'

'They didn't have to die.'

'Better them than me. That's my regimental motto.' Nocks laughed, an ugly sound, but one in keeping with this place.

Duncan hardly had time to take in the dead bodies, ignoring their accusing, wide eyes; these ones, his. Not dead from the distant artillery, the guns of the south or the Vandian war machine. *Dead by my hand*. There was a shudder as the *Wolf* crashed straight through a mound of soil, screams of crushed and buried men, and Duncan's hand seized the turret's hatch handle to stop from spilling over. He righted himself and peered through a firing slit in the rampart. Duncan watched royalist cavalrymen peel off beside the war machines as the column gained the piecemeal network of ditches and embrasures outside the city, more than four hundred mounted soldiers sweeping like thunder across the defensive line.

Riflemen inside the trenches appeared on fire-steps and opened up on mounts and men, a volley like splintering wood cutting down some of the lead riders, but Duncan could see that the rebels' numbers had been depleted by the artillery bombardment, the majority withdrawn behind the relative safety of the curtain wall. *And we're about to spoil that illusion of safety for them*. Leaping horses cleared the first ditches, sabres sweeping down as others fired into the ditches with pistols and carbines. *My brother-in-law may be a dolt, but he's an eager one and no coward*, thought Duncan. He doubted any tales Wallingbeck carried back from this savage day would impress the nobleman's troublesome wife, however.

'This is your first time, ain't it?' said Nocks.

'I've seen dead people,' said Duncan. *We had to fight for claims in the sky mines with nothing more than pickaxe handles*. 'I was in the slave revolt.'

'How'd that go for you?'

'I was shot in the heart by Jacob Carnehan. He left me for dead.'

Nocks seemed to find this greatly amusing. 'That was mighty inconsiderate of him.'

'What's so funny?'

'Nothing much. Just occurs to me that there's a man who mightily needs killing.'

Yes, but who's to do it? Perhaps ten tanks jounced in front of the *Wolf*, and with a throaty battle roar from their engines they mounted the final soil embankment, only slowing a fraction on the slope, before each machine struck the heavily damaged curtain wall with the impact of a four-hundred-ton sledgehammer. The first three colossal fighting machines pushed through with a landslide of brick and stone collapsing around them, the others mounting the smoking rubble and dipping down as their turrets opened up on Midsburg's exposed interior, before rumbling forward and inside. The *Wolf* followed and as it bucked over the mound where the curtain wall had stood, Duncan saw that the first vehicles through the breach had slowed enough for their legionaries to dismount from the ramparts and fan out.

It was complete chaos inside. Shooting. Rebels running. Burning buildings. The infantry spread out, moving to protect their steel charges from Weyland grenadiers running to toss fused charges against the drive sprockets, a spirited defence by regiments held in reserve behind a wall that no longer even existed in this section of the city. The *Wolf* came down slow over mounds of stone, as broken cannon platforms and half-buried corpses churned below its tracks. Duncan's legionaries dropped down the steps and hurled themselves into the smoke. They moved in disciplined units of four called quads, each legionary covering their comrades, and where anything moved, twitched or fired back, their electric rifles poured bullets into the smoke; walls and entire houses collapsing as bursts tore through them. With the legionaries disembarked, the huge war machines shuddered forward again, ploughing through the cheap houses in the lee of the curtain wall, every gun trained back along the ramparts, clearing the wall of riflemen and cannon platforms. Anyone kneeling behind the unprotected parapet and on the wall-walk side of the defences shuddered and fell, cut down in the open beneath a storm of bullets. Shots fell against the *Wolf*'s armour, clanging where they struck, and Duncan added to the melee, aiming over the parapet and firing his pistol into the soldiers along the curtain wall. One of the Vandian war machine's armoured skirts was circled by protruding pipes connected to spherical steel barrels and Duncan saw their purpose when a vast hoop of flames jetted out in all directions, buildings bursting apart in balls of fire. It took the lead of the armoured column, tracking down the wall and incinerating a passage for the other war machines to follow. The opening in Midsburg's defences hadn't gone unnoticed on the hill. Duncan could hear a distant roar as thousands of royalist soldiers came charging across the battlefield, heading for the breach along the wall.

'Down we go!' yelled Nocks. 'Our business ain't on the city wall.'

'We should stay with the *Wolf*!'

'Your Vandian friends' strategy is sound enough,' said Nocks. 'Leave defenders along the outer wall and you'll be fighting your way through the city with rifles aimed at your back as well as ones aimed at your front. The rebels will surrender quickly enough in the streets once they see the king's standard fluttering from every tower along the battlements.'

They dismounted and ran through the streets towards the heart of the city. The artillery shells falling on the city had lessened now the royalists knew friendly troops had gained Midsburg. *Thank you, Father*. There had been enough carnage earlier, however, to make up for it; smoke from fires burning out of control, the shadows of townspeople moving through the fumes as they tried to escape with whatever money and possessions were most portable. It was like being back in Northhaven when the slave raider had struck the town from the air. *It's a lot easier when it's not your neighbours and friends doing the dying, though*. Occasionally they caught sight of rebel soldiers running panicked through the ruins, but it was as if the soldiers were on a stage, part of a play and separate from Duncan's existence. Once, a young soldier came sprinting out of a side-street and went hurtling past them, not even looking at or seeing Duncan, although he surely felt the shots in his back when Nocks gunned him down.

Duncan looked in disgust at the cowardly manservant but Nocks just laughed. 'One less, boy. One less.'

Duncan coughed as he blundered through the smoke, using the cannon fire against the curtain wall as a compass, the distant thuds of breaking masonry sounding like a drum. 'I can hardly see a thing.'

'Must be why it's called the fog of war, boy.'

Nocks strode up to the soldier's corpse, knelt alongside and started patting down the bleeding uniform and pulling out coins and keepsakes.

No. Anger swelled inside Duncan. That young soldier hadn't asked for any of this. Probably been pulled from a farm by some northern landowner, had a rifle shoved in his hands, then pushed into Midsburg to defend it. And now what little he'd once owned was being stripped from him. 'Leave the money!'

'For what? The worms, or the next soldier who stumbles across the body?'

Duncan flourished the heavy pistol. 'I mean it.'

'Your clip is empty. You emptied it on the war wagon.'

'I wouldn't bet your life on it, Nocks.'

He snorted. 'There's an ammunition indicator on the side of the gun, you idiot. It's red!'

Duncan turned the pistol. A drum-like indicator he had thought was ornamental had rotated around to reveal a red line across the steel.

'Don't bother reloading,' said Nocks. The servant raised his pistol, pointing it directly as Duncan's head. At this range, he'd need to be blind to miss. 'This is just perfect.'

Duncan stared at the servant as though he had gone insane. 'What for? Because I won't let you loot?'

'Let's just say if old Nocks has to risk his neck in a city's sack, he'll rescue willowy Willow first,' said Nocks, spitting to the side while keeping the pistol barrel poked towards Duncan's face. 'Your sister owes me a sniff of her sweet flower, and as much as I'd like to take the same liberties with your imperial girl, I don't reckon the emperor would be too happy if I did. Never does to have an emperor pissed at you.'

'I'm your ally! Your duty – I saved your life back on the *Wolf*!'

'And I'm sure I said I'm obliged, so I'll make this quick for you. You're the best kind of ally of all, boy . . . the dead kind who can't betray me.' Nocks gestured with his pistol. 'Ease that imperial hand cannon into your left hand and toss it over there. Drop your belt with the spare clips, too.'

Duncan switched the gun, held the pistol out and lobbed it to the ground, then unbuckled his ammunition belt and let it fall to the ground. *I underestimated you, Willow. I thought I'd finally put you in a position where you had to help me. But this was your plan all along. You've murdered me at last.*

'So Carnehan senior already shot you in the heart,' smirked Nocks, 'and I can see how well that worked out for him, so I'm going to put one right between your eyes to make sure. A nice little hole for the maggots to crawl through.' His finger tightened around the trigger. 'Just as easy and painless as—'

There was a crack of a distant pistol and Nocks went spinning, his shot going wild and hitting Duncan in the centre of his chest armour with a violent crack, splinters from the round scarring his face. Duncan yelled as he was thrown back through the air, a sledgehammer driven into his gut, his face torn against hot, burning rubble as he hit the ground. Duncan's vision streaked red with blood coming down into his eyes. He pulled himself around, desperately searching for Nocks, but Willow's perfidious manservant had fallen into the ruins of a smoking building and vanished. Duncan touched the breastplate with two fingers, buckled in the centre where an odd green gel leaked from beneath the rent material. A figure came limping out of the smoke of war, a civilian whose face lay hidden under a foreign merchanteer's cloak, a Weyland revolver clutched in his hand. *No, not a civilian. Paetro*!

Duncan recoiled in shock as the hoary old soldier drew closer. Paetro's face had been rendered into a bleeding mess of cuts with his green silk shirt soaked in blood from similar chest wounds. 'Sweet saints!'

'You should see the man who worked this evil on me,' coughed Paetro. He lifted up the Weyland revolver in disgust and tucked it under his belt. 'Luckiest shot I ever made with an antique. I thought the hounds in blue uniform were on our side, lad.'

'Willow betrayed me,' said Duncan. 'This ambush was her doing.'

'I warned you about trusting her back on the ship. It's your sister's day for treachery, all right. She's played me false again too,' said Paetro. 'Willow cleared off with the outlaw priest, Carnehan. Left us hanging in the wind.'

The pastor's here? A sudden vision of Lady Cassandra tied to Jacob Carnehan's saddle spun through Duncan's mind, explosions flowering around the killer as he galloped through the siege. The scar on his chest burned in shame at the memory of how easily Carnehan had emptied a round into his heart. Despite himself, Duncan felt a superstitious shiver of fear. 'Taking Cassandra with them?'

Paetro shook his head. 'It was a ruse all along, lad. The little highness was never here. Carnehan packed her off to Rodal long before the siege started. I came out to where the Twelfth Armoured said they'd dropped you after I got through to a Sig on your column. Didn't want you risking your neck for a fraud.'

Rodal! Cassandra, how are we ever going to find you in the caves and canyons of that gale-tossed place? Duncan retrieved his rocket pistol and carefully inspected the ruins where Nocks had disappeared. There was a smear of blood there where the manservant had fallen before dragging himself away. *Wounded; but I'm not nearly lucky enough for it to have killed him.* Duncan thought of Cassandra and a mixture of relief and regret flooded in as he realized his mission in Midsburg had never stood a chance from the start. 'This was all for nothing, then.'

'I wouldn't be saying that,' grunted Paetro, leaning against the stump of a lamppost. 'The emperor's given out a few lumps to the slave revolt; pride and honour are restored, for whatever that's worth. There'll be a grand triumph laid on in Vandis when we return.'

Not for us. For Prince Gyal and his beautiful wife to be; curse the arrogant nobleman. 'We'll see what the princess's alliance with Gyal is worth, now. Helrena won't go back to Vandia, not without Cassandra.'

'I know. And neither will you or I. Not till this is done.'

The haggard wounded bear of a soldier didn't say they still had business with the pastor and Willow. He didn't need to. Duncan holstered his pistol. 'You look like you need to go home . . . you look like hell, Paetro Barca.'

'Only fitting after encountering a few demons, lad.'

Duncan's chest scar burned like ice. Northhaven's pastor, Duncan's treacherous sister and her murderous manservant ahead of him; Prince Gyal taking up the rear. *And how many more of them are still on the loose?*

It felt like home to Jacob, riding with the Royal Sharps Greys. *Just men with rifles and bad intentions. It's amazing how far you can go in such company.* Vandian helos skimmed through the smoke of Midsburg's burning skyline, dipping down to land raiders to harry the men on the battlements from the city side. That was the kind of mobility it was hard to oppose with squadrons of horses and rampart-mounted cannons, but luckily for the invaders, it didn't look like the assembly's army was really trying. *Now I know how those Nijumeti nomads up north must feel when they charge the Rodalian Skyguard with horses and spears.* Timber and stone fountained into the air as the wall's batteries fell silent one by one, the counter-fire needed to give the gunners on the south's cannons something to occupy their minds seeping away. Bullets whizzed past Jacob's head, angry wasps seeking bodies to burst, but never the pastor's. It was only the good people who died. That was the lesson of war. The good. The kind. The meek. They were always first to be swallowed by the ravening maw of battle. Men like Jake Silver; they got spat out, too tough to digest.

'You're fine with what needs doing?' Jacob asked Arick Densen.

'I know I don't much fancy the idea of charging those steel fortresses on tracks,' said the cavalry sergeant. 'Even if Hard Charging Houldridge can scrape together enough horse regiments for a second attempt. That doesn't strike me as much of a winning strategy.'

'I think Captain Carnehan would agree with you if he was here.' Jacob was more than grateful that Carter wasn't. *For once, fate has taken my impetuous son out of harm's way rather than carrying him towards it.*

'Talking about old friends: that mad one of yours, Sariel, is he able to do half of what he claims?'

'Maybe even more than half.'

'Well then, let's go and make sure we keep the captain in the skinning game.'

Jacob and his cavalry company found the general staff holed up in the half-collapsed assembly building, just as Mrs Sackville had said they would. *Guess even a treacherous old torturer has to slip and tell the truth once in a while.* Nestling behind a ruined wall with no ceiling, the officers of the Army of the Spotswood stood hunched over a series of field tables nestled among cots filled with wounded soldiers, surgeons treating the injured, runners stumbling over the dead to deliver messages and carry new ones to battalions scattered around the city, hard-pressed defenders manning the battlements and trench works surrounding Midsburg. One of the wounded was Field Marshal Houldridge; his litter leant at an angle across a ruined wall so the army's commander could bark out orders to staff officers and runners with a little more dignity than a bedridden patient. Judging by the blood seeping from his burnt and blackened tunic, Jacob would say he'd only just survived the suicidal cavalry charge. Prince Owen still seemed as sickly and distant as he had the last time Jacob had seen him. *It's like watching a sailor new on ship ride out his first storm.* And this was a hell of a storm. *But don't worry, Your Highness. This isn't your war anymore. And all it cost to take it away from you was a couple of hundred thousand dead Weylanders.*

Field Marshal Houldridge's demeanour turned as dark as his wounds when he caught sight of Jacob and his soldiers riding in. 'What are you doing here, Carnehan? You've been dismissed. Is that the Second Royal Cavalry Brigade behind you? What in the name of the saints are they doing away from the field?'

'Oh, we had to come and admire the genius of your defence up close. I tried to spy it from the city walls, but all I found were the screams of dying men and horses drowned in burning mud.'

'Why are you here, Father?' demanded Prince Owen. 'There's no place for you in Midsburg now.'

'There will be after what's left of the three armies is ordered to retreat north.'

'Not this idiocy again,' barked the field marshal. 'We yet may have to fall back, but if so, we shall withdraw east. Link up with the Army of the Broadaxe, combine our forces and face these cursed invaders united.'

'So you can repeat the siege of Midsburg in a second city? As fool an idea as I've ever heard,' said Jacob, 'even if the Vandian armoured vehicles weren't swinging around your eastern flank and smashing through the city walls, cutting off your main avenue of retreat.'

'I am still alive and I give the orders here!'

'You're about fifty per cent wrong, don't make it a hundred,' warned Jacob.

'You dare to threaten me with mutiny, you abhorrent criminal!' Houldridge's hand dipped for the pistol in his belt and Jacob didn't hesitate; the revolver's grip was hard in his hand before the officer's had cleared his belt, the gun bucking once as Houldridge slumped back into his cot, a neat hole drilled in his forehead. Half of the staff officers leapt for their rifles and belt guns, the few that weren't staring in shock at their commander's bleeding corpse, but Jacob's cavalrymen had already swung up their carbines, a clacking of rounds being chambered as the horsed soldiers moved their rifle barrels threateningly between the motley assortment of grey-uniformed majors and colonels.

Criminal? You'd be surprised how many pardons a victory brings. 'Some people just won't listen. To be a mutiny, it'd still have to be your army,' said Jacob.

'What have you done?' shouted the prince, his face draining white. 'He was wounded, wounded.'

And now he's dead. 'What I should have done when you threw me out of your council of war,' said Jacob. 'You're appointing me as your new field marshal, a battlefield commission just as legal and as proper as you like.'

'You're crazy! Field Marshal Houldridge was a good man, a family friend, my most loyal ally inside parliament's army—'

You think that's crazy? I haven't even started yet. I haven't got time to waste, not with Carter in danger up north. Damn Thomas Purdell. If ever a man deserved to die twice . . . Jacob waved his smoking pistol at the field marshal's corpse. 'All Houldridge was good for was getting better Weylanders than himself killed. Sariel's in the forest north of here opening one of his sorcerous gates up into Northhaven. I'm taking any troops left alive in the city through it, and ordering what's left of the three armies to fall back towards the high north and the Rodalian Mountains.'

'You'll abandon Midsburg to be burnt by the south? And what of all the innocents in Middenharn, Creedlore and Gunisade?'

'This city's going to burn anyway, the only question you need to answer is do you want your army's ashes to be among its ruins? As for our other prefectures, the usurper's regiments will be too busy chasing us to put the torch to every town and village they pass.'

'I won't do it. I'll sign a warrant for your arrest before I sign any commission for you in the assembly's army.'

'Oh, but I think you will,' said Jacob. 'Because before Sariel brought Carter's riders back to help me, he took your friend Anna Kurtain from the hospital. Healed her pretty good, I'd say, given how many injuries she took protecting you from your stupidity.'

'Healed? Anna's healed?'

'She was well enough to take a trip through Sariel's gate. But Miss Kurtain won't be going to Northhaven. I'll drop her somewhere safe on the other side of Pellas, so far-called that it'll take a thousand years for her messages to pass through the radiomen's relays. You will never see or hear from her again. Or Anna can travel with us to the Rodalian border, for the price of that battlefield commission.'

'You're a dirty *bastard*.'

'So I've heard. And unlike my predecessor, I'm the kind to win battles, not lose them.'

'Everyone in Midsburg will die.'

'No, I figure most of them will end up as slaves, at least the ones that can't run fast and far enough. Either taken by the empire or seized as indentured labour for Marcus's rich friends in the south.'

'Stand and fight here,' said the prince, half begging, half commanding.

'I only fight battles I can win, Your Majesty, and this one was all on your *good* and dead friend.'

'Then help the people of Midsburg escape north, too. If you're taking the regiments you can take the townspeople.'

'So I can watch women and children starve, leaving a trail of corpses behind us every day we retreat? No. I'll have enough trouble supplying the army from Havenharl's farms and winter grain bins. At least Marcus and his Vandian friends will feed any prisoners they chain up. Dead slaves don't work as hard, or so I've been led to believe.' Jacob unrolled the battlefield commission he'd prepared and passed it to Prince Owen. As he expected, the prince crumpled and signed the paper before returning it. *Too weak to rule, too strong to be ruled. Well, that'll be Weyland's problem, not mine, after I've laid out a fine thick red carpet of corpses for him to walk across to his throne.* 'The Vandians are about to find out that the girl you've got in the assembly isn't Lady Cassandra, Your Highness. I expect the bombardment will grow mighty fierce, then. Fall back through the north gate.'

'I'm staying here,' snarled Prince Owen. 'With my people in the city. I won't abandon them. Carter will return with Lady Cassandra soon. I can force them to terms using her as a hostage.'

'A hostage is only any good if you're willing to nail her to the battlements, which I know you won't be. Besides, Midsburg's people will be slaves long before my son flies back. You want to see Vandia's sky mines again on the wrong end of a whip?'

'I'm staying *here*!'

'As you like,' said Jacob. *He's a master of the grand gesture, I'll give him that. But as long as the south has a usurper, the north needs its pretender.* Jacob drew his pistol smoothly and shot the prince through the leg, watching the young nobleman fall screaming to the cold ground clutching his smashed thigh. 'The prince has been wounded by a sniper. Put him in the back of the wagon and dress his wound as you head to the forest.'

'You treacherous dog!' yelled Owen, struggling as he was helped to his feet by the cavalrymen.

Jacob shrugged. *I suppose I'll have to listen to his bleating for a while longer.* Willow waiting with Sariel was enough of a conscience for the pastor. He hadn't wanted the weight of her scruples in Midsburg. 'Treachery? That's no way to address your new field marshal, sire. I reckon if I wanted to be king, I might have shot you to begin with, and aimed for your thick skull. Crowns are heavy things, all that gold and silver. I prefer simple and honest lead.' He waved his pistol at the survivors among the general staff. *No way for me to tell which are the courtiers and placemen yet, and which are soldiers. But there'll be plenty of opportunities to shake out the grit, Marcus and his allies will see to that.* 'Anyone who wants to live, follow me north. You'll need the stomach to follow me and the stomach to fight better than today. Anyone with different ideas, save me the trouble of hanging you. There's still Vandian steel left east of the city for you to mount a last, suicidal charge.'

Some officers came and some stayed, and in truth, it didn't much bother Jacob either way. *I can only use the ones smart enough to follow me.*

'Reckon Midsburg was a hell of a defeat,' said Arick Densen as they rode out.

I hope the usurper believes that, because victory teaches little. 'No,' said Jacob to the sergeant. 'Defeat never finishes an army, only quitting does.' He listened to the shells falling from the guns of the south, watched helos fleeting above the smoking city like angry wasps. *This is the last time the Vandians and Bad Marcus will be fighting on my side. They've given me my army. Now I'm going to show them just how to use it.*

Turn the page for a preview of
the final novel of the Far-Called trilogy:

The Stealers' War

ONE

AN AUDIENCE WITH THE GREAT KRUL

Lady Cassandra Skar moaned with pain as the nomads dragged her from her horse towards the tent where the King of the Plains awaited her. Of course, the word tent was a bit of a misnomer. It was closer to a palace woven from colourful felt-lined fabric, staked toweringly high with wooden lattices and roof ribs. Multiple tents arranged together like a series of stretched foothills. In fact, as Cassandra gazed at the nomads' faces – expressions ranging from the curious to the openly hostile – she realized that the term *king* might be a bit of a misnomer too. *What would do instead, I wonder? Rag-tag hairy-arsed barbarian war chief lording it over a bunch of roaming savages? Best you keep such suggestions to yourself, lady.* From the way the nomads manhandled her, they clearly didn't see many Vandian noblewomen out here. She didn't take it personally. They clearly hated the other two prisoners in her party even more than her. Sheplar Lesh was a pilot from Rodal, the clans' mountainous neighbours to the south, and as close to an ancestral enemy as the plains people possessed. Although in fairness, they probably regarded everyone with the bad luck not to be born in a saddle among the clans as their ancestral enemy. Kerge was a forest dweller from the far side of the peaks, an oddity that only reminded the nomads that while they commanded the endless steppes, they'd always been beaten back from the rich, prosperous nations on the other side of the mountains.

Cassandra heard Alexamir's shouts of protest ringing out behind her. The love-sick young nomad had promised her his protection. Swore that he would release her if and when she chose to leave for home. *What a joke.* Leave for home? How could she do that with a broken spine and her legs paralysed by the plane crash? She should have cut her wrists rather than suffer such a dishonour. That was the way of her house. For someone born and trained from birth to rule over millions, Cassandra had ended up not even being able to leave her bedroll unaided. The Vandian Imperium was power and strength or it was nothing. Maybe Cassandra would have ended her life if Alexamir hadn't removed and hidden her dagger. *Or maybe these people will cut my throat and save me the trouble.* Like so much else, it seemed that Alexamir's boasts of his importance among the clan had been somewhat exaggerated. *Or maybe this is how they greet all honoured guests under the protection of one of their so-called greatest warriors?*

She caught a brief glimpse of the witch rider, Nurai, standing by the entrance to the massive tent palace. A look of satisfaction twitched around the margins of her face. *It makes a difference from jealousy, I suppose.* Nurai clearly regarded Alexamir as her property, and would be only too happy to help Cassandra shuffle off this mortal coil; preserving the dashing, insanely reckless nomad for her sole attentions. There wasn't a future Nurai had prophesied where Cassandra's presence among the people of the plains wouldn't end up in despair and the gnashing of teeth and lamentations for the clan. *Maybe that means I'll live a little longer with Alexamir pining after me. Although perhaps the witch rider just foresaw my death here?*

Lady Cassandra was dragged like a haunch of meat, cursing her dead, useless legs, deep inside the palace of tents, ending up in a wooden-frame-vaulted throne room. The throne itself was composed of propellers taken from the planes of their Rodalian enemies, fallen skyguards who had broken every nomad horde to attempt the invasion of Rodal. She gazed up at the man who sat upon the throne. So, this was Kani Yargul, the warlord who had declared himself Lord of Clan Lords. The clans called such a king their *Great Krul.* Cassandra suspected that anyone capable of unifying the quarrelsome, ever-warring clans of horsemen was going to prove an equally great nuisance to the nations surrounding the steppes. Physically, Kani Yargul looked every inch a warlord. Strapping, even by the standards of the strong

Nijumeti tribesmen, perhaps two normal men wide, a shaved head, dark, short beard, narrow eyes, and a notably bulbous nose that had been broken many times. On the warlord's left stood an ancient witch rider, presumably the priestess to whom jealous Nurai owed her training and allegiance. On the right was an even queerer sight. An obviously foreign golden-skinned elder weighed down with the heavy rune-embroidered robes of a sorcerer. The way the robes covered his protruding spine make him look like he might be hunchbacked. His hair was naturally curled in a way that would have made many of the ladies of the Vandian imperial court jealous; a high forehead with dark, brooding eyes belying a superior, erudite manner. The sorcerer looked younger than she'd expect a man of his position to be.

'Hear me, Great Krul. I have given my word to Lady Cassandra, offering her the protection of salt and roof,' said Alexamir, pushing his way to the front of the crowd.

'*Your* word,' said the warlord. 'Not mine. Am I to extend the hospitality of the clans to every beggarly intruder who despoils the grass sea? So much trouble from you, Alexamir Arinnbold. Always. You leave to raid Rodal and prove yourself a man and you come back not with thralls to serve the clan, but with *guests*?' Kani Yargul chewed unhappily on the last word as though it was unexpected gristle on a haunch of meat.

'These two I have taken as thralls,' said Alexamir, pointing at Kerge and Sheplar Lesh. 'But the golden fox I would take as my wife.'

'Then marry the girl as a saddle-wife. Throw her inside your tent and go raiding for more.'

'Indeed,' said the priestess by the warlord's side. 'One saddle-wife is a vexation. Three or four is a goodly number.'

Cassandra pulled against the hands of her captors. 'I am no common prisoner.'

'It is true,' said Alexamir. 'She is the daughter of a princess, granddaughter to the Emperor of Vandia.'

'Another empire?' said the warlord, puzzled. 'I know of the Empire of Persdad to the north. Fine raiding for those willing to brave their legions.' He glanced at the sorcerer. 'What is this Vandia? Have you heard of them, Temmell Longgate?'

'I have, Great Krul,' said the sorcerer, nodding on the other side of the wooden throne. 'The Vandians are now allies of the king across the mountains. They fight in the Kingdom of Weyland's kin war, brother against uncle, for control of the land. Vandia lies far-called to the south, a rich and powerful empire which they boast of as the world's greatest nation. Their forces rarely travel as far north as the Lancean Ocean. I find their presence so close to us to be most disturbing.'

'So, an emperor's granddaughter? It's hard to take a wolf cub without bringing in the whole pack. Still, although they know it not; these Vandians are also my allies. Let them rip each other apart in the south,' scowled Kani Yargul. 'Let their kin war lay a thick red carpet of corpses for us to crunch over when the clans ride. Every dead Weyland soldier is one less for us to face when the time comes.' The warlord stared at Cassandra with his cold green eyes. 'And how much is the Vandian emperor's granddaughter worth in ransom?'

'Nothing,' said Cassandra. 'Not as I am . . . broken. A Vandian noblewoman must be able to fight for her house when challenges are issued. I cannot stand in any duel now. I am worthless to you. My house will expect me to end my life honourably. There will be no gold for you in exchange for my person.'

'At least she is honest,' said Kani Yargul. 'Useless, but honest.'

'She is *dangerous*, Great Krul,' said Nurai. 'She saw what we are building when we rode into the camp. The girl and the rice-eater and his forest man friend, all.'

Yes, that sight had come as quite a surprise to Cassandra. But not as much, she suspected, as to Sheplar Lesh. This was the young witch rider's best chance to have Cassandra executed, and the woman knew it.

'Do you expect this broken girl to gallop south and warn the nations of the Lanca?' said the warlord. He sounded amused, but Cassandra sensed the undercurrent of menace in his tone. 'Have you seen this in your visions, witch rider?'

'I have seen many things concerning this one's presence, Great Krul,' said Nurai. 'All of them leading to dark fates for our people.'

Madinsar fixed her understudy with a beady glare. 'Then why have I not seen similarly, my acolyte?'

'The true sight shows many paths,' was all the answer Nurai had to give.

Madinsar pulled her priestess robes in close and eyed Alexamir suspiciously. 'As does the heart. Never confuse the two.'

'This foreign whelp has cast a spell over Alexamir,' accused Nurai. 'How else can you explain his willingness to carry her here, the girl unable even to clean a tent or cook for his family? She is a burden, not a saddle-wife.'

'She was given my protection before her wounding,' said Alexamir.

Even Cassandra thought the justification hollow. There was more to it than that. She had experienced the tenderness with which Alexamir had cared for her when she had been injured. How eagerly he had tried to distract her from her plight and duty. He might be a fool, but he was *her* fool now.

'If a spell it is, I believe it a very ordinary enchantment,' said Madinsar. 'And not one you care for, Nurai.'

'I would ask you to heal my golden fox, Temmell,' said Alexamir.

'I am adviser to the Great Krul,' said the sorcerer. 'You seem to mistake me for some wandering healer.'

'Yet such you were when you first arrived with us,' said Alexamir.

This was clearly not the right response; reminding the strange-looking adviser of his humble origins here. The sorcerer's irritated expression turned to fury. 'I once regrew the arm of the Mark Lord of Simaria after he lost his limb in a joust. Am I now to be the medic to a common mounted thief?'

'Careful, Temmell,' cautioned the warlord. 'It is a fine thing to be a thief among the Nijumeti. To be an unsuccessful thief, however, is quite another thing. Your raiding party took many casualties, Alexamir. And you have returned with a bare handful of thralls and a hostage who has lost her worth.'

'Lesser men would have perished a dozen times where I survived,' said Alexamir. 'We were attacked twice by the Rodalian skyguard, their flying wings swooping down on us, dropping bombs and giving us the bitter taste of their cannons. The golden fox was taken from us and locked up in Salasang. But I broke her out and left the rice-eaters a burning town for their troubles. Then I escaped in one of their planes and claimed two propellers from the rice-eaters' pursuing skyguards. And when these two fools tracked me to recover the girl, I ambushed them and took them as thralls. If any bard was brave enough to travel with Alexamir, people here would be singing for months of my bravery and audacity.'

'Why would we need a bard, when we have you to sing your own songs so well?' asked Madinsar, wryly.

'I dreamt that Alexamir would scale the walls of Salasang and leave the town in flames,' said Nurai, speaking in defence of the reckless young nomad.

'I do not doubt it,' said Kani Yargul. 'You are truly the blood of your father, Alexamir Arinnbold. He danced with death every day until it found him. He tried to get me killed on his adventures a dozen times a season, and this is a hard thing to do, as the spirit of every broken-necked clan lord hovering above my throne will testify.'

'You honour me, Great Krul,' said Alexamir, his chest puffing with pride.

'Do I? The bravery expected of a rider and the recklessness of a clod are easily confused,' said Kani Yargul. 'Sometimes I can barely tell them apart myself. We shall see. Paltry though your booty may be,' said Kani Yargul, 'I shall claim the right of the Krul and take the rice-eater as my own thrall. You have a use for him, do you not, Temmell?'

'Officers of the Rodalian skyguard are rarely brought down on the plains alive,' said the sorcerer. 'I have many uses for such a servant.'

Cassandra winced. *That does not sound good for him.* Although Sheplar Lesh had been prime among her captors after she was seized from the Imperium, the Rodalian pilot had treated her honourably and risked his life twice to save her from the nomads. *You should not show such weakness, lady. One captor less is no bad thing for you.* Except she had no home to return to now. Not as she was.

'You would put him to use against the mountain people, Great Krul?' asked Madinsar.

'And where would you have the clans turn their attention instead, priestess?' retorted the warlord.

'North. Towards the Empire of Persdad.'

'Your ambitions are limited, Madinsar,' said Temmell. 'The nations of the Lancean League are the richest, fattest kingdoms in all the Three Oceans. Poultry left unplucked by the clans for too long.'

'Left unplucked, but not for lack of trying,' said the witch priestess. 'You were not born in the saddle, Temmell Longgate. Wander the camp at night and listen to our ancient songs. Hear of all the Great Kruls who raised their hordes and led them against Rodal, smashed them into the mountains, urged them through canyons and were left with nothing but bleached bones in foreign passes for their plunder. There are countless sagas that end sadly in Rodal. Or perhaps you would prefer those that end in the bogs of Hellin, whole clans drowned in quicksand and never seen again? North lies Persdad, protected only by hills and steppes and mortal men with timber palisades. That is where we should ride.'

'And rich only in wheat and lumber and thick-headed legionaries with blades to protect their wooden walls,' growled the warlord. 'The league lies on the southern caravan routes, littered with trade metals and the bounty of machines and mills, the Guild of Rails carrying treasure in every direction. Ports on the salted sea heaving with vessels packed full of plunder.' He slapped his thick muscled legs. 'This Vandian girl is a sign from the gods. What we seek is seeking us. Her people have joined the kin war in Weyland. Our enemies are disunited. The Lanca turns in upon itself. There is no better time to strike south.'

'You speak wisely,' said Temmell, his eyes gazing slyly at the priestess. There was obviously no love lost between these two, the left hand of the throne as jealous of the right as the reverse was also true.

'No Great Krul has ever breached the Walls of Rodal,' warned Madinsar.

'I am no mere Great Krul,' said the warlord. 'I am Kani Yargul. I shall make the god Atamva weep in envy at how thoroughly my foes are smashed. I will forge a victory crown so heavy that only my own sons will be able to bear its glory without being crushed.'

'Atamva always remembers,' whispered the priestess. Then Madinsar raised her face and looked at the warlord. 'Claim the right of the Great Krul again, my lord, and give me the forest dweller as my thrall.'

'What use do you have for this creature?' said Kani Yargul, staring down contemptuously at Kerge. 'I thought him half a bear and half porcupine, walking upright like a man when he entered my tent.'

'He could dance for us. Or perhaps the high priestess wishes to use the spines from his hide to pick meat from her teeth,' said the sorcerer. 'I hear the care of teeth becomes of great importance when one reaches such an inestimable age.'

'One of a great many nuisances I would rid myself of,' said Madinsar, staring down the sorcerer. 'If I could. This one is a gask. A twisted man, and the people of the forests possess many gifts, including that of dreaming the future. Such a thrall would be useful to me, and of service, thereby, to the clans.'

Kerge looked like he was going to say something, but didn't. Cassandra guessed the gask was going to point out that he had lost his gift of prophetic vision, but on second thoughts had wisely decided to keep his loss quiet less he end up with a far worse fate. *Poor Kerge. If you could still see the future, you would have never come after me with Sheplar. You would have stayed safe in Rodal and gone back to your shaded city in the trees.*

'I must have something so you must have something,' said the sorcerer.

'As long as our clans grow stronger,' said Kani Yargul. 'So be it. Now bring me my feast. No more talk without action. I have a hunger and I have a thirst.'

He waved away the foreigners and court supplicants. Cassandra was dragged through the crowded tent until Alexamir caught up with her and lifted the weight of her body from the two guards. Nurai manoeuvred through the crowd to make sure she was there too. A knowing look on the young witch rider's face that Cassandra wished she could wipe off by breaking her proud nose. *If I could just take the step towards you, I would.*

'You came back from the raid with three thralls,' said Nurai. 'And you leave the tent with just one.'

'I leave the Great Krul having made two gifts to him,' said Alexamir. 'And the golden fox is the only prize I value.'

Those words struck Nurai like a slap. 'Fools' gold for a fool,' she growled and stalked off.

'The witch rider is right,' said Cassandra. 'I am no prize worth possessing.'

'Her words drip with envy,' said Alexamir. 'But then, what woman would not be envious? I am already a legend among the clans and my saga has only just begun.'

While mine is doomed to end here, it seems. 'And what of me?'

'I gave you my word that you would be free to return to your people if that is what you wished.'

'You gave your word to a different woman.' *One who could walk.*

'You shall be that woman again. I will talk to Temmell. Beg him to heal you. Offer him my life and loyalty if he heals you for me.'

Cassandra felt her heart sink. This golden-skinned outsider, Temmell; he was clearly an itinerant medicine man whose wagon had been seized by the clans trying to cross the plains; an ex-clan slave who had used science and his canny knowledge of herbs and powders to bluff his way into a minor position of power. Not even the imperial surgeons attending the emperor and the imperial family could mend a broken spine. What chance did some travelling peddler who had landed on his feet here have? 'You are wasting your time.'

'It is my time to waste,' said Alexamir. 'Come, I shall take you to meet my family.'

As if I have any choice in the matter. 'I am sorry to hear your father is gone. Does your mother still live?'

'She became one of the Great Krul's wives and lives inside the palace. It is the way of our people. If your friend dies, you take in the wives of your fallen brother. My Aunt Nonna keeps my household. You will like her.'

Cassandra suspected nothing would be further from the truth. Survival out here in the grasslands, cooking, cleaning, finding water, keeping the animals alive that helped feed mouths and give the clans their hides and wool for clothes, leather, saddles and tents . . . that was a full-time occupation. A pampered Vandian noblewoman, raised for power and made a cripple, that was only another burden.

Cassandra glanced behind her to the palace. No sign of Kerge or Sheplar. It was strange, when that pair had been her captors and there hadn't been a day held prisoner in Weyland when she hadn't dreamt of escaping and making her way back to Vandia. But now the pair were thralls, slaves to the clan, she couldn't help feeling sorry for them.

She gazed out to the east, beyond the hills where acres of camouflage netting helped conceal the clans' greatest secret. Perhaps this Kani Yargul would be the first war leader of the hordes to do what had never been done before. Conquer Rodal and push into the rich nations of the south. *So, Vandia is now involved in Weyland's civil war?* The Imperium had come at last to punish the slave revolt in Vandia. Her people were across the mountains in force. Ridiculously close, given the scale of distances the Vandians must have flown to reach Weyland. *Is my mother there? Paetro, Duncan, others from my house?* Almost certainly. Cassandra knew her mother. Nothing in Pellas would stop Princess Helrena Skar from seeking out her kidnapped daughter, punishing the escaped slaves who had humiliated her by snatching the daughter of her house as a hostage. Lady Cassandra had to stop herself from laughing at the irony. All this way and did her grandfather's legions but know it, it was only the indignity of the slave revolt they had left to punish. *With me, there is nothing left to save.* Only to avenge. Better she stayed here among the savage nomads. Lost to her house. Let Helrena Skar think her daughter dead. *For I am. If I only didn't have Alexamir's affections to remind me that I'm alive.*

Alexamir lifted Cassandra on to a horse so she could pass through the camp with more dignity than being carried like a sack of meal.

'You should have let me end my life,' declared Cassandra.

'Then you would have ended two.' It was clear Alexamir would brook no interference with his plans for Cassandra, no matter what her wishes.

There were thousands of similarly sized and shaped tents in the busy encampment, although there was no chance of the nomads getting lost. Each tent's exterior had been dyed or embroidered with unique runes and symbols, prayers for success against rivals and protection against evil spirits. Children played outside while adults cooked on low stone ovens, cleaning weapons and brushing horses, picking stones from their steeds' hooves. She reached a tent, or rather, three connected circular tents formed into a triangular formation. It had been staked on the top of a low hill. Down on the other side was a stream where nomads squatted by the side of the frothing water, beating clothes clean against rocks.

'I return from the raid, Aunt,' said Alexamir, pushing aside a woollen flap acting as a door to the tent.

'Yes. Yes. I heard the cheers from the palace,' said Nonna. 'I shall cook their applause at once to make a fine feast from the great words of such heroes.'

The nomad woman standing inside sniffed, irritated, watching Alexamir bear Cassandra in and laying her down on a simple bed of sheep skins in the corner. Nonna had the same blue tint to her skin as all the nomads. The same twisted blood that allowed Alexamir to walk around Rodal's frozen heights bare-chested. Alexamir's aunt must have been close to her sixtieth year, but she was still a handsome woman, with the muscled tone of a woman a third her age, dark leather riding clothes belted with twin daggers swinging on wide hips. To Cassandra's eyes, Nonna appeared a gladiator born to battle, not a housekeeper. *Perhaps that is the way with all the Nijumeti.*

'And what else have you carried back from your raid? Sheep with no pelts and a stallion that only gallops backwards? A sword hilt with no blade attached, perhaps?'

'This is the Lady Cassandra of Vandia, granddaughter of a rich and powerful emperor,' said Alexamir, a touch too haughtily. 'She has been given my guest oath.'

Nonna bowed ironically in Cassandra's direction. 'Then I live to serve. As *always*.'

'She will be no burden on you. Not for long. Temmell will heal her. I know it.'

'That one? That foreign *degg*? That golden-skinned spell-sucker? Promise him your soul for a saddle-wife if you must. He shall not have mine.'

'My golden fox is to be no thrall or saddle-wife,' said Alexamir, setting matters out clearly. 'She has my protection and we will honour her with all the traditions of roof and salt. She is free to go among us as she wishes.'

Cassandra couldn't help but feel her heart soften at the young nomad's words. Few men in this land or any other would have held to her in this state. *But he has*. Nothing had inhibited his yearning for her. Not being held as a prisoner in Salasang or being shot out of the clouds by the Rodalian skyguard. Alexamir was a savage, a reiver and a common thief, but he possessed the nobility of a prince of the plains.

'How splendid. Then I shall be witness to a miracle of the gods . . . I shall see a fox walk,' said Nonna. She waved her hand indifferently around the connected tents. 'Welcome to your new kingdom, then,

Lady Cassandra of Vandia. You will find we have fewer servants than an emperor's offspring is used to, but what we lack in numbers we make up for in spirit.' She snorted and picked up a leather drinking bottle, uncorking it and tossing it to the little-welcomed guest.

Cassandra sniffed at the canteen and then took a gulp, swallowing a pale white liquid that tasted of almonds. It burnt her throat like acid before moving down her gut as a stream of liquid fire. She only just resisted the urge to spit it out again. The young Vandian woman experienced a strange, dizzying warmth coursing through her veins. 'What in the name of the ancestors did I just drink?'

'*Cosmos*,' said Nonna. 'Distilled and fermented milk of the mare. Only the finest. Sent by my sister-in-law from the leavings of the Great Krul himself. Milk of the mare gives a woman the strength to see out the day and work like a devil.' She laughed. 'Drink too much and I shall lose my legs as surely as you have lost yours. Or perhaps I shall go blind first?'

Cassandra proffered the bottle back for Nonna to take. As Nonna reached over, she grabbed Cassandra's wrist and turned it around, inspecting the guest's fingers and hand like a palm reader. 'An emperor's granddaughter, you say? On whose word? These hands are hard and calloused, not soft and coddled.'

'I speak the truth,' protested Alexamir. 'The rice-eaters and men of Weyland held her hostage in the kin war across the mountains. I rescued her. I freed her.'

'Indeed. So, you could not resist stealing a burning brand from the fire,' said Nonna. 'Every day you walk into the tent and I glance up and see you and think you are your father, returned from riding the heavens. Like two peas in a pod, in bad manners, poor wisdom and fine features. Truly you are my brother's blood, Alexamir Arinnbold.'

Cassandra broke the aunt's grip. 'That he may be, but *I* am Vandian. The Imperium's celestial caste does not have soft hands and fat chins. We are raised to battle and trained to rule. No house that carries weaklings survives long in the Imperium.'

'Then perhaps your people are not so different from ours, after all,' said Nonna. 'You certainly show enough pride to be a Nijumet. But is it false pride? Never in my day.'

'Your nephew would be dead without me,' said Cassandra. 'I flew the flying wing we stole from Rodal. It was crashing it which broke my back.'

'Indeed? Well, even foul water may put out a fire.' Nonna shrugged and lay a hand not unkindly on one of Alexamir's boulder-like shoulders. 'Yet, where would I be without my Alexamir and his hot air to warm my tent? Winter would have claimed me an age ago.'

If winter tried, I suspect it would end up with a dagger shoved through its eye. This was Cassandra's fate, her future. Worn fabric walls stretched over a wooden frame, her bones warmed by a dried sheep-dung hearth. Before, she had been a prisoner in Weyland. Now she was a prisoner inside her own body. *Where is my escape to be, here*?